EAGLES WHERE I WALK

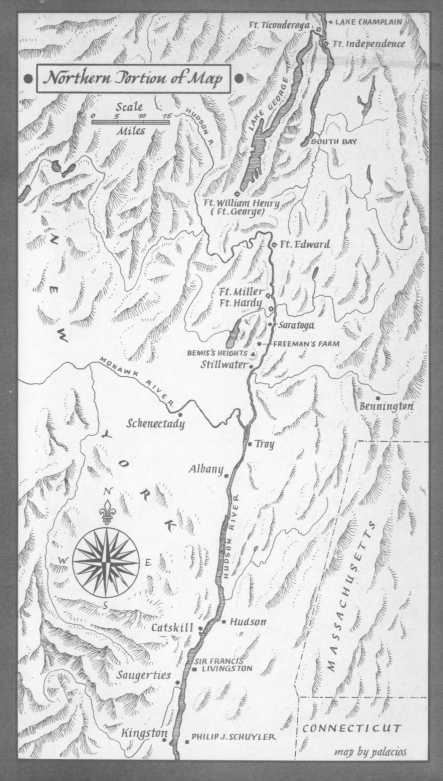

Books by Stephen Longstreet

FICTION

DECADE   THE SOUND OF AN AMERICAN

STALLION ROAD   THE PEDLOCKS

THE LION AT MORNING   THE BEACH HOUSE

MAN OF MONTMARTRE   THE PROMOTERS

BURNING MAN   GEISHA

GETTYSBURG   EAGLES WHERE I WALK

NON-FICTION

CHICO GOES TO THE WARS   NINE LIVES WITH GRANDFATHER

SISTERS LIKED THEM HANDSOME   THE BOY IN THE MODEL T

THE REAL JAZZ OLD AND NEW

TRAVEL

THE LAST MAN AROUND THE WORLD   THE WORLD REVISITED

LAST MAN COMES HOME

PLAYS

HIGH BUTTON SHOES

Methinks I see in my mind a noble and puissant nation rousing herself like a strong man after sleep, and shaking her invincible locks: methinks I see her as an eagle . . . kindling her undazzled eyes at the full midday beam.

—JOHN MILTON (1608–74)

EAGLES WHERE I WALK

STEPHEN LONGSTREET

Doubleday & Company, Inc.   Garden City, New York

1961

Library of Congress Catalog Card Number 61–12549
Copyright © 1961 by Stephen Longstreet
All Rights Reserved
Printed in the United States of America
First Edition

FOR MY SON—A WORD BEFORE

Dear Harry,

The world of the great land-owning patroons—here put down as living along the Hudson River during the War of the American Revolution—actually existed. Most of them were of Dutch descent, either directly or by intermarriage. The Schuylers, Philipses, Van Cortlandts, Livingstons, Van Rensselaers and others still survive, not only as name places for roads and streams, houses, and parks, but in living descendants. I have used the actual stuff of history to tell my story, but most of the people and some of the places are treated as fiction, so that, with a stronger reality and for a greater freedom of mobility, they may fit more tightly into this retelling of the just gone past.

Historians must not look to this novel for a precise rendering of facts. At the same time, the events, dramas of love and property, turmoils, and battles of this book are all based on actual documents, journals and surviving evidence—rather than on modern popularizations. The two battles—one for New York and the other to wear down Burgoyne's invasion from Canada—took place as here described. If the mood and the actual historical figures and attitudes do not often resemble their counterparts as taught in schools, the fault lies with the warping and dressing up of the historical process that has been going on for a long time, and which scholars are beginning to rectify.

This remains a story, a novel, of how we were and how things happened. The author has always objected to the classifying of this special form of story telling as "historical novels" and "modern novels." Whether a writer creates from what happened that morning or from events a hundred or so years ago, he is always in one sense historic—he is spying backward into time—and if his observations on the interplay of human society have any validity, they are modern, no matter in what costumes the dramas are attired. There are only interesting and uninteresting novels. With time all modern values acquire the patina of history—and history is the lives of people who become forefathers.

S.L.

Contents

BOOK IV, AMERICAN ISLAND 145

BOOK V, BRITISH ISLAND 199

BOOK VI, AMERICAN RIVER 235

BOOK VII, FROM THE NORTH 279

BOOK I

Americans in London, 1774

CHAPTER 1   In the chilly morning of a London day in October—during the Hanoverian reign of the third George—a sea coal fire had been laid in the main room of the chambers of Harvell Livingston, on St. James Street. A grimy sun tried to push through the pea-soup fog and the blue silk hangings, as the master of the chambers sat at his brief breakfast of beaten eggs and Yorkshire rusks. His shaved head was hidden in a yellow sleeping cap, the crepe-de-chine dressing gown hung loose on his bony frame. It was apparent to the old servant Mickle that his master was not hungry. He brought the milk pitcher from the Duncan Phyfe side table.

"The eggs are fresh, sir."

"I didn't say they weren't."

"Shall I reheat the rusks, sir?"

"No. Get me the claret."

The old servant in the dark blue livery, his clubbed hair gathered in a black ribbon in back, crossed the room to the sideboard and the crystal containers of spirits.

The young man pushed aside the dish set before him, and frowned into the French mustard cup. He was tall, very lean, his long face plain but regular, and had the pallor of a man who dissipated much and had not taken good care of himself for a long time. At twenty-five Harvell Livingston was neither in robust health nor steady in his movements; his hand shook as he took the glass of claret from the old servant.

"I'm expecting some people, Mickle. Show them into the picture gallery."

"I will, sir. You'll wear the tie-wig and the blue jacket, sir?"

"Yes, yes. What difference does it make *what* I wear? And I'm not at home to—well you know, the usual people. All but Jack Bounty."

The servant nodded and at the door he turned. "If I may speak, sir, as one who has served many of the Livingstons when they visit from the colonies—if I presume, sir . . ."

"Oh, damn you, Mickle, no sermons."

"This thing you are going to do tomorrow, it's no longer fashionable, or the mode, to be involved in them. You could be on the Dover coach in an hour, and there the bark *Mary Survey* is ready to sail for Boston with the next tide. Or the perfidious French across the Channel, sir, might amuse you."

The young man laughed in a mockery of despair and plucked his nightcap off his shaved pate and shook his head. "What a welcome I'd get at home on Long Island, fleeing a duel after what I did to the prince's friend. Leave me. Go down and get me a newsletter—a *Gazette* if it's out."

When the door was closed behind the servant, Harvell finished his drink and went to the spirits tray and refilled his glass. How cozy the chambers were with the clatter of traffic from St. James Street coming in the windows, the bell striking the morning hour at St. Sepulchre's Church near Newgate Gaol where some wretch in the reeking prison effluvium also was going to die; was getting the greasy parson's pious exhortation, and the nosegay, before they sat the condemned man on his coffin on the wagon for the drive through the crowd to Tyburn Hill and its gibbet.

And now, tomorrow morning, he, Harvell Livingston, would face death too. Ball and pistol or sword and slash; Captain Gannon of the Life Guards; the prince would pick no one else to fight the colonial clod.

Harvell walked to the window and watched the sedan chairs pass, then two idle apprentices smoking short clay pipes, a street musician fiddling dismally, a chimney sweep dark as ebony crossing to the red brick house across the way where Harvell had once had a collation supper and danced the minuet and the Sir Roger de Coverley.

It seemed strange that people should go on living with trivial things when such a crisis had come to Harvell Livingston. Three years he had lived in these chambers, idling when he should have

been reading law at Lincoln Court, drinking at Tom King's Coffee
House, while the Blackstone volumes cracked and gathered dust and
he ran into debt beyond anything he admitted in those long letters
home to Lloyd's Neck, Long Island, to Sir Francis Livingston, his
father. Letters of progress in law only imagined, of learning never
acquired. Trusts broken, friendships betrayed, and now *this*.

The young man groaned aloud and looked up at Mr. Wren's new
cathedral (they called anything built since the Great Fire new here).
He turned from the sight of St. Paul's and rubbed his plucked head
and studied the framed plates of Hogarth's Marriage à la Mode; the
small Gainsborough, Stubbs' horses, the old books he collected. He
tenderly touched a volume of Butler's *Hudibras*. He tried with some
effort to remember the events of last night. The meeting with the
usual bucks at Button's Club, the intimate detailed talk about
Jonathan Swift with the little man in the brown fustian coat who
had taken them all out one day last week to the Bridewell House of
Correction, to see the town bawds in Tothill Fields pound hemp for
the royal fleet.

Also last night the painter of small ribald conversation pieces had
been with them, yes. They were not fully drunk yet. They had gone
to the pit of the Crown Theatre to see—what was the name of the
thing?—*Fair Views of Vice*. There had been talk of the Lord Mayor
putting out a new ordinance for the suppression of vicious practices
in the theater, against lascivious and scandalous plays and comedies.
But of course with the fat prince so taken with the Green Room, no
one really felt anything would be done. They all had come from
Ridotto's: sedan chairs, three miles a shilling.

Harvell remembered now—between the acts the smell of beeswax
candles, the Green Room full of color and satins and lace and gilt
swords. The cups of strong iced drinks passed on silver trays. And he,
damn fool, at the elbow of Mistress Nivell, the French piece the
prince was rolling eyes at, ogling, spreading the pleasure of this, his
conquest, this perky large-breasted baggage, among his friends. And
then he, Harvell, the colonial bumpkin, very drunk really and leaning toward the two white breasts straining at the peek-a-boo waist,
had done *it*. . . .

His groan of self-pity was cut off by a discreet tap on the door and
Mickle came in carrying the blue jacket, the plum-colored breeches,
the great tie-wig.

"May we suggest we get dressed, sir?"

"Has my cousin David Cortlandt come around of late?"

"Not for about a month, sir. May I suggest the white silk stockings and the small silver buckles on the shoes, sir?"

"Anything you say, Mickle. Have we Cousin David's address?"

"He's still living, I believe, at John Hunter's medical school, sir."

Harvell watched his image being dressed in the full-length pier glass; the ruffled shirt, the good canary-colored waistcoat, the white silk stockings, smooth on the thin but well-turned legs. He sat as Mickle put on the buckled shoes, and with Truefit's best brown wig in place Harvell felt more confident he could somehow face the day. The night would be a horror, and the next morning he did not think of. The captain of the Life Guards in his jackboots who would kill him tomorrow and celebrate over whist and partridge at White's.

Harvell closed his eyes as Mickle fluffed up the lace cuffs. He imagined the city of New York and the Hudson in flood, the golden maples of fall and the good Dutch estates at Yonkers. How alive he had been there, so young and excited. A week at Philipse Manor, hunting the river grass for the sage hens at Van Cortlandt Manor, or Mynheer Peter Schuyler smoking a churchwarden full of burley, a Virginian tobacco, and saying, "You just wait, Harvell. Some fine fat Dutch girl in a wall bed—she'll marry you and make you a farmer yet."

How far away it all seemed now; Amos van Rensselaer and his father on the good blooded mares riding under the oaks, the morning they took the sailboat up the river from Ackerman's Landing toward West Point. Sir James Tropp, the royal adjutant general of the colony, red-faced and jolly, and the farmers in their smocks haying in the Staten Island fields, and the cyder mills turning at Colen-Donck.

He was aware that Mickle was tapping him lightly on the shoulder. "Mr. Bounty, sir, in the picture gallery."

Harvell turned, pushed back his shoulders, and went into the gallery; the London tailors always cut the shoulders too tight. He could hardly breathe. Lieutenant Jack Bounty was in the gallery, wearing his gilt sword, his short wig—a little worn—and the high-heeled shoes well varnished but scuffed in the back. He turned from inspecting a spotty Italian Holy Family.

"Well, pippin, you've cut the apple now, Harve."

"Don't be so cheerful, Jack."

"Cheerful?" Jack turned his too-pink grinning moon face away from the sunlight flooding in over the Chinese screen from St. James Street and wriggled his fingers in a gesture of dismissal of the idea. Actor, fencing master, Latin tutor of sorts, Jack was the younger son of a dull noble upland family. They had cut him off, and he lived fairly poor at his various chores.

"I'm not cheerful, old boy. My head aches and I still can't believe you did it. All I remember is a bear dancing in a night cellar to pipe and tabor."

"There were witnesses. I was very drunk, Jack."

"So you pitched a cold drink down between the fat bubbies of the prince's favorite. Really, Harve . . ."

"I must have done it. It's all very vague."

"And splattered the prince like a carelessly aiming greyhound. *And* called out, they say: 'I've wet the royal jade!'"

Harvell turned green-white, sat down, and put his face in his hands. "I didn't know about *that*."

"You mumbled so, I hear, it's only an interpretation."

Harvell looked up at the gallery's Dutch still lifes, Stubbs hunting scenes, the Old Cromes—why had he bothered to collect it all? "Captain Gannon will meet me—isn't it so?"

Jack Bounty took up some grapes from a bowl. "Yes, he's to represent His Highness' honor. Of course, Gannon will claim you stomped on his toes in the Green Room and refused to beg his pardon. That's the play, Harve, old boy. Face it chin out, tail up. Grinning."

"Pistols or swords?"

Jack bit his large lower lip. His big brown eyes grew larger as he tossed away the grapes. "Christ's gore, it doesn't make much difference really, my poor friend. Gannon is just a brutal animal skilled in official murder. Half the debauchers and voluptuaries in high places have used the captain to get rid of a nuisance."

"I wish I'd never seen this damned city or come here to read law."

"Gannon fought last week—that Dutchman who pulled the *sauter la coupe*, that cheating card trick, at Lady Wilkes'. A pistol ball right through the liver. How do you shoot, Harve?"

"Fairly well. Back home I could hit a squirrel off a branch a hundred feet away. I've never handled pistols much."

"I've had you two years as a fencing pupil. You're not bad, old boy. Take the sword. He'll mayhaps be satisfied with a little blooding from a point prick. It's a clean thing in one's lung and light, not a filthy lead slug. The cold steel, Harve. A gentleman's wound."

"Thank you, Jack."

Mickle was back. "Captain Sunder Batherden and Lord Queensbury."

"Show them in, Mickle."

"Easy," whispered Jack. "Bright-eyed and bushy-tailed, eh?"

Harvell stood up and pulled his jacket into place. The two men in great three-cornered hats over white tie-wigs, with yellow lace and smart long-tailed jackets, bowed from the rosewood doorway.

"Gentlemen," said the taller of the two—the man with the large jutting teeth.

"Jack Bounty at your service. My principal, Harvell Livingston of Long Island, of His Majesty's American colonies."

There were bows, as Mickle stood in the background, rolled his eyes at the ceiling. "Captain Batherden, gentlemen, and Lord Queensbury, acting for Captain Gannon in the matter of the incident at the theater, for which he demands satisfaction."

Jack Bounty said crisply, "If my principal were to offer the excuse that he was in liquor and regrets the whole incident, how would that sit with Captain Gannon?"

Harvell said nothing, flaring his nostrils as if in pain.

Captain Batherden smiled, grinding his teeth together. "Certain remarks were made about the taste of a certain person of rank, who does not enter into the matter for the purpose of this duel. We firmly regret—no. Swords or pistols?"

Jack looked expressionless at his friend and said, "Swords. The place?"

Lord Queensbury, supercilious and dandified, lisped and blushed. "The fencing school over the night cellar of the Lion's Rest, if that is satisfactory?"

"Quite," said Jack crisply. "Will there be a doctor?"

"A barber-churgeon," said Captain Batherden. "Sews you up neatly like a sack of cockpeas, if there's anything worth stitches. Gentlemen, everything is then arranged?"

For the first time, Harvell spoke. "A drink, sirs?"

"Thank you, no. No offense. Too early in the day."

They bowed and were gone, the Frenchy scent of Lord Queensbury lingering behind. Jack Bounty was cracking his knuckles, his wide moon face cheerful again. "I don't think they intend to kill you unless by accident, Harve. You heard about the bloody barber. Nice of them to think of patching up."

"I don't know, Jack. I have a feeling the prince is very enamored of the bitch."

"What a damned fool reason to fight a duel! An insult to the dugs of a royal prince's whore. Old boy, why the devil don't you go home, thumb your snoot at us? After all—no offense—you're not an English gentleman."

Harvell smiled suddenly. "No, *just* a lousy colonial."

"Don't think you're not a problem there, too. I had breakfast at the Horse Guards officers' mess. There's talk of regiments to go to America to take some impudent rascals, some Committees of Public Safety or Liberty, down a peg."

"There's always talk, no real seditious strength."

"Some damned American Committees of Correspondence say they're out to protect what they call the people's liberty, and now talk of independence."

Harvell waved off the idea. "We're all loyalists in our class, Jack. We're not against the administration of the Crown, and we don't think British troops should be withdrawn from the colonies. Besides, all I can think of is this duel. I'm done in."

"It's going to get to armed colonial resistance, you mark my word, Harve. All this denying the jurisdiction of the king's agents, and now they're raising militia all over the bally map; local yeomen and farmers to force the repudiation of England's colonial rights."

"Swords—you felt that was better?"

Harvell looked away, seeing his cozy chambers, so neat and so filled with his special treasures. He couldn't believe he was seeing them for the last day, perhaps.

"What's it to me, Jack, what the bumpkins say in Carpenters' Hall in Boston, or whether they call a Continental Congress to gather in Philadelphia? I'm going to die tomorrow if I'm unlucky. I'm not the soldier sort. But I'm no coward."

No, of course not—no ineffectual, apprehensive thoughts. He mustn't act like the bourgeois parvenus. After all, he was a Livingston, as good as the best in the crown colony of New York. The Heathcotes, the Pells, and the Archers on their estates up and down the river. And as good as the proud, fat patroon families in their rich Dutch comfort. So solid in their virtues and so rich in their trading and farming and that happy Dutch cunning at collecting gold coins they counted so carefully into their leather moneybags.

It didn't matter that in London they were all held in some ill esteem, as bumpkins of an insular culture, full of naïveté, often inept on the dance floor, and unable, as Jack had once said, "to call off the fashionable articles of female lingerie by their proper names. It's the first test of a man of the world, Harvell, old boy."

How fine it would be to be back there, very young again, with David Cortlandt, drifting with the hard brine tide off the Kill van Kull into the murky harbor, and the impressive sight of the buildings around the Battery, with the shad running, and on the Jersey side the tall palisades topped with green and the report that Indians still hunted the varmints there for food. Payonia, Yonkers, the landed butter-rich estates worked so well and so cheerfully under the firm hand of the patroons. Newburgh, Kingston, those summer journeys up the river to the huge Livingston holdings (even if Sir Francis preferred to live at Lloyd's Neck). And beyond was the land around Albany, the vast Rensselaerwyck, so big that beyond were only the Mohawk and Hoosic rivers. One summer he and David had paddled a birchbark Indian craft up there, and lived a smoky outdoor life. He had given it all up for this damned town's alcoves, boudoirs, marquetry-cased cabinets, and a great deal of inconstancy and vice that now seemed as dismal and fruitless as a mouth full of sand.

Jack broke into Harvell's reveries of the Hudson River Valley. "Must run and get the proper gossip about *this* 'round the town. Can't give any chance to talk you've shown the white feather in a funk."

"You're a true friend, Jack."

When Jack Bounty was gone, promising to return and have dinner with him, Harvell sent Mickle down to the Rose Tavern to hire a chaise and horses.

CHAPTER 2   The hired coach stopped before 24 Jermyn Street, for all its Ionic pilasters a plain and simple enough looking place, with a polished brass sign: HUNTER SCHOOL OF ANATOMY. Harvell got out and tugged at the bellpull. He looked at the fanlight over the door and shivered. A perky little maid opened the door, wiping her nose with the back of her hand. She seemed to be suffering from a bad cold in the head.

"What would yo' be wantah, sirh?"

"I want to see David Cortlandt."

"They be too busy. You can't cum in nowh."

"Busy?"

"Master Davey and Mr. Hunter. Busy in the amphitheater. I don't dare interrupt the dissecting."

Harvell put two shillings into her grimy hand. She grinned, sniffed, and opened the door wider. "Will you cum in sirh, nowh?"

He followed her into a hall crowded with large paintings of serious-looking men, dipped in oil rather than painted. There were the backbones of some great fish hanging from the ceiling. Jars of anatomical specimens in yellow fluid seemed carelessly left on tables.

"This way," said the maid, and Harvell followed her through the house and along a passageway smelling of strong brine, spilled chemicals, and badly-tanned, reeking animal skins. They came out in a great shed of a hall, the walls lined to the ceiling with large glass jars holding fearful segments of human anatomical details. Higher up hung skeletons of once-condemned men, now stripped of their flesh and used here to teach young men the systems of bones. Filling in were collections of strange fish, apes, fragments of fossils. All was lit by skylights in whose glow the trapped smell and dust were strangling Harvell.

The maid wiped her nose on a corner of her skirt. "The Hunterian Museum, they say there's seventy thousand pounds of money put into it now. Watch yer head, sirh."

Harvell ducked down into a short low hall and the maid pointed to a red-painted door and suddenly fled down some side passage before Harvell could stop her. He stood alone in the odor of chemicals (and something worse), his hand held up to the door, and then he knocked. No one answered and Harvell turned the silver handle and went into a brick octagonal amphitheater, whitewashed, with great sperm-whale oil lamps hung on cords over scrubbed tables. On one table was the severed brown leg of a man. Bent over it were his cousin, David Cortlandt, and John Hunter, the famous surgeon, toxicologist, and anatomist.

"Cut ye down to the femur," his Scotch bass said. "The obturator internus, Davey laddie. That's it. Now do ye see how it divided into three portions, eh? This one, laddie, is the coccygeus." The cracked walnut of a Scots face looked up at Harvell. "Who the devil be ye now?"

The famous surgeon had a quick temper and a feverish stare— and no wonder. He often infected himself as an experiment.

David Cortlandt looked up with the end of some obscene tendons held in his wet fingers. "It's my cousin, Harvell Livingston, sir."

"Medical fella? Looks like his lymphatic vessels don't function."

"No, a lawyer," said Harvell. "At least I've been reading some torts at the Inns of Court."

"Aye. Come here, young fella, and look at yon bone of the coxendix, the ischium. Prettiest thing ye did ever see, eh?"

"I'm sure it is."

Harvell looked down with horror at the skillfully dissected leg and wanted to be ill. He saw the mocking face of the anatomist and he said stiffly, "If I could speak to David for a few moments, sir."

"We're through. What a bonny leg. Belonged to Murgittrude, the Thames Robber, ye know. The laddie that broke into Moses Pedlock's private bank on Cheapside and outran the rozzers of the watch for three miles before he was felled by a load of shot in the head. A grand runner. See what it did fer his leg muscles?"

David was washing his hands at a slate basin, grinning at his cousin's discomfort. David was taller than his cousin Harvell, and much broader, with red hair, a strong square face, and great hams of hands. Very handsome in his early twenties, in a back-country way, Harvell thought; all those fine white teeth, and good health just bursting from him. Odd to spend one's youth cutting up poor felons.

"You look peaked, Cousin Harvell. Maybe Mr. Hunter will prescribe some of Turlinton's Balsam of Life, or Mrs. Bannister's Venice Treacle."

The surgeon was writing in Latin on a label stuck to a jar of spirits floating a spleen. "Never bother with the quackery of special dram. You get the pox or anything, I'll cure ye without the fancy Tatnall's Powder, or Deimer's Ointment. Would you care to shuck off yer garments for an examination?"

"Thank you, sir, it's nothing like that."

David was getting into an unfashionable gray jacket, dismally tailored across the shoulders. "Come along, Harvell, and you can buy me a cut of the best mutton at the Sailor's Port."

Once in the street, Harvell sucked in air deeply and followed his cousin to an ale and cook cellar that sold hot mutton, good wheaten bread, great pewter tankers of bitter beer, and bumbo-mimbo—which was rum, hot. Seated comfortably in the back, David took a deep pull on his tanker.

"Cousin Harvell, you look terrible. I'm almost a full medical man and I've a mixture that can cure tetters, wind colic, scurf, morphew, and scurry. Or is it a woman?"

"It isn't any of that, David. I'll be dead before morning."

"Oh, now—"

They were served large sections of fat mutton and David carefully used the mustard pot on the meat, frowning. He looked up at Harvell. "What nonsense are you talking?"

"I'm fighting a duel at morning."

"You'll be hanged for murder if you come out of it alive."

"It's a matter of honor among London's best society and perhaps you wouldn't understand."

David dug the two-pronged fork into his mutton and cut off a mouthful. He chewed thoughtfully. "You've done right coming to me rather than to some barber-churgeon. I'll stand by you tomorrow, and if it's God's will you'll live. Eat your mutton."

"Could I have a geneva?"

David nodded and motioned to the barmaid. "A gin for my friend."

"David, I'm going to make a will, and you, as one of my witnesses, will see it's carried out."

"Drink your geneva and don't talk so fey, Harve. We've been through a lot together. Storms off the Sound in the ketch, bear hunting in the snow near the Indian camp on the upper river near Troy. Ah, yes, and I'm sorry I haven't been seeing more of you here."

"Our worlds here, I fear, don't mix. You're the red-haired man with the book in your hand and a true student. I've been a fool and a fop."

"A lively one. Running with the beaux and swells, the ragtail and bob of the prince himself. What'd this duel result from?"

Over another gin Harvell told the story. David finished off his beer and sat shaking his head. "It doesn't seem possible that such a world of hellracks and fools are important to die for. Over the milk glands of a Drury Lane wench and the fickle favor of a noodle-headed prince. Damn it, Harve, you can't fight for this wretched thing."

"David, listen to me closely. It may well be I did what I did to get back at her for a Covent Garden actress friend of mine, who was snubbed badly by the French bit. I don't know. And what the drunken mind acts out, who can tell?"

"I don't follow."

"Three years ago I took on an intrigue with an actress and singer of ballads at the Star, one Peg Munday."

David shook his head. "I don't go to the theater."

"She became quick with child. The upshot was we were secretly married by a drunken preacher at Harrogate. The boy is two years old now. My son Daniel. No one of the family knows of the marriage or the child. Look."

Harvell offered his cousin a nip of Kipper's snuff from a gold box. On the inside of the lid was set a miniature painting in ivory of a blonde young woman with too much chin and a boy with the same color hair.

"Peg and the boy, painted by Cosway."

David held up the open snuffbox and nodded. "Sir Francis doesn't know of any of this?"

"No, he doesn't. Father was stern in his warning against actresses. You know his pride in family and all that."

David closed the snuffbox with a snap and handed it back. "Harve, this boy is the heir to the Livingston estates, isn't he? I mean after you, of course."

"You're beginning to understand, David, how meanly I'm boxed in. If I am killed in this duel you must get Peg and the boy back to the colonies and New York."

"I've another part of a year of my medical and anatomical studies at the Royal Physicians' and St. Bartholomew's Infirmary. Besides, you need a lawyer, not a young sawbones."

Harvell looked into his drink. At the bar a large drunken man, unbuttoned, stocking slipping, began to pound the table. "First of all, you can tax Englishmen, tax 'em for windowpanes and wagon wheels and dressing their wigs, but a freeborn American the likes of me now, no!"

David nodded his way. "A fellow countryman. Botts is his name; runs the local Sons of Liberty. Nice when sober, a wild man when drunk."

"And drunk now. David, I depend on your help in my private life."

At the bar the soused voice went on. "Grenville's Navigation Act, the new Molasses Act, I tell you the whole British mercantile system is impoverishing us colonies."

"Stow it," someone shouted. "You bloody colonies owe us a debt of over five hundred million pounds right now."

Harvell looked disturbed. "We'd better get out of here. I don't want to mix in this."

"We can't go now, he'll grab us. Botts represents John Hancock the smuggler here in England."

"Now, me buckos, your blasted Stamp Act failed, didn't it? And the tar-and-feathering of the stamp agents learned you all a lesson, didn't it? Bristol and Liverpool face bankruptcy."

"Mr. Botts, you will leave this place. No treason talk 'ere."

"I'm a freeborn American, half hoss, half alligator. I dance to no tyrant's tune."

David pulled on Harvell's sleeve. "Don't attract attention. He'll see us and ask us to join forces. He's notorious hereabouts for the boldness of his fists."

It was too late. Botts, sweating and unsteady, was bending over their table. "Fellow colonists, David lad. What think you of the Declaratory Act binding us to the whole bloody mess, and what did they do to a poor nigger and honest citizens in the Boston Massacre just a few short years ago? Cold-blooded . . . cold-blooded General Gates—bang—bang—bang!"

"Go away, Botts," said David. "You're drunk again."

"Drunk on glory. Have ye heard, lads—they're calling a Continental Congress in Philadelphia."

A barrel bung in the hands of a small wiry man crashed down on

Botts' head. The bung swinger said, "Sorry gents. 'E does get out of hands at times."

The unconscious Botts was dragged out. David said, "You see? Everyone has his problems."

CHAPTER 3   David Cortlandt believed that one did not just decorate an era, but that one could motivate one's time. It was the common conceit of youth. Jermyn Street was home to David in London. He lived on the third floor of John Hunter's residence in a brown pine room slanted in on one side by the roof. In return for room and some board and a great deal of teaching from his master, the young American mounted and numbered the thousands of pathological specimens, helped in the dissecting theater and examination diagnoses. He also did nocturnal errands—to collect bodies—with some of the bully boys always willing to earn a bright coin on a moonless night. He remembered the night the twelve-fingered man had died of an aneurysm of the popliteus. David had taken him away from under the rival collecting team of the pathologist, Sir James Paget. And there was that great victory when John Hunter bought, while still alive, the bones of "The Irish Giant" Charles Byrne, eight feet two inches in his torn stockings, his feet fifteen inches long, hands fourteen inches from wrist to middle finger. Twenty-one years old, at Cockspur Street, and going fast of the lung ailment and drink. Five hundred pounds it had cost John Hunter to get the giant's body when the last big drunk was over, and now the amazing bones were the pride of the museum's exhibit of the species man. It had been an odd way to pay for a medical education.

David closed the door of his room, and he turned back to look from his one small window down on the busy London day. The smudge of rooks flying over London Bridge, the beetle crawl of oared wherries on the river. His mind was over a thousand miles away on the Hudson River, where the sumac was red now, the streams cold. In less than a year he would be going back. A full-fledged young medical, proper surgeon, anatomist, a prober of the inner secrets of the human body and its illnesses. Lord, if he had known the struggle of it, and the poverty, the despairs it would be, he would have put the Kentuck' rifle of his father on his back, whistled to the hounds, and gone with the men who followed Boone tracks into the bloody forests.

Being born a minor Van Cortlandt was fine enough, born into that river society of spinets, tabby velvet, of the patroons and big estates. But not to be a descendant of a younger son who held only a few grubby acres on the fringe of his relatives' fat lands. David's father had died an officer of colonial troops when the lobsterbacks of Braddock were defeated in that French and Indian ambush. His father had died for Colonel Washington, the Virginia planter who commanded the colonials—a collection of tanners, coopers, weavers, and smiths gone to war to help the Crown.

David had been educated on the scant kindness of relatives, the boy working the land and repairing the stone fences, running errands for old Dr. Garrick Pelham, harnessing his gray mare for the winter calls in the sled, saddling the doctor's red gelding Peter. Running with bottles of medical bitters, Renier's Orange Oil "for wind cholick," to sick folk. Or holding a farmer's twisted limb full of barnyard muck and turned black while Dr. Garrick Pelham sawed on the bone and the farmer was held firm by four strong men.

"Assurance and diagnosis is all you need, Davey. Bury *this* out back."

In the summer David had explored the Hudson River country with Harvell Livingston and Old Sam, an Indian wrinkled and very aged, who claimed to be a Seneca. He made them kinnikinnik, Indian smoking tobacco from osier leaves, beanberry, sumac, and willow bark rubbed finely together. It was a deadly smoking mixture but David got to like it, lying and puffing among the woodbine and fox-grape hills above Yonkers, listening to hounds (followed on foot) run a fox in the Schuyler woods. He and Old Sam also hunted varmints for fur among the swamp maple and bull-brier patches. When it came fall they shot the wild ducks and clamoring grackles, all bronze and black, shooting them from the oak trees below Acker-man's ferry.

David learned to cook out-of-doors between two stones, to join the few Indians digging lily roots, and to wake in the morning under a great tree and listen to the mourning doves cooing their velvet dirge and the bleat and *baa* of the Philipse sheep cropping among

the wild geranium and dogtooth violets. There was no better place
on earth.

It all gave David a feeling that this rich river land and lofting
hills and still tangled woods of blooming shadbush, the crackle of
cicadas in manor gardens, was the best place to be rooted. Nights,
riding with Dr. Pelham in his sulky, were fine, while the hawk moths
darted among the joe-pye weeds and the late raucous mocking of
crows settling down for the night gave an eerie sound to the darkened
world. David the boy sensed a deep kinship with earth and place
and time, but lacked as yet the language to express his feeling to the
old doctor.

David was also a water child. Much as the meadows and fields
and secret parts of the forest drew him, he enjoyed the lap of the
river with the shad bubbling by and the tide runners coming in
from the sea.

Everyone knew Davey Cortlandt, the orphan with the red hair
and the wild woodsy ways, and his willingness to earn a shilling or a
bowl of cracklings and corn mush for hoeing, wood-splitting, roof-
repairing, bellow-pumping, or driving sheep down to the city market.
He knew the lobster holes, the nest of the wild goose, the place the
trout slept in the blue watery shadows of elms.

He was available for sailing pinnaces, sloops, and shallops around
the Great South Bay and along the salt sea tides of the Sound, the
guttural *gawk* of gulls overhead and a faint pencil scribble of Connecticut coast to the lea. Taking up his father's rifle, he went in
solitary woods to the pine barrows and, lying in the reeds and grass,
listening to the grasshoppers sing, he felt the earth turn, an earth
warm and smelling of green thoughts growing under a sun low
enough to bite. He was a rangy, shaggy, red-haired boy, growing too
big for his breeches of worn buckskin, studying hard in the cold
attic of the doctor's river-front house—under a farthing candle—the
worn learned books that made him want more of this medical art.
Earning a shilling here and there, working at the crossroads ordinary
for travelers—an inn by the road that led past Yonkers down to dusty
Broadway and into the city. Holding a horn lantern for the late
night-comers arriving at meetings of the Sons of Liberty to talk
against tea taxes, shipping laws, or repeat the wild words of Sam
Adams. He went tankering golden sack from the oak butts in the
inn's stone cellar. He hand-lettered, in gilt on a scarlet background
that showed a unicorn and a lion, with care:

RIVER INN

Drink for the thirsty
Food for the hungry
Lodging for the weary
And good keeping
For horses.

He classified herbs on local meadows: pennyroyal, bloodwort, purstain, coriander. In time David was a strong sixteen, carrying baggage on board ships at the Battery for the embarking gentry in their full-bottomed mohair, foxtailed, or drop wigs. Prosperous folk sailing with the turn of the tide at Sandy Hook for England. David saved enough splitting roof shingles with a beetle and wedge to buy a medical anatomy, and at seventeen he signed as apprentice seaman on the Schuyler vessel *Greetje's Pride* for London. He hoped he would come back a doctor with a gold-headed cane, into a position high in the Hudson River Valley society.

The voyage to England ended on a wet gray day. He had the letter from Dr. Benjamin Franklin that Dr. Pelham had added to his own. Both were addressed to John Hunter, who late that night looked at David, thin and lousy from the ship's bunks, his clothes rags, his red hair uncut, standing on the Jermyn Street stone steps. Hunter read the letters then and there.

"A devil of a medical man ye be making by the flea-marked look of ye."

"I'll work hard, Mr. Hunter. I know the bones. I've seen a Vesalius anatomy of the *De humani corporis fabraoca* and have it all copied out and drawn."

"Ah, the colonial rag heap knows Latin, does ye now?"

"I've picked some up from Dr. Pelham, whom you taught yourself, and I've all the drugs in Latin memorized—or shall. Shall I recite you the bones of the metatarso-phalangeal joint? The first internode, the . . ."

"Shut yer mouth. Go down to the kitchen and have some hot food, and I'll find ye some better clothes. You'll do to sweep the laboratory and dispose of the dissecting leavings. Come in, come in."

Four years had passed, the lanky unkempt seventeen-year-old boy had become the twenty-one-year-old man. Slowly, daily, in long hours he had mastered it all. The Latin was still stiff but of the rest his mind crawled with knowledge. The pelvic measurements he had learned from Willie Smellie, the great master of obstetrics, the notorious male midwife. Oh, the shame of the first time David attended him in a case, Smellie wearing his woman's dress as midwife, hooted by the street lads. Then had followed John Hunter's lessons in the use of the cather, scalpel, forceps, gorget, the threaded needles.

David was almost a medical man with the proper certificates, a doctor and surgeon ready to go back to the colonies, and now this mess with Cousin Harvell. A rich spoiled youth, this taster of sophisticated London, Bath, Brighton, Epsom; all the vice that England had to offer. The reckless life of clubs and stews, of parties and orgies. David had glimpsed it often, from the medical side. He must do something. David picked up a book, thought, put down any idea of reading, even Hunter's great work *The Disease of the Articulating Cartilages*. He put on a worn black seaman's jacket, the battered hat that had long ago done service for Sir William, John Hunter's brother, and taking up a blackthorn stick (David owned no sword) he let himself out of the house by one of its many side passages, so well adapted for secret entrances and exits.

In a chaise, Harvell took him across town to Mrs. Gray's Lodgings on the Strand. It was a good building but run down a bit, and there was the odor of liver and onion and cats on the stairs; not all cooked together, David hoped. On the second floor they went to a suite facing a garden of lilac and now-dormant crocus in the back; a cheerful room in blue wallpaper, a small fire in the grate, and furniture expensive but a little vulgar; too much Delft and Persian china, bayberry candles already burning. A fat maid had let them in, she still chewing something from a late tea.

A little boy came running into the small hall. Brown-haired, face too pale, and dragging one leg slightly. "Daddo!" he shouted and leaped. Harvell caught him up in his arms and kissed him.

"Daniel, this is my cousin David, Mr. Cortlandt from the colonies."

"He be a Indian?" the child asked.

"No no, but you'll see real red men some day soon."

"He's a handsome child," David said.

"He limps, as you see. Some difficulty at birth, I've been told."

David felt the thin leg, patted the boy on the head, and smiled.

"A slight clubbing of the foot from a tension of the long tendon. A well-fitted shoe will make it almost unnoticed."

"Harmony, dear," said a musical female voice, and they entered the big blue room. A young woman rose to greet them; the original of the miniature Harvell carried in his snuffbox. David saw the artist had smoothed and played down the strong chin, a chin just a bit too marked with personal desires.

Peg Munday was of tallish height for a woman, rounded, and her face made up too white and the lashes too black. She was wearing pale green brocaded gauze silk, a high-waisted gown then the mode, Greek in feeling, that artists were making so the fashion. Frizzled and powdered hair, stiff with pomatum, completed her toilet.

"Ah, you've brought someone."

She kissed her husband's cheek and held out a firm white hand to David.

"My wife Peg. My cousin David Cortlandt. We haven't seen much of each other, but now, David, you know my family."

"So good of you to come, Cousin David."

Her voice was that of a trained singer, controlled and aware of its range even in conversation. "So now I'm to be let out of my gilt hothouse a bit? You *are* red-haired, aren't you? Isn't he, Harmony?"

"No hiding it, I confess, madam."

"She calls me Harmony—a pet name."

The child said, "I wanta Bartholomew Baby." (The fair at St. Bartholomew's was famous for its miniature babies.)

"You're too old for it, Dan'el," said his father. "And besides, you may be going over the sea to see Mohawks and Hurons and other red tribes."

Peg made a mock bow. "So even that is now promised us, Harmony." She turned to David. "I dislike Harvell as a name, so I call him Harmony in front of close friends."

"So I hear." David suspected Peg had a temper and a will and made Harvell's life a bit of a trial. He felt uncomfortable in her company; she was too vivid, perhaps vain.

"Either you have been ruined at the gambling table or you are now the full heir. News of some sort from the colonies?"

"No. Sir Francis, last I heard—God protect him—was alive and well. No, no, just that conditions exist that may take you, us, all of us, home."

The plump maid was back. "Time Master Dan'el should take his nap now."

"No. Aw!"

"I'll see him to bed," said Harvell, carrying the protesting child out.

Peg stirred the fire with a gesture David was sure she had learned wearing nankeen and satins on the stage. Addressing the small fire, she said, "I am not supposed to know of the duel?"

"That is correct, Mistress Livingston." He felt clumsy and ill dressed without the wig he usually scorned.

She turned. He saw her eyes were blue, her small breasts flung forward by some emotion. "Mistress Livingston? Me? You mock me, sir?"

"No, believe me, I only call you what you are."

"Oh—you are an earnest young man."

She put one hand to her cheek, leaned over, and put down the fire tool. She turned half around and said crisply, "I don't say it hasn't been worth it, but it's been cruel on the child. You notice he is not perfect. The leg. It's a sign of our sin. Oh, I don't want you to think Harmony was my first protector. But I did feel, with no pious exhortation, I must change. Are you really his cousin?"

"Yes, a most distant one. And he may be dead tomorrow morning. If so, I have promised to take care, to get you and the boy back to Long Island. The boy would be heir to a great estate."

"Damn me if I care of that now." She opened and closed her fingers, working a cambric handkerchief between them. "Have you seen me play in *The Harlequin's Invasion?*"

"I almost never go to the theater. I am a medical student and not too loaded with coin."

"I was not bragging. I just want you to know I am a good actress, and if he wants me not to know of this duel,"—she laughed, the laugh just a bit forced—"why, I will not know. I'll get up the last bottle of Madeira and we'll drink." She pinched David's arm. "Help me or I may fail in this part yet."

David pressed her arm to show he would help. Harvell came out of the boy's room adjusting his lace at throat and cuffs. Peg set herself down with a swirl on the sofa, leaned back revealing blue calamanco slippers with mauve ribbons, crossing her fine ankles. Peg had large feet, David saw, for so well-made a young woman.

She sent Lizzie Patch, as the fat serving woman was called, down for the Madeira.

CHAPTER 4   Near dawn David slept in fitful bursts with great snoring. He came awake to hear St. Sepulchre's bell ring out five o'clock. Night still darkly held the streets, and he saw from the small window only a faint pink edge of light toward the east. He plashed water up from the icy bowl into his face, got into his clothes, picked up a battered medical case, a serge capuchin cloak and his only hat off a nail, and tiptoed downstairs, carrying his shoes in his hand. From the hall rack of deers' antlers he took down John Hunter's sword and hanger and belted them on. He let himself quietly out into the biting brown fog. A lamp blinked somewhere ahead, high in a house, and he began to run to the Lion's Rest.

Arriving, David looked up at an expanse of small leaded windows over which hung a sign. *Lovat's Man of Fashion Fencing Academy. French and English Styles. Pupil of the Great Angelo.*

He found a door that opened to a dark staircase smelling of moldering plaster, going up, and he thumped his way to a double door of fumed oak, badly scarred. David knocked and it was opened by a one-eyed hunchback with very handsome teeth who asked, " 'Oo now?"

"Mr. Livingston's medical man."

"Aye."

He was permitted to enter a long narrow room with mirrors at one end; masks, foils, épées, sabers, and some Italian's engravings of swordplay tacked to yellow walls. Two large oil lamps were lit overhead. At the far end of the fencing gallery stood some people, and David walked toward them over the floor covered with loose gray canvas.

A large man with a look of crafty violence said, "Captain Batherden at your service. Second to Captain Gannon."

"David Cortlandt, medical man for Mr. Livingston."

"Brought his own sawbones, eh? Well, meet Captain Gannon, Lord Queensbury, and Barber Leadbetter—bleed you, and so help me, shave you for half a crown. This is Mr. Cortlandt for Mr. Livingston."

Captain Gannon, handsome as a prize horse, and almost as large and stupid, made a throat noise, said no word.

David returned the bows of all but the bowlegged little barber with two combs stuck in his long greasy hair, who was laying out some grimy tools on a stool. A leather bucket of dirty water stood on the floor.

The one-eyed hunchback asked, "No fire, I suppose?" He pointed to the huge fireplace in which torn papers and broken bottles were piled. He showed an amazing mouthful of teeth in a wide smile. "'Arf a crown extra."

"No, no fire. Mr. Livingston *is* late," said Lord Queensbury.

David put his medical case on the fireplace mantel. He looked at Captain Gannon for a hasty appraisal—dressed in tight-fitting black, feet in Hessian boots with yellow tops. Wide-shouldered, the beginning of a paunch, balding of the golden hair, unnaturally strong wrists. Small blood vessels bursting under skin of his nose.

"Damn me," said Captain Gannon, "I have breakfast waiting for me at St. James Palace."

There was the clatter of shoeleather up the staircase and Jack Bounty came briskly in, followed by Harvell. Both were in dark blue, a little lace, with heavy cloaks. They dropped their cloaks and stepped forward, Jack Bounty a little in advance with a seeming lackadaisical grace. "Gentlemen, we are ready to proceed."

David was aware of Harvell's expressionless white face, a slit of closed mouth, and he wondered if the bright large eyes meant Harvell had taken a few brandies. He hoped not. David had noticed spirits make a man careless and slow on his reflexes.

A rosewood box of swords, thin-pointed rapiers, had been brought out and Jack Bounty was soon holding one up, whipping it through the air with a sinister swishing sound. He turned to David. "I'm Jack Bounty, standing for Harve with you. He's too bemused to introduce us. Good sign, *very* fine sign."

They shook hands and David muttered his name. Jack handed him the sword. "This please you? It's weighted neatly in the hilt and has deuced good lash to it."

"I'm sure it's fine if you pick it, sir."

"Well, I hope Harve remembers all I taught him. He's fast on the circular parry but I wish we'd practiced more the envelopment of quick blinds and the cut-over, or coupe as we say."

David nodded, trying to appear the calm expert.

Jack walked over to Harvell and handed him the sword. He

picked up another sword from the box with an épée point, and David saw that Captain Gannon was armed and Lord Queensbury also had a sword.

Harvell and the captain faced each other, sword points just touching, and at right angles to the duelists stood Jack Bounty and Lord Queensbury, their sword points on the canvas floor.

Jack said curtly, "When we knock up your swords, attack. The duel will go on until first blood is drawn. Lord Queensbury and I will then knock up your swords to desist and the thing is done. Your man ready, Lord Queensbury?"

"He is ready, sir."

David stepped back. Captain Gannon, a smile on his heavy handsome face, stood easy, sword held firmly. Harvell faced him, expressionless, no tremor in his sword arm. David noticed the twitch in his neck cords and the throbbing of the temples.

Jack Bounty and Lord Queensbury lifted their swords, driving apart the duelists' weapons, and then jumped back. David was aware of the spark of meeting steel in the light of the lamps, the thump of feet as the two men parried and thrust. He knew enough of swordplay to see Captain Gannon was a fine master of the murderous art. Harvell was lighter, faster, much more active. Gannon directly began a lunging attack, then went into a match, and ended with a jump and a fast thrust. Harvell, just in time, moved out of the way of a throat wound. Harvell feinted, did what was called a blind beat, and drove Gannon back. The striking of booted feet on the loose canvas, the dust columns in the light of the two big lamps, made a picture that David would never forget. Captain Gannon was moving forward again with a wrist that never seemed to stop moving. It was an envelopment of quick blinds and cut-overs, the coupe just missing as Harvell caught it on his own blade. Captain Gannon followed with a riposte after Harvell's return parry and Harvell drove forward a counter-parry.

David glanced at Jack Bounty, who was smiling, arms folded, sword trailing under his arm. Captain Batherden was chewing on something he had found between two teeth. There was a hard thumping and Harvell began to breathe with an open mouth. The captain was driving in hard counter-ripostes, following with a redoublement on Harvell's parries. David suddenly became aware this was the most scientific kind of skill imaginable, and that the bloody brawls he usually thought of as swordplay were not that at all.

Harvell almost fell, recovered, and parried, a deadly point near his right eye. The captain at once fell back and saluted to give time for a recovery from the near fall. Harvell nodded and held his own with a circular parry.

Jack Bounty looked at a watch and fob he pulled from a waistcoat pocket. Captain Gannon lifted one arm to wipe his damp brow and send in a cruel lunge after a fast feint. David thought Harvell was stabbed like a held goose, but Harvell had stepped back just in time. Again now the captain faced Harvell to parry, feint, and lunge fast into a jump. Harvell was in desperate straits. He was no match for the strength of the solid, beefy captain, who handled his sword as if exercising foils. Harvell was losing co-ordination and fast responses to the quickening attack.

The banging of blades, the heavy beat of the boots on the canvas, went on. Harvell was going back, back . . . almost the whole length of the fencing hall. The captain was beating Harvell's blade aside and down, then parrying it upwards, coolly waiting for that split second that David saw had to come, which would give the captain the time for a last cruel lunge and a splitting of Harvell's body on the faster blade.

The hunchback had circled to the fireplace and now, his one yellow eye sparkling, he was making mewing sounds like an amorous tomcat. David felt his hands go damp and sweat pour out of his armpits and roll down his body. Harvell was showing clenched teeth and making painful efforts to fill his lungs.

"Ah!" suddenly shouted the captain in a great, almost unbelievable marching attack, his swirling sword blade producing multiple images before David's eyes. Harvell threw himself desperately to one side, cut over, banged against the enemy steel. The captain, with a powerful flip on Harvell's sword, sent his own swift blade into Harvell's left breast. Harvell screamed and lunged forward like a sleepwalker. The captain moved back, his booted heel hitting a wrinkled roll of loose canvas. He stumbled forward directly onto Harvell's still outstretched sword—which went through the captain's throat like a hot wire into butter. It came out behind his left ear.

Captain Gannon fell like a brick wall overturned. Harvell staggered down to one knee, holding a bloody hand over his chest.

"No!" shouted Lord Queensbury.

"By George!" said Jack.

There was for all of them a moment of awe and horror, ultimate consciousness, an instant of unbelief, before anyone moved. In David's mind—like a clock ticking—ran the lines of the poet Grenville:

> *Oh wearisome condition of humanity!*
> *Born under one law, to another bound;*
> *Vainly begot, and yet forbidden vanity,*
> *Created sick, commanded to be sound.*

He was aware someone was screaming like a woman in labor; it was the barber. Captain Gannon's seconds were lifting him up by the shoulders, the vibrating sword still firmly set in his throat. The barber-churgeon was dancing around them, shrilly screaming. "Don't pull it out, *don't* pull it out!"

David had a moment's glimpse of the weapon, like the antenna of a fearsome insect growing, so thin and deadly, from the throat of the Captain. Jack Bounty pulled on David's coat skirts, and bent down over Harvell, whose head had fallen over to his collarbone; his hand was soaked with blood where he held himself tight, clawing at the dark cloth.

Jack Bounty said, "He's caught a bad one in the brisket."

"Captain Gannon is dead or dying," David said, touching his cousin's face. "Right through the neck."

"That's *their* problem."

David slid a hand under Harvell's damp shirt and felt the small puncture to the left of the breastbone. It was not bleeding very much now. From his medical box he took two pads of linen, placed them gently over the tiny hole, and asked Harvell to hold them there.

"You can walk, can't you, Harve?"

Harvell nodded. He spoke with effort. "I hope he's satisfied."

"Who?" asked Jack, brushing his knees briskly with the palms of both hands.

"Captain Gannon and the prince."

David saw Harvell had no idea of the grotesque and terrible accident that had happened to Captain Gannon. He turned to Jack. "We must get Harve out of here. If Gannon is badly hurt or dead, Harve will be arrested for murder."

Lord Queensbury, his face green-yellow, his Adam's apple moving, was standing stiffly over them. "I beg of you, Doctor, to see to

Captain Gannon. He appears to have attained a sadly mortal wound."

The captain was stretched out, spread-eagle, on the canvas, the sword still erect in his throat. David bent down and saw the strong bleeding, the dark blood, the deadly position of the sword and where it came out behind the head.

He glanced up at the two seconds and the hunchback looking from one to the other. David held the captain's wrist, hunting a pulse. He pushed back an eyelid and looked up again, shaking his head.

"The sword severed the great main vein in the neck. Most likely cut the spinal column on its way through. Captain Gannon died of that and drowned almost at once from the condition of the lungs filling with blood. I regret this, gentlemen."

He said it as calmly as presenting a case to John Hunter at St. George's of some poor wretch dead of the throat-ail or the coughing sickness. He stood up and rubbed his fingers together. The seconds nodded grimly and Lord Queensbury said, "Would you have the kindness to remove the weapon?"

The barber started to say something and changed his mind.

David grasped the still-warm sword handle and plucked out the blade. The dead man's head fell to one side and the last of the air in his lungs escaped with a ghoulish sigh. The barber screamed again and someone slapped him very hard.

Jack had Harvell on his feet, his cloak on and his three-cornered hat placed on the back of his loosely shaking head.

"Better move," said Jack, "before the day gets much lighter."

David saw it was an early white morning. Between them they brought him down the stairs and into the interior of a waiting yellow coach.

Jack shouted out to the coachman: "Jermyn Street. Twenty-four. And don't go directly. Go by the way of the outskirts of town."

CHAPTER 5   In the candle-pricked gloom of Hunter's, there had been a dreadful ten minutes over the shape on the low table. John Hunter looked up from the work and snapped his wet fingers to attract David's attention. "I don't know. I don't know. Can you feel any pulse at all?"

"Very, very faint. A thin thread. Irregular. Now it is gone, sir."

"It's all over, I fear, Davey."

"You sewed the surface tissues up neatly."

"Aye, I did."

"The heart just stopped."

"It went so well, too. Death, what can it be? With all our inquiry it is in the end a fearful, clumsy step in the dark."

David held a bit of mirror to Harvell's nostrils. The smooth surface of the glass remained clear. John Hunter shook his head. "It weren't the cut. It weren't our handling. The shock to the system, I would say. Little is commonly understood of the condition of the person under operation. There is a nervous shock sets in that poisons, I am sure, the body. I have some notes somewhere. Aye, somewhere."

David covered the still, now indifferent, face of his cousin with the coarse gray cadaver sheet and began to wash up in the wooden basin by the side of the surgeon.

"Ye will tell the wife? And his friend Mr. Bounty?"

"I will, sir. I thank you for what you did. It was beyond mortal mend."

"How do we know, lad? It's just this poor Scot who failed with his clumsy hands. And not enough experiments. If I had had more of this practice . . . Aye, more."

"Good night, sir." David dried his fingers and went out into the hall, where jars of specimens stood around. Jack Bounty, wrapped in his cloak, was asleep on a black leather sofa, his cocked hat over his eyes to keep out the dim glow of a gutting candle set at his elbow. He came awake at David's footsteps and said in a husky voice, "Davey?"

"Jack."

"He rests with God now, eh?"

David nodded, too full to say more.

The mortal remains of Harvell Livingston were interred on a rainy morning in the old Moravian burying ground in Chelsea. It was the only spot that dared give his body space because of the still shrill disfavor of the prince. And the added fact that even the lead-encased casket was unpaid for. The Livingston chambers and art collection were being seized for unpaid debts.

They stood in the rain, a close cluster—David, Peg, Jack Bounty—
under the brown façade of the little church, and watched the rum-
red faces of the two gravediggers as they used shovels in the wet
clay over the casket. A thin parson wrapped in wet black robes proceeded to do a hasty job of committing the departed from this
world with a reading of a fragment from the Old Testament. No
one had informed the parson of what the late Harvell Livingston,
Esquire, had died of, and David, holding Peg up by her arm, was
amazed to hear:

> *"For he was cut off out of the land of the living;*
> *For the transgression of my people was he stricken."*

Peg was locked up, tied to her own thoughts, and David looked
across at Jack Bounty, standing red-faced and damp, his arms folded
across a huge military cape borrowed for the occasion.

> *"And he made his grave with the wicked,*
> *And with the rich in his death."*

David leaned over to Peg and said, "We can go now. It's about
done."

> *"Because he had done no violence,*
> *Neither was there any deceit in his mouth."*

Jack took out some coins from under his cape and gave one to
the gravediggers and some to the parson. David motioned the
hired hackney coach to come forward. Peg clung to David's arm.
"What was the parson saying? I didn't understand it."
"Something out of the Book of Prophets."
In the hackney Jack said, "Filthy weather. We need a shin of hot
beef and a few drams of gin."
Peg began to shake and shiver. David put his arm around her.
He felt for the first time an alien in this smoky stone city of yellow-
gray house fronts, of indifference to him and his hopes. The Sons
of Liberty were right. He was really a colonial and now he wanted
to go home. The lines from the Prophet's lament—in memory—
sang with the rain in his ears.

The people also shall be all righteous
They shall inherit the land forever
The branch of my planning, the work of my hands
That I may be glorified.
A little one shall become a thousand
And a small one a strong nation.

David felt Peg move closer, and he thought of the new problems he had acquired. Life was no longer all *materia medica.*

The once splendid St. James Street chambers of Harvell Livingston had been stripped by the moneylenders—two oily Greeks, a firm of dour Scots, and one fat Cockney, all usurers who plundered the flat of its art, its furniture, taking out even the silver doorknobs. The Adam desk, commodes, bureaus, and Chippendale chairs, the encoignures, the very nails that hung the small Hogarth oils. They ripped up the last dusty inch of the Ferghana *guli hinnai* carpet, took the tin kitchen dipper beside the Georgian Irish silver service, the dinner porcelains of Chelsea and Derby.

Mickle, the old *valet de chambre*, reporting on the household rape to David at the Brown Bear on Bow Street, said, "Everything is gone, sir, even the rat traps and the empty wine bottles. I tried to save a pair of silver candle sconces he gave me last year at Christmas, but everything went."

"You are owed wages, I believe."

"Eight months, sir," said Mickle, swallowing some cow heel and tripe. "And he borrowed ten gold guineas besides."

"I'll try and get a settlement from the family in America."

"I'll be living in Wapping, sir, with my brother. If you should need a valet, sir, I would be more than willing to serve."

"I much doubt the need, Mickle, doubt it very much. I'm returning to the colonies soon."

"I wouldn't care for it, sir. All those native red fellows, I mean."

David had no watch, but he heard the church clock near the King's Bench prison strike two. He walked to Peg's lodgings buried in thought.

Peg, in the big blue room, was bent over a large red leather trunk inspecting wrinkled female garments while the fat Lizzie Patch sat feeding a dish of bread and milk to Daniel. The child looked pale but alert.

"Uncle David," he said, a mouth full of soggy bread, "we're going to live out in the street."

"Stow yer bread and milk, lovie," said the nurse.

Peg slammed the trunk shut and faced David, arms on her slim hips. "Not only are we being put out in the streets, but Harvell didn't pay my tailors. They've seized my new wardrobe and what I have left I couldn't wear as a ballad monger in Cheapside. Not a thing left to take to the Three Blue Balls to pawn."

"I'm sure everything will work out," David said. "I could try to see Sir Francis Livingston's London agents."

"What will that do?"

"Sir Francis' factors and bankers in London might meet your obligations till he is ready to advance you passage money for young Dan and yourself to go to the colonies."

Peg gave David the close, searching look of a woman in doubt and said crisply to the maid, "Lizzie, take Daniel out to the park."

"He is still eating, marm."

"Don't let him play with the ragamuffins. And keep him away from the duck pond."

The child wiped his mouth on his sleeve. "May I stone the swans?"

"Not unless they hiss at you, lovie," said the nurse.

When the woman and child were gone, clattering down the stairs, Peg turned to David and made a mock low curtsey. "Have you any money, good sir?"

"None but what Mr. Hunter allows me for helping him in his work."

"How much have you right now?"

"Ten or twelve shillings. More or less."

Peg stopped pacing the worn wooden floor from which the Turkey carpet had lately been removed. She faced David very closely, searching his features as if wondering if he were jesting. "You mean to tell me, David Cortlandt, you never have more than a few shillings in your breeks?"

"I have little need for money."

"Can you borrow some, then?"

"I suppose Mr. Hunter would advance me a guinea or so."

"Or so! You can't even borrow big!"

She was angry at him and she just pushed David with both hands into a chair and knelt down facing him—looking, he thought, pretty and enraged, and suffering what John Hunter might call *systema nervosum maxime irritabile.*

"You're a colonial bumpkin, David, for all your damn medical knowledge. And no more belong in London than a black niggrah chief in all his colored feathers. You may be able to live flea-proud, like a dog in a barrel, but I need clothes, food, furnishings, a pleasant chamber. Any of that hinted at in your damned chirurgical writing?"

"Of course not."

"And I can't wait for a packet of guineas to get me to the colonies, or a letter to come. I'll be up before a judge in Old Bailey and in Bridewell by then."

"I'll go see the agents."

Peg's face was very close to his. The spleen and jaundice mood drained from her. "You don't understand, David. I am most desperate. Harmony left me only debts. The friends I had I have no longer. Most of them dropped us because of Harvell's wild excesses."

"I am your friend, Mistress Peggy. What do you suggest, as to your friend?"

"I know you are, dear boy." She took his hand in hers. "I know it deep in my heart. Yet as a pretty woman I can make other new friends. I can get money to take up my life the way I once lived it."

David looked at her, aware she was talking with some purpose of her own.

"I don't understand, Peg."

"You booby, I can be some noble's fancy woman. A toy like his favorite clouded cane, or a fine silver-hilted hanger."

David supposed he should have been more shocked. He was only upset and was driven to express himself before he could think the matter out too clearly. He blurted out: "But, Peggy, no!"

"Besides," Peg said calmly, "there is Daniel, you'll say. The heir of the Livingstons. The only heir now. It would not be seemly, would it?"

"No, of course not. You mustn't think of it."

"The true ways of the world, my dear David, are hard, and pleasant sentiments are for rich poets, for warm family beds safe from want and the threat of being turned out into the street—the way a chandler's shop on St. Martin's Lane turns his barrows of stuff out on the curb."

"I'll get what I can this afternoon." He rose from the chair and she stood with David and put her arms around him. Peg kissed him on the cheek and rubbed her face against his.

"Oh, David, you are my only true friend. I think of the dark river, of the peace in the old burying yard. And then I look at poor Daniel, and your kindness, and I say to myself, 'Do not give in to the distemper of despair. Not yet.'"

She smelled to David so much better than poor Bitsy the little housemaid, the only other kisses he had had in London. He stepped back, flushing at having such sensual thoughts about his late cousin's wife. Peg did not let go of him and her hand patted his strong, trembling throat and her voice was very low and very weary.

"I can't go on unless you help me. That is the plain truth of it."

He started to say something, felt he would say the wrong words, and stammered out, "You're a colonial now, Peggy. One of us."

"Yes, if you want me to be, dear David."

He pressed her hand hard and took up his hat.

When he was gone, Peg went to the empty bookcase, not worth reclaiming, and took out a stone bottle of Holland gin. She filled a small handleless cup and sat low in the chair, sipping it, staring into the empty fireplace. After a while, after the second cup, she felt better. At least the country cousin was earnest and touched. She kicked off her slippers and put her feet on the battered brass fire fender. Images and impressions floated through her mind. David Cortlandt dominated some of them, and Peg brought herself up sharply; she had assumed she knew just how far she wanted to go with him, yet that had always been her weakness since the age of twelve. She sighed. Involvement with a handsome male at the wrong time. It must not now destroy her plans for her son. She poured another gin.

David had no way to raise money. He was living on what John Hunter gave him for cataloguing the collection of scientific and odd items in the Hunter Museum. The orange bills of kingbirds, the backbones of monkeys, the fluted seashells from far places. He sat and pasted paper stickers onto items labeled in Latin, and entered them and a number in a ledger under the headings of *Animal, Mineral, Vegetable,* and *Unidentified.*

Jack Bounty was no help either. His luck at the faro tables was amazingly bad, but he hoped it was a sign "the law of averages" would "come around soon." Her fancy friends would have no more of them. New favorites, more exciting events, were going on in London.

After a fearful summer, cold winds brought the first taste of fall, then came the winter snow. David sat in his cold attic room, having sold whatever he had so Peg and Daniel and the nurse could have wood and coal for their plundered room. He was reading with very little scientific interest the London mortality figures for the year in the *Annual Register*. They seemed to fit his mood. "Colic & Gripe, 15 dead; Flux 9; Livergrown, 21; St. Anthony's Fire, 2." (The word fire made his chilled fingers colder.) He slapped his shoulders and tied tighter the old yellow wool scarf around his throat. "Thrush, 39; Water in the Head, 110." (Imagine the ignorant louts bunching everything they couldn't understand as Water in the Head.)

There was a solid tap on his door and he went and opened it. Two men bundled against the cold stood there, rubbing their red ears, their breath like animated lace in the cold passage.

"Thunder," said the very handsome tall one. "Colder than a snow-woman's dugs. I am Morris Manderscheid of Philadelphia. You know Botts, I believe."

The fat figure of Botts, sober and neat in potato-brown, held out a big hand.

"Yes, we know each other. Last few times we met I was a bit full of the grape."

"Yes, you were," said David. He pointed to his lumpy bed. "It's all the extra chairs I have."

Morris Manderscheid nodded and sat down, breathing on his mittened fingers. "Later we can go to an eating house and talk in more comfort. But just now this is the best place. No neighbors?"

"In the summer I have pigeons. They're all Cheapside meat pies now."

Botts nodded and looked over the mean room. "Mine isn't much better. Lad, you're well spoken of by Joseph Philipse of the Hudson River Philipses."

"I used to take him fishing up Yonkers way for shad in the spring."

Manderscheid put a hand on David's knee. "He's one of the Sons of Liberty. We trust you if he does. We are agents for the Sons working here in London."

"Botts has made no real secret of it."

"Aye. When in the power of the cup I prattle. But I've sworn off the grape till there is a liberty pole in every colonial village."

"Mr. Cortlandt," said the Philadelphian, "you can say you are with us, or you are not, before we go on."

"I'm a colonial. I've run errands for the Sons back home. I will not betray you. I approve of the aims of the colonists."

"Good. Now then, the times are coming to a climax. Things are in flux, settling into one side or the other. We are ready to use arms, if we need to, to gain our rights to decide things for ourselves. The Continental Congress sits on much that is as dangerous as gunpowder drying by a fire."

"What can be done from here?" asked David.

Botts put a thick finger to one side of his red nose and winked. "Our ships are busy. There is smuggling of much into our warehouses, known to the good citizens when it will be needed. Powder and ball, even brass cannon. But what we need now are what you can get us with your special knowledge and connections."

"Me? I've even sold my sword. My cape."

Manderscheid took a list from the inside of three waistcoats. "We shall need drugs, medical supplies of all kinds. Surgeon's tools. Manuals for the treatment of diseases and wounds. You follow me?"

"Yes. But you can buy them in any shop set up for their sale."

"No we can't—not in the huge amounts we need. Besides, we are followed. We want to do business with small, safe firms, or those with our viewpoint. We want deliveries to certain ships, in certain places, on certain nights, of harmless-looking boxes. We are in touch with the proper arms smugglers. But we need someone loyal with knowledge of what drugs, what instruments, what medical volumes. We have funds; at least some of us are using our own money. So we want to see it used for the proper stowage of the proper items for the colonies."

"I see your problems, Mr. Manderscheid."

"If you so desire, we will pay you for your connections with the medical trade," said Botts.

David said simply, "Sir, you insult me. But it's too cold to heat my blood. I shall serve the colonies without charge but what I lay out. I am without funds of any sort."

"Ah yes," said the Philadelphian. "I must get to Friday night services in an hour. Rabbi Pool is at the East End *schul* for the

Sabbath services. It is good to have you with us, David Cortlandt. We have two small ships due soon now at Portsmouth harbor. John Hancock of Boston arranged them for us. Only our own men are on board."

David looked up. "You can do me one favor. Transport to the colonies for the widow of an American and her small son in one of your ships when it sails."

The two Sons of Liberty looked at each other. Botts nodded. "I don't see why not. Boston please you? Now, let's get to a cook shop and at least have some hot mugs of tea. We'll manage to talk so no one knows of our business, now you know the main things we want."

David was pleased to get out of the cold room—the swirls of snow beginning to batter at the window and drift the hard white silt of its icy particles through the cracks.

"The British are stiffening their demands," said the Philadelphian on the stairs down. "General Gage has threatened to march out from Boston and seize the colonists' supplies. He has his spies out too, you know."

David asked, "You think there will be open warfare?"

Botts shook his wide bulk. "We have friends here. I'm for an open fight. We'd soon show them we mean business."

Manderscheid said, "A little boldness now could lead to settlement of the long disputes with the colonies. After all, we only wanted the right to run our own lives."

Botts added, "You'll come to our next meeting and hear the true facts."

It was late when David left the two members of the Sons of Liberty and walked to the lodgings of Peg and the boy. Peg had been out. David waited while Lizzie Patch put the boy to bed. Peg came in very late, her face made up, she wearing a pale blue costume, cut low in front. She smelled of wine, and grinned at him and snapped her fingers.

"Been waiting any length of time, lovie?" she asked, dropping a red cloak on the floor. Her costuming looked new.

"An hour or two. You've been out."

"How observing you Americans are! Yes, I managed to get some credit from a new dressmaker, and there was a chance to see the

new play at Covent. It's been a marvelous evening. Everyone asked
where I'd been."

"I'm pleased you've managed to get out, Peggy."

"Don't you want to know with *whom* I've been?"

David was too bursting with his own news. "I've arranged passage
for you and Daniel to Boston."

"Boston?" She sat down suddenly, giggled, and held her head in
her hands. "Oh, it was good to be out again and not stare at these
dismal walls. I'm a little blinky, of course. You said Boston?"

"There is a ship to New York from Boston. We'll go together.
You, I, and Daniel. You must be ready to leave on a few days'
notice."

"Really? I'm just beginning to live again. You're nice, David, but
you're full of duties and feeling. You spoil things."

He went over and took her hand in his and kissed it. "It's a new
life for us in the colonies and everything will be fine once you meet
Sir Francis."

"You think he'll ever accept me as his son's wife?"

"I'm sure of it."

"A fat lot Sir Francis Livingston will believe if he doesn't want
to."

In the gray moonlight of John Hunter's dissecting room the early
students had gone, after a short history of the major human bones.
John Hunter took out his square steel-rimmed spectacles and hung
them over his blue eyes as he stared at David re-hanging the exhibits.
"Get me quill and ink, Davey. I have something for ye."

From an inside pocket of his stained waistcoat, John Hunter took
out two enscrolled squares of paper.

"The College of Physicians sent over one. And when I sign the
other you're a master surgeon, as good as I've ever turned out."

David flushed and beamed a tight smile. "It's been a long time
coming, sir. And I feel without you, I'd never have made it."

"Aye, I've had to push ye up a step by the tail here and there."
The quill scratched his ragged signature across the paper. "I haven't
had the full education I should. But it's my legal full-blown signature. Don't disgrace it, Davey. Here, respect it."

David held the certificates in his hand. "Words are futile things,
sir—and I'm too old for tears of gratitude. Thank you for putting
up with me."

"You're a medical man and can wave the scalpel with any sawbones here or in the colonies. Raise ye the right hand. And repeat after me, *I swear by Apollo, the physician, and Aesculapius, and Health, and All-heal, and all the gods and goddesses, that according to my ability and judgment, I will keep this oath and this stipulation . . ."*

David repeated it in the echoing empty dissecting theater, in the dusty enclosure of its plaster walls, under the bird-soiled skylight, with the bones of long departed highwaymen attached as anatomy lessons to oak panels. David repeated the words of the great oath seriously and slowly, feeling the emotion the ancient ritual brought to him. Word by word he heard John Hunter go on, and he repeated it section by section—close to tears, aware he was leaving the protecting shelter of this great man.

"With purity and with holiness I will pass my life and practice my art. Into whatever houses I enter, I will go into them for the benefit of the sick and will abstain from every voluntary act of mischief and corruption." They embraced in the clumsy manner of men.

A month later, the secret meeting of the Sons of Liberty was held in a large back room of a warehouse below Black Friars Bridge. David smelled the vast tuns of tobacco leaf stored there. Benches had been pushed together and when David arrived after giving the password—"The Tyranny of Kings"—the air of the place was thick with the smoke of clay pipes. Some twenty men were present. Botts was up front in a large blue coat with brass buttons, Morris Manderscheid was busy writing on a paper placed on a crate under an oil lamp that was attracting many moths.

A white-haired middle-aged man with regular features wrinkling prematurely and blue eyes, was thumbing through a pile of newspapers. Botts rose and said in his blustery, husky voice: "I want you to meet Abner Hightower of North Carolina, who organized the Regulators down there. He has just debarked from a ship from the colonies. He brings us amazing news."

Standing on a stool, Abner Hightower had the smile of a man who was content with his news; only the busy movement of his hands showed David his taut inner excitement. David sat among men in journeymen's dress, some with the inky thumbprints of their trade. Others were men with gentlemen's dress, carrying swords, and also men in snuff-yellow who had the appearance of lawyers. And one mahogany-colored man who could be only a seaman of rank, a red

kerchief around his throat, a blackwood cane topped in silver in his
weathered fist.

Abner Hightower spoke up in a clear, slightly slurred, voice. "The
Committees of Correspondence under Sam Adams of Boston have
been issuing reports that show the thinking of the Caucus Club
there has lit a flame in the colonies that can not be put out by what
is to us all a foreign *directoire*."

There were cheers and someone shouted: "Hear! Hear!"

The speaker held up a newspaper. "I have here the *Boston Gazette*,
which states, and I read: 'Unless the patriots' liberties are immediately restored, we are determined to become an independent nation!'"

There was more cheering. Hightower lifted an arm to stop them.
"We all know that his mother said to the present royal head: 'George,
be king!' And we know he has tried too hard to be. They have
tried to make us pay tax on their tea, but we have been smuggling
in our own tea from Holland. John Hancock, whose vessels are so
employed, has said, '*This* is imperial browbeating, and the blood of
our forefathers demands resistance to this new outrage.' Three tea
ships came to Boston, and fifty Sons of Liberty, dressed as feathered
savages, dumped the tea into the harbor. The Port of Boston has
been closed. It must be opened!"

David listened to what this man was uttering in a tone of violence.
He felt hard breathing around him.

Standing on his stool, Hightower went on. "The first Continental
Congress has been in session since September. Patrick Henry stood
up and said, 'I am not a Virginian but an American!' Stood there
in Carpenters' Hall in Philadelphia and spoke for all of us. The demands of the delegates were direct. I was there and I heard it myself.
No restrictions by the administrators of the Crown. All closed ports
to be opened. The British army of occupation to be shipped home
to England. . . . All objectionable laws to be immediately repealed."

They had to be told not to cheer so loudly. Hightower held
other papers in his hand. "These are the Suffolk Resolutions that
have gone to all the colonies. Some say they are an invitation to
armed resistance. I will not foolishly say they aren't. They are! And
more! They proclaim the independence of the Commonwealth of
Massachusetts. They deny the jurisdiction of the king's agents and
of the king himself!"

There was no cheering now, only the sudden intake of breaths at these daring and shocking resolutions. A mutter of undertalk passed among bench sitters.

"Jurors and constables who obey the king's justice will find themselves hanged. Every town is to raise up a militia. Those that say this is sedition are right! Colonel Washington of Virginia said, 'Blood will be spilled!' And I heard him."

That made them cheer again.

"The natural rights of men call for final action. The Continental Congress before adjourning was written a Declaration of Rights. It repudiates England's colonial jurisdiction. The men of that Congress have said it: we must fight!"

They were all standing, mouths open. Botts was on his feet speaking: "The Continental Association has been organized to stop the buying of all British goods, the importing of anything at all from Britain. We here and now are disbanding our organization in London. We can do no more here. Only certain vital supplies to aid our fight will leave on the last ship we shall load here. Three cheers for the Continental Congress! And to hell with King George!"

They were given with a will. David found Morris Manderscheid at his elbow. "Strong talk. Colonel Washington is right. It will not be an easy victory. Can you get the last of the cargo you have been assembling for us ready in four days?"

"Most of it."

"Good. It must be on the ship *Bear* at Portsmouth harbor on the morning of Thursday. Will you sail with the ship?"

"You are not coming, Mr. Manderscheid?"

"I go to Paris for Dr. Franklin. But I have arranged for the lady and child to embark with you on the *Bear*."

"Thank you, sir."

"May we face each other in a new nation, David."

The meeting had broken up into groups of excited, gesturing men.

CHAPTER 6   After weeks of hard work collecting the secret supplies, there was now in David a feeling of smuggler's pride and a sense of destiny. He, in his small way, was fighting for a good cause.

It might only be the procuring of packets of tincture of opium, or cases of fine steel surgeons' instruments from Amsterdam, but it all added up to aid for those who would soon have to fight with more than brave words. David had always suspected that oratory was the most fraudulent of talents, yet the fervent speakers at the secret meeting had stirred him.

Smuggling was so plain and to the point; neither subtle, suave, nor tortuous. David was no fool. He knew there were those who saw the scheming as only a plan by certain American merchants and smugglers to break free of tax controls. That was true, but only part of it. The Americans *were* a people, and the constant presence of stiff-laced royal governors, of binding unprogressive controls, gave the colonial journeyman and squire a feeling of pressures and controls not in keeping with the open horizons, the green wilderness, behind the coastlines of the long continental shores. No wonder some Americans packed up their pots and gear, put a long rifle on their shoulders, and went out to Kentuck' and Ohio, and beyond, able to feel free only in the dangerous Indian lands.

Peg had at last promised David to be packed and ready for a ship journey. The coach for Portsmouth would be leaving the Blue Bell Inn yard in the morning, two days before the sailing of the ship *Bear* for the colonies.

"I shall be seasick," she told David while Lizzie Patch packed the two trunks, the three leather carry-alls, the hatboxes Peg would be permitted as baggage. "I vomit when I cross the Thames in a wherry."

"I'll be here with a hackney coach at dawn to take us all to the Blue Bell." He smiled at Daniel. "Better be prepared for a pirate attack. How does the foot feel, boy?"

"It feels good. I will see the savages—the red ones?"

"Boo," said the nurse. "It's not glad I am to be sailin'. Not pirates I fear—I kin handle anything in breeks—but they do say the rats on a ship are *that* bold they carry off your shoes in the night."

"But not you, Lizzie. Never get you off the deck."

"I'll miss the Hockley-In-The-Hole taproom."

David smiled at Peg. "We're going at last."

"So it seems. You'll join Jack Bounty and myself for dinner tonight at the Duke of Marlborough's Head. I'm going to miss everything in London the devil of a lot."

"I'll see how my last hospital rounds go."

David felt the proper worldly man as he hurried down the stairs into his last few journeys through the smoky, dirty city—this London with its crowding, hustling bodies, the smell of river and horse life, the neat green squares and the dignified Georgian façades.

Greenwich, Deptford, Woolwich, Lee—he had seen it all as a young medical man, a city alive and kicking, sick and smelling. He suddenly understood Peg's nostalgia for it, her reluctance to leave. There might be ease and comfort across the seas, but this old and new, gilt and eroding city and its bridges that laced the muddy river had a flavor and a style that captured one's loyalty to it for all its bulldogged countenances of parishioners and rakes.

It was late in the afternoon that Botts, of the Sons of Liberty, found David washing up in the cellar of St. George's Infirmary. Botts was dressed in rough gray woolens against the cold, a red scarf across his throat and his battered three-cornered hat tied down against a rising wind. The crimson carbuncles furbelowed on his well-spread nose glowed like rubies.

"Have you had a sense these last few days of being followed, Dr. Cortlandt?"

"I haven't had time to notice. I've been making my last hospital rounds."

Botts rubbed his unshaved chin. "Some loyalist understrappers have crept in among us Sons, we fear. The *Bear* is going to stand off Portsmouth, with a lighter at Pingill's Wharf ready to carry you and your party on board. But it seems better you separate."

"But why?"

"You'll be carrying that last chest of medical supplies—three hundred pounds of gold coin they cost us—besides that trunk of surgeons' instruments. It seems safer you hire a fast private chaise."

"Damn it, Botts, this is all play-acting."

Botts grinned and unloosened his jacket and tenderly pulled aside his dirty shirt. Bloody bandages ran from his right shoulder down his side. "Efaith, Doctor, somebody has been very interested in us. I surprised some swabber looking for our secret papers in that tobacco warehouse."

"Who treated you?"

"Never you mind the wound. It's just a bullet through me fleshy parts. We dropped the niggardly whore's son's body into the river last night, weighted with a bag of stones. So you see it's not at all play-acting."

"You think it's safe to send the women and boy to the ship alone?"

"Yes. We don't think they know anything about that part of our plans. The Sons' meetings had no part in that scheming. But let them go by common coach. And you in a fast chaise three hours later, innocent as a smock-faced parson."

David rolled down his sleeves and shook his head. "How can things come to this? I'd better go see Peg, and . . ."

"No," said Botts firmly. "Write her. I'll take it to her. Say you will join them at Portsmouth, on Pingill's Wharf. We shall have a man there. That's all. Write just that. Nothing else."

David wrote, and Botts read it and put it inside his jacket. "Now, go off to get your two boxes. We'll have a chaise at nine for you outside the Dog and Duck, with a trusted driver."

"I have my own baggage and instrument cases and medical jars. I've managed to buy back my own medical box, or John Hunter did for me."

"The chaise will hold four large chests." Botts took out a heavy flintlock pistol and handed it to David. "Take this. It has two barrels, two triggers. It now carries balls that will stop anything human you'll meet on this earth. You have your papers, the money?"

"Everything Mr. Manderscheid turned over to me."

"You have no predeliction against killing a man—in the non-medical sense?"

David laughed. "I'm not delicate about it."

Botts nodded. "It's going to be a wild night and cold. What I'd give for a pint of the best brandy! Well, there's no good cause and bad habit that go together. We must get drunk in the colonies sometime, in the Coach and Horses on Wall Street."

"I know the place," David said, shaking the big man's hand.

"They make a fine suet, marrow, and raisin pudding."

Botts pulled up the scarf around his neck and went out. David sat down on a stool and stared at the heavy pistol in his hand. He peered around the under-lit hospital cellar with its flaking walls. It looked about as usual. He would never, after four years of its dirty intimacy, see it again.

David had said his good-bys to the Hunters, Mrs. Hunter wet-eyed and Miss Hunter a little coltish and shrill. John Hunter was stern and tight-lipped. For the first time, he appeared to David old and tired. As a last gift, he gave David one of his wooden tubes for listening to heartbeats and lung action.

"Partings are foolish times, Davey. We sigh over our passage through life, saying as ye know: time flies. But time stays, laddie. It's *we* who are flying."

David got soft and sentimental. Bitsy, the little housemaid, had one of her colds, but she snuffed back tears when David gave her a gold coin—a very small one—and best wishes for a good and long life. The two porters who were to carry his own boxes, well tied with ropes, were on the stairs, and he followed them down and out and across town to the Dog and Duck. Good-by, Jermyn Street. Good-by, youth.

David had once removed a large infected tooth for the innkeeper of the Dog and Duck, so he was well known there. The smoldering inn fire revealed the usual half dozen drinkers, spitters, smokers, and a casual liar boasting of some feat of studship or horse race; David was too keyed up to listen with much care this windy, chilly night.

The inn owner told David to put his boxes in the buttery and David paid off the porters and made sure the other two chests for the Sons of Liberty were already there. They were made of heavy walnut wood and held with leather straps and brass bands. David had no papers or bills of sale. He wouldn't want the watch or the coastal revenue officer to see their contents. Pure—and rare—drugs and such fine surgeons' tools were hard to come by in the colonies.

Near morning David came awake stiff and with pain in his knee joints. A wan sun—humble as a beggar, he thought—came through the unwashed square of leaded glass, showing off the unswept inn floor and its streaked blue walls.

After he had eaten and sucked up tea with rum, his nerves began to bother him. He stood in the doorway in his three-tiered cape, his fairly good boots polished, the tricorner jammed down over his own clubbed hair. The innkeeper saw an earnest, very large, handsome young man who kept feeling in his right flap pocket where the deadly shape of a double-barreled pistol rested. Nat never questioned a gent carrying a loaded hog-leg.

The two-horse chaise was ten minutes early, driven by a shiny black Negro muffled in a violet-colored traveling cloak with a high standing collar, a red woolen seaman's cap anchored to his head by a yellow-brown scarf that ended up by being wound around his throat and shoulders. One hand held a slim and elegant whip that waved in the wind and the first silvery rain.

The Negro's accent was as sharply English as that of a Grenadier Guards officer.

"Dr. Cortlandt? Caesar Paxon at your service."

David remembered certain orders. "How is the weather this morning?"

The Negro looked at the windy, rainy day and said with a grin, showing huge, very white teeth, "Mr. Botts says it is a *most* fine day for it."

"Good. Come in and help me with the chests. Will you have room for them? They're large."

"Plenty of room under the leather cover out back, Doctor."

It was a matter of minutes to get the boxes and chests into the back of the chaise and tied under the heavy weather hood up back. The rain, hard as nails, beat into the street. Nat waved to them as Caesar cracked the whip and the two shaggy but powerful-looking horses started off down the storm-beaten street. Reflections of houses filled the pools between the cobbles. David looked around but saw nothing that could seem out of place. He turtled his head down into the cape, his hands deep in his pockets, chilled fingers on the walnut butt of the pistol.

At nightfall, muddy and soaked, they were in Fareham, Caesar having decided not to take the direct road into Portsmouth. The harsh rain had fallen away to a steady silver lisp and the puddles had calmed but for the rippling vibrations that scummed their surfaces when the cold wind swooped low. The chaise smelled of wet wool and tired horses. The bobbling village lamps made an ache in David's nodding head.

Soon they could hear the bumble and crash of the sea and the running tide bang into the bay. They came skidding down stone streets and saw a fringe of masts, a tangle of ropes, the spider webbings of rigging. Caesar drove as if he knew the town and its alleys well.

"You think the coach got through, the one with Mrs. Livingston and the boy?"

"Don't see why not, Doctor. They had six horses, and three hours' start. Your pistol loaded?"

"Yes, I hope the priming powder is dry in the pan."

"I hope we won't have to find out. Just remember, if we have to run for it—it's a hanging matter."

"Thank you, Caesar."

They were clattering down to the wharves and David saw the swinging of a lighted lantern in the drizzle, a butterfly of orange in the blue black night. The wheels of the chaise hit a wooden roadway and the hooves of the horses pounded with a hollow thudding sound as the chaise ran out onto a pier. The geometry of masts and spars appeared ahead. David was stiff of limb as he swung himself down from the chaise. A burly seaman in short white canvas trousers appeared. He was carrying a horn light and a club.

Caesar said, "The tide is fast tonight."

The sailor answered, "Aye. Fast for liberty. This the gentry with the boxes?"

David rubbed his freezing hands together. "The women and the boy get aboard?"

"Shipshape and in their cabin. We're piping up the anchor, soon as you're stowed on board. We go by tender to the ship. Wind north by northeast."

There were other sailors to unlace the leather boot behind the chaise and the boxes were soon disappearing into the blue gloom that led down toward a low boat in the water. A sailor was leading David onto slippery planks, and he smelled the odor of ports: tar, bilge, rope and wet wood, the mixed mush of old cargoes, the muddy tide gurgling under the pier.

The harbor was packed with dark shapes of shipping, and men were climbing down into the tender with his boxes. David found himself seated in the boat and four sailors went to work moving their oars in crab-like gestures over the dark bay waters.

In half an hour they were bumping against the weedy hull of a ship. The rising day showed her to be green-streaked and unpainted but looking sturdy enough. The sea roll was worse; white crests creeping over the tidal waves. David's boxes were snaked up with lashed lines, and he himself came on board hand over hand on a rope ladder sparsely set with slippery wooden rungs. A smart-looking young man, mackerel-jawed, badly in need of a shave, held out a hand and asked, "Dr. Cortlandt? Captain Rodger. Pardon my lack of ceremony."

The young captain turned to the sailor who had put down his

club. "Mr. Chase, you will walk up the anchor and get the top main-
sails on her."

"Aye, sir."

There was activity as sailors in a motley arrangement of sea gear
and peacoats, some under tarred hats, walked the windlass that
brought up the muck-dripping anchor. David could see the land slant
away as the waves rose and fell and punched at the plants of the
Bear.

He was led to the captain's cabin and sat there drinking as hot a
cup of tea flavored with rum as he had ever swallowed. The ship was
heeled over and running before a sharp, snapping wind that cracked
the sails like gunshots.

"We're delayed, Doctor, but we're running down the Channel
and I think we can outrace anything but their fastest cutters. I want
to get out beyond the light off St. Alban's Head and Weymouth. If
we slip past there I'll pretty much guarantee our safety, once we show
our stern to the Lizard Head."

"Could I see my people, Captain?"

"They were most tired last night. But should be rested now. I'll
get the cabin boy to chart the way for you. We've bales lashed everywhere." The captain put his head out of the door and shouted
"Ben!"

A very dirty boy with a wet red nose appeared carrying a tray of
tin cups and pipkins.

"Show the doctor to the passengers' cabin."

"Aye, sir."

David knocked on the door pointed out to him after following the
cabin boy past a narrow, crowded passage and ducking a swinging
lamp. There was no answer. He knocked again. He turned the door
handle and found himself in a narrow yellow cabin with two wall
settees guarded by a low brass railing. The child Daniel was asleep
in one, wrapped in a red wool knitted shawl. In the other he faced
a wide back and spreading woolen rump. The ship shifted as a blast
of wind caught its sails and the bulk turned and David saw the green-
gray face of Lizzie Patch the nurse. She moaned, fluttered her large
lips, then gasped and groaned.

"Holy Mary, I'm a dyin'!"

David went over and shook her. "Where is Mistress Livingston?"

The wretched nurse opened her bloodshot eyes and groaned again.

"You, sir?"

"Where is your mistress?"

"I'm dyin', that I am. I want to pray for me soul."

"It's just a touch of seasickness."

"Just!"

The fat nurse retched, and dug splayed fingers into her great bosom. When she withdrew her hand it held a warm and crumpled letter.

David tore open the red wax seal and held onto a railing that ran hip-high around the small cabin. The weighted lamp in the ceiling swung, turning to deep upright no matter which way the ship dipped.

Peg's almost childish scrawl spread across the sheet of paper he held to the dim yellow glow of lamp flame. The words began to focus on his understanding and register in his eyes.

Good Friend David,

I have bean two ways about going out to the colonies & I take pen to hand to say I have decided against the matter. I entrust Dan'el to yr. care nooing full well you wil deliver him to his father's family & that you will see his rights are fully respect'd for which he is. I enclose all papers pertaining to the marriage & his birth record. Rite me of yr. safe arrival in care of Drury Lane Theatre. I have decided to go back to the stage. Lord Gibney has been most attentive & I am giving up these retch'd chambers [the nurse began to choke in dismal rolling sounds] and take better ones. So it would be best not to rite me there. Keep my Dan'el and God see you both safe. Goodie Patch's wage is five shilling a week. [Daniel was up and weeping.]

Yr. most obdt. & grateful friend & servant,
Peg Munday, the late Mrs. Livingston.

"Davey, I's so sick," said the child.

David folded the letter and thrust it into a pocket. The nurse was being very ill in a revolting manner. He picked up the boy and, wrapping him tighter in the shawl, took him out of the cabin as the nurse fell like a stone, lamenting and choking, from her settee.

On the tilting deck the day was turning penny-bright, and gleaming highlights were pin-pointing cliffs and flag standards and edges of houses fast being left far behind. The ship was moving past the Lise of Eight, the steersman said. The crackle of the taut canvas overhead, the creak of cordage, and joggle of masts in their stops all pointed to a fast ship moving properly under skilled hands. The sailor at the wheel stood motionless, moving a spoke of the tiller from time to time.

Daniel put his thin arms around David's neck. "Ridee?"

"Yes, a long ride."

"Mummee not coming?"

"No, not coming. Uncle David will take care of you, Dan."

"I love Davey."

The pale, shivering child kissed his cheek and David held the thin body close to him, and looked back at the spinning sea spume of their passage. The diving gulls in a shrill geeking were darting in at the fanrail. Far off, growing dimmer, were the green and chalk-colored shores of England, as Captain Rodger beat out of sight of land as fast as he could. As it fell away, color drained from the jutting cliffs.

David felt alert and torn by mixed emotions. A large part of him had tried to escape and was now safely back inside his chest and body. It would feel hollow for some time. He knew the reputation of Lord Gibney.

The faint smudge of land was gone now in the fog and heat haze of early day. The vessel heeled further over, harried by a rising wind. A kind of fury and unreason held David, a thing engendered by a sense of pride in being something many were so proud to be—an American. His heart thumped like a trout on a dry shore.

The child, too, was warming into the day, close-held to David. His cape was fluttering in the wind. David looked up at masts rattling in the crisp breeze smelling of salt.

He thought of a poem he had read lately:

> To see the world in a grain of sand,
> And a heaven in a wild flower,
> Hold infinity in the palm of your hand,
> And eternity in an hour.

The child whimpered: "I's hungry."

"We'll see."

As they crossed the deck David looked up again at the masts. There was as yet no flag.

BOOK II

New York

CHAPTER 7   Mynheer Peter Schuyler and his wife Anita were giving a ball at their spacious stone mansion on the Hudson. Their estate was set in locust, elm, and oak between the villages of Yonkers and Tarrytown. A house moored under its copper and slate roofs in a green salad of river shrubs and emerald tufted lawns that reached its Dutch stoeps above well-worked farm fields. Though the prominent Schuyler family held no patroonship (its great landholdings were to the north, at Poughkeepsie and Albany), Mynheer's estate was often pointed out as what a patroon's holdings could be and usually were not. Now the dusk had come, to the sound of harpsichord, flute, and strings, and fireflies signaled to each other across the rose garden and through the orchards of pear and peach and apple. In the outbuildings, set well back from the house, the cattle and barnyard stock were settling for the night, indifferent to the varnished carriages full of peruked and spencered gentry coming up the blue stone drive between the gate lamps. The bustling mutter of low Dutch and Yankee oaths was coming from the kitchen out back. The house slaves sweated and panted over the great barrels of oysters. Lobsters were hissing on the red-hot coals. The brick ovens steaming with the basted bodies of turkeys, grouse, meadow-hens, chickens, and three huge geese. In the clay yard-ovens bread was baking, and two thin little Negro children were watching a vast iron kettle of boiling water and seaweed steam its load of Sandy Hook blacknose clams and Blue Point crabs.

"The beef! The beef!" screamed Helga, the Dutch cook of ample girth, and she banged an iron spoon on the wool of Maxon, the vegetable garden slave. She ran to pry open an oven door in the huge brick kitchen, pulled open with fingers that she burned and then sucked. A special tidbit of spiced beef held her attention before she pushed it back into the belly of the oven.

"Mit the black ones who can cook, who can prepare?"

On the main fireplace a whole side of beef was turning, and two huge dogs ran inside a wire wheel off to one side to keep the beef revolving on its smoke jack. On tables the salads and pickled delights stood and the soup tureens were out. A dozen flitting slaves ran about and dodged the heavy iron spoon with which Helga kept order and sped the progress of the party's preparations. She was so wide that a special oak chair had been built for her, and she sank into it from time to time and fanned her really remarkable breasts with a fat hand while a little Negro girl, her wool tied up in hex knots, handed her a tankard of newly brewed beer.

"The *reken* books—the account books—are all mixed. The gentry is already coming and the fish sauce not seasoned yet. Maxon! Max you loafer, is the wine come up? I need a bottle for the sauce."

Maxon ducked back out of spoon range behind a mound of lettuce and small pale green gherkins from the hothouse beds. "Nero, he go fer it, Missy Cook. He go."

An explosion from the smaller fireplace turned Helga into an animated bundle of flesh and she rushed to the black soup pot on its pothook, lifting the lid with a long fork, already aware it needed just a pint of sack wine.

All the cooking was done on open fireplaces or ovens built into either side of the fireplace. Cobirons and firedogs with latten brass fittings were the supports of Helga's art.

Far down the river there was the firing of a cannon. Maxon said, "Must be the royal governor on a man-of-war celebrating something."

The slaves looked at each other with the big shiny eyes of some secret satisfaction. White folk was havin' a heap of trouble among themself; up near Boston way there had been killin' and the town was playing fox and hound, with the Gener'l Howe playing B'er Fox and colonial militia playing B'er Hound.

Mynheer Peter Schuyler was sixty-eight. He was a powerful man with a large paunch and little hair left under his great tie-wig. He was pink-faced, round-cheeked, with a hawk nose under little blue eyes. He stood in his embroidered satin dressing gown, smoking while Tim, his crook-backed old valet, brushed the jabot lace into place on a well-cut coat he had just taken from a disordered wardrobe.

"You are late, Mynheer. The carriages are already arriving."

"*Dunner*-damn." Mynheer put down the long clay churchwarden pipe he was smoking and allowed himself to be disrobed and the jacket and lace fitted around his round form. As soon as he could he put the pipe back into his mouth. It was the vice of his old age, this greedy slavery to a good cured dark Virginia leaf. In clouds of pungent smoke he permitted Tim to readjust his wig, load him with a huge watch in his waistcoat pocket, and at last push low-cut shoes with fine paste buckles on his gouty legs.

"I hate these balls and their quadrilles, Tim. I'd rather play cards or sit on the front piazza and count the boats. I'm getting old. Life isn't worth holding on to—but health is."

"Old Martha she want to see you, massa."

Mynheer's face showed ambiguous, contradictory emotions. "What a night she picked for it." He put down the pipe and admired himself by the spermaceti candles reflected in the pier glass from Venice his great grandmother had brought back in one of her ships. A fine figure of a man yet, he decided, with the good Schuyler stomach, the Schuyler color, all raised on the Schuyler landholdings on the river and back on the creeks. The last items caused a frown to break in on his good nature as he thought of the future. He had little use for his son Culbly—at thirty still law-courting, whoremongering in New York, running with the horse breeders, cock fighters, mixing with French dancing masters to the tune of violins and tambours, and the friend of British rakes sent in exile to the colonies. And the nephew Homer, two years younger, mixed up with that rebel rabble of barn burners and tar-and-featherers, talking of a commission in the crazy mob the Continental Congress was calling an army of rebellion. It was enough to make a man tear out his few remaining hairs. He had Tim refill a fresh pipe. Flicking the lace of his ruff and admiring his stout, not too puffy, legs in yellow silk stockings, he went to visit his mother.

The Schuyler mansion had been built seventy-five years before of good honest native stone. A splendid gray-green granite older than history. Mynheer admired the mansion. Philipse Manor was very fine and its plantation well worked, but together not as fine as his holdings. Cornelia Schuyler, the other important branch of the family, had inherited seven thousand acres and added thirteen hundred more; true, but her son Philip was already committed to the Continentals, while Mynheer's own was still merely talking sides.

He had a proud mind, full of names. Perhaps going to see his mother brought them all to the front. The Schuylers were related to *everybody*, everybody that *mattered*. The Van Schlichthorsts, Der Dorcks, Van Rensselaers, Van Braams, Van der Lyns. He caught himself and smiled at this pride in good Dutch names. Below in the hall and entry he could hear the noise of the ball being prepared, the first guests arriving. "No early guests are important," Mama had told him often. And when Mynheer was young and had been most foolish, she had added: "Peter, no one should mind responsibility. You have only to do what seems proper to a Schuyler, and if it turns out badly, it is the fault of nature for not having made you clever. Never be a *verklickker*—tale bearer—and remember always to walk with your shoulders back. You have a strong spine—use it."

Those were the years of calm before Lexington and Concord, and when the river was still so Dutch. Shrovetide was a time to go spaking the girls, and the burgomaster permitted riding the goose, and there were cocking mains in the yard behind the spring and ice house.

The mood of nostalgia was broken by fragile feminine sounds below and the smell of pomatum on fresh-done hair, the odor of fox-gold and marigold from the gardens. The music makers in the ball-room were tuning up, and the house slaves ran about as they always did at a party almost beyond their control.

Mynheer felt young in heart and adjusted in his mouth the set of carved seahorse teeth that Dr. Matzer had fitted him with two months before in New York. "The best hippopotamus ivory, Mynheer," he had said, and they felt too large for weeks. Now he accepted them in public, even if he could not accept the new times. It had taken the Schuyler mansion several generations to accept the English, and now it would have, perhaps, to adapt itself to another change. This house of great oak beams cut on the land, of home-slacked lime and solid brick kilned in their own yard. It was spacious, cool; and, in several thrifty yet well-living Schuyler generations, imports from London, Amsterdam, Paris, Rome (and even from China) had filled it with treasures.

Mynheer stopped to watch the bustle below, then hurried in a cloud of good tobacco smoke along the upper gallery. He passed the blackening portraits in oil of his ancestors. All those Rudolphus, Uldricks, and Fredericks. Their taste in art had been simple and uneducated. Most of the pictures were large, but of little value, he had been told. But here and there was quality—a Copley painting of Anita, Mynheer's wife, painted when she was still a Philipse. And some really fine Italian primitives so dark under their skins of aged varnish that little was exposed to the passing eye. Outside of his mother's room were hung two Rembrandts, "Uncle Nicki" and "Aunt Fredka": so several generations of Schuylers had called them. No one could actually identify them. Some Schuyler had bought them with a small Titian and a Rubens' orgy while making the Grand Tour in 1713. He had shipped them home, dying himself in the notorious epidemic of plague in Lisbon the following year. He was the only Schuyler who ever had an eye for art, and during his short time as head of the family, Mynheer remembered, he was the only Schuyler who did not add any major acreage to the family holdings.

Mynheer knocked once and turned the silver doorknob. He went with wary toes into a large square room overlooking the river and the row of elms that followed a steep path down to the boathouse. It was a dark, olive-green room, lit only by silver candle sconces on the wall. There was the great bed with its valance and tester and hood of cochineal red blocked linen, a wide low chair, and Martha Schuyler at eighty-eight staring up at her son. A little yellow maid was putting morocco shoes on her.

Martha was short, wide, with a brown wig covered by a lace cambric cap. She had sunken cheeks in a mouth lacking most of its teeth, yellow-green eyes that seemed to glow in the semi-dark, and a hooked nose of old age that appeared to have taken on a wild growth of its own. Mynheer didn't remember Mama having such a nose when he was a boy and she dressed in dove-colored tabby cloth. Her hands, short-fingered, ringed with jeweled and gemmed bands, were dry and wrinkled, but firm around a gold-topped cane. She wore a dark brocaded nankeen dress.

She looked up and peered in his direction. Her eyes had been failing for thirty years, but the slaves said she saw what she wanted to see. "It's you, you lummox?"

"You're looking well, Mama."

"A man close to seventy calling an old woman Mama. I want to *blakkernye—*"

"You're disturbed by this ball? But we have to have it. It's a yearly ritual with the Schuylers."

"I'm coming down. It's my last ball. I'll not miss it."

"You've said that for twenty years."

She grinned and lifted her cane and knocked the smoking pipe from his hand. It broke and fell onto a yellow and blue rug from Arabia. The little yellow maid came forward quickly and swept it all up into a silver dust-catcher.

"Smoke coming out of the nose, fire dropped all over the house. Men and their nasty habits. A *huysvrouw* has a lot to take."

"I must go down, guests are arriving."

"Sit down, Peter." Martha motioned to a chair opposite her and sighed. "I don't know what will happen to you all when I am gone."

"You'll be here a long, long time, Mama."

"It isn't amusing any more when you're old, so old. The head pounds like a fulling mill. How is your gout?"

"Nothing, nothing at all. I've got my dancing pumps on."

"No fool like an aging one. Now listen, Peter. Things will get much worse. What plans are you making for the safety of the family? The farms, the Rensselaer silver and my jewels?"

Mynheer pulled on his waistcoat and smiled. "There is no danger. The royal commissioners when they come from London will blow this rebel collection of fools off the earth in a few weeks. There will be no fighting around here on the Hudson."

The old woman closed her eyes and sighed. When she opened them again she looked sternly at her elderly son. "Don't take sides. Don't favor one side over the other. A good lover loves the fields. In this fight have a foot in each bed."

"I don't understand. We're loyal subjects of the king."

"Loyal, fiddlesticks! Those Hanoverian pig-eaters from some German sty! You call *them* kings. They can fool the Britons they have a royal house—not me. In this world guilders and stuyvers count."

"Mama don't talk so. It's dangerous these days. Van Hoolen's farm was burned only last week. And all he said was that apprentices were using the trouble to escape their work to go dancing away to meetings."

"Peter, divide the house. Let a son support the king, the nephew the Continental Congress."

"I'm shocked, Mama."

"You were always dense, Peter—and yet a good son, but not too much given to thinking. And with your looks and figure—or what they once were—who could blame you? You do as I say. So whichever side wins, the Schuyler property remains in the end. The loser can go to the devil. The winner carries on in the Schuyler way. We belong here, dead or alive, on the river. The Domine Everardus Bogardus will bury us on its banks, so we can guard it even when dead."

"Your sentiments shock me, Mama."

"Sentiments are for fools and poets, for Sam Adams and fanatics like him. I believe in the family, the land, and a respectable sin-punishing God. The rest is nothing but talk. Philosophers, politicians, and dreamers—they make all the trouble in the world. Moka, my blue lace scarf and bring me my jewel case. Diamonds, the yellow Schuyler diamonds tonight. Go, Peter, and check the wine. And remember what I told you. Sit two horses at once, and don't change buttocks in midstream. Moka, help me up."

The little yellow maid ran to help the old woman to her feet. Mynheer kissed his mother's dry cheek and avoided her yellow-green ironic eyes.

She said, "I'm not ready yet for the gravestone marked: *In Den Heere Ontslaapen*—Sleeping in the Lord."

The ballroom, smelling of pennyroyal maidenhair fern, was Georgian, or at least as fashionable and modern in that style as Anita Schuyler could make it. It was a very beautiful room, added onto the older house, which itself had been often added to from time to time. The mansion presented many such changes made by several generations from the first simple stone square to the newest grand staircase that led to the upper chambers.

Now the large, two-storied middle hall was filling with guests being helped off with their capes by the Negro servants in white cotton stockings, knee breeches, and white wigs. The Schuylers were not quick to change from the old ways. There was always a sense of solid conforming to what was good enough for their forefathers; but they liked well-dressed servants. The slaves were not field hands but bred —for generations of living at their tasks of serving the family itself— to valeting, barbering, housekeeping, coaching, and waiting on table. On the drive the noise of arriving chaises, chariots, and landaus increased.

Mynheer had come down to the foot of the grand staircase, greeting people, in his blue velvet jacket with gold buttons a most majestic figure, fluffing up his lace, standing with his paunch well forward, his smile wide, and his arms out to greet the guests. "Ah, Sir James, welcome to Schuyler Mansion. Good of you to come."

Sir James Tropp under his full-bottomed mohair wig, agent for the Crown in the colony, bowed. In his late thirties, foppish in white silk and black sateen breeches with a leg lacking much of a calf, he was a striking-looking man with his long and perfect nose, his thin ironic mouth, and a way of looking just slightly above the person he was addressing.

"Damned glad to be here, Mynheer, although I was warned not to venture my person this far out into the country."

"My dear Sir James, we mustn't let this shouting rabble frighten us."

"I don't intend to. And dear Anita, where is she? I must pay my respects."

Servants passed with silver candlesticks burning pungent bayberry candles. Mynheer looked up the staircase and turned back to Sir James.

"Always late. She'll join us soon."

Sir James leaned forward for Mynheer's private ear. "We have word they are raiding the farms for supplies, as they call it, for their militia outside Boston. Washington may be their general."

"General, Sir James? Make *him* a general?"

Sir James bowed to a pretty girl wearing a thumb ring. "We'll hang him at the yardarms of one of His Majesty's tallest men-of-war some fine morning."

Mynheer touched his gold sleeve buttons for luck. "May it be soon."

Dozens of candles burned and servants took more capes. The Hudson River society prided itself on its fashions, yet Sir James, the traveler from London, could only smile at styles already several seasons old. These piled-up hair arrangements were there replaced by the mode for winged affairs, and a three-tiered cape was no longer seen on the best Mayfair ladies. He looked over the ribboned queues, the indigo-dyed serge suiting, calamanco shoes, and damask mantuas so favored by these people. Shiny and prosperous enough for colonials, Sir James decided. He was no snob, he liked the full, fat country life of this class. Besides, his debts in Briton were so large it would be years before he could go back.

Someone tapped him on the back, and he turned. He faced a tall, handsome couple; by their looks they could only be man and wife.

"Ah, good evening, my good Philipse. And Mrs. Philipse." He bowed and took Greetje Philipse' hand. In her late forties she was still one of the most beautiful women in the colonies. Sir James didn't mind older women. ("Adds a bit of the over-ripe to the sport," he used often to say. "As Samuel Johnson says, 'Maidenheads are for plowboys.'")

Jonathan Philipse, aware of his wife's ample charms, smiled. "Sir James, I don't trust your interest in our welfare."

Greetje patted her husband's arm. "It's fine to be lively again."

Jonathan, as head of the largest Philipse holdings, on three sides of the Schuyler estate, his manor house being just north of Tarrytown, was a man who looked taller than he was because of his thinness. His marriage to Greetje Schuyler, favorite niece of Mynheer, had brought the two greatest landholding families together. But not to a close friendship. The Philipses did not like the easy, cheerful ways of the Schuylers.

Sir James was looking down Greetje's gown. "Damn me—pardon my language—it's unfair for a man to have so pretty a wife."

Anita colored down to her satin smallclothes. Her beauty, everyone said, hid a conceited goose's mind. "You mustn't talk that way, Sir James, of a woman with two grown children."

Sir James smiled. "Little Roxanne's not grown up?"

Jonathan Philipse beamed and motioned to a young girl with her corn-colored hair in powder, and a young man with a head of brown curls—his own hair rather than a wig. The girl in crayon-blue seemed amused, the young man over-bold as their father made introductions.

"Sir James, you remember little Roxanne—she's nineteen this week. This is our son Joseph. He's just back from the Grand Tour. Got that hair-do in Italy, I believe. Sir James Tropp, His Majesty's agent for the colony."

Roxanne made a curtsey and smiled as young girls will. It didn't fool Sir James. He was an expert on young girls. This child would outshine her mother in looks, and already had more brains. There was a cold observer under that blue silk, that powdered head of hair, apparent in the way she extended her white hand with the grace of a king's courtesan.

"Sir James, is it really a war?" Her voice was firm, yet not set.

"From His Majesty's side it's merely a punishing of rabblement."

Joseph said, "You have not been reading Thomas Paine, I gather, Sir James."

"The devil I haven't, you young spark. I read everything these hotheads print that I can lay me hands on. It's all there in my letter press, to be used to hang them to the tune of 'Yankee Doodle.'"

Joseph, called Joey, folded his arms in the stance of a Roman statue he remembered from the Forum. "Many of the young gentry are joining the Continental Army."

"Now Joey," said his mother. "We don't talk about it."

Roxanne took her hand away from Sir James. "Aunt Anita is coming down. I must pay my respects."

Sir James bowed. He was not the hurrying kind of womaner.

CHAPTER 8   A Schuyler ball, Anita Schuyler liked to say, had a personal scent. The smell of hair powder, of lavender, of French essences, of the beeswax candles. There was a powerful and pleasing odor in the great hall as Anita Schuyler joined Mynheer at the receiving line. She was a well-curved little woman with small hands and feet, and after so many years of marriage she still retained the Philipse proud stare and firm mouth. It was said by old ladies in chimney corners that the exchange of brides between the two families had been to the Schuyler advantage. Anita certainly was an asset to Mynheer, "who has a good brain but is too lazy," his mother said, "to take advantage of it." Anita, in her best jewels and a London-cut gown of goslin green, smiled at the guests as they passed, putting in just the right word or two to compliment Mynheer's laughing snort of greeting or ribald country remark.

Sir James said directly in Roxanne's ear, "You need have no fear, my dear. I will not arrest your brother Joseph."

"I should hope not." Her hazel eyes flecked with gold turned on him with a touch of temper. "Joey has done no wrong."

"Organizing the recruiting of rebels is not the best way to prove oneself loyal to His Majesty. However, as yet London does not take this matter too seriously. I am ordered not to arouse any more anger or feelings at the moment."

"Good evening, Aunt Anita, Uncle Peter," Roxanne said, making a deep bow.

Anita pinched the girl's cheek. "*Such* natural color."

Roxanne kissed her aunt under one eye. "You know Sir James, of course."

Anita, deep in her sixties, nodded and smiled. She had been a faithful wife, but it was pleasant to hold the hand of a notorious rake if gossip did not lie. "Good of you to come, Sir James, with all the trouble in the district."

"Let us not think of it tonight."

The fiddlers and the flutes, were playing a tune from *The Beggar's Opera* in the ballroom off to the right. Mynheer said with a portly, overdone bow, "Anita, the first dance."

Sir James offered his arm to Roxanne. "If I may, Mistress Philipse."

"I love the long quadrille."

The ballroom in its white and gold with the big Adam fireplace, the silver and gold crystal chandeliers, was a beautiful room. The long French window overlooked the dimpling river below. From the garden came the scent of roses and herbs and the tangy memory of new-cut field crops once gorged on sun. The stately quadrille showed off the several red coats of British officers among the dancers —light dragoons and fusiliers. Not as many, Roxanne remarked, as is usual at a ball. Sir James said the garrison in New York was standing by either to march or leave the city, whichever the commanding general, or London, would order.

Everyone was over-polite, Roxanne noted, or laughing in a key pitched a little too high. She explained that it was only because a Schuyler ball was an important river society event, and that one must act as if these times were like other times that had brought out so many of the best families.

Sir James dipped in the dance—"You see things clearly."

The music makers on a platform at one end of the ballroom were fifing, fluting, and fiddling. On buffets set against a long wall, tables held fruit and coquetel—a kind of ice cream—bottles, and bowls of punch. Several white-wigged house slaves, all gloved, were handing out the glasses, plates, and cups of cherry bounce, flummery, bohee tea, and the little round biscuits made of muscovado sugar to nibble with port or perry cyder. The men took a stronger wine. There was none of the native pot whiskey the journeyman farmers brewed from fermented maize. Gentlemen had no taste for its strong raw bite. Brandy and rum took its place at the ball as a minuet was followed by a Sir Roger de Coverley, then a *contredanse.*

Culbly Schuyler had come to the ball late—to pay his respects to his parents' party. He was just in his thirties, with a legal-looking sleepy head shaped like a pear, given to fat jowls. He was a fine lawyer, when he attended chambers, and his round body was more muscle than fat as those who tried to Indian hand-wrestle him found out. He was tailored in the best English fashion. His popping, cunning round eyes and his suet pudding shape kept him from being handsome. He handed his heavy Spanish cape of shiny yellow to Nero, the old butler, at the door.

"Fine evening, Nero."

"Yes it is, Master Culbly. Indeed it is. Don't see you here as often as we'd like. We have your favorite quiddany jellies and sturgeon soup tonight, sir."

"The law courts, you know—the majestic procession of the law courts. Besides I'm getting too fat to sup here."

Culbly looked around, saw the people crowded near his mother and father, still receiving guests. He wandered into the ballroom, bowing greetings, hands folded behind back; he found the position most comfortable. He had dined too well on terrapin, rollickes and sausages, and neck of mutton.

He caught the eye of Sir James, and when the dance was over several beaux made claims on his cousin Roxanne. Sir James came up to Culbly as he took up a glass of rum.

"Ah, Sir James, you carry off my beautiful cuz under the porridge eyes of the country esquires."

"Damn it, Culbly, why don't you marry her yourself? A very beautiful piece. Certain to be a credit to any marriage bed."

"I like them with a little more plump sweetmeats on the pretty bones, and more—well—experienced."

Sir James accepted a cup of punch and nibbled on pickled walnuts. Culbly leaned forward and smiled as if relating a hunting-field story: "There is a raid planned tonight."

"We have had no such information."

"Young Joey Philipse has been talking to some of the local lads, asking them to join. I had tried to stop them."

"Against whom is the raid?"

"Cato Heathcote's place. His flax farm."

"The old stamp agent and lawyer?"

"Yes, I once clerked in his office. A stiff-necked, strong loyalist. He has been attacking Sam Adams, Hancock, Franklin, expanding some remarks he made in court this week."

Sir James rejected a posset cup and a quince-and-rum jelly. "I must send a message to Yonkers Landing. There is a small Tory section of mounted men there to prevent the burning of the ferry. Dreadful mess all this, Culbly. What do they intend for Heathcote?"

"A coat of tar, and feathers added. And his bony arse to ride a rail out of the district—not to come back."

"I'll get a note to my coachman and send him to the loyalists. Where the devil does Heathcote live?"

"On a farm with a serving wench, two half-wit hands, just before the road takes a big bend where the river comes in to make a cove. Called Hendrick Cove, I believe."

Sir James bowed and smiled at a passing couple as if it were all he had to do. Then he went out to find his coachman. Culbly finished his drink slowly and smiled with pleasure as a regal-looking man of about sixty came into the ballroom, walking in a slight limp aided by a thin silver cane. There were those who said that Sir Francis Livingston was descended from one of the Stuart kings of England, and he certainly had the long dark head under the white tie-wig, the handsome features accented by a large lower lip. He had never gone gross as most of the colonials did in middle age. His blue-violet eyes, Culbly suspected, were icy with the weight of just being a Livingston.

"Ah, Sir Francis, you never miss a Schuyler ball."

Sir Francis turned and greeted Culbly pleasantly. He was a reserved man, not permitting his notorious temper to get the best of him more than once or twice a year. "One of the best-looking balls I can remember, Culbly, my boy. Not so many soldiers, however. Pity they don't catch a few barn-burners and hang them."

"They try. Maude is not with you?"

"No. At her youth she feels her sap. She is in Philadelphia visiting cousins. But with that damned Continental Congress and all, I wish she were home. Culbly, why don't you marry the pretty?"

"You are the second to offer me the advice of marriage tonight."

"My daughter is heir now."

"I'm honored."

"It's time we gentry struck together. This talk of making Colonel Washington a general has not been given enough attention in Britain. I've met him, this Washington—a planter. He's a hard, cool head, not like the leather-mouths who talk liberty and rebellion and thumb their noses at our carriages and barouches as they pass. He's a man with cold determination. Breeds Jenny mules—a Spanish jackass with his mares."

"He should be with us, Sir Francis."

"I don't know. He was so enraged at the way he was treated after Braddock's defeat that mayhaps he turned against the Crown. They did treat colonial officers shabbily. Or maybe he is land-hungry, trying to set up holdings he feels would be better off without a royal dictate as to taxes and land deeds."

"Those Virginians are all land-mad. You think we can count on many loyalists down there?"

"About as many as hereabouts, Culbly. The moneyed people will be for the king, mostly. But I don't think we can rally more than half the population to loyalty, if that much. Damn it, get me a chair. My limb aches."

Culbly motioned a servant to get a chair. Sir Francis sat and took out a snuffbox. He and Culbly took strong pinches and brushed their lace clean.

"Between you and me, the king is a great fool. If he lets the colonies slip away, Culbly, by his foolish petty tickling, he will regret it. The people in power never took seriously the flood of words set free here to inflame the people. A few scribblers giving the king's side of it might have stopped this tide. Now it has to be guns and rope. Ah, if Jonathan Swift were still marking out pamphlets!"

Culbly shook his head. "On the surface it all seems the simple folk being used to further special interests, Sir Francis. But have you talked to the young hotheads! Joey Philipse—mind own friends from childhood. Their visions can frighten a man. At least your son Harvell is free of the taint of infection. God rest his soul."

"God rest his soul. Yes." Sir Francis tapped his slim silver cane against the leg hurt years ago on the hunting field. The dancers on the floor were whirling past them. There was the warm excitement of many bodies in motion and in pleasure. Sir Francis got up and walked away toward the hall.

The gayness of the ball carried to the farthest part of the estate buildings. Besides the slave quarters, Mynheer Schuyler had some cabins for several indented servants. They were mostly Englishmen and Irishmen, either freed from festering prisons and shipped overseas, or poor men and women who sold themselves for seven years' service to pay for their passage to the colony. They had been trained as smiths, coopers, distillers, carpenters, of more or less skill. There were plowmen, buttery wenches who milked and made cheese, and even an old crone who was a weaver of a kind of Lancashire woolen cloth, when not mixing fearful herbs or acting as midwife.

The biggest of the cabins, one of the few buildings still with its original rough-hewn planks—for the log house was actually used only much further west in the Kentuck' and Ohio lands—was the dwelling of Silvester Hand, the estate's tanner. It reeked with the ammoniac odors of nearby stables and the leech of the tanning pit. A burly man, Hand combed his limp yellow hair forward to hide a growing baldness. His mouth was always filled with a twist of tobacco, the cud constantly in motion as if he were preparing to talk, but he rarely said anything more than was needed.

The one and only room of his cabin was lit by pine knots burning in a mud and stone fireplace, and some rag wicks floating in crude pewter lamps full of grease. The music from the ball made Hand frown. He was the organizer of the Sons of Liberty on the estate. Into the cabin were crowded about two dozen men, some seated on benches, some on half logs used as chairs. Most were standing, listening to the music, drinking beer. Almost all were wearing the loose linen or woolen tunic cut on the style of a hunter's deerskin shirt, with a kerchief of blue or red twisted around their necks to complete their costume.

Hand, standing by the cold fireplace, folded his arms and looked over the men drinking their cups of beer or chewing on apple slump and crowdy.

"It's no matter fer talkin'. Who's not fer it?"

A young man named Jim, an apprentice groom from the Philipse farms, shouted: "Let's burn every Tory in the county!"

Hand said, "We take orders, Jim lad. Calm down."

"It's time we got harder," said a farmer with a taciturn set of weathered features.

There was a sharp tap on the door, repeated three times, and the leather string latch was pulled from the outside. Joey Philipse came in, wearing a rough blue cape and tricorner hat from which the silver brim trimmings had been pulled. He waved a greeting.

"Friend Hand, are you ready to move? I've just slipped from the ball—they are too merry to notice anything."

"We are. We've got the keg of tar."

Joey nodded. "We have six muskets hidden in the barn, men. Hand will issue them to those he decides can use them best. The rest will be armed with pikes and farm tools. There will be no looting. No molesting of the house wenches. Any man caught carrying off anything will be tried by the Committee of Public Safety—and hanged."

The farmer said, "If guilty."

The men stared expressionless at young Joey. They were unshaven countrymen, servants, small landholders or renters, many marked by smallpox scars. They were local recruits, all ardent for liberty and a chance to give back a little for their grievances against some rich neighbor or landowner.

Jim, the young groom, spoke up, "Sir, Heathcote, the swine, has been flogging his apprentices twice a day, right or wrong. He claims it does them good to liven them—and he makes them bathe even in winter, when he cuts a hole in the river ice and they jump in. He fines them for any reason all their small pay. And the food, it reeks."

Hand took a pistol off the fireplace and stuck it into a wide leather belt. "It's not for that, Jim lad, we're burning the tax agent and informer out."

"Remember that," said Joey. "No personal matters. Heathcote is reporting our every move to the British ships in the harbor. This is our chance to drive out the whole Tory breed. There's a rumor the British are all moving onto the ships. Soon New York will be in the control of the local Sons and their appointed leaders on Canal Street."

There was a cheer and a lifting of beer cups. Some men cut off ling and herring fragments in a clay tray and ate.

Joey said, "Stop feeding yourselves. We'll leave now. In twos and threes."

Jim said, "H.M.S. *Neptune* is patrolling the river up to Tappan. The green dragoons are aboard—no horses."

Hand nodded. "We'll reassemble by the apple orchard on the creek branch. There will be no dogs along. We have a raid going too at Verplanck's Point."

Joey motioned to Jim the groom, and they went out. Silvester Hand gestured to two other men to follow. The lamp behind him crackled. In the loft that covered half the cabin he heard his wife stir on the husk-filled pallets, and he thought of his five children up there. Hand had a firm conviction and a confused idea that he was doing this night's work for his children's future. When Homer Schuyler and Joey Philipse explained it all to him, he knew it clearer. But "Never thee mind" (he motioned two more men out)— the gentry knew the full true reasons for this whole thing. So did the Provincial Congress of New York. A louder strain of music from the mansion ball came to him; they were wearing out the good shoeleather he tanned for them on the dance floor. He motioned a militia recruiter and a vestryman to head for the orchard.

At the mansion, tables had been set on the wide porches facing the river. Candles burned behind wind-shielding glass globes. The crisp table linen, the good silver, and the trays of food being brought out by the sedate and stately house servants made it a picture, Sir Francis Livingston thought, by some small Dutch master, one who painted the inanimate good things of life with a hard, careful attention to detail and textures. We are born *inter feces et urinas* and invent art to hide the fact.

Nero, the Schuyler butler, was at Sir Francis' elbow, bending down. "Sir, Mynheer would like yourself in the library, without disturbing the ladies. Urgent matter."

"What kind of game is he playing now?" The leg hurt; he was of a dark, saturnine countenance tonight.

"There has been a courier of sorts just come from Boston."

"Ah, something has happened, has it?"

"I have no idea. Just a few of the menfolk have been asked."

The music came louder than ever over the crackling of the garden cicadas and the stamp of feet. There was the liquid sound of silk on over-animated bodies. All seemed so normal, and so right, Sir Francis thought as he forced himself to his feet, favoring the bad leg. But damn it, a bilious colic filled the colonies. It was a bad time.

The library of the Schuyler Mansion was a square room, rather neglected as to use, but kept dusted. It was of a good chestnut paneling, with many small paintings of river scenes by an ungifted local artist whose water was like bending glass and whose boats were somehow always out of proportion. There were few books— mostly bound volumes of English newspapers, some farm gazettes, and several shelves of blue morocco classics ordered from England but never opened. The Schuylers were not much given to literature.

As Sir Francis stumped into the library he saw Mynheer bustling around. Sir Francis nodded to Sir James Tropp, cold and correct, to Culbly Schuyler, to Jonathan Philipse, warm and correct, to about a dozen of the most important men on the river. They were standing around a tall, travel-worn man in a brown suit, his face tanned, the red hair worn unpowdered and tied behind in a snake- skin. The features were familiar, and Sir Francis was about to wonder who this was, stirring up the pool of memories, when Mynheer spoke up. "Gentlemen, may I introduce Dr. David Cortlandt. Some of you may remember him. He was a boy in these parts."

Sir Francis made a firm line of his lips. Of course. The orphan. In the shifting light as someone moved a candlestick, Sir Francis saw the hair was as red as ever. But the face was mature and hardly like the simple farm lad's he remembered so many years ago, when David and his own son Harvell were mad for hunting and boating from Setauket, Long Island, to Teller's Point.

Mynheer was facing them, hands clasped behind his wide back, his waistcoat fluffed up in front, making no effort to hold in his paunch. "Dr. Cortlandt has just come from Boston, with amazing news."

The tall, red-haired man, fatigue written on his features, faced them and looked placidly at them, too worn to dramatize his news. He caught Sir Francis' eye, but did not pause in any greeting, not even a nod.

"Gentlemen, I am on my way to report to the Provincial Congress of New York. My horse foundered on the road here, and while a fresh one is being prepared for me, Mynheer had thought I should inform you of events in the north."

Sir James Tropp smiled. "British information, Mynheer, is as fast and good as any. The king's guineas work hard."

Culbly stood silent.

David Cortlandt shook his head. "I doubt if this has yet reached His Majesty's forces in these waters or any Tory ears. I left ahead of any express. Three days ago, on June seventeenth, at Breed's Hill outside Boston there has been a great battle between colonial forces and the British regiments."

"I know the place on the Charlestown spit of land," said Sir Francis. "There is another hill, Bunker Hill, nearby."

"Yes, Sir Francis." He waited for the shocked whispering to stop. "The Americans lost 140 killed, 300 or more wounded or missing. The British losses were much higher. A frontal attack against native sharpshooters. Twenty-seven officers killed; and every British officer engaged either dead or wounded."

Mynheer made an O of his mouth and leaned his head to one side. "And what other result?"

"In the end the Americans retired from the hill. The local militias have been called out, and Boston is going to be put under siege by the Americans."

Sir James was pale, but expressionless. "Thank you Dr. Cortlandt. This means Washington *will* be appointed general now. It's outright civil war. Mutiny, sedition, treachery. Lexington and Concord might have been just raids against rebels. But with a pitched battle, it's war. I must be forgiven, Mynheer, if I leave now. There is so much to move to the ships in the harbor."

A soap boiler and tallow chandler asked, "You're leaving New York town to the mercy of these cutthroats?"

Culbly said, "I'll go with you, Sir James."

Mynheer put up his hands in protest. "No taking sides, Whig or Tory, here tonight. I wanted you all to hear the sudden turn of events. Let us go back to the ball and not alarm the ladies."

Several men were questioning David closely. He shook his head.

"I can tell no more but these bare facts. The dispatches I carry are for other eyes."

"You will stay the night?" said Mynheer.

"No, I cannot. Get the horse saddled as you kindly offered. But I could use some food. I am famished. The fodder in the country inns is deadly and lean."

"I'll have a tray sent in here. And something to wash with."

"Thank you, Mynheer."

Sir Francis stayed behind when the rest had left. He leaned on his cane and looked at David. "You must feel strange toward me?"

"Not at all, Sir Francis." He took off his cape and slapped road dust from his sleeves. "You have refused me an audience for many months. That is your right."

A servant came in with a silver pitcher of water, a basin, and a towel. David poured a basinful of water. "I have been held in Boston by conditions beyond my control. But, Sir Francis, as you refused to answer my letters, I felt little would have been gained by trying to come down to you here. Your grandchild is well and growing like a weed."

Sir Francis sat down and David finished washing. A tray of cold chicken, sliced lobster, fresh biscuits, and a tankard of wine was brought in. David fell to the food with a vigorous hunger. He did not try to curb his appetite. Sir Francis watched him tear into a section of chicken David held in his fingers, biting with strong white teeth.

After David had somewhat appeased his hunger and taken two strong pulls on the wine, he relaxed and ate more slowly.

Sir Francis picked at a loose piece in the rug with the end of his cane. "You were Harvell's friend. You were there. I am still not over the shock of it. The waste and horror of it. I acted as I did from dreadful grief and rage. The spleen of an old man is a fearful thing."

"I knew your hurt." David put a hand into a pocket and pulled out a set of seals patterned as a watch fob. "Harvell's. But I regret the watch went to settle some of his debts."

Sir Francis took the seals and nodded. . . .

Culbly and Sir James Tropp had left the ball at once. Culbly Schuyler understood better than most of the river families the significance of their history. The early Dutch, full of frugal toughness and some pious compassion, came first to the Hudson shores. Young sons with no fortunes and a hunger. They were never real to their descendants in their blackened portraits by third-rate sign painters. They became the milk-herd breeders, maize and tobacco growers with an eye for the main chance. They spread out to old Indian lands, entered the House of Burgesses, organized defense militia, horse races, and cockfights. They achieved a fat respectability and a dignity of rich living. They kept their wealth and fields until they were set in cold pride and mixed with the English gentry and were much respected.

The Livingstons came later, Anglo-French stock crossed with Scotch and later colonial blood. They were no more important than the Philipses among the biggest landholders. Some, Culbly knew, were readers of Plutarch, members of the imported Anglican Church crossed with solid Scotch-Irish Presbyterianism. A few had the Presbyterian belief in predestination. Vestrymen, churchwardens. Many of the Hudson River families were a hard-working aristocracy, unlike the hound-dog Tidewater grandees of the Rappahannock and the James he had visited. Best of all, they had a keen taste for business. Ships, tea-importing, grain contracts, cotton exports. Timber, pitch, Jamaica sugar for rum, indigo for dyes, and pleasure in totting up figures flavored their lives.

The old names passed to new generations. Heligorda van Schlichthorst. Feargod Smith. Rudolphus de Vries. Margaret Filipse. Thomas Pell. James Pelham. Uldrick Heyn. They were church folk, not godly—but in good respect of God as a patroon of them all. Culbly smiled as he remembered it.

("How unmannerly for Judas to have betrayed the Lord with a kiss," preached the Domine Erasmus Everardus Bogardus.

Mynheer agreed, "No real gentleman would be that rude," and winked at his old mother.

"The French," her grandson Culbly had said, "carried off the bells of St. Michael's when they evacuated upstate New York at the end of the Indian wars."

Sir James Tropp, a Sunday guest, had remarked, "Not like them to show such bad taste.")

Culbly Schuyler hoped to preserve this society, a free and casual breed, moving among their alabaster vases and great tinkling chandeliers, proudly occupying their arbors and parterres, served by black men whom they called, from a pleasant fashion, Scripto, Agamemnon, and Cato. And the dark or yellow women they cheerfully named Sappho, Venus, and Chloe. (When Sir James asked, "You sleep with them?" "Why else are they all getting lighter?" Culbly had said.)

It was a simple, lazy life, Sir James Tropp reported to London. Drinking water was fetched still by Negro girls in great jars from the well. An old black man at the Schuyler estate stood all day at the yard well pumping bath water into the great roof tank over the bathroom. A lamplighter moved at dusk to light the smoking oil lamps on the drive—each light proudly topped by a brass river eagle. He had reported to London, "We must keep the passions of the New Englanders at bay, and turn their creative fury towards a new study of the Bible, the newer sciences and inventions of money-making. We must fear these fanatics in Boston, men in badly cut linen. They are not of the ruffled-cuff tribes of the world who live by outdated romantic codes and extraordinary respect for the Crown. These are wild as the forests behind them, cunning as the Indian tribes."

At Schuyler Mansion Sir James sat often, his face that of a decaying Roman emperor (one of those lesser Caesars, his friend Culbly said, after the great and notorious Nero). They often passed the time in a tower of glass and wood over the green Hudson River, looking with a tarnished silver telescope across at the Palisades and the ships.

"You must raise more Tory bands, Culbly, to match those of the Sons of Liberty."

"We have a good agent in Colonel Lemon."

"You people are mostly loyal to the Crown."

Culbly had held up a leather book bound in old polished calf now falling to bits. "I don't know why, for sure. My grandfather was the last of the family to be educated in England. Listen to this from the school he went to: 'A limited Number of Young Gentlemen will be accepted by The Reverend Leon O. Lance's Academy at the seat of the late Lady Starkweather at Wooltan. Boarding for the Young of Good Families who are taught Latin, Greek, Merchant Accounting, Surveying and Drawings, Experimental Philosophy and Astronomy. Twenty Guineas per Annum.'"

"Sounds like a place where the lash was used freely. We cane greatness into our youth."

"'Due regard is paid to Health, Morals, and Behavior.'"

"How did your grandfather turn out?"

Culbly flipped the pages of bound letters and accounts. "He took over the estate at twenty-two. The first year he lists what the Schuyler ménage consumed: 'Thirty-two thousand pounds of pork, thirty-one beeves, six hundred and fifty bushels of wheat, four hundred of corn—for cattle, servants, and slaves. Five hogsheads of rum, a hundred and twenty-one gallons of brandy.' They really dug in their forks and filled their cups." Like all the Schuylers, Culby enjoyed reading the family's bookkeeping.

Sir James reverted to their previous subject of discussion. "That school sounds fairly typical."

"My grandfather liked it. Seniority through a system of student prefects, morning cold showers, black pumps for dinner, a personal handshake at least once a month with the head of the school, a great deal of moral significance, and the duties of a Christian gentleman. It's nothing to be ashamed of, Sir James."

"I'd be happier with hard, cruel bands of toughened bravos, like the Sons of Liberty. Cruel times are coming. It's not easy to brutalize a proper gentleman."

(And now events had caught up with Sir James.)

CHAPTER 9   A dog barked in restrained fury as the party of night raiders neared Heathcote Farm. There was the rattle of chain, and Joey Philipse knew the creature was not running free. Behind Joey the Sons of Liberty bunched low against a row of barberry hedges and boxwood. They carried muskets, farm-made pikes and cruel-looking harvesting tools. Silvester Hand came up to the raiders out of the river mist. "All still on the river side. The dog is chained."

"Is Heathcote to home?"

"In the barn, bundling flax with some apprentices."

Joey nodded and turned to Jim the groom. "Take three men and cover the farmhouse. If anyone rushes out to aid Heathcote, which I doubt, clout them, but don't shoot."

"I'll hit them right between their damned Tory eyes."

"The rest of you come with me."

Six men followed Joey Philipse down toward the old stone barn. Horn lanterns burned inside under the steep-pitched roof. Through cracks in the heavy doors the raiders could see the moving shapes inside the barn. They waited, eyeing each other as if for clues in each other's faces.

It was a warm, damp night and the river eddied and sucked on its banks below as it muttered to the bay. The dog still barking in sharp, short howls of alarm.

A thin, harsh voice came from the barn. "See what Cleo is making the blasted noise about."

"Dog must have smelled a skunk."

One of the big plank doors opened about two feet and a stout youth carrying a light came out. Two men grabbed him and muffled his short-cut cry of surprise with their large hands. He struggled, his big frightened eyeballs staring, and sounds of protest and fear choking in his throat.

The lantern fell from his hands and clattered over the slabs of stone set before the barn.

"You clumsy oaf!" said the harsh voice from inside the barn. "You'll get ten licks with the blacksnake on your bare arse if you broke that horn light."

Joey gritted his teeth together and pulled open both doors. Silvester Hand ran forward, his pistol held up. The interior of the joisted and cross-beamed barn was filled with hanks of ripe bleached flax, gambrels and ox yokes, and stored firkins of butter. A solid, quick man with a red hinge of a nose and powerful-looking shoulders was tying up a bundle of flax, and he continued tying as he stared at them, for a moment too shocked to react.

"You Tory dog!" Hand shouted, moving toward him. The rest waited, weapons ready, arms steady.

The man dropped a bundle and reached for a heavy musket under the table. Hand hit him on the high domed head with the butt of the pistol, and the man fell backwards, showing long yellow teeth as he howled in pain and rage.

Joey pushed Hand aside. "Heathcote, you've come to justice."

The man, dazed among the flax stems on the stone floor, pushed at the wound flowing blood into his eye and mouth. "Aye, I can see that. You Whig scum."

"You've informed on our meetings, you've harassed many—any of your tenants you've suspected of our leanings."

"I've not hit out at them in the middle of the night, with armed cowards at my back."

The Sons of Liberty were standing in a half circle around the man on the floor, their weapons still in front of them. Jim the groom spat down. "Colonel Lemon and his Tory bands have stopped here, in this very barn, for the night."

"Aye. Who can say them no?" said their victim. "No more than I can say you no. But I'll have Sir James Tropp informed of this outrage. There is still royal law and order in the colony."

"Not English law," said Joey, bending down to grip the man by his shirt collar. There was rustling in a stall behind them, and Joey turned just in time to see a yellow-faced Negro come charging from behind a post with a sharp-pronged pitchfork.

"Mind!" shouted Silvester Hand and fired. The Negro pursed his large lips together and rolled his head as if attacked by insects. He fell forward, a side of his face blown away. In the smell of gunpowder he sank slowly, and the fork fell from his hands and struck sparks as a prong met the stone floor. In the light of burning tow dipped in saltpeter and tallow, which hung on a beam, all stared at the Negro.

Heathcote was on his knees watching the powder smoke twirl in the light of the lamp's glow. Joey stood pale and he turned to look around, as if hunting a fresh ambush. Hand put an arm on his shoulder. "Don't rattle, sir. It had to be done." The dead Negro's large and naked feet seemed grotesque in his sudden death.

There was the click of a musket hammer being pulled back and all suddenly saw Heathcote crouched under the table, the musket held in his arms. "I'll take a few of you devil's spawn to hell with me," he shouted, and without aiming he pushed up the gun barrel and fired.

Joey felt something burn him in his right groin as Hand flung his heavy pistol at the bloodied head of the man still staring popeyed along the musket barrel. Joey flung himself forward and leaned against Heathcote. The musket fell to the floor.

"Leave him be. I'm in command here. Jim, go find a pot to boil tar. Someone go to the house and get some feather beds."

Hand stepped back and put his empty pistol back in his belt. "Hangin' in what for, he needs, sir. Did he hit ye?"

Joey pressed on the burning flesh through his thick cape. "A scratch. Drag him out."

Strong hands snatched the man from under the table. His face was unfrightened and his scowl, all bloodied, showed his contempt for them.

"You hoodlums will feel the king's justice."

Silvester Hand opened one of the lanterns and took out the big wad of burning wax. He looked over the packed loft and the baled bundles of prepared flax. The barn was full of flax and well-filled piggins, buckets of maize, churns, and a salt mortar. "Ah, this will warm the cockles of Whig hearts."

Heathcote suddenly screamed at this threat of destruction. "Not the flax. Not the flax! It's worth seven thousand pounds. Three years' crops."

It was a unique scene, and the raiders, all but Joey and Hand, were cowed.

"You think more of your crop, sir," Joey said, "than of your loyalties."

"No flames. I beg of you."

Hand seized an armful of flax and set it on fire. He thrust it into the middle of a pile of bales. "Come on, me boys. Catch yourself each a bundle and set it alight. Fire every corner of the warehouse and barn."

Heathcote fingered his drugget breeches. He no longer protested. He stood wide-eyed with his bloodied head, held firmly by the grip of two members of the band. Jim dragged up a large iron pot used to mix hogfeed. "Just right for the tar. You like it hot, warm, or *very* warm, Squire Heathcote?"

Heathcote did not answer. Despair, the futility of all endeavor, spoke from his every gesture.

From the direction of the farmhouse itself came the sound of china and glass breaking, the screams of farm girls, the kicking in of solidly hung doors as hasps and hinges gave way.

Joey felt faint from fear over his wound and held onto the table. "We're only burning the barn. We'll spare the house."

Heathcote said in a low, husky voice, "I'll not thank you."

The flax bales smoldered with a pungent smell like heavy musk and burning turkey wings and then caught and burst into yolk-yellow flames. The raiders set fire to every corner of the barn and tossed lighted bundles into the packed loft. Soon the spark-filled air was too hot to breathe and great coiling snakes of black smoke ran along the rafters hunting escape in the sod roof. A tonneken of salted shad burst and stank in the flames.

Hand kicked the table aside. "Here's one lot of American stuff that will not see royal London."

Pushing the silent, sorrowing Tory between them, they went quickly from the barn. Jim, coming along behind them, banged on the iron pot with an ox yoke and sang: "Yankee Doodle went to town, sitting on a pony. With a feather in his cap. Call him macaroni!"

The raider began to tear up a snake-rail fence and a maize crib, white-limed with crushed clam shells, to build a fire under the tar pot.

At the house of Mynheer Peter Schuyler the ball was breaking up in the failure of small talk and awareness of the hour. The fiddlers were sawing at a last river jig, their eyes on the pots of beer waiting for them. The carriages were wheeling to the wide front steps. There was little gaiety left. The news from Boston of the battle on Breed's Hill had spread even to those who had not been in the library to hear it direct from Dr. Cortlandt. Linkboys carrying flaring candlewood torches were helping reharness matched teams of horses, and under the big black pine by the river the smell of freshly trampled horse manure, sorrel, and brier roses filled the night.

The kitchen fires were dying; outdoors the last embers were going blind under the clam and lobster pots. Helga, the fat cook, stood red and damp in the shade of the grapevine arbor by the kitchen door drinking a muddled tankard of rum. The Negro house servants, tired now, were doing their last clean-up tasks with listless fingers, yawning and scratching their wool.

Mynheer and his lady were at the front door under the leaded glass fanlight, where the big coach lamps were set in the brick and stone, giving a bright brassy light. Mynheer looked old and his jowls were sagging, the belly dragging. He had undone the bottom three buttons of his waistcoat. The women in silk and summer dimities had lost their fresh look.

"Ah," said Mynheer, "next year who knows if we shall give a ball?"

Jonathan Philipse shook his host's hand, and his wife kissed Anita on the cheek. "Delightful, really delightful. Too bad these rumors had to break it up so early."

Jonathan snapped fingers at his coachman. "I can't find Roxanne —she must have left early with Joey. The young folk these days have no patience with their elders, Mynheer."

"It was different in our youth," his host agreed. "We respected our elders."

Anita sneezed. "It's the roses. I must go and take my hartshorn drops."

Then carriages on the drive began to thin out, a nightbird sang, awakened by lights.

Culbly Schuyler and Sir James Tropp were driving back to town in Sir James' light coach. The events of the evening had not silenced them. It now brought words in which they took stock of the situation that had ruffled that night.

Sir James shook ash off a West Indies cheroot.

"The things that are best about the Hudson River society, and which, Culbly, you can't accept, is their calm, casual adjustment to their world and their life. They make no effusive efforts to change, knowing they have their place; they are never pushing in public, or show any personal emotions in places where others can see them. It is this colonial accepting of themselves at their own worth that differs them from the rest of the English."

"What about the Virginians?"

"They try to show how much smarter or stronger they are than the rest of the colonial herd. But the Hudson River people and their friends play a sort of game of being no different than anyone else, well aware of their distinguishable qualities. But not adjusting them to changing times. We are never, they hint, insulted by those we know are inferiors. We don't display wealth in flamboyant ways, they seem to say, except for boats, horses, and sometimes for bad good—or good bad—women. Poor manners are a larger insult than robbery, and they would rather be taken in adultery than in dirty lace or unpolished hunting boots."

Culbly looked out at the night landscape. "You think them all loyalists?"

"By no means. Isaac Vanvleet has a militia company. Joseph Philipse is a Sons' man."

"But damn it, Sir James, we do differ from the colonial clods."

"The things that separate the world of the Schuylers and the other important families," said Sir James, cold air on his face, "is your way of talking. Your French is no better than any Anglo-Saxon teaching of it, but your English is at its most formal, free of the ugly slurred and broken sentences of the farmers and mechanics you live among."

"We're not freaks. England needs us."

"Your world of the best tidewater families is free of witty or top-ical remarks, except in a few off-key members such as yourself, dear Culbly. No one talks slang or trade jargon, unless it is about the illness of pedigreed dogs, or the curve of a merchant ship's hull."

Culbly laughed. "You're still a London snob, Sir James. We're not as bad as you make out. We speak without breathing moisture on each other. We do not hawk up and spit on rugs, or clutch at someone's waistcoat to make a verbal point. We talk at a slower pace, and use up less words. Latin quotations are for professors. Our ministers are expected to outgrow their early vivid vernacular and revert to Anglo-Saxon monosyllables when they begin to breed their kind."

Sir James nodded. "In mixed company you do not mention the body functions, if one can help it, and to talk of money is as bad as blowing one's nose in a drape. Sexual comment in mixed company might include a mare or a favorite hound bitch in heat, and the fact that some younger son has acquired the clap. I admit it is a healthy society—better tuned than our London lords to protect the colonies."

"We shall, Sir James, save the crown colonies—we, this placid society you mock."

"When will you save them?"

"Tomorrow, if we Tories must."

"After the coffee and port and brandy, and when the cheroots are passed? When the men recite the four-letter words of Fielding and Smollett? While the women gather to talk of clothes, their digestive system, the next ball? And to gossip of what young man has made a fool of himself over a married woman?"

"What makes you brood so over us, Sir James?"

"Your Hudson River society is passive. It can't last more than two more generations. It's the century of the common man. The danger is not that your mob is common. It's when they get power, Culbly. When the rocky-hill-acres son becomes a big shipping man, when the fur hunter and groom and their short stocky litter become intelligent but greedy politicians. Look at Sam Adams! And when the farmers' and coachmakers' sons become retired admirals and generals recruited by commerce. You river landholders will face a new élite you can only control by intermarriage. And blast me if we're breeding enough passionate women who are amusing in bed.

It will be a race of two colonial societies to see if they put you out of existence, or you absorb them. And all you'll give will be a little polish and some rare furniture."

Culbly smiled. "You have been digesting Thomas Paine, Sir James, and he has left lumps. Now how do we save the colonies?"

"We'll go aboard the H.M.S. *Duchess of Gordon*. They may have dispatches for me."

The coach ran on over ruts.

In the library Sir Francis was sipping the last of the bottle of Madeira he was sharing with Dr. Cortlandt. The food and drink had made David drowsy. His joints were stiffening painfully. He sat well back in a deep crimson leather chair and shook his head.

"Strange, being home again, Sir Francis. I crossed the Croton River at Van Cortlandt Manor, but the faces at the ferry were new, and as for my relatives—they've never made me feel one of them. In my haste I did not stop. . . . But to your grandson."

"Yes, since we come to it, what of him? What of your voyage?"

"It was not the kind of voyage home I expected, Sir Francis. First the ship was blown off its course. We were demasted off the Azores. The first mate died out at sea of a swelling of the spleen. When we came to Boston the boy had a bad lung congestion. He's a bright lad."

"Look like Harvell?"

David handed over the miniature of Peg and the boy Daniel. "Of course that was painted two years ago."

"I don't see too much a Livingston likeness."

"He's filled out since. He's boarding now with my landlady on the Charles. I didn't set up as a medical man in Boston. I got involved in secretly moving supplies to the villages, Concord and Lexington among them. But a lot I can't talk of yet. As for Dan, I waited to hear from you, Sir Francis—and suddenly after some months came the explosion on Lexington Common."

"Ah yes, what the devil have the loyalists done?"

"I believe a lot have run into Boston for the protection of General Gage. Some are even talking of Canada, Nova Scotia.

"No, I can't think of doing that, David. Not after Lloyd's Neck. You remember it? It's a beautiful spot. You must come again and visit. If the world doesn't turn upside down. This wife of Harvell's?

You wrote once she would come to the colonies with you and the boy."

David rubbed his chin and slowly finished the wine in his glass. "A very headstrong woman of character, Peg—Mrs. Livingston. When she heard how you felt, she refused to make the trip. She did send the boy."

"A baggage? A whore?"

David rose and pulled the blue velvet bell cord. "I must be on my way. London ways are not our ways, Sir Francis. She moves in good society. I'd rather not say more."

Sir Francis saw the Madeira was all gone. So, he thought, David Cortlandt has had his way with her himself. He's bedded with the jade himself and played at whore's tricks with her and now feels shame at it.

"I don't know what we shall be in the next months, David. I remain with the king, of course. But when there is some kind of a calmness, a sanity, I will take the boy in."

"You will accept Dan as Harvell's heir, and yours?"

"Don't plague me now about *that*. I'll take him in—that's the best answer I can give you now."

Mynheer came into the library. He was panting, open-mouthed, and wiping his brow with a wisp of lacy handkerchief. "They are burning a barn near the cove. You can see the flames in the sky."

Sir Francis stumped over to the leaded casements and opened them. A faint pink blush tinted one corner of the inky sky. "Must be Cato Heathcote's place. The damn rebel rabble."

David Cortlandt was at his shoulder. "It could be Colonel Lemon and his Tory Rangers burning for the king."

Mynheer stuck his kerchief up his sleeve. "I'll have the small sulky and a good stout horse sent around to the side in ten minutes for you, Dr. Cortlandt. Better than getting into the saddle again."

"Thank you, sir."

The three men stood at the windows watching the stain of pink turn to old rose, to a coral red, to a deep turkey tone. The awakened bird somewhere in the holly hedge continued to sing.

The man did not scream when they stripped him by the pot of softening tar. He did not move when they mocked his exposed, withered manhood. Behind them the barn was reduced to the great rafters and crossbeams, like the ribs of some plundered whale. Then everything burned and the flames licked up toward the rafters and they glowed, outlined in dancing flames.

Jim and Silvester Hand dipped bundles of broom corn tied to sticks into the tar and began to slap it on the white skin of the staring, encircled man. He screamed now at the heat and acid of the tar and tried to break free. Strong arms held him, and loose mouths laughed. He continued to scream, but by the time he was a dripping black statue he only whimpered like a sick puppy. The man made no objection as Jim tarred and tangled his unbound hair.

Joey felt very ill. The wound was not bleeding much, but his imagination pictured all sorts of involved damage to his innards and lights. His bowels softened as he waved to Hand.

"You take over. Get him properly feathered and onto a rail and set him free on the county line with a good solid warning never to come back."

"Stay for the fun of making a great hen of him, sir. Jim suggests we capon him with a cane-cutting knife."

"No, just feather and rail him. I've got to get back to the ball."

"You look pale, sir. It's not for gentry, this sort of night raiding."

Joey did not answer. He was gone quickly into the dark, up a narrow path.

Jim was busy with a large plump feather bed looted from the house, tearing it open and sending a cloud of feathers into the air. "Look now, it's a mother hen what needs its feathers, or an old bent cock. Come on, lads, let's get the chicken in marching order!"

With glee, for they had found some hard-cyder jugs—everyone seized feathers and in a choking white feather storm they began to plaster them onto the tarred hide of the man. He twisted and begged, he tried to kneel but they jerked him to his feet. They feathered and patted Cato Heathcote's thin rump into a ball of smeared feathers. He stood at last like a great obscene bird, feathers on his head, lumps of them on his cheeks, streaks of tar gleaming on his flanks and torso. He looked a molting sick bird with large staring eyes.

The glowing ribs of the barn fell in with a sudden clatter and a great shower of sparks. Two men came running up with a long length of sharp-edged rail torn from a garden fence.

"Mount, damn you!" shouted Silvester Hand. "Mount your steed and ride off to tell the king how we treat informers." The feathered creature began to choke.

The ballroom was empty. A cased bass viol crouched in a corner. Broken crystal glasses lay in the fireplace. The buffet table had been carried away and empty bottles were stacked in the hall to the kitchen. Several drunken house slaves were on the stairs leading down to the cellars, finishing off the remains of the drinks, the last few inches left in the bottles. Nero, the butler, had locked the wine bins and gone off with a bottle and a bird to his own room in the buttery building. The buxom cook was soaking her large red feet in tepid water and reading a book on the explaining of dreams.

The group of house slaves sat on the cellar stairs, the younger, bolder ones laughing and carrying on. One of the black footmen was pleasuring a yellow girl who was very drunk. Nero was getting too old to oversee the servants properly.

Mynheer was in his sleeping shirt, scratching his belly and yawning. The valet had gone, taking the soiled linen, the wrinkled suit with him. Anita was in the big bed rubbing her naked neck, shoulders, and breasts with a special mixture of elder-tree water and extract of twig hazel.

"It may be the last ball in a long time, Peter."

Mynheer kicked off his slippers and got into the family bed beside his wife. "I forgot to say goodnight to Mama."

"It's just as well. She would want to know all the details and keep you up for hours more." She rubbed her large breasts and frowned. "I suppose this means the mandilion cloak and the frieze cloth will not come from England, now they need the shipping for soldiers and cannon?"

Mynheer nodded sadly and put on his tasseled nightcap. "We're old, Anita. And suddenly I fear for our few remaining years. I'd give it all up—house, lands—for a guarantee of no war."

She leaned over and kissed him, and he put his arms around her, smelling of her ointment. Mynheer felt tender and sad, but no longer frightened. Yes, he thought as Anita beat up his pillow, they were old. Life had passed too quickly somehow in all those lazy summers and cozy winters, in balls and routs, in hunts and sittings at well-stocked tables. In good talk over grapes and nuts and wine, in the reek of fine cured tobacco. They had harmed no one, used no one ill. Now, when their last years should have been as safe and casual as a country walk over a well-loved landscape, they were facing a dreadful time of thunder and turmoil.

The red glow from the cove had died out of the sky. The two in the bed knew each other as old people know the partners with whom they have shared the same bed for many years, and they needed to say no more. The things left unsaid they both felt deeply, and with a sigh they fell back on the well-stuffed pillows. Anita put out the remaining candles with a long snuffer, and in the smell of scented candlewick, the comforting awareness of each other's bodies, the retained pattern of dancers and guests remembered, their minds grew numb and then empty of images. They slept—Mynheer with a marvelously high-pitched snoring, the damn seahorse ivory teeth watching him from a bedside table.

In the ballroom below, the dark had given way to moonlight coming in through the bank of French windows. It was a delayed moon, but now the sky had cleared of scudding black and the stars sugared the silver-gray sky. Martha Schuyler, old, slow, careful of foot, came down the great staircase, dressed in her best lace-drawn black silk, her jeweled shoe buckles held forward.

"Well, I'm here at last," she said, addressing the old portraits on the walls. "I don't hear the music. I am getting deaf, I must admit it."

She came to the ballroom and stood on the two carpeted steps that led down to it. "Where is everyone? I say, where is everyone? Peter, you lummox, you've forgot to order the musicians."

She stood there, a large old woman, smiling at the things she would say to him in the morning, this big foolish baby of a son. There were times now, like this, when she lost control of the time count and moved freely back and forth into three generations. Was it a birthday ball? When Peter had reached his majority at eighteen? Or was it her own first ball as mistress of this big house, a Van Rensselaer bride from way upstate near Albany, from Rensselaerwyck. And this handsome booby, staring and sweating, was he her bridegroom?

Martha picked up the hem of her gown and with eyes closed she slowly began to dance a stately minuet around the ballroom.

David Cortlandt was tired beyond almost the limits of his flesh. He had ridden hard from Boston, and he was not used to horseback. Now, driving the horse and sulky borrowed from Mynheer Schuyler, he felt as if every bone was topped by burning oil and that every muscle was ready to dissolve into jelly and leave his big body helpless and unable to move.

The road leading south along the river was shaded with old trees, and in the moonlight the silvery landscape was like a setting for trolls and wood gods rather than the Hudson River Valley of his boyhood memories. He slapped the reins on the back of the powerful gray horse and held on as the sulky's wheels hit a pothole and came out with a jolt and went on. He would cross to Manhattan, to Harlem Heights, before morning. There a certain farmhouse was a station for the Sons of Liberty. He would send on by trusted messenger the dispatches with their electrifying news. And he would sleep, sleep, and never think of roads and horses' sore haunches, of colonial wars.

Strange how everything here fitted back into his life, even if he had been away so long. Mynheer, Sir Francis, the valley society, the very smell of the river on his right purling along to the bay past fish weirs and rocks, and ahead the sleepy ribbon of moon-drenched road. A mist was walking on the water, white as cotton, but with a blending and merging grace.

Ahead there was a stirring of sudden movement at a crossroads. David reached for the pair of pistols in the saddlebags at his feet. He pulled out one of them and cocked it. A strange wood creature came floating up from a patch of berry bushes. It was a grotesque hen, five or six feet tall. It had the features of a man bewhiskered by clumps of loose feathers. It ran, this apocalyptic beast, on two thin legs, and its wings—were they feathered arms?—flapped as it ran. Its groin was bloody. Black strips of skin hung from it.

The horse shied at the dreadful thing and flared its nostrils. David took a firm hand with it. The creature in feathers looked around and David saw the mad eyes, glazed with an insane fear. The ungainly bird thing ran away, and to David its croaking sounded like the crowing of a tormented rooster. Then it was gone. He drove on, wary and shaken. The Sons were out tonight.

CHAPTER 10   New York lay bleaching in the summer sun,
and the morning fish hawk, flying in the heated air, saw below him
the long triangular wedge of Manhattan Island. It was thickly settled
by fifteen thousand citizens and laid out into pig-infested streets,
mostly around the Battery, going bravely north to Wall Street, but
giving up and becoming fields and farms in the region of Harlem
Heights. From there it looked across at Westchester County and
the Hudson River where the manor houses, estates, and big farms
of the original (non-Indian) landowners began.

On the east side of the island of Manhattan the indifferent hawk
knew the East River that connected New York Bay with Long
Island Sound. On the western tip of Long Island protruded
Brooklyn Heights. It commanded a view over Manhattan and the
harbor. A fringe of housing and gardens bearded the top of the
heights, and behind it were sandy roads leading past farms and
hayfields. Husbandry was bounded by snake-rail fences, and there
were grazing cattle. On the shores north and south, the fishers and
mooncursers—smugglers—lived along the churning Great South Bay
and the narrow barrier of sand, Fire Island.

The morning hawk, hungry for any eatable, killable, digestible
item, kept his eyes on the ring of anchored ships that lay off the
shores in the bay, sheltered by the Jersey inlets. They often threw
tidbits overboard. The larger ships were near Paulus Hook, already
being called, by a few, Jersey City. These were the ships of His
Majesty's Navy, herding the hulks of the East Indies merchants and
the yachts and ketches of the loyalists. The news of battle on
Breed's Hill had already seeped through, and New York itself was
now left in the hands of the local Provincial Congress. The fish
hawk, his wings not moving, circled and glided lower. The gilt sterns
of the men-of-war becoming clearer to him, the sides of the wooden
sea walls alternately painted yellow and black, the bronze cannon
at the ports. The captain's gig of H.M.S. *Mercury* was being rowed
to H.M.S. *Neptune.*

On shore "the freed slaves to despotism"—the town dwellers—
watched the ships and waited. The *chevaux de frise*, those sharp

stakes and barriers around the fort at the Battery, pointed to a conflict between the town and sea power rolling in glassy swells as the tide came in. Across the bay the Palisades were heavy in green timber; their rock paths led down to the Hudson. Below in the open bay facing Manhattan was Staten Island, gritty with clam shells and mud flats behind which nested farms, cattle barns, and berry thickets. Along Wappinger Creek in Dutchess County, past the white church at Fishkill, past Verplanck's Point on the east bank of the Hudson, to the white salt-crusted roads of the Long Island Rockaways there was a watching and an activity of preparing for something explosive to happen. Today, tomorrow, six months, even perhaps a year . . .

The fish hawk flew on and was lost from sight. The British ships rolled at anchor, sent out picket boats and waited for orders from London. Waited for more ships, more lobster-backed infantry, and asked *what* was to be done with a war of rebellion?

David Cortlandt, having slept away a day and a night, came awake in a plank farmhouse on the Harlem River near Spuyten Duyvil. He looked out through windowpanes turned a faint violet by sun and weather, looked out at King's Bridge toward Westchester. The road seemed animated with a few more wagons than usual; a carriage raising up the choking June dust, and beyond, in a meadow, a local militia company drilling with muskets, Kentuck' rifles, every kind of horse pistol, old sword, or cutlass.

The wraith-like events of the last few days flooded David's mind and he rubbed his unshaved chin and felt again the ache in his kidneys caused by his saddle odyssey from Boston. Pensive, introspective, he ached. He had sent the dispatches downtown to the proper people and had slept. Now there was more to do. Orders not written down had to be transmitted to the local provincial government. He scratched his mosquito-plagued neck.

From the saddlebags, hung on a Hitchcock chair, David took out a good English razor, a present from John Hunter. He found tepid water in a pitcher and a last bit of soap, and he lathered his face and stood stropping the razor on his broad leather belt, its buckle held firm by a knob of the bedpost. . . . He hoped he was free of self-deception.

Here he was, suddenly caught up in the delirium of a war, in the spite and calumny of Whigs and Tories. There would be great need soon for his skill as surgeon, but somehow he had not planned to use his knowledge merely for war. David Cortlandt had certain psychic intuitions that this rebellion was not wholly what it appeared on the surface. He knew that many were using it for their own ends. But it did not matter. He stropped the razor slowly; what mattered was that a new concept of Americans was being born. That some men did not want it he could understand. The moral aridity of merchants made them loyal usually to their ledgers. Yet some, like Morris Manderscheid, would bankrupt themselves for the new ideas. Unique circumstances would test us all, he decided. Injury and ingratitude would occur. No doubt John Hancock would do well now; war was a smugglers' heaven. And what of that poor tarred and feathered wretch he had seen on the road driving down from Schuyler's? Things like that would increase rather than be done away with. One had to believe in final events or one was stranded in the abyss of nothing. He saw with John Hunter now that the perfectability of man was a dream. Life was a short play of tenebrous shadows. David began to shave with great sweeping strokes.

Time plays an essential part in our mortality, and suddenly for no reason he could imagine (or admit) the image of Peg laughing filled his mind—so desirable, so lusty, so full of nuances of pleasure and joy. He drove sensual patterns off, carefully shaving his long upper lip. It is harder, he muttered, to meditate on man (or woman) than on God.

David finished shaving, washed his face clean of lather, and combed and retied his hair. He was proud that he had never worn a wig. More and more of the colonials were wearing their own hair and not using powder. He felt cheerful again, refreshed; presentable in his wide-cut brown suit, the well-made riding boots.

It is so easy to falsify sentiment. . . . In the meadow below, militia officers shouted at their men and on King's Bridge two boys sat fishing. The future would happen; he did not have to hurry it by thinking too much. A man could be tossed outside the dimension of time by a stray bullet these days. He began to pack the saddlebags. *And all this too shall pass away*: it came to him out of some dim corner of memory from a church service when he was a boy—yes, in a white church with a thin spur steeple in the patriarchal Hudson Valley, where a feeling of plenitude was normal in those English-Dutch manors with their well-fed squires. This war would be a wrench to them.

The borrowed sulky was in the barn, and the horse was munching oats and driving off bluebottle flies with its tail. David thanked the wife of the Son of Liberty whose farm this was. He harnessed the horse and drove off, saddlebags and pistols on the floor of the sulky. It was pleasant to drive down the spine of Manhattan, past the farms, the beehives, the kine standing knee-deep in streams chewing their eternal cud. In an hour he came to buildings closer together, to town blocks, sidewalks. He drove by a forge, a fuller mill pounding cloth, many hogs; past a shipyard, where the raw oak side of a hull on the ways stood deep in wood shavings as men with mallets drove wooden pins to hold the timbers together.

On the Hudson, as the river widened and the bay began, David saw the high gilt and yellow shape of a man-of-war. Under reefed sails in the slight breeze drifted the frigate H.M.S. *Scarborough*. Colonial spies had fully reported every ship of the Royal Navy. The Tory governor of New York, William Tryon, was supposed to be on her.

The town itself, under its elms and the heated sky, went about its business. Citizens gathered on corners to read the gazettes, and there were some men wearing the colonial blue and buff, even one with a gold epaulet. The militia was out by now, he knew, patrolling Flushing, Hell Gate, Whitestone Landing. There must be a provost marshal somewhere actively preparing the city for defense.

The sulky's wheels ran over the rough cobbles at Spring and Wooster streets, where Corbie's Tavern stood, and beyond it the Sergeant's Arms. David avoided them. The reports were that they were nests of Tories and could bear watching. He saw the tall gallows set up near the Bowery, and beyond it in the dimpling bay and, far out, the hulls of British vessels.

David found the house he had been told to look for. On Canal Street, two stories of red Dutch brick, white lattices, dormer windows, some mulberry trees in front. A fresh sign read: *American Colonies Trading Company*. Inside at a kidney desk sat a young man with the yellow eyes of a liver sufferer, dressed in tawny summer holland, writing with a feather on long lined sheets of paper. So *this* was the office of the Joint Committee of Safety and Supplies.

David took out a folded letter and laid it before the clerk. The clerk read it, said nothing, and went away. After a while he returned and said, "At the head of the stairs, Dr. Cortlandt."

There was nothing at the head of the rather loose steep steps but a green-painted door. David knocked and turned the latch. He found himself in a square room overlooking backyards and gardens. Muskets and rifles leaned against three walls; parts of a brass cannon called a cohorn were scattered on the uncarpeted floor. A large man turned from looking out the unwashed window, and smiled.

"So it begins, eh, Davey?"

It was Botts, the secret agent for the Sons of Liberty in London. They shook hands, Botts full of a jovial pawkiness. Memories bittersweet flooded David's thoughts. "I gather you've closed out the British branch?"

"Nay, Doctor. Just the smuggling part. We've got our men inside the War Office, and doing other good work in talking up our interests."

"You got my dispatches?"

"Aye. We've been spreading the news. I'd offer you a drink but I'm still on my promise." The big man sat down hard on a chair and looked up at David. "You're to be assistant to the Surgeon General of the Continental Army."

"The devil I am," David said.

Botts nodded. "Dr. Church of Boston will be Surgeon General. I suspect him of Tory leanings, but Washington's friends are in the driving seat now, and he's a favorite of theirs. So let's accept actualities and certainties."

"You think Colonel Washington will become general?"

"Your news of Breed's Hill will make it so. At least he'll show London how wrong Dr. Johnson and his friends were. I remember the old blowhard in my drinking days at the Cheshire Cheese, saying, 'Sir, Americans are a race of convicted felons, and they ought to be thankful for anything we allow them short of hanging.'"

"Ah well, Botts, I've treated the foul doctor for his sores. A bag of pus. Once I said 'Sir, you smell.' He corrected me, 'You smell, sir, I stink.'"

A door on the left wall, which David had not noticed before, had opened. A young girl in a blue riding habit came in and looked about her with the air of one expecting some service.

"Botts, I'm worried."

"Nothing to worry over, Mistress Philipse. Many a bad knock I've had and it was worse than what Joey got. Oh, may I present Dr. Cortlandt. Mistress Roxanne Philipse."

She looked at David frankly and directly, in no mood for manners.

"Be you a medical doctor, a teacher of Latin, or perhaps a preaching fellow?"

David smiled and bowed. "I am a surgeon and medical man with the proper certificates."

"Then you must look at my brother. He feels his whole innards are in inexplicable disorder. His side is all blue and purple."

Botts shook his head. "The lad got a mere blow with an underpowdered slug in a raid the other night. You'd think he were drawn and quartered on Tyburn Hill. Better look at him."

The girl flared up, her little chin firm—a spoiled darling, no doubt about it—and faced Botts, hands on her skirted hips. "You'll keep the flip side of your tongue away from me, Botts. I'm a Philipse, and don't you forget it. Follow me, Doctor."

"You lovely little vixen, I'll paddle your bottom," Botts said and laughed, slapped his knee, not at all insulted.

David shrugged his shoulders and followed the girl through the low door, down a short flight of stairs, and across a small, rather neglected garden of hollyhocks and peach trees, to a small brick building. She pushed open the door and past a short hall David found himself in a low-ceilinged room lit by small leaded windows. There were piles of old Queen Anne muskets, and kegs of what smelled like salt horse—navy pork packed in brine. David bumped his head on the low doorway.

On a low bed lay a young man with a pale face in need of washing. His breeches were unbuttoned, his stockings sagged. He wore no shoes. He lifted himself on one elbow and stared at his sister and David.

"Now don't fret, Joey. I've gotten you real medical aid. Dr. Cortlandt, my brother Joey Philipse."

David smiled. "And I your most humble servant, Assistant Surgeon General of the Continental Army, I have just been told. What's your trouble, my young bucko?"

Joey moaned and fell back on the bed. "I was shot. I feel all my lights and parts punctured, and vital humors sloshing around."

"Joey, you stop talking in that manner to the doctor. If God means you to live to fight for liberty, you'll live."

"Spoken like a good American," said David, bending over the bed and removing wads of linen steeped in an oily yellow salve.

The girl said crisply: "Don't mock me, Dr. Cortlandt. You men are such fools as to think all women as foolish as you are."

Joey moaned. "What a shrew you are, Roxanne. I pity the man that marries you. Oh Doctor, am I undone?"

"Inside us all sits a vulnerable man."

"Yes, I am undone."

"Unbuttoned, I would say." David looked at the bruised white skin, at the healing scab where the slug had gone in and the other wound where it had come out two inches away. "It was a spent slug. Just plowed a bit under the skin till it came out. Nothing vital touched. No intestine, liver, spleen, gall duct, lung, or bowel touched. Get up sir, and get well washed and dressed. You're a blinking fraud."

Roxanne began to laugh and dance a jig in her slim riding boots. "Oh Joey, what a fool you've made yourself look."

The boy bit his lower lip and pushed his soiled shirt into his breeches and buttoned himself. He sat up and looked puppy-dog hurt at David. "It was the first time I've ever been wounded."

"'He mocks at scars that never bore a wound.' Shakespeare, I believe."

Roxanne came to his side—two heads shorter than he. "You don't quote it properly, Doctor."

"Well, I'll be damned. A bluestocking miss who knows the Bard. I didn't know any woman in London who could quote him."

Roxanne looked up at him wide-eyed. "Oh, you've been to London! Tell me. It must be most grand—the damn English, they really walk the golden earth, don't they? All those bawdy society ways and *mésalliances*."

Joey stood up and looked at his soiled hands. "I keep telling her it's just a dirty city. Wild and rotten in high places and full of the pox and the stinks. After all, I've made the Grand Tour."

"Shut up, Joey. You're not very observing. Tell me, Dr. Cortlandt, it's wonderful, isn't it? Not placid and proper, like here in New York?"

"In many ways. My friends call me David."

The girl folded her arms and shook her head. "It's vulgar to call a gentleman by his Christian name. Even in war."

"*La glorie militaire*," said Joey, "is a matter that concerns men, not ballroom beaux. What do *we* colonies do now?"

David was amused at these two bright and rather agitated unsophisticated children. Not that Roxanne—at near nineteen, he suspected—was a child in looks. She had ample breasts, a well-curved hip in the loose-cut riding costume, and a skin so pink he hadn't seen its match anywhere outside of England, among the milking maids. However this was no time to become entranced by a mocking eye and a little foot; Joey was right, she'd make some badgered man a dreadful shrew of a wife.

"The colonies will have a long war, I would venture," David said. "The British can stand a long siege in Boston. They will make an attempt on New York. This city and Philadelphia are, with Boston, the major centers. We shall see men-of-war in fleets on the Hudson soon. Big guns, I wager, on Brooklyn Heights and Staten Island."

Roxanne smiled as if mocking a farm boy. "Really Dr. Cortlandt—David, rather—once we teach them their full lesson up Boston way, there will be no problems here."

"I observe your brother was wounded in local action against loyalists. There are Tory bands out too, and you will see them bushwhacking and burning, and cruelty enough for all in your own front gardens."

"You will come to dinner tonight, David?" Roxanne asked.

He cocked his head to one side. What damned *presence* this girl had! So sure of her family and position and their possessions. To the manor born, of course. "I know the Philipse house on the river. I went there with my cousin Harvell Livingston several times."

"We are in our town house now—for the present—on King Street, number 62. We dine at eight."

Joey, stepping into his boots, sighed and was soon putting on a battered tricorne hat. "We don't have to tell you, Doctor—nothing of all this to the pater. He's a colonial, but hasn't declared himself yet."

Roxanne said, "Nonsense, Daddy is a patriot."

"I shall listen, and eat my dinner," David promised.

Joey seriously shook his hand, and Roxanne made a neat little bow. When they were gone David sat down on a stool and laughed. They were such pleasant, innocent young people, and he was so much older; four or five years' advantage really did seem such a barrier between him and these young sparks' fury of purpose.

Botts came into the room, bending low with old knowledge, to avoid the beam over the door. "Well, Davey, you amused the whelps.

They found you—I quote—'interesting.' Yes, that's what Roxy said: interesting."

"You seem to trust them, Botts. Can we depend on the big land-owning families?"

"Some. But Roxy has been with us since fifteen. Carried letters and packets sewed in her drawers and smallclothes for dispatch to Philadelphia. Joey has been reporting on Tory visitors to his uncle's. I must say it's turned out valuable."

"But it's only a game to them, Botts."

"Mayhaps. Still, had that slug been an inch or so to the left the other night, Joey woud have known just how dirty the game is."

"I've been invited to sup at their town house."

"Go. You'll be able to test the temper of landowners and taste their vittles. I'll have orders for you when you get back. We have some forts we've seized, you know. Ticonderoga among others. It holds the key to invasion of Canada, or a defense against a British invasion from up there. It commands Lake Champlain, the only waterway between Canada and us. A major military point."

"Botts, what are you? Head of intelligence, or what?"

"Don't ask." The big man rubbed his lower lip. "Say I am a drunk-ard held in leash by an idea. That is best for you to know. I test political weather. History has no meaning unless seen through a society, or a culture. . . . There is great illness at the fort—ague, fevers, bloody shirttails. You will investigate and prescribe. Also for me you will file a report as to conditions, loyalties, gossip."

"A spy, Botts, me—on my own side?"

The big man still looked simple, the course features stupid. How he has fooled me, David thought.

Botts sat down on the bed. "This place reeks. Open the window, Davey. This war may not be won on battlefields—but by informers, spies, turncoats. Traitors' deeds, dirty business, drumhead court-martials, hangings; things that will *never* appear in the popular history books."

"You suspect the British are also active?"

"They have information nets and drops all over the colonies. We're ferreting some of them out, but it's not easy. Every Tory farm or house is a hiding place. Every loyalist feels he must send in a report. And London has the gold coin to pay for everything. We depend only on a cause . . . a cause that puts no butter on bread, nor ale in a tankard."

"I'll do my best, Botts. You know, I never heard your first name."

"Better so. I'll brief you later. Now go get your toilet fixed for the evening. You can stay here in the house, but you need clothes."

"I have a fresh shirt in the saddlebags, and some good lace. I need a better hat, stockings, and pumps."

Botts went to a closet and opened it. "Young Joey has things here. His jackets and breeches wouldn't fit your bulk, but try his other gear. Davey, you've had no traffic with Sir Francis Livingston?"

"I talked to him at Schuyler's, near Yonkers, the other night. Private matters."

"About the woman you befriended in London and whose spawning you brought over? Don't scowl. We *must* know these things. It would be best not to get too involved. Sir Francis is head of the Tory Legion recruiting hereabouts. They hope to put several regiments on the king's side. Culbly Schuyler, we suspect, is paymaster to the notorious Colonel Lemon who has been attacking our farms and our militia."

David took some long gray stockings off a peg. "Damn the war, Botts. I'm dining out. Tomorrow I promise I'll worry over the colonial condition."

"Jonathan Philipse has a marvelous claret, I hear," Botts said.

CHAPTER 11   Jonathan Philipse (he could call himself Lord Jonathan Frederick Philipse) besides being the holder of Philipse Manor and its manor house, first raised up in 1683, was owner of one quarter of Westchester County, possessor of almost twenty-five miles of the Hudson Valley from Spuyten Duyvil, through Yonkers, Tarrytown, and Sing Sing, to the Croton River. (His ancestor, Frederick Philipse, had sold some few thousand riverside acres to Mynheer's wealthy ancestors a century ago.) He was a prize for which both the Continental Congress and the Crown made bold bids. Jonathan had held his ideas on the subject private, but now there was gossip he would go with the colonies.

When in town he and his wife Greetje lived at his house on King Street, three-storied, much redone from its original form, and furnished in Sheraton-Hepplewhite, Connecticut cherrywood, Carolean and Georgian brass, and his adored wife's Waterford and Delft glass and porcelains. He himself had rather lush taste in painting; Angelica Kauffmann, Roman scenes by Benjamin West, and upstairs some Frenchie things for private eyes: nates, breasts, and bellies.

Dusk turned from topaz to sepia and the supper was held in the large dining room under crystal candle hangings, ormolu-mounted furniture, addosses sphinxes, mahogany and inlaid satinwood. Everything was a little over-ripe.

David sincerely said to the hostess, "It would do honor to London's best taste, ma'am."

Greetje Philipse smiled and motioned the butler to serve the soup. He was not a slave; but a tall, pale-pink Yorkshireman, assisted by two little rosy-cheeked maids.

Jonathan had introduced David to the other guests after Joey, pale, washed, re-dressed, had introduced David to the head of the house. The two men guests from northern New York colony seemed solid merchant types, tanned by outdoor life, ruddy with overfeeding on hardy fare. Their wives were scented with lavender sachet, dumpy, rather ill dressed, but kindly. Roxanne had her hair dressed tall; her blue silk was low-cut and wide below. She smelled of patchouli and bergamot. It was an age for strong odors.

"What do you treat mostly, Doctor?" asked the host, as a large red river salmon on a plank was brought in.

"Scrofula, *cholera infantum*, lung tubules. But I don't think it's talk fit to grace your fine food."

Roxanne laughed; he had heard her taffeta underskirts rustle when she had walked up to greet him. "Oh, we talk of everything here, don't we, Papá?"

The shorter of the male guests said, "Damn lot of horse croup near Albany, pardon me."

"Not my field," said David, forking the slice of salmon served him.

Greetje smiled at her daughter. "I'm pleased you dressed tonight as you used to."

The roast followed the salmon—they listened to Jonathan fix the position of the Continental Congress. "Whatever we may think of it, good or bad, it has the support of many of the people of the colonies."

The larger male guest shook his several chins. "*What* people, *what* support? Coarse fellows from grist mills, idle apprentices."

"We shall all have to declare ourselves soon," said Jonathan. "I rather think a man must stay with his native soil." He held up a glass. "A toast: May the sword of the parent never be stained with the blood of the children."

The northern guests looked at one another and began to eat quickly. They were not going to commit themselves just for a good dinner and a fine red wine. David wondered if Breed's Hill had not stained *both* parents and children.

With coffee, Roxanne captured David from Joey, who wanted to take him to the top of the house to view his weapon collection. Roxanne—a girl all gold and quicksilver, David decided—managed to lead him to the garden with the skill of someone showing off a prize horse and trying to give the impression the creature was picking its own direction.

It was cool in the amethyst-tinted garden. The brick walls kept out some of the night sounds, as well as the roaming pigs that did the sanitation service in the public streets. The smell of jacqueminot roses masked the river odors of ships, tar, hide warehouses, and wool bales on the nearby docks.

Roxanne turned to David. "I brought you here because I have a problem and a medical man might give me help."

"Cucumber-water lotion is good for the skin, and the London beauties wash their hair in stale beer. I rather dislike that habit."

"No, no. I *can* trust you, can't I?"

"I'd rather not hear any secrets."

She sat down on a stone bench in a swirl of petticoats and made a minx-like gesture for him to join her. She looked at the sky, then back at David, and took his hand. "A girl has few people to turn to. Do political values transcend moral values at a time like this?"

"I don't know. That's an abstraction. I don't work well with abstractions. Or my mind, at least, doesn't."

"If I were to leap into bed with an important crown official—for our cause, I mean—you wouldn't call that immoral?"

"I'd call it damn foolish." He tried not to show his prissy shock at the question.

"Dr. Cortlandt, you're flushing."

He looked at her and pinched her ear. "There are many good causes; none I know of are worth that sacrifice."

"Suppose you were that official? I am worthy of bedding with, aren't I? I mean even a rake like Sir James Tropp is all adrool for me, and he knows much we could use. Information. I might even get him to come over to us, our side."

He patted her hand and kissed her cheek lightly. "Oh baby Jezebel, grow up."

"Damn!" Roxanne stood up and banged a little foot on the turf. "All we hear, Joey and myself, is grow up, grow up."

"Frankly you are not the material for a courtesan."

"Stop grinning. Why not?"

"I am not, Roxanne, a true man of the world. Even if I spent some years in London. But I did know the drabs and beauties who were, well, shall we say bedded rather casually. It's a body- and soul-destroying thing."

"I shall decide. It is a matter of deep concernment, I agree. You're no help at all. You see me only as a child."

David put a hand on the nape of her neck and pressed his fingers lightly on the warm, throbbing column. "Besides, I hear Sir James Tropp has fled to the ships."

"Oh double damn. Treat me as woman. I am, you know. Have been since twelve. But a medical man would know that. Even Joey gets more consideration than I do. He's going with you on some mission, I'm told."

David remained expressionless. "I know nothing of it."

She laughed and held up her face and kissed his cheek. "Dear David, you are an ox at social graces. Botts trusts me to do many things for him. Why can't I get into buckskin breeches and go off with you into the woods on this mission as a boy? Shakespeare's girls all did."

"Yes. But, you see, boys played the women's parts then. It was easy to believe. Speaking as a medical man and anatomist I would say you have developed since the age of twelve certain curves, certain convex and concave parts that would look ill in male breeches."

She suddenly changed the subject; her large eyes were half hooded by her lids. She rose, took the crook of his arm. "Come, you must see our forcing beds. Daddah likes his early vegetables."

They inspected the garden beds under glass. In the glow from the candle-lit windows they admired the grapes ripening. They came to a low section of wall that showed the river and ships' spars. Far out over the water the stern windows of a man-of-war made orange reflections in the bay. Roxanne said, "I wonder if Sir James would swim ashore if he knew what I had planned for him?"

The distant lights twinkled in the tidal pull as if signaling back some lover's answer.

Botts, at his post on Canal Street, looked in the lime-white morning light as if he had done little sleeping. He sat in the weapon-cluttered yard house and stared up at David and Joey Philipse standing before him.

"You're on orders to go upriver in a small sloop we'll provide. Tarrytown, Verplanck's Point, and beyond. But don't land unless you have to. In Albany, at the White Hart Inn, you'll meet one of our scouts. He'll lead you overland through Saratoga, Glens Falls, and to Fort Ticonderoga. You, David, have the rank of captain, and here is your commission as Assistant Surgeon General of the Continental Army."

David took the papers and glanced through their fly-track ink lines. "You have the medical and surgical supplies I listed ready to go with us?"

Botts glanced at Joey. "I have what I could collect. Four chests. You may get pack horses at Albany, you may not. Joey, can you carry forty pounds all day through Indian country?"

"Yes, I can if I have to."

"The aborigines are being recruited by the British. The Six Nations are out on scalp hunts. Mohawks, Senecas, Onondagas, the Oneidas. Damn me if I remember all the Nations."

David said, "The Cayugas and the Tuscaroras. I used to hunt on the estates around Albany as a boy. Had a fat old Indian guide who taught me a lot of the tribal lore, most of it lies."

"I hope he taught you how to save your hair. You understand conditions are mean and ugly up there. Medical aid is badly needed. Besides that, as I hinted, it is a gateway of invasion for them, and for us. You'll both find clothes in the closet and wardrobes. Pick any weapons you want. Your sloop leaves tonight. Foot of Canal at seven."

Botts stood up and mopped his plain, wide face. He was expressionless, only the blue-green eyes showing his reaction to the mission.

"Good luck, Captain Cortlandt."

"Thank you, Botts—do you hold a rank I should call you by?"

"No rank." They shook hands.

Joey spoke up, "I'm a full-fledged soldier now, too?"

"A kind of one,'" said Botts. "You get leftenant's rank if you do well on this mission." He held out a square of thin paper marked in red and blue ink. "It's the best map we have for around Lake George. Joey, you're to mark on it any information you can. Tribal movements, British scouts, or reports of such. Anything you think I should know. Captain Cortlandt will handle anything you feel too big for you."

"Yes, sir."

"The Tory bands are mucking around all along the Hudson Valley. So be wary. And get rid of the map if you're in trouble. I must go see now to other people."

Botts picked up some papers. "You'll carry kinepox, Davey, for smallpox inoculation, some felon lancets and bistoury kits, apothecary jars of stramonium, belladonna, arnica, opium, and whatever else I could find. Not all you need, I fear."

"It will do and thank you. Thank you."

"Good-by." Botts waved and went out.

Joey was plucking at the closet hooks, going over a collection of hunting shirts, leather breeches, battered hats. "They've mostly been worn."

"Should be comfortable."

Joey held up a new blue and buff jacket with brass buttons. "It has a tag with your name on it: *Capt. David Cortlandt.*"

"No breeches, no boots? Well, it will have to do." David picked up the jacket and, slipping off his coat, he put on the blue and buff. "That Botts is a fairly good maker of magic. Joey, it *almost* fits."

David stood in front of a small mirror on the wall and saw himself in the uniform jacket. A moment of discomfort and worry turned at once to great pride.

On the outskirts of Albany a strange figure sat in front of the White Hart, a river inn—sat on a low bench and watched the river spin by. Jack-Tom Swales was blond, tall and heavily built, all six-feet-three of him. He would have been a very handsome man but for the manner in which he did his hair. In a most odd way. He was clean-shaven except for a two-inch fringe of cedar-colored whisker that began just under his chin and ran from ear to ear. Also, his long and narrow head was shaved clean but for a Seneca Indian bush of hair—golden wires—that was three inches wide, three inches long, and went from his brow back to the nape of his weather-brown neck.

"Me topknot," Jack-Tom called it. "I like to give any red varmint that wants to lift the hair a good thing, if he kin get it."

Jack-Tom wore a long deerskin hunting shirt, beautifully tanned and fringed, and his loose trousers were of the same leather. The effect was spoiled somewhat by the fact that Jack-Tom used his clothes as napkin and towel at times. The stains of grease, campfire soot and hunting muck had pretty much dissipated the original condition of the garments. The long deerhide fringes that swept from sleeves and trouser seams were often missing where Jack-Tom had needed a leather thong in a hurry.

The cleanest thing about the blond giant was the long Kentuck' hunting rifle, nearly as tall as he was, its beautiful maple stock having a tiger-stripe pattern burned into it. Over one shoulder hung a hunting bag of tanned elkskin. And it and his belt were decorated with shell beadwork and colored quills; Cayuga squaw work of fine detail and some skill. Both items displayed plumes of hair of different shades worked into the design. In the belt he carried a razor-sharp steel tomahawk made for the frontier trade in Sheffield, England. By its side rested a hunting knife with a heft bound in rawhide. In back dangled a bullet pouch full of lead balls Jack-Tom had run himself from a mold he carried in his elkskin bag. The giant had very large but well-arched feet, and his moccasins were splendid examples of Indian design and decoration.

This morning—his ears ringing with war whoops free of consonants or vowels and audible only to himself—sitting in front of the Albany inn, Jack-Tom was feeling the agony of the damned. He had been drunk for three days and nights and the eve before he had eaten several pounds of venison and wild turkey, Indian fashion, gorging the boiling meats till he felt ready to burst. Somewhere in between the drinking and the feasting he had orgied with a young Indian girl, already ripe at fourteen and amorous as a mink pond in spring. He had purged himself with elder-tree juice and snail water and herbs—it hadn't helped.

The pounding in the big man's ears was like a waterfall of good-sized rocks hitting him on the top of his head. His digestive system growled and protested, and the squaw had bitten him deeply on the right ear in amorous play. He felt for the clot already formed on the ear lobe.

The sun was six degrees off the horizon. When those people arrived that he was to take up north, he'd be better. All he needed was to measure a trail, walk thirty, forty miles a day on the packed leaves of centuries, smell an air free of city smoke, and himself kill his own meat. He'd feel a mite better. His throat burned like Ole Beelzebub hisself was livin' in it. A little pokeberry and sage tea in an Indian village would help.

Jack-Tom Swales was famous on the northern frontier as a wilderness man. He never slept under a roof in summer, never felt really at ease with wood or stone or rug under his feet. It was said he had been born somewhere in Vermont, and that Mohawks had raided his father's farm, killed off the family, all but seven-year-old Jack-Tom. Till he was fourteen he lived as a Mohawk, then he was captured by the Oneidas of the Six Nations and made a member of their campfires. At sixteen he was a *coup*-seeking painted buck, his blond topknot dyed with oak gall and berry juice, only the china-blue eyes at odds with his savage blood brothers. He had killed men in tribal raids, fathered some sons and one daughter on various squaws. Kiyoutan—Lake Eyes—as he was called, would have ended his days as a chief in one of the bark longhouses but for a raid on a British column surveying land for one of those hare-brained schemes for the cutting of royal timber on the Canadian border.

He was sixteen when captured. Too old to teach to read and write—or he showed no interest in the idea. As a recaptured white man he was apprenticed to a blacksmith in Bennington, but ran away. He returned to his tribe, who saw him in all his long-haired blondness and in white man's gear. They laughed and mocked him, threw dog turds on him, and banished him from the tribe. He became a fur hunter, a wilderness guide to royal commissions that went a little way into the tangled woods. One winter he brought out a lost party of English hunters short only several British fingers, a foot frozen off. Jack-Tom disappeared for months at a time into the forests, came into Albany, often smeared with Indian paint, reeking of tepee fires, usually with a bundle of well-tanned furs which he proceeded to drink up and orgy away as quickly as possible. Despondency ruled him then, and he felt his life was lived in an abyss of nothingness.

He had a remarkable mind, but as he spoke badly and as he could neither read nor write he remained what he was, a cunning barbarian with a great love of the wilderness and a powerful knowledge of Indian ways. When despair passed he enjoyed a feeling of plenitude. He had hired out to the Continental Army to guide parties to the

various lake forts. Not for any deep-seated understanding of all the
talk of tyranny and liberty, but because Jack-Tom disliked the Englishmen he had met, and a year before a major had had him flogged
in public—twenty strokes across the naked back—for not saying "sir"
when addressing the officer. Jack-Tom hoped the major was now
fighting on the other side. He wanted to add his British brown hair
to the fringes of other enemies ornamenting his hunting bag and
belt.

The agony in Jack-Tom's throat and stomach was as bad as ever.
But, Indian fashion—living and dying in control of one's being—
he showed by no outward expression the agony he was going through.
He shifted his seat on the inn-yard bench and wondered if he could
get a hair of the dog this early in the inn's taproom. Harry Morris,
the innkeeper, came out of the wide door into the sunlight followed
by a tall red-haired man in a blue and buff Continental jacket and
a youth in a dark linen hunting tunic who needed a bit of filling out.

"Jack-Tom, this is Captain Cortlandt and Joey Philipse. Got in
yesterday. You was to meet them here, but you was too drunk last
night. This is Jack-Tom Swales. Injuns call him Kiyoutan."

Jack-Tom stood up and held out a long narrow hand. "And here
I be. Howdy Captain, howdy Philipse."

The innkeeper looked askance at the wilderness man and went
away to see how the stables were this early in the morning. David
felt his fingers gripped hard and when the pressure relaxed he said,
"Mr. Botts in New York said we'd meet a scout here."

"You just done met him. Got much gear?"

"Four packs and some personal boxes. I hope we don't have to
carry it."

"Harry will get us two pack hosses. Either of you carryin' a little
crackskull, as Harry says? I'm a mite over-powered this morn."

David held out a silver flask. "Peach brandy do?"

"Beelzebub, yes," said Jack-Tom rubbing his blond fringe of beard.
"I reckon it will, jest." He took a big swallow, sighed, and rubbed his
eyes. "Grips a man's cods. The sooner we now git on the trails north
the better. We're avoidin' the river. Tories may be layin' fer you."

Joey was examining the hunting bag, touching the hairy fringes.
"What kind of fur is that, Jack-Tom?"

"That be folk fur. Injun mostly. That reddish one belonged to a
Frenchie I got me near Lake George. He was after me gizzard with
two Injuns—come two years ago spring."

"Scalps?" asked Joey. "Human hair?"

"They ain't forest fern. You both got firearms?"

David nodded. "At the inn. I've got a Philadelphia rifle and Joey an English bore pistol."

"Let's git goin', then. It's a fur bit to Ticon. Walkin'."

It was on the trail under oak and larch and locust trees that Jack-Tom showed himself at his best. He was no mere frontier character. He was a wise and cunning trail boss, aware of every sound, knowing —it would almost appear—every tree and rock. Jack-Tom was only twenty-four, and the regular triangular cheeks, brown features with the fringe of yellow beard and the shaven head with its welt of top hair, Indian style, made him a striking figure. He pointed out sassafras and spicebush, swamp rose, bay, and spoors of animal.

The two pack horses were small but powerful. Joey was in charge of them. Jack-Tom went first, rifle held in the crook of one deerskin arm, the man stepping with care on the trail, his moccasined feet making almost no sound, avoiding twigs, stones. His continual glance from side to side showed he was always alert. He led them under the arched shade of trees, past gushing brooks, and along the looping bends of damp, soft earth of what must once have been ancient deer paths. They had left the last of the farm roads the day before and were going north at a steady four miles an hour. David and Joey had changed their boots for moccasins, but the fast trail pace winded them. Jack-Tom called a halt every two hours. He would take out a red stone pipe, a noble calumet, from his hunting bag and smoke a mixture of willow bark and rank tobacco, while David and Joey lay on their backs among old leaves feeling as if their joints would never function again.

"You'll git back yer jisum and feel just fine another day out. We git to some pretty parts ahead. Nothin' as good fer a man like the woods, and the critters in it. I'll git us some grouse fer supper tonight. Maybe some trout too. I got me a trout line in the bag."

Joey sat up and sighed as he slapped at biting insects. "It like this all the way, Jack-Tom?"

"Shat, no. Beelzebub—it gits real rocky and tangled near the fort. Come through here one year with six Iroquois heeling after me. Raced 'em two hundred miles to save me hair. Night and day never slept more than ten minutes at a time. Outrun 'em all."

David was making notes in a small journal. "Any danger of running into aborigines around here?"

"Don't rightly think so, Captain. Never kin tell, of course. The varmints go on a raid whenever time hangs heavy on their hands. And times are sure unsettled."

"Are they good fighters?" Joey asked, examining a blistered heel.

"Good enough, smart enough. But they'd rather murder, steal, and futz than anythung else. They be real mink about futzin' and capturin' women. I've seen a few ruttin' doin's done you wouldn't want to believe."

"Cruel, are they?" Joey asked.

Jack-Tom ate the end off a strand of grass he pulled up. "Life be cruel, boy, real cruel. Everythang ettin' offen someone else. They're no crueler than what I seen in cities. In Albany and once't in New York. Hangin' a sojer, cuttin' slaves open with a bull-pistill lash. Prisoners chained together, rust eatin' off their hands, farmers beatin' their hired help into ijets with a ox yoke. Injuns just take it more fancy. Burnin' pines splinters pushed under yer finger nails, denuttin' ya with a clam shell, or bitin' off yer finger to show you're welcome." Jack-Tom held up his left hand; the little finger was missing. "An ole Tuscarora woman she fanged and gummed it off when I was sixteen during a little to-do I had winterin' at a village up near the Canuck border."

David was looking at the map Botts had given Joey. "You think a lot of the Indians will join the British?"

"Jine any side what will give 'em rum, beads, guns, and a chance to go futzin'. Them red buggers is mean." Jack-Tom spit out the stalk of grass and adjusted his scalp-trimmed hunting bag. "We better mosey along now. Eighteen miles before we makes camp."

Joey wept that night, the blisters on his heels bloody and broken open. David ate a little jerked meat and watched the campfire coals while Jack-Tom cleaned the spider skillet with sand, and the hobbled pack horses grazed nearby. Every time David woke up, the bells around the horses' necks made soft silver sound.

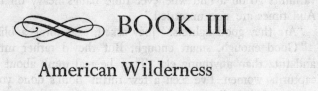

BOOK III

American Wilderness

CHAPTER 12   The late afternoon sun was slanting in—umber as dried dust from the west. The three men and the pack horses were moving along a brown twisting trail soggy with century-old leaves and crisscrossed by timber, blown down by ancient storms and rotting slowly away. Jack-Tom peered ahead. "We use this back track fer safety. Too many things I don't like about the other—the main trail— just now. Git them hosses up, young fella."

Joey banged the haunch of a pack horse with his arm and wiped the sweat from over his eyes. "It's muggy here."

"Want to make Ned Styron's place fer sure tomorrer. Gotta git along."

"Who's Ned?" David asked, balancing his rifle in the crook of his left arm and looking up at the tunnel of trees.

"Powder maker. Got a mill up on Green River. Has to live alone— just a wench fer cookin' and some sons. First, 'cause he makes gun-powder what has a habit of goin' up fer no reason. Second is Shelagh. Seems folks in the settlements don't mind a man pleasurin' with a Nigra shoat—but when a man is sot on marryin' up with . . ." Jack-Tom held up his hand and went suddenly silent. David stood still, aware only of the buzzing of small green insects darting about in front of his face to sting him. Joey leaned against a pack horse to stop it.

Jack-Tom, wary and careful, looked around expressionless, winked at David, and glanced at the firing pan of his Kentuck' rifle. David did the same and hoped the gun powder had not gone damp in the humid forest they had been tramping through all day.

Jack-Tom said casually in a low voice, "Don't pay me no mind. Just keep moseyin' along. I'm goin' ahead fast, but don't try to kotch up to me."

"What's doing, Jack-Tom?"

"Don't know rightly. There been two fellas on this trail not an hour ago. What knocks me off my perch is they was tryin' to walk so as to leave no signs they been hereabouts."

David searched the leaf mold on the trail and the thin grass underfoot. "I don't see a sign."

Jack-Tom swung his powder horn around and hitched his bullet pouch closer. "Ain't none fer most folk. I gotta smell new to me. And then I see the grass bent like it been stepped on, and yet the soft part, the real mushy parts of the trail not stepped in—avoided, see?"

"Indian?" David asked.

"Beelzebub, yes. Only two, three of us white folk kin hide signs like this."

"How many?"

"Two, my guess. You listen to me. I'll *gobble-gobble* like a tom turkey critter iffen I overrun 'em. Two *gobbles*, you freeze dead in yer tracks. Three gobbles means come up fast and be sure yer flints is set and the pans primed."

Joey took a pistol from his belt. "What kind of Indians?"

"Hell, boy, only an ijet could guess now." Jack-Tom sniffed the air. "Yep, smell 'em too. Old grease, dirty breechcloth, camp smoke in their hair. Strong as wood turnip and chockaberry."

David wondered if the tall blond man in the dirty buckskins was making up part of it. But before he could ask Jack-Tom was gone in a bend of the trail, walking with toes in, hardly, it seemed to David and Joey, touching the ground.

David motioned Joey on. "Easy does it, Joey. Don't drive the animals hard. A slow march."

Joey primed his pistol. "Ever fight Indians?"

"I've camped out with them. Hunted with some."

"They're crafty."

"Keep still, Joey."

There was no sound ahead but the scratching scamper of a small animal in a treetop, the rubbing of leaves and branches in the slight breeze from the south. The sun was twelve degrees off the horizon, he guessed—if they could see a horizon. The smell of green growth, of wood rot, of natural animal life, forest pollen, and sun on bark all blended with the sense of danger that cloaked them.

David had an awareness of the closeness of death, and the personal, pulsing surf of blood and heartbeat that separated one from death. They moved slowly on into the dark channel of the trail ahead.

They had been walking for about twenty minutes when ahead they heard the bang of a rifle, not loud, more like a tree limb being snapped. Both knew it was a rifle shot. They stopped, and one of the pack horses relieved himself on the trail while the other ate with yellow, worn-down teeth the lower leaves of a birch. The natural function of the animal seemed to make a splashing din. Then there came through the trees the clear crackle of a tom turkey's *gobble*. Once, twice, *three* times! A pause of five seconds, and again—one, two, three *gobbles*. David motioned Joey forward and they ran, leaving the pack animals to amble along behind them. The trail dipped down; it did not widen, but there was more golden light as the olive-green treetops turned to larch and more birch and a few elms. There was a wide curve in the trail, and David, rifle held at ready, ran quickly, avoiding the great snarls of tree roots that crossed the trail, (so like, he thought, those heavy veins one cut into around the heart of old patients, those whose course is run and their sluggish blood has difficulty making its way around a body and . . .)

The thought broke itself off like a thread, and he caught a patch of red ahead and then a place where a foaming stream crossed the trail and the trees were thinner. There Jack-Tom was standing, legs apart, with the cruelly twisted body of a nearly naked man at his feet. A weathered brown skin, a dead, staring face painted in yellow and white stripes, a head shaved but for a topknot, very much like Jack-Tom's, only this one was black. Jack-Tom did not turn around as David and Joey ran up. The wilderness man's rifle was pointed to a figure of a man—a second Indian seated under a tree calmly filling a stone pipe from a pouch carried in a belt that held a tomahawk, a butcher knife in a bead-and-porcupine-quillwork sheath.

Jack-Tom said casually, "The two buggers lay an ambush fer me. I had to knife this one in the back."

The figure under the tree grunted and said in guttural English, "Kiyoutan is oh so much the trail-master."

David saw a short but powerful Indian given a bit to fat. Young, with a great wedge of Roman nose and heavy cheekbones. The topknot was tied with red ribbon and the scarlet coat of a British captain of infantry, much mucked up with grease, fitted over the broad torso. The legs were naked, the heavy feet were in worn elk-hide moccasins.

Jack-Tom laughed and spat on the side of the trail. "Too bad I didn't coldcock *you*, Half Hand—not this other buck."

David saw that the living Indian had four fingers missing on the left hand, but he managed to handle the pipe and strike it alight with a flint and steel he carried in his parfleche pouch.

"Just huntin', Kiyoutan, just some venison-trailin'." The Indian spoke his thick English quickly but understandably. Jack-Tom never let his rifle barrel move from the center of the seated Indian's chest. He said, "Doctor, you just pick up his rifle, his knife, and tommy-hawk, and if you want to bash in his mangy skull, you go right ahead."

The Indian calmly sighed and smoked. Joey stared, open-mouthed. This was no silent and noble warrior, as some romantic folk described the red man. This was a dirty, powerfully built intellect—with four fingers on his left hand missing and looking rather barbaric in the red and gold British military jacket. A necklace of bear claws and a large gilt medal of George II in a leather case on a string were worn around the wide throat to complete the picture of a savage in his glory.

David picked up the rifle. It was not cheap trade goods, but a fine English thing. David lifted also the knife and tomahawk and stepped back. The Indian certainly smelled high even if his glance was sensitive and perceptive.

The smoker puffed up smoke in three directions slowly, taking his time as if they were only errant, delusive phantoms. "Half Hand is your friend. I no harm any white settlers, and my tribe is berry-huntin' and killin' meat for the winter smokin'."

David asked, "Why are you wearing a British officer's coat and carrying an English-made rifle?"

The Indian shrugged. "Big fight with British long time ago. Kill six red-backs, take coat, take rifle." He smiled and wiped his wet lips. "Take much rum. You give Half Hand a dollop of drink?"

Jack-Tom shook his head. He looked around as if listening for fresh sounds. "You lyin' bastard. You're in British pay. And I'd cut yer throat like a shoat's at chittlin' time, but yer tribe once sheltered me when I was a young 'un."

"You are one of us, Kiyoutan; of the Senecas and Cayugas." The Indian stood up—he was too stout to be impressive as he knocked out the pipe on his palm and walked quickly away through the trees without a backward glance. Jack-Tom lifted his rifle to follow the retreating back, and then lowered it, and the Indian was gone, except for the smell of the willow-bark tobacco and a faint scent of stale body grease.

Jack-Tom said, "Git the hosses, Joey, we gotta vamoose in case Half Hand contacts a war party." He bent down over the dead man and took out his knife and made a fast circle through the shaved scalp of the dead head at his feet. The blade went around the topknot. Joey gagged and ran off to get the pack horses. Jack-Tom grasped the topknot and with a sudden jerk pulled it free of the skull, the crackling and tearing of skin clearly audible. Jack-Tom shook off a few drops of blood from the scalp and stuck the thing under his belt.

David, unimpressed, looked around, aware how blind he was to direction in this wilderness. At his feet the brook purled and sang over stones. Jack-Tom wiped his fingers on the seat of his buckskin pants. "They wuz waitin' fer me just as nice as two kittens fer a mouse. I got on their flank and picked off this varmint before they knew I wuz on 'em. Half Hand just said, 'I give up to you, Kiyoutan' —that my Injun name."

"Who is Half Hand?"

"A chief of the lake country Senecas—a sachem. Not a big chief, but a risin' young fella. I guess he was just huntin' fer deer spoor. But then again he *might* be scoutin' fer the British. So let's make tracks."

"Isn't it a disgrace for an aborigine to get caught as you caught him? Tribal code or something?"

Jack-Tom patted the scalp in his belt. "That sure be the kinda nonsense I hear in Albany about how Injuns feel about things. They ain't much more than very crafty animals, killin' and futzin' among the tribes, torturin' and cripplin', crackin' the skulls of their wives and tormentin' children and breakin' the legs of their dogs. They just want to do you in 'fore you do them in. Remember that. Beelzebub, ain't nothing like Injuns fer liars either. Come on."

Joey was up with the pack horses and they went on past the crumpled-up dead man on the trail, the top of his head bearing a watermelon-pink circle, his unseeing eyes on the treetops. Jack-Tom put the extra two rifles and gear on the nearest pack horse and went on at a fast pace in the gathering dusk as a pallid coal of a moon grew stronger. Once they stopped while Jack-Tom listened to the cry of a lake loon.

"*That* be Injuns, making out like loon birds. Don't they do it mighty pretty?"

"They after us?" David asked.

"Could be. We'll jest go by stream."

They stepped into a cold brook, pebbles rattling off its hard bottom, and they followed it for a mile and then found rock on one bank and crossed that, and found another stream, this one colder still, and the day was gone. The blue-violet of a cricket-mad night made the forest a lost world of night sounds and animal cries: hunting or avoiding each other for love or food.

They didn't rest that night, but drove the protesting, winded pack animals on. They cut sharp sticks and jabbed the pack horses every time they refused to move. Joey's feet were a bloody mess. He and David were ready to drop onto the trail and refuse to rise again. Jack-Tom looked over a stony marl bank and said, "I ain't heared no loon calls for three hours now. We'll tuck in here. No fires. Just some dried jerky and corn cake. It's one hour to dawn, and we move on." David was already sleeping.

A genteel security bounded his dreams and the agitation of man against man was far off. Then he felt a wrenching sensation of shock that even in his deep, tired sleep jarred him away from the safety of some passing fragment of a dream. It was a rifle shot that made him vulnerable to reality. Close to his ear. David came quickly into waking, fumbling into a consciousness of the image of Jack-Tom Swales, who had fired his rifle into the bush and was now reloading, jamming down the lead ball wrapped in a patch of linen made stiff with tallow, ramming it down with an oak stick on the powder he had spilled into the long barrel from the powder horn a moment or so after firing.

David asked, "What—?"

Joey struggled awake, rubbing his tangled hair. "Indians again?"

Jack-Tom pulled free the slim wooden ramrod and shook his head. "Missed him. Injun was skulkin' 'round us. Only thing fer us to do now is run fer it. There's a war party or war parties out fer us—sure of it now."

Joey struggled to his sore feet, and the bell on one of the pack horses clanged softly in the already blossoming day. The sun was in the east, riding up almost with a snort from behind trees.

Far off to their left and also to their right the mad cries of the lake loon sounded. "War parties fer sure," said Jack-Tom. "We didn't slip Half Hand like I thought. That was his scout I took a pot at." David was sniffing the morning heat, already uncomfortable and wet.

"What do we do now?" he asked. "Stand 'em off? We have three rifles, two pistols."

"Captain, we run, and we forget the pack horses. Shuck down to runnin' shape. Drop yer rifle here. I'll take mine, but you and Joey carry a pistol each."

"I can't leave the medical supplies—the surgeon's tools."

"You'll carry yer own loads."

The loon sounds were converging, and suddenly David felt his breastbone vibrate with a dread of the scalping knives. "All right, I'll just take my own medical kit on one shoulder."

Jack-Tom was pushing some corn-meal cakes, dried pumpkin, and deer jerky into a pouch. "Let's git. And don't stop 'less I says so."

David looked at the packed medical cases in the grass, at the still grazing horses. Jack-Tom took David's rifle, and, holding it by the barrel, he shattered it against a rock. He did the same for the two captured Indian weapons.

"Their lootin' our camp will hold 'em ten minutes maybe, fightin' over the truck and roustin' out the rum. Better leave yer coats."

Jack-Tom was off running down the trail, loping along at a great pace, the big, heavy buckskin figure with his blond topknot exposed. He wasn't carrying any hat in this race, his bullet and food pouch flying behind him, tomahawk and knife in his belt. David watched Joey follow Jack-Tom, big pistol in his belt. He took one last look at the medical supplies and went after the two swiftly moving figures ahead. The merging loon calls were only a half mile away now, he figured, and somehow he sensed the crackle of brush and leaves under moccasins of heelless leather-covered feet after him as in a nightmare.

At first their running was easy. It was cool and fruit-green under the trees, and fear salted their heels. Jack-Tom ran without effort, his toes hardly seeming to touch the trail. For a large man he ran light. Joey kept up with him, but his shorter legs had to move faster. David felt his second wind, heard the tide of blood go faster as it passed and repassed into his heart. Here he was in the wilderness, running from dirty death; how far away were the hopes and the years of London and all the healing wisdom packed inside himself! What use now was a diagnostician and healer? Joey tripped, picked himself up, and ran on, his cheek scraped and cherry-colored blood appearing through the bruise. It was an hour before Jack-Tom held up his hand and they fell over to lie on moldering leaves, their chests rising and falling like the agony of fresh-caught fish tossed onto a shore.

Jack-Tom wiped his face with the back of a hand and fingered his ginger fringe of beard. "They are delayed by drinkin' the rum and the medical alky, I reckon. But they're after us." He put his ear to the trail and seemed undecided as to what he heard. "Danged woodpeckers thro'n' all sound off. Ready?"

Jack-Tom didn't wait to see if they were, but was off on his steady loping run that caused their heel tendons and hams to ache and become agony. David felt he could not ever run again. His body was bathed with sweat and the gnats and hunting insects drowned in it left acid patches of burning.

Joey was showing the whites of his eyes and breathing with a whistling sound. His feet were bloodstained. As they climbed out on a stream bank, Joey sank down and gore began to flow from his nose. David poured water on the boy's face. Jack-Tom shook his head. "Don't let 'em drink. Both of you just swoggle the watter round yer mouth. Spit it out. I'm goin' back to bushwhack a bit and lead 'em off on a deer trail back thar. While you two keep north."

"No, let's go on together," David said.

"Cholera, no. They'd run us down in half an hour *that* way. Never run straight from 'em."

Jack-Tom went off down the trail the way they had come. Joey sucked air and rolled his face in the stream and David said, "Don't drink it. Just keep it in your mouth and spit it out."

"Looks hopeless, David."

"I don't know. I don't aim to just wait here to become a scalp, smoke-curing in the rafters of an Indian longhouse. Let's go."

"My joint's re-locked, David. I can't stand. The skin is all off my heels."

David helped the boy to his feet. "Run barefoot. Keep moving."

Behind them down the trail there was the bark of a rifle, followed by a harsh, shrill outcry, like a pack of wild dogs.

"He's bushwhacked them," said David, and pushed Joey ahead of him.

They ran till the sun was directly overhead, and an hour past that. Then David fell down and the great, intolerable pain in his side was like live coal. He shook the sweat from his head and panted open-mouthed, unable to get much air to stay in his lungs. A kind of inordinate dementia gripped him.

"Joey, I don't know. I think they over . . . ran . . . Jack-Tom. If so . . . they're right behind us . . . you . . ."

"My left leg—it's locked in a cramp. Oh!"

"Beat it with your fists. Hard. Listen . . . you go on . . . leave your pistol with mine. . . . Going . . . to bushwhack a few for myself."

"No, David. You can't stay . . . not . . ."

David rolled over and buried his head in his arms and his lungs worked like bellows. "Orders. . . . soldier. Try . . . reach the powder mill. Warn . . . Indians scouting . . . Go along."

Joey's pistol dropped at David's feet and he looked up to see that the boy was weeping, his hair in disorder over his dirty face, the cheeks scarred by beating bushes and touched with fire by some flounder against leaves of poison sumac. "No, not alone . . ."

To the left the bushes began to rattle and move and David raised a pistol in each shaking arm. The low *gobble-gobble* of a tom turkey rose from the thickets. Jack-Tom came pushing his way through to them.

"Hell, you most nearly let me have a gizzard slug or two, eh?"

"How did you get here?" David asked. He was still breathing in agony but *some* air was staying down.

"Got a varmint, but couldn't stay to take the scalp. Saw 'bout ten of 'em, heard others—all movin' low and fast. Led 'em way off to the east through a deer track and then swum a bit in a lake and got out by pullin' myself up onto a tree by a branch. I reckon we got fifteen, twenty minutes' head start at this here point."

Joey wiped his face with his shirt sleeve. He had discarded his moccasins. David also had dropped his heavy belt and in shirt and stockings and breeks looked up at Jack-Tom. The wilderness man was haggard and drawn but his breathing was easy and he kept looking back over his shoulder with big blue eyes.

"Too weak, you two, to swim a lake I'd say, and I can't git you to use the reed."

"The reed?"

"You lays on the shallow lake bottom, maybe two feet down—more among the weeds and breathes up through a holler reed. But you two would drown unless you knew how to do it proper. Lay there two, three hours iffen you knowed how. Let's git on. Tricky trail hereabouts and lots of deer and elk runs. We'll confuse 'em."

"What's the use?" David asked. "Where do we run?"

"We're right near Ned Styron's powder mill."

"They must have burned it out by now."

"Ole Ned, he's made a real fort of it up on a bluff over the river. He and his boys kin hold off an army."

"How far?"

"Fifteen, eighteen miles, if I got my sights in order."

Jack-Tom moved off, running, and Joey followed, game, with head back to keep from having another nosebleed. David put his feet forward and ran without knowing it.

They ran slower than they had, but the effort was worse and they had to stop from time to time to rub cramps from their legs and thighs. It was afternoon, and the insects carried knives under the low-hanging branches of the forest. Jack-Tom turned and twisted, down deer paths, moving up little streams, rattling on fast or slow through mud and black muck and billions of gnats. They went on, pulling clinging leeches from their skin. The horror of their journey was becoming bigger as their hopes fell away. Only Jack-Tom remained expressionless, his mouth open, breathing in regular gulps, like some swimmer a long time in the water. To the west there were pitch-pole trees, thin and graceful with green feathered limbs scarred by old lightning. From nearby came the cries and jabbers of bluejays.

Jack-Tom held up his hand. "Them's not real jays. A fresh war party they picked up. Movin' ahead of us to get between us and Ned Styron's. Just about ready to ambush us too, as easy as suckin' a sugar tit."

David sank down, feeling every joint bathed in acid. "Let's just wait and fight."

"Be over in a minute, then. No. Let's git on."

Joey said, "Suppose they're ahead of us now?"

Jack-Tom pulled on his fringe of wet whisker. "Injuns allus take the easy way. They expect us from the south. I reckon. And hope. We come in some other way."

He ran on again, and David could see the forest man could keep up this sprinting game for a week, and most likely had. He ran on ahead of them, flies attracted to the fresh scalp on his belt where the gore had turned black on the fearful object.

It was gray marshland now and blue-brown bog and ponds, in one of which stood an elk eating bottom greens as he stared at them, chewing stupidly, and they went on. The ground grew hard and the blue- and red-leaved bushes were thick and prickly. The afternoon was settling into dusk. Jack-Tom held up a big hand and ahead they could see, in the east, a river cliff and on it a kind of fort with log walls and a blockhouse, all covered with heavy clay that had washed out here and there, showing old planks. Smoke came in lazy, sinuous curls from a chimney, rolling in easy patterns into a sky tinged with the first signs of sunset.

"The Injuns may not expect us from the west. Let's hope they are hoot lazy and layin' fer us south of Ned's."

They walked on, now so weary that sleep often tripped them and their minds numbed over and they came back with a jolt to the world, unaware they had left it for a few moments. They passed old tree stumps, crude sheds and handmade farm tools left around. They followed a crude beaten path. David found himself standing under a wall dabbed with red clay and Jack-Tom was scratching at a heavy narrow door set about three feet off the ground.

"Damn you coots inside, nobody on watch?"

The door opened inward and a young man much in need of trimming his face fuzz looked down. "Hully gee, Jack-Tom, it's you fer sure!"

David had a sense of climbing, of the smell of candles, and of a strong drink in his throat. He fell into sleep on corn husks.

CHAPTER 13

Styron's Mill
Twixt Forts George & Ticonderoga
11 July, 1775

My dear Botts,

It is with great regret & some shame that I must write that all the medical supplies and instruments destined for Fort Ticonderoga are lost, being destroyed on the trail by Indian action, and Joey Philipse and myself have had a miracle performed to let us escape with our lives from red savages in the services of the British. We are much worn & battered, but thank Providence that we are alive at a place called Styron's Mill. This is an establishment in the wilderness that makes gun powder for the Continental army. We shall continue to the fort as soon as travel can be resumed, with little more than my personal medical kit. I shall write in greater length when we are more recovered, but work now with pen in haste as there may be an express south to bear this dismal letter to you.

Yr. *servant,*
David Cortlandt,
Capt., Continental Army

He put down the yellow goose-quill pen and sanded the letter. David sat very still; inside his head he was still feeling the jarring concussion of running so near collapse on the trails. He sat in a large room built of hewn planks, at a rough-cut table on a bench of split oak logs. At the other end of the table Joey, his feet wrapped in linen rags smelling of hartshorn-leaf ointment, was eating hasty pudding and johnny cake, served by Shelagh, a large and very pretty Negro woman. David wondered just how much white blood there was in her and what unique circumstances had produced her.

"Master Joey," she said, "You ain't stopped eatin' for two days. From our corn porridge samp to quiddany jelly."

"I'm that hungry," said Joey smiling, "and glad to be alive."

"Well I got you a mess of elder buds and mushrooms stewed for midday."

A large round man—with a great moon of a belly, a bald head fringed with brown hair, and a long beard out of the Old Testament—came in, his hands deep in the pockets of a blue jacket of sailcloth cut full. He was followed by two oversized spotted hounddogs that stuck to his heels, trailing him with tenacious love.

"Captain, good morn to you. Getting your letter done?"

"Yes, it's finished. You think you can get it down to New York?"

"One of the boys is going through to Albany with a listing of powder on hand. If they want cannon powder they'll have to send me linen bags to pack it into charges. I can't guarantee to get bulky kegs through with Indian raiders about." Ned Styron winked at Shelagh. "That's right, feed them up till the skin is real tight."

"Any sign of Indians?" David asked, sealing the letter with a wad of spruce gum.

"Nary a feather. Just some spoors at an old campfire, four days old. My son Malachi, he's almost as good a tracker as Jack-Tom Swales, found nothing out there."

"How is Jack-Tom?"

"Been drunk on perry cyder for two days, and is gloomy and low as a hound-dog's crouch. He gets that way two, three times a year. Jack-Tom, he's lost between the Indian's camps and white ways, and it makes him inordinate touchy at times. He'll be out of his irrational ways by the time you go up to Ticon."

It was strange, the fort-like place where this round man lived with his brood of mulatto sons and common-law wife in her linsey-woolsey gown—and mixed up sulphur and charcoal and saltpeter into a thick black mud and ground it coarse or fine for rifle or musket or cannon use. David sipped the parched rye coffee. Ned Styron shook his head as David reached in a pocket for a tobacco pouch (and remembered he had dropped it on the trail).

"No smoking of the weed here, Captain. You could blow us heaven-high. The philosopher may say, 'Whatever lives deserves to die,' but what's *our* hurry?"

"I'm sorry. Mr. Botts would like to hear me report you're going full blast here."

"I would like to say it too, but we're running short of flowers of sulphur—brimstone some folks call it. It's heat and vapor produced on islands in the West Indies, and we need more. The saltpeter now, there are native limestone caves in Kentuck' and Virginia that give us all we want, and frankly I have some caves near here that are producing it. But I don't want the British to know *that*."

"That's all you need for making gunpowder?"

"Nay, there's willow and poplar charcoal, and that wood is nearby too. I pulverize the charcoal and make what I call the Yankee Doodle Mix. Come and see. You too, Joey."

Shelagh said, "You let the lad be, Ned. His heels and toes are something cruel hurt."

In the walled yard, under a low shed of bark laid over poles, four of Ned's sons, light yellow in color, with handsome laughing faces, were bent over a series of hollowed-out hardwood logs standing upright. Carefully from bags and baskets they were mixing gray and yellow powders.

Ned fingered some of the powders and nodded. "To make Yankee Doodle Mix the best powder I use seventy-five parts of saltpeter to fifteen parts of charcoal to ten parts of sulphur; that's the yellow stuff."

The boys began to pound the mix smoother with log pestles. Ned nodded. "You keep it grinding easy like that, moving it together even, and adding a bit of water till you have a nice cake." He held up a slap of black cake as big as a country cheese. "Now we break it up and grind it again. And here is Samuel sifting it for size."

A teen-aged boy was sifting the powder through a series of copper sieves. Ned patted the boy's head. "The coarse stuff is for cannon, the fine dust for rifles, and the very fine for pistols. Of course the polished grains are the best against moisture spoiling the powder. The polish keeps the powder drier."

They stood in front of a closed barrel mounted on an axle attached to a big handle. Two young men with the telltale features of Shelagh's strong skull were turning the crank. A rattling, rolling sound came from the barrel. "It's filled with a coarse powder and several hundred small brass balls. And every time it turns, the brass balls polish the powder grains. Open it up, Adam lad."

From the top of the barrel Ned Styron took out some hard black grains shining with polish. "See? That doesn't soak up the damp air like unpolished powder. It's prime stuff. The saltpeter is well leached with wood ashes and washed and strained. The charcoal has not a bit of rotten wood in it. It will never flash in the pan. Always be a sure shot for liberty. Forty cents a pound, the British agent Lemon offered me for it. I said no. I feel safe here. But they may try and capture or blow up the place."

"I'll see you get some soldiers from the fort."

"No need. I've iron cannon at the corners of the place and pistols and carbines loaded, 150 grains of powder to every one-ounce ball. And plenty of knapped flints from the Brandon quarries."

It was a busy place with the mixing and pounding and sieving. The sun was warm and river breeze cooled it down to a bearable level. David felt again his love for the woods and wilderness, the love he had had as a boy, loafing and hunting on the great Hudson River estates of the patroons. He wondered how the best families were dividing their loyalties.

"I'll move out as soon as Jack-Tom sobers up."

"I'll cut his whiskey down. We make it ourselves from corn and rye mash, fermenting the buck and distilling it through the copper worm. Twice distilled and the mean fusel oils taken out. A year in the charred oak kegs and it tastes like nothing you ever had in London or New York, Captain."

"I agree. Last night I had too much. Get Jack-Tom away from it for the good of your country."

Ned Styron laughed. "Never hurt a man if used in moderation. And I'm a man of moderation, unless it's the matter of Shelagh. Twelve children we've spawned us here in twenty years. And only three were girls. High-stepping yellow wenches too. Married them off to the farmers up by the lake who think it's prime stock. Come, let's try that whiskey before the midday meal. Opening a new five-year-old keg."

The afternoon was a bit hazy for David, but by noon the next day he was packing his personal medical kit—all he had saved—and thanking Ned Styron for the loan of a deerskin shirt. The buff and blue coat of office had been discarded on the trails.

"Now you'll need weapons, Captain." Ned led David to a strong door held closed by a huge padlock and opened with a toad-strangler of a key. Inside were stacks of weapons on rough racks. "It's my hobby horse. I collect them, and in time they'll fight for the Continental Army. That eight-inch Ketland horse pistol came off a British officer captured last year. The Whately and Kirkland trade guns are English. Made for Indians. I carry a lot of them.

But this Charleville French musket; heft it, Captain, it's going to win the war—it and the Brown Bess."

David held the heavy gun, avoiding the thin bayonet at its end gleaming in bacon grease. "I prefer a rifle."

"Sure you do, Captain. But they are hard to come by. Musketoon and carbine is what armies carry. In peace now, I'd trade twenty beaver peltries for one gun. And earn me twenty guilders a pound selling my powder to the Algonkin, Huron, Montagnais. They use mostly flintlock fuses. But now I fear they are all armed by the British."

"You think the Indians are a force in the field against us?"

"I figure there are thirty thousand of them tribes ready to take the king's shilling and the free smooth-bores and brass blunderbuss. Honniasont, Montauk, and Mahican among them. The best pelt hunters there were too."

"It's a lot of Indians."

"And a cruel power for the British to use to cut up settlers, burn out villages, and carry off the women for forced pleasuring. Here's a gift to you, Captain. It's a Bates of London pistol, octagon barrels, and *what* a balance."

David took the beautiful weapon. "It's too good for the wilderness."

"Almost as good as a Clarkson set—a pair—I sent to General Washington. Well, let's see if Jack-Tom is over his black mood. He has an irrational guilt—his conscience turned in reverse."

They found the wilderness man sitting in the sun, on the ground, his back against a wooden wall, a gourd dipper of well water by his side. Two hound-dogs sat watching him, and he would look up at them and moan and close his eyes again and sip from the gourd.

When he saw David and Ned Styron facing him he scowled. "Don't be fer to hassel me. I take my good time taperin' off a drunk."

"I want to go to the forts as soon as we can, Jack-Tom."

"Didn't I say yer goin' to git there? Jack-Tom Swales said so. What's my word worth, Ned, when I give it?"

"Your bond and heart on it, I always say. But don't ask for a cup of hard tongue-wetter. The captain wants to start with the sun high and get to the fort before dark."

Jack-Tom looked up and shaded the sun from his face. "Well, the captain is a good man to be on the trail with. Just let me shave my head and face and I'll be ready. Better leave Joey here for a few days. His feet will not take it."

Ned pointed to a wall where a loop of willow branch twisted to a circle was surrounded by buzzing, feeding flies. "And take your damn scalp with you. This is no tannery for savage habits."

Jack-Tom laughed, his black mood of despondency gone. "Beelzebub, there wuz times I thought me and the captain and the boy would end up that way, our hair dryin' in some Injun village." He stood up, creaking his joints one by one, as if testing their vitality.

4 October, 1775
Fort Ticonderoga, Lake Champlain

My dear Botts,

Lake Champlain is rough today & the fort is slack to the drilling & I am having problems in getting the men to set up their jakes away from the main lines & to bury their refuge. It is not a healthy fort. There is much black gum and coughing & throat-ail—some of the sods have brought with them the old rale from the Indian camps' women & I have isolated them, but lack the stuff for treatment. I lack most everything in the way of supplies & have never regretted so much all those things we had to leave on the trail. What you sent after has been put to good use.

Fort Ticonderoga stands just where Lake George empties into Lake Champlain. The fort is in thickets on the western headland; the majestic lake is here narrowed to a mere quarter mile. The buildings are mean & the logs rotting away, much of it going back to 1755 when it was the French fort Carillon. Lord Jeffrey Amherst took it from them & he blew it up & retired. It was rebuilt by the British & we have inherited it in all its broken & rebuilt parts as a strong point.

I can see when Ethan Allen & Benedict Arnold stormed it & took it & nearby Crown Point, they faced a hard task well done. Enough of this, as I want to report what you may know better than I. General Washington is having a hard time before Boston & needs heavy guns. There is talk of a scheme to wait for the winter's snow & sled over the Berkshire hills & on to Boston over 80 pieces from here—4 pounders to 24 pound guns, mortars, howitzers, 30,000 flints and tons of cannon balls. It sounds a harebrained scheme to me. But Henry Knox has said it can be done & he will do it himself. Going from Fort George to Albany, Kinderhook,

Great Barrington, to Springfield & so to Cambridge to throw iron into British Boston. Twelve oxen to a gun in the mountains is the least that will do it Jack-Tom Swales says. He wonders if they will be there in Boston in the spring of 1776 for the battle for the city.

Of a more personal nature, Joey Philipse is now a proper leftenant, a great smoker of tobacco & has become a good wilderness man. The skin on his heels is all back. Pass on to his family his greetings. He is not much given to letter writing. & to his sister, Mistress Roxanne, my own best wishes to her continued health. I hope you will get me away from here, & if I am really a helper of the surgeon-general, I want duty where my services are of more value to the army.

I dread this winter with my limited supplies, if there should be a serious illness or some baffling surgeon's task. I have become again skilled with the hunting rifle & am sick of venison, hope to get a bear when they take to the caves this fall. Any gazettes & news-letters you can spare will be something to give us some reading matter beyond the volume of Caesar's wars & Mr. Milton's pious poems or Mr. Defoe's Moll Flanders, which is ticklish reading full of the devil's itch to lift linen, when the nearest available Jade is coated in Indian cooking grease & wears leather skirts. We badly need the Peruvian bark for the ague among us.

Yr. most obligated friend,
David Cortlandt

With the first white sign of winter the chill came with sharp, dark wind, and the lakes turned sky-blue then gray, and the curling little waves ran with a snarl onto the shore shelving before the fort. Sitting wrapped in a greatcoat, David looked back over his shoulder at the fort, the weathered high log walls, the tall corner blockhouses, the bronze snouts of cannon, unpolished but ready. The soldiers were tattered and ill uniformed. The smoke of wood fires had turned their eyes red, and now winter would be upon them soon, and David was aware that men in barracks, gambling, cursing, or even (a few) praying, with little outdoor drill, would bring many illnesses for which his talents would prove little help. Scurvy would come unless he got some Dutch kraut juice, and the men disliked it and clammered for rum and the local whiskey called crackskull.

Major Homer Schuyler came stomping along the shore in his horseman's cape, the brass helmet and its blue feather worn high over the big face. A man of sensitivity to stresses and loyalties.

"Well, Captain Cortlandt, taking in our view?"

"I've seen it too often. I want to get away."

"Ah, you miss the true value of this cursed fort. It will see action soon. They'll come down from Canada, or we'll go up—and this is the cork in the bottle for them, and us."

"How is your arse? You haven't been riding, I hope?"

"I had to. Ned Styron wanted an escort for his powder train. If they strip us of cannon for Boston, he says they'll be no good without gunpowder. Oh, I ache."

"There are shreds of bone still coming out of your hip. And, I believe, fragments of that arrowhead rusting inside your buttock."

"My tail will teach me patience, Captain. It hurts in the morning and it hurts when I go to bed. In the day I ignore it. What an inglorious-placed wound. Scurrilous."

"I'll look it over tonight."

"No, you'll go to Fort George. The men there are broken out with blisters, run a fever, and their shirttails are bloody from the flux."

"All I have for them is some flummert jellies, wind belly powders, loosestrife tea, and sassafras bark."

"I'll give you escort of four men and horses. Any news from New York?"

"I hear in a letter your uncle Mynheer has declared for us."

"But my damned cousin Culbly, and Sir Francis Livingston, are organizing Tory Legions. You think they'll try to seize New York?"

David shrugged. "I'm no general or military expert. But it would be sense. Who holds the New York valley holds a great share of the colonies' shipping, wealth, farming, supplies. It's a good harbor, and the Tories are strong around it. The test will come when the guns boom and the patroons have to say yea or nay to seeing their barns burned, their houses looted. And we sit and wait."

Major Homer Schuyler nodded and looked at the lead sky. "It will be a most miserable winter here."

There was some excitement along the frozen landscape and a break in the dismal routine of fort life when Henry Knox came in early December, in a weather so cold that one could hear the sap freezing solid in the trees and the hawks' feet froze to their perches in the morning.

Knox—solid, square, red-faced, loud, began with sixty cannon, lowering them with pulleys and ropes from the high wall emplacements. "I hope to have these darlings for His Excellency, General Washington, before Boston in seventeen days."

Captain Cortlandt, wrapped in everything woolen he had against the biting cold, shook his head. "If you do, sir, you'll have matched Hannibal's crossing the Alps with his elephants."

"I shall use oxen. Elephants would break through the ice—and I expect to cross the Hudson four times on sleds with these guns, getting them away."

The dismounted guns were carried across the swampy ground to a wooded peninsula and loaded by sweating men, steaming in the frosty air, onto a scow, a bateau, and a pettiauger. Ice was forming on Lake George when the strange fleet set sail with cheers from the gun-raped garrison. The tattered sails caught little wind and the boats floated in the blue chill of the day. The scow ran aground at Sabbath Day Point and was a leaking wreck on a sunken rock. Everyone turned out to unload the guns, and David had chills to treat and smashed fingers to repair. In the end the scow's cannon were put in the other two vessels, and off they sailed loaded very low in the water. Head winds came up and it was touch and go to Fort George. From here oxen took the task of moving the bronze snouts.

When the guns were gone to General Washington there was nothing to do at the fort but live out the coming shock of northern winter. Snow began to fall, the lake proceeded to freeze solid for two feet down, and every morning the winds grew stronger. At night around a never fully heating fire the officers sat wondering how well or badly the cannon were being hauled on cattle-pulled sleds over the Berkshires. And everyone kept repeating much too often: "Better here in this dismal hellhole than climbing those goddamned mountains in this mucking weather."

Christmas at the fort was a blue windy day with blinding snow swirling sticky and smothering over every object. The naked cannon looked colder than the hinges of an icy hell. Half the men were down with grips of the long gut from eating too-fat elk meat. The rest were wrapped in blankets and rags, and their red noses were hopeful of a bigger whiskey ration.

On their Lord's birthday the good Christians in the fort were roaring drunk and some fool fired off a cannon and was punished

by having to ride a wooden horse outdoors in the cold night, and
caught water in the lung before morning.

The officers had a huge clay bowl of fair punch, very powerful
and raw, and Jack-Tom came loping in with three hen turkeys and
a brace of great white hares. Joey sang several obscene comic songs
learned on the Grand Tour, and Major Homer Schuyler produced
two wrinkled lemons, to everyone's amazement, to slice into the
steaming punch. An old soldier played the fiddle badly. Past oiled
linen windows and barred shutters the lake wind came roaring down
from Canada to polish the stars—a wind that would chill them to
the bone before morning.

David, full of punch and the ache of memory, went tipsy to his
rope-mattressed trundle bed of corn husks, and piled over himself
all his clothes and a bearskin given him by Jack-Tom. He slept fit-
fully and dreamed first of Peg Munday and later he was ardently
kissing Roxanne Philipse in the garden by the wall and taking
liberties, and he was ashamed as he awoke to find himself in a state
of aroused animal sensuality. Near morning he slept again and
was wakened by the wild Indian howling of Jack-Tom, who had
become roaring drunk, had stripped himself naked, and gone
swimming in the icy lake. He was pulled out by a boat crew—a giant
naked man with his ginger whiskers and topknot crusted with mush
ice. They carried him struggling to the dismal hospital hut, where
David came to wrap him in blankets and pour hot root tea and vile
burning drops into him. Two soldiers rubbed the frozen wilderness
man's feet warm, and Jack-Tom slept, none the worse for his night's
madness, to wake a day later with a clear eye and an innocent stare
when told of his adventure.

January froze the last lake and David's dreams grew desperate.

CHAPTER 14   The morning of middle March had turned
from topaz to sea-blue, and some ice was still on the lake near where
the fort hugged the slopes. The men were on duty, working with
drawn shavers and chisels on log walls in the shadow of a still
lingering late cold. And somewhere, Dr. Cortlandt suspected, some-

one was secretly at work with coarsely ground maize distillate, making a dreadful whiskey.

There were crows over dead trees, coming in against the wind from the north, lumps of blackness trying to scratch a living from the still iron-hard ground. Dr. Cortlandt walked in his tattered uniform, unshaved, stamping his feet on the chilly parade ground; the past is dead, he thought, but never at rest, and the flesh has its own spirit. (Ten more minutes walking and I'll go in.) I have tried to understand, rather than believe, and here I am like a fish out on an icy shore and a war is declared and here nothing happens. Spring never comes. I am part of an awe-inspiring death of an epoch and all I think of is that my boots are worn and the food is beginning to stink. (Seven more minutes and I'll have done my morning walk and then back to reading Gibbon.) What did that old teacher in medical classes on the nervous system say in London, a million years ago? "*Materia appetit foremam ut virum femina*—material seeks form as woman seeks man." It's no jest; this man seeks woman, not the other way around. I'll not end up with the squaws like the troopers, rutting with animal grunts in the damp hay of a horse barn. Gibbon's Romans had the right spirit. The strongest man stands alone, and to stand alone one must live without illusions. Only, to lack illusions would have kept me from this war. (Two more minutes and I'll leave this landscape to the crows hunting corn kernels in the balls of horse droppings by the stables.)

He should ask Roxanne to marry him, even if she were a sweet shrew, next leave to New York. He must order his life with prosaic deliberateness. Get the boy Dan and the nurse Lizzie Patch over to Long Island to Sir Francis, set up a practice once this damned war is over. (One more extra minute in this glum day breathing hard to show I'm not just a speck in the wilderness, but a man in relation to aspects of eternity.) Time's up.

David Cortlandt turned quickly toward the officers' barracks, beating his cold hands on his red ears, moving fast for shelter; to create definite action quickly—*that* is grace.

Inside the disordered room he shed his cloak and stamped his over-repaired boots in front of a butt of a tree burning in the fireplace.

Major Homer Schuyler was busy with pewter knife and fork in a poplarwood trencher eating salt horse, a dram of rum at his elbow. "Spring in a few days, David."

David picked up the Bristol glass bottle on the table and poured himself a quince juice-and-rum. The breakfast of suppawn and milk wasn't sitting so well. He sipped. "Maybe there will be action now."

The major gave up feeding and threw the pork on the puncheon floor, spat, and cut himself a slice of rolliches—a headcheese from a farm nearby. It smelled too high for most of the officers to try. "My father set a great table, David. Now it's deer suet and moose fat, and what I'd give for a pipe of Madeira. My lower guts seem encumbered."

"I'll send you a measure of medical rhubarb, Major."

There was military shouting in the parade yard and the raw sound of voices at the guard posts. The door opened and Jack-Tom Swales came in, shaggy in a wolf-pelt jacket over his hunting shirt, a red fox cap—with tail attached—on his shaved head and its top-knot.

"Beelzebub, Captain, pour me a ballswarmer. I got bad news fer you. Mornin', Major."

The scout swallowed the tin cup's content and then the big man sighed. "Been moving along the creeks last few days and stopped off at Ned Styron's powder mill. Trouble there."

"Indians?" asked Major Homer Schuyler.

"Shelagh. She run from a party of two British officers and some Indians when she was out huntin' a house cat that got scared out of the cabins by a loose dog. Got hit."

"Badly?" asked David.

"'Bout two weeks ago it happen. A slug of lead in her left leg. Been swellin' all the time, and now it's so swoll up it's ready to bust. I seen it."

David turned from the fire. "Is it red, angry, or black?"

"Green-black like. And smell? Hully Joe, it smells."

"Damn! Why didn't they bring Shelagh into the fort?"

"First they feared an attack. Then the weather got unseasonal. Ned, he said fer you to come, Doctor. She's far gone."

Major Homer Schuyler said, "In this weather, with a late snow any minute? What about those Indians and British agents?"

"Come down from Canady on snowshoes. I seen their tracks. Onondagas by the shape of 'em."

"Major," said David, "I can make it overnight unless complications set in. It's mortifying, that leg, and it may have to come off to save her life."

The major stared at his plate and pushed it away. "Marvelous-built woman, that Shelagh. I'll give you four men, Captain, and I hope you can walk on snowshoes. Jack-Tom, how much time do you need to rest up and lead Captain Cortlandt to Styron's Mill?"

"One more tin cup of this eye-popper and I'se ready fer bar. Brown or grizzly. I warn ye—a spring blizzard is comin' up."

David went to get his medical kit and a whetstone to oil-hone his lancets. Somewhere he had John Hunter's notes on the subject of leg wounds. It was a hopeless business once the mortifying of the flesh had set in. If it reached her mound of Venus and groin she'd be dead.

They left the fort in an hour. David, Jack-Tom, and four cursing troopers, all wearing snowshoes. In the east snow whirled off the heights, forecasting a deep fall soon on the old January and February crystals. David's legs ached from the snowshoes—soon it was agony to move on them.

They camped that night in a howling storm four miles short of the powder mill. They had fought the spring blizzard all day, and now in a blue-black dusk they bunched together, ice forming on their eyebrows and cheeks as they lay under the overturned trunk of a forest oak. It offered some shelter from the cursing wind, the stinging ice particles driven like sharp sands in blasting force on their shivering bodies. No fire could be lighted. Jack-Tom stuffed snuff powder under his gums and David gave each man an inch of rum in the bottom of a tin cup. One man licked the metal and lost some of his tongue in the instantaneous freezing process.

By morning only the deerskin case of Jack-Tom's long rifle barrel was in sight in the snow drifts. They came awake weeping and groaning. David had trouble getting life back into his numb ears. His fingers were so senseless he beat them like sticks against his legs.

The party went on after David made them rub snow on their ears and blossoming noses. The weather had let up some of its fury, but the trees dropped heavy loads of snow on them from time to time in the crunching snowshoe parade. The forest was silent but for the beat of snowshoes, the rush of wind drifting the snow, the creak of branches whose heart sap was almost solid with the deep chill.

Here and there a broken bush tried to stand, and no bird nor animal was seen. They came with steamy breaths to the mill at noon. Its roofs were two feet thick with crusts of ice and snow. One narrow path leading up to it was almost lost in the drifts. A smell of cattle came from a smoky shed. At the main cabin door Ned Styron stood under a vast bearskin cap, his hands locked in tension in his long beard.

"Doctor! She's pert ill!"

"So I hear. We're almost dead of cold and crippled by snow-shoeing, but take me to her."

The fireplace inside was filled with sparking logs on fire, but the corners of the place were chilly. Half a dozen silent sons sat staring at their hands—hands raw and chapped by work and weather. David threw off his wolf pelts, his jacket and mufflers. He followed Ned Styron into a bedroom. The sickening sweet decay odor almost knocked him down. On a wide bedstead slung with rope and raw-hide were set two feather beds and on them blankets. In the center lay Shelagh, her eyes glazed, her big, powerful arms picking at the ruffles of a linsey-woolsey nightgown.

David moved over to the bed and felt the fever on her damp brow. He pulled back the blankets and exposed a stained bundle of linen strips wrapped around the left leg.

"It's been powerful bad," said Ned. "And stinks like fish. It happened two weeks ago."

"Two weeks? Bad, bad. Blood poison first, and then gangrene. I don't have to smell it close. Better step back. I'm going to undress the wound. Did you get the bullet out?"

"Got that out. But the leg spoiled."

Shelagh said weakly, "He's got me, got me, the devil is pullin' me down. By the legs, the sinful legs of a fornicator; ah, devil!"

"Now, Shelagh." David flipped back the gown to above the pubic area and slowly unwound the leg wrappings. Red streaks led from the knee to the inner thighs. He felt the groin glands, touched the vulva. Hot, dry. Fever. Very high. Below the knee the leg was a disaster. It was swollen and hard and cracked with the flowings of noisome fluids. He put the blanket back on it.

"My fingers are still stiff, Ned. Get my medical case there. Open it. Get out a jar marked *Tincture of Opium*. That's it. Don't let it fall, man. There isn't another drop of it north of New York. Pour a half inch into a glass. Now, make her drink it. I can't. My fingers are still frozen. Slowly, all of it. Don't let her cat it up."

"You'll fix her limb, Doctor?"

"Ned, I've got to take it off right away."

"Damn you! No, no!"

"It's for you to decide, Ned. She'll be dead before nightfall if I don't. She may die anyway. Those red streaks, see them? Once the black decay follows them into her reproductive glands, it's all over."

Shelagh said softly, "Ned, you let the doctor—he knows, he decided."

Ned began to weep into his long beard.

David ordered wooden boards to be placed under the woman in the bed and got his notes by John Hunter. He began to read:

> You shall certainly know that a Gangreene is turned into a mortification, and that the part is wholly and thoroughly dead, if it looke of a blacke colour and be colder than stone to your touch. There be a great softnesse of the part, so that if you presse it with your finger it rise not again but retaines the print of the pressure. If the skinn come from the flesh lying under it and it a strong and great smell exhale and a sanious moisture, viscide, green or black-ish flow from it, and the part be quite destitute of sense and mo-tion, whether it be pricked or burnt then the mortification of Gangreene is complete and Amputation must be made.

David looked up to find Ned Styron standing over him. "Ned, get a great many towels sopping in hot water, and you and Jack-Tom are to hold her down. Can you face it?"

"I can face it. She will suffer?"

"The opium will help."

> Let the patient be placed as it fit and drawing the muscles up-ward towards the sound parts, let them be tyed with a strait liga-ture a little above the member to be cut off. Now cut the flesh even to the bone with a sharpe incision knife. You will note that there usually lyes between the bones, a portion of certain muscles, which you can not easily cut with a dismembring knife. Wherefore you must carefully divide and seperate it wholly from the bone

with an instrument with a deeply curved blade for soft things. As flesh tendons and membranes can not easily cut with a saw. Then nimbly use a little saw a foot and some three inches long to severe the bone as near to the sound flesh as you can.

He put aside the notes and opened his instrument case and took out the sharp steel knives that he kept neat and clean in soft soap. Carefully he threaded four long needles with thick yellow silk. Shelagh was quiet on the bed, her lips dry. Ned and Jack-Tom, standing over the bed, waited for him to proceed.

David went over to Shelagh and, taking up John Hunter's listening tube, he felt for the heartbeat between the fine firm breasts. There was a regular *thump thump*. The pulse at the wrist was strong but a bit swift.

"Ned, send the boys away to the barn."

When the powder maker was gone from the bedroom, David turned to the scout. "I've done it often, but never alone—always with help, or helping other experienced men."

"There is strength in you, Captain."

"It takes skill. Will bone-sawing unset you?"

"It's no worst than pullin' a scalp to me."

"You're to hold her firm to the boards. If Ned fails us, you'll be alone. She mustn't stir when I cut and saw and sew. There will be some blood. But I'll clamp a tight belt around the leg above the knee to hold bleeding back. You've seen naked women before, I'm sure."

"I be no puritan, if that's what you mean."

David pulled the nightgown up under the armpits of the woman, and lifted an eyelid of the prone head with a finger and studied the dilated pupil. Shelagh spoke in a hazy, deep voice. "Send the children away . . . the cow's milked . . . what's the matter?"

"Sleep, sleep. Try." He took up a gourd for whiskey and from a glass jar of the amber liquid gave her two huge sips. Jack-Tom looked down on the large, curved soft body below him, the breasts big, the stomach strong, the thighs firm. He reached for the gourd himself and swallowed. David took it from him. "Not too much, Jack-Tom, I need you."

Ned was back, staring open-mouthed at his naked wife lying on two large planks. David uncovered the swollen, mangled leg and poured civet perfume and rose-water over it to cut the stench. "Ned, you're to hold her down firm on the boards with Jack-Tom, when I give the word. We'll give her a minute more to feel the whiskey and opium. And bring in about a dozen big candles, lit. Set them around."

He picked up John Hunter's notes and went on reading. He hoped he appeared calm and collected. Ned began to whimper, his big beard shaking, then he thumped his chest and stood very still, waiting over the bed.

Let the Veines and Arteries be bound up as speedily as you can, by taking hold of the vessels with a Crows beak. When you have tyed the Vessels draw together the lips of the wound with four stitches having taken Good hold of the flesh—so the wound may be the more speedily agglutinated.

To conduce green wounds use an ointment of Album ovorum uj bole arm. sang. drac. gypsi, terrae sigill, aloes, addendo olei rosarum & myrtil . . .

Place the member in a comfortable posture upon a pillow stuffed with oaten husks or chaff. It must not be stirred after the first dressing for four days in winter, but somewhat sooner in summer. For the ligatures wherewith the vessels are bound they must not be loosed. Patients imagine at times they have their members yet entire and doe complaine thereof of a pain. Give remedy of this symptome by lauri & juniperi Liniment. . . .

The many candles cast shadows in all corners. David put away the notes and stood up. He shucked off his jacket and shirt. On a wet huckaback towel he put out his sharp tools, his needles and threads, the saws and ointments.

He said softly, "Look away, both of you, if you can't stand it. But goddamn the man who lets her stir her hips or legs." Quickly David began to tie a narrow leather band above the knee and draw it very tight. He heard the breath whistle from Ned's lungs and Shelagh gasp for air. He lifted the broad curved knife and attacked the flesh of the knee joint. . . .

Ten minutes later David was covered with muck and pus and blood. The room stank like a butcher's shed and the severed limb was under the bed wrapped in blanket. David was tying off the last of the blood vessels with slippery fingers. The woman had turned a pale-lime color. She was muttering and rolled her head, making little drugged screams that choked her. Ned had closed his eyes, but nothing missed the bright stare of Jack-Tom. Four strong hands held the woman firmly to the wide boards. With sensitivity and speed David tied off the largest knot.

"Christ!" said David as he brought the prepared flaps of skin together over the freshly cut-through bone and muscles. "Ned, I've tried to give her a solid, healthy stump." He stitched quickly and then stood up and very carefully loosened the leather band above the knee just a small bit. Not much. There was no seepage beyond a little pink oily liquid. He rubbed on some ointment, not sure how much good it was to the healing process. From a small jar of pitch, using a wooden sliver, he took up a heavy tar-like substance and plastered the stump and knee. There were doctors who called for red-hot irons to sear the flesh for quick scabbing, but John Hunter insisted the shock of that was greater than the aid.

David sat down and wiped his hands on the fearfully soiled towels. "Jack-Tom, tie her hips and thighs to the boards. So she can't move them."

He turned away and took a deep sip of the strong whiskey. Then he led Ned from the room and patted him on the back. "Go out in the yard. Jack-Tom and I will finish off. Don't be ashamed to toss your dinner if you have to."

Jack-Tom was still busy with the straps. David listened to the woman's heart again and felt the pulse. It was slower and seemed weak.

"Bury everything under the snow, Jack-Tom. I'll sit with her now."

The last storm of the season was breaking up. Outside beyond the closed shutters David could hear the soft lisp of driven snow, falling away to silence. He felt tired, depleted, but pleased. The pulse, however, remained weak. A hell of a business if he had completed the job and failed now to keep her alive. He blew out the biggest candles and put on his shirt and covered the woman's body. He sat a long time listening to her breathe and came to himself a long time later to find Ned shaking him.

"Doctor, Doctor, she's muttering something."

He had dozed off. Shelagh was struggling to breathe and whispering unconnected words. Her head felt a bit too hot, but the pulse was stronger now and faster.

"Ned, she's holding her own. Sit with her. I'll sleep a bit more. But be sure you wake me in an hour. Before, if anything changes. If there's bleeding wake me at once."

It was two days before Shelagh began to complain of the fearful pain in her missing leg. David cheered up. "Good for you, Shelagh, we'll have you on your way doing your household duty in a couple of weeks."

"But how will I get around?"

"Ned will carve you a pair of crutches, at first. Then a good stout oak leg with a padded knee. Your knee joint will work. Now don't be shy at me caring for your natural needs. There isn't a damn woman around, but Ned is getting a half-breed girl in to take care of you."

"That's just fine—fine."

She sank back into sleep and the stump smelled tarry and not at all tainted.

Two days later David and his party left for the fort, warning Ned to follow his orders fully and have a couple of the boys ready to run to the fort if any trouble signs showed.

"Doctor, you don't know what a woman, the right kind, can mean to a man."

"I'm getting the idea, Ned."

There were signs the season was changing, now that the freakish last storm had come to the end of its fury. The melting snow was soft and slushy. The escort and Jack-Tom walked ahead, carrying David's cases, and he looked up at the deep green of the firs and walked wary on the rotten ice of small streams.

As they came near to the fort they heard cannon fire, and overhead was the snap of the fort flag flying, an insignia of a coiled snake with the words: DON'T TREAD ON ME!

"I don't see any attacking forces," David said.

"Not an enemy within miles," said Jack-Tom, "or we'd a seen some signs."

On the platform over the main gate stood Major Homer Schuyler beaming down on them. "Good news, David. Great news."

"What is it?"

"General Howe, who had replaced General Gage in command of the British, has evacuated Boston! And General Washington holds the city now for Liberty and the Continental Congress!"

"The devil you say!" David shouted as his party entered the parade ground full of celebrating soldiers.

"Dispatch came in this morning with the tidings. God bless our cause," said the major, grinning down on David. "And the cannon Knox carried away from here, to frighten off the British, blessed it a lot more."

Inside the fort David found great bonfires burning in the slush and soldiers shouting in red-faced glee. He felt a galvanic energy in his tired limbs and a break in the fleetingness and enigma of life. Oh, to become, and live, in the fullness of one's being! He opened his mouth and shouted with all the rest.

"For Liberty and the Continental Congress!"

The uncertainty of the future, the opaque cawl on the unresolved items of his life—both were pushed aside. Jostling and stumbling in the filthy snow of the parade ground he cried out with heartfelt enthusiasm: "Hurrah, hurrah!"

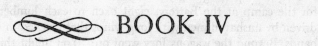

BOOK IV

American Island

CHAPTER 15   The season of spring, a green steamy warmth, was far advanced on Manhattan Island. The tree buds had opened and the bees in their hairy yellow breeches were active among the May flowers. There was a sense of tension now that Boston was captured and the war was moving south; New York was hard to defend. Every day more regiments of colonial troops were coming to the island, joshing and pushing, young boys with beardless faces, and oldsters who would have been better off at home.

David and Joey Philipse riding down from Philipse Manor at Tarrytown on the Hudson moved past the morning lines of soldiers in their homemade uniforms and hunting jackets. Often there was a group with regular pattern of blue and buff, but mostly it was make-do—even occasional captured British uniforms recut or added to.

Joey Philipse was no longer the callow and nervous youth of the year before. The winter at the fort, the hard scouting in snow and wind, the detailed trailcraft he had absorbed from Jack-Tom, and the tough soldiering he had known under Major Homer Schuyler had created a weathered, solid young man. Growing broader and taller. His new uniform would have hung loosely on the boy of last year. An officer in service as well as rank, he rode beside David Cortlandt, who was also in new and neatly tailored blue and buff.

"Damn it David, you can't be serious in courting Roxanne!"

"Why the devil not?"

"Because you're my friend."

"I don't understand."

They were passing huge, clumsy farm wagons loaded with supplies for the camp at the Battery, eight oxen to each lumbering wagon, driven by unshaved men with long whips that cracked in experienced hands. Beyond the wagons Joey went on: "You might think I object on foolish ground, such as her being a Philipse with an estate and . . ."

"And me being a poor pot doctor, or rather an officer who hasn't paid for this uniform, and has even borrowed this horse from her father."

"No, and you know that isn't what I mean. But you need a hard, strong wife to cook and sew and go with you wherever you open practice. Roxy—well let's face it, she's flighty, opinionated, and given to having her own way."

"I think I wouldn't mind any of that; besides, she loves me."

They had stopped to water their horses in the stream at the dip under Harlem Heights. A little brook ran clear here, and the horses sucked up the bubbling silver water. David looked over the green slopes and the heights behind them. Plum and apple trees were in blossom and David felt light and easy after a hard winter. If nature had trapped him into the mating dance, he did not mind. Several times he had taken Roxanne for a ride along the Hudson on swift horses of the Philipse farm, and she seemed to him to have all the graces and charm that womanhood should have. He was aware, in his scientific mind, that his knowledge of the subject of respectable love, wives, and marriage was slim. Women had been few in his life. He dared not think in so purely carnal a way about Roxanne. Desire was covered over now with manners, social procedure, and the fact he did not know fully just how she did regard him.

The two men rode on past tented fields where brass cannon stood at the head of wooded lanes, and they went into the city itself, a town that seemed as always busy with business. There were more tents on corner fields, and the shout of whores came out from smoky inns; they saw a reeling drunken soldier muttering along a curb, his tie strings falling to his knees. There were also the swift movement of a detail of troopers marching somewhere for guard duty, the raucous street cries of hawkers and peddlers selling ribbons and cool drinks, and pen and paper and apples and brass buttons to the soldiers and their frowsy women. (Each regiment had at least nine to a dozen women camp followers, listed as "laundresses" mostly. It worried David, not for moral reasons, but because as a medical officer he was trying to keep the Continental units free of the clap, the soldier's disease.)

General Washington had set up his headquarters in midtown in a neat white house of two stories, behind a white fence that girded simple yellow and red flower beds. Two dragoons, with horsehair-topped helmets, white trousers, and short carbines, stood guard before the walk.

Joey waved his arm at David. "I must attend a family gathering. See you tonight in camp."

David nodded. The dragoons stiffened and presented arms, and David tied his horse to the iron ring set in the curbstone and went inside. There was a neat wallpaper in the hall, and several young staff officers, well tailored, shaved, polished, were laughing over some scatological ribaldry. David asked for Botts and was told to go upstairs, first door to the right.

He knocked, and Botts' thick voice said, "Enter."

The room was the usual careless untidiness to be expected wherever Botts made his office. Great leather saddlebags, wardrobes filled with odd assortments of clothes, weapons propped on chairs and sofas. Botts himself in ill-fitted clothes, halfboots and open shirt, sat at a kidney-shaped desk writing quickly on gray paper.

He looked up, solid and coarse-gestured, but freshly shaved—there was even a dab of soap left under one ear.

"Well, Davey, was it cold up there by the lakes?"

"Yes, it was. I've been back about a fortnight."

"I've been in Jersey, trying to ferret out the Tories from the good folk. Your reports were fine. The British are scouting deeper and deeper south from Canada. Well now, I suppose you're ready to take on the organizing of medical units for us here?"

"I've already begun. And with what, I'll be damned if I know. Drunken laundry women, filthy bandages not even properly washed between uses. As for drugs, grandmother's herbs and Indian messes is about all we have left."

Botts during the harangue took up two long clay pipes, offered one to David, and pointed to a blue china jar of tobacco. As they filled and lit up the pipes Botts kept sorting the papers on his desk.

"Not a bad native tobacco. Of course a bit of Turkish and Irish added to it would help, but that will have to wait for peace. Davey, I'm aware we're short of drugs and shorter of medical men. But you know the surgeon general himself, Dr. Church, turned out to be in the pay of the British. He had to be arrested. But he escaped us, worse luck, and joined the British. Now I could have gotten the position for you, but you wrote no, you wanted to join a regiment and work within the battle lines."

"Those are my words. I'm not the man for ambiguous high position."

"Yes." Botts smoked and blew smoke at the ceiling. "Very well. We have landed the boy Dan Livingston and the fat nurse from the Connecticut shore last night."

David stood up. "No! Wonderful! Where are they?"

"In lodgings at Boyd's Inn." Botts walked to the window and looked down into the back garden. David joined him there. "It's been a long time since I've seen the boy. He's all right?"

"You'll see him later. Yes, he's fine."

Below them in the garden a middle-aged man with reddish-brown hair turning gray was walking between the rose beds. The neatness of his uniform, the good quality of his sword showed he held some rank. A short woman given to plumpness was snipping roses into a basket, and the officer would hold a branch down for her when the position of the flower was hard for the lady to reach.

Botts blew smoke out of the open window. "You plan to send the boy on to his grandfather, Sir Francis Livingston?"

"Yes, I promised I would—to Lloyd's Neck on Long Island."

Botts nodded. "How would you like to deliver the boy yourself?"

"It's rather a bad part of the island right now. Tory bands out, and a lot of odd things going on there. The Tories have a palisade and fort at Jamaica."

"You'll not go as an officer. We hold most of the island. By day, anyway. But at night, as you say, the Tory bands are out doing damage. Davey, there's a big fleet of warships, with Hessians, thousands of British troops, due soon to attack New York."

"When?"

"We have some sources of information and swift ways of knowing, sometimes. But not everything. That's why I want you to go to Lloyd's Neck and get me some facts on the Tory strength, and what Sir Francis is doing and what Culbly Schuyler, and the notorious Captain or Colonel Lemon—or what rank he has—is doing."

David watched the officer in the garden below take the basket of roses and bow the lady into the path toward the house. David asked, "That's General Washington, isn't it?"

"Yes. And his wife. The lady is leaving us soon for home. She proved rather stiff with the local hostesses and is going back to Mount Vernon, their farm in Virginia. They say he married her for her money—richest widow down there—but the truth is he's also rather fond of the little butterball." Botts knocked his pipe out carefully on the window sill. "The boy Dan is at the inn on Water Street. You'll start for Lloyd's Neck in two days. I want to wait here for reports from one of our agents. Take Joe with you."

"Joe?"

"Joe Philipse. He's too weathered now to be called Joey, don't you think? He asked me to stop doing it. He made a good officer?"

"Yes, he did. You think Sir Francis is the chief agent for the Crown in organizing Tory bands on Long Island?"

"We've known something like it for some time. But I need better information. Let me show you some maps of the region. Correct me if they are wrong in detail."

David nodded and stood at the window finishing his pipe. War was such an enveloping dementia and Dan so close—stirring so many memories.

The streets were full of a fervid assertiveness, a sense of business as usual and many uniforms. There was a tightening of David's chest as he walked up the inn staircase and knocked on the blue-painted door. He heard movement beyond it and a latch being thrown back. Lizzie Patch's broad face stared out at him, with Cockney touchiness writ boldly on it.

"Lord love us all!" she said, throwing the door open wide. "It's Dr. Cortlandt! Now hain't that nice. Danny boy, lookie!"

"Lizzie, you old coot, you're wider than ever."

A bright-haired little boy who had been making marks with his saliva on the windowpanes turned with a shriek and came running. "Uncle Davey, Uncle Davey! Lizzie doesn't let me walk alone in the streets."

David caught up the handsome boy and hugged him. "And rightly so. Soldiers and boy-biting hogs, and heavy wagons that could crush a boy."

"It's not London, lovie—don't come near it either," said Lizzie, hands on hips of her clean green dress, a cap on her disordered graying hair. "No toffs, and nought to drink but this dismal native beer and what they call corn spirit; it don't 'it the spot like a nip of gin once't did."

"Shame on you, Lizzie. Well in a day or so we'll all go out on the island and you two will be safe with Dan's grandfather. A big place, lot of space to walk and run."

"Do they have any 'osses?" Dan asked.

"'Osses?" David said, puzzled.

Lizzie made a gesture of pulling on reins. "'Osses, you know 'osses what pulls carts, and what the gentry goes riding 'igh-arsed on."

"Oh 'osses," said David, "we'll have to start the young chap's education to call them horses. And give you, Lizzie, some *h*'s."

"A fat lot good they'll do me." She pulled a crumpled letter from between her large melon-sized breasts. "I got me this letter from London, oh a few weeks ago. Come through by smuggler, delayed. A pig-gelder that read it to me said so."

David took the letter and saw Peg's writing, her scrawling penmanship. It was a large sheet of paper written on one side and folded and sealed and addressed to: "Mme. Lizbeth Patch. Seek at Dolfin Inn, Bosston, Massuchetts."

"You want me to read it, Lizzie?"

"It's from duck's mutter, it is. I ain't 'eared it since it was last read. I don't read writin' nor write readin'."

"You didn't say," Dan interrupted, "if they had riding stock."

"Oh yes, your grandfather owns horses and ponies, and breeding jackasses and even oxen. And you'll ride them all."

David walked to the window and unfolded the letter and read out loud.

Dear Goodie Patch,

I take pen in hand to rite you across the see to ask of how is my dear Dan'el, his health & comfort & his welfare with his grandfather the old helot. Things are much the same here in London butt for the war with the dastardly rebels which has made it a most livly place. Butt costs my dear have gone climbing. I do hope God in his mercy is protecting you and dear littl Dan'el. There is good hope I may myself be on yr. shores in a not so distant future. Beeing that my protector has bought himself a Major's rank in the Green Dragoons & if they sail to Canada I will go long. This is all to be decided yet butt there is in our destinees many changes as Lord Alban was just saying the other nite when he punted the bank at Celos and went down his entire estate & the poor buck is now reduced to appearing only at night, in his cloak, all he has left, & a pair of boots, after he was stripped by the roozers & the Greeks. Rite me care of the Duke of Dorset Publik House, Portman Square, hugg and kiss my darling Dan'el & say his fond mother sheds tears at missing him. The Duty is now 6d. per pack of playing cards, 20s 6d on Four Wheel carriages of which my fancy keeps too.

> *yr. faraway mistress,*
> Peg Munday

Lizzie sniffed despondently and wiped a large eye with the corner of a sleeve. "It's like years since we wuz all together takin' the good with the bad, the fat with the lean."

"Get your bonnet, Goodie Patch, and I'll show you and Dan the town and get us a cut of the mutton joint at a good eating house. May I keep the letter?"

"Lord, yes, I don't aim to learn readin' at my time of life. Dan washee, washee, and we're ready."

"I'll only get dirty again."

"Never you mind, you're gentry and your grandfather likes clean boys, of that I'm sure."

Protesting Dan was led to the pitcher and basin for a husking with a rough towel and a combing of his corn-colored hair. He was thin but wiry. David stood with Peg's letter in his hand and wondered at the burden of memory. He was meeting Roxanne in two hours and hoped to convince her that in time of war amorous people married in haste, on short notice, and that love was the practical application of the senses to a continuing faith in society and the race. Was it hypocrisy to remember old passions?

The favorite trysting place of David and Roxanne was below a gun emplacement in the middle of Manhattan island overlooking the Hudson, and called, with no imagination, Gunners' Point. The soldiers were either helling and deviling in the tent towns that had sprung up to teach them vice and gambling, or cutting hay for extra wages in the meadows to the north. David usually met Roxanne near her house on King Street, she mounted sidesaddle and he on a strong chestnut nag once from some upriver Tory stable. He did not like to have her ride out alone now. The island was becoming a gathering place for soldiers. General Washington was marching them in to protect New York. Many were roughs and drunkards, or farm boys debauched and turned to nasty ways. It was these bad pennies that gave a poor name to all the soldiers, most of whom were honest and earnest and given to little more in the way of crime than wringing the neck of a curious straying hen, or trying to kiss or fumble a housemaid while she knelt to wash down the front stoeps of the town.

Roxanne in an orange velvet habit, with a pert little yellow feathered black tricorne pinned to her hair, sat her horse skillfully, a slim whip under one arm.

"David, you don't have to herd me around the island, I've been native to it since I could totter. I could meet you at Gunners' Point."

"My dear Roxy, let us say I wanted to see more of you."

She grinned, got her whip in her gloved hand, and flipped the dark gelding's flank. They rode well—two handsome people, David's red head of hair tied tight behind under the new hat, his blue and buff uniform as yet unwrinkled by any battle.

At Gunners' Point he tied off the horses to a bush and they sat on a grassy slope against the trunk of a beech tree and looked down at the Hudson. There was the busy activity of sloops and barges from the Jersey coast, the moored shape of a hulk to which two back-masted privateers were attached like nursing sharks, taking on powder and stores before going off to harry British merchant shipping to the West Indies.

"Roxy, I may go off on duty again soon. I want us to get married."

"Now, darling,"—she sank into his arms and amused herself by tickling his nose with a grass blade. "It's *not* that simple. You inspire passion in me, and you're a handsome brute. But I haven't traveled: Philadelphia is nothing, and I haven't seen the world. Am I ready to settle in and breed your brats?"

"You can't travel for many years. Besides, it isn't as fine as our own Hudson Valley."

"I'd dislike believing that. Rome. Paris. All the swank, posh ways in London. A girl has to think these things out before she's to be slave to some brute like you. As for that, I dislike children, you know."

"No mother does hate them once she's held them in her own arms. But isn't *all* that in the future? I want to wed you, and I can't wait till you make a Grand Tour or outgrow dolls for babies."

She laughed and kissed his cheek and his mouth. "You are a man who knows his own power, aren't you? Oh Davey, it isn't that I'm against marriage, but it's so dull as I see it. Mommee and Daddy, they might be two sticks that bow and meet and eat and listen to each other talk. I want our love to be wild and full of fire and on a level not possessed by people I know."

"You've been reading novels, Roxy. The novel is a debased collection of nonsense. Three weeks. That gives you enough time to feel I'm not rushing you? Your minister can post the bans or what they do hereabouts, and we'll be married in your church, Trinity at Wall Street, and set up housekeeping till the war is over."

She pouted and pulled away from him. "Really, Davey, you want a mere baggage for your lusts and a housekeeper for your chambers, I sometimes think. Damn it, I'm a Philipse."

"And I'm a Cortlandt, and a patch-pants one. So names don't impress me. What a tempered, spoiled darling you are."

She stood up and brushed small leaves off her riding habit. "You irk me at times. A surgeon doctor, handsome enough, manly, adored by me, but I suppose it's love that will keep us?"

David smiled and went to get the horses. "I'll flog you, once we are married, to get those la-de-da notions from your head. I'm not asking dowry. Money doesn't matter now in this new nation. It's what a man is, what he can do, what his hands and shoulders can perform."

"Oh dear, solid-headed Davey! I see I'm to be the realist. Money is a fine thing and buys comfort and ease and causes no sweats at night and no fears of creditors in the morning. You can be sure *I'll* insist on a dowry."

Leading the horses, they walked arm in arm up to the road. "I've a good mind once this war is over, Roxy, to pack a solid strong wagon and put you on top of the load, and head for the Kentuck' and Ohio lands. Damn me if you'll not lick into shape over smoky campfires, and Indians skulking around your corn-husk bed."

"You'll never find *me* in the wilderness in buckskins, scraping your boots free of mud. If I marry you, you'll be a prosperous New York surgeon and medical man."

"That your promise, to marry me?"

"What?"

"To marry me if I set up my sign here?"

"And it's not *just* to own house slaves, and a collection of the good furniture and china Mommee will spare me. No, Davey, I also love you and adore you and I want our love to be strong and not tame. But is it wrong to want a *proper* setting for it?"

"I suppose not." After all, he felt as he helped her mount, cupping fingers for one slim boot, a girl who had been raised as Roxy had been, and had temper and was so beautiful, was like other girls, only *more* so.

They rode down the yellow road by the river, passing gun crews moving cannon to vantage points; Roxanne patted the gelding's neck and the creature spat foam from his silver bit. "They seem to be preparing to hold the island."

"Yes, there is rumor of an invasion fleet, and a massing in Canada, and there is terror in the south, off Charleston, from English raids inland. I think the waiting phase is over."

She grabbed his arm with her gloved hand. He loved her to touch him—so perfectly alive, so full of vigor in her fingers, her lips, her limbs. "I shall pray for us, Davey, that we will live through this and come out of it well and whole. You think General Washington would stand up for you in church on our wedding day?"

He gasped in shock, and then laughed. "Lord love you, Roxy. You have a fool's courage. I wouldn't dare ask. And don't let your father ask either."

They rode on and laughed, much in love, and were amused.

CHAPTER 16   The activities around General Washington's headquarters in New York had increased. When David reported on the morning he was to start for Lloyd's Neck on Long Island, he found the house ringed in by soldiers and he had to wait in the hall until his name was taken up to Botts. A sense of testing of loyalties and attitudes was in the air. Once he had been passed upstairs he found Botts talking to a tattered Jew peddler in a soiled brown coat, the long rabbinical beard untrimmed, the face and hands unwashed.

The peddler turned and grinned like a stage Shylock and pulled on the long greasy curls that grew over his ears, "Ah Dr. Cortlandt, any pins, notions, two-penny nails? Needles, thread, perhaps a shilling handkerchief?"

David stooped and stared at the soiled figure of the peddler and then turned to Botts. "It can't be? *Not* Morris Manderscheid?"

The peddler rolled his eyes and laughed. "If I can fool you, no wonder I fool the Tories!"

"But where is the Philadelphia gentleman, the Hebrew scholar I knew in London?"

"Some place under this lousy shirt, under these real and filthy whiskers."

Botts nodded, "Morris has turned out to be one of our best agents on Long Island and in New Jersey."

The peddler lamented, "And a filthy business it is, and everyone kicking an old peddling Jew into the ditch or turning the dogs on him. But now they know me, I am part of the landscape. A child of chance, naked as a needle to their low humor."

"What's all the extra guard doing here today?"

Manderscheid shook his head. "There is a plot to abduct or murder General Washington. That's why I came to report."

Botts scowled. "And that's why, David, you must keep your eyes open on Long Island. We don't know all of it. We suspect several people here in New York close to headquarters—in the mayor's office—but we expect the actual people who will try to perform the deed are from Colonel Lemon's Tory Legion on Long Island."

"Kill General Washington! People close to us . . . on our side?"

"It points that way," said Botts. "Morris is going back tonight to Long Island. You're leaving with Joe Philipse and the boy at noon. There's a boat ready to ferry you and the sulky over to Brooklyn Heights."

"Then what? I mean after I contact Sir Francis?"

"Wait till you hear from Morris. He may have information as to names and places about this plot by then."

Morris Manderscheid began to gather up his bundles and packs. "And if in two days you don't hear from me, Dr. Cortlandt, better run for it. Colonel Lemon's drumhead court-martials always end in rope. And Botts can't weep for us." He laughed and winked. "He doesn't give a damn about his agents—only the cause."

David tried to feel amused, but he cracked his knuckles. "Gentlemen, I'm planning to be married. I'd like to *return* from this mission."

Botts waved off the idea David wouldn't be back (how cold he is, thought David) and looked up from a list he was reading. "The death or abduction of General Washington would cripple the colonial war. The defense of New York, the general and the Congress feel, is vital to our cause. It all ties in. Tories are preparing guide beacons for the expected fleet from England, and if they do land detachments in force we want to know where. You two are not the only agents we have out. Detailed information must be gotten."

"Nor," said Manderscheid pulling on his beard, "are we the only side to use agents. So, Doctor, beware of sudden friends. Unless Botts or myself proclaim a man safe, avoid any personal contact. Remember Bacon's remark: 'A crowd is not company, and faces are but a gallery of pictures, and talk but a tinkling cymbal where there is no love.' "

David fingered the edge of his hat and said, "I'll be ready with my charges at the proper time. It is all right if I carry pistols?"

"Use your head," said Botts. "It's always a better weapon than a shot of buck and powder. Take what you want."

The peddler scratched under his arms. "Oh what I'd give for a bath, but it took me two months to get a body patina filthy enough to be accepted on the roads."

It was past noon when the sulky and its two fast-moving bays was rolling along beyond Brooklyn Heights, down country roads past Dutch farm buildings and workers in green fields hoeing and weeding. David in tawny jacket with gilt buttons drove, and Dan sat beside him, *geeing* the horses. In the back seat sat great Lizzie Patch with a bilious green sunbonnet from which her large reddish nose peered out to test the country air. Beside her in a blue gentleman's suit was Joe Philipse (David, too, had come round to thinking "Joey" no longer fitted the young man), arms folded, chiding Lizzie for her fears of Indians.

"Now Patch, old girl, they never scalp fat juicy ones like yourself."

"Oh, don't they now?"

"They'd marry you off to a big chief and try and breed you."

"They better not take 'igh liberties with me! I'll marry no bloody naked savage."

David clucked at the horses and said without turning his head, "Keep the blunderbuss handy, Joe. We're crossing over to the north of the island and it's mixed company there. Ours, or the king's, and no one neutral. But so far we've managed to control the roads."

"Don't worry, I've got the old barrel loaded with nails and small shot on some of Ned Styron's good powder. And there are a brace of pistols behind me in a bag."

"No shooting unless I signal by dipping my whip."

"Lord love a duck, *what*," Lizzie asked, "have you two gotten me and the angel boy into?"

"A sunny ride, a view of the Sound soon."

Dan shouted, "I see water!"

In the afternoon they rolled on past the blue expanse of the Sound, the waves like overlapping fish scales in the sun, and here and there a bone-white sail turning and tacking in a light breeze. At two o'clock they stopped and ate a picnic lunch from a hamper under old apple trees. Dan caught a knobby toad and was warned against warts, and then the boy sat on a bee and howled. Lizzie with her teeth in a chicken wing said, "Never sit down, Dannie lad, without lookin' first. Come and show me." But Dan said, no, he was too old to expose himself to a woman that way, *there*.

When Joe reharnessed the horses the sun was in a slow dance far to the west and Lloyd's Neck still lay some miles off. David beat up the horses and Dan shouted, "*Gee gee*. Run, run!" It was a well-packed sandy road and they raced along past white villages and through crossroads where there was usually a loafing, spitting outpost of Continental soldiers to look at David's pass and wave them on. That the pass listed them as "merchants for timber" seemed only fair, David felt. It wouldn't do to drive up to Sir Francis Livingston's estates in blue and buff uniforms. He had been unable to gather just how Sir Francis stood with the British loyalists. He was too far out to be fully under American control, and at the moment it was the procedure to leave alone those suspected of loyalties to the king *if* they remained quiet, or were beyond active observation. There was much raiding, and crude and often unjust hearings and punishment on both sides. Tories called "cowboys" lurked in many thickets, acting more like bandits than loyal men. David wanted to be off the roads before dark and whipped up again the now tiring horses, which were moving with wet, shiny hides on a narrower road that led out to the point of land called Lloyd's Neck between pines and elms and a snake-rail fence.

The fields looked as if they had once been well cared for, but there were many weeds now and certain of the sheds were in bad repair. The road to the big house over the water was full of ruts. As they passed between the stone gateposts in need of whitewash, the sun slipped out of sight and the blue-purple dusk was spattered with the blinking flares of fireflies. Late birds gave raucous farewell sounds. Dan said sleepily, "How do the fireflies set fire to themselves, Uncle Joe?"

"It's a secret art," said Joe, and the sulky made the full half turn to the wide steps of Livingston Hall. It had been built and rebuilt for half a century, and was imposing and much grander than the earlier Dutch river houses that had not been modernized. Several good marble and lead garden statues of Greek gods stood in the formal gardens, gardens in need of trimming and spading. The wide steps of the house were unswept. No lights gleamed from any part of it.

David brought the bays to a halt and he looked around and stuck a pistol in his belt. He stepped down onto the unraked crushed bluestone drive. A dog barked in another county.

"Keep your eyes open, Joe; I'll try and knock someone up."

Lizzie shook her head, "Don't look like they got any 'ot supper waiting for the boy."

David walked over the wide squares of white marble to the big double doors. He banged the green-patinaed copper knocker in the shape of a sea beast. He waited. No lights came from between the chinks in the closed double shutters bolted on all the windows. No sound echoed from inside the house. He knocked again, and in the darkening gardens the throat throbs of frogs at evening joined the buzz of insects and the night music of crickets. A late bird sang and stopped. Somewhere a night-blooming plant was sickening sweet.

David was just about to turn away when from the door issued metal groans of a lock turning, and yet the hinges (oiled most likely) were without a sound as they caused the one door to open, part way. A ruddy-faced old man, wrinkled with deep etchings of time and wearing a badly washed wig, looked out at them.

"No one at 'ome, no one at all, sir."

"I'm David Cortlandt. Sir Francis is expecting me."

"No one 'ome at all."

"I've Sir Francis' grandson with me."

The little old man sucked on toothless gums. "Do wait. But I assure you, no one 'ere at all, no one at all."

He went away and David waited.

Joe helped Dan and Lizzie from the sulky and tied up the horses to a ring in a block of marble bearing the Livingston coat of arms deeply cut into it. *Esse quam videri*—to be rather than to seem.

David said, "I've gotten someone to answer. He's gone to tell Sir Francis, I think."

"That's better than nothing," said Joe, tucking a pistol out of sight. The old man was back on the other side of the door. "Come in and foller me. Mind the dark now, sir."

It was a strange procession they made. First the old man carrying a feeble candle in a bronze holder, then David, and Joe herding Lizzie wide-eyed and in panic, she holding onto a sleepy Dan, all casting eerie shadows on the black and white stone floor of the grand hall. On either side old paintings reported dead varnished faces trimmed in lace and rimmed in armor or honors. The crystal chandeliers were hooded in linen, and on either side were rooms resting in linen shrouds. The house smelled of unaired, shuttered-away furnishings, rotting apples, of a grandeur now hooded and unused.

The little man opened a narrow door to a set of steps going down. "Watch the second step, she be a bit loose."

They went down into a vast cellar made of boulders and walled with many cases and boxes. They walked across a stone floor to a door to a wine cellar which was open, and into the wine vault, smelling sour and grapy. Racks of bottles not at all cobwebbed as David had expected, but clean, with only a thin film of dust on them. They faced another door of solid hickory on which the old servant knocked, and it was opened.

They were in a chamber fairly large, cut into the living earth and buttressed with raw pine planks bleeding rosin. At a rough table two men sat drinking wine from silver cups. A small pot of charcoal was under a bubbling large kettle of what smelled like stew well seasoned; garlic and bay leaves had not been spared.

Sir Francis—one of the two men—stood up, leaning on his cane.

He had lost weight and his face was tanned by weathering new to him. "Welcome Dr. Cortlandt, and you too, Joseph. This is Culbly Schuyler."

David made a curt bow. "I knew your cousin Homer Schuyler."

The stout and bald young man laughed. "Hell, yes—*Major* Schuyler of the damned Continental Army, eh? And you two, I believe, are in the same forces?"

"As of now," said David warning Joe with a look, "—tonight we come as plain citizens." He turned and took the little boy by the shoulders. "Dan, this is your grandfather, Sir Francis Livingston."

The boy rubbed his eyes and stared open-mouthed. The big man limped over and placed a hand on the boy's head and smiled. "Ah, he has the look of Harvell when a child, the same slope of shoulders, the same tilt of head. Doesn't he, David?"

"I'm sure he has, Sir Francis."

"I'm hungry, sir," Dan said.

"Good hunter's stew is ready. Culbly, dish it up."

David had a feeling there were many men around. Somewhere in the cellars or just outside this earth dugout he sensed there was an exit to the north, facing the Sound.

David said, "My duty seems done, Sir Francis, since I have performed what I promised Harvell I'd do so long ago in London. These are strange times. This is Lizzie Patch who's been with the boy since his birth. A good woman."

"Yer servant, Sir Francis," said Lizzie making a clumsy bow. "'Ere to serve you I'm sure. Goodie Patch knows 'er place and duties."

"I fear times have changed at Livingston House. We've closed it so as not to attract raiders. And we live here in what was once the vegetable cellar when we're not elsewhere. But now to stew. There's plenty of that."

David could see there was—enough stew for at least ten men. He felt something odd in the atmosphere here. And Culbly, in russet hunting serge—burly, unshaved, bright-eyed, and very intelligent—watched them as they ate, and said little.

Sir Francis observed the boy eating. He fingered Dan's childish limp hair. "Yes, he does look like Harvell."

David nodded. "It grows, the resemblance. I'll take my way back to town in the morning. I have duties."

"Stay," said Culbly. "It isn't often we get visitors of such rank among us. 'Be not righteous over much,' says the Old Testament. 'Why shouldest thou destroy thyself?'"

Joe was spooning up stew and looking first at David and then at Culbly. David took up a bit of bread. "You bake your own here?"

"We have a yard kitchen out back," said Sir Francis. "What Culbly means is that he can't let you go back just yet."

"Why not, Sir Francis?"

The grandfather continued to stare at his grandson, then looked back up at David. "These are mean years. There is much doing here, and so elsewhere."

Culbly banged down his knife. "Sir Francis, there isn't any sense in explaining events. These are enemy officers."

"Damn you!" said David rising in anger. "We came here to bring to Sir Francis his grandson. We are not in uniform, and it seems to me we were all not so long ago good neighbors."

Sir Francis pursed his lips and motioned Culbly to remain seated. "In this house it will never be said I did a mean thing. But David and Joseph, there will be a delay in returning you to your own lines. It is war, you know, full of ubiquitous functionaries who like power."

Joe had loosened his pistol under the table. "We'll leave in the morning," he said. "You may have the men to stop us—then again we may have men too."

David sat down and looked across at Dan. The boy was sleepy and his mouth was stained with food; Lizzie wiped the mouth and said, "If it's all the same, I'd like to find a place to tuck in the laddie for the night."

Sir Francis rose and said, "Follow me."

When the nurse and boy and Sir Francis were gone, Culbly said, "It's a weakness an old man has for a grandchild. But I don't give a damn if you brought a dozen grandchildren, you're prisoners and I'll take no blatant arrogance from you."

David looked at Joe. He had made a bluff of having men with him and he waited for Joe to say something more. The boy had become a man and was neither angry nor afraid, or so he seemed, sitting there, his hands under the table. Joe said blandly, "It's a thing I didn't expect—you always being such a gentleman, Culbly, when we met at your father's, Mynheer's, place. But two can play at this nonsense. Our men will move in by nine tomorrow morning if we are not on our way back."

Culbly laughed. "They'll sup in hell if they do. I have six companies of Tory Rangers in the woods all around this estate. All trained, armed, and with cannon—three brass four-pounders."

David folded his arms and sat back. He was tired from the day's drive. The sun and air after several weeks in New York had affected him. "You talk as if you were in contact with Colonel Lemon, the notorious Tory leader?"

Sir Francis's voice came to them. "Culbly *is* Colonel Lemon." Sir Francis stood in the low doorway smiling, a candle in his hand. "The boy is sleeping pleasantly."

Culbly went red with rage. David stared at the fat young man with the high bald forehead. He laughed. "I can't believe it. *This* the cruel and deadly Colonel Lemon? Who leads the evil Indian raiders and burns women and children alive in barns?"

Culbly bit his lower lip. "They are the usual lies of war. But if hard measures are to be taken I don't shun them. Sir Francis, you're as gossipy as a woman tonight."

"I don't like this sulking in woods and hiding in cellars. When the fleet gets here and . . ."

Culbly stood up to stop any further information. "I order you, Sir Francis, to retire."

The old man stood proud in the flickering candlelight in a clay cellar smelling of roots. "Sir, this is my house." Outraged, he waved his cane at the Tory leader. "You're my guest, don't forget it."

Culbly sighed. "I dislike melodrama. It's so true to life, yet vulgar." He took a silver whistle from his pocket and blew it. "You leave me no choice, Sir Francis. You've become a babbling, senile old man at the sight of a child."

A plank door to the outside opened and two burly men came in carrying Brown Bess muskets. They were followed by two more armed with pistols.

Culbly said without turning around to face the men, "Sir Francis is under arrest. And these two enemy agents also."

David looked at Joe, who stared back, saying nothing. Sir Francis glared at the men and then at Culbly. "Very well, act your damned part, Colonel Lemon. When the king's regiments land here, I'll see you're given what's coming to you. I'm a personal friend of the king, you forget."

"I said hold your tongue, Sir Francis. I hold a commission from that king to recruit these loyalist regiments. And whatever I do is approved by London."

Sir Francis spoke with a gloomy voice. "We'll see, sir." Turning to David and Joe he added, "I can do nothing for you gentlemen. I am undone here—to outquote the colonel—'Babylon is fallen, is fallen, the great city because she made all nations drink of the wine of the wrath . . .'"

David expressed their situation by showing his hands palms up in a gesture. "It's an odd way to treat friends who only tried to aid you."

Culbly, trying desperately to control his temper, shouted, "Get these two into the stockade hut. Sir Francis is a prisoner in this house. And send scouts out to see if there are rebels in any number in the surrounding farms."

"Very good, Colonel."

David stood up and Culbly came over and took the pistol from him, and then he held out his hand to Joe, who gave over his weapon. "You will be tried by legally appointed representatives of the Crown. You'll find royal justice unimpaired, undiminished."

"You are serious about this charade, aren't you, Colonel?" David asked.

"I don't intend, my dear Doctor, I assure you, to see the king lose this war because of any sentimental weakness on my part."

Sir Francis stood leaning on his cane, his mouth made into a thin line. David and Joe were marched out. The night was butter-warm but dark. They were paraded down a lane between apple orchards, their guards cursing and assisting them along with a kick or a cruel punch in the kidneys with the butt of their muskets. They soon came to a clump of pine trees; in their dark, olive-green shadows a series of weathered gray tents had been set up. Several dozen men were seated around campfires, cooking, drinking, making the usual banal camp jests. Sparks flew upward to die in the lower branches of the pines.

A lean, handsome man dressed in the well-worn red coat and white breeches of a British officer rose to meet them from a log bench. He was holding a stone bottle and his once-white wig was in disorder. The red face was a bit twisted by drink, but cheerful and friendly.

"Sir James Tropp at your service, gentlemen. Prisoners, I seem to sense. Ah, Joseph."

"Dr. Cortlandt—we met once at Peter Schuyler's," said David. "You know Joseph Philipse."

"Ah, yes, how do you do." Sir James shook hands a little too heartily, a bit unsteady on his feet. "Know all the Philipses, sir. Know your lovely mother. Miss the city, you know. This blasted camp life isn't for a gentleman."

David said, "Your leader, Colonel Lemon as he calls himself now, seems to think us dangerous criminals. We hope you can make him understand we're nothing of the sort. You are king's agent in this colony."

"My dear fellow, I can't do a thing with the brutal monster. War has disarranged his clear brain. He enjoys it, the bite of cruelty, better than a woman on a bed. Have a drink. One of you sods get two cups for our guests."

David accepted the dirty cup, so did Joe. "You are still king's agent in the colonies. He wouldn't dare go against your position."

Sir James drank and David sipped the strong rum. Sir James nodded and sat down on his log bench. "By Godfrey, I am. But you know he doesn't admit to the accepting of my office. Says I lost it, lost it when you rebels drove me out. Sad, sad. I feel drunk, Doctor. Fizzy drunk I am."

David rubbed his chin and looked over the camp, its tents, the many men and stacked arms. It was no collection of local Tory farmers. It was a military force of real strength and training. He would, if he could, get some information for Botts out of Sir James. "We have been told by Sir Francis that soon Colonel Lemon will have higher rank—over Sir Francis. When the royal fleet arrives."

Sir James nodded and brushed the loose hair from his wig off his face. "In late June, or mayhap July. It's all planned. We attack New York, thousands of Hessians coming. Guns, men-of-war. Then I'll be king's agent again and that damn Culbly—Colonel Lemon indeed—I'll have him skinned and his hide made into a drum. A dirty native Nero, nothing else. Pardon me, gentlemen, no offense to you."

"None taken, Sir James."

Joe looked around him. Sir James turned over the empty bottle. "Not a drop. Well good night, gentlemen. Sergeant Bloodbetter? Where are our guests staying?"

"In the smokehouse stockade, sir, colonel's orders."

Sir James shook his head. "I regret it all, gentlemen. Filthy hole. However, cheer up, no one stays there long. He shoots so many."

The sergeant pushed them away from the fire. "This way."

At the end of the camp was a heavy little building of square planks. It had once been a smokehouse for the processing of bacon and hams. They were pushed into the windowless place and fell over old chain used for lifting swine sides and hurt their knees on gritty charcoal. The heavy oak door locked behind them with the click of a padlock being shut. In total darkness they sat elbow to elbow smelling soot and stale lard. A sorry pair of spies, David decided.

CHAPTER 17   Close to terror, David in his darkness was haunted by fragments of old lines:

> *Great Empedocles, that ardent soul,*
> *Leapt into Etna, and was roasted whole.*

It was desolately and desperately clear to David Cortlandt that he was a fool. *Hang there like fruite, my soule, till the trees dye.*

A fragment of a poem was no help in this stinking darkness, confined by soot-covered logs greasy to the touch. His teeth edged with fear.

He heard Joe's voice, "You can say this for Botts, he doesn't care whom he uses in his fancy business."

"You really think he sends people to their death? Into hopeless conditions on the chance something might get to him?"

"Yes, damn it," said Joe, striking a log in the dark. "It's all passionless, for a cause. I wonder if he was so cruel when a drunkard?"

David rubbed his grimy fingers together. "I knew him in his drunken days in London. He was a cheerful loud fool. Of course it may all be part of a plan for us to betray ourselves."

They could hear the passing clang of metal, the trot of booted feet, the hoarse sounds in the night, all the noise of a camp at rest, free of the fear of attack.

Joe let off banging the log wall. "Have you thought much of death?"

"Not yet. I will before morning."

"It's a vulgar thing—Christ!"

David laughed. "I suppose. Certainly not a dainty thing, and all the poetry on it sounds false."

"They'll shoot us?"

"Hanging, more likely. We are spies."

Joe made a retching sound and sucked in breath. David lowered his head to his knees. "I don't fear death, Joe. It's all negative, John Hunter told me—the absence of all things including memory—what I dislike is the process of dying."

Joe did not answer. It was warm in the old smokehouse. Soot entered their noses and made gritty their mouths. They tried to climb the log walls but they were smooth wood and set close, slippery with old lard, rancid to the smell. They hunted in all corners with touch and feel. They bumped each other aside. It was hopeless. Solid oak beams set with great nails made up the floor. There were no windows.

It was—by guess—near dawn when they heard the crunching sound of rats on the roof, or what David thought of as rats gnawing.

Joe's voice was nearby. "What is it, David?"

"Something on the roof."

"It's chewing on the shingles."

There was a tearing, crackling sound and a hole appeared in the ceiling letting in, after the jet total blackness of the interior, a milky bit of atmosphere. Neither spoke.

A voice, muffled and softly projected into the smokehouse, came from above.

"Make a noise of some kind, you damn oafs."

David said, "Who is it?"

"Morris Manderscheid. And it's a solid-built jake."

"It's a smokehouse."

There was more tearing—their friend must be using an iron bar.

"Can you climb up?"

"No, the walls are too greasy."

"I suspected that; *grab*."

A thick knotted rope fell on David's head. "It's knotted every two feet. Better hurry. Be morning soon."

David said, "You first, Joe." And before there could be a protest he slammed the rope into Joe's arms and lifted him up and pushed him high. "Climb, you monkey."

In a moment he heard the creak of weight on the roof shingles and the rope came down to his waiting grasp. It was not easy to climb the swaying thing—nor to muscle one's body through the torn corner of the roof. In the pale milky light he saw pools of mist sifting through the camp, the mackerel-mottled sky, and the bearded face of Morris Manderscheid grinning at him. A soot-stained Joe was looking off toward where a dog barked. Joe was holding a three-foot iron bar, the one used to pry a hole into their prison.

Morris said, "Easy, now. They're drunk and sleeping but beware of dogs. We drop feet first into grass—then follow me—leave the bar, Joe."

David jarred his spine in the drop to the ground, but was off after Joe and Morris under spreading black pines. And then there was sand underfoot and they were moving along a beach, moonlight drenching the white-bearded waves that broke at their feet.

By sunrise they were several miles to the east, sitting by a brook under a thicket of blueberry bushes full of wasps, trying to remove the soot and grime from their bodies and clothes. Morris in his tattered brown coat, his low-crowned hat over his tangled curls and beard, was smoking a short clay pipe.

"You'll never get really clean for a week. Now listen with care. They're after me and I'll never get through to Manhattan. I'm too well known to slip by. I'm going to go out to Sag Harbor and try that way. However, you two must get through in the next two days."

"What's so important?" David asked, inspecting the ruins of a once-white shirt.

Morris handed him a soiled square of paper folded and refolded. "Here is the information—names, dates, and details of the plot to kill or kidnap General Washington."

"The devil you say," Joe said looking up from laundering his stockings.

"Yes. Here is some coin, and one pistol—I need one for myself. Get to Jamaica—the Dolphin Inn. Hire a carriage there. It's safe."

"And you?"

"I must run for it. I'm marked."

"Botts can't let you be run down—like, like a fox by the hounds."

Morris smiled and pulled on his filthy beard. "He can and will. A man in his position can't spare sentiment and still do his work."

David put the paper away inside his jacket. "We'd better start. Any other message, Morris?"

The peddler shook his head and closed his eyes. "No, you don't know my family—besides it's better they don't ever find out how dismal my condition had become *if* I don't survive."

Joe began to pull on his wet stockings. Morris looked warily around. "A few more runs with the hounds—then, if, if, I'll shave off this beard, change my clothes—on the off chance I can get through. *Mazel tov.*" And he was gone, only the clashing and breaking of bushes to mark his passing.

It took them eleven hours to reach Manhattan, dodging back and forth along back roads, seeing Tory bands in every field of innocent farmers, suspecting all innkeepers of being crown agents, frightened by the mooing of a herd of unmilked cattle, and snapped at by stray curs they thought it better sense not to turn the whip on.

In Manhattan at Botts' headquarters at last, they stood before Botts and Major Homer Schuyler while the two men read the note Morris Manderscheid had given them. They felt tired and drained of any desire to spy again.

Botts looked up blandly, "As you know the contents, I must ask you not to leave this house. We are arresting all those involved tonight."

The major shook his head. "A man from General Washington's own Life Guards and the mayor of New York! And you also met my cousin, Culbly?"

David nodded. "Sir Francis Livingston identified him as the Colonel Lemon commanding the Tory Legion."

Botts looked up, "What!"

"Culbly Schuyler seemed very displeased," said Joe, smiling, "to be so identified."

Botts beat his fists on his desk top. "And you two pinheads just remembered to tell me this?"

David nodded, "Yes."

"We've been trying to identify Colonel Lemon for months. And you two just stumble into it and sew up your mouths."

"We've been through a great deal," said David. "We're tired and filthy."

"You'll find wooden tubs in the next room and I'll send up hot water and a gourdful of soft soap."

"You've done well," said Major Schuyler.

Botts began to write on rough squares of gray paper. Without looking up he said, "Not badly at all, for such rank amateurs."

David scowled. "You don't seem to give a bean's interest to Morris Manderscheid."

Botts went on writing. "He's a very remarkable man, that Hebrew. Courage and wit."

"Is that all you have to say, Botts?" David felt rage and acid bite at his stomach.

"You have three weeks' leave, Captain Cortlandt—you wanted to get married. Congratulations."

"You cold-blooded son of a bitch," Joe said, and moved toward the desk and the writing man. David gripped Joe's arm and stopped his progress. Botts' large cheeks colored, his brow grew cherry-red. When he spoke it was in his usual calm, noncommittal voice, "Leftenant Philipse, you're being posted to a battery on Brooklyn Heights. Don't bother to apologize when you recover from this matter. Men under stress are permitted certain outbursts." He picked up his papers and went out, followed by Major Schuyler.

The traitorous member of General Washington's Life Guards was hanged one fine summer day in the middle of a square of regiments, drums banging and the gallows in view of all those citizens of Manhattan who cared to view the event. The mayor of the city, just as guilty, but with friends in the right places, escaped the military rope and was put into jail.

David Cortlandt and Roxanne Philipse were to be married the day after the execution—rather an anticlimax to the town, but not to the Hudson River families who gathered at Trinity Church on Wall Street for this break in a rather dull social season. There was much talk now of the British invasion. It was unlikely there would be much more going on of any pleasant nature till the war was done with.

Mynheer Schuyler and his wife came down from their estate in the yellow family coach—Mynheer in last year's blue with a poorly recombed wig, but with the diamond buckles in his shoes. "Damn me, a man must live as if life goes on. The least I can do is bring down a dozen bottles of the good wine to the wedding."

His wife wasn't listening as their coach crossed the town, its streets littered, the buildings unpainted, ungainly, slovenly soldiers boldly staring at her high-lifted bosom—she laced tightly.

"It's not the same place, somehow. People shouldn't marry in wartime."

"Appetites go on, my dear. You wouldn't want to encourage a group of bastards on our girls, would you?"

She didn't answer. Men had such barnyard minds.

The Philipse town house echoed with the march of servants' feet moving bedding for guests who were staying a few days. Slaves from the manor were setting tables, pulling corks, bringing great pans of beef and mutton from the bake shops—the Dutch ovens of the house were over-used. A great excitement prevailed.

A pale Jonathan Philipse with dignity greeted the guests, and after the usual salutes and wishes the men mostly lit West Indies cheroots, swallowed rum and water, and walked in the gardens discussing the war, prices, *and* the failure of youth to show much of their parents' wisdom, fortitude, and strength of character—in that order.

Mynheer inhaled on four inches of prime black leaf. "I live excitement all the time—will the damn Continentals persist? Or the rotten crown agents succeed in reversing all the nonsense we live through?"

"You're a good colonial patriot, I hear," said Jonathan. "No?"

"The devil I'm not. My best horses pulling their hearts out on the guns in this town, my bins emptying to feed the guts of these town loafers."

"You're being paid, Mynheer."

"Paper promises, but,"—Mynheer sighed—"I have to make up for my son Culbly's actions. You haven't heard any gossip of his capture and shooting?"

"None," said Jonathan crisply. "He was involved in the plot to kill General Washington, I hear."

The sound of arriving carriages and the gush of female greetings filtered out to the garden.

Mynheer mopped his large red face with a lace handkerchief. He had reached the third most popular subject of the day. "Children are like sticky burrs under a father's saddle."

David in a new blue and buff uniform, gilt buttons, a borrowed sword, his red hair tied well back, came into the garden, bowing to greetings. His father-in-law soon-to-be smiled, took David's arm, and had him face Mynheer.

"The captain makes a very un-shy bridegroom."

Mynheer pumped David's hand, "Congratulations, my dear boy. I've known Roxanne since a child—well, I'm sure she'll make a proper wife once you've shown yourself a proper husband. I had a devil of a wedding night. Too much rich pork. Ill as a cat."

"I'm not as calm as I look," David said, accepting a glass of pale red wine from a passing tray. He was sweating in the new and uncomfortable uniform that Joe's tailor had put together in rather a hurry. And the prospect of marriage seemed both delightful and awesome. His independence was slipping away quickly. . . .

Alone the sun arises, and alone spring the great streams.

But the words of poets were no help now in this fine garden among all these fine Hudson River families come to see him (and Roxanne) wed. Here was a religious sense of man's relationship to his society and his neighbor, here was the opening door, the manifestation of some mysterious ideal of family and generation. A ritual to produce a mating game. To release the stored-up energy of love in individuals and humanity. He almost tripped over the borrowed sword at the seriousness of his thoughts.

He went calmly with Joe and Botts (the Botts of ill-fitted brown jacket and clumsy hands and the odd-trimmed head of dark hair) in a carriage to the church. Pigeons preened on old graves, the interior smelled of moss and cold stone. There were many uniforms and the usual strange woman, related to no one, who sobbed and sniffed into a small handkerchief.

Joe took David into a small side room, while in the church a leaking organ played Handel rather well.

"No, David, there's no escape but I can get you a strong rum dram."

"Thank you, but sober will be fine."

Botts came and nodded. "We'll begin. The general has just come in."

"The general?"

Botts smiled. "Cold-blooded as I am, I felt it safe for him to come down. He wanted to see you wed."

"General Washington?"

"You did help break up the plot on his life. He is grateful."

Joe peered through the door, slightly ajar. "What swank! The staff—lots of ruffs and military lace."

David felt himself propelled out into the church, into a garden
of faces. The general stood at ease with members of his staff. Tall,
pock-marked, the narrow mouth expressionless, powdered hair ma-
thetically in place. His huge hand reached for David's.

"I offer you, Captain, the example of a happily married man—
may your own years be as full as mine."

David said something—he never really recalled what—and soon
stood, Joe on one side, Botts on the other, watching Roxanne in a
foam of white lace kick at her train, held by two small, indifferent
Schuyler cousins. The minister cleared his throat, adjusted his
strings, his collar, and his pale long hands. Roxanne stood firmly at
David's side, one corner of her beautiful mouth curled ironically,
and he saw by the tremor of her hand as she took his during the
ceremony that she too was emotionally more involved than her
cool exterior showed. The strange woman lamented, as if for
Babylon, and since she was only a disturbing interloper someone
led her out aided by a cane.

David heard little of the ceremony, but he seemed to respond to
Joe's nudges and nods properly. He heard Mynheer cough loudly,
saw Jonathan Philipse carefully wipe a corner of one eye and grip
his lower lip with his teeth.

The minister closed the small morocco-bound book in his hand
and finished the ritual in a hushed, tomb-like whisper as he came to
the words, ". . . man and wife."

Roxanne said briskly, "Darling, you're too stern-looking."

He kissed her cheek before they all closed in and he was aware of
General Washington and the staff leaving by the little side room.
Remaining were the Hudson River families—all the cousins and the
uncles and the aunts, and all those not related but part of the life
that made up the society he was now firmly wedded to. The fears,
the regrets were gone from him as he shook hands, made small
talk, and bowed.

Too sweet is the rind, too bitter the core seemed no longer to
apply.

Roxanne swept up her skirt with one graceful movement. "If we
can get to the vestry, my darling, I would like a glass of Madeira."

She took his arm and, bowing and steering, they made the bare
cool vestry where Roxanne's mother was weeping and the immediate
family were lifting crystal goblets of tawny wine.

"Sir Francis Livingston," Joe said, "has somehow managed to send through a silver Queen Anne teapot and a note of good wishes."

There was more to marriage than a ceremony and too much to drink and certain leering comments.

David had taken over from a Major Woolfan two chambers at Goodie Bejens', next to the Sailor's Rest. The major had been ordered to the Jersey side to ferret out some Tory bands harassing the Morristown hills. It was late afternoon when David and the new Mrs. Cortlandt broke away from the wedding guests at the Philipse town house and got to the new chambers.

With the setting of the sun and the lisp of a night rain on the low roof overhead they had gone into the wide bed and the physical ritual of married love. It was pleasant, violent, unabashed, and much prolonged.

Roxanne looked up, her eyes half-closed in pleasure.

"I don't try your strength?"

"No, Roxy."

"You are a handsome thing stripped down, my darling."

"There's no need for me to comment on your own charms."

She laughed and rumpled his already disarranged hair. "Of course there is—tell me, am I wild enough?"

"Splendid."

"Bold?"

"Very."

"Ardent?"

"To suffice."

"Beautiful to your eyes?"

"It's getting darker."

They were neither shy nor jaded and in the morning they took hold of each other again and David was aware this stranger was no longer a stranger and he was no more alone.

That afternoon he went on duty and returned with a brace of ducks to find Roxy damning the servant girl for the condition of the sheets and giving lip to Goodie Bejens herself because their servant was not permitted to use the fire at all hours. One of Roxanne's wedding presents from her father had been two house slaves, a very black couple called Cake and Bread. Cake was a lazy maid, a fair cook, and Roxy boxed her ears a great deal. Bread was good with David's horse, showed signs of being able to care for a uniform, and could polish a sword—Joe had given David a good blade and hanger for a wedding present.

They settled in to housekeeping at the chambers, found out each other's secrets, likes and dislikes. Roxy was spoiled and opinionated but beautiful to watch taking her bath naked in the tin tub Cake had half-filled with tepid water. She was demanding in her love rights and marvelous to please. He loved her as he had loved no other thing before.

She could be trying; not caring if there was a war, times were at sixes and sevens, supplies short.

"It seems to me, David, you'd demand better hours. Mommee wants us at table at least three nights a week."

They were at breakfast. He put down the teacup. "I am trying to set up medical centers. Once a battle begins, it is too difficult to do these things then."

"But I miss you so."

"It's mutual." He seized her fingers, smelling of butter and jam, and kissed them.

"Other officers find time to prance and parade down Broadway. Popinjays and their dismal wives! I have no one to take me to tea on the Mall."

"I'll take it up with General Washington."

She stood up and scowled, in her thin dressing robe, curls all in disorder. "We Philipses have little sense of humor."

"Then I'll tickle you, my dear." Which led to a set-to and much laughter and rolling on the floor and upsetting the table and Cake finding them in the bed again. And Captain Cortlandt a half hour late in inspecting some medical stores just brought by ship from Holland.

Often when Roxy's high spirits and desire to play were prolonged he was happy to escape to the outposts, to talk with Joe on Brooklyn Heights, or spend hours with Botts over maps that only fairly reported Staten, Long, and Manhattan islands.

"Any news of Morris Manderscheid?"

Botts shook his head, "Nothing. But also no information as to any capture or executions."

"He'd be a dreadful loss."

Botts changed the subject. "I've got Long Island under observation. Your friend Jack-Tom Swales is going to command a company of scouts, and I've agents Gilly Buke and Nathaniel Hale acting as farmers on the scene."

"I hope they're better able to take care of themselves than Joe and I were."

"I use what I have at hand. Our privateers report small boats from Tory harbors sweeping the sea lanes."

"Waiting for British men-of-war?"

"Yes, they were to have sailed several weeks ago, our informants on the Continent told us."

"And we wait."

Botts put his hands in his pockets and looked his most casual. "There will be big news out of Philadelphia and the Congress in a day or so."

"The town buzzes with gossip. Well, I must go and take my wife to dinner."

Botts nodded, "I forgot. I wanted to ask you to walk with me along East River. I wonder if the guns are well placed, prepared against a landing."

David never did find out if they were. Married men had social duties.

CHAPTER 18   On a heated July day, with a clear sky overhead and the wash of bay tide firm against Manhattan Island under the guttural scolding of seagulls, the drums were rolling among the American regiments drawn up in hollow squares at the Battery. General Washington had been assembling more and more of his troops. Now, in positions facing the bay, in the camps at King's Bridge, and on the Brooklyn hills, the men stood at arms and the citizens surrounded them in their holiday best. It was a moment of pride, David Cortlandt felt, and of certain fears. But mostly of great pride.

The officer facing his commanders on Manhattan Island unrolled the sheet of paper and in a clear, strong voice that carried over the parade ground began to read.

"When in the Course of human events it becomes necessary for one people to dissolve the political bands . . ."

The cheering began. The women waved and the horses reared to loud hurrahs. The men in the ranks stood very still, eyes front. David, Roxanne at his side, was among the civilians. Joe was at the head of his regiment. Silence held them all—but for that one voice. The reading went on in hushed interest. This, then, was what the Congress of the United States—no longer the Continental Congress, David remembered—had labored over. The Declaration of Independence of the thirteen states, once thirteen colonies. For so warm a day, sudden chill ran through many of the listeners. They were cut off, slashed free of the mother country.

"And for the support of this Declaration, with the firm reliance on the protection of divine Providence we mutually pledge to each other our Lives, our Fortunes and our sacred Honour . . ."

The loyalists in the crowd, Roxanne noticed, had glum faces. The Whigs, however, felt an expansion of their chests, and some wept. Many turned away, burdened with great fear. "The thing is done," said Jonathan Philipse. From the camps cannon were firing a salute to the deed. The soldiers joined in the cheering. There was embracing and a keg of foaming beer was bunged. Many pretty girls were kissed. The officers in their new blue and buff fingered their sword knots.

Roxanne in yellow silk clung to David's arm. "Let's find Mommee's carriage and get out of the mob."

"It's an American mob, darling."

"Really, David, I'm as loyal as you are, but smells are smells." She held a small kerchief to her nose. "They just upset me more."

"Of late—have you been feeling oddly mornings?"

She looked up at him. "Don't play doctor with me, Davey. If we've made a baby I'll tell you in good time."

"I should examine you and . . ."

Roxanne waved off the idea with her sunshade. "No clinical questions, please. I'd hate to be tied down with a brat just now."

It was a pushing, cheering crowd they were trying to force their way through. Everyone seemed to be leaving the parade grounds at the same time. It wasn't easy to walk. Two great hulks of men suddenly barred their way, one smiling. David saw Jack-Tom Swales and a large farmer, by the looks of him in a too-tight uniform.

"Beelzebub," said the wilderness man. "Iffen it ain't the doctor."

"Roxanne, this is Mr. Swales, one of our scouts. Jack-Tom, my wife."

"Honored, ma'am, mighty pleased too. You sure got a man who can cut offen a leg slick as pie. This is Silvester Hand—he helped organize the Hudson River Volunteers."

"How do," said the man. He lowered his eyes and then looked up. He didn't appear to like well-dressed gentry.

Jack-Tom in his fringed buckskins, the ginger-colored topknot covered with a black felt farm hat, looked around. "Too many folk to suit me. But some place they must have likker. Nice to have met up with you, Doctor, ma'am."

"We'll meet again, Jack-Tom."

When the two large men had gone off into the crown Roxanne said, "What a handsome wild man, the blond one."

At the Philipse town house that night some of the guests brooded. Old heads, too old for battle, too unused to the ideas of liberty, said Congress had been too hasty in shutting the door against reconciliation. David took Roxanne home early.

Gang warfare broke out that night. Tory diehards were tarred and feathered and put riding a rail through the streets of New York. Tory farms held meetings and American barns were burned. In the morning black plumes of smoke trembled in the hot July sky. Men lay dead in Long Island hedges, grimy hands clutching musket or spike. Wounded men were hidden in barns along the Hudson. Some dead were buried. All along the Hudson Valley gang warfare expanded its terror. Joe Philipse went out to lead soldiers against Tory bands.

More troops came from Boston; the Americans began to organize. Larger camps went up in the summer grass, between the rivers, in Brooklyn, on Long Island. From Harlem to the Battery soldiers became pets of the natives. The Twentieth Connecticut, the Twenty-sixth Massachusetts, the Rhode Island Brigade. New heroes on prancing horses—Israel Putnam, Henry Knox—were cheered from along Broadway and up into Gravesend. Pickets walked lonely beaches, heights were measured for gun pits. Landings of massed British troops, all were sure, would take place soon, and backing them would be the heavy tiered guns of the fleet.

Best of all the citizens liked to cheer the commander-in-chief. Cold, stern, perhaps because of his mouthful of hand-carved teeth.

A man to inspire confidence, David felt. Very tall, his reddish-brown hair turning already grizzly, soon to be white. His lodgings were at the Abraham Mortier house in Lispenard's meadows. His wife Martha, small, dumpy, cool to the northern society, kept to herself mostly, poured a few cups of tea from Mr. Revere's best silver pot, and watched the guards that protected them. They were not soldiers now but sailors in blue jackets with flaring white trousers—Maine Marbleheaders under a John Glover. Soon she left for Virginia and the general went part way to the waterfront with her.

David organized two warehouses into hospitals, trained dressers, and asked for all women to roll bandages.

The streets were in holiday mood, fifes and drums were never still. There was much drinking and chasing of wenches. Fights, too, and the camps filled up as more and more of the defenders of the island poured in. Bay Staters in brown coats, folk from way back in fringed deerskin with hunting tunics. Hairy men and smooth-shaven, country bumpkins and the sons of Maryland landowners. Virginians with their rolling liquid speech. Dutchmen, Yankees, Jews, Irish, Germans, half-breeds, runaway slaves, indented servants turned free to handle a gun. National troops and state troops, not yet in conflict, camped side by side. Tents, sheds, and warehouses held them, and David toiled over their health.

The soldiers fought and drilled, they drank and drilled, they complained and avoided drill and guard duty and fatigue. Provost marshals fought bloody inn brawls. Morals broke down as vice and gambling appeased the boredom of the waiting soldiers. A reeking tent-and-shack city festered into a foulness of sordid women, drunken hangers-on. Bordellos and blind tigers did their greedy business. Clubbing and knife fights took their toll and the morning harbor tides washed loggy bodies up on the fringes of the town's beaches. Nighttown, or Holy Ground (as some mocker named it) was filled with deserters and old convicts, still scarred by lash and chain. Unmarked graves filled many empty fields.

The officers put the men to digging to take some of the spit and vinegar out of them. Forts of dirt and stone, redoubts and flèches began to hem in the island. The Hell Gate channel was commanded by a fresh-set battery. Log breastworks held cannon dragged all the way from Ticonderoga. And where the ground was rock, men sweated with picks to cut into the island's prehistoric flanks. Fort

Washington was carved from living stone. A tidal moat from Wallabout Bay along Gowanus Creek was extended by forts into wooden thickets past Dutch farms, Fort Putnam, Fort Stirling, and armed, conical Ponkiesburg Hill.

Lieutenant Joe Philipse, Jack-Tom Swales, and twenty scouts came ashore on the west side of Staten Island two hours before dawn. Two small boats had taken over a ferny cove. They lay among cat reed and canebrakes as the night shattered into fragments and morning rose over the island.

Jack-Tom, his buckskins greasier, his topknot longer on his shaved skull, listened to the morning birds hunt insects for breakfast. He slapped at a wasp. "We better be atraipsin', Leftenant, it's a fur bit, tit-to-tether, to that boatyard we're goin' to burn out."

Joe nodded and looked over the twenty scouts. They were in linen hunting smocks, buckskin skirts, a dozen kind of hats—feisty shaggy men with good clean rifles—and all waiting for Joe to start the march inland.

"The way Botts explained it, Jack-Tom, is if we cut across here we come to a place called Roman Nose Inlet. Basil Coe has a shipyard there, and if information is correct, he's built a dozen barges for the ferrying of British troops to New York."

"A daisy-do if I ever heared it. Just go in an' burn 'em, eh? And how about the pursy bastards of Tories we have to fit to do it?"

"I don't know. Two men, Jonah and Watson, you stay as boat tenders. The rest follow me and Jack-Tom."

"It sure gives me a wild hair up my arse the way they order you to do a thang in this army."

"Jack-Tom, if we run into any big opposition we'll pull back without a fight."

A scout with no front teeth, called Whitey, said, "That suits this yere catamount. I was born yere. Foller me."

They passed through the reed and cane, in black mud to their calves, and came to solid ground, half the sky still a deep blue garnished with star fragments. They moved alert, and Whitey led them, pointing to old landmarks he remembered. There were several Tory camps on the island and they knew just where—they hoped— these were.

As morning brought the sun up for a hot day's work they were pushing through pine barrows, the trees marked with old scars where

turpentine slashers had worked them a few years before. There came
the hoiking hoot of geese, the smell of barns, and the sight of elms
moored over old farmhouses. Much of this they bypassed, tearing
through huckleberry bush and swampy ground where flying insects
bit and sucked blood.

As they cleared through the wild grapevine and odorous puffballs, Jack-Tom held up a hand and they froze, rifle barrels on the
ready.

"Not so fast. This be the blue-be-Jesus place, Leftenant?"

Ahead and below ran a swift surf over scoured sands, and they
saw a small bay sheltered behind wet black rocks, a wharf, two piers
on stilts, and a shore on which a dozen barges in various stages of
completion rested on greased ways. Six men and two boys were busy
shaping wood or driving in dowels and pegs to hold the sections
together.

"They ain't lallygagging," said Whitey. "They really buildin' them
barges."

Joe looked up to a large white house over the cove. "Jack-Tom,
you take half the men and seize the shipyard. You'll find pitch and
coal oil. Burn all barges and sheds, and destroy the tools."

"I'll skin all their carcasses, they try any high-toned rumpus with
us."

"The rest will follow me—I'll point out who—to the house. All
right, Jack-Tom?"

"Fun's my failin'. Pick yer boys."

The sun was climbing as Jack-Tom and his men descended to the
shipyard. Joe didn't wait for results but led his group up a path of
crushed oyster shells. Below them the sea heaved, white tops raced
along glassy, slick ridges of purple water. A dog refused to wag his
tail as they passed through the house yard, but did little else to stop
them. The front door was open and Joe and two scouts entered.
The rest, under Whitey, surrounded the house.

It was well furnished, but simple. A breakfast table laden with
dishes of corn mush still warm, a massive plate of griddle cakes, a
side of pork, and pitchers of milk.

"They ran for the bush when we came up. Stuff's still warm.
Keep your hands off it till we're sure it's no trap."

Joe kicked open the door to the kitchen, where milk had boiled
over in the fireplace. A yellow tabby cat licked its bottom and stared

at them with cold green eyes. There was a cough down a passage to the right. Joe listened, pistol in one hand, sword in the other.

From the little bay shipyard came the *bang bang* of rifles and answering musket, then silence.

Joe motioned the two scouts to stay where they were and went into the passage. A low door opened into a room with drawn drapes. He was aware of breathing in the room. As he pulled the drapes apart, light, strong and white, filled in details and he saw a girl in a flimsy nightdress on a low trundle bed. She was blindfolded.

Joe said, "Why didn't you run with the others?"

"I be with measles."

He bent over the girl. She was pretty with wavy brown hair and well-formed breasts, but very young. "You're not spotted."

"I be past *that* stage. But if light meets my eyes Dr. Bacon says it will injury them."

"So I hear. What's your name?"

"Sally Coe."

"Your husband own Roman Nose shipyard?"

"Daddo do. He's gone to Perth Amboy for timbers."

There was more firing now from the yard. Joe looked out of the windows. Great greasy columns of black smoke were rising from several parts of the boatyard. The firing was too heavy to be only Jack-Tom's group. It was steady musket fire—a controlled, trained fire. Jack-Tom and he had better get away quickly.

The girl was sitting up, eyes bandaged, unaware her beautiful breasts were exposed. She had a delicate blushing skin. "What is it, what is happening?"

"Now Mistress Coe, calm yourself. It's just a raid. Your father's shipyard is being burned out by a colonial band."

"Who would dare!"

"Me—I mean Leftenant Philipse. Sorry."

She stiffened—her little bosom grew firmer with anger. Joe couldn't resist. He bent down and delicately kissed her between her breasts. It was impulse and he didn't regret it, but he was amazed at his action, his boldness, and his lack of remorse at what he had done. She went rigid with surprise, then pulled off her bandage. Her eyes were hazel, with dark violet flecks—the dilated pupils tried to focus in the strong light.

Joe tipped his hat. "We'll meet again, Mistress Coe—I hope."

She stared open-mouthed at him, then saw her state and sank laughing into the bed and under the covers.

Joe ran into the kitchen where the scouts were cramming greasy mouths with food. "Follow me—Jack-Tom's in trouble."

Outside rifle and musket fire was blasting the day. Whitey had his men behind a low barnyard wall made of clam and mussel shells. They were firing over the heads of Jack-Tom and his men as they retreated from the burning shipyards. Several of the barges were burning briskly and others were catching fire. The shed full of paints and oils was exploding into a vast, expanding rose of noise and fire. Half a hundred men in Tory Ranger green were converging around the bay in a spreading circle to trap the raiders.

Jack-Tom came up with his men, two of them with bloody badges of bright red.

"There be a hull camp full of Tory boogers over the sand dunes. We better git. Sanders is dead; we had to leave Matt Monter with a gut wound."

"Back to the slashed pines," Joe said. "First ten men set down to fire—then fall back and reload. Second group take up position to fire when they reach the pines and fall back to reload. All clear? Fire and move back in turn."

"We'll piggyback that way to the boats," said Jack-Tom.

The green hunters were spreading out slowly and with care. They had no rifles, only muskets. In the hot, sandy pine grove the smoke of rifle fire was acid and biting as the first group fell back after firing.

Joe wiped his face with a sleeve and took up position with the second section. The line of green Tories came across the salt hay meadow, muskets at ready—strong, brown-faced men just like themselves, only loyal to the king. "*Now*," said Joe.

The rifles went off almost all together, and men dropped in shock, faces and features torn away.

Joe motioned his followers back and Whitey spun around, clutching at his collar as if it were too tight. From between his yellow teeth black blood seeped. He fell forward on his face and Joe stepped over him, and smartly they all ran to where the first group, now reloaded, waited in firing position.

Jack-Tom said, "Maybe we ain't goin' to jubilate this here burning back in our own camp."

"We'll separate north and south, Jack-Tom. Come in on the boats from different directions."

The sun was blistering, the sand under the pines was dusty. It was with desperate breathing they separated and the wild bush took them over. They tore past burrs, fell into gullies, and fired at the steadily advancing Tories, who hung grimly on all around.

Joe had three badly wounded men with him. It was noon before he splashed into the muck under the cat reed and canebrake and saw the two boats waiting. They were partly filled with worried, panting men. Jack-Tom, standing in a clump of bull lilies, said, "I don't reckon any more kin get through." To west and north there was still firing—uneven and in bursts.

"Eleven missing, Leftenant. Four badly wounded here."

"Let's get away."

As the boats swung out, Joe wondered if they could avoid Tory search boats. The wounded did not moan.

In Manhattan, General Washington drove his preparations for defense. When not enough soldiers could be found to handle all the points that needed to be readied for battle, able-bodied men were conscripted in many sections of Long Island. In the summer heat sour-faced Tories, Negro slaves, and farm boys swung picks, scooped up the golden sands, turned the old turf, piled tree trunks, under the eyes of brisk young officers with plans on long rolls of paper.

There was a sense of waiting, of coming war, of the need for hurry, of uncertainty. Was this the right place to stand to fight, to arm, to set up the packed earth and timbers?

Soon there were twenty thousand soldiers to feed, but food there was as yet in plenty from the farms. From France had come gunpowder—fine silky grains, Lavoisier's best black pungent stuff. Brass and bronze guns took up battery positions. The cynics asked David, "How does one get an enemy to land just where you are prepared to meet him?"

Tory bands under "Colonel Lemon" continued their raids; farmers were murdered—those who had taken the colonial side. And the militia also made trips off the roads into the brush and hilly acres to hunt out suspected loyalists. It was a deadly serious game. There was only a surface approval of what the Congress had done. In many districts Joe Philipse found at least sixty per cent of the population were Tories. They were strong too, Botts knew, on the fringe of Westchester, and along the route to Philadelphia, in New Jersey, through the pine barrows and on the red clay roads. Each farm was often a small crown fort. Men banded together in larger and larger groups against what their side thought of as the common enemy. Both parties waited, with over-extended imagination, rumor, and gossip, for the expected English fleet and British army, the Tories sanguine of a final defeat to bring the rebels, now treasonable traitors, to heel.

As all waited, with summer providing its usual torrid and humid weather over Manhattan, Roxanne lay gasping in her petticoats on the sofa of their front room, their chambers in disorder. The maid, Cake, was weeping from a slapping her mistress had given her for scalding the milk.

Roxanne had retched and vomited again that morning. She was two weeks past her period. She knew now she was with child. And she resented it. Her young body would swell, and David would look at her more often with that guilt in his eyes, as if they had committed some great crime out of their pleasuring intimacies.

From the street below came the bang of iron-rimmed cart wheels. They never stopped. Cake had carried the tale of a fishing boat which had run in before the wind to say it had seen vague shapes out at sea and claimed it was the royal fleet. It might be imagination, it might be true.

David came in at noon, tired and drawn, his boots dusty, his linen frayed. There was a dearth of needed drugs and trained wound dressers, and the medical students and old doctors he had found in the ranks were medieval in their healing procedures. Their knowledge of battle wounds stopped with the belief that well-chewed tobacco plastered on a wound took care of everything.

David bent over Roxanne on the sofa and kissed her brow.

"You don't smell nice," she said crossly.

"No, I don't, Roxy, and I must go out again soon and get smellier. How are you, my dear?"

"Breeding like a brood mare, damn it!"

"I've been aware of that," David said, smiling. "I'll leave you a set of powders. Take one in milk every three hours."

Roxanne stormed, "Oh, look at the proud stud! He's done his

male duty. But what am I to do here in this heat, hatching like a brood duck?"

"I've talked to your father. As soon as he can get some wagons down from the manor he's moving everything and everybody up on the Hudson."

Roxanne, in panic, held out her arms. "No you don't, my fine buck! I stay here. Lovie, don't send me away." Hugging him, she closed her eyes. "Love me, Davey, when I'm clumsy and bloated, love me as you did when I was slim and quick. Love me, that's all that matters."

He promised, and went out to inspect his staff of dressers. It was a foolish time, he decided, to replenish the race.

CHAPTER 19   Lieutenant Jack Bounty came on deck of H.M.S. *Tiger-Cat*, his regimentals unbuttoned, his feet in frayed slippers. To the horizon stretched the fleet of men-of-war, supply ships, horse lighters, frigates, sloops. All were wallowing in a south-west breeze that lifted spindrift and spume under gilt bows and banged on the yellow and black sides of vessels already needing an overhauling of their barnacled bottoms bearded in seaweed.

His head ached from the stink of bilge, tobacco smoke, the stench of three hundred Germans, four hundred Irish and Scots, and forty-two horses—twenty steeds had died at sea, refusing to stale, and with burst bladders had gone over the sides, royal horseshoes gleaming in the watery sun of the North Atlantic.

He had been gambling in the wardroom all night and now owed twenty-six pounds debt to fellow officers and Royal Navy personnel.

Zounds, would the American shores never show? Six weeks, or seven, blown and battered by the damn sea? Jack Bounty hated this ship life, the beefy marines in buttoned gaiters, pipeclayed cross-belts, the officers on the quarter-deck watching gleefully the army officers spew in seasickness over the rails.

He looked off to a hoist of signal flags on the mizzenmast of the flagship. An Admiral of the Blue was aboard there. Some more nonsense of running chain through the hawsepipes and exercising the damn guns in drill. He looked up to where their jib boom and spritsail had been carried away. The lookout up there was searching the empty sea with his spyglass. Jack Bounty hoped they didn't tack and wear any more. This old store ship rolled so and the mizzenmast riggings over their cargo of victualing stores were rotten and gave way so often. At least she was an old three-decker with lines of carronades that could fight back if the Yankees attacked. But the Yankees had no real men-of-war for that.

The bosun's mates ran past and also the gunner's mates. The ratings were flogged into place with rope colts. The forecastle men, surgeons, loblolly boys, and snotties were soon standing at attention, just because the admiral had sent up some flags.

Jack Bounty felt ill, his stomach full of beef six years in the salt keg, oatmeal called burgoo, and weeviled biscuits. The larboard watch called them "meat-and-cake." Jack Bounty thought of the fetid lower decks full of Germans, and in despair looked over the rolling sea and the herding fleet. How had they been able to come this far with poor, pressed sailors, paid twenty-five shillings and six-pence a month? And all the time blown and battered, tossed and arse-turned on this bloody sea that Homer called wine-stained (his throat puckered in memory of the raw green wine guzzled last night) and that was really bile-green under the rail in this dizzy rolling pitch.

H.M.S. *Tiger-Cat*, a converted frigate ripe with teredo worms, her copper sheathing torn and flaking off, made into a transport, was a desolate, uncomely thing beside the neat, clean ships of the line herding the fleet of motley vessels west. Jack Bounty turned a bloodshot eye toward H.M.S. *Ajax*, *Caesar*, *Sully*, and *Dragonfly*. Signal flags stiff and flapping, the white breasts of canvas taut, it was a once-impressive sight gone weary. H.M.S. *Brighton* had put a jury mast in place of the foremast carried away in the blow a week before. Sea birds were gathered around the H.M.S. *Brunswick*; they were throwing dead horses over, great bloated carcasses on which the sea vultures fell with guttural cries and the crisscrossing of wing spans.

Jack buttoned his jacket as Captain Corky—veteran soldier— came puffing on deck, wiping his fat shaved head with his wig. His face was burned scarlet with forty years of rum rations. The captain hawked the morning slimes into the sea and shook his head.

"The bloody blasted dragoons will walk to battle if we lose any more hoss."

"Looks that way, Captain."

"Jack, me boyo, what the divil are the admiral's flags reading?"

"It's still beyond me." He hallooed to a naval rating on the upper deck, "What do the flags read?"

The rating grinned, "Fleet to fall into danger position; two enemy ships sighted."

Captain Corky replaced his wig. "The rebels have men-of-war?"

The rating put a glass to his eye and hunted the horizon. "Low black craft nearly hull down north, northeast—brig rigged— privateers most likely—*Wolf* and *Dover* in pursuit."

The action sank over the razor's edge of the horizon and the badly aligned, ill-assorted fleet, hardly in battle position, spread out again, stragglers scattered over leagues of water. The men at action stations were dismissed.

Captain Corky leaned his fat arms on the rail. "Watter, watter, green as Kelly's breeks. I can smell land somewhere."

"Can you, Captain?"

"Aye, Jack. When we lay off Calcutta in '62 lost in fog, I could smell the wog shore. And have you ever sailed the Sandwich Isles?"

"No, never." Jack's head ached and he closed his eyes hoping for a cool sea breeze—but the day would be murderous hot—and from below the dreadful stench of horse droppings fermenting in piss and of unwashed Germans already was rising with the day.

"The major was at dinner with Admiral Howe last night—a mighty tureen of turtle stew and a peach brandy punch were served —and it's less than a day away, this America."

"A hot day, Captain."

Sailors were pumping salt water onto the decks, spraying with canvas hoses the whitened holystoned planks. Captain Corky began to disrobe. "Let's get under the pumps for a soaking. Hey, you oakum pickers, look ye sharp and turn your spray this way."

In a minute, naked and shouting at the shock of cold sea water, Jack Bounty and the stout captain were dancing and sputtering under the glass-green columns of water the sailors in their tarred hats were drenching them with.

Breathing open-mouthed and tingling after the showers, Jack and

Captain Corky stood naked at the rail. A new set of signal flags were going aloft. High up in a crow's nest a raucous voice hurled itself down at them, "Land to starboard." Jack saw nothing but the kicking geometry of the sea's horizon.

The signal flags were again changed. Jack Bounty, naked and cool in the light breeze, watched the great three-decker H.M.S *Revenge* next in line to them break out into a scurry of activity. The jibs and staysails came tumbling down. The courses—the low big sails on the fore and mainmasts—were clewed up and the topgallants lowered. Captain Corky had to admit, "The monkeys do it neatly now, don't they?"

"They do, Captain."

The helm went alee to bring the heavy ship into the wind and the main topsail backed, all in a skilled balancing of wind and canvas to push her astern. Other ships had done the same, and the fleet lay hove to, now that the American shore was clearly seen as a thin line in gray mist. Here and there a point of land higher than the rest rose on the bumpy horizon.

Now all over the fleet the drums were beating to quarters to the tune of "Hearts of Oaks." The crews moved barefooted to battle stations, tarred hats over tied pigtails. Below, hinged bulkheads were being secured or taken down with much banging. Decks were being sanded and wetted. Jack Bounty could hear the steam hiss as the galley fires were put out.

"Captain, while we do nothing, do the Navy boys expect to fight the Yankee fleet?"

"Aye, who knows what's out here fer any of us?"

Battle lanterns were being strung ready. Carpenters moved past with sounding irons and shot plugs. The gun captains looked to their powder horns and priming irons. Slow matches were lit and hung over half-filled water tubs. Fire screens of wet blankets were being strung and powder boys were lugging cartridges up from the magazines. The gun lashings were taken off, tackles secured, and bronze guns were run back ready to load.

Jack Bounty looked over at the American coast. There was no sign from it or sound and, standing in the shade of the fore topgallant, he saw nothing but an unknown land and a suggestion that here he would find fame or a grave. The damn admiral was signaling again. Jack's hangover was gone.

Major Homer Schuyler, Botts, and David stood on a Canal Street roof, strong spyglasses to their eyes. It was morning as the summer haze lifted and the sun swam up behind it. The great invasion fleet was exposed—over a hundred sails. It could be seen from the upper window of any seaward-facing house. Sir William Howe in command, Botts said. The town militia ran below them buttoning up their coats. The regiments stood to battle order in the camps. The fleet lay just outside of cannon range.

Would it land on Manhattan, Long Island? Botts wondered. Or go tacking up North River and the wide green Hudson, making contact with a British attack moving down Lake Champlain. What were British plans?

Botts shut his spyglass. "We wait. They move."

The British did not rush things. Their patrol boats at a slow pace crossed Kill van Kull, they set up camp on Staten Island where no defenses had been prepared against them. Ashore to New York, under a white flag, came Sir William Howe—with his medals and gold lace and white wig—to bow to General Washington. He politely offered terms. Terms no American could accept. General Washington bowed back, and delayed and talked on while the Americans came down into the lines through King's Bridge and every soldier dug harder now in the trenches as the men-of-war swung at anchor, their ports open and the bronze cannon winking across the bay in the strong sun.

Transports and convoys came in to enlarge the British fleet. With a powerful glass David could see troops in dark blue. These could be nothing else than Hessians. So the king was buying soldiers to fill out his invasion forces. The town waited. In early August there were reinforcements. Three thousand more men—the spies reported to Botts—under General Cornwallis.

General Washington had his twenty thousand men, worn out and tattered with so much digging; powder was on hand, so much that storage for Ned Styron's wagons was hard to find. General Washington rode his sorrel through the streets, doffing his hat and remaining stern-faced and outwardly calm.

Joe Philipse, walking near the Battery (where his men—moved from Brooklyn Heights—were behind high walls of log and stone), was going toward David's chambers when he saw a pretty girl stop and look at the filthy street puddle at her feet.

Joe smiled and lifted his head. "So we meet again?"

The girl, her hands full of green cotton skirt, looked up in wonder, then she began to giggle. "Oh, it's *you*. You *bold* man."

"Sally Coe, what are you doing here?"

"I've come to stay with my Aunt Ann now the boatyard on Staten Island is burned out."

"You know, I caught the measles from you," Joe said.

"A grown man all spots for a week? Really."

"Yes."

"Serves you right," she giggled again. "Seeing me like that. And doing, sir, what *you* did."

"Did you mind so much, Sally?"

"No, I didn't. Of course I wouldn't admit it, being a proper maid. Isn't it dreadful, all this marching, and ships all over the bay?"

Joe assisted her over the puddles in his arms. She was nothing to lift, but so soft and warm. "Isn't your father loyalist?"

"Oh yes," Sally Coe said, safe on the other side. "But Aunt Ann is for liberty and everything. Her late husband was related to the Jeffersons of Virginia. Poor Papa, his yard burned, his daughter here. Well, it has been fine to see you again, sir."

"Philipse, Joe Philipse, Leftenant."

"Oh, I see *that*. Aunt Ann runs a hat shop next to the Bull and Boar. Do come by. I'm learning to trim felts."

Joe said he would indeed and watched the trim girl go off across a brick walk, looking back at him to laugh and wave. Yes, he would drop by if the blasted battle held off. He went on to David's (whistling "Drink to Me Only"), where Roxanne was fretful but refusing to leave town, using her power as a mother-to-be to bully everyone into doing what she demanded of them. Major Homer Schuyler was there and two other officers. The conversation was all of the coming battle and how it should be fought, or not fought. Joe thought it all talk and very dull.

David heard many opinions in the next few days. There were those who claimed to know the science of war and were a little doubtful of General Washington's placing of his troops—on Manhattan, on Long Island, even in Jersey. In letting them be so divided by bays and rivers, it was said by some, the general was parceling out his strength so it could not be collected in one firm, united army to meet an attack. Others told David this was wise— the armchair experts. The general stayed calm.

The British controlled all the bodies of water. Their ships began to probe up the North River, going around Brooklyn Heights to Haverstraw Bay. American and English cannon snarled at each other, sent spinning iron balls across rippling water, or thudding into bough-laced earthworks. Congress wanted New York held, and General Washington and his generals did not object to the idea. For most Americans it was the first great test in a major and formal war situation. The army was in most ways a blind one made up of guns and infantry, and when someone wanted to raise up a body of horse he was sent away by Washington's staff, which claimed there was not enough fodder.

Roxanne still refused to leave the city.

In late August the crops were ripening, wheat and maize, and vines were heavy, the root plants ripe underground. At New Utrecht, Flatbush, and Flatlands the farmers worked the fields between the meadows dotted with tents, and soldiers filled the lanes and drilled under old oaks. Jack-Tom and his scouts were active in small expeditions against Tories.

Then came the alarm. The British at last were making their move. On the morning of the twenty-second, warships and bomb ketches were seen moving for invasion. From English-held Staten Island nine barges loaded with troops were observed moving over the brass-colored waters. There was a sense of drama heightened by the music of fife and drum, the color of uniforms. It seemed a gay prelude, David felt, for bloody death and wounds to come. All stood out in the clean sun of day. The bright red jackets, the tall caps of grenadiers, skullcaps of infantry, the plumed brass helmets of the dragoons.

Joe Philipse stood under the wooden awning over Aunt Ann's millinery shop and Sally Coe held his hand. "You're really not coming in?"

"Sally, damn it, you know the British are on the move."

"Oh, yes. Aunt Ann's gentry friend, the captain, didn't stay the night."

"So you see. But I'll be here soon as I can get away."

Sally leaned over and kissed him on the cheek. "I don't know why I am so fond of you, Leftenant." She put a small paper-wrapped packet in his hand. "A lock of my hair."

Joe felt the ache of denied manhood in his loins and ran down to the waterfront where troops were lining up. He put the packet inside his shirt, and saw the barges way out beyond cannon-shot. He got to his men at the Battery and found they were alerted, and he leaned against an old brick wall and thought of Sally and her giggle which wasn't at all silly. Cannon were booming somewhere out at sea and in Great South Bay.

Jack-Tom Swales was sitting with his band of scouts on a Long Island stone wall. Orders were late getting to him, and he wasn't going traipsin' all over God's little acres till they told him *what* they wanted.

"You kin talk about cloth," Jack-Tom said, fixing a chaw of tobacco into his jaw, "but skins is the best fer clothin'. You don't see no bear, no elk, wearing a pair of breeks, do you now? Best pair of leggin's I ever did have I got me when we overrun a Huron Injun village whose braves killed the McMurtry family and hacked up the two girls somethin' fearful before they died. I got me tommyhawk into a big fat buck—he was a sky-buster, this Injun—and I skinned his thighs, just made a circle cut round each leg high up and peeled off the hide right down to the ankles." He spat and reset the chaw. "Had 'em tanned and wore 'em for years as leggin's." A rider had appeared carrying an order and Jack-Tom took it and held it out to Silvester Hand. "What is writ here?"

"Move down to locate landin' parties on the bay."

On the south shore of Long Island, American units waited just beyond the tidal sands and coastal reeds. Major Homer Schuyler searched the bay with his spyglass. No enemy barges were yet in sight here. He picked up the little book he had found in an already looted house. *The Rites of War—translated from the Chinese of Mao Tzu.*

He opened the book and began to read. "When the enemy comes from the East, build an altar towards him, eight feet high, also a hall with eight sides. Let eight men eighty years old take charge of the ceremony. Have them hold up a blue banner with the Blue God painted on it."

A man behind the major said, "I see something buggerin' round out there."

The major said, "Let me know when you make out what it is." He read on:

"Have eight men, eight feet tall, use eight bows to shoot eight arrows—no more, no less. The general of the army must also be dressed in blue. When the arrows are in the air, sacrifice a cock."

"Barges, Major, up to their arse in soldiers."

He closed the book and put it carefully away.

Barges filled with men. The spyglass showed the feathers and kilts of the Forty-second Black Watch, the Thirty-third West Riding proud in their war gear. Drum and hautboys proclaimed the dark blue of Graf von Donop's Hessians. Silly-looking toy soldiers, the major thought, as from a distance he counted copper-topped helmets with woolen pompons. Jaegers with rifles—deadly shots it was said—and the slant of bayonets silver in the sun hit his eye.

"Stand by to fire," he ordered.

The barges grounded on Long Island a mile from the major's forces, and the sand was soon trampled there as the red- and blue-clad soldiers came on shore under the barking of their cane-lashing sergeants. Their officers pulled jackets into place and set sword hangers for the proper stylish pose. It was a hot day and would get hotter as the British tars took the barges back for reloading.

Ahead the British saw pine thickets, little Dutch roads, the roofs of farmhouses, the stare of a boy herding lost or strayed milk cattle, the half-idiot drool of some hired hand. Resistance at most points was merely an exchange of fire with Pennsylvania riflemen who withdrew, as did Major Homer Schuyler. By dusk the British had landed fifteen thousand troops, all moving slowly inland on Long Island. It had been perfectly timed and performed with ease.

Night came down to see opposing armies at rest. Their campfires were in sight of each other. Sentries watched from behind walls and barns, tree roots, and along stone-fenced roads. Both sides waited for morning. The wind had favored General Washington. It kept the British from moving ships between Brooklyn Heights and Manhattan. All night Americans were ferried across to Brooklyn. Connecticut men, New Yorkers, more Philadelphians. David went with his medical unit and set up in an old apple-storage shed.

General Cornwallis took over Flatbush and pushed his camps from Gravesend and New Utrecht to Flatlands on the west. General

Washington continued to divide his strength. The best-uniformed Delaware men and brown-smocked Marylanders were sent ahead to Brooklyn. The wind continued to keep the British ships away from the Heights. General Washington had weakened Manhattan by his own orders. He had two water-divided armies now. Not one strong one.

Jack-Tom and his scouts, after killing Germans from ambush, came falling back from the south shore to the growing maize fields and took a breather under the shelter of a stone wall to drink what they had stolen from a cyder press and chew on large chunks of bread fresh from a deserted bake oven.

Silvester Hand wiped his high bald brow with his hat and looked south and east. They could hear the tramp of British infantry on the march.

"They're every place, damn them, we hardly got time to eat a bite. Thousands and thousands of them."

Jack-Tom nodded and smiled and began to reload his rifle. "Mighty smart lot of sojers. Can't shoot a blue-be-Jesus, but real pretty."

A scout turned from watching the winding road. "Somethin' comin'! A passel of men."

Jack-Tom waved all the scouts down on their faces and they lay between the maize plants, their rifle barrels pushed out to face the road. A column of men, by twos, were moving quickly. Jack-Tom held up his arm. "Them's our'n, poor boogers, worn to a frazzle."

"They sure be."

Jack-Tom let out a "Yahoo!"

An officer rode forward. It was Major Homer Schuyler and he looked down at the scout. "I kind of expected it would be somebody like you, Jack-Tom. Well, it's begun."

"How's the war goin'?"

"Very good for the British. I've orders not to engage fully but pull back. What's doing near Manhattan?"

"The general he's got everybody he could roust across from New York up in the Heights. Say, ain't them lobsterbacks just dandy dressers?"

Major Homer Schuyler wanted to say something to his men and swung around in his saddle. There was a whine among them of metal moving fast. The major looked up at the sky, then crumpled in his saddle and fell slowly into the arms of Jack-Tom. There was a great bleeding gash on one side of his neck.

The scout began to fire. The major's men turned and looked about them and fell with heavy feet into the ditch. Somewhere nearby there were crisp English orders from the underbrush and a line of red coats, blue coats, and a few green ones began—in perfect line—to come up to the maize fields. The high pointed helmets, the white-powdered hair of the officers, the gleam of gold braid, and the cream of lace seemed somehow to Jack-Tom out of place in battle. "Them lallygaggin' sojers."

The major opened his eyes and felt Jack-Tom wind a scarf around the hurt neck.

"Blooded, major, but don't seem real serious. Better not git back on the horse though."

Silvester Hand shouted. "They got the bayonets on fer a charge!"

The English units were moving on a run now, needle steel well forward. The major in a rasping sick voice ordered his men to fall back, and the scouts stayed and fired to cover them, then they too crawled away through the maize fields to hide in a knot of elms, and watched the British sweep by, yipping like fox hunters. The officers sat their horses calmly, lifting their swords as if on a military exercise.

Jack-Tom carefully raised his Kentuck' rifle against an old stump smelling of turtles and took a slow bead on a fat red head with a most curly white wig. He squeezed off the trigger and split the Englishman's skull at nearly a hundred and fifty yards.

There was a prolonged yelling on three sides of the scouts. Jack-Tom dropped powder and a lead ball into his rifle barrel and used his oak ramrod. "They got us boxed in, boys, it's every son of a bitch fer himself."

The scouts scattered into twos and threes, and when it got hard going they became units of one man creeping between trees and past barns to save his own hide. Major Homer Schuyler's men were mostly not so lucky. They had many killed, and over half of them ended up the day as prisoners sitting sulkily under trees, guarded by Hessians who nudge-bayoneted one of them from time to time just for the sport of it.

Captain Corky walked up and down the loose beach sand on his short legs looking over the Scotch and Irish faces forming up in line, and behind them the jabber-jabber of the Hessian officers slapping faces and snarling at the hired soldier-peasants, strange men staring at the strange land.

Jack Bounty came walking through the beach kelp, his sword under his arm, carried like a cane.

"Captain, we're to advance west at a good steady trot, and if the kraut-snappers don't break, to meet up with the other beach parties and then move north. It's developing into a fine rumpus."

Captain Corky shook his head. "I didn't expect Ameriky to be at all like this. Fairly decent-looking place. Anything good in spirits?"

"It's farming country. Shall I start to pace them off?"

"Get any horses, Jack?"

"Dragoons got whatever was on the ships, and whatever we pick up we'll hold. Anything worth drinking?"

"Keep your eyes peeled, me boyo, the goddamn Black Watch would loot the drawers off their mothers to turn it into a dram."

Lieutenant Jack Bounty turned to the sergeants standing stiffly in the hot sun. "Columns will march in fours to the west. Send out advance patrols and follow in five minutes. Look smart, Sergeant."

"Yes, sir," said Sergeant Dickens. He turned and began to shout orders at the other sergeants. The guttural German commands went off behind them, and a top-heavy Hessian officer came up to Captain Corky as the advance patrols began to drift west on the damp sand—red coats, white leggings, tailed hair under bucket helmets.

"*Donner-und-Blitzen*, Hauptmann Corkink going wir advancing now, ja?"

"Hello, Fritzie, old lad. Keep your hair on," said Captain Corky. "Mit the moving now, yah, we're going on. Yah. Ober west. Yah. You follow what I'm saying?"

"*Danke*." The Hessian saluted and Jack Bounty said with admiration, "You've a hell of an ear for language, Captain."

"It's nothing, Jack me boyo, always could pick up a language among any of the wogs and naggers."

"*Die Luft ist rein!*" shouted some German officer, and across the sands the columns of red coats and blue coats went in regular lines, crossing the battered beaches where a small wreck rested, and skating past rocks and wading streams that wandered through shore bogs before reaching the bay. On the right were the low farmlands,

on the south the bay, and beyond it the sandbar, Fire Island, and
overhead a heavy sun on all this lace and pipeclayed belting and
heavy headdresses and gaitered legs. Seapod, kelp, and sand fleas
were trodden down.

Ahead was a blur of scribbling lines moving in glints of silver
and scarlet and it turned out to be other troops getting out of
their barges. They all joined up at noon and waited in the sun.
There was some firing to the north and there were dead men on
the beach—six of them lay near an overturned boat. Pale green-
white features and glazed eyes staring at nothing. They wore hunting shirts and torn stockings and someone had lifted their shoes.

"Americans?" asked Captain Corky.

A German officer said, "*Die Natur weiss allein was sie will.*"

"I'll wager it," said Captain Corky. "Yah mit a hell of a way
to die, nein, yah? Say, any of that Kümmel bottle left, Fritzie?
Mit drinking eins you know, old chap, yah?"

"*Nein,* just finished . . . muckin' 'ot what? *Der Krieg ernährt den
Krieg.*"

"Oh sure, yah, I'm spitting cotton, it's that dry a day."

Lieutenant Jack Bounty came up with two plump knot-headed
horses, miserable saddles on their backs. "The horses aren't bad, but
I don't speak for the saddles, Captain."

"You're a bloody genius, Jack. Where did you snag the steeds?"

"Back a bit in the fields. We're moving inland, I hear."

"What's it like in there?"

"Oh, a proper bit of country, really, quite civilized. Caught a look
at a bit of a girl. Wide in the rump—but clean. A might thick, but
a shapely bum."

Captain Corky got on a horse with a gesture, "I'm a breast man
meself."

The drums were beating and fifes began to sing. "It's inland,
Captain Corky."

"Keep yer eye on something to wet the throat. The buggerin'
Dutchies have swilled all their spirits without a thought of their
allies."

"*Das Seitengewehr pflantzt auf!*"

"What the bloody ballsup is he crying, Captain?"

"Oh, something about keeping their hats on in the sun."

"It's amazing how you know their jabber, Captain."

There were over two thousand men in the section now, and as they moved inland they filled the roads and the paths in open order and their feet kicked up the dust. Their eyes were all staring ahead, wondering if there were an enemy near. There was heavy firing to the east, so someone was putting up a resistance.

Several snapping dogs were killed, and twice someone fired on them. All wells were visited by the thirsty troops. Late in the afternoon they ran into real resistance and they faced several stone walls from which heavy fire held them up. Several men fell. Captain Corky waved his sword and shouted, "On the double, cold steel, lads!"

They overran the walls, coming in with bayonets down on farm boys clubbing muskets at them. It was soon over—a bit of butchery; these were not trained troops able to face British infantry moving in line. Among the dead Jack Bounty found one with a stoneware jug and he tasted its contents.

"Damned if I know what it is, Captain, but it's spirits."

The captain put his naked sword under his arm and tried it in turn. "Blow me, lad, no wonder they rebel. But it sure cuts the slimes. Bring it along."

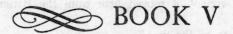# BOOK V

British Island

CHAPTER 20   For three days David shouted at his dressers, trying to get them to understand wound treatment, and for three days he worried over Roxanne's refusing to leave Manhattan. He had taken over a large garden shed on the top of Brooklyn Heights and filled it with wounded men. They were walking in from Long Island, a few were carried on doors and shutters. There was little enough he could do. Lop off a leg, sew up a flap of face-skin sawed at by a British bayonet, and not think too much of the men with gaping stomach wounds who would pass on in a day or so begging for water.

There was great digging all around him and David went out to escape the smell of drying blood. Men were moving down into dusty trenches dug all along the heights. David walked down to an officer placing troops in position. Far out there was smoke clinging to the trees and brushland, and the popping of muskets came from east and south.

"They're still ferrying in men, Captain?" David asked.

"Hell, yes, barges coming in and going back to Staten to refill. Dutchies too, big ones. And cannon."

"It looks pretty fine up here. A solid position."

The captain smiled. "You know battle procedure?"

"No, I'm a surgeon."

"Oh," said the captain, looking over his men, peering down at the smoking landscape. "At our back is the river, and in the bay is the British fleet. What would happen now if we had to fall back to Manhattan?"

David said he didn't know. He went on and found Joe Philipse directing the digging of trenches under the strong sun.

"Morning, Davey. Got moved here from the Battery with my men."

"This seems to be the spot."

"You think they'll come this far?"

"They seem to be coming. It may take a few days for them to build up their strength, but they're coming all right."

"Did you get Roxy, that stubborn wench, to leave?"

David shook his head and wondered how he'd move his wounded in case of a retreat.

Culbly Schuyler, the Tory leader known as Colonel Lemon, was in a rage. He had been assigned to guide British troops behind certain American positions. It had been a dry, crisp order delivered by a tall, thin major. Colonel Lemon had expected to be invited aboard the flagship. He had not been. Sir Francis Livingston and Sir James were with the Admiral of the Blue, dining with the generals and attending the staff meetings. But Colonel Lemon had merely been ordered to meet advancing British units at Churchyard Corner and provide guides that would lead to the rear position of the American troops.

At midnight the measured tramp of marching feet announced the arrival of the British units by the old Dutch burying grounds. Under the spreading elms, among the splintered gravestones, Colonel Lemon and his men in green bowed to the three British officers who came forward. Colonel Lemon ordered the horn lantern put out.

"Major Gillespie? Colonel Lemon of the Tory Rangers at your pleasure."

Perhaps it was too dark for the major to see the hand Colonel Lemon held out.

"I believe you understand the plan, Colonel?"

"If you want to be in position by morning we'd better move at once."

"Oh, there will be two regiments on my left. You have enough native guides?"

"We're not butterfingers here, Major. I said there would be enough guides. Natives, sir, are Indians—we are loyalists."

The major sniffed, rubbed his huge hinge of a nose with a finger of a gloved hand and nodded. "You'd better inform Captain Rawlins of your routes. Rawlins, carry on here with the colonel." He laughed. "And don't call them natives."

They moved on in ten minutes, Colonel Lemon too outraged to speak much.

The weather remained fine for more barge trips and most of the Germans crossed to Long Island standing at attention, muskets on shoulders. The British officers wondered why General Washington had divided his army, and how he hoped to hold Long Island.

On the twenty-sixth Jack-Tom could report about ten thousand British moving on the American lines around the Flatlands. It was a night attack, the shadowy forms of various English units—guns ready, bayonets forward—moving to the clang and clatter of gear, and twenty-eight field guns on their limbers cutting deeply with heavy iron-rimmed wheels the narrow dirt roads. Not a frontal attack. The Americans had no horsemen to scout for them. The British, swinging in a great curve, led by local Tory guides, went through Jamaica and came upon the Americans from the rear and waited there for the signal to attack.

The sun was not yet up when British cannon began to stutter and roar. Hardest hit was the American right. Small frontal attacks, mere feints, probed the right and center. The British in position behind the American line waited. General Putnam commanded his colonials to fire back at the British, and the raw soldiers, most for the first time under fire, held and stood.

The sun rose to disaster as the rear of the American positions was hit and hit hard. It was surprise, it was shock, and it was easy. The colonials had not expected this sudden fury of battle from their rear. The unexpected brought panic. Eastern Brooklyn saw the tattering of units, the running away of frightened new-made soldiers, the flash of English bayonets, the horror of death by slug or steel. With the clattering of running boots each man thought of his own survival. Squads, platoons, companies hunted for escape in trenches and gun pits, behind bushes, past trees, and along stream bank. The dust rose yellow as pollen, the sun went higher. Many men began to drop their arms, to strip off their jackets.

Major Homer Schuyler rallied what remained of his men, and also the new soldiers that had been put under his orders between two stone barns. They were being attacked from the front and from the rear.

"Steady, steady. Keep firing!"

The men looked at him with powder-stained faces and loaded and reloaded, but it was deadly business. Ahead were the moving rows of bright red uniforms beginning to come closer, and behind there was shouting and they could hear their comrades running away; the sound of panic an army makes when it breaks up. They heard the toss of gear into the roadside, the tearing of cloth as the body was driven through underbrush without a care for uniforms or flesh. Horses rolled into ditches in tangles of harness and shattered limbs.

The major's painful neck had swelled from his wound and he was losing his voice. He looked about him, the white smoke of battle rolling in lazy swirls over the countryside. Every lane seemed to disgorge more red coats. He admired abstractly the way the British lined up and moved forward, their officers running by their side, white stockings neatly pulled up, powdered hair in place; then reality came with the thudding brutality of lead slugs seeking and finding flesh to lodge in.

The major's men did not break as the other American units did. But they were dreadfully hurt. Dying men unable to catch their breath clutched at his boot heels as he walked about, and a young man with amazed blue eyes was staring in wonder at where his arm had been. The British cannon were doing damage and the boy, lips shaking, let someone twist a scarf around the shattered stump; but it was no use, the major observed—it was the life blood, rich and shiny, escaping.

"I'm sorry, Major," the boy said, and his face was very white under the battle dirt and powder marks. Ten minutes later they were overrun, it was all over. They were standing surrounded by enemy soldiers and the survivors were laying down their arms. Major Homer Schuyler, in great pain, held out his sword to a short, stubby fellow with a red face who waved it off.

"Wouldn't think of it. Gallant enemy officer, code of battle and all that. Captain Kevin Corky of His Majesty's Guards."

"Major Homer Schuyler of the Continental Army."

"This is Leftenant Jack Bounty. He'll see to getting your men back to the prison hulks. You look as if you could use something liquid. Try this, some native brew."

The major was dead tired, the pain in his neck was descending to his chest and numbing his arms. He took the stoneware bottle and had a long pull. "It's the local whiskey, made from maize."

"Damned strong," said Jack Bounty. "Have your men march out and we'll get them back to the barges."

"How's the battle going?"

"It is an arse eye's view we have here," said Captain Corky, "but you are all running. No shame. Everybody runs from experienced British infantry."

"There is something the matter with my neck."

"Don't tell our sawbones, they use the dullest military needles in the world. The Dutchies will take you all back. Oh, Captain, mit raust raust gong thesen prisoners, back back, you yah me?"

"*Das ist kein Kunst. Das freut mich.*"

"Good-by, Major."

The prisoners walked gloomily off, some limping, two badly wounded being carried. Major Homer Schuyler was beginning to suffer from fever.

The British lines were re-formed against isolated groups of Americans skulking among the trees. Captain Corky said, "This whiskey as he called it, damned powerful, a buzzing like bees around my ears."

"Those are bullets, Captain. We're moving up in a frontal attack on a series of farmhouses they still hold."

Here and there Americans were trying to rally. Powder-stained, bleeding, gathered in clumps of pines, near barnyard gates, to face the enemy. They were overrun by the lines of bayonets; many died or were hurt, or ran. Some fought with the butts of their muskets, but everywhere the word was panic and they were speared, spitted without mercy, and overrun.

For a time it looked as if the center would rally enough to hold. But reloading was a problem, with the Scots and British and Germans so close with their naked steel. The Americans were trapped on swampy land, in thickets of burrs and thorns. They screamed as they were pinned to the trunks of trees. Colonial cannoneers stood firm at their guns till they were run through by massed bayonets. The guns were abandoned; of the gunners only a few stayed to die yelling at German faces, struggling to keep cockney iron from their entrails.

Prisoners were herded back to the barges on shore. Little groups of beaten men, hurt men, a few hysterical, and one or two driven mad by this fearful day of defeat.

Late in the morning General Washington came over from Manhattan and stood on the strong works on Brooklyn Heights. He stared at the dust and confusion below, the sounds of men moving, soldiers dying in battle, the thud of horses dragging guns forward or backward. The British fleet again tried to come between Brooklyn and Manhattan. Again the wind was against them. Frigates and sloops gave up the contrary wind passage.

The Americans still held firm their strong works along the Gowanus Road. The torn remnants of their forces fought from behind trees and fences, from burning barns, from the remains of grist mills. The smoke of black powder hung in the air. Farm animals moaned in terror, full-uddered cows ran about unmilked—in pain and animal fear. The sporrans and bonnets of the Scots could be identified as they were held up for the moment by skirmishers. But now the biggest Royal Artillery guns were being put into place, closer for strong fire.

Jack-Tom and his scouts, delayed by volleyed rifle fire, advanced then fell back. The British attack moved on and the Yankees fell back and back—those that were alive. They were no match, in their shocked condition from the dawn attack in their rear. Not against the steady, ordered rank of the British forces. Soon only the lines along the Gowanus Road held, and behind the road was only the purling blue of the bay. General Cornwallis, mounted, was up in person to command as part of the Americans tried to escape across marsh and bog, and the rest stayed to hold off the red coats and the blue.

Five times the remaining Americans threw themselves against the British line. Almost they broke through, then fresh English flung them back, too battered to try again. In the end there were only two hundred and fifty of them, and only nine reached safety, but they made possible the retreat of thousands of their fellow soldiers. The American commander gave up his sword to a German, who accepted it eagerly.

The Americans on Brooklyn Heights saw on the plain below the British massed for battle. A general began to write a report to London of victory that day over the damned rebels now behind their last earthworks. The winds still kept the naval force from attacking the American rear. Engineers made plans for the British. Sappers began to shovel up redoubts and trenches. Farmhouses and barns were torn apart for building material.

The British missed their chance. An attack might have won the day. The Americans had few bayonets and fewer men who knew how to use them. Gloom sat in American eyes. Men bled, held tenderly to broken limbs, and let David help them. Men stared at the enemy so close below, glanced over their shoulders at the East River and the bay that separated them from Manhattan.

General Washington held them in their places. Calm, at least on the surface, and expressionless, he dismounted to inspect a gun battery. He made small talk with Joe Philipse. He seemed not at all flurried at their heated and dismal defeat.

The men began to sort themselves into some kind of order. Guards were sent out. David operated all day.

Botts, in his weathered cape and battered tricorner hat, came to the ridge of Brooklyn Heights looking for Joe Philipse. He found the young lieutenant encouraging his men to raise a little higher the brush and earth piled up in front of them.

"Joe, you look proper busy."

"It's all wasted if we don't stay on here."

Botts motioned him aside. "That's up to the general, and he's as stubborn as one of his Virginia mules."

"We're not beaten yet."

"I'm not a military mind. Not about raw troops against trained infantry in solid line, against mechanical precision and rigid dependence on orders. And firing in volleys on command. Well, lad, it's given our troops a bit of a shock, hasn't it?"

"We're holding."

"We are. But if the fleet gets between us and New York there will be no more Continental Army. Now, Joe, I want to pull you and your men out of here and come with me. I have the papers for your movement."

"But the fighting will be here."

"I'm moving my papers and my chests out of New York. You're to be the escort part of the way."

"You don't think we'll lose New York!" Joe's eyes grew big and his fists closed. "How can you think so, Botts?"

"I don't think of anything just now but of my organization. If's butter no parsnips maybe, but I think in *if*'s. If we lose New York—my papers mustn't be captured."

Joe looked over the heights and heard the Highland pipes of the Black Watch below skirling a paeon. "They are close."

"Let's hope General Washington hears it too."

"Dreadful sounds at any time."

Sporadic shells from British guns below the heights were beginning to hit close. Joe called out his men to stand ready.

General Washington, on the heights of Brooklyn—brooding, silent, angry—was determined to hold New York. To do this, he told his staff he must hold and dominate Brooklyn Heights. He was, the staff knew, the kind of man who when he decided a thing could be done did not change his mind. He did not admit the danger of the British being able soon to get their warships between him and Manhattan. As to the fact that he had divided his army and put the major part of it ashore on an island from which retreat might be almost impossible, he refused to face the possibility of such a retreat coming about.

If the sun did not shine then on the Americans, something better happened. A great storm, all thunder and lightning flashes, came up suddenly in the heated August air and a blustering northeaster drenched both armies and wet the powder. The colonials had no tents and no shelters, cooking fires were impossible, and the guns and muskets became useless. The wind howled over Brooklyn Heights, the rain in driven sheets went scudding past pickets at country crossroad. In miserable condition the foes faced each other as the surprise of Nature's chilling storm tore at men engaged in savage games of their own.

The rain continued to fall in gray lead columns. There were reports that the British vessels were again trying to get their hulls behind the Americans on the heights. Now General Washington, bowing to his staff's pleas, knew he must get away. The wildest rumors spread through the colonials' line. The filthy, untended wounded lay gasping and damp. The dead stared without interest at the sodden skies. And all the living began to collect in shivering companies and look back to where Manhattan lay under its pall of storm; the proper safe place to be.

On the night of the twenty-ninth the boats and scows, the bateaux and barges came grating against the Brooklyn wharves and plowed the tidal muck. Maine men and Massachusetts men rowed them—full of sea knowledge. They began to prepare for the retreat across the river to the island of Manhattan. On the heights with no flank guards, in the weariness of foreboding, the Americans waited to go down to the boats.

The long lines began to move into the retreat. The problem of a night retreat—of getting the wounded away from Brooklyn Heights —was a pressing and difficult one. Captain Cortlandt had had the wounded collected at a damp cooperage shed at the end of a battered wharf. In pleasanter times, he thought, it must have been a cheerful place of barrel staves and shavings, of seasoned oak and hickory. Now in the light of three battle lanterns pilfered from some ship, David, stripped to his shirt, was operating on men supported by boards laid across two wooden horses.

A huddle of broken bodies, most of them white-faced with pain, lay or sat on the floor. A desperate soldier with a fearful face wound tufted with raw cotton made grunting sounds ending in screaming whistles. A blond boy with little chin and too-prominent teeth aided David as a dresser, and an old horse gelder with red-rimmed eyes and shaking hands assisted David on the ghastly operating table.

Moths dashed at the battle lanterns, and outside the beat of running feet in rain puddles gave no hint as to how the retreat was going. David wiped his face with a filthy towel as a red-coated soldier was put on the planks.

"A damn lobsterback," said the hose gelder. "Git one of our'n."

"Keep him where he is."

The English soldier was an old sod, weathered in many wars, his rum-burned face rolling from side to side.

"The muckin' chest, governor. It's like on fire."

David pulled open the wet red coat, cut away the sweated vest and shirt. White ends of ribs, the bubbles in lung tissue, the bag around the racing heart—all were exposed like an anatomy chart.

"Still does it, old cock." He took the threaded needles from the dresser and closed off two bad bleeders. It looked hopeless but one never knew—if by a miracle poisoning didn't set in. He trimmed away fragments of ribs and quickly put in two wick drains of cotton. No use trying to repair the lung.

"Lord love ya, sir—I'm as busted as a kite. Never see 'Anging Sword Alley agin."

"Near the Castle and Hound?"

The staring eyes rolled round to focus on David. "You know it, sir? A bit of all right, eh? A snug public 'ouse."

It was a scabby slum, but this filthy old soldier, runted, warped by it, was crying. "A muck' lot of lads I've recruited there for the king's shilling. And here I be—"

"Don't talk."

"Did you . . . know muckin' Nobbie Walsh what beat Dutch Jew Sam . . ." The eyes were glazing. "Twenty-four rounds bloody muckin' fight . . . it . . . was . . . too . . . ten bob I won . . ."

David said, "Take him away. He's gone."

The place smelling like a slaughtering pen, the lanterns with their rancid grease gave him a headache. It was no use, David's lancet and bone-saw were held in numb fingers. It was the hacking off of such strong young legs that was the worst. Boys screaming not to do it, or too far in misery and terror to protest.

The young dresser said, "You've been at it six hours, sir."

"Any boats?"

"All for the soldiers with arms, sir."

David lit a West Indies cheroot to kill the odor of offal and blood. "Goddamn it—I was promised boats!"

The horse gelder wiped his mouth after swigging rum from a canteen. "We're takin' 'em down now, them what can stand it. Have a swig, Captain, you need it."

The raw, strong rum cleared David's head, but the weakness of hours of operating in this butcher's pen came through. "We've got to get out of here. Across the river. Move them all. No more dressing here. To Henley's warehouse across the river in Manhattan."

He wiped his tools, looked at the broken and hurt men still waiting for his help. "In Manhattan, lads. The British may soon be here."

Outside, roars enveloped the heights behind him. A pea-soup fog rode low over the river, and fleets of rowboats and cutters, fishing smacks and barges, were loading and starting across in the fog. A gun team came roaring down onto the wooden wharf, the horses whipped to a frenzy. It piled up without stopping against great wooden posts and David heard the snapping of horse bones and the screaming of disemboweled animals. Soldiers were shooting the struggling horses as others loaded the gun and its carriage on a barge. A large rowboat turned over, tossing men into shallow water full of floating ammunition crates, dead mules, and stale slops.

The dresser had David by an arm, "We're holding a boat for you, sir."

"The wounded all off?"

"Them what could be moved."

"All of them?"

"Hereabouts. They need wagons for them left on the heights."

He looked up—a desperate combat was taking place there. The night sound of guns, swordplay, oaths, the agony of hurt horses. He turned, his medical kits and surgeon's tools under his arms, and groped his way aided by his two assistants into a cutter full of bandaged men. The horse gelder was drunk. Four wounded men still able to sit dug oars into the black water. Nearby, gun crews were breaking the legs of artillery animals with iron bars rather than let them be left for capture. David turned away, sick, and hopelessly tired.

The oars bit water, a wounded man vomited. Around them boats passed or fell back, filled dangerously heavy with dirty-faced soldiers.

A dog swam around hunting a place to cling to—heavy oars beat it off. Its strength was going, its thick fur soaked and weighing it down. The dog's head disappeared—then came up. David grabbed the dog's ruff and dragged it aboard.

Someone was firing into the boats. He saw splinters break off from the near oarlocks. The horse gelder began to gag and one eye was gone and part of his jaw. He fell out of the boat.

It was a mile across in this fog. He wondered if they were pointed in the right direction. A wrong turn and they'd be among the British sloops gingerly probing the river approaches.

The young dresser said, "I see lights." It was only other boats. The fog held and choked them. Then the keel scraped sand, there were flares of pitch pine, and a stone jetty.

Disembarking was not easy. The place was fearfully crowded with boats and pushing men and officers roaring orders and stragglers drifting off without helping their comrades.

"Take the wounded to the warehouse. I want to get my other kit before the British come over."

The young dresser opened his mouth in shock. "You don't think the British will take Manhattan, sir?"

"That's General Washington's problem. I'll join you at the warehouse." David walked on shaking legs past women feeding bread and tea to exhausted soldiers and officers trying to line up stragglers. He passed furtive figures bent over dead or wounded men, going through their pockets. An old woman pulled on his arm.

"How's it goin'? How's it goin'?"

"It's going wildly, mother. Get off the streets."

The panic had begun. Wagons and carriages passed loaded with household goods and boxes. Negro servants trotted along, loads on their heads. Someone threw a brick through a shop window. Near David's chambers a young officer was lining up six bronze cannon, his men piling up timbers from a nearby yard as protection.

"Canister," the officer said. "Canister and chain is what they'll find waiting here."

"More work for surgeons," David said, passing on. He came to his chambers and went up the steep flight of stairs. A bucket of water stood on the landing. He plunged his arms in, poured water over his head, and wiped himself on his soiled shirt.

The door to the chambers was open. He went in and hunted a fresh shirt and put it on. He combed his hair with his fingers and heard a sound from the front room. He went in and saw Roxanne standing at the shattered windowpanes watching the street. Far off the guns of the heights could be heard. When a salvo went off from the British men-of-war in the lower bay, the sash rattled and bits of glass fell away.

"Roxy—why are you *still* here?"

She turned, in a traveling cape and a little three-cornered hat perched on one side of her piled-up hair. "Oh Davey—we're losing the war."

"No, no, just fighting one battle."

"It's not at all like the prints and engravings of war, is it?"

"No, it isn't. Don't come too close. I'm covered with muck."

"The Danzers' carriage will pass by soon—we'll all go to Philipse Manor."

"You will, dear. I'm a soldier and a surgeon."

She held him close anyway, he aware of the gore and tissue fragments and bone dust clinging to his skin and stockings. The world exploding outside it was no time for philosophy or easy words, and neither said anything.

In the street it was all one way now—north—a milling of carts, carriages, and bundle carriers. A large blue coach with four bays was fighting its way through the packed roadway, two Negro coachmen swinging whips.

"The Danzers," Roxanne said. "Come with us."

"And get shot? No, you'd better hurry."

He picked up a small leather case Roxanne had packed and his extra medical kit and went down the stairs, leaving the door open in the chambers where they had first been man and wife. Like swimmers in a tide they fought their way to the coach and he pushed Roxanne inside among pale, worried faces and stepped back as the coachmen swung their long cruel whips.

"Git up—make way; git up."

Thinking every man is adrift and every action is hazardous, "Colonel Lemon" came smartly up the side of the big three-decker and saluted the sergeant of Royal Marines in white-clayed crossbelt who met him on the rolling deck. Colonel Lemon's stomach was a little queasy after the rough row across the bay, but he pulled his jacket into place and pushed his fingers deeper into new gloves.

"Colonel Lemon reporting on board."

"This way, Colonel." He was led along the holystoned deck past great bronze guns on their heavy wooden carriages to an ornate carved door which the sergeant opened with a word of warning in a Yorkshire accent. "Watch yer head, sir."

Some smoke-smelling oil lamps lit the heaving corridor and Colonel Lemon caught the intimate odor of all ships that always made him ill—bilge, old rope, tar, rancid stores, and worse. An armed sentry stood outside the main cabin as the Tory officer was passed into a large cabin, gold and white, and shiny with polished oak presses, toward an expanse of table set with damask already soiled by wine, fruit peelings, and the drippings of a huge punch bowl in which lemons and spices floated on the amber steaming brew of Barbados rum. A dozen officers of high rank were busy drinking and talking.

Sir William Howe, wide in his unbuttoned uniform, his wig pushed back on a balding brow, came forward. "That the fellow?"

"Aye," said Sir James Tropp. "The backwoods cockerel. Good to have you here, Colonel. Sir William, Colonel Lemon of His Majesty's Tory Rangers."

"Actually my name is Culbly Schuyler, Sir William."

"Deuced confusing, isn't it?" Sir William said.

Sir Francis Livingston turned away, refusing to meet Colonel Lemon. There were several young officers and an elderly Scot in gold braid with a wooden leg. The drinks were being consumed as fast as a rating and a midshipman could ladle them out. Several officers were smoking long china pipes.

"Well now," said Sir William, as Culbly held a cup of steaming punch. "You've done the Crown a neat bit of business."

"We like to think of it, Sir William, as only our duty to our king."

"Admirable, admirable. Wish the other felt that way."

Sir James Tropp, sleek and trim in a new uniform, fluttered his lace with thin white fingers. "What the lords would like to hear, Colonel, is how long do you think the damned Continentals will hold out?"

"A few more days."

"Good," said Sir William. "I've been saying that in dispatches. We've caught the thing and ended it."

Colonel Lemon took a small sip of his drink. He was feeling dreadfully dizzy. "I meant *here*, Sir William. I don't think the rebellion will be put down for years."

"Damn me, Colonel, you talk like Burke and those pale-livered sops in London who favor this rabble!"

"It's a big, wild land, and if I may say so, the crown officers—excepting you gentlemen—do not use us loyalists the way we should be used. We are at the mercy of chance—so chance must become our God."

An officer of the Guards showed large teeth in a smile. "Really, Colonel Orange . . ."

"Lemon, Major."

"Yes, well, you forget we have no use for chance, but only for

British infantry and royal cannon, never defeated yet in any war within memory of man."

Sir William patted the colonel's shoulder. "Some agree with you in Whitehall as to a long war . . . and are planning an invasion from Canada. We to push north, they south. Crush the rebels like nuts between us."

"It's a good plan, Sir William, if properly executed."

"So. We need men in the next few months to organize the savages into active bands from along the border and through the upper lake country."

"It is practical, Sir William."

"We have men like Brant and Johnson to do the major dealings. But we need also someone like yourself to inspect the tribes, count their number, see to their arms. We shall, of course, have plenty of weapons on hand for the red buggers to use."

"I'd consider it an honor to do this thing for the Crown."

"As soon as we get this matter of New York cleaned up and the port is open, you'll get fuller orders. Meanwhile you can drift around and continue to recruit those bands of, ah, loyalists, you would want to take with you."

"We are regiments, Sir William. Bands puts us in the class with the savages."

"Yes, I see. Have some more punch, Colonel."

Colonel Lemon was feeling the punch. It was over-spiced and had been seared with a red-hot loggerhead poker and it settled poorly on his stomach. He walked toward Sir Francis Livingston and bowed to the large man leaning on his cane.

"I hope your grandson is well, Sir Francis."

"He is like the green bay tree—and I'd consider it a favor for you not to speak to me unless it's business for the Crown."

"You still resent my methods?"

"I resented your manners toward me at my own house. I dislike your treatment of our fellow colonists, no matter what mistakes they make in rebelling. You are, however, fully worthy to recruit savages."

"If you, sir, were a younger man, I'd have you out at pistol length, Sir Francis."

Before Sir Francis could answer, Colonel Lemon felt a rising tide in his throat and he ran on the reeling floor to vomit in a red leather bucket reserved for fire-fighting on board ship. As he retched and the men edged away to avoid his soiling their white silk stockings, he knew the evening of social mingling with officers on the flagship was a failure.

CHAPTER 21   On the Brooklyn shore was ignominious retreat, panic, and disaster. Loading had become difficult and fear spread. Men began to rush the remaining boats. Bodies smelling of wet cloth, unshaved faces reeking of battle sweat, began to jam together in the river mud and on the piers. It looked as if the final embarking would destroy itself, as it became so locked in fear and fury that the major bodies of troops might even fail to get across the mile of water to the other side.

The boatmen made some kind of order, and in the dark night boats and barges began to pull across the engulfing blackness that hid them from the British watchers. All the torturous night the boatmen, worn and tired, made the two-mile round trip. Danger-ously overloaded, they carried torn and tattered men, soldiers with the first taste of a lost battle in their powder-stained mouths, men in fear, in rage, and boys who whimpered and wondered why they had ever followed the music of fife and drum.

The enemy began boldly to send out pickets. Any moment might see the screaming up of flares, the explosion of rockets in the night, exposing boats filled with attacking British. The guards on the heights began to thin out; at one time no one was left there. Then a last guard was ordered back up and everything that could be carried off was transferred down to the boats. For six hours of the night the round trips went on. At dawn the white mercy of fog kept the enemy from knowing what was being done. Only a few cannon were abandoned, spiked and worthless. General Washington, silent with some personal preoccupation, was helped down the slippery path and carried away in the last boat to leave the lost heights.

Ten thousand men, or close to it, were carried across to the damp cobbled streets off Coentie's Slip, and further up the island. It was a gray, cold welcome. Unhappy, haggard faces wondering would

Manhattan be another trap to escape from *if* they were lucky? Steam rose from the defeated ranks; most of their rifles and supplies had been discarded. Soggy and torn, they clustered into unmilitary mobs that waited and shivered in the wet.

In his littered room at Washington's Manhattan headquarters Botts was burning many papers in the small fireplace. Joe Philipse and his men loaded stacks of others in a cart just outside the garden gate. Joe picked up a bundle and glanced out of the window. General Washington and his staff were riding up, the men humped over, only the general ramrod-stiff. He dismounted and handed the reins of his horse to a guard and went quickly inside, slapping his boots with a short whip. The staff followed in their wet capes and from the river came the sound of cannon.

Joe turned to Botts cramming maps into a saddle bag. "The general isn't running."

"His problems aren't mine."

"You think he'll hold here?"

"He may well try."

"Damn it, Botts, how can you be so calm, everything falling apart like this?"

The big man studied his hands and wiped them on his breeches. "It's only a small part of the whole we see. An important part, but the war isn't going to be won by battles only. It can be lost by them but not won."

"What do you mean?"

"It's going to be a long war, the British trying to wear us down, and we trying to stay out of their way after this mauling, I hope."

"That's no way to fight a war."

Botts shrugged his shoulders and began to repack his maps. "We'll move up to White Plains as soon as everything that's going is out of here. You want more men?"

Joe shook his head and pressed Botts on the shoulder. "Forgive me. Everything is such confusion. I want to come back and fight."

"You can." Botts nodded and calmly went on folding papers and stuffing his saddle bags. From the bay came the boom of heavy naval guns. The flame in the sperm-oil lamp began to dance.

Below in the staff room some of the military minds around General Washington were firm.

"Get out, burn the city, sir, to keep it from the English."

"It's of no use to the Americans now."

General Washington looked over the Council of War at the Mortier house. "I agree, gentlemen. The British with their sea craft could attack us from a dozen places in our front and rear. But I have to hold here. Dispatches from Congress informed me I could hold or not. And I answered I would try. We will, however, begin to evacuate the vast stores piled up here."

The staff looked at the tall Virginian and decided they would try to hold the island. A wigged slave passed glasses of yellow sack.

The British, as September began, started to move forward for the kill. If the damned colonials wanted to stay in the trap of Manhattan they would begin to tighten the noose. Their troops advanced. The Union Jack held Brooklyn Heights, the shine of British guns and bayonets reflected in eyes of the town's citizens below. Astoria, Blackwell's Island, other important points, all echoed to the beat of English drummers as Britons and Germans moved into position around the doomed city. Gun pits were dug, dirt flew as Royal Engineers placed the Hanoverian bronze siege cannon in place. Flushing Bay, the North and East rivers, all flew the lion and unicorn banner, the Union Jack.

Sir William Howe invited a Congressional Commission to meet him on Staten Island. Mr. Franklin, Mr. John Adams, and Mr. Rutledge ate British food and listened to the terms of peace. But Sir William could offer nothing but pardons. The Americans—as one said—had eaten of the apple of liberty. It all ended in handshakes and the war went on.

The colonials massed their major forces on the north end of the island, and General Washington was now in the Jumel mansion on Coogan's Bluff, three miles from the tip of the Battery, where four thousand Americans waited for the major British attack.

The fifteenth of September was a clean, lovely day, crystal clear; every flag on the five British men-of-war on the East River stood out in full detail like perfect miniature painting.

Roxanne lay fretting in the great bed at Philipse Manor, sweating lightly, her morning sickness upon her. She spat up bile into a blue china jar held by Cake, the slave girl, and wiped her mouth with a cambric handkerchief. She was getting thick in the middle and when alone she wept at her clumsy new self—and the worst would yet come. She would grow big and awkward. Her face would bloat. Already her breasts were tender and nipples pinker, and the nights when David was up from New York she lay in his arms, frightened, angry, outraged that nature should do this vulgar thing to her.

She looked up at Cake. "Dr. Cortlandt hasn't left yet?"

"Me ain't seen him, missy."

"Don't just roll those eyes at me. Go look."

"I better leave this jar."

Roxanne lay back. It was warm, the sun too bright, and beyond the descent to the river the water flowed and broke into shards of reflected gold when the light was just right. Somewhere to the south there was the far booming of cannon; the British men-of-war were on the prowl. Oh, devil take them all and blast them and their war! This was no time for a husband to be away so much and come back smelling of medical things and stale gore.

She turned her head quickly, bird-like, as David came in, buttoning his blue and buff jacket, looking thinner, browner than she remembered him. His lips were tight together, the eyes had that far-off look that meant he was full of worry over his wounded, his medical supplies, and his clumsy assistants. He carried his hat, which meant that he was about to ride back to Manhattan.

"Oh, David, please do stay the day."

"Now you didn't call me back just to say that."

She took his hand and gripped it. "I'm going to die, I know I'm going to. I'm not made for this thing."

"You'll outlive us all."

A rage of resentment of this idea rose in her. "Don't be so sure. You yourself said I have a narrow pelvis and I don't seem to be carrying right."

He kissed her cheek. "You're fine, and your pelvic arch is a noble structure. Now I must go. The British have been very active in the last few days. It's a big attack coming."

"Stay, Davey. They'll push General Washington off Manhattan and we'll be well out of it."

"What has happened to my little patriot, the spitfire-roaring girl I first met at Botts'?"

Roxanne bit her lower lip and began to weep. It gave her time to think, it delayed his departure. She raged at the ninny she had become. She turned her back as David looked out of the window.

Finally she controlled herself. "I'm sorry, my dear. It's my condition."

He kissed her again and held her, he smelling of cheroots and war and just Davey.

"I'll try and get back soon." He turned to the slave girl who had come into the room to get the slop jar. "Cake, you make your mistress laugh and there's a new bonnet for you."

"Yes, Cap'in, blue's mah color."

When her husband was gone Roxanne lay listening to the guns from downriver and she was sorry for men, the poor foolish dears, playing at their games of sword and musket, marching up- and down-hill. Any idiot could see woman had the hard job, bearing children and running a house, and really directing all the important decisions and making out to the men it was all *their* ideas that ran the world. But oh, how wonderful they were, these creatures, if they were like Davey! And how grand it was there was something like love, man and woman love, in the world.

She sat erect and said crisply, "Cake, I'm getting up. My yellow robe, my morocco slippers, and lift your feet or I'll flog you myself! I need the exercise, Doctor said."

The organized Tory forces had grown bolder. With the Americans so busy trying to hold New York, they were moving about at night on back roads, attacking a convoy of wagons, burning out a supply depot, paying off a few personal scores with hangings and stabbings and a little ravishing.

There were also colonial bands, half-outlaws, loud patriots when they came to be counted, who ruined a few Tory farms and paid back in kind the various Tory rapes. Militia, earnest and sweating, could do little but guard the main crossroads and the more important villages.

A large Tory band had been reported near Mynheer Schuyler's holdings, and for several mornings there was heavy smoke on the horizon, showing that the burning brand was active in the neighborhood. Once a farmer drove by in a cart and there were two dead women in it, their faces beaten in and clothes disarranged. Mynheer didn't want to hear of the details. He just pushed a gold coin into the farmer's hand and told him to bury anywhere in the Schuyler churchyard below the ferry landing.

Mynheer had spent a bad morning with his mother. Martha

Schuyler was older and deafer and louder; her tongue wagged as actively as ever.

"Peter, lummox, did I not say the war would come and did I warn you to make everything into things that could be hidden away?"

"Mama, you can't turn milk cattle and grain into coins."

"Ah, and what has happened? The Americans, they took them and gave you silly paper."

"So they did. But it is a just war."

"War, war—just or unjust, it ruins the landowner."

"Mama, I must do my part. It's expected of us Schuylers."

The old lady banged her gold-headed cane into the rug. "When God asks for a finger, don't give him a whole hand. The Lord likes a good bargainer. What news of the battle?"

"We still hold Manhattan and hang on."

"We, we. What do you do but give away the farms and the beef and the corn? Get me sent up the black coffee and the little cakes."

"Black coffee is bad for you, Mama."

"At my age only time is bad for me. And make it strong."

"Mama, we're out of the real java and mocha. But I'll have it made strong."

It was good to get away from Mama and go sit on the great front porch and smoke a pipe of rough-cut tobacco. He was smoking Connecticut cured leaf, not as good as prime Virginian, but it would have to do. He inhaled and exhaled and sighed. The firing downriver was growing in volume. Either they were getting closer, or there were more of them. Any day now a man-of-war would sail up to his front garden and Lord knows what would happen to the house and the old family silver. Yes, Mama was right. He'd bury the silver in the rose garden. Tomorrow.

A flight of crows rose from a field of late maize and cawed out alarms, warning other crows of some danger. He'd have to take a shotgun and get a few of the black varmints. Rook pie with plenty of spicing was a goodly dish.

Men were coming out of the maize field at a walking pace. Hard-looking fellows carrying rifles and powder horns across their shoulders. A dumpy man in a red coat was viewable among them, like a gold coin among dull silver.

Bushwhackers, but everyone knew where Mynheer stood. The Americans had but to ask and . . . he stiffened and knew suddenly that these were Tory raiders. And that the man in the red coat he saw now—peering with old eyes as the men crossed the box and holly hedge by pushing through it—that man was his son, Culbly. Raiding his own papa's place, his place some day. No, it was fantastic to even think there was any danger of fire to this old house and its treasures. He'd feed them some suppawn porridge and samp —kill a few chickens . . .

Culbly had lost weight, but he would never be thin. How like a tom turkey he looked in his red uniform and the cocked tricorner hat over the unpowdered, thinning hair! He had let it grow and discarded the wigs most people wore.

"Good morning, Mynheer." Culbly always had a mocking tone for his father since he stopped playing boys' games of tip-cat and stool-ball.

"Good morning, Captain."

"Colonel. Colonel Lemon of His Majesty's Rangers. How is Mama? and Grandmama?"

"Oh fine, fine. Can I offer your men anything?"

Colonel Lemon laughed. "Don't fear, they'll help themselves. Have you any drugget cloth or saddles?"

The hundred-odd men were already moving toward the barns and springhouse and the maize cribs. They differed little from the farmers who fought with the colonial side. Really, if he didn't know Culbly were his son and had called his men Tories—really, they could be anybody.

"Come in and I'll have breakfast set for you. Battered eggs, hominy and milk. A ham steak."

"No time. Militia are a few miles behind us. I'll want horses, harness and carts, and blankets and linen."

"What can I say, Colonel?" (Might as well play this game of titles.) "Help yourself."

"We will. I'll go in and say the good morn to Mama." Colonel Lemon turned. "Sergeant Bloodbetter, you're to take all the young stock and horsecarts that can hold together in a fast march. Keep the men from rum or hard cyder. No burning."

Mynheer said, "It's almost all gone, the rum."

"Yes, I'm sure your American friends swilled the lot of it. By the way, we've captured my dear cuz, Homer Schuyler."

"Your own cousin?"

"A Yankee officer. Wounded. He's on the prison hulk *Jersey* in the harbor. Don't bother getting up, I know my way."

"Yes, you should."

Colonel Lemon stopped by the doorway and turned around with a smile, "I'm taking the family silver for the Crown before your friends need it."

Mynheer dropped his pipe from nerveless lips and watched it shatter at his feet. "Culbly," he said, using his son's name for the first time. "You can't do that. Not to your own kin."

"And why not? Because it's old? Because it's my heritage to keep and cherish for my children?"

"Because this is your home, my son."

"This is also my war. I'm loyal to my king, and we need silver and gold to buy supplies, to bribe men of business, and to keep us Tories doing our part. The damn British regulars think we're amusing barbarians, but we'll show them."

"Culbly, this will kill grandmother. The silver, it's been in the family for so long and means so much to her. I don't care. I've suddenly outgrown possessions. I'm an old man. For me a pipe and a bit of food on the table is enough. And a view of the river. But you're the family now—don't destroy your birthright."

"Sentimental twaddle. I'll leave you a hunting cup or two."

Mynheer heard Culbly's boots go inside along the waxed floors and he sat staring at the broken pipe smoldering at his feet. From the barnyard came the grunt, then the howl, of a stuck pig, the creak of cartwheels being moved out from the sheds. It was a half hour before Culbly came down from the house. His face was dark with rage. He was making a great effort to control himself.

"Game me no games, Mynheer. Where is the silver?"

"Didn't your mother tell you? She has the keys."

"She's hysterical in bed, and the tableware bins are empty of anything but pewter and brass!"

Mynheer shook his head. "Empty? But how could that be? Nero polishes it all once a month and . . ."

"Ah, Nero! That damned black bastard. Filling the place with yellow brats isn't enough. Bloodbetter! Sergeant Bloodbetter!"

The hard, square sergeant ran up and offered a ragged salute. He wore soiled deerskin and dragoon breeches stuffed into Hessian boots. "Yes, Colonel?"

"Find me a little old nigger with white wool. Name's Nero. Tie him up and flog the hide off him, or till he tells you where the silver is buried!"

"Yes, sir."

"And put a dozen men with spades in the gardens to dig down. Nobody shows much originality in hiding things. Move smartly there."

"Yes, sir."

The sergeant went off howling orders to the men loading the carts. Mynheer felt his limbs shake. "Don't do this thing, Culbly. I never tied up the house servants or flogged them with a lash."

"And they mocked you and went lazy."

"Listen to me—if Nero hid the silver, grandmother put him up to it. She's a shouting old vixen and has a way of getting things done. Nero wouldn't tell you."

"We'll see after the cat takes off his skin."

From the barnyard a man screamed, an old man screaming in misery and pain. Mynheer felt his heart skip a beat as the sound of lash on flesh came to them. Culbly stood rubbing his hands together, his mouth in a thin, angry line. The voice no longer screamed. The lash went on with its dreadful thudding sound for another five minutes. Sergeant Bloodbetter came over and saluted. His sleeves were rolled up and he was breathing hard. "Beg to report, sir, the blacky is dead."

"He say anything?"

The sergeant chewed on his big lower lip. "He asked the Lord to make you a good squire of Schuyler House. But he kind of was not right in mind after the first twenty lashes."

An hour later American militia was reported nearby on the next farm and the Tory band went off without having found the silver.

The British men-of-war were also up on North River. Would there be a pincer movement, landing in mid-island to cut the American forces in half? The guns on the ships began to pound the shores as lines of carronades fired—old bricks were flying, hunting tender flesh under weathered shake roofs. From Newton's Creek on the Long Island shore the enemy barges loaded with troops began their crab-like crawl, rowing to Manhattan. Fences burned in the clear day. Green fields and little woods made a pastoral of some of the island. A few of the British officers sketched the landscape and made watercolors call stained drawings. The ships tacked and wore, and bosun's gunners pointed the guns and fired.

The island looked less pretty to the soiled colonials behind fresh dirt parapets, old trenches, defenses strung too loose, points held by too few. The ships' guns continued to roar and the first British and the heavy Hessians began to come ashore on Manhattan through the river mud and the stone landings. Kip's Bay heard the steady volleys of English infantry, and then came the long rows of bayonets in a walking charge. The Americans broke and fled. As the colonials retreated in confusion British bayonets captured the earthworks that were to have held them back.

Inland the retreating forces met new horror—the angry mounted fury of General Washington and General Putnam waving swords and shouting. "Stand!" "Take cover!" "Hold the orchards! Behind the stone walls!"

Reserves came up, but they, too, caught the panic of the rout. The infection of fear spread, and larger and larger companies of men ran back, deaf to their officers' pleas, to the commander-in-chief himself.

Northwest went the retreat. General Washington lost his poise. He began to wave his sword at the fugitives.

"Back, back!" In fury he turned his horse's head and started alone for the advancing Hessians and red coats. His shocked officers forced his horse into the wake of the now full retreat up Manhattan.

David put what wounded men he could on carts and moved north before the breaking army. General Washington had done a good job with them but they never had met British regulars and the blond hired giants from Hesse-Cassel, Anspach, and Brunswick. General Washington had been firm, had even threatened his men with the gallows, the wooden horse, the *strappado*. But they were farmers and clerks mostly and the lines of British advancing columns had proved too much for them.

David was worn thin. He coughed. He had fevered nights. He had set up what hospitals he could, and only the night before General Washington himself had made the rounds of the wounded lying on hay. He had said to David, "Captain, our hospitals—or rather houses of carnage—begger all description, and shock humanity to visit."

"I agree, General." David was tired; his hands were bloody and he had still to take off two legs, and an arm at the shoulder, after the general left.

"Can it improve?"

"I doubt it, sir. Supplies and trained men are lacking."

"I shall write to Congress."

"Thank you, General."

And now he was on the run with carts of wounded, many barely kept alive by what little he could do for them beyond surgeon's patching and the usual military bleeding, clystering, potioning, and plastering. It was no better with the British. They paid their doctors four shillings a day. Few good men would work for such a pittance, serving the king's common scum in red coats.

David found two old barns and emptied his wounded into them and fell asleep on the floor, fever making his face damp and his breathing labored. He awoke to gunfire and, in his mind, the beat of a London medical school rhyme:

> If you want the bowel to go,
> Scammony, Jalop, Cinchoni, and lo.
> But if you want a regular starter,
> Use St. John's Cream of Tartar.

Fresh wounded were being carried into the barns.

CHAPTER 22   Lieutenant Joe Philipse came awake, over Aunt Ann's New York shop, his head throbbing and heavy after a night of drinking and fun. He smiled without opening his eyes very wide and reached for Sally, lying spread-eagle in the bed beside him. She smelled of sleep and love and she spoke softly, trying to keep her own doziness from breaking into full awakening.

"Oh Joe, lad, don't fumble me."

"Will if I can, I would if I could."

He kissed her naked shoulder and felt his head throb, an ache like a spear-probe. It had been a wild night. Three bottles of rum, several fruit cakes, much beer, and a half a keg of lobsters set to boil over Aunt Ann's fire. The millinery shop, called Modes and

Fashions, had become a wonderful retreat for several of the young American officers, a place to carouse in rather than at the taverns. Aunt Ann was broad-minded and fun-loving, and the two girl apprentices not at all shy. Oh, with Sally how wonderful it was to go up to her bed and talk half-drunken nonsense and hear her giggles turn to passionate mutterings as they fell to making the ardent, thoughtless love of youth!

Below, in the room behind the shop, Joe heard movement. Aunt Ann would be making tea for herself and her lover, Captain Barley, and Joe and Sally would be down soon in robes to join them, lamenting their heads and perhaps taking a half glass of something strong to face the day among the profusion of millinery mirrors.

They were firing again on the river. Sally stirred against Joe, soft, yielding, amorous again.

"You love me, don't you, Joe? I mean you don't think less of me."

"Why should I, love?" he asked as he nuzzled her ear.

"I mean because I've given you my maidenhead."

"Come now, darling, I haven't treated you like a town bawd, have I?" He kissed her eyelids, her throat, and buried his head between her breasts. "You are my own, my one true love."

"Oh Joe—my, wasn't it a night? And when Captain Barley put the leeks and carrots in his . . ."

There were rough steps sounding firmly on the stairs. The door opened and Joe felt that Aunt Ann should have knocked with the tea. Sally was staring open-mouthed, and Joe turned his head. A British officer was standing in the doorway, bloody sword in his hand, pistol in his belt, and two Germans in blue, with great mustaches sweeping around fat lips, were pushing bayoneted guns into the room behind the officer.

"Damn me. What a sight for any *cognoscente* of the flesh," said the officer, smiling. "No time, is it, to break in?" He looked to Joe's sword and pistol and uniform on a chair. "I must say, a delightful vision. Mars bedded and unarmed."

Joe sat up, aware he was naked. Sally still just stared at the officer, forgetting to cover her breasts. "What is this?" Joe asked.

"Leftenant Bounty of His Majesty's forces in America. You are my prisoner."

"The British are on the island!" Joe leaped up naked, not caring, and the British officer held up his pistol. "I beg you, sir, no gallant gestures. I had to cut down a captain downstairs having tea with a likely-looking over-ripe bit of goods."

"Oh," said Sally, "that's Aunt Ann."

Joe stared down at his nakedness. "Could I dress? Leftenant Philipse is my name."

"Very well. Take up your clothes, but leave the weapons where they are."

Joe picked up his smallclothes, his breeches, shirt, and jacket. "I'll be right dressed."

"Yes," said Lieutenant Bounty, smiling cheerfully at Sally. The two Hessians grunted and just stared. Joe crossed to the wash closet and went into the small room with its basin and jug. "I should not," said the British officer, "*not* close that door, Leftenant Philipse."

It was too late. Joe had no sooner entered the wash closet when he flung himself shoulder-first against the oak door and slammed the wooden bar into place in its slot. He heard the officer's body hit the door, the musket butts of the Germans bang into the wood with well-delivered blows. Then there was the sound of Sally's hysterical giggling, ending with hiccoughing sobs.

Joe looked around him as he pulled his shirt on. A basin, a pitcher of stale water, a night chamber gamely announcing its contents. A small leaded window. He banged out the window glass with the basin. It made much too small an opening, but the door behind him was giving way. Wearing only his shirt, he muscled himself out of the small square, blood warm on his thigh from the jagged glass. Joe dropped onto the low roof behind the shop, jumped to the ground, and went over the fence headfirst, naked tail in the air. He landed among late hollyhocks and ran down an alley. Behind him he heard the firing of muskets. He peered out at the street. A column of Scots were moving up toward him, their steel alert. He ducked back into the alley, turned and ran to an open door of the next house. It led down to a cellar full of fermenting root plants. He found a window at the other end which he forced open and, scraping through, came out in a vegetable patch. Crossing over rotting tomato plants with bare feet, he came to a large yellow brick building and turning the corner he ran into the arms of a sergeant and six red-coated soldiers.

The sergeant said, "'Ear, 'ear, what's *this?*"

Joe smiled and shook his head. "I am glad to have met you. I've been held prisoner by the Americans in a root cellar. Just escaped."

"What's that?" asked the sergeant. "—And that gore on you."

"I'm a Tory—belong to Colonel Lemon's men. I must find him. Special information. It's just a cut, nothing."

"Tory? Ain't any telling where anybody be. You try findin' some officer, sir. And better loot yerself some breeks. Try *any* shop." He held up some silver spoons. "Ain't nobody 'ere to say you nay."

Joe nodded and moved closer to a ship chandler's shop, its windows broken in. He should be able to get some sailors' slops there. No one seemed to doubt his story, and why should they? The streets were full of British and German soldiers—Hesse-Cassel and Brunswickers by their crests—all moving north. General Washington must be in full retreat. Joe's leg burned and he saw it was a bad jagged cut, but not dangerous. A battery of horse-drawn guns ran past on the cobbles and the gunners hooted at Joe's naked legs. He ran into the shop.

The streets were in confusion. British commissary officers hunted food and hay, and cane-bearing sergeants drove the soldiers north without too much looting. The Sixteenth and Seventeenth Dragoons had ferried some horses across from Staten Island, and under brass helmets (with a Greek crest of red horsehair) they were sabering cheerfully among Yankee cannoneers. Fusiliers advanced in swallow-tailed coats with regimental colors on their facings. The royal regiments carried blue facings, others were goslin-green and plelemot-yellow. They maneuvered in aligned drill. The island was a battle-field.

The Jaeger sergeants kept up a Teutonic shouting to their men and the Waldeckers and Anspachers heard rumors of beer, but found little as they overran some inns.

The oboes and drums of the line regiments rang out an English air, "The Darby Ram," as the Americans fell back. The prison hulk *Jersey* in the bay was soon packed with captured colonials. Jack-Tom and his scouts fell back, singing before the carnage:

> "*Come along Jack*
> *Come along Joe*
> *We'll rove the banks*
> *Of the Ohio!*"

David was out of drugs as he loaded the last cart available with some wounded. One long-neglected soldier needed an operation for saccocele, but he would not get it here. No stramonium, belladonna, arnica—and the salve jars were dry. He mounted an uncurried brown horse and rode north, his medical kit held across the saddle. Some of his assistants had found an old barouche and were getting drunk on medical alcohol as the wheels rumbled by in retreat.

From the rooftops one could see barges coming from Paulus Hook, and Tory soldiers; Ferguson's American Riflemen, the Royal Greens, and Simcoes' Queen's Rangers were reported as already joining the British advance up the island. Citizens buried their Spanish dollars, English crowns, French half crowns and prepared to make the best of British occupation. Royalist sympathizers began to settle old scores. The Spanish Sephardic Jews—not a Tory among them—fled with their ritual shawls.

As the day grew, as noon ran past, the British were in no hurry. They advanced a good halfway up Manhattan, past closed houses, farms silent but for the snarl of a chained dog or the sudden wail of a frightened child. They drank up a few wells, pocketed hastily neck-wrung pullets and lined up to await further orders. Sir Henry Clinton, in command of the invasion, came ashore with the proper fittings and drum rolls and salutes. He and his staff trotted their horses to Murray Hill and set up pleasant headquarters in Mrs. Murray's fine household.

A brigade of colonials had rallied to protect the retreat of that morning's rout. There was no counterattack. Sir William Howe joined Sir Henry Clinton. Mrs. Murray was a pleasant hostess and the tea and food was in the good Murray tradition. There might be death and disaster out there but Mrs. Murray's interest was not in the new nation. She was bent rather upon being the proper matron with all the social graces, the perfect hostess to these high-born gentlemen in lace and gold braid and the king's scarlet in her best parlor.

Sir William smiled at a staff officer and lifted his teacup. "We have reached our planned objective?"

"We have, Sir William."

"Ah, good then."

"Do we advance?"

"We've done our day's work. I'm waiting reports from a Colonel Lemon."

The British did not cut the island completely in half. They seemed unaware that several thousand Americans were still trapped in the southern end of the island. It was time for tea and brandies and wines—at least for the generals and their staffs.

With no roadblocks to the north, the pocket of trapped Americans, under a dandy and social charmer named Aaron Burr, were led west and north through wooded land and wild country. Their stores were lost. All those heavy cannon. Soon, without hindrance, the Americans turned full north.

Joe, in sailor's trousers picked up in a looted shop and still without shoes, joined the soldiers escaping through the woods. No one paid him much mind. Most of them had lost their muskets and many their jackets. Joe marched, hoping to find a dead soldier to relieve of his shoes but with no luck, even though he found dead men. He sat to rest his hurt feet. The British fire was getting closer. Men in buckskin appeared and Jack-Tom Swales hallooed to him.

"Some daisy-do, eh? Still got yer hair, I see."

"But no shoes—got out of bed too fast to dress."

Jack-Tom stopped four scouts carrying a wounded man, pale as wax, lying on a door. "Ed don't need his shoes fer some time. I'll borrer 'em fer a friend."

The trail moccasins were a tight fit but Joe was happy to have them. Jack-Tom said, "Hully Gee, we bin takin' a lickin'. Beelzebub, yes!"

"Don't worry, General Washington will think of something."

"Never knew a sachem yet didn't have a reason, even fer a whoppin'."

Their feet scudded through the dry leaves as the boom of British guns resounded closer in their ears.

General Washington had an eye for high defensive places. The united American forces—those that survived—were drawn up on Harlem Heights. It was high ground with sudden dips and falls. In the low center it was wild and overgrown, a wilderness tract where dead trees stalked among the living greenery and swamps, and low hillocks were blanketed by undergrowth of which only small darting animals knew the heart.

In the clear hot day the afternoon would carry its climate till dusk, the Americans hoped, with no more fighting that day. Then was heard the sound of military music, and then came the shock to the eye of surging British red and deadly bayonets reflecting in the west-riding sun. Sir William Howe had departed from Mrs. Murray's tea and was on the move. The Boston Road was packed with the marching English forces. More sounds reached the height, more dust, and on the Western Bloomingdale Road were other troops; this time they were colonial, the men that Burr had led to safety from the toe of the island. Joe Philipse was among them.

On parallel roads the two enemy forces, a brace of miles apart, marched north, as yet unknown to each other. McGowan's Pass was the key. Whoever got through that green tangled gap first would be able to spread east and west. Burr's men were not yet safe. A small group of Americans went down to their rescue, firing and fighting to delay the British long enough for the last man to scramble up to safety, to be reunited with the main American force on Harlem Heights, its back to Westchester County.

Night fell slowly and warm on the two armies bedding down for the day—their campfires, Joe Philipse thought, like eyes of watching cats facing each other across the gorge that separated the foes.

"One more day," Sir William said, as he talked with Sir Henry Clinton, with General Cornwallis, and his German commanders in a comfortable farmhouse under the heights. "The whole blasted campaign will be over."

"We've had the men briskly engaged, sir."

"*Alle meine guten Kameraden.*"

"I repeat, gentlemen, *one* more day."

David Cortlandt slept on the ground wrapped in his cape. He was too worn out to remain awake. Nearby the staff was meeting.

In the night, under lanterns, General Washington talked with his officers, Nathanael Greene, Henry Knox, Israel Putnam, and others.

"Will Howe attack?" The stern face was worn but still appeared impervious to the day's events.

"Why not?"

"What do you think his troop disposal is?" The general looked from one to the other as if asking for an assurance of their worthiness.

"Howe has more than enough. On high ground and low."

"Gentlemen, we cannot wait till he moves and the heights are overrun with red coats. We must find out just *where* his forces lie."

No one answered the general.

"Someone must go and find out."

"Just who, sir?"

"A small compact force."

Knox nodded. "I have the man for it, sir. I'd say young Major Knowland. He was at Breed's Hill, you know."

"Very well. Send scouts along."

From various Connecticut regiments about a hundred picked men were awakened and told of their purpose. Jack-Tom Swales swore but went along. Down into the dip they went in the echoing night through bush and bog and up on the heights to the south. Morning light showed their unshaved faces, the torn and slept-in motley of their uniforms. In extended order they moved up the southern slopes. Jack-Tom whispered, "Damn crazy thang—but you sods keep wary. Foller me."

Suddenly musket balls banged and whistled past their faces and they settled down where they could to fire back. Jack-Tom said, "I knewed it would happen."

Two battalions of British light infantry had come awake early. Extended all along the front the English were alert and preparing to finish the battle in the coming day. The men under Major Knowland held their ground until the bagpipes of the Black Watch announced, with awful sounds, that the attack was up in force with the morning sun. The colonials drifted back, firing as they went. Winded, they rejoined their comrades in revolution and Jack-Tom went to hunt rum.

British officers rode up and blew hunting horns and Captain Corky spread the cheerful news that "The Yankees are the foxes we will run down this day."

General Washington ordered a major attack. The two armies met in the low hollow between the two facing heights and fought with banging brutality in the smoke.

Joe Philipse in borrowed jacket and breeches, wielding a knicked sword, moved down among the first Americans. Smoke, confusion, and accurate rifle fire filled the world. This time it was the British who broke and ran. Banging through marsh, stumbling into trees, the various English units fell back. General Washington on his sorrel bay called off the pursuit. As the day ended the two opposing armies sat again each on its own ridge glaring across at the other.

Joe Philipse had an arm wound and Jack-Tom was drunk among his scouts, a blond English scalp hung on his belt.

The British feared to make a frontal attack. The colonials brought up more guns and dug in deeper on Harlem Heights. General Howe huffed and puffed and knew he would not end the thing as he had planned.

On the twenty-third they were still facing each other when behind the British lines there was the alarm of bells, a bronze clamoring, and signaling black plumes of smoke from New York town in the toe of the island. The British swore. An enemy in front and the town two miles behind them burning. A shed had been first—had gone up like tinder near Whitehall Slip. Now ashes and flying sparks drove the birds from the city trees and choking brown and yellow smoke began to eat its way through building after building. Diver Street, Bridge Street, Fulton Street—the flames ran like Indians through fence and roof. Dutch houses, gin shops, mansions, shanties and lean-tos, stables, bagnios, warehouses, all burned. The conquered town was one flame. Shipping and supplies began to pull quickly away from the docks.

Buckets and wells were all there were, besides some coughing little hand-pump engines. Soldiers, sailors, and citizens fell to work under a blistering rain of sparks to pass the contents of leather and oaken buckets onto the spreading flames.

St. Paul's Church steeple caught, but men climbed out on it and beat out the brands. The fire ran past and up Barclay Street. Mobs began to spread the rumor that it had been set on purpose. There were always those who could point to someone as being guilty. Victims were seized and lampposts were used to hang the protesting, struggling prey. As the fire at the foot of Wall Street ate up Trinity Church till its rafters glowed like bones, the frenzy of the mob grew and they threw several suspects alive and screaming into the flames.

In the back of Aunt Ann's millinery shop there was a little private party in progress. Lieutenant Jack Bounty had come with six bottles of wine and a Dutch ham "black as a nagger prince"—and with two fellow officers, Jones of the Guards and Porterhouse of the Dragoons. Aunt Ann was pouring the wine and blowing her own loose brown hair from her flushed and laughing face.

"Well now, Americans one morning and Englishmen the next day. It's hardly what I'd call decent."

"Oh," said Jones of the Guards, putting his long arms around her large hips and kissing her hot pink neck. "It's just what we've said, Annie girl. What's the reason for it all? We're all related like, more or less."

Sally, sitting on Jack Bounty's lap, sipped her wine and giggled. "It tickles my nose, and I look a fright."

"Ah, my dear, that's the vintage bubbles, and you'd grace the best Covent Garden table. You're a little beauty."

"I am, Jackie?"

"Zounds, I said it, didn't I?"

Porterhouse of the Dragoons pulled another cork from a bottle and said, "I smell smoke."

"The scent of glorious victory," said Jones of the Guards, boldly investigating Aunt Ann's vast bosom. "Ah, to be *au mieux* with *all* of you, my dear."

"It is warm," said Jack Bounty pulling off his neckcloth.

Sally became hysterical, "Fire! I *know* it's fire!"

Porterhouse of the Dragoons went to the window and flung back the drape. Two streets away, a row of houses was burning briskly. "Well, the wind is the other way. What a sight all those buildings cracking their knuckles."

Jones of the Guards and Aunt Ann slipped upstairs "for a better look."

Jack Bounty kissed Sally's ear. "You'll forget your Joe."

Half an hour later they all fled outside, barefooted, as the flames engulfed Modes and Fashions. The streets were covered with hot ash, and, rather drunk, they ran yelping and laughing under the falling brands.

In many sections of the flaming city the British fought the fire with the citizens, but it was a hopeless fight till contrary bay and river winds shifted. Soon the fire began to burn out. Here and there a house still went up like a torch, but in time the embers turned black, the reek of burning filled the streets, and the smoldering day sizzled, but no new sections of the city caught fire.

The Tories who had been returning or had come from other colonies stood with their bundles at their feet, wondering now how they would fare that winter. Soon snow and sleet would harry the island, and much of the town was now burned out, desolate as Egypt after the biblical plagues.

The next day there was a hanging in the middle of the island where Howe's artillery park was set. Jack Bounty took Sally to the public event. In the full sun, with the smell of charred timbers floating on the sooty breeze, a hollow square surrounded the rough-made gallows. Blinking in the sun, arms tied behind him, stood a stocky man, blue-eyed, blond, not listening to the busy details of the formal procedure of hanging a spy as practiced by the Crown's military forces. He was one of Botts' men.

The sergeant in charge—a Lancashire man—read out the name of Nathan Hale and his crime. The young man kept his composure and said, in a voice so low that Sally hardly caught any of it:

"I think it is the duty of every good officer to obey any order at all times by his commander-in-chief."

He looked at the spectators, some still blackened by fire. "I hope those of you that watch are also at all times prepared to meet death in whatever shape it may appear."

He was twenty-one—so young, Sally said to Jack Bounty—had been educated at New Haven College.

He stood waiting and remembered in tragic awe—the rope already around his neck—a line from a play he had once read. By changing just a word here or there it would be his last words. "I regret that I have but one life to give for my country."

The drums began to roll. His support fell away and he dangled for dreadful minutes, till final darkness was a complete release from life and duty.

Sally was very ill in public.

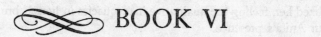

BOOK VI

American River

CHAPTER 23   Roxanne knew she was not supposed to drive out alone in her "condition." She looked at the clock again and got her wide country hat from Cake, who brushed it neat with her sleeve. In the buckboard Roxanne drove south along the river a few miles, past the gardens and the big white church and up the drive of Mynheer Schuyler behind its hollyhock hedges. There a white marble block-lettered SCHUYLER was the base for a cast-iron colored boy used as a hitching ring.

The Negro houseman who opened the door for Roxanne had white wool hair and a pale lemon skin. He said, "Why, Miss Roxanne! The ladies are in the garden having teatime. Walk right back, missy."

"See the horse gets watered."

It was such a pleasant house, with the good French wallpaper and the hanging crystal chandeliers that sang like birds when a wind from the river stirred them. The heavy mahogany furniture was waxed smooth and shiny. She came into the garden through the open doors off the hall. Under the elms overlooking the river two hammocks were strung and a white tea table was set up. Anita Schuyler was pouring. Mynheer's mother, old Martha, looked older than ever, Roxanne thought until she heard the brisk, positive voice say, "You're carrying high—means a boy."

"Thank you." She was too heavy, she felt, to say it was all nonsense, this carrying business. At Belltinkel's—the *Good School For Refined Young Ladies* on King Street (*Deportment, French and Simple Adding*)—they taught you not to talk back to the older folk.

Even to Anita Schuyler, who was often foolish, given to tears, a bit long in the jaw. Roxanne suspected that she had a temper, but she liked her, feeling the qualitative inadequacies in herself brushed away in Anita's presence.

"The fighting is going badly in New York."

Martha grunted as she took the teacup and blew it cool with her leathery cheeks. "Well, the soldiers haven't been here for some days. Not neglecting the war for us, anyway."

"At night I can hear the cannon."

"Hope it doesn't mark the child."

Roxanne flushed. Her color and her corn-toned hair were among her best features. "Now Granny, that's old wives' tales."

Anita asked, "Your father is well?"

"He's away—he'd have a fit if he knew I drove over in my condition."

Anita handed Roxanne a cup of tea. "Talk, talk, all the time of war, battles. And now so close."

"War," said Martha in twanging discords. "I remember when the French monseers burned our place at Green's Crossing, and got two of the servant wenches with whelps. Red-headed niggers all over the place for years."

They all lifted their heads from above the teacups. A shift in wind brought clearly the sound of guns from the battle for New York. (Roxanne from the corner of her eye watched old Martha snatch cakes and hide them in her gown.)

Such warm days in September were called Indian Summer here, Sir William Howe had heard, and the sumac was starting to turn red. Behind the British lines the fields of buckwheat were being harvested. The two armies still faced each other on the northern tip of the island across the gap and drop called the Hollow Way. With the end of the year so close, most of the American enlistments would be out. There were already deserters. Looting of farms and worse was taking place. The army staring across at the British over the gap had lost the early confidence of the battle that had given them these heights to hold to. Equipment was almost all gone. New recruits, and few there were, came with a musket and cartridge box and powder horn, and if lucky some blankets and a spider skillet. The commander-in-chief was standing, arms behind his back looking across to where the enemy lay in bulk, heavy with supplies, waiting.

"Such is my situation," said the general, "that if I were to wish the bitterest curse to an enemy this side of the grave, I would put him here where I am—to change places with me, with my feelings."

"Sir, their sharpshooters are up forward. Step back."

"Call a council. We must decide something. Here we rot away." His assurance still existed even here in the bitter nest of his present troubles.

It was not a happy council meeting in the Morris house. The uniforms were still fairly passable, the setting a well-appointed dwelling. But the final result was crisp and sour.

Charles Lee of the staff said, "I can only give one final answer, sir. Get off Manhattan and get up Westchester way."

"I suppose you're right." Outside the dusk turned from gold-umber to sepia. The night sounds of camp were clear.

"Get off Manhattan and get off quickly. Lord Howe has already set out a flotilla in our rear at Throg's Neck. If he takes King's Bridge behind us, we'll be trapped here, sir."

"I shall issue orders. Thank you, gentlemen."

On the fifteenth of September the Americans were moving back into Westchester. Tired horses, few wagons, loose wheels. A full-scale retreat.

It had been an uneven fight. Sir William Howe had twenty thousand trained soldiers, fifty-six men-of-war. General Washington's army at the end of the battle, worn down by casualties, by deserters, numbered a scant five thousand. And what had the British won but a burned-out town? Over a thousand chimneys stood where houses had once been.

General Washington, assembled his strength at White Plains; moved into a semicircle of running hills between the Bronx River and the lake to the west, and here he waited.

At Philipse Manor there was a period of recovery. Joe Philipse's arm did not heal well and David dressed it every day. It was a bad saber cut just above the left elbow, and it drained slowly and was red and puffy. David himself suffered from some slow fever that left him weak, a camp fever of which he found no record in the medical books he had brought from England.

Roxanne was at times placid, growing larger, accepting now her

role of the pregnant woman. David was with her. He was too weak
with fever to go back to the camps. He was on leave, under orders
to recruit members for the medical service. Where these persons
were to come from he had no idea.

He and Roxanne lay late abed watching the white sunlight creep
higher through the slatted windows. The fall winds sent leaves
golden red and brown down to the gray river, and the larch and
locust trees bent before it.

"I could feel him stir last night," Roxanne said, her arms folded
on her belly.

"They generally begin to quicken into life about this time."

"Quicken? He *kicked!* Here, feel."

David held his hand on his wife's swollen stomach. "What makes
you so sure it's a lad?"

"I had Cake draw me a charm in the earth and sprinkle pennyroyal and tansy. And look into an egg with a blood speck in it."

"What has all that juju got to do with it?"

"Men are so damn practical," Roxanne said with dignity, closing
her eyes, "that they can't see the tip of their own nose."

He kissed her—his fever not bad this morning—and rumpled her
a bit, being careful not to exert her, and then he dressed. He sat
with Joe after breakfast watching a patrol of American small boats
and wherries go up and down the river.

"It's going to be a hard winter for the army," Joe said, gingerly
touching the sling on his arm.

"There is talk General Washington will hold on the Hudson while
moving for a campaign into Jersey. Now they want to hold Philadelphia. It's a war for towns."

Joe shook his head. "He's having trouble recruiting. We'll be lucky
to have twelve thousand men ready for any battle before snow flies.
Let's go to the ferry tavern. At least we'll hear some exciting lies
there."

David knew Joe was depressed, not only by his wound but about
some girl he had been bedding with in New York. It was Joe's first
real love and David knew better than to mock it.

"Joe, I haven't seen your father in several weeks."

"He's gone to Connecticut on some special mission. He doesn't
tell me much, but he must be buying supplies for Washington.
We're lucky the Tories didn't burn us out in a raid. Mynheer

Schuyler's place lost its stock and carts. They say the silver was saved. Come now, I need an eye-opener in this chill weather."

Kill-Devil Tavern, just below the old burying ground, was on the river a few miles south, and they sat indoors and watched the wench make flip for them, mixing the beer and molasses and rum and running the loggerhead poker into the mugs till the drink hissed.

"Here you be. Rum is hard to get, and as for rum-fustian with its sack, gin, and nutmeg, we've stopped serving it."

"Now, Mary," said Joe, "you're getting rich here serving up bumbo mimbo, and I wager you have a cellar of Medford and Barbados rum."

"How people *will* let their tongues run to gossip."

Joe sipped his drink and looked at David. "I'm going into New York."

"That's a damn fool mission, Joe lad. You'll get the gibbet hemp at dawn, like others who tried."

Joe shook his head. "I've talked to Botts. He'll help me."

"Where is Botts?"

"In White Plains sending hotheads and fools through the lines as usual. He even talks of taking men out of the British prison ships."

"You can't go, Joe. Your arm needs my attention. I warn you an amputation isn't much joy."

Joe didn't answer, just scowled, and David said, "I know how it is with a girl."

"Damn your sordid past," said Joe. "Mary, remake the last and in a larger pewter."

After that David kept an eye on Joe. Jonathan and Greetje Philipse were away in Connecticut and the great house was much too large for the three of them. Roxanne hardly ever left their room now that the cold was in season and all the fireplaces were no longer heaped with good logs allowed to roar their lives out up the chimneys. There was a sense of bad times, a feeling of a new battle forming on the fringes of the estate. Every day groups of men in shabby dress, muskets and rifles on their shoulders, passed on their way to General Washington's army. Also small groups and stragglers going the other way—men who claimed their enlistments were up, and some who were just plain deserters and didn't try to hide it.

It was a crisp, cold day with weather outdoors that filled the lungs with vitality, a feeling of strength. David had heard the loose hounds running a fox the night before. Early he took two of the unexercised Philipse hounds and with a shotgun under his arm he went up the cold beaten trail to the north where old trees still stood scarred by ancient lightning. It was good to get out of the house, even from the domestic trap of Roxanne's lovely warm arms. His breath smoked before him, the short clay pipe in his mouth drew well. The stiff-tailed hounds sniffed and circled, lifted their legs in the ritual of dogdom at stumps and other meeting places of local canine culture.

At last the dogs picked up a scent among burdock and wild cherry saplings and went running off, tails up and dewlaps and noses to the frosted turf. David followed at a slow walk, excited and elated to be walking a trail again. But the hounds lost the scent among woodbine and bull brier. They circled and picked up only a rabbit that went into fireweeds. At noon David walked back, opening his scarf. By a field of old maize stalks a large man stood, wearing a tier cape and showing a yellow waistcoat.

"Morning, Botts," David said. "You're not the hound-dog type— I mean, out for small game."

"No, Davey, I'm not. I wanted to talk to you. But not in the house. It seemed a good day for a walk. Crisp."

"Very. There's nobody at the house but my wife and brother-in-law. Joe wants to go to New York, and I say no, not even if you want him there."

Botts smiled. "Aye, I'm sure his arm isn't well enough for that. Davey, it's you can help me."

"No. I was once too close to a noose on Long Island."

"We're all close to the rope if General Washington doesn't hold the army he has together—and it's a small pitiful one—for this winter and next."

"Still think it's a long war?"

"Aye. Now David, there's a group of Hudson River nabobs who seem to have turned loyalist. Oh, we have friends among 'em, and some work hard for us collecting supplies. But this plot is to capture the river fords, burn out supply trains, and try and take our leaders for a drumhead court-martial on some man-of-war, General Washington and the rest, all dangling from the mainyards of the admiral's flagship."

David smiled. "You live in a strange world, Botts. *Always* plots."

"Yes, don't I? We've captured one of their messengers, a tall man with a narrow face and red hair worn uncut."

"I've no relative alive, if that's what you mean."

"His name is Pelham. Says he lived on City Common. Comes now from the Levering Plantation we seized up past Albany. I don't say your father produced a wood's colt, but you could pass for him, if people went by description and didn't know either of you."

"No. Roxanne is soon to be brought to bed with child. I owe her something. Down, Prince. Down, Rattler."

Botts petted the drooling hounds and nodded. "It's a mere night's work. You appear at Yonkers Ferry and show a paper to some people from Coentie's Slip and Ranelagh Gardens. You will be taken to a place where you will meet the leader of the secret loyalists and report on the upriver plans. I will coach you for them as to what to say. They've not been north of Tontine Coffee House or Murray's Wharf I'd wager."

"No, Botts."

Botts looked over the autumn landscape and the leaves falling. "It's a fine place to live, isn't it, Davey? I'd like some day to come here and get a small farm and sit watching the river and the fields grow. Shad and trout, would you say?"

"Yes, trout, and sturgeon sometimes."

"Davey, I have reason to believe your father-in-law, Jonathan Philipse, is the leader of the loyalists."

"You have any real proof?"

"Eleven of his letters intercepted in a house at Queen and State streets and then sent on. The handwriting seems to bear it out. But we are not fully sure. I felt it would do the family some good if you helped prove this thing, one way or the other."

"Botts, you have no social sense at all. I couldn't try and trap my own father-in-law."

Botts held out a snuffbox. "The last of the Kippens stuff. A pinch?"

"No."

"If it is him the estates will be seized. Congress will take everything away from the family. Oh, Joe may get a small bit for his services, if it . . ."

"You don't also suspect Joe? Or me?"

"Yes, I even suspected you, Davey," said Botts, not smiling.

"I'll be damned if you don't! You're a humorless man, Botts, and I think you a little mad."

Botts patted David's shoulder. "I certainly shall not retain any friends, will I?"

"What will you do now?"

"Risk it with someone with a red wig."

"You didn't really expect me to go through with this? You just wanted to see my reaction. Trap me if I was involved. You're armed?"

Botts shrugged his shoulders. "I hope Mistress Cortlandt has a fine delivery. And would you want it to be a son?"

"I don't care either way. Just so Roxy has an easy time of it and the infant be born fit and in proper parts. Are you married, Botts?"

"I have nothing but what you see on me."

They walked a little way toward the river and Botts made his good-by. David whistled the dogs back and went in, scowling at what Botts had told him, and brooding over the events in men's lives that lead them to act the traitor, or from their viewpoint, to risk all for a loyalty to an old society.

It was not a good lunch. Joe's mind was on the girl in New York, and Roxanne was moody in the afternoon as the wind rose and the trees were denuded of more leaves. She threw a pillow at the maid, Cake, broke her favorite cream pitcher, and said her beauty was ruined, her figure destroyed, and that David could not love a lump of ugliness like her any more.

That night David sat long by the fire, smoking, listening to the wind and the creak of cold boughs. The logs were burning yellow in the fireplace, cracking and flaring as the heat reached pockets of pitch. Near dawn a cold rain fell and in the morning everything was gray and drab. The river ran with whitecaps and the men in the patrol boats had their hats tied on with scarfs. They blew on their cold mittened hands and were miserable by gesture, and full of curses.

The Americans went to forging a great iron chain to string across the Hudson at Bear Mountain. It would, they hoped, keep the British men-of-war from attempting to sail up the Hudson. It would be a disaster if the fleet could sail at will up to the large river estates, land troops, and attack the American forces from the rear.

Blacksmiths and horse-shoers, workers of ship iron had been

collected in several large sheds at the ferry landing. At first it had
been planned to forge a great single chain with massive links, each
one a yard across. But there was not the iron on hand or the material
to work out such a chain. Then it was decided to make a great
barrier of various chains tied together, several strands of them,
in sections to be carried north when assembled.

Jack-Tom and his scouts guarded chain-gathering parties that
went raiding along the river, and along the Sound, to break out any
rusting chains they could find. Mynheer Schuyler located several
ancient chains from old ships the family had owned when they went
into shipping and trade. The vessels were long since lost or broken
up, but a barn on the estate had sheltered the chains for many
years.

Wagons carted the sections upriver to Anthony's Nose, then
barges carried the strands of chain from heavy timbers, sunken into
the shore, out to an anchored raft. Large hasps were driven into the
logs and the chains attached. From the first raft chains were carried
to the next platform, and the next, until the river was closed off
by chains across the Hudson; everything sunk, just below the surface.
There was a short section padlocked and bolted that could be swung
open for the passage of American ships should such a need arise.
But at the moment the colonist had no ships powerful enough to
go beyond the barrier of rusting submerged links that barred the
way to British men-of-war.

For a time Jack-Tom and his men guarded the chain, and Jack-
Tom got Mary of the ferry landing inn with child on one of his
stops near Philipse Manor overnight. And, drunk one night, Jack-
Tom went raging out to the farms to hunt Tories, shouting that his
leggings needed fresh scalps for trimming. After that the militia
guarded the great chain and repaired it.

Joe was making up his mind to do something desperate. He
played cards a lot with the militia officers whenever a group of them
stopped at the inn near the ferry landing. He lifted his head as the
dawn gun downriver, in the harbor, went off.

"I'll get the house niggah," Ned Perkins, the militia officer, said.
"He'll run us up a breakfast. Can't ride on a hollow stomach, Joe."

Joe nodded. "We had twenty hogshead of tobacco on that Dutch
boat captured in the harbor."

Ned opened the first button of his linen breeches, cut French style—wide and flaring around the hips and narrow at the knees. "I'll have prawns and some rashers of bacon."

"Marcus," shouted Joe, and the inn slave came in. "Get us some breakfast, and if you have bacon and prawns, fine."

"And some rum. Clear your head for riding, Joe."

They ate as two healthy young men eat who have partied, carded, gambled, and talked loudly in youthful excitement. Swallowing large mouthfuls with relish. They were sopping up their bacon grease with good soda biscuits, sharp and hot with the smell of their ingredients. They sipped their rum to taper off the hard drinking of the night. They had not yet discovered their full maturity, and halfway through their twenties they were set in their background and the manners of their society. Times were exciting and their manhood, Ned said, was a pleasant problem to be solved by simple orders, intrigue, or straight barter.

"Got a good red fox, a vixen, out our way," said Ned Perkins, swallowing a big mouthful. "Run her any time, Joe, you want to try your horse."

The morning light was breaking sharp and white on window-panes, and Marcus blew out the beeswax candles. Joe rose from the table feeling confused and lost. The loneliness of a hard war was near. He called for his horse to be saddled. Ned, an arm around Joe's shoulders, walked him to the smoking stable yard. "Try and get back for the cock-fighting."

The river houses, stained with the smoke of breakfast chimneys, were yellow in the morning sun. Beyond, the river dimpled and heaved slightly with the flow that sucked past the ferry landing. Joe, dressed in white—a chevel, and wearing a catamount waistcoat, riding home to Philipse Manor on his Morgan red, let the horse carry him away from a night of cards and much wine and raw rum. At the card game near dawn he had lost too much money. He was not a true reveler, he knew. He did not dislike the card table and its pleasures; it was expected of him. But he preferred living. He was now an agitated, perturbed young man with the harsh geniality of a weather-tanned countryman. All that seemed to matter was the memory of Sally Coe and the times of their love-making. And the images would not fade. A twinge of conscience made a grimace of Joe's handsome, angular face as the horse stumbled on the way to the last creek crossing before Philipse Manor.

"Watch your step, damn you, Shannon," he said twisting the

horse's head up high till foam dripped from the silvered bit. He was slightly drunk but firm in the saddle from many runnings with the deerhounds and from riding out in gray-mist dawns to the dove shoots. Crossing on the creek bridge, the cold wind on his hot head, he exchanged no word with Hannibal, the old Negro bridge tender, but rode off on the road past the scarlet camellias, the cat-clayed cabins of the slave quarters, until he saw the gates of Philipse Manor. In the yard he handed the horse to a stable boy, dipped his head in the chilled water of a freshly drawn cedarwood bucket, and went in to sleep.

At dinner he and David and Roxanne sat around the huge polished Chippendale table of his father's house. It was a place Joe loved, its prong of green fields smack on the shore, fertile, low, indented by the inlets and estuaries of the Hudson. But he had decided now on his plan of desperate action.

Joe disappeared two days later. A horse was gone and a saddle, and his uniform hung in his wardrobe. David had heard no more from Botts. He didn't want to go to White Plains and leave Roxanne, who was staining a bit, and he had to be with her to make her lie perfectly still. It was certainly to be a winter of discontent.

There was no trouble getting through the lines, Joe found. In his snuff-brown jacket and on his good horse he got to the ferry at Ackerman's Landing, took a barge across, and then hired a boatman to row him to Manhattan. It was risky, with men-of-war on patrol and guards at all dockings. But Joe came ashore below Canal Street and found a wilderness of burned-out areas from Bowling Green to St. George Square. Tents and shacks were filling in where buildings had once been.

He was not challenged even once. But finding Modes and Fashions was impossible. It had certainly burned down. And no one could tell him of Sally Coe or her Aunt Ann. There were many girls on the town, and courtesans in their rustling taffeta and other frou-frou with face patches covering pox, and much drunken pleasure. While Joe had money everyone was happy to help him drink it up in the dram shops. The British officers were pleased Joe had once been in London.

"Ah, a bugger a lot this damn damp land is, compared to a good evening at White's or a party for lobster at Blackfriars, and the Green Room after a play at Covent Garden."

Joe ordered more rum. "It may be a short war."

"That it could be, sir. Your health. To the king."

"To our ruler," said Joe, expressing no dislike.

"How come a likely lad like you is not in the Tory Rangers?"

Joe held up his arm sling. "Only one good flipper."

"Sorry. Didn't mean to pry."

"Another round?"

"Well, we should say so. Were you ever in Mother Needham's bagnio?"

It was not good to see so much drinking and entertainment and womaning, and not be able to find Sally Coe. Joe drank too much and got careless.

The Wild Boar, loud with banging of pewter and copper pots, was a disreputable inn on Canal Street. Out back it sold potent raw spirits distilled from maize and potatoes. The commissary women were there often for a tot of geneva, and there was an upstairs room that was a rendezvous reserved for officers who didn't want to be seen tippling spirits or entertaining the women of the town.

In the back room one night Joe sat fuddled and indifferent to the quarreling at the next table. A woman said shrilly, "Don't make mock of me. I'm respectable. There isn't any better hat trimming than I do. I had a shop of me own till the fire. So I'll thank ye gentry to keep your ideas I'm to be had easy for some pickled cowheel or black and white pudding."

Joe stood up and went over to the table. He put his face between two British sergeants of the Twentieth Foot. Aunt Ann looked up at Joe, damp and laughing. "Well, if it isn't Joe. Now isn't it?"

He pulled her away and said to the sergeants, "My dear old aunt. You two have a mug of Teneriffe wine on me." He tossed down a coin and took Aunt Ann by her elbow into a corner. "Where is Sally?"

"Well now, why don't you ask how I've been? Badly, thank ye. Shop gone, money gone. Respectability the laughing stock of plain soldiers."

"I've some money. Where's Sally?"

"Do you have a bit of snuff?"

"No. I must find Sally."

"Oh, she went off with some redcoat leftenant. He bought her some silk and callemancoe things."

Joe passed her some coins and eyed the sergeants scowling at him. They would make their rush on him in a moment. "Listen, Aunt Ann. Tell her Joe Philipse says if she ever needs help to come to Philipse Manorhouse, up above Ackerman's Landing. Philipse Manor. Will you remember?"

"What's hard about remembering it? But weren't you, say, in another uniform? Seems to me . . ."

Joe ran into the street as the two sergeants rose, knotting as dreadful weapons their buckles and belts around their fists.

CHAPTER 24   It seemed strange to be in New York—an enemy-held New York. Joe had never before surrendered himself fully to anything but soldiering. He never gave all of himself to Sally or to his family or to his friends. There was some secret corner where he faced his problems and certain emotions alone. He was a hard man to comfort. The Philipse pride may have been at fault.

Joe's character was becoming more pronounced. He was already attempting more—as in this crisis—than one man could fully carry out. He had a serious, conscious faith in what he was doing and a bright focus on the goals ahead. A soldier is always, if he is a man of vision and fears, prepared for his failures. Joe had that gift of disregarding those things that might more sensibly remain unfinished. Such as looking for Sally.

The drive of things to be done was strong in Joe, and if he had a flaw it was the bad one of often not acting with the full consent of the people he worked with. A good soldier does not hunt in an enemy city by himself.

New York, Joe saw, had prospered in many ways and gone downhill in others. The hundreds of houses destroyed by the fire were replaced by whatever could be put together. Many of the town mansions, including his father's, had been looted and windows broken, doors torn out. But trade was brisk. The Tories were the pattern-setters now. Most of the Hudson River families had fled and their great town houses held British officers and lace-trimmed naval men of rank.

The river families had most of them decided for liberty, the Continental Congress, and for General Washington's forces. Here and there a family was tragically divided. Some, like Sir Francis Livingston, isolated in a clan of eminent Whig patriot Livingstons, were fanatical Tory loyalists down to the last slave.

Cunning men with hard faces, Joe saw, had taken over trade. Sly bargains were made, goods were delivered late at night, little boats slipped in and out, and the river anchored reinforcing fleets from England and Canada. More Germans were landing. Officers were drunk everywhere, in the theaters, and they rioted in the brothels. They made mock of their Tory allies, and sported in the open part of the island on their well-kept horses. Winter was near. Prisoners were coming in from the last fort that General Washington had left to hold the river lines. Three thousand miserable, tattered men had been captured.

Joe was picked up on the third day by a patrol and taken to a large white house on Church Street. The questioning was brief and conducted by a round little captain who kept looking at the standing clock as if late for some appointment.

"You admit you are Leftenant Joseph Philipse of the Continental Army?"

"Yes, I am."

"And you claim what you wear is a uniform?"

"We are short of uniforms. I came ashore here in a boat for some private non-military matter. I am not a spy."

"We'll see what a military court has to say to that. Sergeant, take the prisoner to the gaol."

"It's full up, Captain Corky. We got them hundreds what come down from the fort."

"All right, I'll write an order for the *Jersey*. He's to be held available there for trial."

Joe found himself in heavy hand irons and with a guard of four not too sober infantry men. He was marched down to a stone dock and pushed into a boat which rowed to a shabby old hulk swinging in the trembling change of the tide. A once fine three-decker, her masts had been sawed off, her guns removed, the hatches and ports set with bars. Now old and wormy with great beards of sea growths trailing from her rotting sides and bottom, the *Jersey* was a dismal sight. A detachment of Royal Marines paced neglected decks, black with grime.

"Ahoy, *Jersey*. Got some meat for storage for you."

"Come alongside and be recognized."

A slippery sea ladder nailed to the sides was pointed out to Joe and he climbed up it, aided by his one good arm, and stood on the rolling deck. Filth and rot were everywhere in sight. There was a stench such as he had never smelled—as if all the personal filth of unsanitary conditions, all the rotting rags and stale food in the world were escaping in a gagging vapor.

A hairy guard with two front teeth missing skillfully searched Joe's pockets. "You'll get used to the perfume, laddy. Hell-and-blue-jesus, not a thing on you. They've skunked you out of everything already. Not a brass farthing."

Joe was directed to climb down a hatchway. He heard the drone of cursing and weeping and wild song. Barred doorways held in hairy men with gesturing arms outlined by stinking rags. Wicks smoldered in dishes of rancid fat. As Joe went lower the odor was deadly enough almost to cause him to faint. It was a world made up of dung, dead rats, decay, wood rot, and the smell of a wretched humanity, unwashed, diseased, and breathing for months the same stale air.

The guard opened a barred oak door and pushed Joe in. "Here be a passel of your friends, you American——."

Joe fell on his one good hand and felt the greasy mush of a horrible obscenity soil his fingers. A feeble light burned blue in a pewter plate where a rag gave off smoke and little light. He saw eyes framed in wild growths of hair, saw arms streaked with——, and sour rags long lost to color or shape.

A face, curly-bearded in inky whiskers to the eyes, came close to Joe. "Welcome to our water tomb. You wouldn't have a crust of bread, a bone with an inch of meat on it?"

"No." In horror Joe pulled back and found damp, decaying straw to sit on. He had heard of these prison ships. It was all true.

So rested the rotting river hulks—the *Jersey* was notorious—all of them dismasted old ruins, unpainted, ports barred, hatches padlocked, the stink of their refuse turning and returning to their sides with every tide, tangled in the long seaweeds and kelp that had long since fouled their anchored bottoms.

Many died here, he knew from gossip, in the deep lower holds. On rancid straw, on their own foul excretions. Ill fed, brutalized by the low men in power, by mad brutes. Overgrown with hair, naked, and reduced to bone and gristle, few men, Joe felt, had the courage to hope here. Beasts and madmen, it was said, prowled against their own kind and exploited the last miserable death rattle of an American soldier on a prison hulk.

The man, all curly beard, was back at his side. "I know you. You're Joseph Philipse."

"Yes. Yes. Who are you?"

The prisoner had turned away.

"Major! Major, it's Joseph Philipse."

A large man, his yellowish hair all tangled, was pulling a heavy chain that was padlocked to the wall, yet he still tried to reach Joe.

"That's as far as I go. I'm Major Homer Schuyler. I think I know you."

The first, curly man said, "He's being disciplined, the major, for lunging at the sergeant of the guards for feeding us hog slop. He's a bit,"—it was a low whisper—"he's a bit off, the major, from being chained up so long."

"Yes, of course, Major," Joe said. "We met at Mynheer's many times."

The curly man said, "I'm Morris Manderscheid."

"One of Botts' men! You freed Dr. Cortlandt and myself at Sir Francis'."

"Tell us, how is it going? We hear such lies of the rebellion."

A deep voice shouted, "Stow the gab. Let us die in muckin' peace." Joe was aware now of at least a hundred men in this compartment lying on the foul straw, aware of rattling chains.

He whispered a long time to Manderscheid, and the major seemed full of sense and nodded. Later, when Joe tried to sleep, he heard all around him the revolting details of the shameless intimate life of long-kept prisoners, and the scratch-scratch of fingers and nails probing under arms and into the crotch for insects. Soon Joe, too, was scratching, and what felt like burning drops of acid walked over him and bit him everywhere.

A reeking open bucket for natural needs gained in foul strength as the night proceeded. Faint shadows moved as dawn groped at the slits of the barred ports, but there would be little daylight this deep down in the ship. Near noon—as Joe guessed—the door opened and a soldier slid in an iron wash basin of gray muck stained with brown spots. The men threw themselves on the revolting mess of spoiled oatmeal, moldy peas, broken sea biscuits full of weevils, and several large horse bones with a bit of gristle but no meat. Friends helped the chained men to eat by passing clay pans of the slop to them. It was truly revolting and Joe gave his share, held on a wooden plate, to Morris Manderscheid.

"Joseph, you'll be licking the plate clean in a few days. We're beasts here . . . not men . . . living in lice and muck."

Joe found his shoes stolen, and his jacket, which he'd used as a pillow, gone. In britches and shirt he sat shivering as a cold wind came up the bay. He hoped it would at least clear the air. But nothing could ever destroy the terrible stench. The prisoners settled down to gnaw bones, scratch, and curse each other.

Near dark the door was opened again and the guard shouted, "Joseph Philipse! Trot up, man, and don't keep me waiting or I'll start you with a rope colt."

Manderscheid whispered through his curly beard, "Lord, lad, if you can get word to Botts, or mention an exchange, do so. The major can't last much longer and keep his sanity."

"Joseph Philipse, now! You comin' out or you want free rent 'ere?"

Joseph followed the guard on deck, where he was pushed down the sea ladder and rowed to a gilt-pooped man-of-war, clean and bright in yellow and black. He climbed up to a white deck where marines with side arms stood stiffly on guard. A midshipman took Joe below to the captain's cabin, neatly fitted in teak and gilt, with fine solid furniture. A man in shirtsleeves was writing, dipping ink from a silver set. He looked up and smiled.

"By George, you seem *always* to be a prisoner."

"Sir James!"

Sir James Tropp smiled and held a handkerchief to his nose. "You smell of the hulks like the very devil. Well, sit down. It was a hasty mistake, my boy. I'll break the captain that sent you there. She's no rose, the *Jersey*, is she?"

"No," said Joe taking the glass of Teneriffe wine offered him.

"Well now, we'll get you tailored and fit and bathed in orange water and cinnamon spirits. Sir William Howe would be happy to have you to dinner tonight on the flagship I'm sure."

Joe slowly put down the glass. The aspect of things was confused. "I don't understand, Sir James. I'm a Continental officer. I was captured out of uniform."

Sir James nodded and winked. "My dear boy, stop playing the game. Your father's work for us has been called to the attention of the king himself. Surely you don't think we'll accept your acting the innocent? Of course it was sense not to blurt it out to the first captain or sergeant you met."

"What about my father?" Joe felt the pain in his hurt arm go to his heart and push needles into his brain. He bit his lips together to keep from shaking. Agony, he decided, goes one way—into the marrow.

Sir James picked up his papers and looked them over. "Jonathan Philipse has done marvelous work in weakening the defenses of the river forts. And he's kept tons of supplies from Washington. I suppose he's too modest to give his own family the full details. Help yourself to the wine. I've got to get these damn papers on the dispatch boat for England. Paper work, paper work, the war will be buried in it. Ah, when war was an exquisite intangible!"

Sir James went out, and Joe sat staring at the copper lamp in the ceiling turn and sway with the shifting of the ship. He heard the forecastle men go up on deck for their watch, the march of marines on the quarter deck, and someone adjusting the chains in the hawser pipes. If he stopped breathing, Joe felt, he would not think of his father, not accept what Sir James had said, not be the son of a traitor.

He put his arm down on the table. His head sank on his arm, and he wept—wept as he had not wept since he was a small boy. And he smelled in his sleeve an odor, the fetid horror of the prison hulk. He continued to weep until he heard Sir James' returning steps. Then Joe rose and went to the long bank of slanting windows in the stern and looked out at New York town across the heaving waters. To the north, upriver, there floated only an opaque mist. . . . First the loss of Sally—now this. The serene sureness of youth had seeped out of him.

"Your clothes have been spoiled," said Sir James. "I'll get one of the ensigns to fit you out with something your size."

"Thank you, Sir James," said Joe, not turning around. "You've been more than kind tonight."

A row of lights were going up on the signal halyards of the frigate anchored downstream under the swarthy sky. The world, Joe decided, was a mad and empty thing, bizarrely balanced on the most illogical of fantasies, called loyalties and consolations.

Mynheer, unbuttoned, strings untied, sat on his river porch smoking a bitter pipe. The world was turned upside down. New York lost months ago, Jonathan Philipse locked away in an American gaol somewhere in Connecticut like a common indented servant—chained, most likely. His vast holdings seized by Congress, and who knew if his son and daughter would ever be able to get back even a small share of it all. Who would think Jonathan Philipse would play the double game, smile on the Continentals and all the time be foot-and-hand, tongue-and-groove, with the British? One of the great river families in disgrace. And what did Mynheer himself have left? The paint was peeling from the double portico, several of the barns had been burned out. The best of the blooded stock was gone, run off or slaughtered. He had an old sway-backed nag or two and a creaking gig and a carriage. What had been a thriving well-equipped estate had now only a few crippled old servants, the slaves who hadn't gone off to frolic or been put to digging trenches for General Washington.

Even the land looked different here from the porch. Still beautiful, with the sumac and the staghorn bush pushing ahead, and the hawk moths among the roses, so full of joe-pye weeds now. The damn raucous mocking of the crows made him angry. He still had the single-barrel shotgun hidden away and he'd go for them some day. There was a he-coon down by the stream too, a nice change from the hog haslets Zopyra the idiot maid cooked up these days. Culbly had once said: "Some think one must create chaos to make over a world." And it seemed so. The mullioned windows lacked glass, a corner of the coffered Corinthian ceiling had fallen down, the Rimbaut clock no longer ran, woodbine and foxglove were now more of a crop than maize and flax.

All along the river the big houses were closed—Beverwyck, Van Braans', Wurdemannwyck—welcoming either the Americans or the

British as protection. There were no real fighting lines that said *this* was for liberty or *this* for loyalty to the Crown. Everywhere there were raids, ambushes, picket lines, and every so often the bark of cannon in the night to challenge the buzz of the crackling cicadas. *That* would be a small battle. The Senecas no longer came to dig lily roots. They were armed and going out for scalps upstate. The peeping of bullfrogs, the velvet dirges of the mourning doves were often interrupted by the curses of marching men, unshaved and brutalized, hunting rum, breaking china, and doing worse in the barns and outbuildings. How right the historian Gibbon was to say, "History is little more than the register of the crimes, follies and misfortunes of mankind."

Only nature was indifferent, Mynheer noticed, when—costive in the morning—he walked back to the neglected flax fields to do his intimate business in an old stone outhouse his grandfather had built. The shadbushes still bloomed, the horsetail reed went to black spore, and the fat dogwood buds, yellow-white as good candles, never minded the war. The bronze-black grackles still mated in the oak trees to produce speckled eggs. Tea was hard to get and in the big house they drank an infusion of the oswego plant.

He heard his mother (most likely in her lace bodice and wide pannier skirt) stirring in the hall. His wife, Anita, was still asleep. An old man and two old women waiting for peace. Living their lives out, three Robinson Crusoes, he thought—on a desert island made up of worn Adam carpet, untuned harpsichord and spinet; some of the young bloods that had last danced the gavotte or the minuet to their tunes were dead, or rotting alive in the British prison ships in the bay.

Anita came out on the porch. So she had not been sleeping. He felt sorrow for his wife. That she was old and her beauty gone, that her brother Jonathan Philipse was in an American gaol, that their son Culbly was a cruel young man with high ideals of crown loyalty, that they would have no calm old age of peace among grandchildren and odors of Cherokee roses, cape jasmine, and white japonica (somehow the flowers seemed more real than the unborn grandchildren).

Anita said in her nasal voice, "I must go upriver to Philipse Manor."

"No, no, not in these times, Anita."

"Roxanne's time is near, and no one knows where David is. And her mother is in Connecticut near the gaol."

"Some say we'd better not have too much to do with disloyal families. But it isn't that. The roads are unsafe."

"Don't jaw at me, Mynheer Peter Schuyler. Go find some horses. I saw the old covered phaeton under a shed. Drive out the stable hands to harness it. Zopyra will drive."

It was better not to argue with a woman. And if he went out to the sheds and found one of the few indented servants left hanging around to harness up, he'd miss his mother's senile cackling and protesting against conditions.

As he harnessed the two bony nags himself (no servant in sight) he thought: what a time to bring a child into the world. And Roxanne—so trim, so saucy she had been as he last remembered her. Now lying in labor in a traitor's house, and her husband off somewhere in the war.

Wandering in slippered feet in the upper hall Mynheer's mother, old Martha, smiled to herself, holding an old *rekenboek* to her thin, bony chest. Nobody kept up the records properly any more. The hog reeves were gone to war, the slaves were lippy and talked back, and then one morning were gone with a side of bacon, a braided jacket, or the gold-backed comb. All the *krankbezoeker* she had done in her youth, visiting in the cabins of sick slaves; and when you needed them they were like St. Peter's wreath after a holiday—gone. But she was fully alive and wary. She'd keep the place going, even if that big lummox of a son just sat and smoked his pipe, like a *voorleezer*-sexton, with nothing to do but watch the old family gravestones marked: *In Den Heere Ontslaapen.*

Ah yes, the Vanvleeks and the Verplancks and all the fine Dutch families that used to live in the old homesteads between Rhinebeck and Kinderhook, what had happened to them?

People now thought her hollow-headed and senile, did they? But she, Martha Schuyler, knew Van Gaasbeck had a militia company that took all the good Dutch young men to war and didn't bring them all back, and Jonathan Philipse, the fool, had got himself pitched into gaol. As if it mattered *what* side one took—all that mattered was the land, the fields, the houses. And when one was young one made love, skin to skin.

The old woman heard the clatter of hooves, the creak of ungreased carriage wheels. She pushed her dried old head out of a hall window. Her daughter-in-law and the crazy black wench that had fits were driving off.

"Thou fool!" she shouted. "This is no time, no time at all to go for riding."

The dust spun under the wheels, the old horses, feeling a small part of their old strength, moved down the neglected drive with a rush of speed.

"You're a disgrace to all the old families—the Van der Lyns, the Provoosts, the Van Schlichthorsts, the De Vries!" Old Martha pulled her head in and felt her ancient heart in her bony chest stir like dried parchment being rolled. There was no meat on her, certainly no juices. Why was she trying to save anything? The Domine Everardus Bogardus long ago had said, kissing her ardently in the grape arbor, "You have no soul, and you lead men to sin. You will die empty and I shall repent and kill myself some day for my lusts."

"But not today," she had said laughing.

What a fool the Domine had been. Such a splendid body, such a great thrashing nakedness to his sinning and lamenting over the wallowing with the Venus parts. To think they two had conceived that big lummox downstairs, her son, and passed him off as a real Schuyler. Fed him and held him—so red and angry. Rose-water on her milky teats, a smile on her face.

The Domine had drowned himself in a grist-mill pond, little fishes nibbling on his cod it was said, when she had taken up with the English lord. But of course those were the great days for passion, the real olden times of grace and poise when a woman knew her worth and men knew she was not above rubies. "You will die empty," the Domine had said feeling her naked thighs, and Peter Rensselaer had seen them there on the violets. And never said a word to their hosts, the Uldrick Heyns.

The old woman shook off memory and opened the recording books and began to try and read the faint ink lines. "16 barrells perry cyder, ten gallens persimmon wine, six pds loosstrife tea, 19 sides bacon, 14 lge sturgeon, 82yds osnaburg clothe, 16 yds lockram, two flagons Renniers orange-oyl, 2qts Turlingtons Balsam Treacle . . ."

They could survive. She looked at the date: 1734 A.D. Was that this year or last? Her memory *did* wander a bit.

CHAPTER 25   She had been dreaming of leaves scattering on the river like a muted benediction. She was a child again and she and Joey were playing in the garden and she had hidden from him in a big gardener's basket. It was close and warm in there. "Roxanne! Roxanne!"—she could hear his panicked cry as he hunted her. Up at the big house they were giving a party and she had heard the clatter of well-bred hooves on the bluestone drive and the polite hiss of people's footwear as they went up the steps to the front doors where her father stood in welcome. Over all there was the sound of decorous violin music; the orchestra from New York was already there. It was cozy in the basket, yet uncomfortable with Joey crying "Roxanne," for Joey sounded very scared.

The basket was getting smaller and tighter and she struggled to get free of its creaking grip. Her neck hurt as the basket shrank and Roxanne cried out and came fully awake, still struggling.

She was lying in early morning sunlight, deep in the bed, her neck bent against the pillow. She rubbed her neck to ease it but the ache only bit the deeper as the flesh was pressed under her hand. The dream went away, detail by detail; soon it was lost. Pains gripped her belly.

She did not open her eyes. That would bring reality. It was better to go on and try to conjure up another dream. She was home, in her old rosewood bed. Something had happened, something strong, and dreadfully sad. She didn't want to remember that. . . . She smelled the palsy drops on the night table and someone had put a pokeberry plaster on her brow to cool her.

The sunlight was warm on her lowered eyelids, but she refused to let the full light come in. She was her own secret, locked away in her own mind. She owed this clumsy swollen body nothing. It had taken all the physical pleasuring and betrayed her into this.

Now she had a new dream, or was it real? David was with her. They were walking slowly across the fields in the first pale light of morning. A mottled mist rode the ground, just about knee level, and there was no more cannon-firing. The battle was over. Sometimes the morning fog hid the remains, the fragments of war, the bodies of the dead. Sometimes they had to walk around the path that led to the manor house.

"How is it going to be with us, Davey?" she asked him.

He twisted his hat twice around in his gloved palm and shook his head. "It's going to be two human beings who don't expect perfection, who will be grateful for love and . . ."

"Just be grateful?"

"I don't think, darling, we have to talk about it. Talk means nothing."

Roxanne said, "By the way, am I your prisoner?"

"You mean prisoner of war?"

"Yes."

"Damned if I know."

They walked on, arm in arm, filled with that painful glow of wonder and worry that is love, the feel and taste of existence colored by passion and doubt. And if they had no illusions, Roxanne thought, we do have each other. This battle is over and this war will be over in time. But a man and a woman have a war, too, and it's harder for us, for we fight it without guns, banners, or marching songs. Now she knew it was only another dream. She came fully awake, screaming, and the final labor to get the child born had begun.

Anita Schuyler untied her cape strings and went into the room where Roxanne lay crying out in agony on the large canopied bed.

"No, my dear," Anita said, taking the girl's damp hand. "It has to be gone through, loud or quiet. And Auntie will help."

"But it can't happen, not *yet*."

"But it is. How far apart are the pains?"

"Five, ten minutes."

"There, there. You see. It's coming."

"But it can't. Two weeks more—we were so sure—at least of waiting."

"No, no. Hold on tight to me. Push, when the pains are closer together."

"No. David isn't here. I can't give birth with him away."

Anita shook her head at the panting girl. "We're not, it seems, waiting for him. I'll just tie some towels to the bed rail and you pull on them. It helps."

Anita turned to the slave girl cowering in a corner. "Don't stand there like a cow. Prepare a basket with some blankets in it, and some winding cloth. And go get some sweet oil from the kitchen. My girl is there. Have her collect a pot of hot water, and basins. Run!"

Cake ran. Roxanne shouted, "Oh, oh!"

Anita Schuyler sat back in a high curved chair, gripping the girl's slippery hand. "There, there. The world has been going through it, at least the female part, for thousands of years. Ever since the Garden of Eden. But I suspect men wrote the story, not women."

"So unfair," cried Roxanne. "So unfair."

"No, it's the begetting and begetting they record in the Bible. Now just rest between the pains."

"They're getting closer together."

"Where is Dr. Cortlandt?"

"Gone to White Plains. Oh, oh—something's broken."

"That's the water, dear. Where is that slave girl!"

Roxanne began to scream in terror.

Mynheer Peter Schuyler had found an old family ledger with a great many blank pages left in it and he was jotting down notes for a new project that he had seized upon—*A History of the Hudson River Families.* He was copying out the words of one Robert Juet, who in 1609 had been with Henrik Hudson when he first sailed up the river.

The thirteenth, faire weather, the wind northerly. At seven of the clock in the morning, as the floud came we weighed, and turned foure miles into the River. The tide being done we anchored. Then there came foure Canoes aboard; but we suffered none of them to come into our ship. They brought great store of very good Oysters aboard; which we bought for trifles. In the night I set the variation of the Compasse, and found it to be 13 degrees. In the after-noone we weighed, and turned in with the floud, two leagues and a halfe further, and anchored all night, and had five fathoms of soft Ozie ground; and had an high point of Land, which shewed out to us, bearing North by East five leagues off us.

Old Martha Schuyler came into the room where Mynheer wrote. "It's time you took a firm hand to your wife."

"She's gone to Roxanne Cortlandt."

"You should have said her no."

"I did. Mama, listen to this I found in an old book by a sailor who first came here with Henrik Hudson."

"Henrik Hudson? I don't remember him around the place."

"No, no, Mama. It was long before your time. Listen, he writes:

The people of the Mountaynes came aboard us, wondering at our ships and weapons. We bought some small skines of them for Trifles. This after-noone, one Canoe kept hanging under our stern with one man in it, which we could not keepe from thence, who got up by our Rudder to the Cabin window, and stole out my Pillow, and two Shirts, and two Bandeleeres. Our Masters Mate shot at him, and stroke him on the breast, and killed him. Whereupon all the rest fled away, some in their Canoes, and some leapt out of them into the water. We manned our Boat, and got our things againe. Then one of them that swamme got hold of our Boat, thinking to overthrow it. But our Cooke took a Sword and cut off one of his hands, and he drowned.

Martha Schuyler scowled. "A grown man copying out such nonsense. I'm hungry."

David Cortlandt, wearing a captured British captain's uniform, looked into the pier glass of the shabby room that was Botts' headquarters in White Plains. He saw a tall, wide-shouldered man in a curled white wig, well-cut red cloth uniform, the white breeches form-fitting, pushed into shining black leather boots.

"Damn it, no, Botts. I can't play the part. And why me?"

Botts, busy examining English letters and military forms, did not even bother to look up. "You are Captain Squires Wilton of His Majesty's Twenty-ninth Light Infantry. Now on duty with the provost courts in New York. I have arranged for your proper papers to fit that part."

David shook his head. "Still, why am I the choice for this mission?"

"Major Homer Schuyler is losing his sanity in the prison hulk, *Jersey*. Morris Manderscheid is starving to death. No hope of exchange. We can't wait. If we are to get them off the hulk we must do it at once. They are your friends. Morris Manderscheid saved your life."

"I'm well aware of all that. And how you use the fact! But I'm not a romantic harum-scarum hero type. So why me?"

"You've spent four years in England, and speak like a proper English officer should. We have few such men."

David pulled off the wig and threw it on a chair. Botts neatly put it on a wig block and rearranged the curls. "We went to great bother to outfit you properly. You've protested enough. Here is the plan again. Memorize it."

David sat down and scowled. Botts slid some papers into an oiled silk envelope. "Every Tuesday at five o'clock a boat from the British military court in New York rows out to the *Jersey* to take off those prisoners who are to be tried the next day before an English court-martial. In the last seven weeks it has never failed to pick up from one to five prisoners to take back to gaol in Bowling Green. An officer and two privates are rowed out to the prison hulk by a navy boat and present papers for the prisoners who are to be picked up."

"The guards would know the officer, wouldn't they?"

"No. The duty on board the prison ship is so irksome the marines are shifted from the ships in the bay for two-week periods of duty. The officer who goes out to the hulk is usually changed every fortnight or month."

"He is this time, I gather, Captain Squires Wilton?"

"Yes, a drinker, a rouster, and related to General Clinton. Tomorrow he will drink more than usual. Our agents in New York will ply him with rum and Frontenac wine. He will start an hour late for the boat trip. When he gets to the dock his boat will have sprung a bad leak. A loose plank. It will take him, we hope, at least a half hour to get another boat. In that hour and a half you must present yourself at the *Jersey*, with papers for the release of the major and Morris Manderscheid. They're all properly made out."

"It sounds *so* easy," said David. "As if you do this kind of thing every day."

"Not every day," said Botts dryly, "but often. Now when you get back into the boat—don't worry, it is repainted and crewed with men dressed as British tars—all you have to do is to remain calm. The boatmen will take the boat to an inlet below Hoboken. There you will be met by my agents with horses, and all of you will be taken to safety."

"And if anything fails and I am captured? I will be shot as a spy?"

"Most likely. Very likely," said Botts, handing David a small flat pistol. "Besides your proper sidearms carry this up your sleeve. In case you have to move quickly and can't reach for the big pistol in your belt. Here is a copy of the *London Chronicle*, only two months old. It should refresh your memory of London. You sure you want Joe Philipse as one of the British privates?"

"He wanted to go, and frankly I'd feel more at ease with him. I'm frightened of your expeditions, Botts."

"You start downriver in two hours. How is Roxanne?"

"Big with child. According to our figures it should be born in two weeks."

"Well, you're the doctor," said Botts, unaware he had made a jest of sorts. He handed David the papers. "Here are letters and personal things that will identify you as Captain Squires Wilton. Here is the release order to move the prisoners, properly sealed and signed by Lord Cornwallis. You can rest in the next chamber, but don't wrinkle the uniform."

David picked up the newspaper and went into the small room next door and lay on the bed, in his shirt, or rather the shirt Botts had given him. He looked over the paper and its London news.

A perruquier advertised his new-styled Ramillies wig, and a tailor off St. James Street was proud of a tamboured waistcoat. Mr. Wilkes, in the House of Commons, had made a speech. "Force avails nothing. The support of the American cause is a vindication of the rights of Englishmen." A well-known town mopsy and street woman had been ravished by a French dancing master in Kensington Gore opposite Prince's Gate, sometime, as she claimed, between Matins and Evensong. Dr. Johnson was reported indisposed in his chambers, having overeaten of veal pie with plums, salt buttock of beef, and mackerel with fennel sauce. . . .

David came awake, the newspaper by his side, to find someone shaking him. The afternoon sun was slanting into the west and Joseph Philipse, dressed as a British private, was looking down at him. "You sleep like a wintering bear in his cave, Davey."

David swung his booted feet to the floor. "I've been sitting up with Roxanne the last few nights. She is sure the baby will breech almost at once. Women get foolish as their time quickens."

"Get your wig and sword, we're ready. Silvester Hand is play-acting the other British soldier. He's a good man in a mix-up."

"No mix-up, Joe, or we're gone as a hedge parson and done for."

David put on his British officer's jacket. "As Jack-Tom says, they do dress pretty with all their gear and accoutrements."

Joe did not answer as he inspected his cartouche case, spatter-dashes, gaiters, and knapsack. He had withdrawn into himself since his father's arrest and, except for trying to prove himself a true American soldier, he was moody and sullen. That girl in New York—even she hadn't improved Joe's temper, David suspected.

The sun's power was dimmed late in the day by a bank of low, scudding clouds. The three men had come in a small cutter manned by oarsmen to the Jersey side and there under a dock had found a jolly boat of British man-of-war design with four sailors in royal naval gear—the wide white canvas pants, the tight peajackets, and the tarred hats.

Silvester Hand was a little too large for his British infantry uniform, but he and Joe handled their Brown Bess muskets as if they knew them well.

Joe nodded to the seaman to get out oars as church bells began to ring from the New York side. "This is the moment."

David sat facing the rowers and the suck of tide spun them into the bay as the oarsmen put their backs to it. They rowed up-bay and then came down with the current as if approaching from the city. Dispatch boats and a captain's cutter were out. Sea gulls fought and scolded over some water-logged tidbits and the three men-of-war at anchor all rolled to one side together and then back again as the tide raced toward the Kill van Kull.

The hulk *Jersey* was permanently fixed near the Staten Island shore, as if isolated as a shameful-looking wreck. The men rowed and David's nerves leaped like crickets and he had to close his mouth tight and grip his hands together. The dark, unsavory-looking ship lay low in the water, pitched to one side, long green seaweed floating from her timbers, her unpainted sides rust-stained, her mast cut off short. Already they could smell her and see the boarded-up ports and portholes, the iron grillwork over once gilt-carved trim.

One of the sailors hallooed. "*Jersey*, ahoy!"

Two high-capped marines leaned over the rail, muskets held at port. "Ahoy, below. State your business."

"Captain Wilton with papers from the military court to pick up two prisoners," Joe shouted.

One of the guards said, "Got any 'baccy, mates?"

"Not a leaf. But," said Joe, "I'll show rum."

"Stand by to board, Captain."

The boat came near the stagnant debris floating near the hulk. David quickly climbed the broad sea ladder, followed by Joe and Hand. On deck he sniffed with disgust and looked at the two marines standing at attention. "Damn smell, worse all the time." He banged the order paper sharply into the chest of one of the marines. "Get these two prisoners up here at once. The tide is turning."

"Yes, Captain." One of the marines turned and went off down a hatchway shouting, "Sergeant Gullymere, boat to pick up two prisoners."

David put his hands behind his back and tried out a pursy self-complacent strut while Joe and Hand spoke to the remaining marine.

"Rotten bit of duty it is here."

"Better than going north to bed with hair-cutting savages," said Joe.

"It give me the grue, being here on this ship."

"Burn some asafetida to clear the air."

"Nothin' can clear the air. I'm so done in I don't care to eat. Could I be having a bit of that rum?"

Joe handed over a small flask. David looked down at the boat bobbing below, held away from the ship's ladder by a sailor's oar. Nearby a ship's boat was being rowed by six sailors and an officer was adjusting his cocked hat against the offshore wind and leaning on an amber malacca cane.

It seemed to David as if the thing would never be done. Down below were shouts, the clang of iron, and always that smell like an obscene gas permeating everything. The boat with the officer was very near. David could hear voices and a curse from a rower as his oar caught a crab, a faulty stroke. The officer with the cane called him a "damned rattle and a clown."

Chains clashed and a sergeant with a patch over one eye came on deck and saluted. "Captain Wilton?"

"I haven't all day, Sergeant. Where are the men I've come for?"

"Right behind me, sir."

Two wretched figures came up, prodded by the marine. David would not have known either of them. The bigger had vacant eyes and a condition that sent a tic up one mottled cheek and caused his mouth to open and shut like a fish; saliva drooled from it. The other prisoner seemed bowed and broken-backed, and only the live and alert eyes, though yellowed and bloodshot, showed the intelligence left in the creature. Both were gyved in heavy leg and foot irons and were dressed in rags. Their dirty naked feet, flat on the deck, were smeared with offal.

David nodded. "All right. Get them down to the boat."

"Ahoy, *Jersey!*"

It was the other boat with the officer with the malacca cane David had noticed before. His boat was lying against David's, the officer looking up.

The marine sergeant said, "We must be getting popular, two bloody boats in one day, sir."

The officer below spoke crisply, "Damn it, Sergeant, can't you manage things better or do you want the awkward squad?"

"I will have it all shipshape, sir, soon as I get this lot off. Prod them sods over the side."

The two shaggy prisoners were ordered over the side and Joe and Hand helped them down the dangerous sea ladder to the waiting boat. David tried to put a leg over and a cheery voice said, "Ods trigger. Half a mo, I'm coming up."

David looked down, aware he knew the voice, stepped back, and pulled the cocked hat down sharply over half his face. Lieutenant Jack Bounty came up over the rail and looked about him.

"Well I must say, prick my vitals—a busy day what? I've come for a prisoner for the court. Here's my papers. One Neddy Murphy. Look lively now, Sergeant."

"Never before had two court boats in one day," said the sergeant.

"Drunken sot who was to do this job diddled out and I had to draw this smelly thing. Leftenant Bounty, sir." Jack was holding out a hand to David standing in the shadow of the stump mast. "Captain Squires Wilton," said David, moving the sleeve pistol down into his hand. Jack Bounty smiled, then was puzzled, then opened his mouth as he felt the small pistol David was pressing against his heart. The sergeant turned to get the prisoner from below.

"Of course, old cock," said Jack Bounty. "Felt I knew you, Captain Wilton. Getting so dark I didn't catch the face at first."

David tried to smile, but couldn't, his lips and teeth were too dry. On the butt of a cannon on deck he read the raised letters: *Georg.*

Rex III, Die Gra. Britt. Omn. etc., etc. . . . His eyes blurred to the rest of it.

Jack Bounty put his hand behind his back. "Well, one meets all people in the service. Who would fancy it, eh?"

"That's right. Who would have thought."

"Well, it certainly comes as a surprise."

Joe had climbed back over the side followed by a grim, cruel-looking Hand. David shook his head at them. "I've orders," he said to Jack Bounty, "for you to join my boat with your prisoner and send your own men back."

Jack Bounty looked at the pistol and laughed and went to the rail. David followed, while Joe talked to the remaining marine on deck. Jack Bounty shouted down to his boatmen, "Cast off, lads. The captain here is taking me and my man back. Report to dock and then to your ship."

The boatmen nodded and one old salt said, "Aye aye, sir," and the boat with the six rowers pulled away. David spoke softly. "Over you go, Leftenant Bounty."

"Be simpler if I remained officially to take my prisoner over. Just suggesting."

David's hand now had a tremor and he could hardly catch breath. Joe seemed calm, and Silvester Hand looked at the marine guard with murder in his glance. The one-eyed sergeant was back from below with an ape of man, all red hair over an Irish face. David had never seen such a Hibernian cranial formation, and the legs were bowed and hung with chains, the arms long and shoulders hunched over so that the prisoner's knuckles almost touched the deck.

Jack Bounty said, "We'll all be going back in one boat. Get him over the side."

The sergeant nodded. "Could all 'ave done with one boat in the first place."

Jack Bounty followed the prisoner, Joe, and Hand down the sea ladder. As David descended, the harbor and shipping seemed to be spinning in his vision. He knew now the true test for heroics was much simpler than he had thought.

CHAPTER 26   The boat with its freed men and rescuers—
and new prisoner—pulled for the New Jersey shore with lusty strokes,
the water splashing from the banging oars. Homer Schuyler lay on
the bottom boards staring indifferently at the sky. The Irish prisoner
said nothing. Morris Manderscheid took a pull of the brandy flask
and combed his curly beard away from his mouth with a black,
dirty hand.

"It was a close thing, Doctor. Close. We couldn't have held out
much longer in the hell of that hulk."

Joe looked down at Homer Schuyler. "I wonder if we were in
time?"

David was watching the Jersey shore and worrying at the number
of boats and cutters active in the bay. Jack Bounty leaned his head
on his cane as if watching a play he found mildly amusing.

"Davey," he said, "you know I wouldn't have tumbled you weren't
with the Crown *if* you hadn't used that Wilton name. After all,
why wouldn't you be for the king?"

"Jack, it's a miserable thing running into you like this."

"I hear your prisons aren't better than ours. I'll soon know."

Silvester Hand growled, "Let me stop the gentleman's gow and
knock his head in."

David shook his head. "No. We can't take him along, and yet
he's an honorable prisoner of war. Jack, can you swim?"

"Dog-paddle, but actively."

Homer Schuyler began to moan and roll his eyes.

David looked at the British store ships anchored in a row two
hundred yards to the south. "In a few minutes, Jack, I'm going to
toss you overboard."

Joe put his hands into his pockets: "You'd better get rid of your
boots and jacket, sword and cane."

"I shall miss the cane," said Jack Bounty, beginning to take off
his boots. "Hurley's on Threadneedle Street made the boots—and
not paid for yet. Odd, Davey, our meeting having to be like this."

"Never question destiny, Jack."

"Yes, any other Yankee showing up in your place would have given me the quick funeral march. How is the boy, Dan?" Jack Bounty retained his calm good humor even in his smallclothes.

David measured the distance to the shore. "With his grandfather, Sir Francis. Any news of Peg?" David felt he shouldn't have asked and regretted he had. But something awkward in his memory had made him shoot the question.

Jack folded his jacket and tossed the cane and sword onto the boat bottom. "Last letter I heard of her, Peg had sailed for Canada— Quebec—with Lord Alban. You know General John Burgoyne, M.P., keeps a rather fancy nest of chickens around him. This water looks blasted cold."

"It's tarnal crazy," said Silvester Hand, large hands on his knees, "letting this redback go."

Joe motioned to Jack Bounty. "This is as good a place as any to get into the drink. Keep left—to counteract the tide."

"Righto," said Jack. He patted David's shoulder and leaped overboard with a great splashing into the gray bay. David watched him paddle along with much kicking. He wondered if Jack Bounty had overestimated his ability in the water. How different this was from their old times playing picquet in Peg's chambers, with the tallboy and chest of drawers containing their last resources—a Geneva bottle and some red herring—and Jack frizzed and cued, with his dress rapier and quizzing glass, and Peg in low-cut gown ready for some muzzy evening gambols at Covent Garden!

Joe pointed ahead. "The inlet. Can the prisoners walk?" The red-bearded Irishman, who had been sulking, rattled his irons. "How do we, sor, get these bogies off?"

"We'll find a blacksmith waiting soon. Can you all do a bit of walking if we have to make a bolt of it?"

Manderscheid shivered. "It's chilly, but we'll manage." David draped Jack Bounty's coat over the man's thin shoulders. "And see if the boots fit."

They were rowing into a salt water inlet surrounded by acres of mud flats smelling of clams and sea silt. Late water birds were gathering for the night. Cat reeds grew to a great height all around them. The seamen seemed to know the place well. They rowed down one narrow open lead of water into another. The sea birds were standing in the mud, all facing one way.

Homer Schuyler began to mutter something. He refused the rum flask as he mumbled, "Blasphemy, tippling, and lechery. Profligate are the times, foul viragoes walk among us . . . help us, help us . . . quirk and quiddities of law, all are fetid, odious . . . vermin."

Manderscheid calmed his fellow prisoner. "Now, Homer, it's to be all right. It's all right. We'll have the chains off us soon and a snug fire." In the gathering dusk they were pulling for a low plank dock set in reeds and canebrake; behind it crouched the sloping sides of a lopsided, settling hut. Two savage dogs with spikes in their wide collars stood silent on the dock. Several men ran out and helped bring the boat in. Gulls and sandpipers were settling down all around.

David climbed from the boat. "Have you a smith?"

"Not here, mate," said a man carrying two pistols in a dark leather belt. "They're getting along out of here. Before the blasted Tory Rangers start combing the reeds for them. And better doff the king's scarlet, all of you. There's a slop chest inside full of clothes."

Joe helped Homer Schuyler up, and Manderscheid followed, feeble but alert. He grabbed David's hand. "It was a gallant thing you all did today."

David found himself carrying Jack Bounty's cane.

"It was Botts. I still don't know how I let myself be patterned into it. It has turned out well, so far."

There were horses chomping behind the hut. The three released prisoners were assisted to mount, Manderscheid having great difficulty from weakness. Homer Schuyler seemed indifferent and in a trance. The group of liberated and still-manacled men, and their escort, went riding down the muddy path among the reeds at a canter. Joe handed David Jack Bounty's sword. "You might want to keep this. I hope he made the swim. It was a far bit."

"Yes, it was. What are the plans for us after we change clothes?"

The man with the pistols in his belt rubbed his rough chin and spat into the brackish water alongside the dock. "You're as much a problem as they were. But we'll get you back upriver after it's real dark. The long way 'round."

There was booming of cannon from the bay and the sea birds stirred. The pistol carrier grinned, showing large teeth with spaces in between. "Alarm guns. They've discovered your little tricks, I'd say. We better get away too." He turned to the sailors who were changing from their natty uniforms into buckskin and hunting shirts. "Sink the boat. Stove a hole in her and in five minutes we'll walk out to the north where we'll meet a guide." He turned back to David, "I reckon we'll have to lay low in some cellar for a day or two till the manhunt is done with. They'll turn every privy over and knock all the farmers' haycocks apart."

There was silence now from the guns, but they could hear the drums beat to quarters. Joe said quietly, "They will be angry. I don't think anyone has ever before escaped from the hulks."

David wanted to say the escape wasn't complete yet but he didn't. All he felt was an ominous uncertainty. Joe looked glum enough as it was. As for himself, he felt wrung out, but not depressed. And not at all heroic. It had been simpler than he had anticipated, and now that the main part of it was over the excitement seemed drained from it. He lacked understanding of just what had made him act the way he had, yet he was aware of the incomprehensible intensity that had seen him through the adventure.

By night stages David, Joe, and Silvester Hand made their way back to the American-held river banks. Jaundiced and often in irritable temper from their dangers, they tippled spirits and spent the nights in different friendly barns. (David realized the courage accessible to people in wartime.) Rendezvous were made, they dressed in strange breeches with worsted stockings, missing victuals and forage when they had horses. They were attacked by odious vermin as they headed for home. Smallpox was raging in many places and David inoculated folk in a primitive manner, by injecting fetid matter from a sick person under the fingernails of the healthy. Usually it worked. But he detested this clumsy way of doing it.

They listened to angry farmers who said, "A Tory is one whose head is in England, whose body is in America, and whose neck *should* be in a rope."

It was not a healthy season—quinsy and contagious disorders raged, and for dysentery David could only prescribe the old Royal Navy remedy, iron-rust drunk in brandy. If it didn't help, it cheered. He wanted to get back to Roxanne. Her time was very near. And yet they had to go a roundabout way, for the British were howling in hue and cry after the prisoners and their rescuers. Outrage filled the British camps at this escape of three men from the prison hulk.

Spent, thin, and weary, they were made welcome by the Continentals. David was pleased to see the new American flag—the bars and mullets that some were calling the stripes and stars, being ignorant of the proper terms applied to a coat of arms. The flag was frankly based on General Washington's family arms. It was a tonic to the heart, David felt, to see it flapping over an American outpost. A corporal let them through the pickets and an officer welcomed them.

David, riding to Philipse Manor with Joe at his side, was aware how worn and racked and tired of the mad business of war he was. He remembered a line of Montaigne's that the coffee-house hackney writers in London had liked to quote during his medical student days. "Man is frivolous, complicated, changeful and elusive as flowing water, and to draw a clear conclusion from him is difficult."

When David saw his four-day-old son, red and sleepy, the grue left him. He kissed Roxanne, proud there on the wide bed, and said, "Oh my darling, and me away during your lying-in time!"

Roxanne, combed and brushed and sassy, mussed her husband's hair as he bent over her and smiled. "You men always run, darling, when a woman is left to face things."

"He's a bonny lad. A good seven-pound weight, I'd wager."

"So he seems. Darling Davey, I thought I'd never be alive and in love with you again."

"You feel fit?"

"I'm eating like it. He's a splendid thing, isn't he? All man and alert, with a red-haired poll to scare a sunset."

David kissed his wife and held her in his arms. "You're the old Roxy again."

"Am I, now!"

He stood admiring his wife with the blue taffeta ribbon tied in her corn-colored hair and his son with the red fuzz on a very large round skull. "We'll call the lad George."

"After the king!"

"No, after, General Washington. You have no objection?"

Roxanne shook her head and made a thin line of her mouth and David knew she was thinking of her father in the Connecticut gaol. He resolved to ask the minister to christen the boy George Washington Jonathan Cortlandt.

Joe was impressed with his new nephew. He peered into the old Philipse family cherrywood cradle. "Are you sure, Davey, their hands and feet are meant to be so small? I never heard of any Philipse who birthed a runt."

Roxanne asked for the baby to be lifted to her waiting breast and ordered her brother Joe from the chamber as a boor.

Mynheer was very busy now working on his projected A *History of the Hudson River Families*. He had dug up old manuscripts, letters, lawyers' contracts, legal forms. On a visit to Roxanne and the new baby he had come back with much Philipse material. He wrote:

Vredryck Flypsen, or Frederick Philipse, was born in Friesland in 1626, of parents who fled from Bohemia to escape persecution as followers of John Hus. He came to New Amsterdam, a young man without money but with skill in the building trades, acquired from his father, who was a roofer. He had a determination to get ahead. In his early years in New Amsterdam he worked as a carpenter for the Dutch West India Company. Later he was employed by Director General Peter Stuyvesant as a master builder, to build houses and churches in New Amsterdam and military fortifications across the Hudson.

In 1662 he married Margaretta Hardenbroek, the widow of Peter DeVries, a woman of wealth, carrying on trade with Holland in her own ships. At the time, he was thirty-six and well established in the community. Margaretta had a daughter by DeVries named Eva. In 1691 Eva married Jacobus van Cortlandt. By Margaretta, Philipse had two sons, Philip and Adolphus, and a daughter, Annetje who married a Jan Schuyler.

Anita Schuyler came in with a tray of food for her husband. "It's going fine, Anita. We must find more old family papers."

"David and Joseph are missing. That's more important."

"They'll turn up. We Schuylers seem to have intermarried very early with all the old families."

"Roxanne all alone in that big house—with two slaves."

"Let me read you something about the Philipses:

"In 1664 the Philipses took the oath of allegiance as British subjects and immediately established friendly relations with the British governors. With remarkable agility and the payment of a tax on a fortune of 80,000 guilders they survived the Dutch reconquest of 1674 and the second conquest by the British.

"Frederick Philipse prospered under the British. He became the largest trader with the five Indian nations at Albany. His ships touched port at Amsterdam, Bristol, Hamburg, and both the East and the West Indies. In the sixteen seventies he built a manor house at Yonkers to serve as a seat for his newly acquired land holdings in that area. He sold a large riverfront holding between Yonkers and the present Tarrytown to the Schuyler family in 1674."

"You shouldn't write such things down. I mean about dealing in slaves."

"I've worse things about him."

"You forget I was a Philipse."

"No, my dear, but you are now a Schuyler."

"Still, we're all so closely related here on the river."

"In 1682 Philipse began construction of the Manor House at Upper Mills, where the river runs through level land in its journey from the hills to the Atlantic Ocean. It was a natural location for a mill pond and a mill. The bay formed by the streams afforded safe harbor in waters where tides rise and fall three or four feet. The harbor was large enough and deep enough for vessels as well as for river boats engaged in trade.

"In 1684, bargaining with wampum and tools, rum and beer, Philipse acquired all the land lying between the original purchase at Pocantico and Yoncker's Kill. In 1693 his estate was raised to a manor and Frederick Philipse became Lord of the Manor of Philipsburg, a title not denoting royalty but which carried certain privileges.

"In 1679 Margaretta Hardenbroek died. In 1692 Frederick Philipse married Catharine van Cortlandt, sister of Jacobus van Cortlandt and widow of John Dervall. This was one year after Jacobus had married Eva Philipse. The Van Cortlandts were already linked to the Van Rensselaers and Schuylers. These marriages united the four wealthy Dutch colonial families. They also established a direct connection between the Van Cortlandt Manor House and the Philipse Manor House. Frederick Philipse was the richest man in the colony."

"And look," said Anita, "what has happened to them."

"Yes, the head of the family, your brother, in gaol."

"Who is the book for?"

"For my own pleasure."

"You promise not to have it printed."

"I wouldn't dare. Listen to this:

"Rumors persist that Frederick Philipse was at times engaged in traffic with pirates. Unlawful in the outside world, he maintained a peaceful, orderly life at home.

"Frederick Philipse, first Lord of the Manor, died and his wife Catharine made an entry in the family Bible: 'Anno Dom. 1702, the 6th of November, Sunday night at 10 o'clock, my husband, Frederick Philipse died, and lies buried in the church yard in the manor.'"

Major Homer Schuyler did not long survive his escape from the prison hulk. A week later he sickened into melancholy indifference. There seemed nothing wrong physically in the prison-punished body. But the mind was clouded and had a deficiency of understanding. The will to live seeped out. He died in silence, staring with unseeing eyes at things no one could guess.

His body was brought to the Schuyler burying ground by the old churchyard below the ferry landing. It was the first day Roxanne had been permitted to travel. David was in his best blue and buff. General Washington and his staff were present, under an old graveyard elm. Botts in rusty brown stood by the honor guard made up of survivors of the major's regiment. Behind them were soldiers drawn from the Maryland, New York, Pennsylvania, and New England regiments. Major Homer Schuyler was being properly buried with full military honors.

Mynheer and his wife had come; Joe Philipse was there, too well aware the Philipses were in disgrace. Many members of the other Hudson River families had come, the young in uniform, the elders in their best surviving clothes. Even some suspected of Tory leaning had come out of respect for the Schuylers.

Roxanne clung to David's arm. "It seems such a fine sunny day to be buried. And dreadful, too."

David rubbed her arm tenderly and nodded. "It seems a waste of so much effort, and so much mind and agony."

The casket draped with the new flag of stripes and stars was being brought on artillery wheels to the graveside. It was lowered to the ground near the heap of fresh-turned earth.

Jack-Tom Swales, freshly shaved, his topknot hidden by a dark hat, stood in a new-made suit of deerskins, its fringes as yet untouched. By his side was Silvester Hand, in uniform, slowly chewing a cud of tobacco, but refraining from spitting. Botts crossed over to Morris Manderscheid, dressed in neat blue that was too large for his ravaged body, a body that seemed mere bone and loose skin in the strong sunlight.

"Too bad, Morris."

"At least he didn't die in the filth of the prison ship. Family graves, together, are a kind of last fidelity."

The grave in the churchyard was red and raw near the tallest group of marble headstones and granite shafts. It was a fine day, all agreed. The sun was high in noon and made marks on the grass wherever it could break through the willows and elms. There was a scent of cold earth mold and new-cut flowers. Mynheer, David and Roxanne, the river families stood to one side. Many farmers David had never seen before kept pushing forward. General Washington, looking older than David remembered him, stood in the full sunlight, arms clasped in front of him.

The folk all along the river had gathered, a circling ring of mourners. The oak casket stood on trestles and the voice of the minister spoke out with the cold comfort of ritual over the dead soldier.

The relatives stood staring at other graves, at the graves of the major's sisters and brothers, the last of the old brood. The major's father's grave—his mother too was dead—there under that stage set of a marble urn. The major's son-in-law lay over by a pine tree; his daughter dead. His elder brother dead by pistol—suicide. Soon, thought Mynheer, more of their family would lie down for a coat of mold, and fret no more about wars, raids, decaying times, and bad manners.

The minister's voice rang out:

> "My soul thirsteth for thee,
> My flesh longeth for thee,
> In a dry and thirsty land
> Where no water is."

Botts stood by the side of General Washington—the general tall and neat in blue and white, head down; the cocked hat was off, seeming too light for his big fist. His hair was almost all white now.

"A fine funeral, Mr. Botts."

"It seemed most fitting, sir."

A very thin breeze stirred the uncombed hair of the two grave-diggers. Their blue-veined faces stared up over the torn turf. Their liquor-numbed features were expressionless in a proper full-dress respect. The soldiers became restless; their muskets fell out of perfect line.

The minister said:

> "To see thy power and thy glory
> So as I have seen thee
> In the sanctuary.
> Thy right hand upholdeth me
> But those that seek my soul to destroy it
> Shall go into the lower parts of the earth,
> They shall fall by the sword.
> They shall be a portion for foxes."

His hand fluttered in some signal. Mynheer stiffened and looked off to the large stone marking his father's grave in the next plot. "Everyone that sweareth by him shall glory."

The gravediggers moved briskly. The casket went into the ground. The first clods hit the oak casing; the earth, wet and sticky, was pushed quickly by the shovels. The grave filled and the gravediggers patted the mound smooth with their shiny tools. They looked in pride at their craftsmanship, mopped red necks and wiped their brows with ragged arms, and stepped back.

The army honor guard lifted its muskets. The volley sounded small until it echoed back from the river. Distressed birds fluttered in the elms. The smoke dissolved and drifted, torn and phantom-shaped among the fir trees along the old cemetery wall.

General Washington reset his cocked hat. The people, creeking in unaccustomed best clothes, began to flow away quickly down the hill.

David, Joe, and Roxanne walked away from the grave and Anita Schuyler came over.

"And the baby?"

"It thrives," said David.

General Washington and his staff were mounting behind the wall. On the road, among the clattering sounds of his mounted staff, General Washington scowled up at the treetops then turned to the

Frenchman riding by his side. "Fighting the war and living the times, it gave our mind space to clean itself. You understand, my dear Marquis?"

"I think so, sire."

"We have got a fine thing here in America. No, I'm not waving the banner. There is always the danger that Congress will not be able to find the right courage in us, or the men with it."

The wind came up and the topmost branches of the trees stirred. The staff rode on. The general said to the young Frenchman: "A man has to act in his society as if everything he does is stained by a love of this vast new land. A man can do what he has to do, even if he's aware he may only come out the leader of a great defeat."

"You do not believe in defeat, sire?"

"No. The true, sad thought about life is that we reach the peak only for a little time. Yet the view is worth it. Up there responsibilities become monsters, sir, unobtrusively accumulate and swallow us. The things we feel deeply about, ideas called truth, honor, victory—they seem most irrelevant when they most apply."

The young Frenchman said as he quieted his horse, "Sire, we all live full of evasions, intolerable demands, inevitable failures. But this world is no dream. It has much coherence, plausibility. You are lucky; your people—you—have the power to elect, the right to face your responsibilities. A man searches for the right way to live, and we all choose according to our chances, our capacities, and even our temptations. War is a temptation to power."

The general touched his mount with the spurs—so that the staff had to catch up. "You've been thinking a lot about this for so young a man."

"Yes. I saw in France that if I went into this thing the involvement must be complete, the issues significant. This liberty may be so big, so heavy, that it could defeat any profound sharing of the full experience. But I have come round to thinking that life without conviction and compassion is nothing. I am, sire, one of those, I've realized, who is imprisoned in a preoccupation with the changes of his own time."

The general nodded. He was not a man much given to abstract thoughts, and only to this young Frenchman (or to Hamilton and one or two others) could he relax in such talk. He rode on thinking of the war he had yet to fight, and all the dead there would be whose sacrifices would some day look easy, when all that were left of them were monuments. The weather turned grayer. He spurred the horse again.

Not all rode away from the graveyard. Some men of the dismissed companies made their way from the burying ground to the inn, Kill-Devil Tavern, by the ferry station. Joe had left his horse in the courtyard there. He did not feel any desire to go back to the manor house just yet. He would perhaps ride along the river and if he were lucky he might see an otter. They were getting scarce, and no one had seen a sturgeon for some time. Soon he would be leaving for the north, where General Gates was collecting forces to block the reported British invasion building up in Quebec under General Burgoyne, M.P.

Several soldiers were already active in the process of getting drunk, if the volume of noise coming from the inn rang true. A young girl was sitting in front of the inn on a log bench. She was dusty from long walking. The bottoms of her brown skirts were torn and tattered, her face wind-burned. Beside her was a bundle made of a yellow scarf, its four corners knotted. She stood up.

"You told Aunt Ann this was the place I should come."

Joe said simply, his voice husky: "Sally," and stood looking at her. Her face was drawn and there was a small bruise on one corner of her mouth. Shabby and dusty as she was, his heart beat faster. He took her hand in his.

"What took you so long?"

She looked away and lowered her head to one side and made a biting gesture with her mouth as if trying to gnaw on her collarbone in humiliation. "Oh Joe. You'll send me away when I tell you everything."

"No," said Joe. "No, I can't send you away."

"If it's not too late I shall be faithful. The conditions of the times spoiled so much. But I do love you, and you only. The way things happened in the town and . . ."

"No, Sally. No confessions, no spooning up the past. All that matters to me is that you were lost and now you're not. Is this all the baggage you have?"

"That is all of it."

"Come along and see the manor house." He lifted up her bundle and smiled properly for the first time in months.

BOOK VII

From the North

CHAPTER 27   General John Burgoyne, M.P., was returning to command in Canada with the power to move the British invasion forces into a direct battle with the Americans; he was going south by the lakes. There had been much talk of meeting Lord Howe in Albany after he broke the river chain and invaded from the south. Now a fleet from England bringing the last reinforcements for the scheme came past the rough, cold shore of Newfoundland and ran into rolling weather at the wide-mouthed St. Lawrence River. The officers and their ladies, the soldiers and their doxies, the sergeants and their camp wives—all looking at the rugged shores and the big black pines, hearing the sinister cry of hawks, became aware this was a wilderness, that a deadly war lay ahead and in it some climactic battle. Bateaux appeared with rough men in buckskin speaking a dreadful un-Parisian French, and soiled-looking aboriginals in huge canoes, twenty paddles to a side. They came out of the river mist to meet the fleet, the savages almost naked, streaked with war paint of ocher, reds and yellows, with here and there a chief smoking a calumet. The river grew narrower and swifter.

Peg Munday came on deck with Mrs. Lewis, and smelled the wood smoke drifting from the shore.

"About time to see land," said Peg, tying a blue silk scarf over her blowing hair. Mrs. Lewis, given to more weight, a lush piled-up golden beauty, laughed and arched her thin eyebrows. "Oh, Johnny will take glory here! He'll drive them in the quickstep, a hundred regulation paces the minute."

They passed victual and forage barges and a band of men in front buckskin out on reconnaissance. The river grew still narrower and louder and they had to send the fleet, to avoid the rapids, slowly around islands held together by black rocks and tree roots. There were French Canadian pilots on board, dirty men who smoked and spat and shouted, "By gee, you go that way you keel this ship *de plus belle*."

Lord Alban would come to walk the ladies and the general's dogs in the evenings. His rather lean figure in his green dragoon uniform looked in need of padding, and his pitted face, the result of a childhood smallpox attack, was red and appeared almost foolish at times. Mrs. Lewis, mistress of the general himself, queened it over all the women on board, aware her husband, the good man Lewis, was busy somewhere making a fortune in army supplies and well pleased that his wife had bedded Gentleman Johnny Burgoyne, poet and playwright, who traveled with his own wine cellar and a collection of well-bound volumes of Smollett and Fielding and several of the Latin poets.

The cabin was close and hot and Peg in her cambric shift lay with Lord Alban, listening to the river sounds. "I never thought Quebec was so far inland."

Lord Alban killed a night insect buzzing at his ear. "It's a grand place, I hear. High up, and Papist though it be, remarkable women."

"Neddie, there are enough hell-rakes in this army to pleasure all they have."

Lord Alban rubbed his insect bites.

In the great teak cabin of the general, Mrs. Lewis in her night clothes was opening wine, and Gentleman Johnny, unbuttoned and in his white stocking feet, sat writing with a good quill pen under the swinging lamp.

"My love," said Mrs. Lewis, bending over to brush her exposed and shapely breast against his shoulder. "You write too much. Scribble, scribble."

"Listen, my rompish, debased girl. I've a war to win."

Mrs. Lewis handed him the glass of wine and kissed his rather large mouth. "And you will do it, Johnny."

"But not if I think I'm back in London at the Turk's Head, or watching Macklin in *Love à la Mode*. What do you hear from good husband Lewis?"

"He has built carts here for you, hundreds of them, to haul your supplies through the wilderness."

"Efficient man, Lewis. We should sight the Citadel, the pilots say, tomorrow sometime."

There was a knock on the door and Mrs. Lewis called, "What now?"

"Ensign O'Crump, madam."

"Come in."

The door was opened by a handsome young Irish officer very tightly breeched in crisp white. He was the general's favorite aide, and he showed no surprise at the undress of the two lovers or the young dog playing under the bed. "Begging your pardon, sir, but the pilots want to lay over for the night before they attempt to get us through the gorge ahead. It's a swift and dangerous one."

"Go speak to the proper naval rating, O'Crump."

"*Curlibet in arte sua perito credendum est.* Good night, sir, madam."

"Handsome hams and leg," said Mrs. Lewis. "And *all* that Latin, too."

The general reset his wig. "Go have the sentry wake Peg and Neddie. I want to read them what I've written to read to the savages and the troops. But don't wake the Dutchie baroness; she's an old she-lion."

"No fear. She and her three girls are snoring away in German, I'm sure, dreaming of meeting their sire and father. Do you really need these Hessians?"

"The king thinks so."

The ships were slowing and the sound of anchor chains was heard. It was nonsense, the general felt, to be so full of talent as he was and decide to use only the military part of it, while ideas for plays and poems crowded his head. The general was an intelligent man, opinionated yes, wellborn, in no great need of money, a proud man, indulgent and given to the pleasures of the bed and Priapean bliss. Sometimes he looked in a mirror and shook his head. How he acted the fool at times.

The little dog barked.

The general carefully scanned his manuscript as he had been taught at school, subduing a too-purple passage, and adding several Roman military terms, out of Caesar's *Gallic Wars*, he suspected.

Peg and Lord Alban in slippered feet came into the cabin. Neddy shook his head at the offer of wine. "My digestion is ruined by this sea trip. Costive or in flux all the time."

Peg sank down on a low divan built into the wall of the cabin. "It will be nice to eat good greens again and put one's bum down on something that's built on dry land."

The general rattled his manuscript to show he was serious and ready to read.

Mrs. Lewis said, "Johnny has written something."

"*Indian allies of the crown—*this is for the tribes—*by your magnanimity of character joined by your principles of affection for the king which I hereby proclaim—I ask your invariable observation during the coming campaign of certain rules of conduct.*"

Lord Alban sneezed during the reading.

"*I positively forbid bloodshed when you are not opposed in arms. Aged men, women, children, and prisoners must be held sacred from the knife or hatchet, even in time of actual conflict. Base, lurking assassins, incendiaries, rapers, plunderers of the country shall be treated with—*"

Lord Alban decided he was coming down with a cold.

Mrs. Lewis asked as the general read on, "Will you proclaim it in English?"

"Translated into their base dialects, of course. For our own troops I have something stirring. Yes, like thus—*This army embarks to approach the enemy. We are to contend for the King and the Constitution of Great Britain, to vindicate Law and to relieve the oppressed.*"

Lord Alban nodded and blew his nose.

"*The services required of this particular expedition are critical and conspicuous. Occasions may arise in which no difficulty, nor labor, nor life are to be regarded. This army must not retreat.*"

Peg said, "Beautiful, sir."

The next day the general's fleet was met by more painted savages in their birchbark canoes, howling, and also by other boats. In the bend of the river was the high misty Citadel of Quebec.

On deck Peg cheered with pleasure. The general's dogs barked. . . . It is tall, she thought, it is impressive with its green-topped rocks and man-made walls. Troops lined the rails to cheer or jeer as they came up to the warehouses and the buildings of the Lower Town. There was music ashore, fife and drums playing "The White Cockade," and Grenadiers in their bearskins, garters, and knapsacks saluting the general on deck, in red and gold, smiling at this town.

Lord Alban, who had knowledge of such things as a former gunnery major, pointed out in nasal tones the batteries, the palisades, and the serpentine roads.

"Where, Neddie," Peg asked, "are the Plains of Abraham where gallant General Wolfe fought and died?"

"Off to the right. Across the river there is Point Levy where he had his camp. And there is Cape Diamond, it's a thousand feet up."

"You are so full of knowledge, Neddie."

"I must be getting on to duty, Peg. You'll be escorted to lodgings and we'll see the town. Bring my pillbox, will you?"

It was an amazing town, Peg decided. Mrs. Lewis was also on deck with her maid and baggage. Cheers in English and French from the docks were good to hear. The ladies came ashore with their baggage, Mrs. Lewis' trunks, and the general's private library. A soldier, a lieutenant, saluted them. "Ensign O'Crump has been assigned to see to your comfort, ladies. He's gone to get carriages. You stay in the Upper Town. The Right Honorable Leftenant Dudley Brown at your service, as it reads on my papers."

Peg smiled up and leaned on the Right Honorable a little more than she had to. "Solid land at last. Do you know a Jack Bounty? Some regiment of the Line, but I've forgotten the number."

"Captain Bounty? Of course."

"Captain?"

"Promotions all along the line for those with connections. Lord Howe admires him. He's off with some companies arming the aborigines, the Wyandots, Oneidas, and others that will join us."

"It will be nice to see Jack again. A captain, *my!*"

The ladies had lodgings in an old stone building near a nunnery of Ursulines and a bit away from the Castle of St. Louis shining yellow in the sun, a castle now the residence of the governor, where the general had formal official chambers. Peg inspected the town on the arm of the Right Honorable Lieutenant Dudley Brown. She had her first sight of a Papist cathedral and she went into its musty interior, which smelled of candle wax and old clothes and smoke. There were some shops on Mountain Street and the guard was smartly on parade at St. John's Gate. Lieutenant Brown arranged for a picnic to the Plains of Abraham. It was going to be an amusing war, Mrs. Lewis said. Even if the slinky Jesuits were to be seen around—Peg had been warned about them as a child. Otherwise the Canadians seemed like other people. The women solid and bold-eyed *par complaisance* and already arm in arm with the Dutchmen of the Landgrave of Hesse. All around the town troops were bivouacking, and Peg got out her dress with the true taffeta rustle for the dinner at the governor's house welcoming General Burgoyne back to North America.

It was a gay ball, with the dress uniforms adding to it—the yellow facings of the Ninth, the white of the Forty-seventh, the red of the Fifty-third, the blue of the Twenty-first. And the Guards and the rest in their best scarlet, white wigs curled, silk stockings taut on well-formed legs. There were Swabians who called Peg *Liebchen*, and officers from Rhetz, Specht, and Hanau regiments. The British were putting a well-trained army into the field. There was talk, by Lord Alban, that there were too many guns to pull through the wilderness.

"Always better too many of a thing than too few," Peg reminded him as they danced.

Later a few of them dined *en famille* after glasses of Malaga cordial, and Lord Alban played at the clavichord, and the general pretended amorous dalliance with some of the women there, the wives and mistresses of the officers. Peg, maudlin with too much wine, came back to their chambers wrapped in a great blue frieze coat and thought of her son somewhere in this wild land, and she ached for him, little Dan.

The continent was all a great forest, Captain Jack Bounty had heard, right down to the wild gulf country of tropical monsters that washed onto the land of the Aztecs. The land was broken here and there, of course, by fields and clearings, and along the coast by plantations and the maize fields, and lower down there was cotton and tobacco and the indigo. Huge lakes, roaring rivers, and in the dank shadows the Indians, these smelly naked savages. Captain Jack Bounty had led a party of soldiers and Indians through the villages of the barbarians, recruiting, handing out the trade muskets and the brass wire and the beads and the Sheffield-made hatchets. It was then he had been shocked at how much wild land there was. It was not neat and small or park-like, like England. The aspect of things was hard to capture; an inner essence was needed to feel alive and important in these hasty camps around a smoldering log fire, gnats eating one's neck, the cough of a loon over deep black waters on some uncharted lake. Necessity, he felt, brings the ordinary man into the category of heroes, or he would die here in this tangle of bush and rock. He sat at night among creep-cedar and tamarack, the resinous tree trunks burning in his face, and the Indians feasting on deer guts and moldy partridge berries. He could not stomach their food. His men, half a hundred wretched lobsterbacks, were ill of malarial fever, and they ate the gruel from their Salisbury cooking kettle without interest. Jack Bounty had made them eat pennyroyal for colic and he had shot some grouse for them. Now he felt fever in his own bones, but he had still a last mission to accomplish.

They would soon have to march an army through here. Men, guns, camp followers, supplies. And no roads, just trails for small carts. He looked up high over the trees and saw the red god Arcturus overhead. Once he had shown interest in the stars and studied some charts. But it was all wrong up there in that sooty sky—the stars were turned around somehow over these damn antediluvian forests, and this unfixed sequence in the heavens was strange to him. Midge and sap-fly plagued them all, even the Indians under their grease. There was a fearful insect that Half Hand, the Indian leader, called the Buffalo gnat.

"Oh they drive man and horse and cow and deer crazy, clean crazy."

Half Hand was a short, solid Indian, four fingers missing on his left hand, and very cheerful, dirty, and greedy.

Captain Jack Bounty turned to him. "How much further do we have to go?"

"We meet with Tory party over in Berkshire mountains."

"That I know, but how will we get there?"

"Walk. You like fat Indian girl? I catch one for you."

"No."

The Indian laughed and spat into the fire and took out a whetstone and began to hone his hunting knife. The sound mingled with the bass counterpoint of frogs and hoot owls hunting in the woods behind them. Jack Bounty got up and inspected his men. They were shivering, their teeth chattering in fever. He gave them a rum dram and a quick, easy word. He went back to his blanket and looked again at the sky. In its inky dial he made out now the Big Dipper, the Pole Star, Ursa Major—the Big Bear. Damn the forest, damn the war—these same stars looked down on comfortable London.

In the morning the party of British went on behind Half Hand and his score of disgusting savages. Every deadfall of old timber had to be climbed over, every clearing was a place to rest and beat at the insect life. Mud-daubers and wasps bit them, and thistle and blackberry tore their uniforms. Sometimes they came to a forest cabin, the plume of wood smoke twisting with the turn of the earth, or so it seemed to Jack Bounty. These were loyalists' cabins, but it was hard to keep the Indians from burning them, violating the women, and scalping everything with hair. The party came to swampy places where a rank primordial ooze and puffballs were underfoot and they walked knee-deep in algae-scummed water—a soup of fish and frog eggs floating on the surface. Jack Bounty decided cause and effect rule nature; it draws no morals. Attack and competition was the way; survival was all. They came onto drier trails, went past hemlocks and poplars, cottonwoods scented by mint and horse-balm weed.

Half Hand called a halt. He was smoking his pipe and he squatted on his haunches. He said, "Ahead, big farmhouse. No fire our guns. We attack him at dark. Surprise."

"Aren't they loyalists?" Jack Bounty asked.

"Not here. We come far bit by now. Soon you meet the Tory messengers."

"Can't we go around the farms?"

"Braves come long way, belly grunt with hunger and excitement. Scalps, woman, rum—they keep warriors very pleased to fight for King George."

"You red son of a bitch," said Captain Jack Bounty, and turned away to look over his men. They were camped among heavy deciduous growths, among lacquered berries and quaking aspens. Their fever was worse.

At dusk the Indians, in hideous war paint and naked but for breechcloths, slipped away making happy grunting sounds, throat, and entrail noises. Where, Jack Bounty wondered, were the silent, noble red men London talked about? Half Hand had come to him just before the start of the raid. "Hunter Moon. Full, very good for attack. We don't walk into trap . . ."

Then the Indians were gone and later he heard the whoop of the bittern, their bird signal to each other. Jack Bounty sat in the dark —they had lit no fires—and listened to his men grouse and call out in their fever. How a full army would get through here became an obsession with him. It seemed a foolhardy thing to try.

He must have slept. He came awake to the sound of katydids and to the smell of woodbine and benzoin spicebush. And the noise of the Indians returning. They were reeling drunk, and Jack Bounty alerted his men. They primed their muskets. Half Hand staggered up, drunk and giggling. He flung some sodden bloody hair on the ground.

"Ho ho! Americans never saw warriors at all. Just we come up quick, push in door, and crack heads like butternuts."

"Get your filthy objects out of sight. And keep your men quiet."

"You come next time. Much futzing. Two girls. They dead now. Torture men long time. They run around pole all on fire, then we geld them. You count scalps for me?"

"I'll be damned if I will." Jack Bounty refused to look at the objects on the ground.

"Johnson he say we get paid, one big gold coin every American scalp."

"Take them to him yourself. I'm no paymaster."

The Indians, very drunk, shouted a string of dreadful obscenities. Jack Bounty touched his pistol and wondered what would happen if he shot down the savage. But he couldn't. He was on a mission to meet Tories. He needed guides, and his men were ill.

Half Hand held up some blond scalps. The hair was very long and shone golden in the gleam of the Hunter's Moon. "Much pleasuring, much screaming." He came up close to Jack Bounty and slapped the officer across the face with the wet scalps. "Ho ho! You like woman now?"

Jack Bounty ground his teeth together and turned away ready to vomit. He wiped his face with the back of his hand. He slapped at mosquitoes and black flies. His sergeant, Old Ed Sour, looked up. "Blinkin' lot of murderin' swine the lot, sir."

"Keep two men on guard, and the arms primed."

"We could give them a volley and knock their blinkin' 'eads off."

"You know the way back, Sergeant?"

"Not blinkin' likely, sir."

Jack Bounty sat down and in great disgust and rage again wiped his face. Images, revolting, horrifying, of what had happened filled his head. He had seen as bad in India and elsewhere, to be sure.

But somehow, here, against people of English descent, it seemed depraved beyond anything imaginable. He'd kill Half Hand some day, of course. But first they would meet the Tory messengers. The average man in this new world must soon sound whatever depths he had, and die, or come through it.

The savages were howling and dancing or roasting chickens, feathers, entrails, and all over a huge fire they had built. Colic overcame him and he gasped in agony.

CHAPTER 28   It was on the sixth day of May, 1777, that General Burgoyne had set foot in Quebec. But he was not yet fully written out, for he dispatched to General Howe, in New York, a message that he had no view but of joining him in Albany in a juncture of their two forces. By the middle of the month he was in Montreal with his staff (and Mrs. Lewis) trying to get started. There were on hand hundreds of the two-wheeled carts, many made by Mr. Lewis, or at least he had purchased them for resale to the army. Thirty were needed for the general's wine cellar alone. Lord Alban mentioned they were made of green wood and would not stand the wilderness journey. Lord Alban was feeling pettish. Some pollens he believed native to North America were causing him a great sneezing. Also he found the Canadians were wary of enlisting for the war.

It was June before the general, in new bag wig and gold-laced hat, having celebrated his fifty-sixth birthday, began to assemble his troops on the Richelieu River to the north of Lake Champlain. He had six regiments of the Line, the Grenadier and Light Infantry companies. The British totaled close to 4000 men. The Brunswickers and four other regiments of Germans came to 3000. There were only 148 Canadians, who proceeded to get drunk and trade off a lot of their gear. About 500 Indians under several chiefs also served—all commanded by a Le Corn St. Luc, a tough old Frenchman who stripped himself naked as any aborigine, streaked his body and face with war paint, refused to comb his white beard, and tied a topknot on his shaven skull.

He was usually shouting, *"Brutaliser les affaires—il faut les brutaliser."*

He was the most notorious Indian leader in Canada, and enjoyed the scalping, killing, and a bit of rape. He was a well-educated man, a Knight of St. Louis, of a noble Auvergne family, who had degraded himself for many years as a barbarian leader of Indian allies. He was very much feared on the frontier.

The general toasted in cups of negus his thirty-eight pieces of field artillery, two twenty-four-pounders, six twelve-pounders and four howitzers. Major General Baron von Riedesel commanded the Germans, and was commanded by his wife the Baroness, who accompanied the troops with their three small daughters, Lili, Putzi and Marlene, in several carts. It was a well-womaned army. Mrs. Lewis and Peg Munday traveled with the general's baggage. Many officers had wives along, and many more mistresses. The rank and file contained laundresses, sergeants' wives, sulters' widows, out-and-out whores, and children without count, many still babes in arms taking suck of maternal breasts while the regiments, cheering the sight, marched past. It was a healthy, well-disciplined army. General Burgoyne was esteemed, respected, and hurrahed whenever he appeared. The men had oiled their feet and shoes. The general, not overlooking any item, ordered:

"New and convenient Necessaries are to be made in the Rear of every Encampment . . . and the old ones filled up—at least six inches Depth of Earth should also be thrown in, when in use every Morning."

On June twenty-first the General Advance was beaten out on the taut drumheads and the army moved on American-held Ticonderoga. It was an impressive advance up Lake Champlain, Indians scouting in full war paint, their canoes cutting the blue lake waters ahead of armed ships of small size. The Germans were staring at the wilderness on the shores. It was a gay advance, British infantry in their scarlet, Germans in blue, the Jaegers' green blending in with the pines, and the tall bearskins of the Grenadiers and the black leather caps of the light infantry seeming just a step away from their original parade grounds. In the rear came the camp followers of both sexes, the dealers in drink, in card play, the blowsy and already tattered women and wailing children. It was no place for salon beaux and boudoir spirits. If they had character it was usually bad.

Colonel St. Clair, worried and undermanned, held Ticonderoga for the Americans with twenty-five hundred Continentals and nine hundred surly militia who wanted to go home. St. Clair was under another Schuyler who had remained loyal to the colonies, a distant cousin of Mynheer's, Major General Philip Schuyler, wary, cunning, brave.

In the warm day Colonel St. Clair was fussy and neat, Major General Philip Schuyler large and calm, and Major David Cortlandt, unbuttoned and smoking a clay pipe as they stood over the main gate at Ticonderoga and looked up the lake, tranquil and smooth as a sheet of tin. Here and there a fish jumped to the surface and dimpled the perfect floor of blue water.

"I can't hold," said Colonel St. Clair. He was facile, gregarious, but lacked pliancy and flexibility of mind.

"You'll damn well have to," said Major General Schuyler. "I'm going out to prop up the other forts. Doctor, have you many men unfit for duty?"

"I had. I moved them out yesterday. To Albany, I hope, if they can be gotten that far. No smallpox, but a lot of flux and some swamp fever."

Major General Schuyler nodded. "Send me Captain Philipse." He walked away and the colonel rolled his eyes and pointed at the lake. "The whole damn British army coming and I've got a few bare-arsed Continentals and some grousing militia who want to go back and plough their land. I ask you, Major . . ."

David shook his head. "Don't ask me, Colonel. I've still got fifty very sick men I want to get out of here."

"Don't take my wagons and carts. I'm not staying myself. And I'm certainly not leaving my furniture."

David knocked out his pipe on the palm of his hand and went to look at his hospital. He was sorry for Colonel St. Clair, stuck here in an impossible situation. The British would take the fort, no doubt of that, but the least the colonel could do was to try and make a gesture of holding. The lancet windows were open in the log building where the sick lay. It was not a pleasant place, but at least David had several good dressers now, and there was as yet no sign of smallpox. The quinsy he could handle, and dysentery—that was always present in a war. Dryden's line came to cheer him: *If you think the world worth winning, think, oh think it worth enjoying.* It would be hard advice here.

In his room he sat at the rough-topped table and wrote a long rambling letter to Roxanne. He asked of his son George, described too much camp humor, the surrounding forests, the dull life at the fort. He would leave soon to organize the entire medical situation of all the forces north of Albany,

which, my dear, is more impressive than it sounds & not to be laugh'd at or impress'd as being of much honour but more of hard work with little to do it with, and the ill demanding yarbs and Deimer's Ointement and Drops of Spirit of Venice Treacle, which is as harmless at least as anything I can give. There is much jaundic'd & irritable tempering here as we wait the invasion, but I shall be moving out to the other forts before it gets here. . . . I miss you, my love, & the daily small contacts of domestic life more than mere words on this wretched gray paper can tell. Neither the joys of Bacchus nor the pleasures of xenophobia—travel —are the delight you are to me. . . ."

The slab door to the room opened and Captain Joe Philipse came in, removing the weathered cocked hat, and skillfully slid his sword to one side to prevent falling over it.

"I've drawn a sticky thing, Davey. You will keep an eye on Sally."

"If she'll come with a train of sick. I'm leaving here tomorrow."

"I'm leaving this afternoon," said Joe, sitting down and extending his unshined and worn boots before him. "The major general wants a scouting group to go into the Berkshires to the east to see if they can capture some Tory messengers who are carrying some sort of dispatches—a list of loyalist available to the Crown—to the British forces moving south. I have a detailed paper of instructions but little information."

"It's a bit off the route?"

"Some of Botts' doings, I wager. All the major general could write down is that there is word the Tories are to pick up Indian guides and go to a village called White Corners, near Mount Greylock. How do things look here?"

"I fear, Joe, we'll lose the fort. As for Sally, you shouldn't have brought her here. With the fort bawds and riffraff."

"I lost her once, Davey, and I'm always in fear of not having her near me. If you go, take her along. We'll meet in Albany."

"She'll be all right with the sick train. But I can't take her to Albany myself. I've the other forts to see to, Joe."

"She's been a bit under the weather."

David nodded and put the unfinished letter in a small book of medical texts. "Now I hope she hasn't been doing the Indian on us —like some camp women—and tried to procure abortion with sumac flowers."

Joe laughed and stood up. "No, damn it. I'd want to keep any pup we two engendered. Any news from Roxy and young nephew George?"

"A two-week letter. Both fine. All right, I'll take Sally along. Take care of yourself in the Berkshires. The Green Mountain Boys are a feisty lot, even if on our side."

Joe fingered his sword handle. "Thank you, Davey. If General Howe comes up the river and this Johnny Britannia comes down and they meet in Albany, I have a feeling we'll all go see Jack-Tom's country, Ohio."

Sally sat on the small cane chair cheerfully sewing on a skirt she had cut out from some trade-goods blanket. She liked being Mrs. Captain Joseph Philipse and being with her husband in this fort and in late afternoons often taking a boat with him and going out on the lake. It was much different than it had been in New York, and Joe had asked few questions. Just married her and taken her into his arms. It was in many ways a confession of how much he needed her. Sally did not hunt too often for motives or enigmas in life. Here she was and if she didn't run out of the brown thread she'd have a fine skirt, at least for this wilderness.

When Joe told her he was off on a march with some scouts and soldiers, Sally kissed him and clung close to him, and promised to obey Major Cortlandt, and do as she was told. "So pack your trunk and kiss your husband good-by," Joe said. "In Albany stay at the Nelson Philipses'. You'll see me there soon, I hope."

Joe kissed his wife, driving out any doubt as to Sally's trustworthiness when left alone. Her damn lovable nature just overflowed at times.

Major General Philip Schuyler had the mean problem of defense, his men being spread out too thin behind the fort, with detachments trying to hold Skenesborough, Fort Anne, Fort Edward, and of course Albany.

General Burgoyne's forces landed four miles north of Ticonderoga and on July 3 took Mount Hope north of the fort. St. Clair tried one ineffectual attack, then fell back to Skenesborough with a brilliant march, but it was, of course, a pullback and a loss of the important fortress. Burgoyne's troops followed the retreating Americans and St. Clair had to move back to Fort Anne in the summer heat. The Americans and the British and Germans fought hard among the trees and suffered and many died. Major General Schuyler scowled when he got the dispatches and ordered St. Clair to withdraw further, to Saratoga, evacuating Fort Edward as he went.

General Burgoyne had two choices. He made the wrong one, Lord Alban thought. Instead of returning to Ticonderoga and crossing Lake George by boat, where he could have surprised the American forts and seized great supplies of carts and draft bullocks, he said no. Yet he would have been down on Albany before the scattered Americans were collected enough to oppose him in force.

Instead, with martial drumming and his dogs at his heels, he pressed on by land, through the tangled thickets, over hard-held ground. He had won so far, and this wilderness could not stop a British force, he wrote. He would take Albany this way. And entrench there while Sir William Howe came up from New York to meet him along the Hudson. The war was as good as over. He ordered one of the wine carts opened and under tenting he and Mrs. Lewis and Peg and Lord Alban and some of the staff drank to victory. Below them along a creek bank the Indians were howling and roasting some milk cattle captured on a farm where they left six scalped Americans.

But the swift advance failed; the British soldiers did not take Fort Edward at once as planned. They were short of tents, Lord Alban reported, short of food, short of powder and balls.

Under the red tent with the long fringes the general sat surrounded by the ladies and his staff, and he waved off Lord Alban. "Of course, of course, we're short of things. But damn it, it's a war in a wilderness. . . ."

"I'm aware of it, sir."

"We don't expect a fruitery and a pheasantry, do we?"

"Just breeches, sir, and worsted stockings and gun powder."

Peg yawned and looked away at the huge trees and the blue smoke of the Indian camp. Somewhere in this wild land was her son, little Dan. He must be growing healthy and tall here, with all this space to expand in. When they got to New York she would put on her best blue silk and go visit Sir Francis Livingston in Lord Alban's carriage (he'd have to get a carriage in New York) and be properly received, too.

Later, when the night sounds of the camp and forest merged, she lay with Lord Alban in their tent under sweetgum and tupelo trees, in discomfort at the heat and the insect bites.

"Neddy dear, is there to be much more of this?"

"I fear so. It's a long way to Albany."

"It's not the peccadillo we expected, is it?"

Lord Alban lifted himself on one elbow. His nightcap was tied on to protect his ears; a gnat had caused him fearful agony one night by flying into one of those organs.

"You don't want to go back to Canada, Peggy?"

"No, I want to get to New York. I have some people there."

"You have? Oh yes, Sir Francis Livingston. I forgot. And the boy."

"You wouldn't mind, Neddie?"

"Lord, no. Will you rub some Turlington Balsam on my chest? I fear I have the rash again . . ."

Outside in the night the cicadas made their sad song in the spruce, the aspens and white pine. The smell of honeysuckle in the bush helped kill the fearful odor of the balsam salve that Peg firmly rubbed into the pale white skin over Neddy's breastbone.

Roxanne drove over to Mynheer Schuyler's with the baby George in a large padded basket. She had a long letter from David, who was involved somewhere to the north in the great maneuvering of forces.

"Ach," said Mynheer. "The British are really there?"

"Yes," said Roxanne, "And they are driving toward Albany, David writes."

She read the rest of the letter and Mynheer and Anita felt old and out of step with the times. They never spoke in front of others of their son Culbly. Everyone now knew he was the notorious Colonel Lemon. The entire neighborhood was divided between the loyalists and those who gave their strength to the Colonial Congress. Raiders from both sides, called cowboys and skinners, were active all around them. The settled, solid way of life that had lasted so long on the river among the great families was broken up. Mynheer suspected it would never be the same.

Anita went with Roxanne and little George to the vine-hung arbor by the river, and there they sat and talked of womanly things, of children—little George was teething and fretful at times.

"I shall have ten children," said Roxanne. "At least."

"If this war ever ends. If the men come home."

"Nothing can happen to David. Nothing. I couldn't go on living without him. I'm hot-tempered and shrewish sometimes with him. But he knows me best."

"Mynheer as a young man was always taking me to balls along the river and suppers in the old houses. He rode much—a fine figure—in those days. I wanted many children too. But after the first it seemed it would be impossible, the doctor said."

They discussed the illnesses and trials of women, the intimate life of wives, and Roxanne felt old and settled. As the sun went into the west, she exposed a perfect little breast and fed George, who pigged and tugged at her nipple and made sounds of gas and pigged for more.

Roxanne felt sad and thought of David in danger and their love. But that would not do; it would, she knew, spoil her milk for George.

Mynheer had retired to his room and gotten out the old ledger, copying out items into it from notes and old papers he was collecting. There was no end to this history of the river families. He wrote on:

> Captain Johannes Schuyler built a mansion, a house large enough to be referred to as a "castle" by the fashionable, and rugged enough to withstand attacks of men or weather. Captain Schuyler lived the life of a feudal lord. The captain was looked upon as a sovereign in power and wisdom, a man of shrewdness and, above all, benevolent to the people, slave or free, on his estate. The Mansion House became a focal point for the estate, a center for activities not proper to the church.

The last line didn't please him. He'd rewrite it later. All the meetings, and wild times, and serious times, and times of weddings and births. In that order, or course. And all the rows of ledgers old

Martha, his mother, had in her room. He must get hold of more of them. They recorded all the business that had made the family so important.

Captain Schuyler, while keeping up his interests in shipping, made the land an extension of his commercial interest. With Indian and Negro slave labor he cleared land and put up buildings. He brought in tenants and allowed them to settle on his land a stipulated number of years on a rental basis. Farmers planted corn and wheat in the fields Indians had planted before them. They cleared land and built stone walls to separate fields and pastures. They cut timber for the export trade to the West Indies and England. The men built their houses, most of which were primitive but rugged. They raised what they wanted to eat, or did without, except for the articles brought in the captain's ships from Holland and New York. Their grain was ground, their surplus products were disposed of. The Schuyler estate became the center of trade for the region.

Roxanne left for home as the miller moths gathered around the first lamps of the evening.

The next morning there was news that the British were still advancing, and that many forts were lost. Some put them fifty or sixty miles from Albany. A call went out for militia and men to join the defenders in the northern forests.

To calm himself Mynheer worked on his history.

One of our outlying farms, Hawes House, where General Washington stopped to rest after the battle of White Plains, had an incident. Just after he had gone on his way, British pursuers arrived. In anger at his escape they slashed the door frames with their sabers. The boards with saber slashes will be preserved.

To continue my history: Records of the Dutch Burying Ground mention Hulda the Witch, a local character said to be a Schuyler born on the wrong side of the blanket. Unable to speak English, believed to be a Bohemian, she was called a witch because of her strange appearance and actions. She lived by herself, raised what she needed, and wove baskets for sale. She kept a cow and raised dried herbs. When British raids on livestock became intolerable, the farmers fought back. In a skirmish on Battle Hill, Hulda the Witch took her gun and fought shoulder to shoulder with her neighbors until she was killed by a British bullet. She was given a Christian burial, near the northeast corner of the Dutch Burying Ground.

He ate a hasty lunch and went back to his notes and ledger.

To go back—Between 1685 and 1699 Frederick, Vredryck Schuyler and his wife Catharine built what is now called the Dutch Schuyler Church. Erected for his family and tenants, it stands on an elevation within a short driving distance of Schuyler Mansion. It is close beside the river and only a little way from the old Albany Post Road. An ornamental bell, cast in Holland bears the letters VS for Vredryck Schuyler and a motto in Latin now too worn to make out.

Mynheer looked out of the window. Men with muskets and rifles on their shoulders, carrying packs, were moving up the river road. Going, he supposed, to join the American forces retreating before the British advance. He closed the ledger. Somehow it was no day for writing family history. He went down to the spring house and got out a clay pot of buttermilk and offered it in gourd dippers to the passing men carrying their dusty weapons.

CHAPTER 29   Major Cortlandt did not delay his bullock teams, carrying the wounded, at Ned Styron's powder mill. He sent the carts on ahead and he and Sally stayed the night for supper with Ned and with his wife, Shelagh, who lifted her skirt and showed a well-carved hickory leg.

"Ned done it for me. Just to match the one you cut off, Doctor. Almost the same color too."

"Any pain from the stump, Shelagh?"

"Narry a hint! Could dance if there was the music for it."

Sally goggled her eyes. "You mean you *let* him cut off your leg?"

"Had to," said Ned as they sat down at the long table. "Was mortifying something unnatural. You lads attend to supper."

The staring boys bent over their bowls of deer-meat stew. Sally had flustered them rabbity; they had few visitors as pretty as she.

Ned Styron pulled on his beard and said a short grace and began to spoon up stew. "I don't aim to stay here. With the fort gone, they're coming this way. I've shipped all the powder I had on hand. I'm burning what's left and taking the family south to get away from here."

Shelagh sighed. "I never had any babies nohow but here, Ned. Don't seem natural to drop one any ole place."

Ned nodded. "She's quick with a whelp again, but don't worry, Shelagh girl, wherever it's born it will be a lusty Styron."

The mulatto woman nodded. "Doctor now, you don't think it will be borned with a leg shy, do you, because I'm short a flipper?"

David looked up from the bowl of deer stew. "No, Shelagh, and I guarantee it will not even come into the world with a wooden limb."

There was laughter and Sally joined in.

Ned shook his head. "It's a good thing the French are sending over powder. It will be a far time before I get back into the milling of it after I leave here. It's going to be hard to get supplies."

David nodded. "I'm going on to the other forts. You'd be doing myself and Captain Philipse a favor if you'll take Sally with you when you go south. Start her on her way to Albany."

"Be delighted to, Mrs. Philipse."

"Thank you."

"Boys," said Ned, "Get the wagons out and greased. Doctor, I've some local maize brew we might try."

That night and the next morning they tried a lot of it. It was strong and David added a keg of it to his medical supplies. He had two pack horses and a Scots boy called Robin MacBean, who had turned out to be a very good wound dresser. David left at noon with Robin for Fort Anne, but before he did he took Sally aside.

"Now my dear girl, you're properly married and a lady of a fine family, so what I'm going to say isn't needed, is it? But just remember you're most attractive to men and they'll want to pleasure you, which is flattering, but a lady doesn't accept the favors of anyone but her husband."

Sally lowered her eyes and nodded. "Yes, Cousin Davey. And please have Joe take good care of himself."

"I'll do that, Sally." He kissed her cheek; she was full of such a sweet reasonableness. He mounted and followed Robin and the two pack horses up the trail.

Sally stood watching the forest swallow them up and she went back to the house where Adam, one of the Styron sons, was tying up chests with lengths of rawhide ropes. His linsey-woolsey shirt was open all the way and his smooth brown skin rippled over well-developed muscles. Adam was well brought up and very polite.

"If you have a chest, Mrs. Philipse, I better rawhide it. The trail is mighty rough and bumpy."

"It's in my room, thank you."

Adam followed her in and walked around the little red leather chest. He smiled and he put his arms around Sally and rusked up her skirt behind and pinched her. She giggled and felt how strong he was. He didn't ask her and she didn't feel it was right to be fussy about such a simple thing. It was splendid the way he carried her, and on the corn husk pallet the sun caught his fine head as he bent over her. Sally had no thought that there could be anything wrong in something so satisfying and delightful as this young stud.

The British were appalled by the unending soggy green of the wilderness. Even with the help of the American Tories—Tarleton's Legion, Ferguson's American Riflemen, and others—the forests awed them. The casual, happy brutality of the Wyandots and Oneida Indians shocked them. The fife and drums kept up the "White Cockade" or Dr. Arne's "Rule Britannia" until the drumheads burst, and the white facings of the Forty-seventh of the Line turned grimy. The Swabian sergeants beat their men brutally with canes, and the hired soldiers from Rhetz, Specht, and Hanau left their dead in untamed woods of poplar and red oak.

General von Riedesel wiped his wide red face and looked at his fat, scarlet-faced Baroness. They sat under a cart among wild growths and drank wine and looked at their three small daughters, Lili, Putzi, and Marline with wonder as they blew on milkweed floss and thistledown.

"We shall get out all right, *Liebchen*," said the general.

"But of course," said the Baroness. "General Burgoyne will see to that."

The general called out on the general a few German army oaths and insults. "*Die Engländer haben keine Intelligenz*," and the Baroness poured the last of the kümmel into her only surviving wineglass. "Ach, the odious vermin the children have to live with."

The general got up and rebuckled his sword. "Keep them away from the troops. How are the lessons going? Marline! Come recite for thy papa."

The pink little girl with golden hair dressed in a blue cloth outfit made a curtsy and began. "*Gebraucht der Zeit! sie geht so schnell von hinnen; dock Ordnung lehrt euch Zeit gewinnen.*"

"Schiller," said the general. "A *great* German poet."

"Goethe," corrected the Baroness. Firing broke out on the left. "Of course, Goethe," said the general, running off to see what his men had blundered into. The Baroness got out her fine comb and began to hunt for nits in the golden hair of her children. Far ahead was heard the barking of Indian war cries.

"Ach," said the Baroness. There was no *Gemütlichkeit* here, and no *Katholische Kirche* to offer up a prayer for safety among these savages, where one could bow down before Him—so blond and Nordic—*lieber Gott,* on the cross under its letters: *Hic est Rex Iudaeorum.* Lili came up to her carrying a beetle.

"Mutti, may I keep it?"

"If you don't take it to bed."

The general, for all his attacks of rheumatism, was too involved in the fighting to take care of himself. It would be dreadful to be left a widow here. She decided to see if she could make over a campfire some smoked jowl and cabbage for the general's dinner.

Schiller—the general was so fond of Schiller. He had recited to her during their lusty courtship; "*Der Wahn ist kurz, die Reu ist lang.*" The firing was coming nearer to the cart. "*Kinder,* come on."

"What is it, Mutti?"

"Everyone into the cart," said the Baroness. She heard the sound of a horse and Peg Munday in a yellow riding habit came by on a bay gelding. "Good day, Baroness. How pretty you keep the children."

"Ach, Fräulein Peggy, it is not easy. Do you think the girls are in danger?"

"I don't think so. The Brunswickers are coming up to the line. You know I have a son in America."

"I didn't know. *Mein Herz,* tell me."

"Yes, in New York. I hope we get there soon. His father is an American."

"Too bad," said the Baroness, crushing a sphinx moth that had blundered into her.

"He's dead."

"Ah, well, in His bosom we all at last repose, *nein?* Children, everyone into the cart."

"Mutti, Putzi stepped on my beetle."

"You naughty girl."

Somewhere close cannon were going off. The women and children turned toward the sound and waited. The guns were fired again and Canadians passed the cart carrying hickory-helved axes in their hands.

Peg quieted her horse. "The Americans are cutting down trees across the trails to delay us." The guns continued to fire. Lili strained her little bladder.

Captain Jack Bounty's men in the Berkshire foothills could go no further. He called to Half Hand when they had camped for the night between two fallen trees.

"I want you to give me guides back to the British Army."

"What about the mission to meet Tory messengers?"

"You go on with your men. My soldiers are sick with flux and fever. I must take them back."

"Not much courage in English heart, is there?" Half Hand said, fingering the stiffening blond scalps he carried in his belt.

Captain Jack Bounty smiled. "*If* you don't give me guides to get back . . ." He took out his pistol and held it against the naked, shiny stomach of the Indian. "I intend to blow your lights and liver out right now. And if I don't get back, do you think the British paymaster will pay you for your scalps?"

The Indian showed worry. He chewed his lower lip and said, "It is not fear of pistol. It is the worth of many reward scalps we have and more we hope to get. I give you half the band as guides and hunters. I take the rest to the meeting place."

"You will send runners with a message to the Tories. You will guide them through the forests to the general."

"I will need all the rum in camp here."

"You will take *half* the rum, Half Hand. I want to start back in the morning. And no tricks. My men can still shoot."

Half Hand nodded and hunted his pipe. He was an involved savage and most cunning. Some foolish warriors might kill off these feeble lobsterbacks for their scalps. But a worthy chief would think of all the British gold to be earned. The interesting thought entered his mind: he could kill the entire group of Englishmen and sell their scalps—one head of hair is pretty much like another. Only it was worthless hair and short under their wigs. Besides, Captain Bounty and his detachment would be missed. Half Hand lit the pipe with a coal from the fire held by two sticks. He grunted. "You start back at sunbreak."

Captain Jack Bounty went over to his tattered, unshaved men. He now suspected smallpox among them but he did not tell that to an Indian. At hint of the disease, the savages would stampede and leave them here to die in these dank woods.

"Sergeant, prepare the men for a march tomorrow. Back to the main army."

"It will be slow, sir."

"We can't go on, and we can't stay here. All arms loaded, and no Indians to be permitted to touch a weapon of ours. The worst-palsied men can abandon their knapsacks and gear. Private Nordland worries me."

The old sergeant shook his head. "He's fagged out. A shirking, stealin' lyin' bugger, sir."

"Flog his fat arse when we get back."

Jack Bounty sat down and held his head in his hands. It was ringing and the dizziness only left him when he closed his eyes. He looked up at the sky. There was old Cassiopeia off to the left of the Pole Star.

Much to the east of the fighting armies Joe Philipse and his detachment were moving down a deer trail to the village called White Corners. The Berkshires were impressive and hard going. Silvester Hand, now a sergeant, looked about him with a pleased expression on his large weathered dial of a face.

"I grew up hereabouts, Captain. Good clean air, but the rocky fields sent me away to indent with the Schuylers as an iron worker."

"How do they feel about the war hereabouts?"

"A letter from me old sister Drusilla says they are all for the Continental Congress. She lives up near old Greylock. Highest mountain in the world."

"It's high, Silvester, but not *that* high. Ever hear of the Alps?"

Silvester shook his head and looked around him. "Can't say I have, Captain Philipse." He remembered the old unpainted church of the Dissenter Rollers among the blue oaks where all sang songs with a clapping of the hands. Sad songs, deep feeling songs, happy songs, and they danced and decked the church in green. Their neighbors thought them devils as they sang:

> "As it fell out upon a day
> Small rain from sky did fall.
> Our Saviour to his Mother said,
> Pray, may I play at ball?"

The odor of wild grape brought back memories of the time his uncle and he had gone into the village to buy seed. Uncle had a mad idea that year of cutting out the big trees and the brush in the sour field beyond his place and cutting off the tops of the apple trees and grafting sweet stock slips on them.

The wild, small apple of the swamp country is so bitter even trash folk can't chew them—but if you graft budwood clippings with good buds of sweet stock they will produce the good big fruit. It's the hard way to get a grove, a poor man's way, uncle said.

It was a foolish thing for an aging man and a boy no taller than the squirrel rifle to try. But all fall they cut brush and snaked out timber with the old Maud mule. They cut the wild trees way down, almost to the roots. Soon the tiny green shoots came up and they hoed dirt over them because the night frost was mean, and that year it was so cold they couldn't keep enough firewood around. Uncle and he on the double bucksaw just cut logs all day and split them into three sections and fed the stove. Every day dig up a hill around the wild apple shoots and see if the sap was still flowing green in them. In the spring, graft the budwood onto the growing shoots, tying it tight with twine, and then, sure enough, out of almost every bud eye there grew a new green shoot, this new one taking sour-root sap and growing into good sweet wood.

They had lived like animals for five years—weeding, fertilizing, trimming that grove, and burning bush. Then one year every head of green tree was filled with sweet fruit. A crop. They had a real grove, a mine of sweet fruit, and only aching backs and hard-shelled fingers told the price. Then, just as they were ready to pick, down came an early winter storm so cold the small seedlings burst apart, tore the wood to splinters as the sap froze in them, and the trees dropped their leaves. Next morning, wrapped in blankets, they crossed the fields. There was snow on the ground. Uncle pulled down a fruit and cut it in half with his frog sticker. The juice was just a solid ball of ice. They stood there sucking the sweet ice from cut skins, and then walked slowly back. The next day the thaw came and every fruit began to rot and the sap no longer ran up the tree trunks. Cut into a limb and it was cold and dark. Every tree limb was dead.

They sat there so sad even the hound-dogs were scared.

"What kin we do?" Aunt asked.

Uncle spat and shook his head. "Roots most likely might still be alive. We could cut down to 'em and start again and bud-graft some more. But I'm not agoin' to—no more. All them years workin', all them short rations we et, and every penny from the hens and the shoats put down in supplies. No sir-ee. To hell with it! To damn hell and damnation with it!" He got so mad he went out to the barn and cried on the mangy hide of the mule, his heart fit to break.

The voice of the captain broke the thread of Silvester Hand's memory. "What do they grow hereabouts?"

"If they can get apple trees to mature, they make a hard cyder. Freeze the core of water out of a barrel of it in a cold winter and the rest is prime hard. But it's a mean, rocky land."

They came into White Corners—a dozen unpainted houses—at dusk and found the militia officer, a tall thin man named Captain Wood, at the village inn.

"We've been feeling activity all around us. Scattered bands of Tories been sighted too, Captain Philipse."

"Why are they gathering?"

"Don't rightly know. Better bed down your men and I'll get some food for them."

"Do you have any scouts out?"

Captain Wood scratched his long shallow cheek. "We're recruitin', and mostly we use the scouts to bring down the detachments of Green Mountain Boys."

"You know a scout called Jack-Tom Swales?"

"Savage fellow, ain't he? Yes, he's been guiding when he's sober. Had a spell of drinkin' that settled him out from the war a mite."

Joe Philipse asked, "Hard cyder?"

"Yes, come in and try a tankard."

Jack-Tom and a dozen scouts reached White Corners around noon the next day, followed by two hundred newly enlisted Green Mountain men, mostly boys trailing the family hunting rifle.

Jack-Tom was pleased to see Joe Philipse. "Beelzebub, been some shady things up hereabouts. No, thank you kindly, I don't aim to take on any crackskull. And I'd advise you, Captain, treat that thar hard cyder with respect. It sure kicks like a Huron squaw with big feet."

Joe inspected his men and had them see to their powder. In the afternoon he sat in front of the inn and looked off into the thin warm air north of the town. Beyond it rose Mount Greylock, and damn, if it didn't look like the tallest mountain in the world. But Joe had seen the Alps on his Grand Tour, and they had said the Alps were the highest.

Jack-Tom sat on the steps, reclining almost on his spine, chewing on a sliver of wood cut from the porch support with his hunting knife.

"Soon as this shebang of a war is over this chile is goin' out beyond Kentuck' and Ohio. Find me a spot not even ever seen by no white folk. Git me a nice fat young Injun gal to wrassel down and raise me up a passel of breed kids. I got no use no more for this part of the country. Hell, no." He spat out some wood slivers. "More folk and their kin usin' the air; a man can't breathe no more."

A boy with tow-colored hair came riding a farm horse, riding wildly up the street to the inn. It was a young lad with a pot haircut, and he fell rather than dismounted, shouting, "There be a fight at White's farm! Four militiamen kilt fer sure."

"Easy, boy," said Jack-Tom. "You just suck air and swaller and tell us everythin'."

Joe nodded. "Who killed the militiamen?"

"Two fellas that wore Tory green. And there was an Indian with some fingers missing."

"How it happen?" asked Jack-Tom tossing aside the wood splinter.

"Ezra White, he farms out there near the mountain, and I work on the next farm, old Missus Harper's place. Whites settled in this part of the country way back."

Joe said, "Damn it boy, give us some facts. I'm looking for Tory agents."

"Well, I hear shootin' this mornin' from White's farm, and I knowed he's got a meetin' of militiamen from the crossroads, three of 'em and hisself, they meet twice a week and drill, hayfoot strawfoot."

Jack-Tom stood up. "We'll never get no sense from this boy."

"I hear shootin' and I run over and this Indian—I'm behind the big barberry hedge—this Indian with only part of a hand, and a big man, and a stocky round man both in green, they're shootin' down Ezra and the other militiamen."

"Seems senseless," said Jack-Tom.

"Ezra has a lot of big dogs and they musta attacked the strangers. The slaves in the field they hid out and wouldn't move so I come into town on Missus Harper's plough horse."

Joe began to shout his sergeant, Silvester Hand, out of the inn. Jack-Tom went to see if the scouts were sober. Joe asked the farm boy, "How far is it to the White house?"

"Come the back road or the main road? Back road she be eight miles. You'll find good ridin' horses in the inn yard here."

The soldiers and the scouts left the village in half an hour and several riders were sent out to alarm the countryside. Joe, Silvester Hand, and Jack-Tom, well-mounted on local stock, kept urging the soldiers on. Ahead the scouts were moving and over all the activity the shape of Mount Greylock looked calmly down, Joe thought, with the indifferent stare of Nature.

CHAPTER 30   The farm boy, excited to silence, rode by Joe's side and held the big pistol someone had given him across his saddle. Twice Joe asked him to point it the other way.

As they moved toward the scene of the reported slaughter, Joe remembered a verse David Cortlandt often repeated:

> All, all of a piece throughout!
> Thy Chase has a Beast in View;
> Thy wars brought nothing about;
> Thy lovers were all untrue.
> 'Tis well an Old Age is out,
> And time to begin a New. . . .

He didn't care for the bit about "Thy lovers were all untrue." Sally had been behaving very well.

The land rose and the riders and militia moved on. Joe Philipse rode, neither pleased nor annoyed now as the Americans moved upward over jarring ruts. The sun was very high and the land was checkered with sparse cultivation.

The slaughter at White's farm had begun in a kind of bloody comedy of errors. Half Hand the day before had left his band of warriors camped under tall trees while he had gone ahead along to meet the Tory messengers at a loyalist farm near White Corners. There he had met Colonel Lemon and his companion, Sergeant Bloodbetter, a large and rather silent man who looked to Colonel Lemon for orders—almost to do his thinking for him.

Colonel Lemon had not been impressed by Half Hand. "Where is the escort of British soldiers? It was promised."

"They take much sick. They go back to the general. I have Indian scouts waiting for us up past the mountain. You want to come to general? You come. You don't want to come, I go."

Colonel Lemon felt the heavy wad of thin paper sheets he carried sewn up in an outside pocket. The damn list of Tories was like a burden of lead on him. Only a folly-filled British general would demand it be brought to him through the wilderness. And what if the English didn't drive through to New York and end the war? If the list fell into American hands, black disaster would overtake the loyalist world.

"All right, we'll start in the morning. Sergeant, charge your rifle."

"Yes, Colonel."

They were dressed in faded green, and the next morning, at a distance, could be taken for hunters. Following Half Hand through the fields and wooded slopes, it seemed to Colonel Lemon this was the easy part of their journey. And then farmer White's chained-up dogs had scented them. The militiamen had gone for their rifles along the fence and the bloody slaughter of the Americans began.

The survivors fell back to the house. One reached for his pistol, and the rifle of the sergeant took him in the ribs like firing into a barbecued side of steer. Calm, arid, and precise, Half Hand dropped to one knee and began to reload.

Two unwounded men grabbed their screaming comrade. They started across the yard. Colonel Lemon finished off the wounded man, the slug catching him in the buttocks and spreading out to mess up his torso. The men dropped the butchered shape and one turned back to fire. He never had a chance. Half Hand was a dead shot. The man went down with a red spray replacing his throat, and Half Hand ran forward as the last survivor escaped in blubbering fear. Sergeant Bloodbetter dropped to one knee at fifteen feet.

"Christ, don't!" shouted the one militiaman. He turned, opened his arms wide, and walked slowly toward the kneeling man, shouting pleas for leniency. The dogs stopped, barked, and snarled deep in their throats.

"Listen," said the militiaman.

The shot caught him under the breastbone. He died.

The field hands did not dare approach too close to the farm house. Colonel Lemon walked around the bodies, his rifle ready. Then he turned to the house. The sergeant looked at the first man killed. Another lay very still, unconscious, bleeding. The dogs now made no sounds.

Colonel Lemon said, "We'd better move on."

One of the field slaves, a Negro, started across the fields. Sergeant Bloodbetter reloaded and got him from an upper window at a hundred yards. Right through both thighs. The Negro fell down and lay there. He wasn't badly hit, but the rest of his life he would lumber awkwardly.

After that the field slaves stood beyond the pasture, not daring to move, holding whispered conclave among themselves. The Tories and the Indian left at eleven, loaded with guns and bullet belts and many packs. They caught horses, mounted, and galloped off shouting something the field hands couldn't make out. The sun went higher.

The wounded man recovered consciousness and began to scream, but the field slaves were too frightened to come near him. The Indian and Tories were now out of sight on the upper trail. The wounded man told a fragment of his story and died.

The sun stood at high noon, balanced in the brass heat of the day as Joe Philipse, Jack-Tom, and the militia came there and stared down at the bodies. Soldiers and scouts were tactfully anxious, throwing glances over their shoulders at the hills.

Joe looked away from the huddled shapes and he, too, eyed the ridges which militia were climbing, their rifles held carefully before them, the dogs unchained or on leashes sniffing oak and bush. The hunt was under way. High in the sun a hawk rested on blue wings as it watched the thickets for smaller game.

Joe said, "Let's join 'em, Jack-Tom."

No one caught any sign of the killers. The mounted men had ridden up Big Bend Brook and swum their horses across the sandy shallows of Big Pine. At four the steeds were spitting foam.

Jack-Tom slid off his horse, "I aim to walk."

Colonel Lemon and his two companions came into the court-yard of Pine Tree Inn at about this time. The innkeeper, an old man with a twisted nose and a slight limp, gave them food and water, and brought a side of bacon from the spring house. He had one horse.

"You be Americans or Tories?" he asked.

Half Hand pushed the barrel of a rifle up and drilled the old man just below his ear. He lived for two hours before he was found by Jack-Tom's scouts. The killers were by then miles away, clanging up and up toward the tall firs.

Colonel Lemon grew daring as darkness fell. He circled back down-trail and hunted a blacksmith, having found that the horse, a stallion, had lost a shoe. Ben North at Black Corner fitted a new shoe and took two silver coins for it, but he didn't say a word to Colonel Lemon, whose eyes almost dared the man standing at the bellows to comment.

The men moved on. In the events of that day the smith was the only man they could have killed or mangled whom they spared.

Militia hunting strays heard the sound of the stolen horse crossing the wooden bridge and hurried forward. A blast of shot stopped them. They fell into the dust but none were very much harmed. That was the last anyone saw of the killers that day.

Joe and the scouts camped out in a hay shelter on the peak of Rock Point where the early hill hay was stored.

Colonel Lemon stood under a spreading butternut tree, the stallion tied to a lower branch. He faced the Indian and the sergeant.

"It's important what I have on me gets to the general, and that the Americans don't get it."

"Only scalps worth carrying," said Half Hand.

"The horse can carry two men, he's a powerful brute. Sergeant, I'm taking the Indian up behind me as a guide and heading west. You stay behind and draw their fire."

"Yes, Colonel."

"When they see you, you lead them north."

The Indian looked at the ground. It was none of his business, this sacrificing of the sergeant. He had little use for men who obeyed orders—this kind of orders. The sergeant seemed indifferent. He opened his bullet pouch and began to examine his rifle balls.

Colonel Lemon fingered again through the lining the papers sewed inside his jacket. "Give us a few hours, then you slip away west and join us on the river."

"I tell Indians and scouts you coming, Sergeant," Half Hand said with a smirk, as if he knew how foolish it was to hope the sergeant would get through. The soldier began to load carefully, wrapping his rifle ball in a small square of oiled linen and sending it down the barrel with a smooth, gentle shove of his oak ramrod.

"If I get away, Colonel, I'll make west for the river. Any other orders?"

Colonel Lemon shook his head and mounted. He held out his hand for the Indian to mount behind him, but Half Hand leaped up and, unaided, grasped Colonel Lemon around the body. The Indian kicked the stallion savagely in the ribs and the last the sergeant saw of them was the horse running up the trail.

Ten miles away in a hay barn Joe Philipse and Jack-Tom were waiting for morning to come. They lay in the hay, listening, but heard nothing but owls, the creaking of tree branches, and the bark of dogs. Joe bunched up against Jack-Tom and twice he awoke and felt Jack-Tom stir in his sleep, muttering something he could not understand. Once Joe went out for a drink of well water from a rusty iron dipper. The night sky was excessively chaste. The water was ice-cold.

It was very still. The militia slept, the wind whispered in the ridges, and there was no moon—only a milk-white mist over the sharp crags.

Dawn was dry, inscrutable, tense. Then the sun came and burned the day into life. It etched the militiamen rising all around. The hills were filling with men. Deer hunters, soldiers, scouts, patch-pants, hangers-on, avenging relatives, even scowling, fresh-made orphans.

It was interesting to Joe to see how eager all the people were to get on with the hunt. They ate a farm breakfast—thick bread and butter, bacon and fried eggs, a parched acorn coffee—and drank rum.

Jack-Tom picked up a wedge of bread and looked about ahead of him into the dark, cumbersome mountainside.

"Damn! Look at the militia. You'd think they were goin' to get free land instead of their heads shot off. I tell you there's goin' to be more killin'. Half Hand is a dead shot. Can hit coins at two hundred yards."

Joe looked up at the soft russet and gray growths on the hills, "Think they'll get them alive? We'll catch 'em?"

"We kin try."

The hunt went higher into the rosy-gold and indigo silhouette of the mountain, the searchers walking now, alert and watchful of all dark clearings. The hours passed with not a sight of the hunted. Jack-Tom discovered the enemy had separated. "We've been trailin' only *one* man all day."

"We'll go on," said Joe. "Send back word for the men below to look for where we lost the other two."

They were very high—almost up to the last tall pine. Above were enormous stones.

Signal shots stirred across the crags at dawn. The body of the stallion was found at Devil Ridge, fifteen miles to the west—his fractured leg doubled back. Colonel Lemon had shot the horse and gone on.

The dogs picked up Sergeant Bloodbetter's scent and followed, their wet noses protruding bleakly, their throats rasping.

Ahead Joe heard the yapping of the dogs. Then suddenly shots, close together, like chain thunder. All moved forward.

The trail dipped and went down about fifty feet before it rose again between huge rocks shaped like broken stars. Joe could see the dip and then the bodies of some of the dogs lying on the trail. A furiously angry farmer with an armful of dog gear ran forward, cursing, and then something snapped and the dog handler lay in the trail, his thigh shattered.

The militia moved down behind a ridge of small stones. One scout rubbed his swollen neck glands and shouted from his red face in exasperated tones, "Come on out—you ain't got a chance."

An echo answered. The dog handler moaned and rolled about in agony. Joe shouted, perplexed, violently earnest.

"You haven't got a chance."

Suddenly, overhead, a voice, derisive and cold, said, "I'll count three. Then I'll shoot."

Jack-Tom said low, "Draw him out to talk. I'll locate him."

"Blasted Yankees—come and get us."

Joe said, "That's Sergeant Bloodbetter, Colonel Lemon's man."

Everyone looked up. Balanced on an overhanging rock stood the sergeant, hatless, holding his rifle, aimed low.

Joe walked forward to where the dog handler moaned. He was very calm and grave—not hurrying, just moving slowly forward.

"Come down. It isn't any use—all this."

"Don't worry," said the sergeant taking a long breath. "A man can only take so much pushing about."

"Come down. We'll not harm you. We'll . . ."

There was a short, sharp bark of the rifle. A militiaman moving forward very skillfully had been trying to flank the sergeant by climbing a higher rock. The sergeant had turned and fired, and almost before the sound of the shot had stopped resounding from the rocks, the big body of the militiaman fell and seemed to collapse like a falling tent.

Jack-Tom ran forward to the body and saw there was a small hole over the right eye. A blue foam came from it. No blood. The other eye was open and was staring into the direct rays of the sun.

The soldiers went forward and picked up the dog handler. His thigh bone stuck out of his flesh like a fragment of white ivory. He was still alive.

Sergeant Bloodbetter killed two more dogs that day and blew the arm off a woodcutter who refused to come along with him and cook for him.

Reports from the west were that there was no sign of Half Hand and Colonel Lemon.

That night it was colder. Joe's party slept in their capes and some blankets, close together in the open. When the full darkness came they lay listening to the clatter of the growing hunt. Pitch-pine flares dotted the mountainside. Fires burned until a rifle ball came out of the darkness and shattered against a rock. The pursuers slept. But there were so many dogs now that sleep came only in fits.

Sergeant Bloodbetter—alone—fighting a rear-guard action, killed his last man the next day.

All day he had been creeping higher up the wild rock lands. The militia with fresh dogs followed him. He had cut himself down to only what he could carry and travel with. He had discarded all gear but the rifle, a blanket, a bit of dried meat, and a canteen of water. The trails of hunted and hunters often paralleled each other.

Militiamen slipped and cursed but no longer talked much. There was an acid, sweaty scent to the men and Joe sensed an almost distilled odor of hurry and hate and desire to kill coming from their skins. Their tongues were coated, their eyeballs were yellow, and they drank raw whiskey and tore food—gulped, swallowed, and went on.

Rock Castle Peak was a sheer wall. It leaped up—no one had ever climbed it, a farmer told Jack-Tom. Beyond it lay rolling hills leading to a wild forest. Once over the Castle the sergeant would be able to make a bolt for it to the west. Word was shouted down to send men up from the other side. It appeared that the game was lost.

At four o'clock across a thousand feet of space, the tiny figure of the sergeant appeared moving slowly up the steep face of the Castle, a small dark blot on the silver and iridescent rocks.

Through a strong spyglass he could be seen with a rifle and a small game bag hanging from him, as he picked his way by toes and fingers up, up, along the wall.

The day would be dying soon, the blue sky reflected from the steep hills to the north. Shadows extended quickly to blot out the remaining light. A phosphorescent twilight began to finish the day.

The militia fired, but the Castle was out of range. It was nearly a deep blue dusk when they got into range. Finding a level area, Sergeant Bloodbetter ran ahead, bent over, running fast, and soon was out of range—and nearly free. Just three hundred feet—a militia-man figured—stood between him and freedom.

Joe shouted, "Somebody get within range."

A party of scouts started across a rock field to flank the Castle. There was a sense of taut hope and a feeling of impending calamity in conflict.

Joe Philipse was nearly done in. The high air, the full throat-stabbing struggle to keep moving, were too much for him. It was all he could do to push on ahead with the flanking party.

They moved slowly, slipping on shale—then descended and went creeping along. The last faint tone of the sun touched the top of the Castle. They could see the sergeant closer—steadily climbing like a human fly, up, up, across a face of stone—the hardest patch he had struck yet. Always moving. At times the wall seemed to overhang him, force him out into space until to Joe's tired eyes he seemed to hang only by his fingers, his heels kicking free. Always he found something to cling to, to haul himself in to safety by and go on climbing. The high place gave Joe a gagging feeling of headachy intoxication.

Through the spyglass he could see the dark red face. It was no longer wild. No longer angry. Sergeant Bloodbetter was smiling. Enjoying the chase. And slowly climbing.

Then the sergeant turned and saw Joe and Jack-Tom and two scouts, about two hundred yards from him, separated by a broken field of great stones. The scouts were panting, too breath-broken to steady their rifles and aim well. Someone fired and missed, knocking off a stone shard above the sergeant's head. Joe shouted, "Take careful aim!" and listened to the echoes of the walloping meter of his voice.

The sergeant maintained his calm. Joe never took his spyglass off him. Bloodbetter had found a projecting stone, tested it with his weight, found it held, and tossed his legs in a grip around it and pulled the rifle from his shoulders. He aimed.

The light was bad. All stood somewhat protected by broken stone. The sergeant leveled off and Joe saw his teeth snap together as he pressed the trigger. Behind Joe someone made a little moaning sound. A body rolled and, still rolling harmlessly as if it were a ball in a child's game, bumped from stone to stone and fell away into darkness.

The sergeant reloaded and aimed again. Joe saw him in the gathering darkness shift his position, twist his legs in a new hold. Then the rifle barrel banged against the granite wall and fell from his red hand. He made one lunge to recover it, failed, and the rifle fell swiftly away from him. He was unarmed. He laughed; mirth came from his big throat.

A voice floated across, malignantly hostile. "Go to hell, you bloody Yankees."

The scouts were all firing now, their gun barrels held steady against the big stones. Joe held up the spyglass. It was hard to see in the fast falling darkness.

The shots were coming closer to the sergeant. The last shred of day left the granite wall. Darkness confused the hunters. It looked as if Sergeant Bloodbetter had made it. He was fifty feet from the top of the wall. The way was the hardest yet, but he moved confidently on.

At ten feet from the top the going was very easy, broken up into huge cracks. The sergeant pulled himself erect and thumbed his fingers to his nose. "Ya can go kiss my jolly arse!" Behind, they were still firing blindly, the slugs making plaintive musical sounds.

The sergeant wriggled his fingers. Jack-Tom, after a careful loading, wet his rifle sight with a finger and took careful aim and fired. "I got some extra powder in her." The sergeant staggered, fell, recovered. Bent way over as if ill. Then he began to struggle up the cliff. He stopped, slowly turned, dropped to his knees and began to slide.

He held tight in a truculent attitude to a projecting stone. Then, calmly and with a certain dignity, he pulled himself erect and leaped forward into space.

All saw the body fall in a long, graceful arc.

It took a long time falling. Joe stood still and watched. When it had fallen halfway down the mountainside, complete darkness swallowed it.

The militia below was firing shots at the end of the hunt.

The scouts went back down to a sheep farm halfway down the mountain. It was too dark to try to descend all the way. A fire burned among the stones of the farm fireplace. They could hear the sheep outside squeechily forming cuds in steadily chewing jaws.

Jack-Tom drank some of the sheep farmer's whiskey and nodded his head. "That's the way to die you know, Captain. In yer prime, full of jisum, with the fat on yer ribs and a light in yer eye. You can have the easy dyin', and the old bones and the doctors tellin' lies about you. Animals die best—in the open, to feed each other. Who the hell is hidin' that jug?"

No one, Joe saw, was really elated at the result of the hunt.

Colonel Culbly and Half Hand got away and reached the British main force.

BOOK VIII

Table in the Wilderness

CHAPTER 31   The British, all banners flying, would not face up to the hardships ahead. General Burgoyne entertained and wrote in an octavo volume: "There is an eternal spiral, exquisite and intangible, a kind of copious incantation that one feels among trees." His officers felt this warfare was a test, a part of one's martial career before one grew portly and was given something like the governorship of an exotic West Indies island, shipped out east, or even landed in Whitehall at a Queen Anne desk. Men act briskly, Lord Alban observed to Peg, in the pursuit of what they may never attain.

Ensign O'Crump took Peg and Mrs. Lewis—in search of fortune-telling—to the Indian camp, and one of the Canadian habitants with the expedition translated what an old Tuscarora crone said were the true signs of the seasons. "She say, you see much fat squirrels, that means the snow, much cold. When there is fuzzy sumac plants, it be damn cold winds coming. And when the leaves they are much brittle, then in January it will be all ice. Starry nights, and the moon when she sit in blue sky, that is the time for fine, oh so very good weather. She say you give her much money. *Cela est selon.*"

Ensign O'Crump dropped some copper coins into the dirty hand. "She is so much great fortune teller," said the Canadian. "She do the looking into the future things."

Mrs. Lewis nodded. "Can she predict the results of this expedition?"

The Canadian jabbered at the old Indian woman, who looked with cloudy eyes at Mrs. Lewis and then began to speak in a shrill voice.

Peg asked, "What billingsgate is she saying?"

The Canadian shook his head and avoided their glances. "She talk too much. I not catch him all. By Jim, but very funny." He looked at Mrs. Lewis and leered. "Indian mind very dirty. Excuse me, *c'est à dire* . . ." The old Indian wrinkled her thin lips in a grin and held out a hand for coins.

Peg shook her head. "I'm sure she said we're sluts who will end up with Indian lovers."

"How revolting," said Mrs. Lewis. "So greasy."

In picnic style the British waited. At a table set in the wilderness the general entertained. The ladies went often to see the Indian ceremonies, and once just avoided seeing the burning alive of several American prisoners. The general was, he admitted, having trouble getting the savages to refrain from making sport of their victims, such as removing vital organs skillfully while the subject's feet charred away in glowing beds of charcoal.

The Americans, slowly retreating, were still cutting down great trees to bar the way. Forest giants tumbled across all trails and Major General Schuyler closed all the roads for miles through the woods. Creeks and marshes bogged the English guns, horses died strangling in quicksand. Forty burned-out bridges, Lord Alban reported, had to be replaced. The picnic days were soon over. The troops toiled with axe and saw, hardwood barriers were cut through, and oxen snaked heavy butts of trees away to clear the road for the cart of wine and the clothes of the women, and all the details of the pageantry with which the general made war.

The carts of green timber fell apart, just as Lord Alban had said they would. The army was down to two days' provisions. Tents and baggage were being abandoned. Peg and Mrs. Lewis sorted and re-sorted their finery and left a goodly part of their fashionable London wardrobe to bedeck the naked buttocks of the gleeful Indians. Only a hundred of the carts could still move, and of the ox wagons only twenty were reasonably whole. Boats were brought overland; it took six horses a full day to move a boat down from Ticonderoga. It began to rain. The weather increased in fury. Everything became soggy; fungus and mold formed. Guns rusted. Muskets would not fire. Transport was hard to get. Horses and oxen could not be found to replace those that died of burst hearts, straining under fearful whippings to move supplies and ammunition up to the waiting army standing in solitary misery in the sodden forests. The drive forward—in desperate effort—began again. On the twenty-ninth of July the British forces had broken through to the east bank of the Hudson River and stood on a rise a mile south of Fort Edward. The shine and the neatness were worn out of them.

Captain Jack Bounty, on inspection of pickets, sat a thin horse and watched the rain beat in leaden fury on the river. Captain Corky rode up to him on a steaming piebald pony. "Silly weather for a war."

"Corky, the whole business is foolish. What do we get out of it?"

"You got a captaincy at least, my boyo. I lack the coin and influence even for that."

"Anything to eat?"

"We have what they call hereabout a buck coon and a stud possum on the coals. I'm willing to risk it if you are."

"Anything you can bite through is food."

The two captains rode their damp horses back to the leaking shelter of a tall pitch-pole pine tree. Several sooty soldiers were tending a fire that gave off much smoke and little flame. Two small spitted cadavers were turning over the indifferent fire. The officers dismounted and were handed fragments of the seared creatures laid on large leaves. With the aid of jackknives they ate and chewed and spat out small bones.

"Jack, bucko, what do you think?"

"I don't dare think. The whole thing is too fouled, Corky. I imagine it's all very cleverly planned."

"Even so, the Americans are running before us."

"They have to stop soon, Corky, and when they do they'll have lots of aid. We don't seem to be getting help. Bad choice, this place."

"We could have gone to serve in Injah, you know. We picked this."

Jack spat out a joint of possum. "Ireland garrison duty was open."

"Fat Catholic tail. Soft on the bone and running to the priests to confess it . . . but doin' it first. My native land, you know, Jack."

"Why you leave, Corky?"

"Younger son of a run-down fox hunting family. Pat and Mike tenants were all barefooted, eating the nose off the teakettle. Six brothers we were, on unpaid horses. The Ould Man, a lecher he was—called by all Himself, repopulating the entire county. And to face it, boyo, there was the matter of the cards I played and the money I owed."

"We should have picked India."

"Injah, yes. You can't knock Americans about as easy as the wogs."

An old white man dressed as an Indian came up under the trees, painted and stinking of grease, the rain falling on his naked hide. He was followed by a Tory officer wrapped in a cape.

"My dear friends," said the old Frenchmen. "This officer, Colonel Lemon, has been looking for you. You have food?"

"Varmints," said Captain Corky. "But you're welcome to a rib or leg. Not a blasted drop to drink."

Colonel Lemon put his cold hands out to the fire and accepted a hind leg. "I expected to find British supply trains up here."

The old man—his nakedness not affected by rain and cold— snorted and broke off a bit of roast coon. "The trees do not bow down to British hopes, eh?"

Colonel Lemon chewed and nodded. "I regret, Captain Bounty, we did not meet as planned. I lost a fine sergeant. But the Indian Half Hand got me through."

Jack Bounty laughed. "What did it cost? He's worse at bargaining than a Greek."

The old man smeared his facial war paint and threw down the greasy bone in his hand. He wiped himself on his long gray hair. "I must go now. We are raiding the settlements to the south."

When he was gone, Corky said, "A naked wet old devil—mad, most likely."

Jack Bounty shook his head. "He isn't human. A kind of filthy animal, running with the savages, torturing women, taking scalps. Tell me, Colonel, you're an American, why are you on our side?"

"I'm loyal to the king."

Captain Corky made an impolite digestive noise. "Aye, George the Three, Gaud bless 'im."

Jack Bounty stared into the fire. "It's a wild place, but when you see the big rivers you sense what it can be and how powerful must be the appeal to be free here."

Colonel Lemon shook his head. "I never expected a British officer to talk like this. I'd like to see the general again to go over the lists I delivered, but I can't get into General Burgoyne's tent."

Captain Corky nodded. "Me ould general used to say, 'Corky,

women who have excelled in wit have failed in chastity.' General
Burgoyne is entertaining his harem."

Captain Jack Bounty looked up at the dripping branches. "I'll
get you through to the general."

"Shall I save the varmints" asked Captain Corky, looking into the
fire.

"Lord no, Corky. We'd have to eat more of them if you did. I've
been promised a Canadian goose."

Colonel Lemon followed the young English officer along a muddy
trail to a group of wet tents. Jack Bounty got them both past the
soldiers on guard. The rain-shiny canvas had weathered to a dirty
brown. The attempts to provide a floor of cut and trimmed saplings
had not kept out the mud. Lord Alban said he'd try and get Colonel Lemon in to the general. "And Jack, be a good sort and go
and cheer up Peg. She's brooding. We've gotten dreadful colds."

He found Peg seated on a trunk, watching a small stream of dirty
water move through the tent. "Hello Jack, it's good to see an old
face."

"An aging youth's face, soggy, not old."

"You know what I mean." She blew her nose. "Got a bottle of
something?"

"No. I hear the general has a few carts of it left."

"He's not sharing it out. Jack, I've decided to break with Lord
Alban. Oh, he's a wonderful boy. But sickly as he is he needs a
dull wife. Being Goodie-nurse with the physic pot is not my style. I
want to live respectable when I find my son."

"Do you now, Peggy? I told you I ran into Davey Cortlandt,
who said Dan is with his grandfather. I hear he's a major now with
the Americans. Not the grandfather—Davey."

Peg nodded and rubbed her chilled hands together and wrinkled
her reddened nose. "Davey was a delight. A proper delight. I may
settle here, Jack. After all I married into the colonies, didn't I?"

"Quite true," said Jack, and felt his leaking boots fill with water.

The British were unaware of it, but the Americans were in a dangerous condition. They had been overwhelmed; their militia had not
held, and there was muttering and crying out of blame in high
places. Congress looked for whipping boys. Fat mouths pointed the
finger at the generals in the field. None of this came to General

Burgoyne. He thought he still faced a foe prepared and waiting. General Washington, occupied in New Jersey, was having troubles. Congress was listening to General Gates, who felt he should replace General Washington and take over the war. John Adams was at the moment against Washington. Worst of all, the Massachusetts regiments deserted to a man, pulling out of the line and going home for the fall harvest. Intrigue and alarms rent the American cause as cumulus clouds and thunderheads hung over the wilderness.

General Washington kept his head. He saw that the passes in the Hudson highlands must be seized, before the British got there. He issued orders to that effect and sent General Benedict Arnold to aid Major General Schuyler. Arnold was the best field general of the war, a powerful personality with a surging vitality, tremendous drive, and a born ability to command and size up a field of battle. Many political claws were attempting to pull him down. Unlike Washington, he could not ignore spite and intrigue. Sensing perfidy and ingratitude, Arnold was beginning to resent those who did not fight but played the filthy game of politics in Congress with supplies and with posts of command. Acids of rage filled General Arnold as he saw the war effort hampered. In dark moods he began to think of the end result of all this—first to the new nation and then to Benedict Arnold. He drank a great deal and wondered if the war was lost.

But General William Howe had no intention of moving on Albany to aid Burgoyne. He wanted to seize Philadelphia. What did a wilderness, all maze and labyrinth of trees, matter when the capital of the stiff-necked rebels, Philadelphia, could be taken? Sir William was city-prone in his thinking. He too was burdened with a mistress and her train, with a court of sporting officers and their camp followers. Philadelphia seemed the place to winter and orgy, not those northern freezing forests. General Burgoyne could take care of himself and march down the Hudson to New York unaided.

General Burgoyne and his insubstantial pageant were in grave trouble. Supplies were his dominant problem. He needed horses to mount his German dragoons. So far they had walked to the war in their great clumsy boots. He needed draft animals to pull his remaining carts and wagons. Perplexed, he decided to send a raid to the Connecticut River country for the much-needed cattle and horses. He was advised by Colonel Lemon, "These folk are mostly loyal to the Crown, General. The local population will arm and join our standards."

"You seem very sure, Colonel Lemon."

"That countryside is Tory, mainly. I vow it."

"Very well. We raid there and raise up the loyal population."

On the ninth of August Lieutenant General Baum, tall, catatonic, sorrowful, who could not speak a word of English—*Das Beste ist gut genug*—was named to command the raid, with Colonel Lemon's newly organized Tory group to scout ahead of him. It was rumored that there were large stocks of horses and cattle at Bennington, thirty miles southeast of Fort Edward. It was a strong force for such a raid. Three hundred Germans, some gunners and their cannon, and a mixed lot of three hundred made up of Colonel Lemon's Tories, Canadians, and Indians.

The German took his time; it was like a walking tour, he felt, in the Schwartzwald back home. The Indians ran ahead, cutting throats, raping and burning, and to the Germans' horror not capturing the cattle *but* slaughtering them for their cow bells! Bells which gave him a headache when the savages came back to camp ringing brass and displaying American scalps.

Before Bennington General Baum found the Americans gathered behind every wall, every barn. General Baum sent back to beg for reinforcements. Five hundred German dragoons and a few cannon started out to help him, bogging down in flooded rain forests. General Baum stopped at the Walloomsac River facing Bennington, entrenched himself in the mud, and waited.

Meanwhile the Americans gathered in the farmers—fifteen hundred of them—and marched into Bennington. The Germans thought they were men intended for Colonel Lemon's Tory forces, or loyalists that wanted to join up. General Baum did not fire on them.

Captain Joe Philipse was active with the farmers in Bennington. He helped put them into position and plan the defense. The local militia leader, Colonel Stark, was not for defense. Rugged, trigger-tempered, and firm, he shouted for all to hear.

"We want to drive them away, and do it quickly!"

"I understand, but these are trained Germans. With cannon."

"Don't matter, Captain Philipse."

"Will you men fight on in face of volleys by trained European infantry?"

"Don't see why not. And a lot more Green Mountain Boys are marching to join up."

"We'd better wait for them."

"We'll fight *now*."

"Very well, Colonel Stark. You're in command."

"I've been up against their General Gage at Bunker Hill. And in the Seven Years' War I soldiered with Abercromby and Rodgers."

"I bow to your rank and position, sir. I'll go and place my men."

Joe rode down the Walloomsac road among fox sparrows feeding on late wild berries, and found Jack-Tom and Silvester Hand among Colonel Stark's men preparing to attack. Jack-Tom rubbed his shaved scalp, fingered his fringe of corn-colored whiskers, and said, "There are, I hear, Green Mountain Boys due soon, Captain."

"I hope so. The Germans have cannon. Keep our men here."

Joe rode back and he and Colonel Stark with two other local officers laid out the plan for attack. Joe felt if it worked it was a splendid plan, and if it didn't it wasn't such a good idea. He had found out that in war success is everything. And brilliant planning on a map was merely a ritual in a game often really decided by accident. He chose to join the attack with his men attached to the central column. Joe thought of Sally, of his pistol priming, and rode out at the head of his men to take up advance positions. The Germans were beginning to fire from the muddy fields and woods where they lay in camp behind damp piles of freshly turned-up earth.

The Americans were divided into three columns, one to attack in front, the others to go around the flanks and take the British and Germans from the rear. It was a hot and heavy march for the flanking columns. General Baum came awake to his poor position when all his Indians ran off, *clanging* their cow bells. Rain and lightning, great rolling chords of thunder filled the battlefield as the Americans attacked. It was a desperate struggle.

The camp fell apart, was torn up. The Germans broke, Canadians and loyalists leading the rout, with Colonel Lemon screaming in protest. The Americans pursued for miles, slaughtering Germans; Jack-Tom's men knifing Canadians, taking many prisoners, all muddy and confused. Joe Philipse tried to get order among the cheering Americans. As he feared, the British reinforcements, stuck in the mud six miles from Bennington, came up at the sound of firing and found the victorious Americans looting the German camp. The British drove the Americans from the camp but the long-expected battalion of Green Mountain Boys suddenly appeared, with Joe at their head, and the British fell back as darkness came down under the dripping trees. Joe kept the Americans alert for a counterattack.

The German commander was mortally wounded. Baum died with his face in the mud, his forces scattering around him. Colonel Stark counted close to six hundred dead. The American losses stood at thirty.

Colonel Lemon rode to inform the general of the defeat.

General Burgoyne took the news of the battle seriously. The Americans were gathering around him too, from farms and shops, from barns and crossroads.

"They can fight," he said. "They could defeat the best Europe put against them."

Lord Alban said, "Sir, you are short of everything. Should you burn the boats, should you stay?"

"Send dispatches back to England to the War Office, blaming Howe and the damned attack on Philadelphia for my present position."

He wrote them himself in a dripping tent. Neatly he worded them, always the stylist, even in the rain beating on the canvas, with Mrs. Lewis and Peg bent under blue capes over a smoking fire, and wild hares for dinner. "I little foresaw that I was to be left to pursue my way through such a tract of country and hosts of foes, without any co-operation from New York."

Lord Alban came in wearing an oiled linen sheet over his uniform. He was feeling some twinges of pain in his right toe. Gout in the wilderness was a bit of too much.

The late corn was in tassel, crushed mint and horse-balm weed flavored the wet forests. Major General Schuyler and General Arnold sat in a leaking hunter's cabin of bark and poles while around them in the rain and storm the Americans re-formed under new discipline as they gathered strength with the news of the victory in Bennington. General Arnold, seated on a log, was drinking, having taken a fresh bottle from his saddlebags on the ground. Major General Schuyler accepted a few pulls on the bottle, but Arnold managed to consume most of it as they stared through the doorless opening into the gray bowl of lead that was the rainy world outside.

"We're out-foxed, outwitted. It's that fat pig Gates that's done us in."

Major General Schuyler looked at the general. "It doesn't matter. I think we can squeeze Johnny Englishman to cry surrender."

"Not with fat-gut Gates—as mean and greedy a face as I've seen —whispering in Congress, trying to replace General Washington. It's enough, sir, to give a man horse-croup."

"Washington is a Virginian fox, General Arnold, and Gates is just a fat shoat to him."

Major David Cortlandt came in through the hut opening, wearing a canvas wagon cover as a cape. It had not done much protecting of his worn uniform. "Gentlemen, if this weather is as harmful to the British as to us, I pity all those wonderful London tailored uniforms and well-bred limbs. My farriers, bone setters, and cow surgeons could do them less harm."

Arnold held out the bottle. David filled a handleless cup found on a log by the map case and sipped the strong brandy.

"I've moved back all sick and wounded I could. I need more carts and horses. I fear lung tubules infection in this weather."

The major general shook his head. "I'd give horses off my farm but the British have overrun it."

"I am sorry," said David. "I hear it was a beautiful place."

General Arnold paced the wet clay floor. "You landed gentry all better see to your war. We *must* get Gates removed from command. He's a lazy, card-playing, blundering coward. And he dislikes to fight."

"That may be, General Arnold, but we still take orders from Congress. If we didn't it would be a war of every commander for himself. Myself first."

General Arnold got a fresh bottle from his saddlebags and went out into the rain puddles. They heard his horse go clopping off up the muddy trail.

David shook his head. "He's right about Gates, of course, but Arnold's a hot-tempered man who shouldn't get so out of control."

"Arnold is the best of all the generals we have on a field of battle. But he's dreadfully harassed on all sides by the easy-living folk who don't do the fighting. Well, Major, get all the sick and wounded back as far as you can. I think we're beginning to hurt Burgoyne in the stomach. He's bogged down, and the loyalists he expected to rally to his side haven't. Not so far."

"I hear your cousin Culbly has a good-sized Tory force with Burgoyne."

The major general smiled. "We Schuylers are at least spared the use of our name. He calls himself Colonel Lemon."

There was a tap on the hut wall and Robin MacBean, David's best wound dresser, came in, rain dripping off the point of his large red nose.

"Sorry, Major, but I thought you ought to know. Some of our cart convoys have been cut off south of Rock Creek by British raiding columns. The Styron wagons from the powder mill were carrying most of our extreme wounded."

David folded his arms and frowned. "If there are Indians among them they'll try and scalp the wounded. I don't suppose, sir, you could spare a column of men to protect my patients?"

"I'll give you fifty men, but that's all. And it's not official, in case General Gates hears of it."

David touched his damp hat, hitched up his wagon-canvas cape, and followed Robin out into the pelting rain. The lichens on the stones were gray-green and the crushed tufted needles of the tamarack were a sharp scent in the muddy forest clearing. The company of men David got were stupefied and brute-tired from much marching, but he quickly set them on their way south.

CHAPTER 32   The two Indians with the British officer had tracked the wagons carrying American wounded across a flowing creek swift with rain runoffs. The wagons had bogged down on the other side in a thick yellow mud. Two had been pried out by brute force, aided by brush laid under the wheels. But one wagon was down to its hubs in the sticky mire. Under the canvas hood two wounded men turned and twisted in wet bandages. Sally, watching their pained unshaved faces, wondered at man's ability to survive, while so badly damaged, all this fearful journey. Ned Styron came around to the tail end of the stalled wagon.

"Sally, we're moving the other wagons up on the shale trail ahead. We'll unhitch the teams there and come back for this one. You want to come along, or wait?"

"I'll wait with the wounded. It looks very wet out."

"It is that. Give the poor lads a drink." He handed her a brown glass flask. "We'll be back for you soon as we get up on firmer ground."

One of the wounded whimpered, "Don't be leavin' us here," and then remained silent. A sense of immobility, of tranquility, held the wagon. It was still but for the drip of rain on the trees and the mutter of the angry-flowing creek. Alone with the wounded, Sally sat still and tried to get warm. Only when one of the wounded men shouted, "They're here!" did she become aware of the Indians.

She looked out past the bow of sodden canvas and saw two painted faces on naked shoulders marked with rain-smeared war paint. A strong dark hand lifted up a tomahawk.

Sally didn't scream, she just stared, no sound coming from her vocal chords. The wounded were too far gone to do anything but roll their eyes. All were actually aware of the cruelty and callousness of war. One with a bad head wound tied in blanket strips tried to roll toward an axe on the wagon floor. He fainted before he could reach it.

An Indian put a muddy foot into the wagon and Sally saw he had four fingers missing on his left hand and that the fringes of his hide hunting pants were trimmed with red and brown scalp locks.

She found her voice and enough air behind it to make it vocal. She shouted for no reason she could logically explain, "It's no time to come calling! *Scat!*"

The Indian turned to the one standing behind him in the drizzling rain and made some quick savage sounds. Sally pulled her hair down and hid her head over her breasts. An English voice said, "Get out of that wagon, Half Hand."

A British officer, his red jacket turned dark with rain, was looking into the wagon. Sally looked up and said, "Oh, sir."

Half Hand spat toward the two wounded men, who were watching open-mouthed. "My tribe is allied with the British. You no stop me in killing Americans?"

"Stay away from the girl."

The two Indians looked at each other and both laughed. "You wait your turn, Captain. We leave you have girl too, but with no hair." A pistol shot went off. Sally shivered—the shot sounding mean and loud in the wet air. One of the Indians outside the wagon fell away. Half Hand—the survivor—whirled around and leaped out. Sally heard a rolling around in the mud, savage oaths and panting. A wounded man said weakly, "Get the axe, missy."

Sally grabbed up the axe and crawled to the end of the wagon. She saw the dead Indian in a grotesque position, two rifles in the mud, and the live Indian and the British officer rolling on the mired trail. The Indian tightly held onto his tomahawk. The officer had his sword up, but as they rolled, close and engorged with rage, they prevented each other from using their weapons. Gripping each other's dangerous wrists, they held death away from themselves. Both Half Hand and the officer were so angered that the fight could have only one ending, and that fatal.

Sally leaped from the wagon, sank down to one muddy knee, recovered her balance, rose, and advanced on the struggling figures, the axe held high. Half Hand brought up his knee into the groin of the officer, who fell away in agony, curled up into a ball. Half Hand lifted his weapon to throw it at the defenseless head, then decided to deliver the blow direct and close up. Sally, advancing silently behind the Indian, swung the axe just as he lunged forward. She spun around, striking only empty air. Half Hand threw himself at the officer, screaming a long-drawn-out howl. The officer brought up both booted heels suddenly and caught the Indian flush on the mouth and jaw as he kicked, lying on his back. There was a sound of breaking teeth and cheekbone, and the officer rolled away and reached in the mud for his fallen sword.

The Indian, fearfully bloody about his crushed mouth and in great pain, retained his grip on the tomahawk. He forced himself to his knees and moved forward again in the mud, crawling. The officer still searched for his sword, his hands in the mire, his eyes on the savage with the deformed face moving toward him.

Sally behind Half Hand got in one weak head blow that stunned the Indian and opened a gash on one side of his wet shaven head. The Indian whirled to throw his weapon at Sally, and the officer found his sword. The Indian's feet gave out beneath him in the greasy mud as he twisted to toss the hatchet at Sally; she felt the thing go sheering past her head like a swift bat. The officer leaned forward with a grunt and drove his sword down through Half Hand, through the back of the neck into the torso. For a moment Half

Hand stared up at the rain falling without let-up, his eyeballs protruding, then he fell slowly forward, the sword still deep in him, and he died with a short choking sound. Sally dropped the axe and the officer stood up, wiping his face with the backs of muddy hands. She lifted her skirt and tore off a length of petticoat and handed it to him. He cleaned his eyes and cheeks with her intimate linen and kicked at the dead Indian.

"I owed the swine this thing, Sally."

Sally now for the first time carefully examined the face being scrubbed clean by her fragment of petticoat. "Why, it's Leftenant Jack Bounty. We met in New York."

"Captain now, or rather was. They can hang me for what I've done to a war chief and ally of the Crown. And maybe they will."

"You must get out of here." She was keenly aware for the first time of the evanescence of human life.

"I will if you'll come along, Sally. I can't help the wounded. But I can take you away. There are other Indians following behind us and they'll guess this deed is by me in a minute. They can read all the signs."

"What can you do? Where can you go?"

Jack Bounty had recovered his pistol and put his sword in place. Now he picked up both rifles and hunting horns and some pouches. "Let's run now and we'll talk later."

She followed him, not thinking it wrong; either the Styron party would come back soon, or the Indians would reach the two wounded men. They ran west on the wet trail. She saw the officer had learned a great deal about forest marching and trailcraft. With Sally's skirts tucked up they went marching west on a fairly good trail, flinty, but drier than the lower creek paths.

They came across no one till they stumbled over the dead body of a large woodsman who had crawled this far from some fatal fight to die. He wore a deerskin shirt and strong linen trousers dyed with butternut. Jack Bounty looked at the corpse with pleasure. "A godsend, Sally girl. How he got this far with such a head wound I don't know. But he's going to inherit a proper muddy British officer's uniform. You may turn your head, my dear, if you care to. Not that you did in New York when I husked."

Sally watched Jack Bounty strip and then dress himself in the frontier outfit of the dead man. Jack Bounty buckled on the wide black belt, stuck in the hunting knife, hung the pouch from it—then stood before her under a wide-brimmed black hat, leaning on a tall rifle. . . . "Well, my dear, I suppose the thing to do now is to keep going west *and* west, till we leave this damned war. It's too rainy to trail me, but they will report my killing of the chief."

"You can't be serious, Jack Bounty—deserting!"

"You don't know what can be done to me for killing an important Indian leader and ally. If the savage war parties desert the general over my little deed, I could be taken to England and hanged, or shot here."

"But what will happen to us now?"

"We'll wander in somewhere soon, and tell some simple story of being run out by Indians. And if we pass for married and keep drifting away from the battle area, we shall at last be free of this damned war and find ourselves a place, eh, Sally? You did like me in New York. You did pleasure with me like a willing girl out for a bit of fun. Well now, how do I strike you now?"

Sally giggled and came and leaned against him, almost hysterical. "I did promise Adam Styron I'd meet him in Albany. But I can't, can I?"

"Not if Jack Bounty is to be your virile love now." He wiped his face and sighed. "I'm a bit shaky yet. Of the thing I've done and am now doing in this mad war. I've been fed up with it too long to relish any more battle or trailing of Americans. And it's just as well I've done this thing under the charge of anger and flight. So stay by me, Sally. It's your wild green land; show it to me."

He held her to him, both wet and muddy, and then they went slowly away from the naked man left dead and desolate on the trail, next to a discarded uniform and a tossed-away sword. When they camped that night the rain had stopped, but it was still wet under the trees. They found a dry cave between some great rocks and ate black dried jerky Jack Bounty had found in the dead man's pouch. The deer meat was hard to chew and took a long time to swallow. They lay side by side on dry and ancient leaves, working on their meal. Sally suddenly swallowed a lump and said, "Oh Jack, I forgot to say. I'm a married woman."

"Forget it. I'm not taking you back now."

"I'm Mrs. Joseph Philipse, wife to Captain Philipse."

"If you like titles, I'll make you Mrs. Jack Bounty in front of the next backwoods hedge parson we meet."

"Can you do it that way?"

He kissed her ear. "Respectable people do like to keep this marriage business well forward. You sleep, I'll lie guard."

When she was calmly sleeping on her arms, Jack Bounty looked out into the damp night and hunted among the stars. The rashness of his deeds was on him now. He felt the power of this large land and the rawness of it, and somehow he didn't care if he had gone wrong.

Our story, Jack Bounty mused—as the London wits would put it (when Dr. Johnson would stop his tavern pontificating and let them talk)—our story is always about time passing and its too stealthy merging of our youth into age, and the blind spots in our own souls—as witness this rash and fearful thing done this day— but in our story there is no waiting, no sitting in a byway; we move and tremble into the darkness ahead, always unwary, blindfolded, unknowing. . . . He lay in contemplative immobility, the girl breathing softly beside him. Jack Bounty felt sleepy, an abdication of vitality overcoming him after the hard day and the desperate deed. Our actions—he dimly thought—are somehow inherent in our circumstances no matter what accident brings them about. The last thing he remembered before falling into a deep, fatigued sleep was the orange disc of the pumpkin moon and his favorite sky—Cassiopeia off to the east of the Pole Star.

Major David Cortlandt and his rescue column came upon the wagons of Ned Styron's party in a rocky clearing, a fire burning damply and a jug being passed to the sound of tree crickets in the piebald maples and white oaks.

Ned Styron was seated on a wagon tongue and he looked up as David came over to him. "I don't like to say it, Doctor, but Sally was carried off by Indians down by the big creek."

"How did it happen? Lord, how can I tell Joe this thing?"

"We went back to her in the mired wagon by the creek with four yoke of oxen to pull it out."

"You left her there, Ned?"

"With two wounded men and it raining pitchforks. And I had to think of the safety of the whole train. Besides," Ned rubbed his long black beard with nervous thumbs, "who thought the varmints were this far south? We found signs of a fight. Blood, Indian truck, the two wounded men dead and scalped. Sally's petticoat in rags all around. I feel deep sorry about this, Doctor. Worse than the burning out of twenty years of my life with my mill and farm."

It was a shattering blow and David could not fully adjust to it. The personal agony for Joe, and the dreadful fate of being carried off by savages (quick death could only be a mercy). All the days of this forest campaign flooded back into David's memory (he was not listening to Ned) just sitting by the fire, and he remembered the forebodings and apprehensions he had felt. He sat in what was already bereavement, under the drying trees, the wagons drawn up around the one bright red eye of the night fire. Melancholia came to David, worse than he had felt it in a long time. What if it had been Roxanne? He pictured her and little George, safe, he hoped, on the Hudson at Philipse Manor.

Shelagh, wide and still graceful for all her wooden limb, came to him, sat down, and held his hand.

"It's no good thinkin' of it, Doctor."

"I don't know any way to not think of it."

"You got a worse task."

"Yes."

"To tell Captain Philipse. This place ain't no place to bring a woman. Any kind of woman."

David fingered the earth, the bronze bunch grass, then picked a cockleburr from his jacket. "You didn't mind, Shelagh."

"I'm middle yellow. My color be best here. Best here away from the raunchy white men, always pesterin'."

David thought of Sally, her peaches-and-cream against the cruel dark skin of the tribal war paint. It was a fearful image. And for a moment all this Priapean business between men and women was revolting to him. He pressed Shelagh's hand. "Better get some sleep. Ned's moving out early. I think you're safe now. But the whole country is a battlefield, fighting and crazy, crazy at war."

"You think it last much longer?"

"No, I don't think so—I mean here. We're rallying men from everywhere. They haven't any reinforcements."

General Burgoyne, at last aware of his dire plight, stood ready to cut his lines of communication. They were five hundred miles of murderous land and water from Canada. He had piled up what he thought was five weeks' provisions for his army. The thought of retreating to Canada never entered his mind. And somehow he still harbored the idea that General Howe would join him from the south in the middle of September.

Meanwhile he heard rumor of events on the American side. Congress had moved in bickering and gossip, in backstairs political whispering. General Washington was ordered—as expected—to remove Major General Philip Schuyler and replace him with General Gates, the sly, loud, born politician, and a rather indifferent general. General Burgoyne on hearing this news called him "an old midwife" and ordered up a wine cart.

The road led ahead to Albany for the British. They now numbered, Lord Alban figured, 2600 British, 1700 Germans and 300 Tories, Indians, and Canadians. The Hudson was crossed to the west bank on a bridge of boats. The ladies were shrill at the danger of the water and the wetting of their costumes. The soldiers were torn and tattered; the carts, reduced in number, carried only the necessities, except for the general's wine and library; the ladies trimmed down their baggage again.

General Gates, waiting for battle, in his pride accepted the aid of General Arnold and his 1200 men, and Morgan's Riflemen; they had come up with 500 deadly frontier rifles. They greeted Jack-Tom Swales, traded tobacco, and talked of Indian fights they had been in.

The Americans were united on Bemis Heights at Stillwater. A Polish engineer, serving with the colonials, began to fortify it strongly. Jack-Tom and his scouts went ahead of the heights and soon heard the bumbling sound of Burgoyne's advance as he moved down the western bank of the Hudson on Bemis Heights. He located the Americans but took a few days to set up his ideas of how to take the American position. On the nineteenth in three attacking columns he moved toward the colonials on their high fortified position.

General Arnold, tense and angry—a wound-up spring—had begun the day by drinking, and now on his bay stallion he rode to Major Cortlandt's dressing station set up in a sagging barn.

"Do we just wait, do we fight, Major?"

"General Gates knows. I don't."

General Arnold cursed, sawed at his horse's mouth, and rode up forward to find Gates behind the fortified mounds of earth. Robin MacBean, David's best dresser, listened to the sound of rifle fire, the boom of cannon.

"They're moving for a frontal attack, sir."

"The British are like that, Robin. They fight by rule. Have you seen Captain Philipse's men?"

"They've been out front scouting. Here come our first wounded of the day, sir."

Two buckskin-fringed scouts were helping a sagging man upheld between them. The upper part of his blue uniform jacket was bright with blood, his starfished hands, grimy as they were, seemed drained and lifeless.

The scouts laid the man on planking set upon grain chests. David saw it was Silvester Hand. His eyes were closed and his breath was heavy and labored. David tried to pour some rum down the wounded man's throat. But little went in; most of it flowed out down his too white cheeks. The pulse was slow.

Silvester Hand opened his eyes. "I be dyin', don't I?"

"No, of course not. You seem to have something in your belly."

"Some exploding cannon balls went up over us. Down in the woods. The rest of my party is dead."

"Was Captain Philipse with you?"

"No, he was up ahead with Jack-Tom when the British bastards moved up quick. The captain is overrun by now, unless . . . he . . . pulled . . . back . . ."

The man had fainted. Robin gave him some more rum. David held the pulse. "Damn, this is a bad thing." He cut away the jacket, the shirt, the tops of the breeches. Two ugly black bits of iron projected from the groin. He touched one ragged sharp edge. There were more wounded now. Young boys holding their shattered limbs, a few groaning. The dressers attended to the lightly hurt. Robin felt the pulse of Silvester Hand. "It's weaker, sir."

David shucked off his jacket, rolled up his sleeves, and began to cut away broken skin and torn muscle. Blood welled up, and he sponged and cursed and the smell told him the intestines were perforated. They usually are when you stop something like this iron with your stomach. He took out the two three-inch slivers and their toothed edge. The other, high in the chest, he left alone. Silvester Hand was bleeding badly. David stitched and sewed the edges of

torn tissues. He tied them off and wiped his hands. Silvester Hand
was staring up at him, his eyes glazing.

"It's like eatin' red peppers . . . Doctor."

"It's not a scratch."

"I'm dyin' of thirst."

David motioned to Robin. "Give him water."

Robin shook his head. The wounded man caught the gesture.
"Water ain't for gut wounds, is it?"

"Just a swallow can't hurt you, Silvester."

"You know it don't matter nohow—hell it don't matter . . .
nohow."

Robin soaked a rag and wet the fluttering mouth. Silvester Hand
panted and shivered. "Don't let me drink. *Don't* let me have a
drop! I seen Roger Bankus drink after his lights was hit, and he died
in minutes. Doctor, don't let them give me drink . . . odd . . .
odd odd . . . the wife, the young whelps . . . who will see to them
now? Liberty . . . talk . . . hot . . . Doctor . . . it's burnin' me in
the throat. It's like red hot iron bars . . . nobody will care . . . don't
have the what thing . . . now be . . . this so . . . *oh*—"

Robin closed the staring eyes. "He's gone, sir."

"Don't bother with the stomach-wounded, Robin. Get somebody
to me I can help."

As they worked in the fearful horror of this hastily set-up hospital, David could hear the battle forming and re-forming beyond
the breastworks.

Silvester Hand was buried in wet haste, given back to the earth
with ten other shapes, wrapped in soiled wagon canvas, placed in
a shallow mass grave dug with effort among the living tree roots.
Robin MacBean, who had studied in Edinburgh for the ministry
before turning to hospital work, read from a damp and tattered
Bible, as a black rain fell under the tall trees:

> "*To every thing there is a season, and a time to every purpose
> under the heaven; a time to be born and a time to die; a time to
> plant, and a time to pluck up that which is planted; a time to kill,
> and a time to heal; a time to break down, and a time to build up.*"

David stood shivering; all their breath was steaming as vapor before them. There were not many present. At any moment the battle

could flare up again and they would go back to their tasks, each to his rifle or musket, his horse or his scalpels. Robin MacBean closed the Bible; rain had smudged the words, but he knew them by heart:

"A time to weep, and a time to laugh . . ."

They were burying a comrade, a soldier. Hasty, angry, hot-blooded, unthinking, cruel, Silvester Hand who had bred up a brood of children no better, no worse than he was, who was dead now under the wagon canvas, and two gunners were pushing shovels full of clay on him and the others. Whatever marks would be placed over them, soon they would fall down or rot away, and the forest would rush in again and saplings try to struggle up. They would be as if they had never been, and yet they had been, and fought and gone hungry, gone lousy, and had abstractions burning in their minds, absolutes they never fully understood, all capped by the word LIBERTY, a kind of sacred personal godhead. And it had killed them, destroyed them, sent them down to the marl pit.

David beat his hands together to get warmth into them. Broken men, still alive, waited for him to mend, or try to mend their hurts.

"A time to rend, and a time to sew; a time to keep silence, and a time to speak; a time to love, and a time to hate; a time of war, and a time of peace."

"Amen," said David, and hurried off under the wet trees.

CHAPTER 33   The British and Germans advanced through the trees, flecks of scarlet showing between pine and birch and elm. General Gates sat behind his breastworks and let the British prepare their attacking lines. General Arnold cursed and said to anyone at hand, "Gates will not fight." He begged to be allowed an attack. Gates smiled, shrugged, and Arnold was permitted to move out with Morgan's Riflemen and Dearborn's Infantry. A close struggle took place among the trees and bushes. Nothing came of it and Arnold and Gates met again.

Gates said, "I hear your progress has been undecisive."

"So far—so far."

General Arnold put spurs to his bay stallion and rode out shouting, "By God, I'll soon put an end to it!"

General Arnold had been drinking but was not drunk. General Gates sent out an officer to Arnold ordering him to call off the attack. But the thin dark-skinned general was flying on ahead, to a farm where Morgan's Riflemen were being hard pressed by the British. Arnold rallied the line and sent men up into the trees to pick off the British officers. "Shoot their eyes out."

The British brought up Germans and several guns. General Arnold sent a message to General Gates to throw in his reserves— he had almost ten thousand. But Gates was a cautious man and General Arnold roared. The British were spared a major defeat.

The night was made dreadful by the howling of wolves who came out to feed on the dead. The Indians had sulked during the day's battle—now they made the night hideous by their scalping of the wounded and dead. They did not care if it were British or American hair they lifted. The British had lost over six hundred men, the Americans a few over sixty.

General Gates, all knew, could not stand another officer gathering any glory that he felt was his own. General Arnold asked that General Gates attack in the morning. Gates, in a shouting match with General Arnold, ended it with, "General Arnold, I remove *you* from command!"

Burgoyne also had bad news. Americans in his rear had captured the greater part of the supplies behind him. He was cut off completely from Canada.

Captain Corky and his regiment lay behind hawthorn bushes on the outskirts of a farm held by the Americans. It was not uncomfortable, but the ground had not fully dried out and Captain Corky lay on a red cape trying to ignore the insects buzzing around his ears. In a long military career of no great brilliance he had been in worse spots. Ensign O'Crump came in the dark asking for him; and English and German voices cursed. Ensign O'Crump lay down by Captain Corky's side and caught at his breath.

"Devil of a time finding you, Captain."

"It's no spot to be proud of. The Americans—with rifles—are in the farmhouse. Can your people spare a cannon?"

"No. The Americans are alongside us now too. I'm looking for Colonel Lemon and his Tories."

"They were on our left at dusk. Stiffish fellow this Lemon-Orange, isn't he?"

"Very. Doesn't think we treat him with the proper protocol and all that."

"Have you got a drop of something sharp, Ensign?"

"Warm beer. I *think* it's beer. Here."

Captain Corky swallowed and spat. "I think, my boyo, it's horse brine."

"I doubt it. Tastes much too foul for that. If you see Colonel Lemon, he's to pull out his men and go to the other flank and engage the enemy."

Ensign O'Crump stood up in the dark, only the glint of the gold lace on the collar of the shirt his London tailor had made for him sending a tiny gleam into the night. A sharpshooter from the farmhouse drilled him through the head with a rifle ball at a hundred and fifty-two yards. Ensign O'Crump fell forward on his face, unaware that he was dead, or had been hit. Captain Corky called out, "Sergeant Dickens! Have two men carry the ensign back. Oh, leave the canteen. It's no good, but it's wet."

"Yes, sir. We sty 'ere till mornin' do we, sir?"

"I'd rather be at the Seven Veils off St. James Street than here, but I don't think about it."

"No, sir. I 'ear the muckin' Germans have kilt a sucklin' swine and roasted it."

"Try and get me a front foot, will you Sergeant Dickens, ole cock?"

"Yes, sir."

The body of Ensign O'Crump was dragged feet first from the battle. In half an hour the Right Honorable Lieutenant Dudley Brown came up to Captain Corky's position.

"Fearful row at the general's. O'Crump was from very posh folk. The general sort of promised the lad's mother, Lady O'Crump, to keep an eye on him."

"Never put your napper up for a look round, even if it's dark. Bullets don't care much for rank."

"You know what the general wants done?"

"Somebody to come drag their arse up here from New York with a relieving army. So don't we all? I hear we're only fifty miles from Albany."

"He wants to send Ensign O'Crump's body back to England, to his folk, in a keg of rum."

"And take it all from our rum rations, I suppose?" Captain Corky was a professional soldier, and as such he thought always of his skin, his stomach, and his pleasures. "Well, they'll never get a buggering keg back in this bloody wilderness. Have you seen Captain Bounty?"

"He went out with a party of savages some days ago to scout out roads for the carts. Hasn't come back yet."

"Leave it to Jack-boy to soldier on the job. I don't blame him. This ruddy ringaround thing is serious, Leftenant. They have us near surrounded."

"The general doesn't admit it."

"No, I wouldn't either in his place. Now get back and don't lift your head higher than your private parts or you'll need a keg of rum yourself, Right Honorable Mr. Brown."

"I'll mind that advice, Captain."

Captain Corky slept the rest of the night on the ground, snoring and dreaming of the rompish, debased times spent in amorous dalliance in Bombay, and his youth on an Anglo-Irish farm with a wild long-haired colt between his legs and the wood smoke from the cottages over the moor, his backside aching from the birching his tutor had given for not preparing his Latin lesson.

Captain Joseph Philipse reported to the American pickets near dawn, and Jack-Tom went to hunt something to eat. David, sitting in front of the barn-hospital smoking his china pipe, let Jack-Tom have a slab of black smokehouse bacon and a pan of cold corn bread.

"It puts grit in my craw, Doctor, to think we got them all licked out and we don't move on 'em."

"Maybe we will by morning."

"They may be breakin' out by then. That Gates is sure a real yellow streak. He's got General Arnold's gorge up."

"Yes, he has. Captain Philipse with you?"

"Up at the general's reportin'. We had us a crock of prime

whiskey. But it got broke comin' in. But I got me a brace of glass-eyed Calahoula hounds we took off a Tory farm. Got 'em tied up with the supplies. You ever hunt with them?"

"My father-in-law had a pack of English beagles."

Jack-Tom chewed the smoky bacon and spooned up corn bread. "I'm tired traipsin' round with the wool hats, eating ash cake and sorghum sweetnin'. I'm gettin' off huntin' soon and get a bear steak and a likely mess of deer brains. And a young randy squaw, sweet meat to the bone."

There was firing as the sun got ready to come up. Jack-Tom wiped his mouth on his hands, and his fingers on his shaved skull. He helped himself to rum and slowly sipped it. He brushed his fringe of ginger beard into place, hunting among his teeth with his tongue. "I better go see what my boys are up to."

David turned and inspected his wounded in the barn; he had two dead men carried out. He was setting a shattered thumb on a fifteen-year-old boy when Joe Philipse came in. He had discarded his military jacket for a white linen hunting smock. He had a week's growth of beard and was smeared with blood down one leg. "It's not mine, Davey. A little close knife-fighting getting back from behind the enemy."

"There's rum in the barrel."

Joe had an iron cupful and sat down and tossed off his hat and rubbed his hands through his uncombed hair. "I can't find Sally. You know who she went back with?"

"With Ned Styron's wagons."

"I was insane to bring her up here."

David sat down on a block of wood and looked at his surgeon's table laid out on a soiled blanket. John Hunter had given him that once fine set—good Dutch steel, and several of them John Hunter had invented himself, sending the designs direct to the makers to create. He looked up. "Joe, you and Sally are an odd couple."

Joe laughed. "I suppose we are. Not many a man would accept her as she is. But it's unfair, isn't it? A man can go wallowing around with the bawds, but for a woman—strict behavior. And we pry as to how many brides come a virgin to the damask sheets."

"I know." David looked over at the wounded men lying on the ground on hay and fragments of uniforms. He dreaded the day ahead. He was drawn thin and his fever-teased nerves were taut. He couldn't add to it all Joe's horror and rage at the news Sally had been carried off by the Indians.

"Gates fights tomorrow, or rather this morning." The sun was out in a haze of golden flakes, catching the forest primroses, the fiddleneck and maidenhair ferns under the buttonwood and elm trees.

"If Gates fights, I hope, Joe, you'll take care. Nothing too brave or foolish."

"I'll keep your advice in mind."

Joe went to get another cup of rum. A perverse, indecisive early firing announced the day of battle. The camp dogs had run down a fox confused by gunfire. It darted across the front followed by every stud dog, bitch, and puppy in the army. Soldiers resting on arms cheered the chase as it yiped past the waiting army.

The once brightly-colored tent had been covered with green branches of fir and beech and General Burgoyne had a feeling that the day was festive and unreal. He had been shaved and dressed and from his tent, with spyglass at eye, he was examining the heights where the Americans lay waiting for battle. His dogs waited for their morning petting. The general was in shirt sleeves and his valet held out his gold-encrusted red jacket, and when that was on the general set his sword and hanger and examined himself in a small mirror. The damn wig needed curling and they were running short of hair powder. As for starch, there wasn't a drop left in the army.

Mrs. Lewis came up to the tent, walking with care on her tiny feet among the horse turds and the soft puddles made by the last rain.

"We'll beat them today, Johnny."

"As good a day as any, my dear. But let's not be too cheerful so early. Have you breakfasted?"

"On what there was."

"I have made plans for you ladies, the Baroness, and her children. You shall all go back to that Philip Schuyler's farm we captured and wait for us there. It's a most civilized place in such a wilderness, from what I saw of it."

"Johnny, you're not thinking of retreat?"

The general frowned. He was no fool, she knew, for all his books, poetics, and sensual foibles. He was also a veteran soldier. General Burgoyne, combining the philosopher and the soldier, looked off to the American heights. "We live in the world of the mind, we only move in this one."

"I'll go back and pack some chests." She kissed him and patted his shoulder epaulet. She was fond of this man, and if she could ever love deeply any man, Johnny Burgoyne was someone to give all to. But life was not a pretty minuet, and one must think of the future and its incongruities. "I'll go collect my things. Peg Munday is talking wildly of going on to New York."

"We will, *all* of us."

There was activity in the fields ahead and between the tall trees. The general began to write an express to London on his situation. There was joking among the staff that he sent off so many packets to London that he had depleted half a regiment that could have been used in the line. He wrote skillfully and with much grace, and he thought how empty of true depth his life was, and how undone was all that he had planned to do. Those unread books, that unwritten play, some poems to bring together in better shape. For a warm moment Mrs. Lewis' generous form, the mellow melons of her tits, filled his imagination. The very smell of her flesh was recreated in his nostrils. The thing was about run. The flesh lusteth contrary to the spirit. Exalted personages, he knew from history, had destroyed themselves for woman, others had submitted to xenophobia and gone to far Tibet and Tartary; he had come to a wilderness and now it was time for a reckoning.

The general gave up the writing of the express and walked in front of his tent. Around him the red coats, the green and blue facings of his command moved up toward perilous positions facing the heights. The staff, chewing a last mouthful, was coming into the tent. He stood and listened to morning reports, nodded, and looked at a crude map drawn by Lord Alban the night before. Most of the staff withdrew. The general took up a volume of John Donne's sermons and turned to the one delivered on Christmas Day, 1627 A.D., before the king, Charles II of gay memory.

He read, ignoring the shrill screams of some of his Indian allies moving by.

Man is but earth; Tis true; but earth is the center. That man who dwels upon himself, who is alwaies conversant in himself, rests in his true center. Man is a celestial creature too, a heavenly creature; and that man that dwels upon himselfe, that hath his conversation in himselfe, hath his conversation in heaven. If you weigh any thing in a scale, the greater it is, the lower it sinkes; as you grow greater and greater in the eyes of the world, sinke lower and lower in your owne . . .

He looked up. Lord Alban was smiling and standing beside a mud-covered little man in fusty blue who held a folded and sealed sheet toward him. Some of the staff drew near.

"A dispatch from General Sir Henry Clinton, sir."

The general took the letter. "How did you come?"

"Tories took me by boat to below Fort Edward, sir, and I managed the rest on my own."

"You are an American?"

"Brewton, sir, is the name—Albert Brewton of New Brunswick, New Jersey, sir. A loyal follower of His Majesty, King George the Third."

"Give the good fellow a glass of wine," said the general to his valet. He opened the letter, breaking the seal and unfolding the sheet. He read for half a minute, then looked up with a grin at Lord Alban and the officers.

"Gentlemen," he said dramatically, addressing the staff. "A dispatch from General Clinton. The British fleet has broken the great iron chain across the Hudson at Bear Mountain, and has taken Kingston."

There was a cheer, and the messenger, drinking his wine in the back of the tent, lifted up his glass. Lord Alban said, "This means for sure General Clinton will join up with us?"

"If all goes well, and all seems to. We've got the Americans in a nutcracker between us. You may issue orders for a general advance on the rebel lines."

"At once, sir?"

"At once, Neddie. I shall be with you." He turned to his valet. "Have my horse around, and get out my great boots."

The staff hurried off to get the orders issued. Lord Alban began to mark up the map. The general felt a great stone lift from his ballooning heart. He felt elated, humble, and thankful to God for

His aid—he picked up the book of sermons. He read while the valet polished his jackboots and the horse was brought around, freshly shod, his hooves blackened.

> In what heighth soever, any of you that sit here, stand at home, there is some other in some higher station than yours, that weighs you downe; and he that stands in the highest of subordinate heights, nay in the highest supreme heighth in this world, is weighed down, by that, which is nothing; for what is any Monarch to the whole world? and the whole world is but that; but what? but nothing.

CHAPTER 34   Peg Munday in unweeping misery was reducing her baggage to one bundle wrapped in red flannel cloth and tied together with a long scarf. Lord Alban, under a bronze helmet topped by horse plumes, coming into the tent looked at her and her task and shook his head. "You seem sure of defeat."

"My dear Neddie," said Peg, brushing blond hair out of her face. "I do not think we are yet undone, but I must be ready if we are. I don't suppose Americans are much different than other men."

"You've known more of them than I have."

"Neddie, it was so wrong of me to confide in you."

"I have never been green-eyed about it like some impertinent coxcomb."

She looked at her scuffed shoes and sighed. "I would be breaking up our ménage no matter what happens."

"You can't, Peg. I mean what else have we in this dismal wilderness but each other?" He examined the claymore he wore as a sword.

"I have a son and I want to be with him. If I can."

"Surely Sir Francis will not accept you into his household."

Peg went to a small red leather chest, picked it up and set it down before Lord Alban. "You will find your white powders for the headaches in the yellow papers, and the pills for the gout in the small blue flask. We are out of the ear oil, and I confess now your London medicine for the sour wind and bloat has been mixed with ditch water for some time. Still, it seemed to help you, darling."

Lord Alban lowered his eyes toward the earth floor of the tent. "I *am* feeling very well, no flatulence. The hard life seems to have at last agreed with me. But suppose I were to regress to my early illness? You would leave me in the forest with no one to put my head against? You are a cruel vixen, Peg."

Peg laughed and put her arm through a long tear in her cape. "And you've provided well for me, I must say. In rags and all my smallclothes in tatters. I'll soon go naked of navel like the Indian wenches."

"I will not try to hold you if you want to leave," said Lord Alban with dignity, and he lifted his helmeted head high and stalked from the tent.

"Poor Neddie," said Peg and went to find the Baroness. She and her three children were seated under their cart of piled-up feather beds, chamber pots, and jars of goose grease. The huge woman rose to her feet and said, "Well, *mein Herz,* how did it go?"

"He took it like a sulky lamb, Baroness. A proud hurt lamb. You are prepared?"

"*Ach, der liebe* Gott forbid us defeat, or the death or hurt of the dear baron, but I am prepared."

"If there is a defeat we will make for the road south and hide. I am sure Americans are no worse than Englishmen."

"*Mein Kind,* that is no recommendation. I curse the day we took service with these beef-eaters. But we are *Bettel* poor."

The three little girls looked clean, tanned, and had many insect bites on their arms and legs. The Baroness eyed the sway-backed horse nibbling tree leaves. "He isn't much of a steed. But I felt him I could handle. I sent the orderly away. We want no men folk if we have to run for it." She thought a moment. "The Americans do not employ the red savages?"

"I suppose they do, some. But not many."

"It is a hard life. Lili, *mein Liebchen,* take that stone out of your mouth."

Peg sat down and watched the soldiers moving by in the tree-shaded trail. They were no longer the pipeclayed, well-dressed parade troops. Rain and sun and camp grime had destroyed their uniforms. Many were uncombed and unshaved. And they had picked up whatever clothing they could from the dead, and from looted farms. It was a tag-bob of an army that went out to meet the Americans.

The Baroness shook her head of badly combed hair. "How it must hurt the baron's pride to go into battle with such scarecrows, such *Lumpen*."

Ahead there was a rising sound as the fury of the attack grew in volume. The horse stopped its feeding and chewed, listening to the war.

General Burgoyne stuck to his one note of hope, the news that General Sir Henry Clinton had cut the great iron chain anchored across the Hudson and had taken Kingston in the middle reaches of the Hudson. The ordered attack on the strongly entrenched American lines proceeded. But it was soon pushed back and his advance badly mauled. He withdrew and for days waited for General Clinton. Despair took over again.

General Arnold was having a bad time in his lines. Without a command and idle on the heights, he heard new battle sounds below and took over a horse, shouting to his aide, "No one can keep me in my tent today."

"But, General, you have no command."

"If I am without command then I'll fight in the ranks."

"You can't do that, sir."

"You watch, the soldiers will follow me. Come on!" Spurring his horse to the cry, "Victory or death," General Arnold rode toward the sound of new battle. He pushed on a brigade, and himself led Morgan's Riflemen forward against solid resistance. The British could still fight. In a rage General Arnold went out into an exposed field toward the British guns—a lone horseman between two armies. He rallied the brigade behind him and pushed back the enemy center. The fire was deadly. His horse snorted, gulped, and began to cough blood. It fell like a stone. General Arnold, on the ground, felt pain in his leg and saw a bad wound in his thigh, the bone broken.

It had been a fearful day. The British, outnumbered three to one, held on. And for six hours the fighting raged in great sheets of fire. The British gunners fired. General Arnold, down and in pain, stayed on the field and kept the Americans active. General Gates did nothing but sit and gossip on the heights with a captured British officer. His entire contribution to the battle of Saratoga—as it came to be called—was his comment on the wounded Britisher, "Did you ever hear so impudent a son of a bitch?"

General Burgoyne in calm despair, the gentleman under pressure, knew he was near to breaking. The Americans were moving around him. He could not stay and fight. The retreat sounded. The British began to march north over sodden earth—held from moving quickly by their supply barges. In the night rainstorms came, torrents that made the retreat fall on muddy ground.

Major Cortlandt looked down at General Arnold—just on the threshold of consciousness—laid out on two doors under a hanging lantern in the barn. "It's the thigh bone, General. The one you hurt before."

"Yes, I'm always breaking the damned thing, it seems."

The rain washed wildly against the thin slat roof overhead, whipped trees moaned in the driving storm outside. A circle of wounded men lay on floor straw and stared at the general sucking up brandy from a small brown bottle, his handsome brow damp with pain and sweat. "No taking it off, Major. Goddamn it, no sawing at my joints."

"No, General. But I'll have to cut some thin wooden planks and set the bone in place between them. Robin, get me some boards. Now it's going to hurt, sir. One shouldn't be ashamed to cry out."

"Blast me, 'going to hurt'—what do you think it does *now!*" He swilled more brandy and some ran down his chin, and he rolled his head and ground his teeth. "So one pulls victory out of battle and lies on old doors, torn open and swilling brandy. And Gates, what is *he* doing, that bowl of suet—following up the battle I have handed him? I ask you?"

"No, he isn't yet following the British retreat."

"He'd better. He can catch Gentleman Johnny with his breeks down and take him with every soldier in his command. Damn you, Major, don't touch me unless you have to. I'm in no mood for pawky games."

"Cut away the general's breeches, Robin."

David began to shape some thin wooden boards with a jackknife. The lantern smoked and the general soon lay naked from the waist down, the white skin of his legs ghastly under the light, the dreadful wound gaping, black with dried blood, tiny white fragments of bone visible. The general refused to look at his wound.

"Christ Almighty, proceed, Major, *proceed!*"

David took down the lantern and held it close. He carefully examined the wound. "Not much bone damage. A bullet wound, but I think the bone went when the horse fell on you. Now you men hold the general firmly. Come on, lay hold."

"Curse you clumsy hinds. Hold me tight!"

David laid wide bands of linen crossways under the leg. Robin held out to the general a rag wrapped around two musket balls. The general put it in his mouth for something to grip and bite on.

David motioned Robin to take hold of the leg by the calf. "We must put the broken bone ends to matching again. End to end where the break is." Robin bit his lower lip with effort and strain. David ordered, "Pull, *easy*, Robin. Now turn the leg just a little to the right."

Muffled sounds came from between the general's rag-filled mouth. David wiped his eyes dry. "Bring the lamp closer. Now Robin, firm. Don't move till I say so—*push*. Two of you help Robin." He thrust his fingers brutally into the wound to guide the bone ends together. The general's body stiffened, shivered, and his head rolled back. His eyeballs, bloodshot and huge, glared at the barn roof. David put the two boards against the thigh. The exposed naked groin, the bunched pubic parts were indifferent to public decency.

"Hold him. Not a move." With the knife David corrected the angle of a board. He picked up a strip of linen under the leg boards. He tightly tied it around the leg. Then he moved down the leg and tied more linen strips; under the knee, the calf, around the leg and the boards. Quickly he tied off the strips remaining in several places.

He said in a voice he didn't know, "Give the general a drink."

Robin removed the rag and musket balls and General Arnold gulped brandy. Robin wiped his face and chest. The dresser's nerves cried piteously for rest—he was brute tired.

David began to put rag pads between the leg and the boards where the bindings did not touch properly. "It's not over yet. I must now bandage the entire leg and the boards so there is no danger of jarring the knitting bone edges. Robin, give me more linen strips."

The general was panting, open-mouthed. Columns of sweat poured off him. It was a good half hour before David felt the mummy-wrapped leg was properly made rigid.

"It will hold, sir. It may be a bit tight when I wet the linen to shrink it around the boards, but it can't be helped."

"Lord in His mercy," said the general, weak and worn. "It will all be so easy some day when they puke this battle, this war out into school books. Fine words and noble gestures. Let me alone, Doctor. I can stand no more."

"No more to do." David held a glass of wine and opium to the general's bloody and torn lips. "This will deaden the pain a bit. You'll be let alone."

"Feed me no pap. The battle is only half won. Until we take every British soldier we have not done our utmost."

"Robin will stay with you. I must go now down below the heights to see wounded men who cannot be moved."

The general lay back and his chest rose and fell with the effort of sucking air into his lungs. He was bitter-browed and in fearful pain, and now it was not the broken bone, the torn muscles, the shattered nerve ends that agonized him, it was the dark green bile of knowing he would never get the credit of this battle—leave it to that fat granny, the politician Gates, to claim this victory.

Moving north in the stormy night Colonel Lemon and two score Tories and fifty Indians walked quickly in the rain, ignoring wind and mud. They were desperate men, determined they would not stay and risk capture. They were notorious for their cruel deeds and the Americans would hang them, or at most their end would be a bullet. Scalp peddlers, rapists, turncoats, Tory fanatics who had done brutal things now recorded against them.

Colonel Lemon had a bandage over one eye. He supposed the eyeball was fully destroyed, but it was no time or place to find out. It had been a fearful blow he had taken with a musket butt, and he was lucky to have survived with a whole skull the hard hand-to-hand struggle. He was tired but also angry and outraged, and that drove him on; temper made him a good pair of heels. The Indians were moving ahead, deserting them in small groups—and most likely would have scalped them all if they had not feared the swords, knives, and firearms the Tories carried.

Near morning under growling thunderheads Colonel Lemon

called a halt. They had no food, but they could not eat anyway. The storm continued and they sat miserable and sodden, stupified and worn down.

Colonel Lemon looked over the beaten, tattered men. "We may have to separate. We must remove all marks of our military formations, all letters and everything else that signs us as Tories. We shall pass ourselves as Americans sent home after victory."

"As you say, Colonel."

"I am not Colonel Lemon. I'm Culbly, Culbly Smithson. We must reach the lakes, steal boats, make for Canada. We may find British at the lakes. But until we do, go wary."

"The British," said a Tory spitting into the pelting, steaming rain. "They didn't look so mighty, did they, in defeat?"

Culbly shook his head. "We have been loyal, we have honored our king. The rest is the fortune of war. We did not fight to be honored by officers or royal commissions. We . . ." The sick, dying eye was like fire, a live coal in his head. He lowered his face in his hands and tried to rest. Sleep was out of the question in his condition.

A watery dawn, sickly and wan, found the fugitives rising from wet ground. The rain had abated a bit. Culbly saw that none of his men had gone off alone, no one had stolen anything of their common gear. He felt an elated pride in them, these fellow outcasts who had fought as well as they could in what they believed was the right course under peculiar conditions. The king would never hear of them, not by name. They would wander now, most likely the rest of their lives, as exiles, pointed out as men who could never return to their birthplaces.

Culbly shook himself alert in his wet, chafing clothes. This was nonsense. They would be back. The Crown would never let this local setback stand in the way of showing these rebels the error of their ways. Standing under the dripping foliage, Culbly inspected his men and then slowly—joints stiff—they went up the trail.

When Jack-Tom Swales and his hurrying scouts came to the spot he had missed the Tories by half a day. They stood under the tree where Culbly's men had rested. Jack-Tom read the ground and shook his head. "No use trailin' 'em any futher. They might have met up with others runnin' away and set an ambush fer us."

A bearded scout kicked at the mossy turf. "We better bogger back if we want to git in on the celebratin'."

"I kinda fret, Moses," said Jack-Tom to the bearded man. "I was hankerin' by Beelzebub to add that scalp of Colonel Lemon to my huntin' fringes. But he was such a half-bald coot, it wouldn't have made much of a scalp."

David rounded up the wounded still left in the fields—and now there were many British among them, who ached and cursed as much as any wounded. Some few among them were pale and did not care. It was little enough he could do. He was down with his recurring fever again; supplies were running out. He hated the scalpel and the bone-saw, the threaded needles, the probes, and the duck-billed scissors. For the first time he felt the mockery of all he had learned, all he had worked so hard with such tenacity in London to acquire.

The night came and the rain fell in spurts, then the stars came out. He sat on a tree stump after a shaking bout of fever, as far from the wretched wounded as he could. Stragglers of the British units still held out here and there in the woods, and it was dangerous to go walking. Robin came out drying his hands on a husk towel. The boy was the only one with any skill. He wanted to be a surgeon. Should David advise against it? Robin sat down on a section of stone wall.

David looked up at the sky. He thought of Jack Bounty, who had an interest in such things and often had pointed out the heavens to him. David made out the Perseids darting through the sky leaving star dust and, unless his eyes were playing tricks on him, meteoric tails. Poor Jack—where was the roaring boy now? If lucky, in New York, roistering in the taverns; if unlucky, making mold in some shallow soldier's grave.

Robin MacBean said, "Gates is moving in the morning, I hear."

David nodded and did not answer.

CHAPTER 35   Slowly the British crossed the Fishkill and General Gates wasted three days, permitting the enemy to retreat a far bit back on the road to Canada. General Gates had close to twenty thousand men, yet he fumbled and blustered until at last he went through the motions of pursuit and on the thirteenth of October banged into the main British rear guard.

The British general made a motion of standing up to the attack, but by now the Americans had surrounded him on three sides. There was a formal council of war among the English.

Lord Alban said, "Let us abandon all transport and guns."

A German general spoke up, "Load six days' rations on the back from der men and we pull out in de night. *Ja?*"

An officer, the Right Honorable Lieutenant Brown, came in to report that the Americans were now on all sides. Further retreat seemed out of the question, and there was no fight left in the men.

"Withdrawal is now impossible," said General Burgoyne.

Lord Alban suggested a flag of truce to General Gates. It went out and came back with grim terms, "Unconditional surrender."

The general shook his head, the staff cursed, the tent flies buzzed. The general petted his dogs and then took pen and paper and asked, "that my troops be permitted to march out of their camp with the honors of war."

General Gates was not a paper-writing man. He answered he would agree to the honors of war and he would permit in the "Surrender Conventions" the terms "a free passage to be granted to the Army under Lieut.-General Burgoyne, to Great Britain, on Condition of not serving again in North America during the present Contest."

The Baroness von Riedesel, her three frightened children, and Peg Munday lay on the bottom of a farm cart, covered with straw and filthy blankets. The farmer who had been hired to drive them was a cowardly but greedy man. He drove through back roads and when they ran into musket fire wanted to go back, but the Baroness held up a few gold coins and said, "Not a smell, *mein Hund*, until you get us past the armies."

They drove on, Peg hugging the smallest child, and soon there was musket fire nearby again and it was directed at them. The patriots in celebration were firing on everything that moved. The driver refused to go further and the women and the children ran toward a stone house in the cellar of which they found several wounded British soldiers. Cannon were still firing and Peg and the children sat on the dirt floor and the Baroness went to hunt water for themselves and the wounded men. It was a dreadful cellar filled with the smell of an overpowering privy, of rats, and of the badly wounded men with their festering wounds.

Peg said, "We may have to spend some time here."

"Let us hope not," said the Baroness, taking dried bread from a bundle. They sat in the odorous darkness chewing on iron-hard crusts. The clatter of gunfire went on around them, the rush of men going by, the adding of another wounded man to those already neglected on the cellar dirt. They could never later decide just how long they were in the cellar. But at last there was stillness. And they knew that the terms of surrender had been accepted. Peg began to tie up her bundle.

"*Ach, mein Herz,* you go?"

"I'm not becoming part of any captured army. I'm going on alone. It's only fifty miles to Albany. And from there to New York is just a boat trip, I've heard."

"*Mein lieber Gott,* may you be right."

Peg kissed the Baroness, hugged the children, and both women were weeping, aware that in war there are always partings and unresolved destinies. Peg went up into the light of day. Far beyond the woods the British were burning some of what was left of their supplies. A tall, lazy column of smoke went climbing into the robin-blue sky. No gun was firing.

There was a lull, a time to rest, to wash, in the barn where David treated the wounded. There had been a steady march of limping battered men, and a procession of figures carried in, clutching their wounds and looking at David with large pleading eyes.

David had not seen Joe Philipse for some time, and when he looked up from taking an arrowhead out of a farm boy's shoulder, there was Joe, looking at David with the same agonized stare of the badly wounded.

"David, there's been some information. Sally—she may be captive among the Indians. I'm taking a detachment out to hunt for her as soon as the fighting is over."

"Wait for Jack-Tom. He's the expert on trailing—knows Indians."

"He's after Tories. I'm not waiting." Joe sat down and put his hands over his face and rolled his body from side to side. The wounded boy looked open-mouthed from the captain to the doctor. David handed the boy the arrowhead. "Here, you might want to show this to your grandchildren some day."

The boy took the arrowhead, but did not lower his eyes. David wiped his hands on a soiled rag. "Joe, at least wait for more news. The Indians are deserting—have deserted, most of them. We may find Sally in one of their camps."

"Don't make me think of what may be—or *has* happened to her."

"It's not pleasant," said David pressing his brother-in-law's shoulder with his cleaned hand. "Don't imagine anything till there's real information."

Joe shrugged and sighed. A man in a long brown jacket came in, wearing a wide wool-felt hat much favored by drovers and hide dealers. David smiled, "Morris Manderscheid!"

"Malcolm Smith is my name, hide and tallow dealer," said the Philadelphian. "Hello, Joseph. I've heard what's happened to your wife. I'm sorry, boy. At such a moment of victory too."

"What makes you so sure of victory? General Clinton may be on our necks."

Botts' agent sat down on a milking stool and began to cut up rough tobacco which he slowly crumbled between strong fingers. "I was sent up here to tell General Gates that General Clinton isn't going to get beyond Kingston."

David snapped his fingers. "Then Burgoyne was cornered and knew it was all over."

Manderscheid pushed the tobacco into a black clay pipe and lit it with steel and flint in a quick skillful movement, sucking the sparks into the brown leaf. "General Gates was properly impressed with the information."

"What now?" asked David.

"The war will be over up here. There will be permissions for men to go home for the winter. But maybe not. There are hard things ahead."

Joe stood up, looked at David, at the smoker, and went out. David told the wounded boy to get up and go sit in the sun. "Morris, what can we do for Joe?"

"Help him mourn. She's better dead than in the savages' hands for a long captivity."

"It's dreadful to think of."

"Our sacrifices, I'm sure, will be taken easily by those that follow us."

"General Arnold said something like that when I set his leg. He's bitter and in great pain."

"General Washington is also fighting enemies in Congress. A man has to stand up to blows from both sides without losing balance. How is the new son?"

"The last letter said he was growing fast."

Drums were beginning to pound. Manderscheid stood up. "It's a pleasure to watch the British march out to surrender."

David took his jacket off a barn peg. "I forgot. I'm to be with the staff when General Gates meets Burgoyne. An English poet once wrote a poem that seems to fit the event:

> *"The whore and gambler, by the state*
> *Licensed, built the nation's fate.*
> *The harlot's cry from street to street*
> *Shall weave Old England's winding sheet.*
> *The winners shout, the losers curse,*
> *Dance before dead England's hearse."*

Captain Corky, neat, gear all proper, went down the line of his men drawn up to march out for the surrender. Not much pipeclay, no spit and polish—but neat—neat as could be.

"Now then, lads, it's a bloody mess and it's a mucking disgrace, but we'll face it like true British soldiers under the lion and unicorn. Are you listening, Sergeant Dickens?"

"I be list'nin', Captain Corky."

"There will be no taking out of any loot you've picked up. The enemy may resent it. You've searched the packs, Sergeant?"

"I 'ave, sir, me own amongst 'em."

"You'll march out soldiers—not besotted lackeys—and right brisk. As on parade before the palace at St. James, and you'll keep your heads high."

Captain Corky put his hand in his pocket for his snuffbox, but the ragged pocket had no bottom and the snuff was long since used up, and the box gambled away.

"You're to act like Englishmen, even if a lot of you are Scots, Irish, and Dutchies. Sergeant Dickens, can the Hessians in line here understand me?"

"They gets the drift of it, sir."

"Well, it's no time to make a speech in German. Attention! Dress the line."

The battered and repaired drums began to beat, the flutes tootled. The staff and General Burgoyne rode past, the general's dogs following the heels of his horse. Then came the swing by of what remained of the regiments of the Line, a bit out of practice. Captain Corky shouted, "Have your men fall in behind the Nineteenth Foot, Sergeant Dickens."

The British asked to meet General Gates, and it was to Lord Alban a kind of light-opera bowing and good manners. General Gates held his troops in camp when Burgoyne's last command of thirty-five hundred men marched out to pile up their arms to the tune of "The World Turned Upside Down."

Lord Alban said Congress would not honor the terms of surrender and the British troops would never return to their native land.

He was correct.

Major David Cortlandt, standing with the American officers, was in a brushed uniform, the stains fairly cleaned out of it (except here and there). In line with the American officers he watched General Burgoyne as he dismounted and held out his ivory-hilted sword to General Horatio Gates.

The American shook his head. "No, no. . . . You may keep your sword, General Burgoyne."

The British army stood in a long column across the field of Saratoga, their swords, muskets, and sidearms on the ground before them. General Gates, done-up as a peacock in his regimentals and gold braid, strutted along the line of captured Britons. David Cortlandt thought of General Arnold at that moment in a dirty farmhouse room, suffering the fever of a healing limb, a draining evil wound, not even mentioned. And this fat man moving along in the sunlight, taking it all as his own victory. Major General Philip Schuyler looked at David and made a tight smile with the ends tucked in, a smile of ironic comment on history as it is lived and how it becomes distorted.

The American fifes and drums were up now in full power, sounding in the brisk autumnal air:

> Yankee Doodle, keep it up,
> Yankee Doodle Dandy,
> Mind the music and the step
> And with the girls be handy.

General Burgoyne, one of his spotted sport dogs at his heels, turned to General Gates and David heard him say, "Are you really a general, sir? You look more like a granny of a midwife."

General Gates turned cheerfully and winked at his staff, and then faced the defeated British general. "You are right, sir. I am a granny of a midwife. Today I have delivered you of five thousand men."

David joined in the laughter shared by friend and foe. The captives began to march off the field of surrender, toward a port of embarkation they would never reach. David went back to his wounded.

CHAPTER 36   The party at Mynheer Peter Schuyler's was in high progress. Compared to the great balls that had once graced its halls it was a comedown to simple farm fare, scuppernong wine, a limited amount of cyder, and demijohns of local brew. But it was joyous enough, a ball given for the men who had returned from the battle against General Burgoyne's forces. And with the splendid news of the surrender of his army. Major David Cortlandt, flushed with the recurring bout of his swamp fever, looking thinner, more worn, was happy with his rosy wife Roxanne in her old made-over green gown. The guest of honor, Major General Philip Schuyler, could fill in for them with some of the more personal and intimate events of the campaign. Colonel St. Clair and several young men from the neighborhood, in their blue and buff, were merry with the local belles.

It was warm and cheerful at Schuyler House for the returning soldiers after the long marches, where men were reduced to small significances in the hostile immensity of the forests.

Mynheer in his fading blue jacket with the gold buttons greeted everyone and pointed to the food which was farm product and not fancy. In the ballroom a fiddler, expert on the schottische, and a boy on the flute, furnished the music. The room was decorated with cut wisteria and jonquils.

Anita Schuyler, not wearing her diamonds (those were safely buried somewhere for the duration of the war) said to Mynheer, "No red coats this time, no officers from the royal fleet."

"These are sterner times. Aren't they, Doctor?"

David agreed and shook hands. "They are certainly times to try men's souls, as Thomas Paine wrote."

"Did he now? I don't know him. How's young George?"

"We're having problems. He's about to cut some teeth and he's fretful."

"Now Davey," said Roxanne, her eyes sparkling, her feet feeling the teasing tingle of the music from the ballroom. "He's a baby and he has to fret and he has to cut teeth or he'll chew corn meal like a granny all his life."

"Where's Joseph?" Anita asked.

David shook his head. "He had to go to Albany for a few days. He's much upset of course, his wife being carried off by the savages."

"Oh, oh!" said Anita holding up her arms in horror. "Dreadful, dreadful."

Roxanne shook her head. "Poor Joey. No matter what she was, she was his love."

Major General Philip Schuyler bowed to Roxanne. "Mrs. Cortlandt, may I have this dance? It's a country dance and the only one I know."

David smiled and nodded, watching his wife, again so swift and slim, so animated and bright, go off on the arm of the general toward the ballroom. David sat down in a Chippendale chair in need of repair and was aware of the fast beating of his heart. The damn swamp fever first contracted in the Battle of New York and now again reinforced in the bogs and swamps of the northern woods, was boiling inside him and making the great hall of the Schuylers whirl before him. Every so often the fever seemed to reach a peak of sweating and chilling, and his teeth would chatter and his strength spin out thin as a thread. He could feel the fever in him now and his limbs begin to tremble. He rose and went into the library and stood with his head against the row of red-bound copies of the *London Chronicle* of ten years before. He had a long leave of absence to recover his strength and he wondered if he would ever take the field again with the Continental armies. It had been a hard life, prolonged for almost two years now. He felt his youth and his vigor had been lost in an ominous uncertainty.

On the dance floor only half the usual sconces of candles had been lit and they were ordinary tallow dips, not the fine scented barberry and beeswax tapers that used to light up a Schuyler ball. But it was as lively as any of the best balls of the good days. The young men were weather-tanned and full of the juices of life, and the young women were alive and alert to the actualities and certainties that they must capture and hold one of these warriors before he again went back to battle. Some *mésalliances* would come of the ball. As for the older people, there was a thinning of ranks, a falling away of attendance. Some had stayed away because of the dangers of the road, some like Jonathan Philipse were in American prisons, or had fled to England, many were disrupted to Philadelphia, to the Virginias. And so many, Anita thought, were dead; destroyed by the natural process of aging in hard times, or carried away swiftly by the pressures of a fearful war.

The general whirled Roxanne in a country dance—no times, these, for the satin rustle of long quadrilles—and the fiddle wailed, the fife trilled. Roxanne laughed. "The last ball I attended as a silly girl, and now I'm a married woman with a child."

"You're still nimble and dance like a girl."

"You say the things I like to hear best, General. And now that the end of the war is near, we shall all dance more. Gay but not frivolous."

The general shook his head. "This war is just beginning. The fighting has a long route to go, I fear. General Washington is cruel-put to keep an army in the field at all. It is a wearing-down process, I sense."

"Oh no, I'm sure the king will perceive we shall not ever bow to him again."

The general smiled. "Let us leave the war to others tonight." They danced on and the floor started to empty and the young men began to move their partners toward the neglected gardens to talk of love, and the brevity of the life of a soldier, under the poplars and red oaks.

The last guests were leaving and Mynheer had escaped to an upstairs room and was working on his history of the river families. He copied from the *Boston Gazette:*

Reasons for stripping a 92,160 acre Westchester and Bronx domain from Lord Jonathan Frederick Philipse 3d are further explained in discovered Philipse's family papers.

The papers mention that Philipse, a British loyalist, spied against the Americans. The "personal tragedy of Philipse" was attributed to his "incredible error of judgment" that came to the attention of Gen. George Washington. Some of the letters of Philipse were written in prison and some of the documents alluded to his smuggling of military information later while he was free on parole.

Philipse had owned one quarter of Westchester County and twenty-four miles of the Hudson Valley from Spuyten Duyvil to the Croton River. After his error of judgment Philipse barely escaped execution by fleeing.

An authentic portrait of Lord Jonathan Frederick Philipse had been located. A Philipse portrait painted by John Wollaston has been identified.

Five of the Philipse letters now publicly disclosed were written to his wife while he was imprisoned by General Washington's soldiers. Writing from Horseneck, Conn., Philipse told his wife of his life as a prisoner and said, "I am really tired and sick of this filthy place."

"As I am conscious," he wrote from New Haven, Conn., "that I have done nothing inimical to the liberty of my country, or ever would, let the consequence be what it will, nothing affects more than to be taken up in such an hostile manner without any crime brought to my charge and without a hearing."

With the Manor at stake and with his own interest in the "real and permanent prosperity of America" he took the Loyalist position, a position shared by many of the large holders in the area. He headed the first list of "suspicious or equivocal" in Westchester County and in August was arrested on orders of George Washington and imprisoned in Connecticut. He was paroled and allowed to return. He then went to New York City, thereby breaking his parole and forfeiting his estate. When some British troops were withdrawn, he accompanied them to England.

His property was confiscated by New York State and sold, the Manor House to his son-in-law Doctor David Cortlandt of the Continental Armies Surgeon-General's Service, the farms along the Pocantico with only a few exceptions to the people who tenanted them. The map of the upper part of Philipsburgh Manor, prepared for this sale, shows that Cornelius Jones held 200 acres; James Farrington, 85; James Requa, 170; John Requa 200; David Requa, 280; David Conklin, 300; and William and James Forshee, 228. These farms covered all the land known as Philipse Hills. Their ownership can be traced back to the original deed Goharius granted to the first Philipse.

Mynheer dried the ink and closed the ledger. There was one more clipping he wanted to copy out. Ah, yes. He hunted up the item about the report of the birth of a two-headed rooster. It was said to be sure sign that the war would be over in two weeks—or was it two months? He took up the clipping and reread it. He re-opened the ledger.

It said two weeks. He was willing to wait two months if he had to. He had so much work to do on this history, and he never suspected it took so much writing and so many words to make a text.

Mynheer finished copying with his goose quill the newspaper item into his ledger and set about filling his late night pipe. It was quiet now and the last guest was gone, and while it had not been like the old days it had been a fine ball, and, if he lived, he would have another next year.

As he sat smoking he heard Anita go to their bedroom and the solidarity and identification with her was pleasant. He wondered where their son was and in what dire straits he found himself, if he were alive. Who would get the Schuyler Manor if Culbly never came back? The major general most likely, as a distant cousin. Still it was better than what had happened to Philipse Manor. David had managed to bid in the house, which would bring him nothing but debts, but the land was gone, sold off. And Joe would most likely get some small piece of the holdings as an American officer, if Congress so decided, but Congress was beset with politics. Ach, it was a time of change, and not a fit time to be born into. Not for an old man.

He took up his tallow dip in its pewter holder and in the yellow glow he went down the hall to the bedroom. On the way he listened at his mother's door. Old Martha seemed very quiet. He turned the white china door handle and held the tallow dip high. His mother was sleeping on her back, small and lean in the great bed, almost lost in a sea of pillows. There was a thin crescent of a smile on her toothless mouth. She had conquered time, and conquered logic and reason, he felt, and would last forever in some grotesque, inexplicable manner. She made a murmuring sound in her sleep and he held the burning candle away from her bed and closed the door. He knew he was still in awe of her, that she dominated him as much as she had when he was a damp, overheated school boy, or the plump young man coming into the estate (at least people thought it was his estate) with the aging woman always somewhere on the scene.

Anita, beribboned and laced, was in bed and lay against her pillows. He kissed her brow and said the party had been a fine one. She smiled at him in agreement. They were old and no longer needed to talk much to fully understand each other. Set habits had at last become the old rituals of a full acceptance of their long life together in which only the moment, the present, could matter now.

David lay till noon, the bed linen wet from his fever, staring at the green baize door, the brass-nail-studded chair. When he came down in his dressing gown, young George was sitting on Roxanne's lap in the kitchen while Zee the slave girl stirred the pots over the fire. George was swallowing a thick warm gruel his mother fed him with a silver spoon.

"Oh Davey, listen to *this*."

She ran the spoon along the baby's upper gums. The sound of metal on a hard surface was heard clearly.

"Davey, George has a tooth!"

He peered into his son's mouth, George protesting, and saw the thin line of white set in the watermelon-pink gum. "Yes he has. Let's hear it again."

"I don't want to wear it out. You will have some battered eggs?"

"No, I don't think I can hold much food. Just some toast, Zee."

"I'm sorry there is no coffee or tea."

"It doesn't matter." He watched George take his gruel, and David sat down, the dizziness upon him. He could get little of the toast and milk down.

When Roxanne took the baby upstairs to change him, he sat in what had been his father-in-law's private closet, a room with a paneled wall, some figures in landscape of the Italian school darkening under old varnish. Lord knew how he would ever carry the house. His pay in Continental paper wasn't worth much, but it had been acceptable so far, and how could they ever reject their own currency?

But in the future (if he had a future) could he keep this house, now divorced of most of its land? It was certainly no place to open chambers as a doctor. But this was no time to think of settling into private practice. The swamp fever had to be tamed first, if it could be.

There was a tap on the door and Joseph Philipse came in. He was dressed in fringed frontier buckskin, a battered black hat in his hand and over his shoulder a deerskin pack, a blanket, and a Kentuck' rifle. In his belt he carried a hunting knife, pouches and a tomahawk. Joe had not shaved for some weeks and there was a golden beard beginning to take form on his drawn and haggard face. An irrational tension seemed to be his only mood.

"I may not see you again, Davey."

"Nonsense, Joe, and besides we need you back here. I'm ill of this hanging fever."

"I'm going back into the woods. Jack-Tom has talked to a Huron who says he remembers a captive white woman in a village on the west bank of Lake George."

"It sounds most vague, Joe."

"It's all I have to go by. Or live for."

David shook his head and looked up at his brother-in-law. He couldn't rightly think of any reason why Joe shouldn't go off to hunt for his wife. It was foolish perhaps to go on hunting like this, and it would be better if he accepted the loss and let time leach it out of his memory a bit. But in matters of flesh and the passions all involved are a little mad. And David could agree with old John Hunter. (Could he still be alive in his anatomy chambers, busy hunting the secret of life in the stench of cadavers?) As John

Hunter had once written, "The passions are more than a feeling, they are a true disease that takes hold against the will."

David asked, "When will you go back on duty?"

Joe shook his head. "I've managed to get Botts to use me in exploring some situations on the lakes. I have a roving commission to study the number of savages who are recruited by the Crown."

David stood up and shook Joe's hand. "You're a damn fool, but in your place I'd most likely do the same thing. Get us back a letter from time to time."

Joe nodded. "Don't tell Roxy I'm off and away yet—not till nightfall."

When Joe was gone David sat thinking of the accidents of life and how banal all thoughts on the subject are. From the leaded window he saw Joe go down toward the river, walking like a trail-master for whom the wilderness no longer held many secrets. When Joe was gone behind the row of pepperidge trees that led to the river, David picked up a volume of texts that had been found in the British camp and given to him by a wounded soldier. He had never read any of the sermons of John Donne.

> We are all conceived in close Prison; in our Mothers' wombs, we are close Prisoners all; when we are borne, we are borne but to the liberty of the house; Prisoners still though within larger walls; and then all our life is but going out to the place of Execution, to death.

He closed the book, keeping his finger in the place. In all the games and pleasures of life, in all the dangers of existence, few could, or would, write it so direct. He went back to the reading:

> Now was there ever any man seen to sleep . . . between the Prison and the place of Execution, does any man sleep? And we sleep all the way, from the womb to the grave we are never thoroughly awake; but passe on with such dreames, and imaginations as there, I may live as well as another, and why should I die, rather than another? . . . What man is he that liveth, and shall not see death?

The buzzing of his fever in his ears made reading difficult. He closed the volume. Upstairs he heard the happy sound of his son laughing and the light steps of his wife as she moved around on old oak floors that reacted even to her lightly-placed foot. There was a wind rising among the roses gone to neglect in the garden, a honking V of geese were moving south under the shifting equinox. Somehow he felt the truth would come to him and this new nation, a salvation to come from reason and not grace. There was much yet to be done in the fields of the republic. Tomorrow he would start by trimming back the roses.

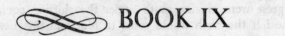

BOOK IX

The Disloyal City

CHAPTER 37   The spring of 1779 came at last after the hard and desperate winter. Morris Manderscheid entered the city of Philadelphia as the British army left. Sir Henry Clinton, the king's general, had given up the city after a season of balls and parties. Young John André also left—he was a major with the English forces, from a family once as French as was La Fayette who served with Washington. André regretted going and he most regretted saying good-by to Peggy Shippen, the belle of the English balls. She was the spoiled daughter of a rich Quaker who steeped himself in perfume; a citizen of rock-hard Tory leanings who had not objected to making gold coin selling supplies to Clinton, or seeing his daughter Peggy followed by the gay London dogs—all in chase. Her eyebrows were famous, her golden hair frizzled in the mode—her virtue suspected but never harmed. It was expected Mistress Shippen would marry an earl. There was a gem-like hardness of purpose in her, and a drive to become part of the English society that had sent such fine officers in so much lace and gold and red cloth to Philadelphia. . . . Mistress Shippen, too, was sorry to see the British depart.

Morris Manderscheid, sitting in a low river front dive making reports to Botts, wrote: "P.S. is still sending letters through the lines to Major John André." Outside the American blue and buff took over the city, the army marching down from the bitter hell of Valley Forge, scarecrows of men with bound rags on their naked feet, the officers on gall-marked farm horses. The wealth of the city caused this army to show their hungry teeth as they moved to billets.

Major David Cortlandt and his assistant, Lieutenant Robin Mac-Bean, took over a former British supply loft as a hospital. The major was leaner, there was a persistent buzzing in his head which the last bout of fever had left. He had an impression that he was becoming hard of hearing as the result of his several attacks of fever.

"Sign chits for everything you grab, Robin. But get me beds, get me linen, get me supplies. I must take off a great many toes long killed by frost at the Forge."

"The folk seem fat here in this town, with easy living."

"They enjoyed the Crown's wags and parties, you Scot puritan."

"They all wave and cheer the blue and buff now," Robin Mac-Bean said, and went out to hunt supplies.

Philadelphia, thought David, is free of most of the gloom of New England's icy emotions, its twenty-five thousand citizens aware of their worth, its Sephardic Jews, its love of pleasure and fetes a by-word in the colonies. Yet from the end of Market Street wharf he had helped ashore relatives of these indifferent folk—broken soldiers, dying men in rags. How could it side-step the war, this city that took pride in its printing of books, its collections of art? Its antique grace somehow hid a desire for the gold from the London Exchequer, and its Quaker farmers had been happy in a creed that avoided fighting and yet allowed the selling of their products to the British, while their own soldiers starved a score or so miles away.

Sir Henry Clinton, replacing General Howe as the British commander, had enjoyed the Philadelphians and their portly charm, his officers in their full-dress sloth and incompetence joining in the pleasures. Yet Carpenters' Hall was here, where the Congress had met: earnest men, honest folk, patriots, and of course the usual venal people, the sly counselors who had badgered General Washington and Arnold, and plotted against the army.

David thought of the dead men on their backs—staring with glazed eyes into the Germantown hills, the marching men with bloodied bare feet on the road from Chester, the desperate fighting around Pennypacker's Mills. These soldiering Americans had missed the soft life in Philadelphia, all the ale and spiced food at the Three Mariners and at the Crooked Billet.

From the small, dirty loft window David could see the well-dressed citizens promenading on Chestnut and Walnut streets, and there were well-kept carriages and sleek horses (which ate better than most of the soldiers) clopping along Market Street, turning at Fourth Street to stop before neat, well-cared-for houses, gentry in their invidious ostentation in the middle of a fearful war, awing the farm boys in torn breeches standing with their worn muskets in public parade.

It was all too much to think of and David had work to do.

Later Botts came into the loft, his red nose redder, his cropped hair grayer, the live, searching coals of his eyes hooded. The Americans, David knew, now had an active and well-organized secret service, and Botts, with Aaron Burr, close to Washington, ran it.

"How's Roxanne, David?" Botts asked.

"Quickening our second child."

"Never send soldiers home on leave, unless you want the country to grow quicker than usual."

"Have you heard anything from Joe Philipse?"

Botts shook his head and sat down in a backless chair. "Not enough to know if he's insane or just sour on life. He's scouting west into the Indian country. But his reports don't tell me much."

"He's still in search of the Indians that carried off Sally?"

Morris Manderscheid came in. He had put on weight, had healthy color in his face, and under the long brown coat he wore a good waistcoat with a show of fine watch chain. "Welcome to our city, Doctor," he said. "We've a few stables of Tories to clean out here and it's again the home of the Congress."

"How did you find your family?" David asked.

"Hannah is fine, the children now read Hebrew, French, and are going into Latin. You must come to dinner if I can find a goose. I'll have you Yankees reciting the Haggadah yet and you can replace the evil Pharaoh with George the Third."

Botts stood up and walked around the loft, picking off a stray splinter from a low rafter. He bit thoughtfully into the fragment of pine. "We've got to find out how letters are getting from our camps, from Philadelphia to the British in New York. Who sends them, to whom they're addressed. And what they say."

Manderscheid nodded. "I have our agents working out the routes. But unless we arrest the friends of friends in Congress, we're not getting far."

David said, "I don't suppose you can round up all those who entertained the British, and put them behind lock?"

Manderscheid shook his head. "It would break the Congress trying to feed them all in gaol. It's hard to know if the letters we copy contain more than just girlish gossip. Do we dare toss Mistress Peggy Shippen in irons?"

"No, no," said Botts. "I want to know how often she writes to this Major John André she entertained here, and see if we can get a full copy of what she writes. Unless it's actually military information, don't try to stop it."

David put on his worn blue cloak. "There's a place called Button's where they serve a breaded soft-shell crab. I will stand for the crab if some one of you will stand for the drink."

"Done," said Botts. "We owe you back pay anyway. You and most of the army."

They went into the cobbled and muddy streets where the small windowpanes of shops were shining in the spring air. Well-dressed people, ragged apprentices were cheering the soldiers marching down the narrow streets. A group of officers rode past at a gallop, flinging up black mud from the curbs, and everyone pushed back against the red brick house fronts under the hanging signs to avoid as much of the foul flying mire they could.

Botts wiped a smear of wet dirt across his nose. "Popinjays wearing out the few good horses we have."

The eating house was warm and clean, and the soft-shell crabs, the white bread, and the fairly decent rum (Botts abstaining) made them feel thankful for the day. All, in memory, thought of those agonizing winter days in Valley Forge, where they ate horse corn— when they had it—ground between two stones, and hope seemed an illusion from another lifetime.

"It's not over yet," said Botts. "The hard times, the evil times, but we're meeting the French soon for talks in Connecticut, and their supplies are coming in. It will be a close thing, but . . ." He looked down on his breaded crab, "But we shall survive."

Manderscheid nodded and grinned. "I want to toast the day the war is over, and Botts takes his first drink of rum. No, not a drink, a *whole* bottle!"

Botts looked at them grimly, his square, ordinary features set, only his eyes amused. "I tell you gentlemen, I've grown *away* from the drink. It no longer torments me—not very often."

There was cheering in the streets, the sound of horses' hooves, the bang of doors. A limping officer, leaning on a white jeweled cane, and two lieutenants came into the inn. The cane-bearer waved his gloved hand at the people cheering him from the doorway.

"Thank ye, thank ye all. Now I need some wet for my throat."

David stood up, "Major General Arnold!"

The general limped over and banged his game leg with his cane. "Gimpy but present, my dear Doctor." He was dressed in a new uniform and wore magnificent boots.

"You know Mr. Botts and Mr. Manderscheid? Attached to"—he thought quickly—"our department of supplies."

"You supply and forage gentlemen can do much better for us." General Arnold sat down and grinned—handsome, dark, with the liquid, passionate eyes of a determined, violent man. David wondered how it felt to be a hero at thirty-nine; the general was famous for his battlefield valor, and was even being given credit now for destroying Burgoyne's army.

"Landlord! Your best wine. And have you a pullet roasted? Good." The general peeled off his gloves. "Ah gentlemen, my staff. Anderson and Clayton. You fellows go amuse yourselves while we older men talk."

David said with an ironic tone to his voice, "A staff of such bright-looking well-dressed young men."

"All on credit from the best tailor in the town."

Botts broke some bread, rolled pellets in his fingers, and looked at the results. "General Arnold has just been made military governor of Philadelphia."

"The devil you say!" shouted Manderscheid. "My best to you, sir, on this honor!"

"The devil almost did me out of it. Some jackanapes in Congress were after my pelt *and* General Washington's. To remove us both."

David tasted the fresh-brought wine and held up his glass. The others did the same. "To the true victor of Saratoga and the north woods."

A whole roast pullet was set before the general. He looked down at it and sighed with sensual delight. "I tell you I dreamed of this sort of thing—but tender and swimming in its own juices. But I also dreamed more of women. I've three sons growing up, but am a widower who never became used to celibacy. I tell you I will taste of the womanhood of Philadelphia." He cut into the pullet and chewed thoughtfully. "I hope *they* are as tasty and yielding."

"They seem willing enough," said Botts, "to refresh the sheets, and accept the friends that yesterday were the city's enemies."

General Arnold fed on his sections of chicken. "Ah, it costs, costs like the very Harry to live here. But it all does—all full living, be it gambling, horses, collecting paintings, and particularly, women. And I have at this moment just about enough to pay for this meal." He banged his jeweled cane on the floor, "Innkeeper! another bottle. This cane was the gift of an admirer to ease my healing bones. So now I have three legs, to get around quicker. You did a good job of it, Doctor, but it aches at times."

More officers came in, more toasts were drunk to the military governor. Cards were brought to him, by messenger, inviting him to balls and dances. David sat watching General Arnold take it all as his due and wondered if the bitterness was out of him. Could the general now accept with honor and grace what he had once wanted? And did it feel fine, or was he let down by having achieved what he had so long desired?

David stood up as church bells rang. "I must see if my other crippled have arrived. I have the grim task of making several men toeless tonight. Good day, General, Botts. I shall keep that dinner invitation in mind, Morris."

"If I find that *Shabbosh* goose."

David pushed his way through the crowded inn and he decided, yes, General Arnold enjoyed fully what he now had, and would go on enjoying it. And he had earned it—as the best field commander in the American Army, and a most brave one.

Philadelphia, 4th of March, 1775
At the sign of the *Three Mariners*, Market Street

Dearest Heart,

This town methinks is too much given to pleasur'd ways but it may be my own remourse at not being with you & little George at this time. There is much ball giving & dancing & young officers often embroil'd with the provost guard. I fear there is too much of drinking. Yet we are preparing for battle, to continuing the war & we have as yet so little. Even here supplies are short for the common soldier & the men are flogged for stealing food. Many de-

serters are brought in and some are shot. So it is not all beer &
skittles, even in this Philadelphia.

The last news of yr. bro. Joe is that he is somewhere in the
wilderness to the west scouting for any sudden British surprises
from Canada, but Botts thinks *that* game is over and the Crown
will now try now & batter us by raids along the coast. These are
still desperate times, and attack'd at will as we can be by their
fleet, let us hope the French aid us more.

I am eating to surfeit & the fever has not come back. I do think
the ringing in my ears is wearing off. Certainly I hear as ever before again. Do tell young George to be the firm master of the
manor & do you think of the most pleasur'd memories of yr. most
obdt. etc. & know I do think of them too. All the Tories that have
stay'd in town are now loud in proclaim'd loyalties to us. So if
one wants warmth and food & drink one goes to look in, sternly,
on them & carve their roasts, drain their well filled cups. Pinch
young George's rump for me.

yr. devot'd
David . . .

Young Robin MacBean came in with a new fluffy shirt. "And,
Major, I have gotten someone to make us both new boots with
yellow Hessian tops. I go to play the buck at some rout. My heart is
not in it, but my Scots stomach demands it. The Shippens feed
well."

"I've promised to go there myself."

It was the best house to give the best parties in Philadelphia,
a tall narrow house with gardens behind—and white rooms full of
the best people.

General Arnold had a lusty baritone, and Peggy Shippen played
the harpsichord about as well as he sang, off-key but earnestly,
sweetly. The general faced the guests, his dark, handsome head
flung back as he sang:

> *"There is a lady sweet and kind;*
> *Was never face so pleased my mind."*

Peggy in yellow and much feathers smiled; all her English earls
lost, almost all contact gone with proper British gentlemen. This
handsome American with the romantic limp was a delightful re-
minder she could *still* capture a man and disarm him with a sigh.

"Her gestures, motions, and her smile,
Her wit, her voice, my heart beguile."

The general pressed on her naked arm and slid his finger along the smooth, healthy skin. She looked up at him, one corner of her arched rosy mouth curled up in mirth, and just the suggestion of her pink tongue appeared for a moment to mock him as she shook her plumes at him.

"I did but see her passing by,
Yet will I love her till I die."

There was a round of applause as the song ended, and Peggy Shippen smiled and stood up in a good rustle of silk. "General, I have other guests, you've had me much too long."

"I'll stay them all out."

"Yes, do stay, dear General." She pressed his fine new uniformed sleeve above the gold braid, and he watched her walk away in a swirl of fan—with grace and poise. Damn it, he was young again, alive again; even the broken bone was aglow with the thrust of pleasure this slip of a girl gave him. True, he was slightly drunk, but so happy. He turned to the refreshment table serviced by Negro slaves in white wigs and stockings. Lieutenant MacBean was there, slicing up a turkey with the skill of an apprentice medical student who had taken off many a man's limb. "May I produce for you, General, some specimens off this roasted subject?"

"No. The major here, MacBean?"

"Yes, sir. He's smoking in the garden."

The general swallowed a glass of wine, and bowing and smiling, making small talk, he limped into the garden. The blossoms were falling from cherry and apple trees and on the gravel path paired young couples walked. David was seated on a marble bench looking at a rain-streaked stone Greek god playing a flute. He was enjoying one of his host's cheroots.

"Ah Major, don't rise. Wanted to get you alone all week."

"I've been out along the Delaware River visiting hospitals."

"Hard to get supplies moving along, don't I know it? I've hired some wagons for mine own use. I need money, as who doesn't, eh? And this cartage business seems to pay very well."

"I've heard," said David coolly.

"Damn it, don't you go stiff on me, Major. We need wagons, we need transport, and we have to have someone haul it."

"I wasn't being critical, General."

"No, of course not. I'm touchy—and full of drink. But if you have some supplies going south, I can rent you twenty wagons and drivers, and fairly good horses."

"That all goes through the surgeon general, and since I've turned down the post I let them worry for transport."

The general sat down by David's side, one leg stiffly held before him. "You've heard things about me? That I like the Tories too much and their parties, and I'm indiscriminate as to whom I dine with?"

"So am I, General. I don't like camp fare either."

"True, I keep a gaudy carriage. I like decent livery on my servants, and I admit my last two balls at City Tavern are still unpaid for. But damn it, I'm military governor and I lack funds to keep up the office."

"I never pay much attention to gossip. Besides a hero has unlimited credit, General."

"Congress owes me, Major, four years' back pay. And yet they cast the suspicious eye on me when I hire some army wagons to earn a pittance."

"Your courtship, however, seems to go well."

General Arnold smiled. "It heats the blood, doesn't it?—her dainty feet, such eyes, and there's a full woman under all that froufrou. Damn it, what if the government goes to pieces as the Shippens and their friends think? Or we have no gold and the exchequer is empty and our army rots and doesn't fight."

David stood up and threw his cheroot into the bushes. "You have been listening to some strange talk, General."

"I listen; I don't swallow it all. Why, these Tories hint they'd make me military dictator—the fools, they'd even topple Washington. They think me the hero, not him."

David said firmly, "General Arnold, you're drunk and I shall not remember your conversation."

The general looked about him unsteadily, and rubbed his eyes. "Not just drunk, David my friend, desperate for a woman, and no means for it. In love with living and no way to get it. They still whisper against me in Congress—and my bones broken in their cause not yet fully healed. And what if General Clinton moves quickly and brings the war to a sudden close? And Washington is taken and we all at the head are made political prisoners? I taste the hangman's rope in my dry mouth every morn I awake."

"General, I'll come over to your quarters soon and test your liver and bile. You're driving yourself too hard and you're risking an attack of nerves. It's no mere lady's disease."

"Nonsense—I am *not* unnerved. If Peggy will have me, I'll have what I want. They can take my fame and hang it on Ben Franklin's nose. A man is only alive when he's human to emotions, to creation, to sensation." The general stood up and leaned on David. "Forget my hot talk. I anger too quickly when drinking and my speech gets florid. I see evil and envy everywhere. I was born with a burdened set of suspicions."

The general pressed David's hand, and went limping into the ballroom aided by the jeweled cane. David wondered if historians were right to think a woman could change an empire, sway men for good or evil, twist destiny like feeble clay in their sweet fingers. He smiled; he had taken on a rather full cargo of host Shippen's wine himself, to think like this of Peggy Shippen. She most likely was only a flutter-brain, just a pretty girl dancing a heated general in and out through emotional hoops.

CHAPTER 38   Edward Shippen, the forgiven Tory, the sly Quaker, spared by the military governor of Philadelphia, one warm April night had all the candles lit in his gracious drawing room. To a select number of local and military guests he served a splendid wedding supper after the ceremony in which his high-breasted daughter married Major General Benedict Arnold. Only a few of the general's officers had been invited.

David Cortlandt, puzzled by Arnold's drunken talk in the garden, had not come to the wedding. He did not want to think of the general as a man so confused as to the purpose of the war; it would be a charity to let the ramblings of a spirited, hot-tempered man (much put upon in the past) be forgotten. Busy with wounded the night of the wedding, David had written in a note to General Arnold: "There had been much fighting in New Jersey, and many wounded needed attending. I wish you and the bride much of joy and life."

The wedding music was muted—French and Italian compositions —and polite, the wedding dinner plentiful and well cooked. There were toasts and much drinking, and the bridegroom, on guard, managed to avoid taking on too much wine. The smooth round face of his father-in-law watched him. Peggy had brought the crafty Quaker around to permitting the marriage, but the little Tory was not unbending too far in admiration of his son-in-law. It would do no harm to have a general in the family if the Americans won the war.

"Your health, sir," said Edward Shippen in mustard-brown but chary of lace—the only Quaker virtue he retained.

"Your blessing on us, sir," said the general, in new buff and blue, lifting the thin fluted crystal glass of ruby Canary wine.

Peggy gave the general a warning glance and he smiled back at her and merely sipped his drink. For he felt he'd break his other leg just to see her smile.

In the stable yard behind the house a carriage was waiting with two black horses, and Lanky the coachman leaned against a polished yellow wheel, his long whip in the crook of one liveried arm. In the red leather boot behind there were trunks and morocco carryalls strapped in place. Two men came up the stable alley from the street.

The larger of the two in a long brown coat asked, "They're still at it?"

"A devil a lot they care," said Lanky the coachman. "And never a pot of ale sent out to the driver."

The smaller of the two men held up a bundle. "We're deliverin' a weddin' gift from the general's staff."

"You should of taken it in by the front way."

The man in the brown coat nodded. "Rush in by the kitchen, Nosey, and I'll have a nip here with coachy."

The green glass bottle he held out gleamed in reflected light from the celebrating house. The smaller man nodded and started for the house. The coachman took the bottle and tilted it, his Adam's apple wrinkling. The smaller man did not progress far toward the kitchen. He went up behind the coach and began to feel the baggage strapped into the leather boot.

The man in the brown coat took back the bottle and looked at it. "You're a two-fisted guzzler, friend, I'll say that. I shoulda kept the drink and given you the bottle."

"I was *that* dry. And when Lanky Wells is dry, he's *dry*."

"You might as well have the last draw at it."

"Thank ye kindly."

"A fine man, the general. And a good strong night to him."

"Ah, that he is, a stallion of a feller."

"And a gracious bride that Mistress Shippen, that's Mrs. General Arnold now."

"To that I'll finish the bottle."

"No telling us, I suppose, where they'll be in honeymoon tonight?"

"No, not a chance to tell ye. Where the devil is yer boy? He could of delivered a dozen parcels by now."

"Slow-witted, you know. I don't see why we keep him."

"Well here's yer bottle back, empty, and here's yer boy. Did you deliver it, lad?"

The small man was back and nodding. "They're dancin' and guzzlin', the gentry is. They give me a silver shillin'."

"Let's hope it's not American,"—the coachman spat—"but good king's coin."

The two men went off down the alley to the street and the coachman savored the spirits he had gulped and banged his whip butt on the ground and the horses *clopped* their hooves on the brick alleyway.

The two men crossed to a small house three streets over and let themselves in by a basement door and went to a low room with all its windows barred and covered. Botts sat in the room, under two gutting candles, writing long lists of names. He looked up as Morris Manderscheid and the smaller man came in.

"Was the wedding going along?" Botts asked.

"Like a greased bird at a turkey pull," said Manderscheid. "Nosey here got into the baggage."

Nosey nodded, "Weren't I the best pickpocket and strongbox man in all London? For that I was transported from Newgate."

"You were sentenced and indented to the colonies for strangling an actor, we all know that," said Botts. "Disgorge."

"I'm as good an American now as any," said the small man. From various pockets he took out letters folded as envelopes, with fragments of wax seals still on them. "And you need not fear. I closed everything up the way I found it. The lady had a small casket of lacquered iron in her red little traveling desk. But the lock was only a matter of a bent wire for me."

Botts took the papers and slowly unfolded them. Manderscheid gave some coins to Nosey, who touched his forelock of greasy black hair. "Thank ye kindly, gents. Any time, any time at all for the Continental Congress.

Manderscheid led Nosey to the door. "You'll be used again soon."

When he returned again to the table, Botts looked up. "Listen to this, from the general to his bride, dated just before the wedding: 'Our differences in political sentiments will, I hope, be no bar to my happiness. I flatter myself that the time is at hand when our unhappy contests will be at an end, and peace and domestic happiness be restored to all.' What do you think?"

"A heated man to a girl he desires."

"And the girl?" Botts picked up another letter. "No date, no signature. From the formation of the letters, I'd say Anglo-French. Look at it. Know it?"

Manderscheid studied the script on the square of stiff linen paper. "Major André of the British forces could have written it. I have some scraps of his texts some place. I'll compare it."

"He was in close attendance once on Mistress Shippen. Read it."

"The American cause, *mon ami*, what if it failed? England has not yet been wrong in its dealings with people of its only blood lines. Look at it this way, considering everything would it not be better to end all this dreadful happenings, this spilling of the precious blood of English and Americans, who are after all the *bon ton*—the same people. . . ."

Botts took the letter and studied it. "I don't know. I suppose she's still Tory, still admiring the British manners, and an officer with Sir Henry Clinton would write in these tones to an old girl of his."

"I agree."

"Let's wish the general a splendid wedding night. And we'll put these away with the letters collected here in Philadelphia. We've other things to look into."

Manderscheid nodded and began to bundle the papers into a roll. With a bit of black chalk he wrote on the packet, "April 1779, B.A. & P.S.A. & J.A."

The town of New Brunswick, in the Jersey midlands, is crossed by a great prehistoric red stone ridge which the Royal Society in London once wrote was the debris left by a retreating ice age. Below the ridge is the shallow Raritan River, which becomes sluggish just above New Brunswick. Good-sized boats could come as far as here from the sea and Raritan Bay. The farmlands around the town were good, the roads and streets still bore royal titles: George Street, George's Road, after one of the Hanover kings. But the countryside was mainly American, loyal to the Congress, minding its colored cattle, growing its crops. Battles had been fought in the town and there were still rusting iron cannonballs, British, embedded in the plank houses up toward Bound Brook on River Road.

A small four-oared boat containing silent, cloaked men made its way in the night up the river and around the bend, so that the few night lights of the town glimmered in the blue-black mist rising off the smooth river. A night bird sounded and dogs barked far off. A lantern was being swung from the shore on the left.

" 'Burnet Street wharf' it's marked on the map," said Captain Corky. "It's the signal all right, Colonel."

A round stocky man in a charcoal-colored cloak, a black patch covering one eye socket, stood carefully up in the boat. "The signal is proper, Captain?"

"Two waves to the right, three times up and down."

"Move the boat in."

Like a large dark spider the boat was oared in toward the town as it slept in starlight. Somewhere a fox barked, and as they came up to the wooden wharf a figure darted out and leaped into the boat. "Pull away. I don't like the shadows follerin' me."

Colonel Lemon looked at Captain Corky. "You know him?"

"It's Lanky Wells, the Shippen coachman."

"The general's now, sir—yer honors."

"Never mind, you have something for us?"

The coachman took out a packet wrapped in brown paper and handed it over. "You can put me back on shore now. Now I've gotten rid of it."

"Too risky if you were followed. Captain Corky, what's a good spot down the bay to drop the man?"

"Perth Amboy. Just before where the navy ketch picks us up for New York."

"The devil," said Lanky. "The skinners will cut me up alive if they kotch me."

Captain Corky said to the oarsmen, "Get down the river fast—pull your backs out, lads." Captain Corky bunched his cloak around his ribs and sat watching the polished silver shores run past in the night light. On the ridge of ancient rock debris here and there a house gleamed bone-white to a rising moon. The night smelled of frogs and pond scum, wet rocks and fish. It would be best to be far downriver when the moon was at its brightest.

Sir Henry Clinton rose early. It was a habit which at forty he no longer noticed. And it was New York—a city he hardly cared for—and he had to get dispatches back to England. This new, fantastic turn of affairs seemed promising. His Irish valet dressed him and he had his tea, but no breakfast. The flesh was filling out too much on this American food. The small white house near Canal Street held his staff, his two writers of dispatches, but unlike most of the British higher officers in the colonies he kept his doxies elsewhere. Sir Henry was fussy, but much more alert to events than his former chief, Sir William Howe.

In the large living room done in knotty pine—really, how savage a way to panel such a gracious chamber—Colonel Lemon was waiting with a neat young woman who had a bold look, a fine pair of green eyes, and a shapely bust. Sir Henry Clinton was a man who liked a neatly rosy bust.

"Ah, Colonel. Your river trip was most successful."

"It was, sir. May I present Mrs. Harvell Livingston. Daughter-in-law of the late Sir Francis Livingston, who was one of our most loyal men in the colonies."

"Pleased, Mrs. Livingston, pleased."

"I got here sir, too late, a widow. Sir Francis was dead of a fever. But my son Daniel had preceded me to the colonies."

"We seem to be always late in the colonies."

"An amazing expanse of land, sir, or so I find it."

Colonel Lemon was annoyed at the small talk. He touched his eye patch and felt under it where an eyeball had been. "Mrs. Livingston has agreed to write for us to Mrs. Arnold."

Sir Henry nodded at Peg. "You see, my dear, we want just a kind of casual, chatty letter from you to a lady of position living in Philadelphia, and bored and wanting to know what is the *ton* in Manhattan and London."

"Certainly, Sir Henry, I write a pretty hand, taught me when young by a—a friend."

"We shall insert certain informations and questions in your letter and then you will recopy it with the new material. All letters in answer from Mrs. Arnold will come here and not to your address."

"I'm sure that's better, sir. I'm a bit cramped in my East River lodging, with a serving woman and a child. And . . ."

Colonel Lemon said briskly, "You'll be paid well. If that's all, Sir Henry, I think Mrs. Livingston can be excused to go write her first letter for our approval."

Peg looked at Colonel Lemon politely but coolly, bowed to Sir Henry, and swept out in a stage walk, her repaired but still stylish clothes creaking.

Colonel Lemon took the letter from Mrs. General Arnold out of his pocket and handed it to the British general. "It's risky, these meetings. We'll need better plans, and I've been arranging them."

"Have you, Colonel?" said Sir Henry, reading the letter.

"Yes, there's a Reverend Jonathan O'Dell who's posing as a chaplain in General Washington's army. He's really one of our agents, and he will bring the next messages through to us on thin paper, held in a hollow bullet."

"Seems rather melodramatic, but it's Major André's game, and yours, my dear Colonel. You know, of course, if we land Arnold properly, he may tear down the whole American defense system on the Hudson before he joins us? Open the gates as it were to end the war."

"We've had that in mind, Sir Henry."

"Thank you, Colonel Lemon."

Sir Henry glanced at Colonel Lemon and reread the letter. It seemed foolish, but also clear that he was dealing with a powerful personality in Mrs. General Arnold—one who talked of a dukedom for the general, great wealth from the Crown, and being honored by the king. Also an estate for Lord Arnold in the English countryside; she had heard Surrey and Kent well spoken of. "My most wise husband has practically decided to devote his sword and honor to righteousness and to Sir Henry Clinton and the King."

Sir Henry looked up from the letter.

"Colonel, instruct Major André for us to also continue his correspondence with the lady, but we must have a letter from General Arnold himself. Otherwise have André say to Mrs. General Arnold we do not know if we are really dealing with the principal in this matter. A dukedom? The personal gratitude of the king? Kent or Surrey? I don't suppose all that too much to pay to break the rebel cause to bits."

Colonel Lemon stood up and said dryly, "I've noticed, sir, that promises made to American-born Englishmen are never fully carried out."

"Don't know what gave you that idea."

Sir Henry waved off the thought and fell again to studying the letter spread out before him on the rosewood desk. He was an imaginative man and could be lifted by a good scheme from the sloth so natural among the British command. And this intrigue was proceeding in a direction that could end this war. If not, it could at least so cripple the American side they would pay heed to reason and a compromise.

The shabby room of Mrs. Harvell Livingston (as Peg Munday now called herself) would have had a view of the East River, if there had been any panes in the boarded-up window. But glass and other creature comforts were hard to come by during the British occupation of New York. She had been fortunate to find her son and his nurse, Lizzie Patch, living in a garden house near the burned-out ruin of Sir Francis' mansion, and get them to Manhattan, where her abilities in striking up friendships with the more gallant of the occupation officers and English merchants (making a good thing of the war) provided the small ménage with at least food, a roof that leaked only on very stormy nights, and some warm clothing.

Lizzie Patch was cooking a watery stew on a few glowing coals in the room's grate. Daniel, grown now to a sturdy little boy, was busy imagining that some dozen hulls of walnuts were the British battle fleet. He was involved in a great sea battle on the dusty boards of the floor.

Peg's footsteps sounded on the creaking staircase and she came in smiling, her outer skirt folded over to make a carry-all.

"Ah," said Lizzie Patch, "yourself was gone so long I feared you were snatched up by them skinners or river pirates."

"Never fear that," said Peg, opening her skirt and allowing a badly plucked chicken, a great green cabbage, a bottle of wine corked with a whittled bit of wood, and a wedge of brown cheese to roll out on the table. "We've had a bit of luck."

"A young lord now? Or one of them merchant captains, lovie?"

"No, I've just seen Sir Henry Clinton himself."

"Oh," said Dan, "a big soldier."

"Gaud bless Sir 'Enry—a fine sojer indeed."

"That he is. Lizzie, have you seen the pen and the ink? I have paper. I must write a letter."

Lizzie was inspecting the cadaver of the hen by holding it over her head. "Nice, nice broth for Dan 'ere from this. Eh? Ink and pen? I been using the inkpot for shoe polish and Dan 'as been tossin' the pen at a pertater. 'Ere it is, and I'll just pour some water into the inkpot and stir it up and that will do as ink."

Peg sat down at the small table that served for all things, even a desk, and Lizzie set down two handleless cups and she and Peg drank the poor and bitter wine. "Not bubbly like we 'ad in London, lovie, but it 'as the bite. No, you *don't*, Dan, drinkin' will stunt yer growth."

But Peg gave the boy a few drops of wine in half a glass of water and he lifted it over his walnut fleet. "To the Admiral of the Blue! Huzzah!"

Peg refilled her cup with a flourish and a shake of her head. "And don't think you'll not have a fleet of your very own, Dan, some day. The Livingston holdings have shipyards and ships, and captains that have traded with the naggers in far-off Chiney. It's all safe, I hear, in some company a smart Yankee is holding for us."

Lizzie was plucking fuzz off the chicken. "A dream. And if this war ever ends! But this bird should last us three days at least."

"There will be more," said Peg, inspecting the twisted pen, and shaking up the brownish liquid in the inkpot. "*Now* to work." She put the tip of her tongue between her lips and began to write slowly in a careful tight script.

Dear Mistress Arnold,

I take pen in hande to ask of yr. health & that of yr. gallant husband. Wars damn'd furies are not for women & yo might care to kno of the newest bonnets in the shoppes here & of how a lady amuses herself in this much soldier'd town this yeare . . .

Peg wrote for a long time, then copied out what she had written on a clean sheet with a neater appearance. She had a good sharp mind and a keen interest in intrigue. She had written her letter as one woman to another, and of those things a fashionable creature would be interested in. When she was satisfied, Peg folded the good copy, finished off the wine, and got her cloak. Lizzie Patch had cut up a part of the chicken for the stew and was roasting the liver on a hot stone for Daniel.

"I'm going out, Lizzie, but I'll be back soon. The stew smells good for a change."

"It's all what goes into it, lovie, that makes anything come out best."

Lizzie spent her time while the stew was coming to perfection cleaning up the room and tossing the debris out of the window. So it was that one of Botts' agents, who had been watching the house, got the first draft of Peg's letter to Mrs. General Arnold.

CHAPTER 39   Lieutenant Joe Philipse came out of the wilderness and found the war settled down to the deadly business of waiting and marching, of attack and counterattack. General Washington was avoiding direct battle most of the time, and the British were doing as much damage with raid and fire as they could in the south, while in the north the opposing foes faced each other and sent out agents to gather information and spread rumors, for it was also a war of gossip, of tall stories, of intrigue, and addled facts that had no beginning and little end.

Joe Philipse had an uncut blond beard that flowed like piles of new-minted coin down over his fringed hunting shirt. He had long since discarded a uniform and dressed as a frontier scout: the greasy camp-soiled leather breeches, the broad belt holding tomahawk, pistol, and knife. He wore a shabby cocked hat free of any trim, and swung on his back was a long rifle and a hunter's pack. He looked hard, dangerous, and those who could see his eyes thought him more than slightly mad.

At Albany Joe got a horse, crossed the river to the east bank, and went down by the Hudson, noting some burned-out houses of the old families, the bones of a straggler, or victim, lying prey for foxes in the sumac leaves of a gully that led down to the river. The Hudson was infected with a kind of freebooter that roved in bands, and claimed first one loyalty, then another, being British in the morning and American in the afternoon if it suited his business. Cowboys and skinners, as this riffraff was called, terrorized the river.

They did not molest Joe. He had little of value, even the horse he rode limped, and Joe looked like a hard nut, and could make trouble. As he neared Philipse Manor he tried again to feel reality, but failed. It no longer bothered him, this inability to command reality. Joe now lived in a kind of fevered dream. He saw accurately and could command events, shape his course, and do his duty. But it was all unreal as dreams and impermanent as snowflakes.

He could not have recited properly the results of his long hunt among the Indians for his wife, Sally. It was all blurred into raids, the slitting of red throats, the palaver in some sort of Indian language with fairly friendly villages, the hunting out of clues and probing the memory of savage minds more disorganized to truth than even Joe's own.

The cardinal acts of existence took place. Joe could drink, he could eat, he could shoot well now, and trail. He wrote simple reports, often on birchbark, which Botts read with great interest and put away in his saddlebags. In those rare moments of rational placidity Joe would wonder, what *if* he found his wife? No matter her condition or her experiences, what then? As time went on he had become a gaunt ghost of the forests driven in some pursuit for which there would be no end, cursed to follow some chase that would never terminate. The images of satisfaction long lost to him kept just out of reach, and when he could almost touch them, or so he felt, they ran faster and he would increase his pace—a large, addled young man with the great yellow beard, running through the forest, screaming guttural sounds of sorrow and rage. Later, worn out, lying panting on the forest moss, only partial consciousness would come back, and he would move on slowly, mouth open, staring at the birds flitting in the branches, aware by some animal sense of the condition of the country and closeness or distance of actual physical danger lurking all around him.

The horse, tired and old (most of the good stock had long since been run off), stopped to nibble at the branches of an old apple tree. Joe pulled its head savagely away and kicked his deerskin heels into the shaggy flanks. The horse responded only with a brief burst

of speed and soon fell back into its usual pace—a slow rather wad-
dling amble which its bad leg made look a little silly.

The family road past the stone gateposts into Philipse Manor was
overgrown with hairy vines, the yellow weeds rioting in the unkempt
hedges. Here and there someone had attempted to keep a rosebush
or a plum tree free of neglect and wasp nests, but it was a feeble
effort and soon given up, Joe could see as he rode past.

Rain had washed out most of the stone on the great circling
drive, the wooden shutters of the stone house needed paint, but it
seemed snug enough. A wispy, lazy brown smoke came from the
kitchen chimney.

Joe dismounted and waited, from habit, for someone to come
take the horse. But no groom came and he took the bridle and the
bit off the horse and turned it loose on the overgrown lawn. It
would not wander far, and if it did, no matter—the creature was
of little value.

The front doors were unused and heavy timbers had been nailed
in a great ✕ across them. Joe went around to the kitchen. A pawky-
looking Negro girl, barefooted with splayed toes in the brisk cold
day, went popeyed at the sight of him and ran indoors shouting,
"Cowboys, de raiders! Lord, lord Massa Dave, Missy Roxy! De cowboys!"

Joe dropped his pack and gun on the red brick kitchen floor and
went into the small room overlooking the river where they used to
breakfast in the days of his childhood, his father reading the London
letters (was he still in prison, or back in British hands and most
likely sailed for Europe?). There was the scarred window sill where
Joe used to beat with his gruel spoon. No amount of paint could
ever hide those dents in the wood.

"Hold still, you. Come around, slowly." The voice behind Joe
was firm and direct in its crisp commands.

Joe turned, not hurrying. David Cortlandt, in shirt and undone
breeches faced him, a pistol in each hand.

"Lower the iron, Davey. It's me, Joe Philipse."

David frowned, then smiled. "So it is, under all the face hay."

"I'm pleased someone still lives here."

"I bought it in, Joe, from the government people when it was
seized. Not all the land, of course, just the house. But damn it, it's
good to see you, Joe."

David's arms were around him and the big bearded man began

to sob and he leaned over weeping on his brother-in-law's shoulder.

After a while they both recovered and stood apart.

David said, "Sit down, Joe. We had no word of you for months."

"I've been away out beyond the biggest of the lakes." Joe sat down and made no pretense of drying his tears. "And past them. But I don't remember much. Lung fever."

"You look fine now, Joe. Shaved and clothed, you'll be the proper Continental officer again."

"It doesn't matter, the appearance of things." He stopped talking, then frowned and drove off the idea he had tried to express and failed. "The war goes on?"

"It does. But the French are active and giving us a great deal of aid. And thank the Lord for General Washington. He's worn down all the hotheads, survived all the plotting against him, or most of it. But it's a hard war."

The Negro girl, open-mouthed, was staring in at the door and David waved her in. "Never mind catching flies, Zee, get some food on the table."

She scooted off and David stared at Joe's heavy, coarse hands, red with weather, dark with ingrained campfire grime.

"David, I didn't find her, you know."

"So it seems, Joe."

"She's alive somewhere."

"I'm not going to try and talk you from the idea."

"There was a white girl living with a Huron chief by the big rocks on the west side of Lake George. I saw her. Blue-eyed, yellow-haired. But she was captive since a babe, and spoke no English and had great fear of us. She had three breed whelps and seemed content."

"Joe, eat something. I'll get a mug of cyder."

"I'm too weary . . ."

The bearded man put his head down on his arms and then fell asleep almost at once. He slept indifferently and deeply, as if he had pulled the plug from reality and it had suddenly all drained away.

Roxanne had been up in their bedroom with the new baby, a large and active girl they had named Mollie, when the unusual sounds from downstairs attracted her attention. She knew at once that Joe her brother had returned. She didn't know how she knew, but an overwhelming surge of blood went to her head, a feeling of pressure filled her breasts—something sang to her that her brother had returned.

She had grown plump with a hurried maturity, and the new baby had widened her hips, enlarged her breasts. Roxanne knew that there would be many other children, yet the thought of Joe come home made her again the slim girl playing in the garden with the little boy, in the golden weather of childhood to which there is no return but in memory.

She picked up Mollie, the pink and round baby, its large blue eyes following the movement of her face. Mollie was bigger and solider than George had been. Mollie had a firmness and was already a demanding creature that did not plead for attention but expected it. George was playing in a corner of the big bedroom, seated on a small bench with a spotted hound puppy licking his face.

"Father—" said George, holding the puppy by its tail. "Father here?"

"Yes, dear, father is home for a few days. He'll be up soon."

"Puppy for father," said George, under the impression he was making a great deal of sense. Roxanne put Mollie down in the cherrywood cradle. The baby made a face of protest and certain deep sounds of anger. But Roxanne was in no mood to placate the spoiled infant.

She turned toward the door, worried and almost in fear. David came in. He was smiling, as he did when he had broken a favorite dish of hers, or had been thrown by a horse she had advised him not to ride. Here now was that special smile with which he padded certain kinds of information.

"Roxy, who do you think is downstairs?"

"Joe. How is he, dear?"

"How did you know? You're a witch and will burn for it."

"Cast me no teacup readings. How's Joe?"

"Temper, temper," said David putting his arm around his wife. "Joe is not well, Roxy. I don't mean he's ill of anything visible."

"What do you mean? I suppose now he's bewitched?"

"It's his mind. The nervous disorders are not my field of medicine. But there is a special melancholy that sits on him. I've seen it in Bedlam."

"Don't say it, Davey. Not Bedlam."

"I don't mean he's a raving lunatic. You know Joe isn't. But he's disturbed mentally now and there is nothing I can do for him."

"We must be kind to Joe. We must give him rest, comfort, and love, Davey. A great deal of love. Oh so much love."

"Yes. John Hunter used to say, 'If we know nothing of a malady, let it alone and leave nature to salve it with time and rest.' Be prepared for Joe's appearance. He's grown a great tawny beard and will not shave it off. And he's taken to forest gear, like Jack-Tom Swales."

"Oh, my poor, poor Joe."

Roxanne turned away and wept silently for a while and then blew her nose. "He will be happy to see the children."

George came over, carrying the puppy by the scruff of its neck. "Hector and George go hunting, father?"

"Yes George, when you're a bit older, both of you."

He patted his son's head, and thought of how like Joe, the Joey he had first known, his own son was in appearance. It was such a mystery, this inheriting of bone and blood and shapes of noses. And there must be more—all the secrets of the spleen and the glands that no one knew the meaning of yet. When he had the time some day he would try and find out some of the stubborn-held secrets of nature. That he would indeed. Now he would go downstairs and try and get Joe to undress and go to sleep in a proper bed.

It was no problem living with Joe, they found out in the days that followed. He was good company during his more lucid moments, and when his mind wandered away he would go off by himself and sit like a monument at an upstairs window looking out at the leaves fall and the river go flowing along. When autumn came he would often take a big wooden rake and go out on the lawns and pile up the fallen oak and maple leaves, and stand there in the wonderful odor of autumnal burnings, his great beard blowing free and dancing sparks endangering it. When the honking V's of geese came flying high from the north, he stood at the river bank and looked up at them. At his feet George played with his puppy and Mollie in her basket made cooing, wet noises. Joe was very good with children, and soon Roxanne had no fear for them at the hands of their strange uncle. David was away a great deal of the time. The French were landing supplies on the Connecticut coast and he had to be there to inspect the medical chests and the drug and hospital gear being unloaded.

Between the sister and brother there was a great, placid peace. Joe was on long leave, and he seemed to have forgotten the war as a distant drum no longer heard. Roxanne would take her knitting out on the back porch and watch Joe and George scuffle with the puppy, or Joe would carry Mollie in her basket into the rose garden and sit there basking in the wintry sun until it became too cold for the children to be outdoors.

As winter came whipping up the surface of the Hudson, Joe had longer periods of contact with reality, but he remained a solitary. He and Roxanne talked endless hours of their childhood, of lost games, forgotten innocence, and little shameful secrets. They never spoke much of their father or their mother; the local opinion was that they were blotted out, gone.

Joe did not sleep well. He broke through the skin of fearful nightly dreams and lay shaking and sweating. Roxanne could hear him come in late and go up the staircase trying to avoid the one creaking step, and then there would be sighs and groans in his room. Past midnight she would often awake to see if Mollie was fretting and free of her blankets, and Joe's pacing would come to her. There would be a candle burning in his window—for his room was in an ell that she could see into when the curtains were not drawn—and the big shaggy man, like a caged animal, would be marking off his strides.

Near morning Joe often went out into the chill dawn. He would come back near noon, soiled by forest mold and covered with dew. He never said much, and Zee, the only Negro house girl left, would serve him and sit looking at him with interest in her wide dark-purple eyes. She was simple-minded and shrill, and between the two of them there was an understanding very hard to define and never put into words. Neither had a full grasp of the visible world and both had some secret ties with a fierce and a special grammar beneath the surface of living that they could never voice. Zee, smooth brown and with gesturing limbs, would sing to herself droning songs with endless tunes, all in a few monotonous bars. She would stop what she was doing and stare into space until Roxanne shouted her into action, or boxed her ears to recall her to duty. "Stop day dreams, Zee, get the pot on the fire."

Joe would often bring a brace of rabbits and a few river hens back from his walks. He liked to sit for hours and watch the kitchen fire and smoke a short black clay pipe almost hidden in his beard. He would take George's puppy Hector in his lap and stroke it and pull its loose skin in his big weathered hand.

Roxanne feared him only in those rare periods when he flung himself into fits of sobbing and spent the night shouting Indian languages, tossing his tomahawk into the ceiling beams of his room. These periods of great emotional unrest did not last long. A day or so, and then he was working again around the neglected winter garden, stroking the puppy, teaching George woodcraft, or plucking a few birds for Zee to cook. They were like woodland animals, these two, almost communicating by touch and smell.

Isolated in the fury of winter, the house took on the atmosphere of a sealed-off world. David, once, riding down from West Point, found the house locked away in a white crystal mound with faint violet and blue shadows on the sugary white snow. He put his horse into the shed and stamped the snow from his boots before he went into the kitchen.

It smelled warmly of apple firewood, baking pears, and drying baby napkins on a cord strung across the room. George and Joe on their stomachs before the fire were drawing Indian villages on large squares of birchbark.

They looked up casually. George said, "Hello, Father," as David came in and they went back to their work. "Now, Georgie, the Hurons live in long bark houses. They look like this."

"Father, see our Indians."

"They look fine, George," said David, warming himself after the long chilling ride.

Zee was staring into the fire where two hares roasted on a spit. David shook her by one thin bony shoulder. "Where is Mistress?"

Zee blinked. "She be upstairs."

David stamped his boots—the big frozen toes were aching into life—swung off his cape, and threw his cocked hat on a pair of deer horns over a spice cabinet. Joe was bent over the birchbark drawings, erasing some detail with a corner of his beard. "The council meeting takes place around large fires. The chiefs sit like thus."

"They are naked, Uncle Joe."

"God made us naked."

David went upstairs. Roxanne was cutting up some of her father's old clothes into patterns to fit George. She looked up as David came in and put the scissors on a mahogany highboy (where no little boy could reach for them).

"I did not see you ride up, Davey. I hope you found fodder for the horse."

"A bit." He kissed her cheek. "How are you all here?"

"We manage. Joe has been of much help. Mollie cut two more teeth. But next time you go off to a far place, we'll all go with you."

He looked at his daughter, asleep in the family cradle.

"No, no. Camps are no places for a family. Teeth, has she? Well now, I must prepare to be bitten." He walked to the cradle. Mollie, bloated with food and rosy with health, lay sleeping with a wet thumb in her mouth. David pulled it out, but she automatically put the finger back.

"It's no use, Davey. She is habited to the pleasure of her thumb."

"So it would seem." David sat down and extended his legs to the small fire of tree burls burning in the low marble fireplace.

"Lord, it's been a cold ride from the Point. I had an escort till White Plains, then excused myself to come back to see you all."

"You'll stay the night, love?"

"Yes." He took some object wrapped in French newspapers and gave it to her. She unpacked it and smelled a pinkish square of some ivory-like substance. "What is it, Davey? It has such a pleasant exotic odor."

"It's from the French ships that brought over supplies. It's a kind of soap the French king and his favorites use. Or so Captain Balbec told me."

"It's so sinful, darling," she said laughing as she sniffed it. "But so delightful."

David, finishing taking off his boots with the aid of the bed posts, pulled her down on his lap. "You're still my roaring girl, and nothing is too good for you, my love, even the king's own perfumed soapings."

"I'll have Zee heat up much water later and get out the sheet-iron bath, and we'll both bathe together right here, after the children are asleep."

He bit at her ear lobe and kissed her tenderly. "You move me oddly, you sinful creature. Mutual bathing like the Romans now at Philipse Manor?"

"It adds a spark to marriage, don't you think so, my dear Doctor?"

They laughed and hugged intimately and made small jests known only to each other. For a little time they recaptured the full rapture of young lovers, for neither was aware how much turmoils of war and the passage of time had changed them from their first images of each other.

CHAPTER 40   Major André, for all his French name was from a family very much Anglicized. Among his pleasures was a love of stained drawings. Water colors delighted him, and he was always sketching with pen and ink, often his own features in the mirror. He sat at Sir Henry Clinton's chambers, a handsome and dainty man in his red and gold-encrusted jacket, very properly tailored, and drew the objects of Sir Henry's table desk. The inkpot in the India brass tray, the ivory ruler on the green leather map case, the silver tray of glasses holding the yellow Spanish wine.

Sir Henry was standing by the glowing fireplace, warming his British bottom—a New York winter with ice floes in the bay was nothing to take lightly. He looked up from the letter in his hand.

"Major André, this is an amazing offer. Is it genuine?"

"It came in a hollow bullet carried through the lines by our agent the Reverend Mr. O'Dell, chaplain—on the surface—to General Washington's troops."

"The handwriting is Mrs. General Arnold's?"

"It's Peggy's, I'd know it anywhere. The general refuses to risk writing in his own hand. But it's dictated in his own words."

Sir Henry read out loud from the letter. " 'If I point out a plan by which Sir Henry Clinton shall possess himself of West Point, its garrison, artillery, &c., I want £20,000 sterling. I think it would be a cheap purchase for an object of so much importance . . .' "

Sir Henry chuckled and tapped his fingers on the letter. "The beggar sets his value high—£20,000 sterling!"

"For the main depot of American military supplies? For the key to the Hudson River fortress and the road to Canada, Sir Henry? High?"

"Damn me, how close to truth is this thing, John?"

"I swear it's as set down. I know Peggy Shippen from our stay in Philadelphia. She's Peggy Arnold now, but still the girl who wants to swallow the world."

"Her hold on him is that strong? What dupes we men are to the lusts of the flesh."

"An aging man," said Major André, sketching Sir Henry Clinton spread-eagle before the fireplace, "mated to an amorous young girl, and she about to present him with the victory of his passions, a child—perhaps the last child of his loins."

"Bring in Colonel Lemon and Mrs. Livingston."

"At once."

When "Colonel Lemon" and Mrs. Livingston stood before the general, he folded the letter and put it inside his flower-embroidered waistcoat.

"Colonel Lemon, I want all information your spies and scouts can give me on West Point and its contents. You know the Hudson River country?"

"I was born on it, lived on it, sir, till the war."

"Good. You know what schemes we are engaged in? I want you to train some men to be prepared to bring a certain personage soon, or in the next few weeks, through the lines. You will support Major André, and you will see to the safety of both the major and the personage."

"Have no doubts of it, sir. I know every stone and backwoods road on both sides of the Hudson. My family still resides on the Hudson. And as we are related to almost all the great families, I've visited their places and know the country. We shall certainly arrange for the safety of all when the time comes."

Major André drew a sketch of the stocky fat figure of the one-eyed colonial. He tried to capture the fanatic's stance, the earnest intellectual twist of the heavy jowled head under its badly curled wig. This adventure, if successful, would have its history told in every officers' club in England some day.

Sir Henry turned to Mrs. Livingston. She had seated herself in a petit-point chair, her hands in black knit gloves folded on her lap. "Well, Mistress Livingston, you have done well with your letters. I must confess I have learned much gossip about the town and my officers; news that my other agents never bring me."

Peg made a bold eye at the general. "It is a lively place if one knows the rounds, Sir Henry."

"Yes, I'm sure. Major André, I don't dare risk you writing direct too often. Mistress Livingston will write a code letter to Mrs. General Arnold of the usual gossip, and we'll get a proper agent to get it to Philadelphia. Major André, explain the diamond code to Mrs. Livingston."

John André leaped up with excitement. "You mean we accept General Arnold's offer and move at once!"

Sir Henry watched Colonel Lemon's expression. "We do if he is able to give us West Point. He's still military governor of Philadelphia. So what can he do to get West Point?"

"Leave it to Mistress Shippen," said Major André. "She'll push him into asking for the post. Now, Mrs. Livingston. I draw on this sheet of paper a diamond shape, thus. . . . Now in it I write this message. *Watch.*" Within the diamond, he wrote: *we accept your offer as in your letter and wait upon you to inform us of your plans and that you will be able to deliver what you promise us. We shall meet any of your desires and carry full protection to you and all you keep.*

Peg Livingston studied the diamond shaped text. "I see it, Major. I write an empty-headed letter around this text using it as part of my letter, working in your words in the position you have them on this sheet."

"That is so, Mrs. Livingston. Properly so."

"But how will Mrs. General Arnold read them?"

"By another messenger—once she gets this letter—she will get a blank sheet of paper which has only a diamond shape cut out of it."

Peg laughed. "She puts that sheet over my letter and all but your message is blotted out."

"Just so."

Colonel Lemon said, "*Most* clever, sir."

Sir Henry nodded and looked over the message in Major André's diamond shape. "Yes, that will do. Better go and get your letter drafted, Mrs. Livingston, and bring it back here tonight at nine. We'll go over it together."

Peg Livingston made a low bow to the general and gave him a wanton, knowing smile that only he could see.

Sir Henry made a curt bow back at her and his eyes made her an answer that a clever woman could understand at once.

After she and Colonel Lemon had gone, Sir Henry sat down at his table, pulled free his lace shirt front, and looked earnestly at

Major André. "You understand, John, we can't fumble away this gift placed in our hands by a greedy woman. You are detailed to forget everything else and give your whole time to General Arnold and this fantastic event."

"There will be no failure, not on our side. Benedict Arnold is a hot-tempered man, and he could betray himself to the Americans. But I think his wife will keep him from error on that account. As for Mrs. Livingston, I am sure she will please you with her work—with her services to you."

Sir Henry refused to rise to the bait. He smiled and said, "I am sure your recommendations of her services were made after careful study."

For whatever reason a clever, greedy woman stoops to folly—or scheming—she must keep close guard on herself. Her friend Mr. Robert Morris, active in the affairs of the Congress, gave discreet little parties in his Philadelphia house—parties with the right people in the right places. Mrs. General Arnold attended his biggest, looking worrisome and out of sorts. The general, her husband, had gone to General Washington's that day again to plead that his life of soldierly inactivity as military governor of Philadelphia was breaking his health. He had promised Mrs. Arnold to mention West Point as the proper place of action for him. General Washington had once said something would be done about it. So far nothing had been.

Aaron Burr and Botts, who had come to talk to Robert Morris about funds for their secret service, noticed the tense and over-dramatic gestures Peggy Shippen Arnold used to answer all greetings. The strain of child-bearing and a husband's career, Burr felt, must have been too much for her. Aaron Burr, a lecherous clever man, had once tumbled her about in a carriage and been slapped for it.

Botts, ill at ease in the fashionable surroundings, only nodded at the guests who knew him. Burr shook his head as his eyes followed Mrs. General Arnold. "Young girls should not marry for ambition, and elderly sensualists should remember they will not lust forever. The itch for living beauty has destroyed empires, historians tell us."

Botts shuffled his shoes on the waxed floor. "The two seem well enough mated to me."

"You don't read that fellow Gibbon's history, do you?"

A young staff officer came in and went up to Mrs. General

Arnold, who had just sat down, and said within the hearing of all, "Good news from General Washington."

Peggy Arnold grasped the arms of her chair and half rose. "It's come! The appointment!"

"General Arnold sent me right over with the news. He's been appointed in command of *all* cavalry!"

"Cavalry!" She screamed it. "Command of horse! But he asked for—I mean . . ." She rose, hysterical, and began to scream. Several women ran to her and held her up. Her head wobbled as if it were held on by a thread.

"His poor leg! It's a plot to kill him! No, no—he can't take it."

"But, my dear, it's a post of honor."

"No, he's not to take it."

Botts did not move toward the hysterical woman.

"It seems odd to reward good fortune by this wailing, sir."

"Do you know much of very emotional women, Botts?" Burr asked.

"Enough to know uncontrollable hysteria when I see it."

There was no comforting Mrs. General Arnold. She was throwing herself to the floor and the people around her were lifting her against her will and placing her on a wine-colored sofa. "They are trying to kill him! That's it, they are trying to *destroy* General Arnold!"

The host pushed pillows under her head and someone went to look for salts. "Now, Peggy, no one is doing the general any harm. It's a fine promotion."

"It was *not* what he wanted! It wasn't what he's set his mind on."

Botts walked over to the sofa and calmly looked down at the thrashing woman, her silks in disorder, her large milk-white breasts almost escaping from their moorings. She was kicking out, losing her blue silk shoes.

"His leg will not permit him to be an active cavalryman. It's a plot! How *could* General Washington do this to him!"

Botts observed the uncontrollable gyrations of the woman. He studied her as a scholar might study some interesting specimen under his lens.

Finally two ladies led a sobbing Mrs. Arnold away to a private chamber and a servant followed, carrying her shoes and scarf. Botts turned and looked at Aaron Burr, and they left soon afterward.

In the bright sun of the early summer they walked slowly down the street. Botts said, "I think you had better report this action to Congress, sir."

"What can I say? You've discovered nothing."

"We've discovered a hysterical woman who acts as if something very strange is going on around her much against her will."

"Of course, General Arnold has just been through a court-martial for appropriating public property—wagons or something. But he was acquitted. Oh very well, Botts, you suspicious hound, prepare me a report on her actions today and I'll communicate it to Congress as a secret document."

They parted and Aaron Burr hurried off to a card game.

Before Botts could finish the secret report to Congress General Arnold again appealed to General Washington, and the honest Virginian, feeling the nation had not redressed all the wrongs done the general, and knowing of his skill as a warrior, said, "West Point shall be yours, General Arnold. You can start on the new fortifications we plan there."

In July of 1780 General Benedict Arnold took over his post on the Hudson as supreme commander of West Point. Peggy Arnold at once sat down to write a letter to Major André through Mrs. Harvell Livingston. A code had been decided on, using the language of chic millinery.

Major André dictated to Mrs. Livingston a letter full of stylish hat jargon and she took it down with care:

"It would make me very happy to become useful to you here. You know the Mischianze made me a complete milliner. Should you not have received your fullest equipment, I shall be glad to enter into the whole detail of cap, wire, needles, gauze, & c. . . ."

Major André looked over Mrs. Livingston's shoulder as she wrote. "Fine, fine. Be sure it's spelled as I've asked."

"I've tried, Major, to improve my spelling under your eye and care."

He patted her soft, shapely shoulder, "You've done well, my dear, very well indeed."

He took up the letter and read it over. Yes, it seemed simple enough. Nothing must go wrong now. He hurried from the small writing room to Sir Henry Clinton's personal chambers upstairs.

Peg Livingston put her feet up on the sofa and closed her eyes. Everything was going well. This nonsense of letter-writing was amusing. Daniel was growing and they would soon be able to take up better quarters. The war would end as soon as General Arnold came over to the British and she would hunt up the Livingston assets hidden somewhere in a Yankee lawyer's strongbox and take her place in British colonial society. She smiled, contented, "like a cat full of butter," Lizzie Patch would have said.

General Arnold stood solidly on one of the gun platforms at West Point, seriously contemplating motifs. He was looking down at the winding blue-green sheen of the Hudson. It was a beautiful view and the river was at its best, the white triangles of sails against the shimmering ripple of clear water. The heights of West Point in their oak and pines, the rocky road up to the fortress were all his. He turned and paced off the platform holding six bronze cannon, four-pounders in a row; and below in the parade yard were a half a hundred men at drill, marching and counter-marching to the rasp of the sergeant's voice. Piles of bricks and stones testified to the work on the new fortifications.

Why not stay here? thought General Arnold, why not serve, why go ahead with the mad plan he was involved with? But even this post could be taken from him. The war was nowhere pointing to a climax, and he thought of his small daughter purling in her cradle in the house nearby, and Peggy's beautiful body and her grace and indolent sultry charm and his need of her. He couldn't leave her like this if anything should happen to him. She was so right. England would see his worth as a soldier and there would be much fortune; gold coins, not the worthless Continental paper promised him. The shame of his recent court-martial burned his face red. Was he a bookkeeper? a clerk with a pen behind his ear to watch everything, account for all the personal actions his position demanded? He turned to an officer. "Colonel Livingston, I'm not satisfied with these guns."

"Yes, sir. I'll have them remounted."

General Arnold looked downriver as if expecting the entire British battle fleet to come sailing up. He began to pace back and forth, his dark, handsome brow furrowed, his hands balled to fists, locked behind his back.

Mrs. General Arnold sat at her small kidney desk in the tiny upstairs room where she kept her traveling accounts under lock and key. Now she was trying to translate military terms into millinery. Sir Henry Clinton wanted to know how much armament would be needed to take West Point. General Arnold had given her the items. She consulted a code from Major André written on thin papers and wrote:

"My needs here would be satisfied by one pr. stockings, 4 pr. white thread, 1 pr. black satin, 2 caps, 1 fan, 1 very light coat." She checked back to her code list. Ah yes, *caps* were heavy cannon, *light coat* a battalion of dragoons, *white thread* a regiment of infantry, so 4 *white threads*, four regiments. Really, she had never imagined war was so simple a thing.

General Arnold came into the room and she turned the letter over and slid the code under a book. He said, "That's right, my dear. I don't care to know the details, just get the damned thing done with."

"My darling," she said grasping his hand. "It's hard for you, Bennie, I know. I've asked for what you feel will be able to take this place once you've prepared it for them to seize."

General Benedict Arnold kissed his wife's cheek. He was surprised at how warm and damp his face was. He had been drinking brandy again, and before dinner. He must get a closer hold on himself.

Sir Henry Clinton was giving a banquet on Broadway to the Tory and loyalist families of New York. It was an irksome, sweaty affair but proper thanks enough for what they had done for England. Colonel Lemon had presented him with a silver tray, the women had at last retired to light wine, nuts, and gossip, while the men and officers were becoming maudlin with strong drink as the soldiers' orchestra sawed out old English country airs. There was something that elated the general and he kept looking at Major André. Once he even lifted his glass and shouted, "And among us all, plain John André, my young adjutant, will come back from a mission soon as Sir John André!"

The young man flushed and Colonel Lemon drained off his glass. The banquet broke up soon after ten and most of the staff, some in carriages and some mounted, went at once to the stews and wine cellars. Sir Henry in his residence gave orders to alert the ship H.M.S. *Vulture* to carry a messenger upstream. He took Colonel

Lemon aside. "Major André goes to West Point to meet General Arnold in person."

Major André nodded. Colonel Lemon frowned: "Is that wise at this time, sir?"

"Letters from him will not do now. We must get information beyond what the code tells us. We have to take West Point with no slip-up. John—Major André—will have a talk with General Arnold and the matter will be settled properly."

"I suppose it's best. But it's a risk."

"Colonel Lemon, you will alert all Tory scouts and Rangers operating nearby to be on their guard, and you will have a waiting unit of men who can be rushed anywhere along the river if the plan should miscarry in any way."

"It's a large river, Sir Henry."

The general patted Colonel Lemon's shoulder. "A general gets *all* he asks for. You once told me you knew every inch of its shores. . . ." He walked over to where Major André was buttoning his military jacket. "My boy, Godspeed, and the beginning of the end of this war."

"Thank you, Sir Henry, for your faith in me."

"Remember, keep your uniform on at all times. Under your cape. Do not take a step in enemy territory out of your regimentals."

"I shall come back with General Arnold's full expression of what is to be done. And in this unpaid-for army gear."

"The H.M.S. *Vulture* will set you ashore at dawn by the landing to Arnold's headquarters. We hope he was given orders the *Vulture* will not be fired on if she is sighted."

Major André bit his lips together to hide the emotions his mission set up in him. He pressed his general's hand and motioned to Colonel Lemon to follow him from the room. Sir Henry turned to inspect a map that hung on the paneled oak wall. He found West Point on the river (he had been finding it on that map for several weeks). It would make a fine gift for the king. It would send English prestige surging up again in Europe. An American hero and general coming over with the fortress of West Point! He turned and sent a servant to see if Mrs. Livingston was still waiting for him.

CHAPTER 41   Mynheer Schuyler was not sleeping well of late. After an hour or so of too-hard slumber he would come awake nights—almost in panic—to listen to his wife's deep breathing and to his own heart racing. All the terrors of the dark remembered from the troubled past of his childhood would try to crowd in. It was best then, he had discovered, to get up and, wrapped in the old dressing gown, go down to the kitchen and blow on the embers still glowing faintly under the white ashes there, and make himself a cup of warm milk. Usually that would soothe him and his heart-beats would feel less like the fatal drum calling him to some last desperate march.

This night, however, his heart had raced and thumped so fast he could not calm it with warm milk, even when laced with a flip of rum. He sat in the dark kitchen in hunched misery—just the glow of a few coals from the banked fireplace lighting pots and pans of copper and pewter that had survived the war years. He felt old and stale and depleted. He had so much more work to do yet on his history of the Hudson River families. At night the old house seemed to be settling with a low groaning of timbers, and the walls (he had never noticed it before) appeared to lean in slightly—or was it because he had left his spectacles upstairs?

And there wasn't really ever a night stillness: there was the whine of wind, light and teasing in the untrimmed trees in the gardens, the scamper of something alive in the walls hunting prey or love—the sound of floor boards; who could be walking about at this hour?

Mynheer was solidly simple about the nature of things. He took no stock in ghosts, poltergeists, or phantoms; besides, the house had had a fairly decent history and there had been no great blood-lettings, no really tragic events, at least not dramatically tragic. The worst he could think of was the grand-uncle who cut off part of his ear while shaving one morning after a heavy night of Holland gin. Ghosts were for peasants and grannies.

Mynheer turned as some one came through the narrow door into the kitchen behind him. It was Martha Schuyler: the old woman stood leaning on her cane, her dark nightdress trailing behind her. How wrinkled and bent she was.

"Mama," he said tenderly. "You shouldn't roam the house late at night."

"Is no one awake, alert?" she asked, banging her cane on the red brick floor. "I just saw a man-of-war, a big ship on the river. Sailing upstream."

"Now Mama, you know even if you're still a vigorous old lady, you do imagine things." He was walking around her—out of range of her cane—trying to get her back to bed.

"Fiddledeedee, Peter. It was an English man-of-war, sailing up the river as if it were owner of everything. There were even a few lamps showing. Isn't there a war on?"

Mynheer waved an arm, knocking over his cup of milk and rum. "You *must* get back to bed. Maybe it was a small boat. But a man-of-war—no, no."

"You go out and look, you hear me? Get out there and see what they want. If they want to buy vegetables or a pig, be firm. They pay in gold, you hear me?"

Mynheer comforted his old mother and wrapped her in a worn cloak from the hall, and helped her up to her room. He promised to go out and hunt the ship. Old Martha's room looked downriver, and he agreed to go see if the man-of-war was visible to the north, upriver.

"Ach," said Martha, sitting up in her big bed. "No one at all to take care of the manor. What will happen to you all when I have to leave?"

Mynheer in slippers, an old hunting jacket over his nightshirt and for some reason a shotgun in his arms (against a man-of-war?), let himself out by the north door of the house onto the uncut lawn. It was a warm night with a milky, luminous quality, and he smelled the late roses and the fresh soil turned up by the night-feeding garden worms. The river itself had a special smell of shore mud and cat reeds, moist ferns and crushed mint. There was no sign of any ship upstream, for there the night seemed to lie thicker. The broad river ran slowly, half asleep, past Mynheer's house as if innocently denying any such thing as a British man-of-war. He sensed he was not alone in this night.

An old family hound came across the wet grass and Mynheer petted it and rubbed its neck. He slowly became aware of a large man standing by the river dock—and a woman—and he wanted to call down to them. The dog seemed uninterested in the strangers and Mynheer decided the dog must know the man. He was about to call out when the man turned and the pale moonlight picked up details. He had a full yellow beard and carried a rifle, and there was a brace of large rabbits hung over one shoulder. The woman was the Philipse slave Zee—she carried a game bag.

"Joe?" asked Mynheer. "What are you doing out tonight?"

"Hunting by the light of the flare. Zee holds it—it attracts game. Did you see it too?"

"See what?"

"H.M.S. *Vulture*. The moon was so bright I could read her name."

"Then there *is* a man-of-war going upriver!"

"Yes, she just tacked around the bend."

Zee pulled back into the shadows out of sight.

"You think it's like the time Clinton took Kingston?"

"No, this was a loner," said Joe. "Just one ship. Scouting I suppose. . . . Don't you enjoy the night, Mynheer? I always relish the night. It's a good time to get rid of thinking—everything is in the dark and in shadows. You get less sharp ideas at night, ideas that don't stab at you and hurt. Some have dangerous points. You ever engender such ideas, Mynheer?"

"Come in, Joe, and have a drink. Shouldn't we report the man-of-war to somebody?"

"Let them scout. I don't drink at night. It spoils the shape of things in your head. I mean the night looks changed then. . . . Good night, Mynheer. Come on, Zee."

He walked away, the two dead rabbits over his shoulder, completely attuned to the night, followed by the yellow girl and her game bag.

Major John André, pensive, overwound, and wary, hoped he could get ashore while it was not yet too light on the river. High up floated the towers of West Point. As the small boat was put overside into the river, he admired with an artist's eye the green salad of the landscape, the perfect pattern of rocks and trees, and over all the morning clouds beginning to dilute the darkness of the first dawn. He came ashore—wetting his boots—at a point of land, as directed in the last letter from Mrs. General Arnold. Lanky Wells, the old Shippen coachman, was waiting there for him.

"Just you foller me, sir."

Tree toads were croaking—an owl sounded its call. Major André wrapped his dark cloak around himself, hiding the British uniform, and began to follow his guide up a fairly overgrown path. From somewhere in the fort there was the bronze call of a morning bugle and the hiss of an early detail marching to the orders of bellowing voices.

Colonel Livingston, the commander of artillery at West Point, had a headache. He had been drinking late the night before in the officers' quarters, and had brought himself awake this morning with a large tot of grog. He was in a mean mood as he paced off the high gun platforms and inspected the guns. He was a man who was most charming by noon, really gay in the afternoon, and a wit by nightfall. But in the early morning hours he was better left alone. A gunner sergeant saluted, standing before his gun crew.

"Colonel, there's a ship out there on the river, just been observed, sir."

Colonel Livingston, a distant nephew of the late Sir Francis Livingston, loyal to the Continental Congress, turned and asked for a spy glass. "The bold bastard!" he sputtered as he looked. "Lying there bold as a wench in haytime."

"She's British, sir?"

"What the devil else would she be! Go have someone inform General Arnold, and get those guns around and aimed—we'll drop a few on her."

The crew went to work on the cannon—gun pointers figured range and angle, and the powder monkeys rushed the powder bags up from the stone hut below. The cannonballs were tamped down and the gun pointers signaled they were ready.

"What do you say, gunner sergeant?" shouted Colonel Livingston.

"We've got her in range, I'd say."

"Any word from General Arnold?"

"Not yet."

"All loaded? We'll fire the first pair. Let's knock her about now!"

"No word from the general to fire the guns, sir."

Colonel Livingston roared (Lord, what a headache!), "I'm in command of artillery here. *Fire!*"

The pair of guns went off over the river, four-pounders firing with a roar and a cloud of white smoke. On the river cream-colored columns of water leaped up around the man-of-war.

"Short! Short by fifty feet. Skew up those sights! Reload!"

There was activity now on the moored man-of-war. She still sat peacefully in the middle of the stream, downriver, but men were running to stations.

The four-pounders went off again and now the columns of pale-green water they threw up fell across the bow of H.M.S. *Vulture*, wetting her decks. Her riggings sang out like violin strings.

"The next set should hit her! A little to the left," shouted Colonel Livingston. The gun crews cheered and began to reload.

In Peggy Arnold's bedroom, Major André listened to the firing from the fort and looked at General Arnold peering out of the small leaded window looking down on the river. Peggy patted Major André's wrist.

"It's all right, John. They'll stop soon."

General Arnold turned from the window. "I can't order Colonel Livingston *not* to fire. You understand he'd find that an odd order, Major."

"I understand."

"Good. Come with me to my study. You have a place to hide some papers I'm sending to Sir Henry Clinton?"

"If not too bulky, in my boots."

Peggy smiled and again pressed the British officer's hand. He followed the general out into the next room. Mrs. General Arnold went to the window and saw the river spotted by clouds of drifting white smoke from the guns. She saw that the man-of-war was setting sails and tacking toward the west shore. As she watched, it came about and began to go downriver, beyond the reach of the still-firing guns. She touched her neck with a hand, and a worried frown puckered her brow.

It was Lanky the coachman who brought them the bad news later. "The ship, she's shifted mooring and then dropped downriver. Not a sight of her now."

Major André bit his lips together and frowned. "I can't stay here till she makes her mind up to return to pick me up."

"That damned Livingston could have damaged her," said General Arnold. "The ship may not return."

Major André thought for a moment. "I need a horse and guide. I'll ride south. Have you clothes to fit me? I can't ride out as a British officer among the river patrols."

Peggy Arnold nodded, "I'll get you together some civilian clothing. The general will order a good horse and a guide. Bennie, darling, explain to John how to get downriver. Should he risk it? Mayhaps . . ."

General Arnold was irked and touchy. He had had a bad night and the firing on the river and the talk with the British officer had not improved his always quick temper. He felt guilty of some great sin—a great stone on his chest—outraged at the destiny that had brought him to this thing. "Should *he* risk it? Damn, I'm willing to risk everything, why not he?"

Major John André turned on his most charming smile. "My dear General, of course. Produce the clothes, the horse, the guide."

"I'll write you a pass. Name of John Anderson. Say you're a young merchant traveling on private business."

"Yes, of course. John Anderson."

"That will get you through the American lines if stopped."

Peggy Arnold went out to find civilian dress and Major André began to strip himself of his uniform. The general sat down to write out the pass. The quill had a bad point and he corrected it, getting ink on his fingers. He finished the signature with a flourish.

Major André crossed a stream with his guide and they rode south from Fishkill, coming up behind White Plains on a dusty back-country road. It was a fine, clear day with the birds singing in the larch and beech trees, and the horses, long in need of exercise, letting themselves out, prancing and foaming at the bit. The guide named Smith (or so he said) was not talkative.

"We're moving beyond White Plains?" Major André asked.

"In that general direction."

The major's mount became frisky and the next few minutes were passed in quieting the skittish animal. There was haying in the fields, and here and there sheep and cows worked slowly across a meadow as they browsed. It was enough to make one stop and sketch, but the major wanted to deliver what he carried in his boots, and quickly. General Arnold was now committed in writing to the deed, and his plans for selling out West Point were admirable. The man was really a fine military mind of great merit.

Smith was becoming worried. They had passed a roadside sentry, one of half a dozen that the major had greeted with gaiety and assurance. Now at Pines Bridge the man called Smith pulled up his horse.

"I can't stand the strain of it, Major, any longer."

"You'd not leave me here?"

"You're in no trouble from now on. Just keep south on these roads."

The major leaned forward on his horse's neck and shook hands with his guide. "In that case, Mr. Smith, thank you for your kindness in coming so far. Good-by to you."

"Good journey, Major."

John André gave his horse the rein and rode on whistling "The Coventry Garden Fete." Damn it, the way wasn't true south at all, the way twisted and went off on branch roads. He should have asked General Arnold for a compass. Which way *was* south? If he were nearer the river he'd know. He was certain he was lost and traveling in a circle. He did not panic, but the horse was becoming winded. Major André stopped to mop his face with his silk handkerchief. He was suddenly aware that this adventure was not sitting well on his stomach. It was neither antic nor exciting, not a witty tale to tell over wine at the officers' mess. He was alone, and there was no one who could get him out of this but himself. He pulled up the horse's head sharply and banged his knees into the creature's barrel with a new and almost frightened cruelty. The problem was, which way to ride? He panted and the green world of trees began to spin before his searching eyes.

On the back road behind Pleasantville, called the town pike, three ragged men in makeshift clothes sat playing cards by the little creek. One wore a red jacket. There were pistols in their belts and dirty playing cards in their unwashed fingers.

"Damn it, Isaac, I never held such poor cards."

"You wouldn't be able to play a good set of pasteboards if you had 'em, Johnny."

The third man, called Williams, smoking a yellowed clay pipe, spat and scratched himself. "Think we'll get anything of value this morn?"

"Why not? Somebody has to pass sometime."

Johnny, who wore a stolen British uniform, said as he picked up some cards, "Now I hope we're not going to bushwhack any more Americans again."

"Devil a lot it matters what they be. As long as they carry something."

"No, no, Isaac van Wart, I no longer will loot the American side."

"The devil, Johnny—so far have we played any favors on either side? It's the only chance the poor have of gettin' a bit of their own back from the quality, and here you go white-livered."

Johnny held up a dirty hand for silence. They all heard it now; horse's hooves coming down from the north. They stood up and pulled out their pistols. A young man in a nut-brown outfit was riding a very good horse, coming down toward the creek. He had a fine lace shirt front, and Johnny had eyes for his beautiful boots. Good boots were hard to get these days. He hoped the fellow was a Tory.

Johnny ran forward and lifted his hand. "Halt, you there!"

Major André pulled rein. He was tired and his nerves were not holding up as well as he had expected. He was a brave fellow with his regiment, but this facing the dirty world alone had much to be said against it. He smiled as he observed Johnny's soiled British uniform.

"I say, there, it's all right—I'm a British officer."

Isaac grinned and winked—"Are you now, sir?"

"Yes—on a special errand."

Johnny was feeling Major André's boots, "Will you get off that horse—dismount, quickly!"

"I must not be detained."

Isaac shouted, "You're in for it, bucko! We're Americans!"

Major André paled, then smiled and pulled a paper from a waistcoat pocket. He dismounted and held it toward Isaac. "I had to say something when I saw the British scarlet on our fine friend here. Let's hurry this thing. I have to get along. John Anderson, American. My pass."

Johnny looked over Isaac's shoulder. "Signed by General Arnold."

"You should of showed your pass at once."

The third member of the road plunderers had said nothing so far; but Williams was not too bright. Now he suggested, "Let's strip 'im."

"Whatever for?" asked Major André.

Johnny pointed down. "Begin with the boots."

"General Arnold shall hear of this damned outrage!"

"The jacket too, then the waistcoat. What nice lace, Johnny."

André undressed slowly, leaving on his breeches and shirt. Johnny bent over the boots, pulled a set of thin papers from one of them. He looked at them and saw the words: *West Point*. He snarled at André.

"Damn it man, you're a spy!"

André gasped as if in pain. He rubbed his dry lips and began to talk quickly, spittle falling from his mouth.

"Look you, fellows, I can see you're simple men. I can offer you *any* sum of money you want to just let me ride on, unmolested."

"Have you got it on you, the money?"

"No, but as God sits above, it's available."

"Who *will* pay? God ain't goin' to."

"Sir Henry Clinton himself. You'll be paid royally."

They all laughed. "Royally! Oh we'd like *that*, puttin' our necks in Sir Henry's hangman's rope. Get on your horse."

"Where are we going?"

Johnny pointed his pistol on Major André. "Up to North Castle. See what Colonel Jameson—he hates gentry—has to say about this, Mr. Anderson, if that *is* your name."

"Colonel Jameson, I don't know him."

"He's the American commander there. Get mounted."

Major André fell forward in the saddle, recovered, and with trembling hand picked up the reins. He tried to whistle some lively tune to cheer himself, but he couldn't manage the pucker. A colonel who didn't like gentry—not even on his own side most likely. Charm would be wasted on him.

He rode on, bootless.

CHAPTER 42   Lieutenant-General Rochambeau, in charge of all French aid to the Americans, came to Hartford, Connecticut, to meet with General Washington and his staff, and with Major David Cortlandt, who was making a nuisance of himself over medical supplies. Best of all to Rochambeau was the meeting again with the

Marquis de La Fayette. But everyone was in such a hurry they had little intimate conversation.

General Washington smiled and shook hands with the French officers. "I must get on to West Point to see what is being done there on the new fortifications."

"We could have another dinner, *mon général,* and talk of the future over a special *cuisine.*"

"To win the war is enough to begin with, my dear Rochambeau. We shall meet again soon."

On the morning of the second of September General Washington and his staff, with Captain Alexander Hamilton, the Marquis de La Fayette, Major David Cortlandt, and a small guard were moving on the dusty road to New Windsor. There was a feeling of great things to come. The horses after a day of feeding were happy again to be on the road.

General Washington turned to Major Cortlandt. "I'm sure you didn't get all you wanted, Major; you must admit, however, they were generous with the medical supplies."

"We can now treat our wounded better, General, but I fear we will never have enough supplies."

"No, I suppose not, but I've had to make do with what was on hand myself." The general set his heels in his horse's flanks and rode up ahead to talk to Alexander Hamilton and the marquis, his two favorite young men.

David, sitting easy in the saddle, began to figure out how to get wagons, carts, and the horses needed to carry his newly promised supplies from the French ships. It would be fine to have drugs and salves and new tools again. The way he had been taught was the *proper* supplying of a hospital service in London so long ago. It was a lovely day and General Washington was laughing at something Hamilton had said.

Colonel Jameson—always in conflict with anyone of the quality on either side—was an unbuttoned crossroads soldier, and he listened to the three captors of Major André in the ramshackle old farmhouse he called his headquarters. He looked up at the pale young man in the nut-colored suit standing in his stocking feet before him. He glanced at the boots on the deal table and fingered the thin papers found in them.

"I fear, Mr. Anderson, you're in a bit of a tangle. You one of those Hudson River family popinjays?"

"No—I'm a merchant, or tried to pass as one."

"These men say you offered them a thousand pounds to set you free."

"I don't think any actual sum was mentioned."

Johnny said, "He said *anything* we wanted. But Colonel, we got our devotion and loyalty to the cause."

Colonel Jameson said, "I wonder *how* loyal you'd have been if he had a thousand pounds on him? I must hold you, sir, for my superiors. Your own kind of gentry."

When the major (still as Anderson) was locked up and the three heroes rewarded with fine words and a promise of glory, Colonel Jameson sat down and thought. He was not a thinking man, and he had never come up against such a problem on such a large scale. He took pen and inkpot and wrote a note to General Arnold at West Point. A little bootlicking wouldn't harm.

"It would seem, my dear general, that we have just captured a British spye who bore a pass from you. I wonder what filthy forger has dared to signe the glorious name of General Arnold to it. . . ."

When he had folded and addressed it he sent for a messenger, a long-nosed country boy with bowed legs. "Nat, you're to ride to West Point, like the very Harry were after you, and deliver this to General Arnold, and no one else, you understand?"

"I do, Colonel."

When the messenger was gone, Colonel Jameson wondered if he shouldn't have written direct to General Washington instead. He could still inform General Washington of the events, but it was time for breakfast and the inkpot was near to empty. He'd look over the captured papers fully after breakfast.

West Point stood out clear as a detailed oil painting in the crisp fall day. General Washington and his party ascended to the lower walls and buildings.

"I would like to inspect the new fortifications," said the general, breaking off a switch from a tree branch. "We'll take breakfast with Arnold later and talk over our winter plans."

The marquis came forward. "Can it not, sire, be done after breakfast? The coffee will be cold if we don't hurry."

Washington smiled and switched at a fly buzzing by. "I suppose, like all the young men, you too are in love with the beautiful Mrs. Arnold? Are you, Major Cortlandt?"

"Only as a married man might admire a pretty woman, sir."

Washington waved his switch. "All right. Marquis, you proceed us. Hurry to her."

The marquis blushed and looked at Alexander Hamilton, neat, tight-lipped, not given much to talk unless he had the general's ear.

"No, no, sire, Hamilton's heart is as susceptible as my own. Let him go and represent us."

Major Cortlandt was amused.

Hamilton bowed from the saddle. "I'll keep the coffee warm, gentlemen." He set spurs to his gray horse and went clattering up ahead to General Arnold's headquarters. General Washington looked out over the river. "I think we can *now* inspect the fortifications."

Life at West Point was informal, almost slack. There was toast on the damask tablecloth, and several china pots of jellies, a large platter of bacon rashers, and the coffee itself steamed from a Revere pot showing that at least General Arnold did not mind paying the price for the best Java berries. General and Mrs. Arnold and his staff of four were just sitting down when an orderly announced Captain Hamilton. The brisk young man came into the room, hand out, smiling.

"Good morn—I smelled the coffee outside."

General Arnold said, "Has General Washington arrived this early?"

Hamilton's stiffness seemed to vanish as he took Peggy's hand and bowed to the general. "Do not give up your breakfast, General. General Washington and his staff will be up soon. I was sent to represent him."

"I should go out to welcome him."

"He forbids it," said Hamilton, sitting down after greeting the staff. "Just make more coffee."

Peggy smiled. "How fine to have him and the staff here! May I pour you a cup?"

"You may indeed. Your brew—ah—and what the French served us, is the first good berry I've smelled in a long time. Your leg is better, General?"

"Yes," said General Arnold limping to a chair and sitting down. "The leg is bothering me, but not too much. Well, what is new?"

"The French are coming ashore with everything we need." Hamilton sipped his brew. "How is the child?"

"Fine," said Peggy, head cocked to one side, smiling at Hamilton. "She is showing signs of more teeth and frets a bit. She looks just like the general."

"Not as dark," said General Arnold, looking off toward the river. An orderly came in and saluted. "A messenger from Colonel Jameson with a packet for General Arnold."

"Jameson? Oh, the farmer in command at North Castle. A slovenly fellow." The messenger came in, his long nose sniffing the delightful odor of coffee and crisp bacon. General Arnold took the packet from his hand and opened it. He read—looked up expressionless, and said, "You will excuse me."

He went upstairs and Peggy and the staff officers made small talk. Lanky Wells, the coachman, came in and said to Mrs. Arnold, "If it's no bother, ma'am, the general would like to see you upstairs for a moment."

She rose and made her excuses (feeling a vise grip and grind her entrails). Cold sweat beaded her brow. She wondered what was happening. She smiled, excused herself, and went up the narrow steep stairs.

A staff officer took out a cheroot. "Why don't we all go out on the porch for a breath of air?"

Hamilton finished his cup and refilled it. "If you don't mind, I'll take this with me."

General Washington spent two hours going over the fortifications and the grounds. Major Cortlandt inspected the hospital and rejoined Washington as they all moved up to General Arnold's house.

Some great turmoil had taken place there. The staff officers were looking at each other with staring eyes, and Hamilton rushed off the porch to the approaching men with a letter in his hand. "General! Colonel Jameson has just sent *another* letter by a second messenger."

"What is it? What was the first?" Washington asked.

Hamilton, unable to speak, handed him a letter. David watched the general. He moved forward; Washington looked ill and as if he would collapse. In a hollow voice, very low, he said:

"Arnold is a traitor and has fled to the British. Jameson's examination of captured papers revealed it all."

He pushed the letter at the marquis. "*Whom* can we trust now?"

They all read the details of the deed in turn. After they dismounted Washington paced the ground under the rolling eyes of a frightened sentinel and his gesturing staff. He pulled at the switch taken from a tree, swung it about, and—not aware of what he was doing—he tore it to pieces with his teeth.

General Washington said, "You will, Marquis, send out a party to capture Arnold and hold him."

The marquis went off to issue the orders. Washington turned toward the house. The wails of a hysterical woman were heard. He looked up and away. He seemed in shock and filled with unreality at the turn of events. A staff officer came out and saluted.

"General, Mrs. Arnold asks if she can see you?"

"I shall be up directly. Doctor, better come with me. We may need your services."

David followed Washington into the house. Hamilton decided to go along. He had a fiancée, Betsy Schuyler, but he had never gotten over his affection for Peggy Arnold when she was Peggy Shippen. The tall general bumped his head as he mounted the narrow steps, and it only made him sterner when he entered the small bedroom. Peggy was rolling on the bed, screaming, pressing the howling baby to her breasts. "You are going to kill my baby! You are going to kill her! It's a plot!"

Washington said, firm-lipped, "Pull yourself together, madam."

"I know! You will murder us *all!*"

David stepped forward and caught a thrashing arm, took her pulse. It didn't seem fast. "Madam must rest now, and I think we'd better put the child in its cradle."

"No, no, I shall never let her go! Never! Kill us both. Now do your worst."

"No harm will come to either of you," said General Washington.

"I am innocent of any harm to you. My intentions are those of a mother and a wife."

"We'll leave you to calm yourself. Doctor, see to her."

David put the crying child in its cradle and took some powders from his waistcoat and mixed them in a glass of water. General Washington and Hamilton went out. David handed the glass to the panting woman. The child was screaming in a lower key. He calmed it in the cradle. It needed changing badly.

The woman on the bed stared into the glass and then flung it untasted against the opposite wall. It broke with a great splash. "No, you'll poison me! You want to do away with me and the innocent child!"

David shrugged his shoulders and went down to the men standing around with General Washington. The general had recovered himself. But it was with an effort. His jaw line pulsed; his fists were clinched.

"How is she?" asked Hamilton.

"She will survive," said David. "She's a sturdy woman."

"But *such* hysterics."

David said softly so the general would not hear, "It is my opinion she is a fine actress. Her pulse is steady, and her hysterical condition that of a fear for the future, not truly a fear of us, or anger at Arnold's action."

Hamilton was shocked. "No. Her tears shred my heart. The sweetness and beauty, the lovely innocence up there are of a tender wife, a fine mother."

David—who disliked fancy prose—decided not to carry the conversation with the infatuated young man any further.

The parties searching for General Arnold returned with shaking heads and winded horses. It was now a fact that the general had actually escaped. He had reached H.M.S. *Vulture* at anchor in Haverstraw Bay, rowing out to her before the pursuit could catch up with him.

Mrs. Arnold that night raved and went into a delirium of grief and fear that convinced all (but Dr. Cortlandt) that she was an innocent pawn in a depraved man's evil schemes to sell out his country. Both Washington and La Fayette consoled her with their faith in her own future. A coach was ordered the next day to take her to Philadelphia, to her parents' home. A mounted guard was provided, and David was sent along, in case medical attention to Mrs. Arnold or her infant daughter was needed.

She calmed down once West Point was left behind and the carriage wheels rolled. They stayed the night at Paramus, the estate of a Mrs. Prevost. Aaron Burr was there, as he was engaged to marry Mrs. Prevost. After the red-eyed woman was put to bed, Burr took David aside.

"It's a damn bit of foolery we've seen. She screamed as she came in, but it's very quiet up there now."

David nodded. "General Washington sent me along to treat her, but I leave the carriage here. She doesn't need medical attention. If I were a crueler man, I'd say she needs the rope."

"You think she was privy to all of Arnold's schemes?"

"Yes, I do."

Burr nodded. "I suspected her some time ago. Both Botts and Manderscheid have had her under observation, but it was too hard to get proof."

Mrs. Prevost, over-colored, over-bosomed, bright-eyed (and a gay widow), came in followed by a servant with a tea service. "I'll go up now and calm the poor creature. I'm sure she's famished."

"Do that, Theodosia," said Burr.

The two men watched Mrs. Prevost go upstairs, followed by the servant with the tea tray.

"My dear Major, I am betrothed to Theodosia, but I wonder if even she has dropped her royalist past. You know her late husband was a British officer."

"No, I didn't, sir. I must get back now to my other duties. I leave Mrs. Arnold in your hands. The escort will carry her on to her family in Philadelphia."

Burr nodded. "She fooled Washington and all the staff. Not any of them understand women. Or has dallied with them and studied their tricks."

"I fear I know them best only medically."

David ate, shook hands with Burr, and went out and took over a horse from the escort, wanting to ride quickly away from all connected with this dreadful deed, this traitorous adventure so imperfectly played out, so miscarried.

Upstairs on the wide, clean bed Peggy Arnold relaxed and sniffed up the last of her tears and blew her nose. Mrs. Prevost handed her a plate of small sandwiches and a cup of tea. Peggy sipped with pleasure and smiled calmly at her friend.

"I am so heartily sick, I can tell you, my dear Theo, of all the damned theatrics with which I made an exhibition of myself."

"I'm sure you did it well. Those sandwiches are filled with our own watercress."

"Who would have thought it would turn out thus?" Peggy sighed. "Was it long planned?"

"For some time the general has been disgusted with the American cause, and all those dreadful fools who managed its public affairs."

"They're no better in England, my dear."

"This, at least, now gives Bennie a position with the Crown, and we shall be loyal to what we believe in."

"But why did he serve the Americans so well?"

"Because he is a brave man. Oh, darling, it wasn't easy at first! I had to use great persuasion, and perseverance. I even had to keep him from the bed, and he such a pleasuring man."

"He always looked it."

"And just when it is all arranged to surrender West Point to the British, poor André is captured and the papers discovered. What will they do to him, Theodosia?"

"Enough to eat? Finish your tea."

"What do you think they will do to the dear boy?"

"They will hang him, most likely."

Peggy shivered, closed her eyes and shook her head. "Dreadful! Dreadful. What have I done?"

Mrs. Prevost picked up the tray. She looked at the woman on the bed and wondered if the old gossip, of an affair between Peggy and John André, was based on truth.

When Peggy was alone, she did not move for some moments. Her torso began to shake as if she were weeping. But no tears flowed. She was all wept out. And yet in her misery and her sadness she somehow had faith that it would all work out. The general would rank high in the British army, and she began to think how they would refurnish their lives with the money he had been promised.

CHAPTER 43   A man's nerve ends—the London medical texts said—can fail him under certain conditions. David Cortlandt avoided attending the captured spy with the excuse his fever was recurring. When it was apparent John André would hang, David wrote a note recommending Lieutenant Robin MacBean as the medical attendant at the gibbet.

"It's not," he told Roxanne at breakfast, "that I don't think the man should be treated as a spy. He is one. But the two plotters who will gain most are not touched. Besides, men dying of wounds or in battle at least go to their fate at the top of their emotions. This stretching a neck—breaking a spine, if the victim is lucky—is not to my liking. Not to watch, prepare for, or treat the wretched victim in his last shaking hours."

Roxanne, busy feeding the baby, nodded. "Dear Davey, you don't have to explain so much."

"I think I'd attend Mrs. Arnold cheerfully if they hanged her."

"You don't mean that."

"She played the Delilah to Arnold's Samson."

Roxanne laughed. "How like a man! His vanity is hurt and he's pouting because a clever minx got a man to do something against his will."

David said with dignity, "I didn't say General Arnold did what he did—betray a great trust—against his will." He rose and took George's hand and said, "Come, son, let us see if your turtle has retired for the autumn."

"That's right. Run away when I scratch one of your shiny arguments."

It was better to walk in the wild-running garden, hunting for the pet turtle under bush and stone. There were times when David felt a man's life fully away from women would be ideal. And then, when he held Roxanne in his arms, all the small differences faded, and the vital, alive, and much desired companionship, the sharing of emotions, even domestic gossip, made for him a world—warmer and certainly more intimate than any other he had. Even his work seemed at such times only a platform for achievements that led him closer to Roxanne. Mynheer—when sampling too much of his own cyder—had once said of David: "He isn't yet tamed to marriage. It takes time. David is still fighting the whip, the curb, the rein of domestic life."

"Peter, go back to your family histories," Anita his wife had said. "You'd think marriage were an animal-taming performance."

"I wonder if it isn't," Mynheer said, but not too loudly.

Major John André had been imprisoned in the Gilbert house in North Castle. He still claimed to be the John Anderson listed on the pass from General Arnold. Jacob Gilbert, a wide-spreading citizen, drinking a bit of gin with Colonel Jameson, shook his head as he pointed to the ceiling. They could both hear the restless pacing of the prisoner in his room.

"That's a soldier's step, Colonel."

"I'd agree with you there."

"You don't yet know who he is? This John Anderson?"

"If the pass is as false as General Arnold, he isn't any John Anderson."

"He's a sweet lad in many ways. Polite; now you don't meet much politeness in our backwoods river farmers. And when he isn't pacing and alone, you know what he does?"

Colonel Jameson shook his head, "I've no idea, Jacob. I never understood gentlemen."

"He jests and laughs and shows us dance steps and sings us gay songs."

"He'll dance soon enough, and high, with air under his heels. Of course there is a chance he may be exchanged. Washington, I hear, might ask for General Arnold in exchange for Mr. Anderson. I tell you he's an important fellow. And might save his neck."

The pacing overhead stopped. "He's going to write now. He writes a lot. But destroys it all."

"Try and get some of it, Jacob."

A plump young man with a dour, thin mouth, saddlebags on his shoulders, came in.

"Leftenant Robin MacBean at your service, gentlemen. I hunt Colonel Jameson."

"Do you, now? I be he."

"I'm sent by Major Cortlandt, as his medical assistant, to see if the prisoner needs any attention."

"He seems healthy enough," said Jacob Gilbert. "Not that he eats hearty. Will you have a gin, Leftenant MacBean?"

Robin MacBean put his saddlebags in a corner and nodded that he would indeed.

Upstairs John André was writing a letter that he had drafted several times the day before, and it now was clear in his mind what he wanted to say. It was to General Washington.

I address you, sir, in this way to make fully known to you that I am in truth Major John André, adjutant-general of the British army, captured behind your lines and now confined and awaiting the sitting of your courts. I have little faith that I shall escape a verdict that will end my span on this earth. I beg of you, sir, as military man to military man, let me dye as a soldier, that is, to be shot, and not hanged.

He stopped writing and shook his head. It was not just right. He must make it a little stronger, and yet remember that General Washington was a gentleman, and manners were important to them both. John André crumbled the letter and began a fresh one. He heard the tramp of the guard being changed outside the house, the voices of children bickering in a stick game in a nearby field, the stable sounds of horses being groomed. He dipped his pen afresh and went on writing.

It was no secret around the chambers of the British commander, Sir Henry Clinton, in New York, that he was in a fearful rage, and yet, as his staff knew, trapped in a situation that would have agonized the wisdom of a Solomon. His valet had cut Sir Henry's cheek while shaving him that morning—and no wonder; Sir Henry had squirmed and twisted so, it was not the man's fault. Sir Henry had a bit of rice paper stuck on the injured jowl, and there was a trace of lather on his left ear; he had left the chair in haste when news was brought of a dispatch below from General Washington.

Sir Henry read the dispatch and looked up at Captain Corky. "It's a genuine document, Captain?"

"Yes, sir. It is. We met the rider under a flag of truce above the Harlem Bridge. He's outside. Shall I send him in, sir?"

"No, not yet. Go get the staff officers at breakfast."

When about half a dozen of the staff were assembled, some still chewing a bit of food, others buttoning their jackets, Sir Henry stood up and clasped his hands behind his back.

"I have here a dispatch from General Washington. He will exchange Major André for—as he puts it—the traitor, General Arnold."

There was a buzz of talk, a rising inflection of voices. Sir Henry held up a hand. "They will hang Major André if I don't agree to exchange. Any opinions?"

"Well, sir, it seems this Arnold person is not a pleasant fellow. And John . . ."

"John *is* our friend," finished Sir Henry with a sigh.

"Also, sir, we didn't get West Point, did we?"

"No. But we may get more American generals if we treat Arnold well. He is a good soldier, but for a few weaknesses. And he has still a great deal to tell us about the American positions and troop conditions. Besides, he has our word of honor. Captain, will you ask the American messenger to wait. We'll call him soon."

The American lieutenant was six foot three, lanky and long-limbed with a lantern jaw. He was staring at some stained drawings of fox hunts hung in the hall as Captain Corky came out.

"Sir Henry Clinton will call you soon, Leftenant. I'm Captain Corky."

"Johnson. Leftenant Abel Johnson, at your service."

"How's the war look from your side? It's a damned bore of a fracas from this side, I can tell you."

"We manage, Captain."

"Do you Americans raise a breed of dog with short ears—so short —and with a sharp bark?"

"White usually, with brown or black spots? Terriers?"

"Fox terriers, Leftenant, I'll be damned. I thought they were an Anglo-Irish breed."

"I have three back on the farm. I'd be happy to send you one through the lines. A six-month pup."

"The devil you would, Leftenant. I've missed me dog, Mikel, that died on the trip from Injah—over ten years old he was. Smarter than any general I ever served under, and a prime ratter."

Lieutenant Johnson had stiffened and was glaring at a man in a new British officer's uniform, heavy with gold lace. It was General Arnold, wearing a London set white curled wig. His face was expressionless and darker than ever. He caught the glare of the American officer and the scorn and hatred in the lieutenant's features. General Arnold did not avert his eyes, but glanced coolly through the stare and went limping down the hall to Sir Henry's meeting. Captain Corky noticed that General Arnold's neck was brick-red and wet.

Sir Henry stepped forward and shook General Arnold's hand. "You've met my staff, General. I must say the uniform fits you well."

"It was kind of you to provide it."

"Nothing at all. I mean we couldn't let you walk among us in that blue and buff. No, of course not. General Arnold, General Washington has made us an offer of exchange for Major André which I am refusing, and I want you to be here when I hand over my answer to the American messenger."

"So that's who he was?"

"I am rejecting General Washington's offer to exchange Major André for yourself. This means, I need not tell you, that Major André will die on the gallows."

General Arnold twitched and rubbed his fingers together. He looked around at the cold, staring faces of the staff. "I most regret it, gentlemen. I know he was your friend and comrade."

"The fortunes of war," said Sir Henry Clinton, beginning to write a dispatch at his table. "The dismal side of the shield—away from the banners and cheering."

General Arnold stood very still and watched Sir Henry complete his dispatch, sand it, seal it, and look up.

"Have the captain give this to the waiting American messenger. He is to be escorted through our lines under the white flag. Well, General Arnold, shall we go in to breakfast?"

Sir Henry, for all his jovial tones, did not look cheerful. General Arnold was as aware as anyone in the room that the image of a hanged man had joined them, and would be company with them for some time.

The warm autumn afternoon was yellow in a swirl of falling leaves at Tappan on the other side of the river. John André had been brought there to a little red brick meetinghouse where the trial was in progress. The board of officers who were trying him sat behind an ink-stained table over which a too-short red cloth had been placed.

The prisoner had managed to get clothes and was splendidly but simply dressed. He faced them from a chair with a fan back, and some of the shutters had been half closed to keep out the sunlight. Flies, late breeders of the fall season, buzzed around the several pewter and brass inkpots.

General Greene was presiding in heavy grace, and the fifteen officers under his gaze were solemn with the sense of duty. Robin MacBean, from the side of the room, watched the prisoner. They had become friendly, and he wondered how a young man faced death with so much unspent life on the wrong side of the ledger. The dull oak pews were sparsely filled—the empty pulpit was depressing, for all the crisp weather outside. The place smelled of candle wax, mice, and damp plaster.

The judge advocate droned past the testimony of the witnesses. John André, musing bitterly on the futility of human endeavor, was aware he was being addressed again.

"This matter is most grave, Major. Could it in any way be proved, and it would please this court to have it so proved, that you were traveling under a flag of truce?"

André shook his head. "No, I cannot claim that saving grace, gentlemen."

"Then there is nothing to set aside the procedures and laws of military rules. No flag of truce; captured in American territory; in civilian clothes; carrying incriminating papers."

John André watched a large fly, wet and slow with fatigue, climb out from an inkpot. The dismal creature crawled across the cloth leaving a black, crooked trail.

"True, you were an honorable spy, causing no physical damage, but the fate of a spy is only too clear to this court."

The fly was trying to clean itself, but it was very weak. John André watched it closely; it barely stirred. He must have been engrossed in the wet, inky fly for some time. He was suddenly aware of someone touching him on the shoulder and asking him to stand.

"It is the verdict of this court that Major John André is guilty of spying, and the penalty this court sets is death by hanging! The time will be set by the provost."

There was a great deal more. General Greene's hand was shaking as he signed the court verdict. John André was still watching the ink-stained fly. It had recovered and was drying its wings. As they led him off John André saw the fly attempt a small, bumbling flight. The prisoner was smiling as he was led from the court. He would hang in a few days.

Roxanne was swaddling the baby. David and George were eating their supper when Joe Philipse came in. He had been gone for two days in the woods. At those times they had to lock Zee, the house slave, up in the shed, for she would go hunting Joe, and neither blows nor threats could keep her mind on her work when Joe was off alone wandering in the woods.

David looked up. "Are you all right, Joe?"

"Yes. I've been down to the ferry landing. The verdict is that Major André will hang."

"Ah," said David, "it's a dirty business, condemning a man, even in war."

"*Bang bang,*" said George, using his spoon as a musket. "I shot a lobsterback."

Joe looked at his sister and smiled. He pulled on his long blond beard. "I'm going away. Going to join the fighting in the Carolinas. I know I've been odd and in a way a burden to you both."

"No, no, of course not," said David.

"Oh Joe," said Roxanne weeping. "Not a burden. But I understand. I'd want to be off to war—if David would let us join him."

"It was John André's fate brought me a part way back."

David said, "I don't understand."

"I've been deep underground. Away from men dying for causes, sides. I've been selfish in my own griefs. There hasn't been much daylight let into me. I wish I could say it all better."

"You're saying it," Roxanne said, taking the baby up on her lap.

"It's like escaping from drowning, Roxy. I remember, when I was a little boy, going down early one morning to swim in the river and beginning to drown, and for a long time sinking and rising, holding my breath and then feeling the solid bottom at last under my cramped toes."

David nodded, "Yes, you've been holding your breath a long time."

"I spoke to a Colonel Martin at the landing. He'll get me assigned to the Carolinas." Joe looked around and bit his knuckles. They would never understand him, he supposed. He loved them so and they were such strangers. He got up and walked away and up to his room.

Zee came in with bowls of hot milk. She looked from one to the other and went back to the kitchen. David picked up a spoon. "Now let's see, George, who can finish his mashed 'taters first. No cheating. *Go!*"

Roxanne rocked the contented baby in her lap. "In a way it's better Joe is going away. There are things going on around here better left unsaid. Now *don't* look at me like that, Davey. You're blind to many things, like most men."

George, breathing hard, face smeared, shouted out, "I won. I *won!*"

CHAPTER 44   On the afternoon of the last day in September
there was a running fight between a fairly large group of Tory raiders
and two regiments of American infantry south of Tappan. The
Tories, depending on surprise, had stumbled into the camp of the
soldiers sent into the region to act as guards for the trial of John
André. A company of horsemen escorting General Greene joined
the fight and all that late day the wooded hills rang with musket
fire, and large horses galloped up and down lanes, their riders hacking
at green-clad Tory Rangers with sabers, till the last straggler was
dead or lost in the dusk.

Only later, when they had questioned a captured raider, did
General Greene write to Washington that it had been an expedition
led by the notorious Colonel Lemon, set on rescuing Major André.
If actually such were its purpose it never came near to success, for
the Americans had moved many troops to Tappan and surrounded
the town.

With the trial over, waiting for his sentence to be fulfilled, John
André seemed at peace. He refused a minister, being, he said, a
skeptic, as, he added, were Washington, Jefferson, Franklin, and
Paine; perhaps, he jested, he had fought on the wrong side. He
maintained his calmness, being full of a natural charm and composure. His life, he saw, had been a futile, empty one of pleasure
and orgy, of parties and wine bottles, of polite adulteries, scented
vices, and the neat, unthinking duties of the soldier. His writing
table appeared to bring him peace, and he wrote long letters of
farewell to his family and friends. He saved the last for his dear
friend and commander, Sir Henry Clinton. Sitting in breeches and
open shirt, in his stocking feet, he wrote:

With all the warmth of my heart I give you thanks for your Excellency's profuse Kindness to me, and I send you the most earnest
wishes for your welfare which a faithful affectionate and respect-
ful Attendant can frame . . .

There was a quick, low knock on the door and Robin MacBean
came in carrying on one arm a dazzling white and green uniform.

"I hope, Major, this will do."

The writer turned over the letter and nodded. "It's an amazing neat thing."

"There are no regimental buttons on it. Plain gilt. And the tailor did his best. There is no red cloth in the district, not enough for a uniform."

"It will do finely, MacBean. I shall be a gaudy sight in my coffin."

"Is there anything I can do, Major?"

"Sit and talk to me. I've never feared death, you know, but I dread the mean process of dying. No, I'm not being witty. It's a poor and vulgar thing, this act of dying, and it's the only thing one must do alone. No friend can do it for us."

"I've arranged a bottle of brandy for you."

"You're most kind. But bring just a tot in the morning. You're a medical man—how means this life, what does it lead to?"

"I'm just a student of the medical branch, and surgery."

For a moment John André was in panic, a momentary lapse of control. "You don't mean to autopsy me?"

"No, no. Be assured of that."

"Ah—thank you—I take my bag of bones with me whole. Do you know Shakespeare?"

Robin MacBean shook his head. "I'm a Scot; we do not hold it proper to read the profane authors. There is too much of pleasure and mocking of morals in these scribblers."

John André shook his head. "No, not *that* Shakespeare. Listen: 'We are such stuff as dreams are made on and our little life is rounded with a sleep.'"

"He speaks like a decent medical man."

André rose and went to the window and looked out at the soldiers camped in front of the house. Some little girls were playing in the road across the way. Without turning around he recited:

> "*Tomorrow, and tomorrow, and tomorrow*
> *Creeps in thy petty pace from day to day*
> *To the last syllable of recorded time;*
> *And all our yesterdays have lighted fools*
> *The way to dusty death. Out, out, brief candle!*"

A scouting party of dusty, saddle-weary horsemen coming in for the night clattered by with the metallic ringing of swords and chain reins.

> *"Life's but a walking shadow, a poor player*
> *That struts and frets his hour upon the stage*
> *And then is heard no more; it is a tale*
> *Told by an idiot, full of sound and fury,*
> *Signifying nothing . . .*

"The same fellow."

"He's brisk enough with awesome words to be a proper Presbyterian preacher," said Robin MacBean.

John André turned around and laughed. "You can have them send up a small touch of that brandy and you stay to drink a glass with me. That's not against your creed, MacBean, is it?"

"No Scot has a creed against drinking."

They stood together in the golden lamplight, and could hear the voices of the guard changing below, the bang of musket butts into the earth as they took the relief. Someone was calling in the little girls from their play.

"It is a beautiful morning to die," Colonel Jameson told Jacob Gilbert.

John André had risen very early. He took pleasure at the sun and shouted down to the guards:

"A most pleasant day."

He asked MacBean to shave him and inquired if there was powder for his hair. He dressed slowly in the white and green uniform, and he took great care with his stock. He gestured in the mirror. "I was always a fusser with these things. You think it sets well?"

"Do you have any more letters to write?"

"Is there time?"

"Not very much, Major."

"Ah." He sat down and looked again into the mirror and began with the pen to sketch on a bit of paper his image in the glass. He had some skill as a draftsman, and he did a very excellent likeness of the slim, elegant young officer seated at the table in his fine uniform with just the faintest trace of a smile on his lips.

When the guards came to take him out he bowed. "My business is all finished. I am ready to go." Taking the arms of the two officers who commanded the guards, he said, "Let us step out."

John André inhaled the crisp air of autumn. Somewhere they were burning fallen leaves and there was an odor of wood smoke and

roasting apples in the air. MacBean followed behind John André.
It was a long way to the place of execution and the fifers were
playing "The Blue Bird."

"I compliment the men on their delightful music."

The curious, the wondering, and the unemployed lined the way.
One of the little girls he had seen from his window the night before
ran up to him and slipped a peach into his hand.

"Thank you, my dear, for a charming gift."

His spirits held till he saw the people on the field, the gibbet of
raw lumber, and the wagon and two horses standing under it. He
turned very pale and Robin MacBean saw him catch at his breath.
His head bowed and MacBean took his arm to encourage him to
recover. John André gritted his teeth in disgust and outrage.

"This is *too* degrading. I've taken all else with fortitude."

"You've been splendid so far, Major. Carry it through."

"To me it's a matter of no importance. But this will mortify my
mother and sisters."

The fearful strains of the "Dead March" were rolling out over the
field. His courage fled, and he pulled back for a moment, MacBean
still gripping his arm as they walked to the gibbet.

"God, must I die like this?"

Colonel Jameson on horseback called out, "Major André, you will
please get on the wagon."

The hangman, his face and hands blackened with burnt charcoal,
waited. John André tried to vault into the wagon but his muscles
failed him. Shamefaced, he put up a knee and raised himself into the
flat wagon bed. The hangman lifted the noose and put it over the
condemned man's head.

John André shouted, "Take your damn black hands off me!"

He opened his own collar, took the noose, and put it around his
neck. Slowly he drew the knot tight around his throat and under
his ear.

Colonel Jameson, still on horseback, said, "Major André, if you
have anything to say, speak out. You have but a short time to live."

The prisoner had recovered his temper and his calmness. "I have
nothing more to say, only this; bear witness to the world I met my
fate as best becomes a soldier."

He took his own silk handkerchief, smiled down at Robin Mac-
Bean, and bound his own eyes. MacBean was aware that he was the

last person John André would see in this world. A light wind came up and as Colonel Jameson read the last orders of the court, the breeze stirred the waiting man's curls. MacBean saw he was biting his lower lip with impatience at the drawn-out ceremonies.

La Fayette and Hamilton had come into the crowd and were standing in the back. The music ceased suddenly. The long fearful roll of drums began. John André must have heard the crack of the whip as it was brutally snapped onto the horses' rumps. The wagon lurched forward and he fell off into space. Several people in the crowd groaned, and a few sobbed. Some threw wild daisies and laurel under the twisting figure. It did not struggle long. MacBean saw the muscular rigidity around the loins and the telltale stain on the white breeches confirming the ejaculation of hanged men. Something dropped from the hanging body's hand. It was the peach, which John André had not let go of until he lost all contact with life.

MacBean waited while the soldiers lowered the body onto a cloak laid out on the grass. He bent down and tried for the pulse, pushed up the handkerchief, and fingered back the eyelids. All life was gone. He stood up, and, before he told Colonel Jameson the man was dead, he kicked the peach aside.

The hanging of the spy left a turmoil of talk behind it and dissatisfaction along the river. There was a war weariness, apparently, setting in. So many had died, so much had been destroyed, and now, with the death of this handsome young victim of misplanning, people talked of his charm and his wit, and the madness of making war. Some of the men close to General Washington had been affected. La Fayette had wept openly in public at the hanging. General Washington, grim-lipped and anxious, remained firm; "There is still a traitor at large and Major André was one of those who encouraged him in his dreadful betrayal of his oaths and his country. We still face a war to fight."

At Philipse Manor there were changes too. Joe Philipse was gone. Casually, suddenly, after a few warnings, his gear was packed up in a blue cloth, his rifle cleaned and swung over his shoulder. Wearing a faded blue and buff jacket of his rank over the hunting shirt, and with a horse found somewhere for him by Mynheer Schuyler, Captain Joseph Philipse went back to the wars.

He kissed his sister, shook David's hand, and went out and mounted. Zee, barefoot on the cold earth, handed him up his hunting bag and some food she had prepared and wrapped in a napkin. Joe kicked the old horse alert and went off down the driveway, the yellow, dead weeds of the season rattling in the chill river wind. Joe did not look back. Zee stared after him, expressionless, mouth open, and then began to run, saying not a word. Joe was galloping the horse and Zee could not catch up. She fell down a half mile from the house in the patch of wild mustard and lay there, not sobbing or howling, just panting and staring at the ants busy among the plants, moving grubs down into their underground caves.

In the house David was also packing. He was going off to inspect the hospitals in the various forts; General Washington had ordered a great tightening up of regulations and discipline. There was gossip of mutinies in Pennsylvania among the hungry, dissatisfied soldiers.

Roxanne packed David some clean but worn smallclothes. He took his wide blue-faced cloak out of the chest in their bedroom.

"You need a new cloak," Roxanne said, caressing the rough cloth.

"It will outlast me, Roxy. You'll be alone here with just Zee, and she seems more unstrung than ever."

"I'll wallop sense into her. And Mynheer drives over a few times a week with Aunt Anita to give us some of their milk and butter for the children. They still have a few cows."

"If things get too remote here, move in with them."

Roxanne shook her head. "I'm a Philipse under it all. This is Philipse Manor. I stay here unless you ask me to join you. It's the future home of George and Mollie and whatever other brood we have."

"Good Lord, Roxanne, *not* again! So soon?"

"Not yet. But I expect to have more children."

"I didn't say you nay, but it's going to be hard enough, just you and Zee here all winter. I put up several cords of wood with Joe before he left. I'll come by as often as I can. Oh darling, I dread to leave you here."

He held her close. Roxanne smiled and touched his chin with a finger. "Go fight your war, and come home."

She was very good about it as David kissed George and made him promise to defend the place against all foes, and Mollie laughed when he touched his lips to the top of her fluffy head. It was the actual riding off that hit his heart, and he looked back and waved a long time, till the overgrown fruit trees, free now of leaves but untrimmed and wild, hid the house.

David rode on slowly, the road packed hard by showers, and he wondered how often he would ride off like this before the war was over. Would it become a stale ritual, an eternal coming and going, the war always going on, always burning somewhere on the horizon? He saw now the greatness of the solid determination that was General Washington, and how he alone, almost, held them together for that abstract principle called liberty. David was tired. It had been a long war, and what difference, he mused, would it really make to him to be under a king or a Congress? Lord, he was thinking like Benedict Arnold! He shook himself awake from such degrading thoughts and rode on, a weathered, war-weary man in a faded cloak on an old gray horse on a windy day. A rider along a river landscape that was indifferent to everything but the cycle of the seasons changing.

There was some fighting before winter came. And much trouble in the camps, so that miserable, suffering men were taken from the ranks and shot before their friends to put down mutinies in General Washington's armies. It was bitter weather, and along the river the houses were hard to heat now that servants were few and men not always available to swing the bucksaws that cut up the logs into chunks for the fireplaces.

At Philipse Manor everything seemed boarded up, hidden away, and the kitchen chimney was the only one that gave off a sign of life. Roxanne had moved the children and herself down from the big room to the small room off the kitchen where, on trundle beds, they shared the heat from the brick fireplace that always had a few coals burning cherry-red. In the morning Zee would rake out the ashes and find the heart of the fire still alive and build it up before Roxanne and the children came awake. Water froze in the washing buckets even indoors—and the pump was often frozen so solid it took days to get it to function again. At such times Roxanne and Zee harnessed themselves to bucket yokes and went down to the inlet and chopped holes in the ice along the shore and filled their buckets.

When the river froze almost solid they had the snow to melt; it fell harder that year, in such clouds that Mynheer Schuyler, sledding over in the old runner with the upcurved blades said, "I don't remember but two winters like it. You sure, Roxy, you don't want to come with me back to our house?"

"No, Uncle Peter, I must stay—so if David should come back we'd be here. He's in Pennsylvania now. Things are very bad there in the camps."

"They are bad everywhere."

When the snow was piled in fifteen-foot drifts around the house, they lived indoors, misering their wood and measuring their food. One night men came to the house and tried to break in, and Roxanne fired her pistols at them. Next morning there was blood in the snow.

They ate sparingly of maize and ground oats and the root plants buried in sand in the cellar—roots treasured as if they were gold. They were more than gold, they were life. When the snowdrifts grew so high that Mynheer's sleigh could not come through with the butter and the milk can, Mollie learned to suck the last of the sugar wrapped in a clean cloth and to drink barley water and take a thin gruel made of the last of their chickens, a pitiful short row of hens plucked and frozen, hanging under the cellar steps. If they measured properly and did not indulge, Roxanne figured, they would last till the spring. The apples in the barrel had frozen centers that turned black on being cut open, and the potatoes seemed all eyes and yellow, obscene growths. There were always the turnips, half-buried in the cold cellar sand. There was little that could be done with them to change their insipid taste and texture, but they were something to chew on. Even the growing pup got tired of them.

Only two letters for her from David came through to Mynheer, and they were full of the misery of winter camps, of soldier's diseases, of the wretched state of the war, of hope for the spring, of dreams of coming home, and regards to the children and love "to you, my own dear love . . ."

For three weeks the great frost lasted. Roxanne and Zee cut their way through the frozen crusts to the barn to feed the horse and hack at a slim side of bacon hung in the smokehouse among the remains of a ham bone and a ladder of pig ribs. It was meager fare to last out the winter.

On the coldest night of blue polished stars and sap freezing in the trees Zee gave birth to a baby boy in the washroom off the pantry.

Roxanne heard Zee screaming and went with the nub of a candle on a brass holder to find the girl sprawled on the stone floor, wrapped in ragged skirts, going into labor. Roxanne stayed with her for two hours and the result, after much screaming and rolling around, was the final agony of birth and a strong-voiced yellow boy. Zee went on moaning, her eyes closed, and Roxanne cut the cord and hid the afterbirth in a rag and washed the child.

She cleaned the boy by the glow of the kitchen fire. He seemed all in order and with no visible deformities, and Roxanne wrapped him in parts of a red blanket she cut up and nested him down in the kindling box, emptied of its contents and padded with some of David's old shirts. The newborn child slept at last, his thin bronze wires of hair and the long head pointing to inherited traits.

Zee was up by morning, weak and open-mouthed, staring at the baby and shaking her head. Roxanne made her feed the child on her flabby breasts, and later George was permitted to look at the baby in its box by the fire. For two weeks they all lived together, with chilblains and frozen fingers, and then the frost broke and cold rains fell. After that the roads were open. Roxanne harnessed the horse to the old carry-all and wrapped Mollie warm and put a long muffler around George till he looked like a plump ball. Roxanne drove over to Mynheer's.

They too had been through a hard time. Old Martha had fallen and badly hurt her hip, and now she lay upstairs muttering and demanding. There was a cheerful fire in the big living room. The few field hands left in the cabins behind the Schuyler house had cut a great deal of wood, and a butt of hickory crackled on the andirons.

"We are killing one of the hogs, one of three Berkshires we have left. You'll take a side, Roxy?"

"Don't think I'll not take it, Uncle Peter."

"We're slaughtering now. You ladies stay indoors."

"Don't," said Anita, "let him squeal too much."

"I'll beg him not to," said Mynheer, getting into an old coat and finding a wool cap for his bald head.

"Can I watch?" asked George.

Mynheer said, "You might as well learn how. If you'll bundle up."

Out in the yard three old field hands had brought out the great iron kettles and water was boiling over fires and a hogshead was mounted on a platform for scalding. From the barn door hung a scaffold, and whetted and ground knives were laid out. George was warned not to touch them. A field hand drove out a large Berkshire boar, and before the hog could shiver in the cold yard a long thin knife was plunged into his neck. There was squealing and much blood. Then into the great hogshead full of water boiling hot, went the pig and was pulled up with gambrels till he hung by his hocks, strung through the tendons.

Sharp tools shaved him clean, till George said, "He's as pink as Mollie in her bath."

"That he is," said Mynheer while the innards were removed and also sheets of leaf lard. George was amazed to see a pig was that complicated inside. The liver, heart, and brains were cleaned and packed in buckets. The intestines and bladders were scrapped clean as casing for sausage meats. The lard was rendered in the iron pots. It was a smoking and greasy scene in the yard. George was allowed to taste a crisp crackling left in a pot, after it was cooled a bit.

"It's good, Uncle Peter."

"Isn't it?"

"There's so much of him."

"All begging to be used."

"All, Uncle Peter?"

"Everything is used," Mynheer said, "but the squeak. This part becomes hams, this shoulder is very good with red cabbage. And when sage and black pepper are mixed with the grinding sausage meat—ah! The Dutch have a saying, George, 'Place little faith in sausages and widows; one doesn't know what their skin hides.' Well, mayhaps you're too young to fully understand. Yes?"

There was a basket of head, snout, jowls, lips, ears, tongue. Mynheer explained how each would be a delectable dish. The tail was skinned and roasted for George, who ate it with relish.

Mynheer saved the headcheese for fried scrapple, and said they would have broth and mush called *panhas* for breakfast.

Roxanne and Anita had to come out and admire the clean sides of pork hanging so pink in the cold air. Somehow Roxanne thought of Major André hanging indecently exposed in public, and she wondered why and turned away and went indoors. Yet she would take a side of the boar home, for the demands of her body for good fresh meat were strong.

It was good to visit, Roxanne decided, to sit by a warm fire without thinking of the wood it consumed, to be able to talk, *just* talk.

"So Joe is gone now, how many weeks?"

"You know, I don't remember, I'll have to count."

"You know we were worried over the boy."

"He isn't a boy any more, Aunt Anita, but a grown man."

"To me and Peter you'll always be children."

"Yes, yes," said Mynheer, letting George hold a lighted paper spill to his big china pipe, puffing it alive. "Somehow it seems unfair for you two to grow up. You were *such* beautiful children."

"And from your father, no news?"

Roxanne shook her head. "There is gossip they sailed. There was a letter, I hear—but that dreadful Mr. Botts I'm sure got it."

"A coarse man. I don't know why David deals with him."

"George, you mustn't play with fire. Now see, Uncle Peter, you've taught him a dreadful game."

George asked, "You have a new baby too?"

Roxanne said George was getting much *too* talkative *and* inventive and sent him to play in the library with the glass paper weights on the desk with the flowers and castles growing in them. She denied that she was with child again.

"I've had no word of late from David. Any news of the war?"

Anita shook her head. "We know only what passing soldiers tell us. General Washington expects to have enough French help this year to drive the British off our shores."

There was the bellow of an old woman's voice from upstairs. Mynheer stood up. "Mama. She dislikes being kept to her bed, but her hip is very bad. I'd better go see why she calls."

The purple dusk was coming down and there was danger of marauding deserters on the road. It was good to be going home, Roxanne thought as the horse plodded through the puddles on the way back to Philipse Manor, George hugging the side of pork wrapped in a linen cloth, and Mollie cooing in her padded basket at Roxanne's feet.

There was no smoke coming up from the kitchen chimney. Roxy drove into the yard and unharnessed the horse and, carrying Mollie, led George, who was crying at being parted from the side of pork. The kitchen fire was out. Zee was gone, so was the yellow baby. Roxanne looked on the shelves in the washroom where Zee kept her few belongings. The broken ivory comb, the bit of mirror were gone. So were her barnyard boots, the thick shawl, and the bundle of nonsense she had collected. Colored feathers, labels off bottles, odd-shaped pebbles, the stones from the gizzard of a goose, and a string of seashells made into a necklace.

Roxanne was left alone in the house with two small children. Zee had taken her baby and fled. There were many slaves loose on the road, fleeing deserted farms, going on to the cities, or hiding out in wood and swamps. Roxanne hoped Zee had learned properly to care for her child.

It was a grim month Roxanne spent alone. Building fires, she black with soot, unwashed, measuring her meager supplies with a thoughtful, hungry eye. Seeing both children through racking coughs and going down herself for three days with a raging fever. She came alive to find the fire out again and George soiled and crying and Mollie sucking on her drained sugar rag and howling. But Roxanne managed it. Survived it, as did many others that late spring. When the cold rains fell in steady torrents, she put a cape on her head and went out to feed the horse the last few moldy pitchforks of hay. It seemed as if the sun would never shine, and then a pale yolky disc came out. The muddy brown fields were exposed in focused details and the dead stalks and leaves were the color of the soil. The river ran yellow with silt from the heavy rains and everywhere, from roof and trees there was the steady *drip-drip*. Standing by the kitchen door Roxanne held Mollie on her shoulder and George petted his dog. They felt the earth dry. They had survived, Roxanne thought, and as David had once said, survival was all.

CHAPTER 45   The ferry service at Ackerman's Landing was irregular, but it was possible to make the trip across the river at least twice a day. It was dark when Major David Cortlandt, and Captain (a fairly new rank) Robin MacBean crossed just below the Tappan Zee, holding the reins of their tired horses.

The spring weather was not yet comfortably warm, but the scent of growing things, of budding trees mixed with the wood smoke from the inn was pleasant to their nostrils as they rode into the stable yard.

"I'm going to have one drink," said David, "and go right out home."

Robin MacBean dismounted, "I'm going to have the like and find a bed. We've been riding for three days and the earth shakes under me, even here on the ground."

The old groom Charlie came toward them. "Even', Dr. Cortlandt. I was just hopin' you'd come along."

"Don't bother stabling my horse, Charlie. I'm riding along in a few minutes."

"There's a fellow in the stable been waitin' for you, Doctor."

David dismounted and shook his head. "You know that can't be so, Charlie. No one knew I was coming home."

"Been there six, seven days in the straw pen. Mighty sick fellow. Kept bellerin' for you. Said you'd be by."

David was puzzled. "This beats all. Come and have a look with me, Robin."

The warmth and smell of the stable was sharp and acid, but David always liked the odor; it brought back memories of when he was a boy, sleeping in stables at times and harnessing old Dr. Pelham's horse for late calls, when they would drive off into the dark pools of the night.

Charlie held up an old horn lantern and led them past munching horses, a solid wall of polished rumps and swishing tails, to an empty area deep in straw. A man lay prone on a folded horse cloth in one corner, his head tied up in dirty gray bandages. Charlie held the light high. The tall figure measured out on the straw was barefooted, wore camp-grimed fringed buckskin breeches and a soiled linen hunting shirt.

"Jack-Tom!" said David, kneeling down. "What the blazes are you doing here?"

The voice that came strained and weak through the bandages was muffled and distorted. "Tryin' to stay alive fer you to pass by."

"Are you mad?"

"Mad as a bull with no tail in fly time. I've been real sick, Davey. Real sick."

Robin MacBean shook his head. "Fortunate we came."

David began to unwind the bandages, which were black with

dried, stale blood and stained with a yellow discharge. They were stuck hard. Robin MacBean went out to get a medical case from his saddlebags. David looked down at Jack-Tom. "What happened?"

"Kotched a musket ball in my jaw about a week ago in a run-in with Tories over in Connecticut." It was becoming harder for Jack-Tom to talk. "Fool horse-leech nearly done me more damage than the Tory tryin' to get the ball out of the jaw . . . bone . . . than . . . the ball . . ."

"I'll have to get some hot water to soften this bandage."

"Couldn't find no one . . . could get the ball out a . . . bone. Got this far. Knew . . . knew you'd . . . come by soon. Had to."

David took some water in a gourd from a bucket nearby and dropped it through the bandages into the region of the mouth. Robin MacBean was back and David set him to cutting away the bandages as best he could.

"I'll go get some hot water. Give him tincture of opium, and, Charlie, get me a table or door to put Jack-Tom on."

Jack-Tom sighed somewhere under the matted horror of his bandages. "Glory be. You'll put me right as a daisy, Davey."

It didn't seem that simple. David wondered. He sniffed the wound and shook his head. There was nothing to do but go to work at once. He got up and went across the stable yard to the inn. A group of men—mostly soldiers—were drinking and smoking in the public room and the two girls serving had a hard time to keep up with the demands. In the small walled-off parlor by the stairs some officers were drinking and smoking long churchwarden pipes.

A large, red-faced officer Colonel Jameson, captor of John André —was banging his pot on the table. "One thing I tell you this war has done is make the river families, the quality, cry out for help. They don't act so tarnal feisty now, do they?"

David walked past the parlor and found the kitchen. He asked the old woman there, Goody Welton, to boil up a kettle of water to send out to the stables. "And Goody, could you provide me some strips of clean linen?"

"Well now, Dr. Cortlandt, that I'll try. How is everything at the manor?"

"I haven't been there yet. Just crossed the river. But there's a wounded man in the stable I must attend to first."

"Have a tot while I get the linen."

David took the drink from the brown bottle on the fireplace. He was bone tired. He had another drink. It went to his head. He hadn't been drinking much and while he waited he sipped, and when Goody Welton came back with some linen rags, clean at least, he was feeling the rum behind his eyeballs and his heels felt it too.

"Bring out the kettle when it boils." He went out of the kitchen and across the main room of the inn. The officers were still busy with bottle and tongue.

"And the damned stiff-necked Philipse," said the red-faced officer. "You'd think they were still the first family—related to the angels. But don't they all have a bit of the blood of the nigger wenches they pleasure with? All of 'em. Touched with the tar brush."

David stopped and looked up at the ceiling. The rum was purring in his bloodstream as he stood listening by the open door.

"That yellow girl, Zee, didn't she come through here a few months ago carrying a brat with the Philipse yellow hair, the spitting image of . . ."

David banged into the room and put his linen rags down on the drink-scarred table.

"I'll ask you, sir, to stand up. I'm Major Cortlandt."

"The devil a lot I care," said the officer. "I'm Colonel Jameson. And I'll not stand for a mere major, gentry or not."

David took the officer by the front of his jacket with both hands. "You have just made certain remarks in public before these officers about the Philipses."

"I know what I said. They sleep with their niggers."

"You inferred, sir, that *all* the Philipses have Negro blood in them?"

Colonel Jameson put his big fists over David's gripping hands. "You hear well. I said it—I say it again. All."

"I am married to Roxanne Philipse."

Colonel Jameson glared at David, in no discomfort at the news. David flung him back in his seat. "I demand satisfaction. Colonel Jameson, I call you out."

"You know damn well General Washington has forbidden duels."

David pulled a pistol from his belt. The other officers made a gesture toward him and David moved behind Colonel Jameson's chair.

"You will give me satisfaction, sir, or I will blow your mangy brains across this table and distribute them amongst your friends."

An officer said, "There is strict authority against dueling. On penalty of death."

"I shall count three, Colonel Jameson."

The colonel laughed. "I faced three battles without any tremor and I can accommodate you, Major Cortlandt, at pistol distance, loaded with two-ounce balls."

David lowered his weapon. "You can send your second to the stables in half an hour. My man there will be Captain MacBean. We have an operation to perform."

David walked out leaving the officers looking at each other with wonder. Colonel Jameson pursed his lips and banged his fist together.

"The damned fool asked for it."

It was only when David got to the stable yard that he realized what a foolish thing he had done. This whole bizarre idea of "honor" . . . He was no purling, romantic boy carried away by some noble creed, or involved in a matter of great importance. The drinks on an empty stomach had befuddled him into a rash and silly action. What did it matter what inn bullies and soaks said? He had indeed gotten himself into a pickle. David rubbed his face, (damned hard drink,) and went into the stable.

Jack-Tom had been resting flat on a rough pine table and Robin MacBean had snipped off a great deal of the bandage, but much still was glued to the face of the wounded man, who made involuntary body movements. "Robin, go to the kitchen. There's a kettle of water coming to a boil. I'll need it to soften these bandages."

Jack-Tom said, "She sure is a lopsided face now. Broke me jaw, eh?"

"I don't think it's a full fracture, but if the ball is embedded in the bone, we've a problem."

With the aid of the hot water, to much groaning from the scout, the gaping wound on the right side of the jaw was exposed. It was inflamed and swollen and the face was blotched and overgrown with unshaved copper-colored hair.

"The horse-leech tried to get the ball out through the wound. I had to beat him off with my fists."

"The damned butcher," said David, feeling the jaw line. "Robin, cut me some small stout sticks about four inches high. I want to prop his mouth open. We'll go in through the mouth. How the devil have you been eating, Jack-Tom?"

"Gruel and . . . whiskey. It's hard to . . . kill a wilderness man."

David got the mouth open and put the wooden sticks in to keep it wide. "Hold the light closer, Robin. Ah, we'll have to pull out a couple of back teeth roots that got smashed. And the jaw is badly inflamed, but I don't think fractured."

"Og, og," said Jack-Tom.

"Quiet," said David. "Give him another dram of tincture of opium. I'm going to have to saw that bullet out."

David inspected his short two-inch saw on the adjustable handle that John Hunter had invented. It would be a tight fit in Jack-Tom's mouth, but the musket ball was deeply imbedded and the bone fragments and tissue were festering around it.

David rolled up his sleeves and began to operate. Robin held the pulse of the scout and wiped away the blood and matter that seeped from the open black mouth.

It took time to do the thing properly without shattering the jaw. The sawing was dreadful, then the probing so that the ball was properly gripped in the pointed forceps. The remains of two teeth with deep roots had to be extracted. They were solidly set. David sewed up the sore tissues around the bone and washed out the cheek wound and drained it and decided it was too late to try and sew up that half-healed skin.

His back ached from bending over and he straightened out. "Jack-Tom, we'll get the bandages on you, but I fear you'll have to grow a beard. You'll have a fearful scar. The edges should have been sewn up soon after it happened. I can't touch the tissues. They're sore enough now."

Jack-Tom lay very still, breathing hard, while Robin finished the bandaging. David was aware of a young lieutenant standing by the table gagging at the bloody rags, the ball, the fragments of jawbone and teeth scattered about on the table. His eyes glazed as he stared at the soiled instruments Robin MacBean was cleaning with a flannel cloth and some olive oil.

"What do you want, gaping there?" Robin MacBean asked.

"Leftenant Barker at your service. I'm Colonel Jameson's second."

David looked at Robin MacBean. "I'm fighting a duel with

Colonel Jameson. You're to be my second, Robin. Arrange the thing like a good lad, and don't stare at me."

"Colonel Jameson suggests at seven tomorrow morning, behind the Schuyler grist mill."

David waved at MacBean. "Natcherly. Natcherly."

Lieutenant Barker nodded, "Pistols."

"Pistols?" asked Robin MacBean.

Lieutenant Barker bowed as if taking that as an acceptance of weapons. He bowed again and went out. Robin MacBean glowered at David. "Of all the mad things, Major, this is the maddest. Duels are for fools and popinjays. What's the duel about?"

"A personal matter. How are you feeling, Jack-Tom?"

"Give me a tot of rum. You got the ball?"

David held it up with the aid of the needle forceps. "You can wear it as an earring."

Jack-Tom closed his eyes as Robin finished bandaging his jaw. "Davey, don't fit no duel. Wait till I get on my feet. I'll drill the bugger through the gizzard from ambush for you some dark night."

"Keep him still. I'll meet you, Robin, behind Schuyler's grist mill at seven tomorrow. Anyone will tell you how to get there."

"I'll not do it. It's against all my Scots principles of conduct."

"If you don't stand by me, Robin, I have no one else. I'll go out there alone."

David rolled down his sleeves, put on his jacket, and went out. Jack-Tom watched him go. "He's got grit in his craw. But he can't shoot worth a plugged shilling."

Robin MacBean rubbed his face with the back of a hand and sat down to think it all out.

Mynheer Schuyler stood in his library, an uplit pipe in his mouth, staring at David Cortlandt, who was seated at his desk, writing on a long sheet of paper.

"What does Roxy think of this mad idea of a duel?"

"I haven't been home yet, Mynheer. I rode here direct from the landing."

"Better if you hadn't stopped at the landing at all."

"I had to perform a surgeon's service. Now, this is my last will and testament to be produced in case I fall tomorrow in this duel."

"Predict me no predictions, David. Stay among the living—go back to the war."

"I leave whatever I have, and it's little enough it is—to my wife Roxanne, and through her to our children, George and Mollie. My medical instruments, my books—oh—it's put down here in detail. Will you witness my signature?"

David quickly signed the sheet and Mynheer peered through his spectacles and sighed. He signed with a slow, boyish script embellished with curlicues.

"What's happened to the river families, David? We were so solid only a few years ago. The world was green and ripe and everything, it seemed to me, appeared it would last forever. Now look about you. Half the houses are empty, some are burned down, and the rest of us fumble about to keep warm and get food. The Livingstons are almost all dead, I hear. Jonathan Philipse a turncoat, his son Joe in the Carolinas, my boy Culbly—well let's not talk about him. Homer Schuyler dead, General Schuyler—his farm burned and the stock run off. And the upriver Van Cortlandts vanished—the rest divided, divided. You think the houses will ever open again and be painted white and green? And children—will they run down to the river crying like birds?—and will we sit on the wide porches and talk in the sun? It can't be—the sun doesn't shine the way it used to."

David folded the paper and handed it to Mynheer. "To the children all our turmoils will seem merely quaint. They will enjoy and frolic as we did at their years, before they in their turn see the recurring words: *This too shall pass away*. Nature, Mynheer, is indifferent to us, but she never changes the rules."

"A stirrup cup before you go, David?"

"No, no more drink tonight. You will hold the will?"

"It's foolishment. Besides, why are you fighting a duel? It's not your way."

"Because of misused human passions, I suppose, that lead to wars and all other disasters."

David shook hands with the old man and went out to mount his horse for the ride to Philipse Manor. Mynheer stared at the folded paper and locked it in the old French desk. He juggled the small gilt key that locked the desk in the palm of his wrinkled spotted hand. Human passions misused . . . It was as good an answer as any. If, as Mr. Gibbon the historian had written, "History is little more than the register of the crimes, follies and misfortunes of mankind," then what little more was left were the few grains of human passion that rose above the follies and crimes and produced ideas and hopes not yet achieved. It was too late an hour to philosophize and he was too old to think it out. Besides the good God had not given him the kind of brains to make solid systems of any thoughts. Happy is the man, the nation, with no history! It would save so much talk, so much space in books. . . . Mynheer put the little key away in his waistcoat and went slowly, stiffly up to bed. It was the one perfect goal of the day.

Roxanne sensed that David was deeply troubled. Near dawn she became aware he had not slept much in the great bed they shared. Early he had been warm and ardent, and made love almost with a cruel frenzy. He had talked foolishly of the country and the future of the children, had mocked the war, had whispered ironically on the destiny of man. But he had not slept much.

She turned to David and put her arms around him. He smelled so fine—just being David, that personal anthology of odors graded like a score of music, made up of his hair, his skin, breath, the various anatomies, all one symphony of being the breathing, moving, acting David she loved. How banal were her images she suspected—yet how strongly she felt them.

"What's the matter, darling? Why don't you sleep."

"It must be too much camping on the ground. I cannot get comfortable in this soft bed."

"Perhaps home excites you too much. You must sleep."

"I will. It is just that I am here now and all it means. I'm sure it's that. You sleep, my dear."

"You can slumber later. I shall quiet the children and lock out the dog."

"No, I must be up at six."

"Whatever for?"

"I have a wounded man in the village. Yes, Jack-Tom. I must see him. You remember Jack-Tom?"

"You can see him at noon. He too must need his sleep."

"It's a badly neglected wound. I can't trust it. If the mortified tissues spread . . . I must be there at break of day."

She held David close and nuzzled his face with hers and rubbed her cheek against his ear. He fell into a troubled slumber and began to mutter in his sleep. Roxanne could make out little of what he said. It was about marching and setting up camp, shouting commands, and some obscure medical details of an involved operation. He was wet with sweat and she could feel his damp skin and the moisture sopped up in his nightshirt.

David came awake with a start, crying out some sound of lament. He sat up in a welter of bed linen.

"David, what *is* the matter?"

He recovered and wiped his face on his sleeve. "It must be a touch of the fever recurring."

She felt his head. "No, it's not the fever. You are in a strange way."

"I've been gone too long this time. It's harder every time to come home and see you all and then feel this *must* end and I must go away again."

He sat hugging his knees, shivering, and she wondered if it was the fever.

"Roxy dear, you are a fine wife—always remember that. I have been happy, you have made me a world in which I would be better off than in any kind *if* I could only have it to enjoy for the next fifty years."

Roxanne got out of bed. He noticed she was filling out now, maturing quickly. She said firmly, hard-lipped: "You need some warm milk. Don't dare to dress."

Outside what remained of the night lay supine, merged with silence.

CHAPTER 46   Botts, saddle-sore since White Plains—riding with an escort of dragoons, Robin MacBean mounted at his side— came in sight of Philipse Manor. It was just as the sun came up and turned the river's overlapping waves to golden scales, like, Botts thought, the back of a giant salmon. Behind the escort came a closed carriage. The morning mist was just rolling away across the already greening fields of spring. Overhead was the piercing cry of swallows. The horsemen and the carriage turned up the rutted drive. Lilac bushes were blooming, the flowers hanging in violet clusters of sweet, overpowering scent.

Botts dismounted and the horsemen pulled in the smoking horses and looked over the boarded-up house. Botts went around to the kitchen and knocked on the door. It was opened after his third knock by David in his regimental blue and buff, but still in his stocking feet.

"What the old Ned are you doing here, Botts?"

Botts pulled out a paper from deep in his dark jacket. "I have here, Major Cortlandt, an order for your arrest, signed by General Greene in White Plains."

"Arrest? You must be demented."

"For fomenting and challenging to a duel, a rite forbidden by an army order from General Washington, and based on a directive of the Continental Congress."

Robin MacBean appeared beyond Botts' shoulder. David cursed. "And I see how this all came about. That was a dastardly thing to do, Robin MacBean."

Robin shrugged his shoulders indifferently. "The life of a great surgeon is of much more value to me than any paltry excuse for a miserable duel."

David turned briskly, angry—too angry to talk. But followed him in. David's sword was on a chair; on the table were a brace of silver-mounted pistols, a cocked hat, and a black cloak. Botts put down the paper and cracked his knuckles.

"Colonel Jameson is also under arrest and on his way to Boston. There will be no duel."

"You interfering block of wood."

Roxanne coming into the kitchen with a basket of baby small-clothes, looked around her puzzled. "*What* duel? What arrests? David, what is this thing?"

"Never mind, Roxy, the thing's undone."

"Botts, what are you doing here?"

"Major Cortlandt is under arrest for preparing to fight a duel this morning."

"David, *no!* How could you? Didn't you care for me, for Mollie, for George!"

"Don't womanize so," said David, turning with a deep scowl to face the window.

Botts added, "You have four hours to pack and prepare to leave the Hudson. There is a carriage outside to take you to Newport where you will board the schooner *Lippincott* for the Carolinas. You will serve as surgeon general of the southern colonies."

"Oh darling," said Roxanne. "I'm sorry I loosened my tongue too much just now. I was horrified—*you* dueling."

David lowered his head and chewed on his thumb. Roxanne turned to Botts. "The surgeon general can of course take his family and children with him to his new post?"

David whirled around. "I've had enough of your ideas! Roxy, plague me no more this morning. I am under arrest, they can thrust me wherever they want."

"No," said Botts. "You can go to Hartford Gaol."

"Four hours?" said Roxanne. "That doesn't give much time to decide what to take. I suppose baggage will be limited?"

Botts nodded. "I'd suggest two fairish-sized trunks."

David shook his head. "It's madness, Roxy. You're not a flighty girl any more."

Roxanne agreed, "No, I'm not. I've come through a winter of hell and loneliness and hunger. I want no more of this house while there is war. I don't want to stare at the dumb face of the river, or live deserted with only a dog and two infants. I may wife you too much, David, but you can't shrug me off now."

She turned briskly and went out. David sat down in a chair and said, "Thank God, Botts, there was no duel. Send in Robin Mac-Bean. I want him to know I hold no grudge for this thing, and he must take over the care of Jack-Tom."

Botts pressed David's shoulder with his large square fingers and went to the door. Upstairs David could hear Roxanne thumping a trunk across the oak floor. The four walls of the kitchen seemed to be whispering together.

Come light, come the rolling day, come reality at the level of audibility as a patch of shouting sun on a deaf wall, come a whole life pushing in—expressed in the slant of curtains all awry, bellied out by a spring wind. Now to collect one's sensations in an old, old body where nothing connected fully, where the functions were atrophied and the sight bleary as sea fog and the world filled with specters, not people. So . . .

Old Martha Schuyler lay small and wrinkled on the large feather bed in the larger teakwood bedstead. Another day gained, another twenty-four hours won from the enigma of existence. The moments of lucidity were getting rarer, but just on awakening, when everything that was most real was in the dreams, and all that was to be unreal was the day to be lived, then would come those gaps in her trance, a state when the clarity of crystal became her mind . . . but not for long.

She was the river purling by, she was the families that had made the fields by cutting the forests, by working the slaves and the indented servants. It was all in line with the procession of ancestors who had carried, in each, something that made this great house. One clutching a pair of copper milking pails, another a tall clock; some with oil paintings, others with leather bags of old coins. There was the stain on the ceiling that was her great-great-grandmother who weighed fish, charted a ship, salted cod, filled ledgers with the large income and the little loss. There was her grandfather, the old rip, his eyeballs swimming in sperm, licking up the last drop of breakfast egg from its shell in his old age and crushing the remains to feed his hens. All of them in the room, all of them represented by every hand-hammered nail, every home-kilned brick (was the stove lit?).

A momentary cloud covered the sun. She was aware of the lack of air in her dried-up leather lungs, of the stiff joints and her hams and breasts reduced to stringy knots of muscle. And the great pain in her hip. She could no longer roll the chalky knob at the end of her thigh bone in its socket, and she seemed to be turning to stone among inflamed tissues (she must feed to live—live to feed).

Damn—double Dutch *damn* they were late this morning! She put out a claw of a hand and pulled on the blue velvet bell cord. Somewhere below she heard sound move on its iron wires toward the bell, and the bell went off, muffled by brick and plaster.

With great effort she cleared her throat of obstructions and, reaching for her cane, she began to bang on the bed posts. Her rage grew, her greed, her hunger, the will to live.

"Coffee! Coffee! Do you hear me? You great lummox! Bring me my coffee!"

She would show them all; just how many there were—faces selected without thought—she no longer remembered. Her son she knew, a large fat lout, and she didn't like him. But at least he would transmit for her the seed for the inheritance, generation to generation. That was all that mattered. What mattered was the land, the crops, the river boats, the wonderfully balanced continuance of the shortness of life; this continuance she had never lost, and if she lasted forever (and she had a profound conviction she might) even then she would never lose it.

"Coffee!" she shouted and enjoyed the scars her cane banged into the bed posts. "With rolls . . ."

The two trunks were loaded into the carriage boot. David said good-by to Robin, who wiped an un-Scots sign of emotion from his eye. David walked past the escort of dragoons, their nervous horses having to be worked back and forth to keep them calm. He climbed into the coach.

He had always tried to curb his sentimental side, but now he opened the gates to emotion as he looked to the trembling sunshine under the trees and among the ruined rhododendrons. He and his were leaving here. Would they ever return to where the ponds lay greased with moonlight on summer nights and a hazy, remote antiquity inhabited every house on the river? It was all up to the fortunes of war. He looked at the bare branches just budding, branches that frayed out at the ends like thinly combed hair.

He remembered a night lined with black velvet, when he first came here with Roxanne and their fill of vision was very personal —made up of each other. There was a certain peculiarity about them yet. They were learning each other then—in ardent lessons, and words would burst around them like bubbles and they would laugh. Later that year they walked, well bundled up, under the frosty metallic disc of the winter sun, aware of the intangible substance of a marriage beyond the promises, the hopes, and the daily domestic decencies.

Mounting into the coach had been like going up to be hanged. And that brought back images he pushed away. We must, he decided, be measured while alive, as to what we are and want. Later it is of no use. He looked at Roxanne and then at the baby with its pink, waxy convexity of forehead, at George hugging the dog, and he knew suddenly the swift charge of time.

They had better start—this introspective brooding was not good for him. The coachman began to drip words, like a leak in a boat, to a dragoon holding the horses' heads.

"Let us get started," David said.

"Go!" shouted George.

The fruity bass of the horse-holder announced, "About ready now?"

David said, "Just about."

Roxanne looked at him and David realized she must be feeling more than he did at this leave-taking. She had been born here.

George held the dog Hector, who panted and licked everyone within reach. Roxanne in traveling cloak and a feathered hat held baby Mollie upright on her lap. Botts rode up outside and bent his head down. "We've got a long ride to Newport. You start. I'm going to Boston."

He saluted with his riding whip, touching his hat, and rode ahead. David never saw him again. The dragoons re-formed on order, the coachman cracked his whip over the pair of roans in harness, and the carriage jolted ahead and went wheeling down the drive.

David, deep in packages, small leather boxes, saddlebags, chests of medical papers, several children's toys, and even the dog's favorite bone, looked out as they turned onto the road. The solid old house, shutters unpainted, bandaged with raw planks across its doors and windows, began to recede according to all the laws of perspective. He hoped Robin would keep an eye on it as he had promised.

Roxanne pressed Mollie against her shoulder. "George, you sit down or I'll have you sent back."

"Can't," said George, dressed as a miniature male in his cocked hat and neatly cut jacket. "Father is 'rested. We can't go back."

David pulled the small boy to his side. "You'll have to come back some day, George. We live here."

The coachman cracked his whip to take the heavy wheels through a bad patch of loose sand. The dragoons jingled by to take up positions ahead. David, Roxanne, and their brood looked out from the dusty carriage window at the river rolling by the shores of bush and tall trees. Were they sure, David wondered, of anything between them and this land, even of the future? The horses settled down to a steady, unhurried pace. They had a far piece to go through the fields of this new nation. Roxanne looked over at David and decided he would do to spend a lifetime with. The coach for some time ran on beside the river, until the road turned eastward. The horses labored up in clouds of dust toward a ridge of blue pine trees.

EPILOGUE

Our time is a very shadow . . .
Solomon II, 5

THE MARQUIS   The three-masted American merchant ship *Cadmus* sailed from Havre on July 12, 1824. After the usual slow summer winds she cast anchor in New York bay on August 15. The city was decorated in festive array and the harbor shipping appeared excited as small boats tacked and filled. On the deck of the *Cadmus* stood the slight, bony figure of an old man, with a peculiar forehead that sloped back alarmingly. He wore nankeen trousers (alas, he felt, the days of knee breeches *are* over). A blond wig fitted him badly and he leaned on a slim blackwood cane to favor a limping leg hurt some time before in a tumble down a flight of stairs.

Behind him stood his secretary, Levasseur, an overgrown lout of a scholar, and to one side his valet Bastien kept opening and shutting his wide carp's mouth. All three eyed the greenery around the Battery, the neat brick housing that rimmed the shore, the bunting flying, and the faint sound of band music carried across the languid bay waters.

A large blue cutter manned by a dozen sailors in white was approaching the ship and from it, when it touched, a fat little man stepped and muscled his way up the ship's ladder. He was followed slowly by other dignitaries. The fat man bounced up on deck, bowing and doffing his tall beaver hat.

He began talking, or rather reciting, almost at once. "Marquis Marie Joseph Paul Yves Roch (not stopping to take breath yet) Gilbert du Motier de La Fayette (a short breath), we, the city of New York, the island of Manhattan, welcome you as an honored, beloved guest of the nation, in the name of President Monroe (a deep suck of air—and a broad ribbon of red, white, and blue placed

EPILOGUE 453

around the neck of the marquis) as the adopted son of the late founder of this republic, George Washington . . ."

There was more, but the old man—he was a wiry but creaky sixty-seven—was observing some limber girls in thin summer dresses, worn loose in the Greek manner, who were cheering him from a small white yawl circling the *Cadmus*.

He replied—aware they expected an answer—not the one he had made so many years ago to General Washington, "*La seule chose que j'ambitionne c'est la gloire . . .*" Glory as the profoundest desire of his heart was only for youth. In his careful English he said, "Each man must some day discover America, under penalty of death. To discover America means to open one's eyes, to become oneself, to be . . ."

THE DEAF MAN   In the narrow white house off Bowling Green the big bedroom fronted the noisy street, but it didn't matter to the man—portly in girth, his face given to the pouches and dewlaps of age—how loud the city must be in its mood of celebration. He was stone deaf and had been for many years. He sat in a stained dressing gown—Lord, how often Betty his granddaughter had asked him not to work in the anatomy gallery in his good clothes! He sat drinking strong black coffee, making notes for his afternoon's lecture on the blood vessels that feed the spleen. Then he remembered there would be no medical school classes that day—the little fop was being welcomed to the town.

He slapped the notebook closed and in his silent world he rested, eyes closed. After a few moments (how much rest he needed now, and how much sleep) he opened his eyes and went back to the notebook.

In his clumsy medically-taught Latin he wrote a bit of remembered Cicero. *Senex ad senem de senectute scribo . . .* an old man I write to an old man about old age. But this would not do. Betty saw it as just more of his obstreperousness (my, what words they taught young girls now) and the growth of his misanthropic nature in his deafness. He began to write something for a future lecture he planned.

It would appear that the nervous system of certain women that I have observed reacts emotionally to certain conditions in their lives for which we have as yet no explanation. Many are sent to the madhouse who with some other treatment could, I feel, become again normal citizens. Some years ago, while treating for hernia a young woman of Trenton who imagined she was in birth pains—she was a virgin—the rigidity of her . . .

He felt a light tap on his shoulder. There was Betty, looking young and lovely in blue watered silk with a paler blue sunshade.

"You give us the fantods the way you neglect your family and your social position."

He could ignore—because of his deafness—most people talking to him, but Betty knew he could read lips. "Is your grandmother up?"

"She has been up since dawn. And you're not dressed. We're meeting the marquis at the big dinner prepared for him, and you're to get some kind of award from the French."

"I have a letter about it somewhere. That paper I did on the theory of bone growth. Damn. And my classes all gone to shout for him—any excuse not to work. What I would have given to have had a medical school here when I was studying for surgeon. The hard cold years, the dismal life, the . . ."

"Boo!" said Betty. "The cruel saga of your youth we all know. People say, is *that* old man your grandfather? Doesn't he ever smile? Why are all the students so frightened of him? Boo—not me, and skip the trials of your beginnings. I'll get your brown jacket with the gold buttons with eagles on them."

"You're just like your grandmother, the same foul temper and wanting your own way under a ladylike varnish."

The girl giggled. "Huh, grandma has a lot to bear from you. Why not wear your old general's uniform?"

"Major, and I'm twice the man I was then, in bulk anyway. I still have my old scalpels, but I lost the sword years ago."

He dressed quickly now that he saw his workday was ruined. The tall hat, the trousers with the straps under the shoes, the flowered waistcoat, and the Italian watch with the thick gold chain Joseph had sent him when captain of the *Sparrow*.

Downstairs the sons and the daughters-in-law and the whole sniffling damp mess of grandchildren welcomed him with those loud open-mouthed greetings one usually gives the deaf.

Roxanne was looking very fine in yellow-brownish silk, and the high lace hid her wrinkling neck, the bonnet cunningly arranged to hide her white hair. How tragic, he thought, as he kissed her dry cheek, it is to watch a beautiful woman fray away under the attacks of age—wrinkling here, a coarsening of the finger joints, a loss of teeth, a failing of breath. Roxy laced too tight. She was having trouble breathing again. There was, he recollected, a paper written by a Russian on the action of pressures on blood vessels, but before he could remember the Slav name, he was out in the sunny day and the city coach he used to go to the hospital was at the door. Black Tom the coachman was fairly sober, holding in the prancing matched grays striking sparks from the street cobbles with their iron shoes. Roxy and Betty sat facing him, and George crowded in at the last minute, having gone out to change into fresh gloves. George was laughing and smelling of spice, which meant he had had a large brandy before leaving the house. George, the popular society doctor with the biggest practice in the whole eastern seaboard, once married to a Holmes of Boston, his son Walter studying in Rome, painting pictures or some such nonsense. His father turned to him.

"Feel any good bellies today, George?"

Dr. George Cortlandt, tall, with a large paunch, his curling hair fashionably oiled and gray at the temples, laughed. "Being a well-liked doctor isn't so bad, Father."

"It is when you have talent for something better."

Roxy tapped her husband's knee briskly with her sunshade handle (he had bought the sunshade for her in Paris when they had gone abroad in 1816). "David, I'll have no plaguing the family with your Tom Paine ideas. I'm proud of George."

The son smiled and pressed his father's hand. They were very close friends. George did not resent his father's idea that he should spend his life in dank medical school cellars hunting obscure nerve ends. George kept horses, a ketch, gave wine parties, hunted mallards in season, and had a taste for the realistic battle pictures of the modern French salon. Napoleon in Egypt, The Old Guards' Last Stand—that sort of *avant-garde*.

The old man closed his eyes so he would have no more lips to read. Damned if he knew what he'd say to the Frenchman. Politics would be best, he supposed, but what was France just then, a republic or an empire?

THE LIVINGSTONS   The cutter landed the marquis in a spattering of oar spray at the Battery and, in the smoke of welcoming guns being fired with blank shot, the cheers of the population gathered under bunting and flowers to shout him huzzah! He stood looking at the neat park, the lines of elm and maple trees, the reconstructed buildings, and the added size and spread of the city. It was not as it had looked in those fearful days when it was a battleground, and a lost one, to the Americans.

A ship's officer was telling him the population was now over ten thousand. He was assisted to an open carriage drawn by four white horses, and they started slowly up Broadway, between people cheering and past old men in faded blue and buff uniforms, and young soldiers in the shakos and feathers of the regular army.

Levasseur relieved the old man of several bunches of already fading flowers. "Shall I have the top put up?"

"No, let them look at me. It isn't much, but it will give them an idea of the passage of time since we fought here."

The valet Bastien was left to see to the baggage, and someone got him drunk, but he was able to dress the marquis for dinner that night in the ornate suite assigned to him.

"There will be turtle soup," said La Fayette. "There always is at American functions."

Levasseur, a nervous young man who tried to appear ironic and world-weary, made a *tutting* sound with his lips. "We must think of our digestion."

"You think of it. I'll have the turtle soup."

In the wide pier glass the old man shook his head and reset his blond wig. "You should have seen me forty years ago—or more. I lived on horseback and the food was poor and scarce."

The valet handed the marquis a well-smoothed beaver hat. Below in the red brick streets a band was playing old military airs that brought back campfire smoke and cold dawns and the shouts of voices long since stilled.

There was also a large night dinner for the popular guest. The Livingstons' mansion on Broadway was well lit and the owner had put up added posts on which the best sperm-whale oil burned behind glass cylinders. The Livingstons, besides owning tea ships, were doing well with whaling in the Arctic and sending their crews across to the Sandwich Islands. In the great hall there were huge cakes of last winter's river ice scooped out and filled with oysters, and the wine was being served with a flourish by the servants Mrs. Livingston had brought back from England years before when she was one of the young matrons around fat George IV at his Chinese pavilion at Brighton.

Daniel Livingston, impressive in his side whiskers framing a handsome face somewhat too lean, stood under the Chinese screens hung against the back hall. He welcomed his guests, who were grateful to be invited to meet the marquis and could overlook their memory that the host's grandfather, Sir Francis Livingston, had been one of the most diehard of Tories.

Daniel Livingston moved forward as David and Roxanne came in, followed by George, helping his father off with his hat and taking the cane and handing it to a servant.

"Uncle David, how fine you could come!" said Daniel Livingston. For this middle-aged merchant king to call the old doctor "uncle" seemed amusing to George. But George said nothing and pulled on his lower lip and looked over the women. George, of all the sons and daughters, had failed in marriage and had a notorious reputation in society as a rogue and lover among women. He had been wounded twice in duels—and "once by Mercury," his father added.

Dr. Cortlandt frowned, "Damn foolery, Dan—it closed the school today. How's your mother?"

"Poorly; the rheumatism is unrelenting. You'll go up and see her, I hope?"

"As soon as I greet the marquis and get the nonsense over with."

The music was being played under the arbor in the large garden, and the living and dining rooms had been made into one, full of crystal and china, displaying the wealth of rich things available to eat, to sip, to gnaw on, to get sticky-fingered about. And that whole cooked wild boar with his skin replaced—better just to look at, Dr. Cortlandt decided.

The marquis came in limping and shook hands and said simple things in his charming English that pleased all. He stopped by Dr. Cortlandt's side, "I hope the ribbon I gave you this noon helps bind our two nations together in a firmer bond, Doctor."

"I'm deef as a rock, Marquis. You'll have to let me see your lips."

"Ah, you have mastered it! Amazing. I knew a nun who could read anything, across a large churchyard even."

"What the devil is the matter with your leg?"

"Not a wound, as everyone thinks. Am I moving my lips properly for you?"

"Yes, yes. But your leg?"

"I fell downstairs some time ago. The torn ligaments don't mend at our age as they once did. I have been using ice on it."

Dr. Cortlandt snorted at the idea. "Worst thing you could do. Mix up a batch of hot wet bran and take it hot as you can stand it three times a day over the joint. And come see me. Yes—I'll write you out some exercises to limber it up."

Roxanne, talking to a big red-haired woman waved at her husband, "Davey and the marquis are talking of the war. They were both with Washington, you know."

"You forget, Roxy, we were Tories."

The company moved in to dinner. The band played French and American airs. The marquis was pleased as the tureen of turtle soup was set down. "Ah," he said to Betty, seated beside him. "Turtle."

"Yes," said Betty, "the Livingstons always have their tea ships stop for turtle. My father and my grand-uncle, Joseph Philipse, were lost in the China sea when the *Sparrow* sank in a typhoon out of Canton with a load of tea. The turtles were captured at Trinidad. Oh!"

"*Pardon?*"

Betty had a feeling one didn't reprimand a French nobleman for pinching one's leg.

THE RIGID WOMAN   It was a large bed set in the full bay window so she could look down on the world outside, and there were mirrors arranged so the crippled woman could see up and down the street. She was sitting up in bed, knitted gloves on her deformed fingers, and pillows bolstering up her stiffened joints that were becoming more unmovable with the advancing neuralgia. She was a beautiful woman still, and there was character and wit in the turn of her chin, the gleam of her eye. She looked up, pleased, as Dr. Cortlandt came in.

"Hello, old crock," she said. "No medical chatter please."

He sat down on a Hitchcock chair facing her and scowled. "What the devil, Peg, makes you so cheerful, locked away here with the lime depositing on your joints?"

"That's better, my dear Davey, more like you, soured and getting so fat between the ears you can't hear any more. How's the party progressing?"

"Brandy, cigars for the men, gossip and sweet wine for the ladies."

"He's not a bad little Frenchie."

"No, he isn't. We used to lie down in the same mud and share the same horse blanket. Here, let me take your pulse."

She slapped his hand away. "Doctor me no doctoring. You were always so damn serious, Davey, especially in London that year my poor wretched husband was killed in the duel with the prince."

"It wasn't any prince that killed Harvell, and you know it. And listen close—Daniel is Harvell's son, *not* the Duke of Alban's as you claim."

"My dear Davey, who's to know better?" She pointed to a cut-glass decanter of brandy on a night table, and David poured two glasses. They spent a pleasant hour, he no longer correcting her memory of what her life had been in London so long ago. Somehow, as he drank and refilled, he had no recollection of all those important names, and those gala events she talked of. She drank in quick, eager sips, loving every drop, and her voice grew loud and husky and her beautiful face grew damp. She laughed in too loud a key.

"They can say what they want about life, my dear solemn Davey, but once you've lived, you have it by the tail. And those who haven't lived, in *what* life are they going to live it? Eh?"

He looked at her deformed rheumatic fingers, covered with the gay knitted gloves, and she rolled her head in laughter and fell back on the bed. Davey adjusted her tortured body and kissed her cheek before he went downstairs and left her to sleep. He was unused to much drinking and he seemed to have trouble finding the top stair. He never thought back much to the old days in medical school and the London of the Third George except to point a lesson. Now a rift was made in a more personal memory, and through the torn curtain of recalled things he felt warm and alive as he had once been in the early stirring of first passions. He regretted nothing, of course. But perhaps George was right to have no rigid values, no scientific morals, just charm and grace and a liking for large fees at good-smelling sick beds.

The idea of George's world evaporated before he got home. He slept with his mind clouded by many shifting images and in the morning he was happy to be his surly and sour old self. Shouting at the servants, talking back to Roxy's advice not to dress too warmly. The students, bent over a cadaver from which they were dissecting out a blood vessel system, got the rough edge of Dr. Cortlandt's tongue.

"The old bastard," said the anatomy room attendant of the school. "He's getting meaner every year. Can't hear a house fall down, and driving the students like they were hogs to market this morning. If I didn't know better, I'd say the old coot was hung over after a heavy night out on the town."

THE RIVER   Doctor Cortlandt forgot to write out the exercises for the Marquis de La Fayette's knee and he left for upriver still limping. The plain people called him Lafayette.

The steamboat on the broad Hudson was an amazing sight, belching smoke black as sin, and sparks flying over all. The party of the Marquis de La Fayette went on board her for the trip to West Point and to Albany among cheering admirers. More music, more shouts. The old man waved. The broad Hudson nudged the boat and played with it, but the engine—turned by steam—cried out its power and the paddle wheels ate into the waters, and soon they were moving against the current with a pounding that shook the boat and the party standing on the upper deck. The Hudson was scaled in gold coins, or so it seemed to the marquis, in the bright sun.

The musing marquis watched the shore, the old stone houses in their nest of greenery and ancient trees. The big estates of the patroons were broken up. There were more small holdings, farms of simple design with wood smoke escaping, from cooking the midday meal; nearby, kine and horses were watering in coves and inlets. Small boats coming out to cheer the old man standing on deck leaning on his cane, sparing his hurt leg—feeling too much his large lunch.

The valet Bastien brought out a chair and the old man sat down and watched the elms and the oaks pass and the snake fences go off in their own pattern across the landscape.

"Make a note, Levasseur—here there was much division of families, some loyalist, some for the American side. It was a tragic time for most, and always the raids and the burnings. It looks so peaceful now."

"A fertile land, I would say."

"Yes, they farm well here."

A little girl, in yellow lace and with silky brown hair smoothed down by water, advanced to the man in the chair holding out a great bunch of yellow tea roses.

She bowed—overdid it—and almost sat down on her little stern. Her high voice shot out some well-learned words, "Welcome, sire, to our country which you so nobly helped to found, and for which we thank you now with all the bountiful harvest of the liberty you aided to full growth, to such fullsome harvest here." Another bow and again almost disaster.

"The moment I heard of America," said the old man, "I loved her. What man has not his little America?"

Boston was more dining, more speeching, more flowers. And looking off to Bunker Hill he was aware, as many were, that the actual battle had been fought on another hill called Breed's Hill, betrayed by history to the shadow of footnotes. Philadelphia was easier to reach than it had been when they all walked on frozen feet (while the British danced warmly in the city) with Washington's men under cruel blue skies, aching for the fire and comfort with which the fat, solid citizens were so happy to entertain the British. Now they were all patriots, even those who had sold supplies to the British and fought as Tories. Sons and Daughters of the Revolution, they were calling themselves now. The old man smiled with a warm cynicism, aware the real soldiers—"the winter soldiers"—had produced few acceptable and well-off descendants to join such societies.

The Masons greeted the marquis at their lodge in aprons and with ritual, and he talked to a few gray heads who gossiped a bit too much of how times had changed for the fat, easy people and how the virtues of hunger, disease, and despair were not remembered by the young folk, who wanted but to enjoy life and pleasure themselves.

Bastien said that night, "The waistcoats are getting tighter, sir."

"Ah, I must rise sooner from the table."

"And the laundry, sir, it is not as good as ours. The white shirts are turning gray."

"It's the water, Bastien. Not like our slow streams. They rush here and eat minerals and become muddy in their hurry."

"Our shirts will not last the tour, sir."

"Perhaps when we get to Washington we shall find an old-world laundress you will approve of, Bastien."

"I have taken to doing our own ironing. They scorch here, sir."

"Do they, now? A wild people still."

THE OLD MEN   Gadsby's Hotel in Washington gave the marquis and his party its best suite, all gold and white paint, so fresh it was still sticky, and the furniture was brushed but sagging. It was a finely laid-out city on paper, but so muddy and so humid, and the night insects so eager for blood to carry back to their swamps along the Potomac, that it took courage to govern here. It was more a plan of a city than a city yet. White marble tombs, cast-iron domes planned, but only dangerous planks to guide one across wide streets all mire and black ooze. The oil lamps on corners were too far apart and the young trees laid out along red brick walks still struggling to gain root strength. It would be a fine city, the marquis could see. He told Senator Andrew Jackson that as they sat in the senator's hotel room and drank whiskey.

"Corn mashed, Marquis, but well leeched."

"I began to prefer it to wine when we were fighting the war."

The senator, his tall cock's crest of hair combed high, nodded. "It kept us alive when the trots took us before the battle of New Orleans. We doubled up and fought on."

"American riflemen from the backwoods—is that the expression? —were always remarkable soldiers."

"No fuss and feathers about 'em, Marquis, but no horse breeders. We need better stallions."

"Yes, but it seems—and this is between us, Senator—the people who fought the war, they didn't somehow do as well as those who sat it out and waited to see who would win."

"Some day we'll breed a fine horse here."

"Jefferson said—" began the marquis, and the two men laughed. "But he said so much, didn't he? He's still alive at eighty-one. I am most desirous to see him. I wonder what he thinks of his country?"

Senator Jackson took the marquis out to see some horse farms.

There wasn't much left of Thomas Jefferson at his house called Monticello. Just skin and bones and a wiry, weary body and this grand house he had built and filled with his scientific toys and gadgets and so many books; there had been more books but there was a time when he was in need of money and he had almost been forced to sell Monticello, so some books were sold.

"I am happy to say, my dear Marquis, this nation is as greedy and ungrateful as any country is to its own past. And that's fine—a nation should look forward."

"You are pleased with its present? Suppose Washington had become king?"

"No, no. No race of kings has ever presented us with one man of common sense in twenty generations," said Jefferson.

"How do you pass the time?"

"I farm, I have the University of Virginia on my back, I have grandchildren, I play with mechanics, and I read philosophy and the classics. For the rest, I sit and wait. It doesn't matter what we think— life has turned its page on us."

They talked on of what old, creaky men will talk, men who had been strong and together in crisis in their youth and vital in some great project. The marquis inspected the farm, tasted of the product, touched old books, and drank a fairly good wine in the largest white room of Monticello.

Jefferson sipped his glass and said with a smile, "I have written out the inscription for my own tombstone. If one leaves it to others, it is usually an insult to one's sense of a good prose style." He took out a sheet of paper from a drawer and read from it. "*Here was buried Thomas Jefferson, author of the Declaration of American Independence, of the Statute of Virginia for Religious Freedom, and father of the University of Virginia. Born April 2d, 1743 O.S. Died* . . . well, *that* is still blank. If there is a creator of the universe and he has a sense of humor, it would be on July Fourth."

"You must show me the weathervane that you can read on the ceiling of your study."

TO THE WEST   Young Sam Manderson, over his seasickness, stood at the rail of the coastal steamer watching the blue-green streak of water the first mate had told him was the Gulf Stream. It could well be. The soot and sparks from the tall black funnel were spotting the deck, and the sea birds, geeking and dipping toward the creamy wake and hunting tidbits, made alive the vast expanse of desolate sea. It was his first trip away from Philadelphia and the

Yeshiva seminary. Sam felt small, astray, and rather uncomfortable. Somewhere in his big blue carpet bag was a letter to the elders of Zion in Savannah recommending him as a young rabbi of deep knowledge—a regular *tzaddick*—and of fine grace, able to recite the high holiday chants on Rosh Hashanah with the proper voice.

If only he looked like a rabbi! He was neither thin nor starved-looking, not broken by spiritual fasting to a sickly green-white. Not crook-backed and red-eyed from study. Not even really bearded or with ritual curls over the ears. Sam had tried to raise a beard, but with no success. He disliked the healthy image of himself reflected in the dining-room porthole: a large brown-haired young man with a vast spread of shoulders, hefty arms, and legs too much muscled for his trousers of cool and now crumpled linen.

Sam recited a prayer, touched the ritual undervest he wore with its sacred fringes. But it did no good. The idea of facing the Jewish elders of the Savannah *schul* frightened the young man. He was nine-teen and his grandmother had wept with joy, her brown wig on one side of her wrinkled head, at the idea of a grandson of the heroic Manderscheids dedicated to the Talmud and the Torah of Israel.

Sam Manderson wandered into the saloon bar and ordered a bourbon and branch water as he had noticed others do, and he stood there sipping the filthy stuff. A square, knobby-faced man given to plumpness stood by his side drinking whiskey by the shot-glassful. He turned to Sam and his voice had the sound of a man who shouted against wind and storm.

"What the blasted devil all this decoratin' and bannerin' all over the hull boat?"

"La Fayette is on his way to Savannah too. We're meeting his boat if we can and are entering the harbor together. At least that's how it's planned, the purser told me."

"All I hope is I can pick up mules and pack hosses, and git out of town before the shootin' starts. The name's Porterhouse, Ab Porterhouse." The plump man wiped his face with a red silk handkerchief. "Buy you another snort of pizon?"

"I don't drink much. But thank you. I'm Samuel Manderson, of Philadelphia—or I was. You from these parts?"

"Texas, there's where I'm headin' back. Space, rich river bottoms, and all fer the takin'."

"Don't the Mexicans own it?"

"Hell, *hombre*, you can swing a cannonball in any direction for a thousand miles and hit nothin' that walks on two hind legs. Course, if you like company we've built up some settlements. I'm kinda dealin' in land—that's my ruckus. Where you aimin' to set down, Sammy?"

"Savannah. May I, sir, be honored by tendering *you* the next drink?"

"Who said you can't drink? Thankee. Bottoms up. You settle any place but west of the Mississippi and you'll make the mistake of your life. Now you look hard-assed enough to handle cattle, clear land, impregnate a family fer some willin' gal. Married, Sammy?"

"No, I haven't thought of it—I mean marriage—till I made my way in the world. To afford a family. I have only limited funds my grandma gave me."

"Barman, bring the bottle. Sammy, you got a randy look and the sooner you get in double harness the better. Now, on the branch of the Salt Fork where I got my landholding and where I'm takin' supplies, there are three, four young heifers—gals just bustin' out all over fer marryin' up. Warm livin' at night, hard workin' in the daytime, and ready fer a row, a deer hunt or a hoe-down, a slap or a tickle. Sammy, you're comin' along with me. I'll show you where to stake out range, sell you gear, and get you title. Loan you cattle on a note against the day we find a way to do more than run 'em down fer tallow and hide. How much your granny stake you for?"

"Two hundred in gold. But you don't understand. I am devoted to, I mean dedicated to, my God. I am one with Jehovah, and must preach in His tabernacles the words of the Judges and the Shekinah."

"Sure, Sammy, you kin preach on Sunday."

"The Sabbath. It is the Hebrew way as put down in the Midrash."

"Sure, you kin preach any day at all you want, fer whatever hoot and holler of God you want to make."

"It's my turn, Ab Porterhouse, to buy. *Sholom Aleichem.* Tell me about the girls. Do you know the Song of Songs that is Solomon?

> *"My beloved to me is a bag of myrrh*
> *that lies between my breasts,*
> *My beloved is to me a cluster of henna blossoms*
> *in the vineyards of Enge-di."*

"You *are* a horny young 'un. You belong in Texas. I'll see your two hundred—gold you say? Not paper? Goes a far piece."

"Thy two breasts are like two young roes that are twins
which feed upon the lilies . . ."

Ab and Sam were very happy when they entered Savannah and took a hack to the mule barns. They bought a pack train, Sam with a share in it, missing the bands waiting at the docks and the people stringing flags for La Fayette. Sam Manderson sold his rabbinical raiment, his small library of theology and holy writ, even the works of Maimonides—and clad in a hunter's jacket and leather pants, singing out at the mules and banging his heels into a half-broken horse, he rode swaying after Ab Porterhouse into the wilderness. The elders of Zion waited for him at the house of Reb Gottlieb till it was nearly dark and they shook their heads and went to *schul* to find a *minyan*—a quorum—and said the prayer for those lost at sea.

Sam Mander (which was the closest Ab could come to remembering his name, and so Sam Mander he became at once) slept that night under dark pines, and he dreamed of burning Hebrew letters that spelled out the word *Texas,* and he saw as in a vision the wild plains and the ancient lost tribes of Israel mounted on untamed Indian ponies, riding like the wind, their huge beards out of Exodus and Isaiah flowing behind them, their right arms, oh Jerusalem, holding high their rifles; with their dreadful war cry: *Kal Mekadesh Shever'ee!"*

ON THE DELTA   The marquis enjoyed the trip to Savannah by steamboat. There were fireworks on the docks to welcome him, and his valet Bastien reported that six pocketbooks were stolen by thieves working in the welcoming crowd. New Orleans was hard to reach through the cypress bogs and the sandy roads and the trees hung with lacy Spanish moss. There were gifts of a tanned 'gator skin and some Indian relics. New Orleans was a rich city and cheerful in its humid grace and its food and its music. There was moonlight on the great muddy river and cold mint-flavored drinks on porches bound in wonderful hammered iron grillwork. The coffee was dreadful.

Coming upriver on the wide stream in the churning steam packet, watching the teeth of the snags reach for the boat and seeing the Negroes on the boggy acres walk behind their mules, the marquis also welcomed the coon hunters coming down to the firewood wharves to cheer. All of this was still primitive forest and river and the smell of ancient mud, and the nut tree groves had been here since before the white men.

There came planters in big hats smoking cheroots, Southern ladies under sunshades, giggling and proud. And the river folk cheered from the keel boats and huge log rafts floating by, and the men drinking and singing to a gourd fiddle and shouting foul oaths in the danger of meeting a steamboat that sent waves over their low bundles of long sticks.

On the Ohio the snags were thicker and the bends shorter, and one night the boat tilted, steam screamed from the escape valves and Bastien, naked as a jaybird, came shouting, "We are undone! We are sunk."

The boat did break up in the turbulent current and the marquis got ashore in a rowboat, but all his luggage was lost. Levasseur lamented: "My dear Marquis, six hundred letters addressed to you are also lost."

"So much the better, my dear fellow," said the marquis, seated by a crossroads inn fire, sucking up a large and very hot toddy, his naked old legs roasted by the burning logs. "Now we shall not have to answer any of them on the next boat. In fact we can claim every letter we got here in America was lost, and so we never have to answer one."

THE OLD MOUNTAIN MAN   The boy Jody came out of the piney woods carrying two dead 'possums over his shoulder; the old rifle was still too heavy for him, but hell, a young 'un had to prove he could carry a man-sized shootin' stick. Ol' Jake was sitting in front of the cabin barefooted, scratching the back of Bogger the old yella hound.

"How you cotch 'em, Jody?" the old man asked.

"They ain't much hard to git in the daytime. Drilled 'em through the eye first try."

"Hell, boy, you're a real deadeye. When I was your age I was shootin' deer with night flares up near Lake George, and had red varmints huntin' *me*." Ol' Jake twisted his toothless mouth to one side and pushed his cud of eatin' 'bacco in a corner and spat. He was a mean and ornery old man, bald as a coot with a long yellow-white beard hanging down to his breastbone; an old man lazy and dirty and a caution of a liar.

"You really kill all them Injuns ya tell about?"

"Been killin' 'em since I was nigh high as you is. Was a scout in the wars an' went west with Jebediah Smith and got my share of Cheyennes, Snakes, the dirty Gros Ventres, Utes—yep, scalped 'em all."

"They ever scalp you?"

"Shucks no—begin to lose my hair when I was a mountain man livin' off the alkali watter up on the Seedskedee River and at Spanish Fork. Oh, beaver pelt was prime high then. We'd cut off their castor glands and use it as bait in our traps. Why once I come in with a big wedge-press of pelts from a cache up on the Snake, packed into Jackson Hole and up to Fort Laramie and got me three thousand dollars fer a winter's work settin' trap lines. Yep."

"Huh," said Jody, "you're the dangest big liar I ever did talk to, Gramp."

The old man spat and beat dust from the mangy hound's hide. "If my misery wasn't so set in my bones I'd beat you as wall-eyed and bowlegged as an Apache or Salish pony sojer. When yer pap come back from keelboatin' he'll do it fer me."

The old man was angry and the boy saw he had been too outspoken. Still, it was hard to believe the old man had ever been anything but just settin' 'round the cabin steps with an old hound, letting pap and maw mosey up his vittles. The old man rubbed his pale blue eyes set in red, raddled flesh and touched off a fly from settling on his bald head, and sulked.

The boy Jody said, to change the subject, "We went down by the canebrakes and set some catfish lines, skinned a rabbit and set a good line in the current, and this here steamboat come lickety split up 'round the bend past the snags, and they yelled out General Lafayette was on board."

"Beelzebub, boy, that pissant was no general when I knowed him."

"You knowed 'im, Gramp? You seen 'im?"

"Like I seen you, only my eye was keener them days. I led the scouts up through the lake woods and the oak ridges when we cotched us some British general in a fox trap."

"No foolin'—you seen Lafayette, and you seen the war with General Washington, all them folk plain?"

"They was just folk then. And I was somethin' then. Raunchy and eagle-eyed, and standin' six foot three in the moccasins and I could outrun, out-wrassle, out-drink, out—well, never you mind. . . . Sassin' an ol' man. Git away from me, you young polecat."

"I didn't mean nuthin'. You tell so many whoppers."

"No whoppers. Just all young folk is lazy and shiftless now. I brung yer grandma out to settle downriver about two hundred miles. There was nothin' here but trees and bears. We had six brats, fast as she could litter, and in winter it was mighty hard livin'. She was a full-blooded Huron, sweet as maple sap and ornery as a wolf's whelp. Sure took time tamin'."

"We got us Injun blood?"

"Yer pap is a breed and you, Jody, be quarter-breed."

The boy frowned and picked at his dusty toes. "There you go, whoppin' again."

The boy picked up the limp 'possums and started for the open doorframe; no use having a door in this weather. The old man took up some apple-flavored tobacco plug and cut off a chew with a honed-down hunting knife. He looked up. "This Lafayette, he's a small young rooster of a fella, wiry and feisty-natured?"

"He was an ol' man leanin' on a cane, and they was servin' him mint drinks in a silver cup."

"Well, he would be ol' by now, I reckon. If it be the same fella I knowed."

"Oh sure," said Jody and went inside the cabin.

Ol' Jake looked down at the hound and patted its ancient and claw-scarred head. "Never mind, Bogger, you know I don't have to tell no whoppers."

Ol' Jake sat pulling at the loose skin on the hound's shoulders, thinking back a far bit to all the world he had known, the big trees of New England and then the exploring in his prime after beaver, reviving images of the vistas of grassy hillsides, alluvial bottom lands, the barrancas of chaparral and mesquite further south, like the time the Spaniards seized their outfit and run them out of town bare-assed. Right after he had been an Injun-hunter collecting a hundred dollars a hostile Injun scalp complete with both ears on it; that was so you couldn't make two scalp locks out of one kill.

Holy cow, it was a long time since that war and Lafayette and Washington, and the later years of just driftin', palaverin' with the skin hunters and tradin' gewgaws and drinkin' lethal whiskey. Playin' euchre and poker on the bullboats floatin' the big Muddy haulin' army supplies. The young 'un Jody took after him as a shot. Time was when he carried a plains rifle with a thirty-six-inch barrel—a Hawkins it was, he remembered, made in St. Louis—and life was fun sittin' round a chips fire eatin' buffalo hump and marrow.

Rosie, his son's fox-faced wife, came out, stumping flat-footed in her bare feet, a young sucker feeding on her dugs. She was all yellow-haired and slovenly like all the McMurtries, her folk, was.

"Come in and git yo' vittles."

"Don't want 'em, Rosie. That young 'un of yours been sassin' me."

"I don't bait if you come to et or not." She shifted the snuffy baby to the other lean breast.

"That young liar been sayin' things like he seen General Lafayette over on the river."

"Yo' ain't no right one to talk about lies—with yo' tall tales about bein' a mountain man on the Colorado and the Gila."

"Git along, woman! 'Fore I take a stick of kindlin' to you."

The hound-dog sighed in his sleep and Ol' Jake thought of all the places on the old maps marked *terra incognita* the officers carried. He saw again the Yellowstone and the time he went right out to the San Joaquin Valley as a fur partisan, and they rendezvoused at that *pueblo* with the big *presidio* and he spent months in that Mex gaol for knifin' that yella girl's pappy.

Ol' Jake's mind sank back back in time and the old man became young and limber again and wore scalps and a red ridge of hair on his shaved head and had a fringe of ginger beard under his chin. It was hard times then around New York and up the Hudson. And they said now it was all lies.

The young 'un Jody came out eating a wedge of cold corn bread dipped in hot bacon grease and he gave the old man a corner of it.

"Thank you kindly, Jody. I dreamed of corn bread when I was winterin' with Sam Bodganis up on the Nephi, trappin' beaver and we near died of hunger fer sure. That spring only me come down from the mountains and first thing they asked me at the fort was 'Where is Sam?' I just winked and I said, 'Meat's meat when you is powerful hungry.'"

Jody ate his corn bread and looked at the old man. "Come me I'm grown, I'm headin' west."

"You do that, Jody. Here is only a pesky neighborhood gittin' crowded. Folks is now settled thirty miles up the trail. Man can't breathe, it's so crowded."

THERE WAS A TOWN   They called him Lafayette and not de La Fayette away from the coast, he noticed. The marquis seemed never to tire. Even after the steamboat wreck and changing to another boat, he went on greeting the people, looking over the river and lake, and talking to the people of the back country on the farms, and in the village streets. Under the drowsy lights of town halls he sat in a smell of night flowers, listening to the welcome of turbulent undisciplined admirers, unbored by the interminable speeches. And only rarely being fed tasty and well-cooked food. It was a land of pot cooking and skillet frying, of wild game eaten singed from the coals, of feeding for hunger and not with any grace. The hawking and spitting and nose-blowing at table, the stabbing of morsels with case knives and jackknives, the ritual of teeth-picking—all left the marquis amused, and wondering when the tidewater grace of the coastal mansions would move back to the hills and to the unpainted towns.

New Athens sat innocent of paint on a sterile sand dune overlooking the windy Lake Erie. It had one muddy street, one brick house (the Judge's) and several wooden ones, a large collection of wandering hogs, some fur hunters, lean farmers, and a great many indifferently bred dogs that spent their leisure time hanging onto a pig's ear, or fighting among themselves for rights to obscene public matings in front of the Judge's Store. The Judge was fat and round at three hundred pounds, and his nose a fine port-wine red. He carried a pistol called a hawg-leg in each side pocket and always held court in the morning before it got too hot. He held local court in the back of his store, under barrels of soda crackers, salt cod, in the smell of oiled mule harness and stored winter apples.

There was a town hanging at least twice a year, and the village

gaol at the moment held an Indian horse thief, an Irishman accused
of stomping his mother-in-law to death, and a peddler of "gold"
jewelry that had turned green.

Judge Bounty called the court to order, spat brown into the box
of sawdust at his feet, and refilled his cheek with cut plug. His sight
was not what it had once been, but he swung a pair of gold-rimmed
spectacles across his rum blossom of a nose and beat the scarred table
before him with a block of oak taken (he claimed) from Old
Ironsides, during one of her trips in for repairs.

"Well, gentlemen, we have to try the peddler, and I'd say ten
dollars and return of the money paid him, but that can wait. The
Kennedy boyo has stomped a bit too hard this time and I guess
we'd better just vote and hang the shanty Irish bastard at high noon
from the top of Bill Hurley's Livery Stable. Does the jury want to
retire?"

Judge Bounty spat into the sawdust box and looked up at the
dozen loafers—the permanent jury—seated in chairs leaning back
against the side of the store.

A little man in a paper collar and no tie stood up in front of the
judge. "It would appear to me, Judge Bounty, with a guest like the
Marquis Lafayette due to pay us a visit, a pair of stinking feet hanging over Main Street isn't what I'd call a welcome bouquet of
flowers."

Judge Bounty pondered and smoothed his great belly. "According
to the volume of Blackstone I've read, and under English Common
Law, which I heard of in London in my youth, the matter of justice
(somebody kick that hog out of this court)—the matter of justice
takes precedence over visiting muckamucks. How votes the jury?"

They sat and listened to the dogs under the store worry the
hog that had been ejected from the court. The leanest of the
jurymen stood up, used the judge's sawdust box, and placed his wide
thumbs under his belt. "It sure seems to me there ain't nuthin' like
a good hangin' to make a celebration come to a boil. Guilty, and the
verdict to be carried out at high noon."

This seemed to be a popular verdict. A tall, bony woman stood up
in back, her mouth pursed tight, her thin arms folded.

"You listen to me, Judge Bounty—there's too much looseness in
this court, and too much running things the way you men folk like,
and not always the way the law reads. I don't want New Athens to

go down in history as the place they hanged a man the day the marquis visited us."

Judge Bounty sighed and rolled his eyes at the jury with a weary look. "Gentlemen, my wife Sally, being of sound mind and firm conviction, feels the matter of public décor is going to give us a bad smell if we have this hanging. Therefore I, Judge Jackson Bounty, of the county of Chatauqua, of these United States, rule the hanging of the convicted woman-stomper be delayed till the departure of visiting dignitaries. Belly to the bar, boys. Whiskey on the store."

Everyone moved over to the long counter where stood an open keg of whiskey and some tin cups. Judge Bounty spat out his cud and went over to his wife. "Well, my dear, he'll be just as dead tomorrow as today."

"You come home, Judge Bounty, and shave, and get the horses curried. Lafayette he's riding in *our* carriage."

The judge rubbed his fat face and looked at the merry group of men around the counter working on the whiskey keg. "You go ahead, Sally, and I'll get going soon as I finish off the town meeting. There's this talk of a full-time school. And while you and I never did replenish the earth with children, there are a lot of snotty-nosed little bastards running free that could use a little culture."

"Don't get too drunk. You're the only man in town who can make a speech in English that has any sense to it."

"That's mere grammar, my dear." He kissed her. "But what can I say? I wasn't his comrade in arms, I didn't fight for liberty, as you well know."

"You shut your mouth, Judge Bounty. We've been here too long—forty years, for anybody to think we're not as good Americans as anyone. And you were wounded in 1812, weren't you?"

"Yes, my dear." He embraced his wife and kissed her again.

Judge Bounty was drunk by noon, but the marquis' party decided to sail around New Athens and go on to Buffalo instead.

SIX WHITE HORSES   The May day La Fayette first saw Niagara Falls was, he felt, the climax of his trip. The marquis stared at the huge flood of water breaking white after it fell to the black rocks below, laced with rainbows and spume. Over the roar he

shouted, "Ah, one would have to be a great poet to say anything of
lasting value here."

By June he was back in Boston and now the formal event of
starting the monument at Bunker Hill was to be done properly. And
the marquis saw it was still planned on the wrong hill. An open
barouche drawn by six white horses ("Where, Levasseur, do they get
so many white horses for me?") took him out in the heated day—
the sky was like brass. The orator of the day was Daniel Webster,
brushed and fairly sober, and the welkin rang and the eagle screamed.
It pleased the marquis to hear such talk. Only a people sure of
themselves and unaware of the decay of nations could take pleasure
in such political platitudes. . . .

Now the marquis was to lay the cornerstone; and they saw a little
old Frenchman with sloping forehead standing in the sun under his
beaver hat, in his best blue jacket, the blond wig in place, the
nankeen trousers properly ironed. He held up the silver trowel and
he made the speech that Levasseur had written out for him. It was
only words, well-meaning words, but what he really sensed were
ghosts all about him. The long-gone wintry mornings on the icy
Delaware and the stains of blood on the snow. The hot fights in
red clay gullies with broken horses and screaming men, dying with
sword wounds in their entrails. General Washington riding with his
head up, after a defeat—the mouth firm over the bad teeth, and the
calm look on his features as he passed the ragged, tired men that
were all the army—so few—so few—that would serve, while the fat
fancy folk waited for the thing to be decided before they put out
the flags. And today they stood here and cheered.

The marquis had visited twenty-four states. He would go home on
the new frigate *Brandywine*, to die of course as all mortal creatures
must—and, unlike Jefferson, he had as yet no inscription ready. He
thought of a line from Homer, "My friends, quit ye like men, and
be firm in battle," and with the silver trowel he skillfully spread
mortar on the native granite.

THE FULL CIRCLE   Allen Schuyler, riding a hired horse he
could hardly control, came trotting down past the red oak and
spice bush swelling with early buds along the neglected trail. He
prided himself on controlling horseflesh (he had ridden on Lord

Wellington's left at Waterloo). He held a tight check on the chain reins, giving the wild brown colt no chance to get the bit in its teeth.

When he came in sight of the old manor house among the second-growth timber, he dismounted and tied off the colt to a rusting horse ring set firmly in an old stone. He walked around the weather-streaked house, boarded up, great sections of cornice fallen away, green streaks on the torn copper roof over the east porch. Old leaves and branches had been blown across the front steps, mud swallows had built among the brown paper-wasp nests under the tall pillars of flaking brick exposing their rubble centers.

Betty Cortlandt was standing on the top step looking at the river below, and she turned and smiled as he came up to her, crunching through the litter of drifted debris.

"Oh, Allen, isn't it a shame, all gone to ruin!"

He took her in his arms and kissed her. "I suppose so, dear. It would be best when we're married to tear it all down and build again."

"No, darling, perhaps I loved you only because you inherited this old house."

"Hardly much of an inheritance, I would say. My elder brother got the up-river place and I had to do with this. Father told me my grandfather used to curse this place every morning before the break-fast prayers, his one bloodshot eye gleaming in rage, and then he'd pour himself a large cup of black tea to drown out the fire of his hate of everything that was left of the family on the Hudson."

"You're not your grandfather."

Betty walked to the boarded-over doors and found a keyhole full of spiderweb. "You got the key from the lawyer's office?"

Allen held out a long bronze key. "If this is it, I did." He turned it in the lock and after much pressure the bolt inside fell back. He put a shoulder to half of the double door and forced it back with much protest of metal and warped wood. They stared into the entrance hall. Light seeped in between the boarded-over windows. They went in. The hall ceiling had fallen; a great pile of gray plaster lay at their feet. Draperies hung tipsily from damp walls. They walked slowly, their eyes focusing in the semi-darkness. They came to the grand staircase.

"It's a beautiful staircase," Betty said stroking the old rosewood. "We can restore it all."

Crystal prisms gleamed down from rotting linen hangings, the rugs under their feet sent up dust as they disintegrated.

"I still say tear it down, or burn it for the nails and roof lead."

"No, no," said Betty. "It's solidly built, needs just some plaster, wallpaper, and a great deal of paint."

"A very great deal."

They found themselves in a glass-walled room overlooking back gardens long gone to the wilderness of small pines and beech grown into a tangle of new forest. The boardings had fallen away here and the bare walls were sunlit—still showing whiter shapes where pictures and furniture had been removed. A long chest, once cushion-covered, ran under the bank of windows. Betty lifted a section of lid, exposing some garments long gone to moth powder, newspapers pulped by mice, and a black japanned metal box.

"Treasure!" shouted Betty, but when Allen pried it open there were only a few ledgers, their gray cloth covers stained by rain leaks.

Betty sneezed at the dust and opened one of the ledgers. "It seems to be some sort of journal, or history."

Allen looked over her shoulder and shook his head. "Everything of value was removed a long time ago. I would have preferred the English furniture or the family silver."

"Listen to this darling, near the back here; whoever is writing has reached the end of the last ledger and is crowding the writing:

"Being in my 82d year and so alone, feeble of breath but still active of limb, I now see I shall never bring my history of the Hudson River families to completion, or even cover fully any part of what I set out to do. Such appears to be the destiny of man; to create more history than he can consume.

In winter the trees are bare and I walk in good weather a half mile to Winterbourne's Hill for a view up the Hudson. The river is easy to follow below the turn at Peekskill; a person familiar with the scene picks out High Tor, Stony Point, the scene of a battle in the Revolutionary War, Croton Point, the rises of Bear Mountain and Anthony's Nose, the entrance to the Highlands hiding West Point. The top of Kykuit was once a signal hill for the Indians. One looks across the stretches of the Tappan Zee and the walls of the Palisades down to Manhattan. I watch the morning sun over the mist that covers the hills and river, the sunset across the water.

The mouth of the Pocantico River drops rapidly down from the hills to the Hudson by Philipsburgh Manor, Upper Mills, and nearby is the Old Dutch Church."

"Respect the old man's wishes, Betty. Let it lay."

"Oh, you have no sense of the past. Don't you feel everything we are and can be is already here, waiting to act its part again?"

"No. All I feel is dust and cobwebs."

"Listen to this:

"North is the place where Major André was captured, and, near me here, Sunnyside. North at Croton is the manor of the Van Cortlandt patroon family, and more such families beyond. In this area a century of American history is on view. I can see relics of the Hudson Valley Dutch, the American Revolution. On bad days when I cannot go out, I have taken to reading books that are not research into the lives of the families. An old Greek wrote: 'Of one power even God is deprived, and that is the power of making what is past never to have been. . . . And what is past is only prologue. . . .'"

Allen took Betty's hand and led her out among the soggy leaves. Below them the river ran cold and blue past the wooden piles of the old boat landing. He said, "Tomorrow, I was told, the shad begin to run."

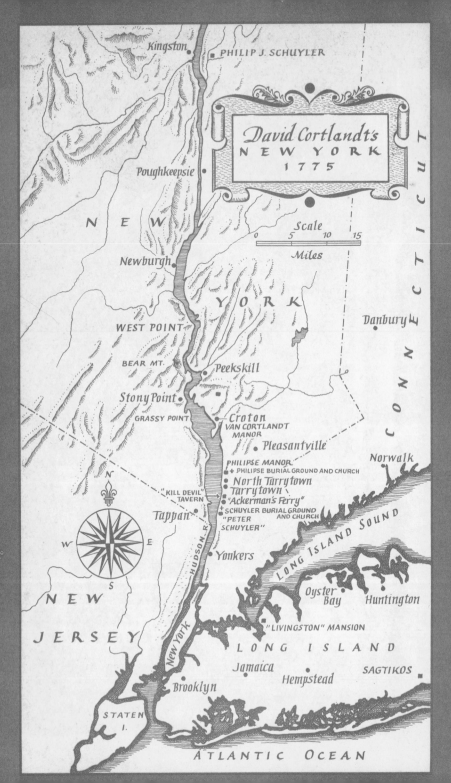